D0458597

ASSIGNMENT: SUSPENSE

HELEN MacINNES

Assignment: Suspense

A THREE-NOVEL OMNIBUS

ABOVE SUSPICION

HORIZON

ASSIGNMENT IN BRITTANY

NEW YORK

HARCOURT, BRACE & WORLD, INC.

LIBRARY OF CONGRESS CATALOG CARD NUMBER: 61–7253

PRINTED IN THE UNITED STATES OF AMERICA

Contents

INTRODUCTION

There are three questions that anyone who reads my novels usually asks me when we meet. *What is true? How much is invented? Did you yourself experience any of those situations?*

I like these questions. An interested reader is an encouragement to a writer. Curiosity, when it deals with books and ideas, is a compliment. Besides, a reader ought to know something about a writer's methods, for he has given his time to considering the writer's words, to thinking about the writer's basic philosophy. If we demand an honest statement of the ingredients of every package of food we buy, it seems odd that we should treat our minds more carelessly than we do our stomachs. False pretenses in the world of ideas (and literature conveys ideas, or opens a new door to the view of the world outside our own lives, or discloses a different light on what we have either accepted as fact or dismissed as exaggeration) can be as deadly in their effect as the adulteration of food. The writer who alters the facts of history, or twists events into a false pattern, to suit his own ideas, is providing his readers with his own package of particular poisoning. The mind is more vulnerable than the stomach, because it can be poisoned without feeling immediate pain.

So there is a particular obligation laid upon any writer dealing with contemporary history; and even novelists who write adventure-suspense stories must be very conscious of it. Unless, of course, their themes and backgrounds are far removed from reality. Then they can be completely fanciful. Whether or not a group of champagne-drinkers in a mythical kingdom feel themselves threatened by the hop-growers in an equally mythical neighboring queendom can be as merry a romp as the witty writer—and he had better be witty—can pull out of his imaginative hat. But a writer who deals with a serious theme, however amusing he can be at times, has to face much research, much comparison of viewpoints and reports, much examination of his own mind and conscience, before he even starts setting his characters and plot into their background.

Background . . . There lies the answer to the first question. The backgrounds of my novels are as factual as I can make them. The physical backgrounds—the places I describe—are fairly simple to reconstruct. They are countries I have visited, customs and peoples I have seen. (This rule is true for all my novels except *While Still We Live.*) Occasionally, in dealing with street addresses or with a specific village, I avoided using real addresses (which might cause trouble, even danger, for people living in an occupied town) or the real place names. (For example, the village of "St. Déodat" in *Assignment in Brittany* does not actually exist, although I have known several Breton villages which it typifies.) I did this in order not to endanger anyone. You must remember that when *Above Suspicion*, *Assignment in Brittany*, and *Horizon* were published, the Nazis were occupying the countries I describe in these novels. If I related the beginning of an underground movement against the Nazis in a small Breton or Tyrolean village, I did not want any real name attached to the fictional place I mentioned. (You may think this was excessive caution. Yet, after the war was over, I met several veterans who—when the fighting ended in Brittany—had taken a free day to track down the places described in *Assignment in Brittany.* They were wryly amused to learn they had spent hours in searching for an entirely imaginary St. Déodat. But the Germans took things more seriously, and were very thorough in working over every scrap of fact about the resistance to their conquest: therefore I tried to give them no such scraps.) Apart from such precautionary measures, the scenes of the novels are as real as I can make them, both from my memory and from my reading.

But there is more than geography in a background. There is history, too: past history, present history, politics, and religion. That is the hard work involved in forming a true background for a novel. It means research: a good deal of collecting facts, comparing various points of view; and yet this research either does not appear in the novel at all, or is only quietly introduced through characters. A novel is not a thesis, or a sermon, or a political pamphlet.

So all this background is accurate to the best of my knowledge and observation. This is the true part of the novel. Against it, I set the imaginary characters and the imaginary plot. Characters and plot—these are invented. That is, I do not take people I meet and put them into my novels. I imagine my characters and their stories, creating people from what I have observed in life. Their actions and reactions develop the plot; and, in turn, the plot develops their characters. There is nothing mysterious or improbable about this creation of imaginary people: we all have, somewhere deep inside us, a reservoir of our unconscious observations; ever since we started being interested in people, in listening to their words and wondering not only about what they said but about why they said it, in watching their behavior and wondering not only about what they did but about why they did it, this reservoir has been gradually filling up. For centuries before Alexander Pope observed that the proper study of mankind was man, the storyteller—whether he was poet, or dramatist, or romancer—had been tapping that reservoir. Two hundred years after Pope, we have all become conscious of the subconscious, thanks to men like Freud and Jung and Adler. But creative writers did just as well, if not better, when they relied on their own observations and meditations about the human race. Actually, if they enquire too scientifically into the subconscious, they may find that their stories change into case-history notebooks, and that they are no longer novelists, but analysts. For art is selective, and instinct is often the selector.

And there is the answer, too, to the third question. The idea that a novelist must actually be writing from his own experience, and that he must experience everything in order to write, is a misconception. How could a man write of the physical pain and extraordinary emotions of a woman in childbirth, if he could not describe something that was totally impossible for him to experience? How could a writer describe death or illness when he himself was a healthy specimen? Birth and illness and death have often been part of the most moving scenes in some of the finest novels. A novelist does not need to be a cripple in order to make a character who is a cripple come alive on the written page. A novelist does not need to be an extremist in politics in order to describe a Nazi or a Communist. He does not have to experience murder or treason or political violence before he can realize what these things mean. Does a surgeon have to undergo all the major operations before he can perform them? With knowledge, and thought, and deduction, and trained fingers, and— most of all, perhaps—instinct, a surgeon does his job. With instinct fully alive and responsive, he could even come close to knowing the actual pains and fears that his patient is undergoing. A novelist is like the surgeon in many ways. He does not need to experience, himself, before he can deal with a subject. He, too, does need to have thought about the subject, to have studied the available facts. But, unlike the surgeon, the novelist can allow himself to feel the pain and the fears: he can become, in imagination, the patient, and he does. In the world of his mind, he can experience anything he describes. It is painful, at times, to be a novelist.

But it has its pleasures, too: for instance, the look on a reader's face when he says (half rueful, half amused), "You know, I sat up till two o'clock last night to finish that story!"

HELEN MACINNES

Above Suspicion

1941

The Song Which Frances Sang

Lully, lulla, thou little tiny child,
By by, lully lullay.

O sisters too,
How may we do
For to preserve this day
This poor youngling,
For whom we do sing,
    By by, lully lullay?

Herod, the king,
In his raging,
Chargèd he hath this day
His men of might,
In his own sight,
    All young childrén to slay.

That woe is me,
Poor child, for thee!
And ever morn and day,
For thy parting
Neither say nor sing
    By by, lully lullay!

Coventry Carol: Pageant of the Shearmen and Tailors, Fifteenth
Century

This song is sung by the women of bethlehem in the play, just
before herod's soldiers come in to slaughter their children

CHAPTER 1 THE VISIT

This June day seemed, to Frances Myles, very much like any other summer day in Oxford. She walked slowly along Jowett Walk, watching the gentle five-o'clock sun bring out the bronze in the leaves overhead. This was her favorite part of the road leading to her husband's College. On her left, the gray walls which hid the gardens of the Holywell houses were crowned with rambler roses. To her right were the playing fields with their stretches of soft green grass, and beyond them were the straightness of poplar, the roundness of chestnut and elm. Today, there were only a few men practising at the nets: most of them were packing, or going to end-of-term parties. Like herself, she thought, and quickened her pace. She was probably late again. She hoped guiltily that Richard would have enough work to occupy him, while he waited for her at College. He generally had. . . . But it was difficult to hurry on a summer day like this: there were so many things to enjoy, like the twenty shades of green all around her, or the patterns of unevenly cut stones in the high walls, or the way in which a young man would catch a cricket ball and lazily throw it back. Little things, but then the last few months had made the little things important.

She entered Holywell, and hurried along its curve of old houses until she reached the Broad. There her pace slackened again, and she halted at a bookseller's window. Richard's new book on English lyric poetry was well displayed. It was selling, too, which had been a pleasant surprise. (The bookseller had explained that away rather harshly: people were buying strange books now, it sort of soothed their minds.) She smiled to herself in the window at her totally unpoetic thoughts. A selling book would be a help towards another summer among the mountains. Another summer, or a last summer, she wondered, and turned away from the window. Once, all you had to do was to decide what mountains you'd like to climb, and then spend the winter writing reviews and articles to cover the train fares, and there you were. But each year it was becoming more difficult. She thought of past summers in the Tyrol, in the Dolomites. Once you could walk over mountain paths and spend the evenings round a table in the village inn. There had been singing and dancing, and light-hearted talk and friendly laughter. But now there were uniforms and regulations. Self-consciousness and uncertainty controlled even the jokes. Now you might only laugh at certain things. Now conversations with foreigners were apt to end in arguments.

Richard had discussed all this with her last night before they fell asleep. He had voted for one last look at Europe in peacetime, such as it was. There were still countries where one could breathe as one liked. Perhaps the premonition that this day was far from being much like any other summer day for Frances Myles had laid its cold finger on her heart . . . Or it could have been the thought of Oxford as it might well be next term. At any rate, the lightness had gone out of her step.

The young college porter was standing at the lodge gate. She tried to make her smile brighter than she felt.

"How is the new baby?" she asked.

He beamed with pride. "Just splendid, ma'am, thank you. Mr. Myles is waiting in his room. He has just phoned down to ask if you had arrived. I'll tell him you're here." He moved back into the lodge. Frances remembered he had joined the Territorial Army in March, just after the seizure of Prague. Nowadays she kept remembering details like that. She hurried through the quadrangle, and began the climb to Richard's room.

The oak was sported. She thumped on its massive panels, and drew back as she heard Richard open the room door first before he could let the heavy oak door swing out. He was smiling, with that guess-what look.

"Hello, darling," she said. "Quite like old times to sport your oak. Why all the precautions?" He wiped her lipstick off his chin as he drew her into the room, fastening the two doors behind them.

"We've a visitor, Fran."

It was Peter, Peter Galt.

He grinned and held out both his hands. "Hello, Frances, you look quite startled."

"Peter! But we thought you were in Bucharest. When did you get back?"

"Two or three weeks ago. I would have written you if I could. I've just been explaining to Richard. I've purposely not written you. And I am not staying with you, either. I am putting up at the Mitre."

Frances turned to her husband in dismay. "Richard, what's the matter with him?"

Richard handed her a glass of sherry. He refilled Peter's glass and then his own, with maddening concentration, before he spoke.

"Peter got into a jam."

"A jam? Peter?" She sat down on the nearest chair. She looked so charmingly anxious under her ridiculous hat that Peter hastened to reassure her.

"Don't worry, Frances. It all turned out rather well in the end. But it did make it necessary for me to be recalled." He grinned, and added, "Ill-health, of course."

"Of course. . . ." Frances was less alarmed, but she was still curious. She waited for an explanation. It was Richard who said in a noncommittal way, as he placed an ashtray beside her, "He got entangled with a spy."

"Well, I only hope she was beautiful," Frances said. "I mean, if you *will* do things like that, you may as well make the most of it." She smiled as she looked up at the correctly dressed young man balancing against the fireplace. She had always hoped that Peter would never get entangled with anyone who wasn't beautiful. She watched his calm face and the shy smile, and wondered. To a stranger, he would seem just another elegant minor secretary to a British Embassy.

"Unfortunately, it was a he," said Peter. "And to be quite truthful, I didn't get entangled with him. He got entangled with me."

"You look such easy meat, really, Peter."

"That was an asset, anyway."

"And so you had to come back to England . . ." Frances was still unable to take Peter quite seriously. "He isn't after your blood, is he?"

"He can't do that. Bucharest dealt with him. But his friends might think I learned too much before that happened."

"But, Peter, you don't mix that kind of—politics with diplomacy, do you?"

"He did the mixing. Now I am waiting for all the commotion to die down."

Peter gave a good imitation of his old smile, but Frances, watching his eyes, was already revising her opinion about this visit. Something serious was behind it all. When she spoke, her voice had dropped all hint of teasing.

"Is that all?"

Richard, sitting on the edge of his desk, gave a laugh.

"Out with it, Peter, whatever it is. It's no good being diplomatic with Frances. She can see through a brick wall as quickly as anyone."

Peter finished his sherry. As he looked from Frances to Richard, he seemed to be making up his mind about something. . . . Or perhaps he was deciding how to begin. They both suddenly realized the change in him. He was an older, a more businesslike Peter. And he was worried. His fingers played nervously with the stem of the sherry glass. He was choosing his next words with care.

"Frances is quite right. I am not in the F.O. any longer: I've been put onto other work. And that's why I am here." He glanced at his watch, and his next words were spoken more quickly. "I'm afraid this visit combines business with pleasure, and we haven't very much time for everything I want to tell you. So you'll understand if I begin abruptly. . . . We haven't the time for any build-up which would enlist your sympathy, and make things easier for me. I'll just have to start with the story, and hope for the best.

"First of all, I didn't want to give anyone the idea that I have been in touch with you. So I didn't let you know I was coming to Oxford, and I can't stay with you. Even the porter at the lodge doesn't know I'm with you: he thinks I am visiting old Meyrick. The reason is—I have a job for you to do, and I hope you'll agree to do it. It shouldn't be dangerous: tiresome, perhaps, and certainly a blasted nuisance, but not actually dangerous if you stick to the directions." He shot a quick glance at Richard, and added with emphasis: "You are just the people we need for it. You are both above any suspicion, and you've a good chance of getting through."

Richard looked at Peter speculatively. "What on earth is it?" he asked. "And why?"

"I'd better tell you about the job, first," Peter answered. "The whys and wherefores can wait until the end. I am sorry if it develops into a kind of lecture, but I'd like you to get all the details quite straight. One of the reasons why I thought of you for this job, Richard, is your memory. If you'd take a mental note of things as I explain them, that would save a lot of time."

Richard nodded.

"The job is simply this. I've been hoping that you would go abroad as usual this summer, and that you'd travel by Paris, meet a man there, and then continue the journey as he directs. At the end of it, you should be able to send us some information which we need very badly. That's the general outline. Now here are the particulars. I'll give you no trimmings—just the facts.

"When you get to Paris, just do as you always do. Stay at your usual hotel, eat at your favorite places, visit the usual mixture of museums and night clubs. Keep on doing that, for some days: long enough, anyway, to establish your innocent-tourist reputation. And then, on Saturday night, visit the Café de la Paix. Sit at an outside table towards the left. Order Cointreau with your coffee. Frances will be wearing a red rose. Don't notice anyone or anything in particular. About eleven o'clock, Richard will upset his Cointreau. He will be glad of an excuse not to drink it anyway, if I know Richard. Your waiter will come and mop up. That and the red rose are the signal. A man will approach your table, and that's the moment for one of you to speak. The sentence should begin: 'Mrs. *Rose* told me we must see . . .' and add the name of some place you've decided on. Pretend to talk, keep it all natural, but be on guard for the number which the man will give you, somehow. That's the key of this whole business. For if you go next day, to the place which you mentioned, at exactly *one hour later* than the number which he gives you, you will get into real touch with him. And he has a message for you.

"It's all very much easier than it sounds. He identifies you by the position of the table and the red rose and the upset glass of Cointreau; reaches your table at the time you expect him; hears the name of the place you've chosen along with the right sentence; and gives you a clue to the time for a meeting on the next day. Have you got all that Richard?"

"Yes. But before we go any further, why choose us? I mean, we shall be such amateurs for that job: we'll probably mess it all up. There must be something fairly important at stake, and it seems to me as if you needed someone with quick wits. I don't know if mine have been sharpened well enough—in that way. As for Fran . . ." Richard shrugged his shoulders.

Frances only looked amused. "Darling, I love you," she said. "Do go on, Peter."

Peter took her advice.

"When you get the message, it will probably be in some code. And that's another reason why I want Richard to tackle this job. I can rely on him to get a meaning out of that message. His brain has had just the right training and discipline for that sort of work. Well, the message will direct you to another agent, and he will direct you farther still, and you will find yourself passed on from agent to agent until you reach the chief of them. He's the last one on the line, and he's the chap we are worried about. That is the information we need."

He paused, and watched Richard pour some sherry into his glass. Again Frances had the feeling that he was once more weighing his words very carefully before he spoke. His trouble was to tell them enough in the right order, without telling them too much.

"I think you'll find the rest of this travelogue more interesting. We are now reaching the whys and the wherefores." Peter allowed himself the suspicion of a smile. "You've heard of what is called the underground railway in Germany, haven't you? It's a version of the old *Scarlet Pimpernel* technique. It helps anti-Nazis to escape, and covers up their tracks. One of the brains behind it is the chief of this group of agents. On the side, of course, he collects information which has been very useful, indeed. Until about five weeks ago, we had the normal reports from him: accurate and regular. But since then, we have had no really informative messages. Two of them, in fact, were dangerously misleading. Fortunately, we had other sources of information about these facts which made us suspicious, and we didn't act on his advice. These suspicions were increased when two men, escaping from Germany by his route, disappeared completely. They have simply vanished into thin air."

Frances put aside her glass, and leaned forward, cupping her face in her hands. Richard held a cigarette unlighted. The eyes of both were fixed on Peter.

"What we want to know is this—before the harvests are gathered in, to put it quite bluntly—: does the man still exist, or has he been sending us false messages to warn us that things aren't just right, or has he been liquidated? So your job is to follow the route directed by various agents, always keeping in mind that you are just the simple traveler, until you find him. The one clue I do know is that he will be an Englishman, the only Englishman in that chain of agents. I can't help with his name or appearance, because he has too many of both. In any case, the less you know, the easier it will be for you to play your role, and the better it will be for all of us. He probably won't seem at all English when you meet him, but if you give him the correct high-signs, which the previous agent will pass on to you, you will find out that he's an Englishman all right."

"But why all this agent-to-agent business?" Richard asked. "Why doesn't the Paris man direct us to him straight away?"

"The plan is his: he invented it to suit his own particular work. And it has been very successful. It's been foolproof for a longer time than most systems. It's simple enough. The Paris agent is the only stationary one, and that's the reason why he takes so many precautions, just to safeguard himself. The others move about as their chief directs. It is just as well to keep moving, for they often work in Nazi-dominated territory. Each agent knows only the name and address of the man next to him, and any information they collect can be posted along the chain of agents until it reaches the chief. Anyone who wants to get in touch with him must begin at the Paris end, and no one can begin at Paris unless he knows how to make the difficult contact with the agent there. There are only two sources which can direct anyone to manage that contact. We are one of them; the other is just as careful as we are. So you see, there is some method in his madness."

"And what about the information which he sends to you? He must have another line?"

Peter nodded. "Yes, and it's a much more direct way, naturally. I knew you'd cotton on, Richard. Anything else which strikes you?"

Richard hesitated, and then, as Peter waited for an answer, he said, "The system is obviously pretty safe, except for one drawback. If the chief man himself is caught, then all information traveling out to him will get into the wrong hands. His agents might even be picked off one by one, if he were—persuaded into any confession. *Not* to mention the fate of the poor devils who thought they were escaping from Germany."

"Exactly. That's why the job has got to be done."

"Your man must have been pretty sure of himself to think up that system, I must say."

Peter said, "I suppose it looks that way, but you've got to take risks in his profession. It has been very much worth our while to take a chance on him. And, strangely enough, it is just this kind of system which gets the best results. Until now, he has always been agile enough not to be caught; he has been doing this kind of thing, you know, since we were being pushed round the park in our prams. You may depend on one thing, Richard: he won't talk. Anyway, you see how vital it is to know whether he is still functioning, before the volcano in Europe blows sky-high. We've got to be sure of him, before then."

"Yes, I can quite see that," Richard said gloomily. "But I still think you need a professional man on the job." It was a good sign, anyway, thought Peter, that Richard was still arguing about it. He was clearly not very much in love with the idea, but he was still at the stage of objections rather than that of a downright refusal. Peter wondered if he should tell them anything more. He thought wearily, "I'm devoted to both of them, but can't they see, in God's name, that I was counting on them to accept, or I wouldn't have let them in on all this?" Yet people changed, and being a don at Oxford might very well make you too contented, too unwilling to act against your own security. Richard was waiting for his answer.

"We sent one," Peter said briefly. "We should have heard from him by this time. When we didn't I suggested to my Chief that we should try an amateur; that line served me well enough in Bucharest. A couple of inno-cents abroad might be able to get through all suspicion. The thing to remember is that you are *not* agents; don't let yourself get mixed up in any sideline snooping. All we want to know is whether an Englishman is there, or not. If things get too hot, then just pull out, using your own good sense. If there's any questioning, then stick to your story. You are just two holiday-makers having your annual trip abroad. There is one other point: your job will be finished when either you find the man, or you've reached the sixth agent without finding him. He never worked with more in a line. You will have a margin of safety all through, because the contacting clues will be vague enough to let you have an out and your amateur status will be an additional help. That really is your strongest safeguard."

Richard said nothing, but Galt, watching him closely, was satisfied. It wasn't a comfortable, peaceful way of life which had held Richard back: it was the fact that Frances would be in this too.

"When you've finished, wire to this address in Geneva," Peter said. He wrote some words quickly on a piece of paper, and handed it to Richard, still looking undecided, worried . . . But Galt knew he had won.

"Better memorize the address, and then destroy it," he advised. "If you find your man, then wire ARRIVING MONDAY, or TUESDAY, or whatever day you actually saw him. If you don't find him, wire CANCEL RESERVATIONS." He drew a deep breath. "Thank God that's over," he said. "Is it all clear, Richard?"

"I've got it memorized, if that's what you mean. But look here, Peter, if you have really decided that I ought to do this job, don't you think I'd better go alone? I'm not running Frances into any risks." His tone was grim. Frances looked at him suddenly. So that was what had made him hesitate.

When she spoke her voice was low, but equally determined. "Richard, I am *not* going to be left behind."

Peter said, "Unfortunately I agree with Frances. Since you've been married, you've never separated on your holidays. It really would be better if you were just to do what you always do. And you'll be safer with Frances, because you won't take risks if she is with you." He looked anxiously at Richard. "I know it's going to ruin your summer," he began, and then stopped. He had said enough as it was.

Richard was staring at the red geraniums in the window box.

"It isn't the ruining of it," he said slowly. "Everyone's holidays are ruined this year. But I don't think we'd really be of any use."

Peter was picking up his gloves and umbrella and his black hat. He was still watching Richard intently. Something seemed to decide him. He moved over to Frances to say good-by.

"I would never have asked you if I didn't think you could pull it off," he said. "And I would never have asked you if the whole thing wasn't so urgent, Richard. I'd have done it myself, except that the people we are working against have got me docketed since Bucharest. I'll be on the files, by this time. I thought of someone else, but your qualifications for this job are just what we need. I didn't enjoy asking you, I may as well say . . . Time I was leaving, now. I see I've kept you late for Frame's party. I met him this morning in front of the Mitre, and he asked me to come along too." He waved his hat towards the invitation card propped up on the mantelpiece.

"How long," said Richard, "should this job take?"

"We allowed two weeks to our man, but he knew the ropes. We'd better say about a month. It will be safer if you don't hurry things. You will have to spend a few days in each place to make it look convincing. Remember, I want you to steer clear of any suspicion, or danger. . . . For God's sake, take care of yourselves."

His voice was normal again by the time he had reached the door.

"Good-by, Frances; good-by, Richard. See you when you get back."

The door closed softly, and left a silent room.

Frances was the first to move. She pulled out her compact and powdered her nose. She readjusted her hat to the correct angle.

"You'll do," she said to her reflection in the mirror. "Come on, my love, we are three quarters of an hour later than I had meant to be late. . . . You've got it all memorized?"

Richard nodded. "That's the least of it. Frances, this is the time to back out. Now."

Frances rose, and looked at the seams of her stockings. She altered a suspender. "When do we start?" she asked. "As soon as you have finished all your teaching?"

Richard looked at his wife's pretty legs.

"Blast Peter," he said, and took her arm as they left the room.

They talked of other things as they went downstairs.

CHAPTER 2 THE PARTY

The party in Frame's rooms had just reached the right temperature when Frances and Richard Myles arrived. They stood for a moment at the doorway rather like two bathers about to plunge off a springboard. Their host, armed with sherry bottles, pushed his way through to meet them.

"I'm *so* glad," he breathed. "Sorry about this *awful* crowd: such a mob." He turned to welcome some other new arrivals. Actually, thought Frances, he was just delighted that the room was jammed with people talking their heads off. She smiled good-by to Richard. This wasn't one of those ghastly affairs where you knew only the host. They wouldn't have to put on their opocial act today, when they would meet each other with surprise in the middle of the room, greet each other warmly and start the vivacious conversation of two friends who rarely met. They always found that others, with an ear for preposterous remarks, would drift towards them. As Richard had said, splendid isolation didn't mix with sherry.

But tonight, Richard had already seen two men he wanted to talk to, and Frances waited in the corner she had chosen for herself as three young men gravitated towards her. They had, in their typical manner, only smiled politely when they caught her eye, and had then, without another glance in her direction, started a quiet but determined progress towards where she stood. She noticed Richard was looking round him in that particularly ingenuous way he had when he was most on guard . . . But Peter Galt had not arrived yet.

The three young men arrived from their various directions, and began one of the usual adroit conversations which sherry parties inspire. They all avoided talking present-day politics with an understanding as complete as it was tacit. This was perhaps the last conversation they would have together for a long time, and they wanted to keep it gay. They discussed the Picasso exhibition in London, and his Guernica, and that led to Catalonian art and Dali. Frances wanted to know if the pineapple Cathedral at Barcelona was still more unfinished. (Michael had been there with the International Brigade—it was a bad show about his arm; Frances had heard that the shrapnel still imbedded there might end in amputation.) But Michael steered the conversation to Gaudi and his architectural fantasies. Frances remembered a chapter somewhere by Evelyn Waugh on Gaudi's telephone kiosks. It was an amusing description and they laughed.

"Eternal Oxford: how delightful it is to return and be so far removed from the rigors of life." The voice had a very pronounced, almost too careful Oxford accent. The speaker was tall, and remarkably good-looking. A dueling scar marked his chin, another his cheek; they gave his blondness a certain formidable quality. His smile was very self-possessed. "Mrs. Myles, as lovely as ever." He bowed low over Frances' hand.

Frances collected herself. "Oh, hello. How are you?" She made hasty introductions. "Freiherr Sigurd von Aschenhausen—John Clark, Sir Michael Hampton, George Sanderson. Herr von Aschenhausen was an undergraduate along with Richard."

There was a pause.

"Charming to return and find Evelyn Waugh and Oxford still inseparable." Von Aschenhausen's voice was friendly. The three undergraduates kept a polite smile in place. Frances knew they were placing his date of residence at the University very accurately. She thought of explaining that it wasn't black-satin sheets but Catalonian architecture which they had been discussing, and then gave up the idea as being more trouble than it was probably worth. Even allowing for the foreigner's favorite indoor sport of underestimating the English, surely von Aschenhausen couldn't be serious. After all he had been to three universities, one in Germany, one in England and one in America. One thing he must know about undergraduates by this time, and that was they were always in revolt. They were never static. The only way they could form their minds was by opposing accepted opinion. Frances herself had seen the swing of the pendulum away from the esthete to the politically conscious young man who Studied Conditions. The esthete himself had been in rebellion against the realism of the postwar group.

George made some polite remark to cover up their embarrassment. Michael was lighting a cigarette. John was gazing into the middle distance. Frances remembered he was allergic to Germany, since that kick four years ago when he hadn't saluted a procession in Leipzig. The conversation limped along, the undergraduates hoping that von Aschenhausen would go; but he didn't. Frances did her best: she talked about summer holidays. The undergraduates were going to France; von Aschenhausen was returning to Berlin. She explained that Richard and she would like to have their usual view of mountains.

"Where exactly were you thinking of going?" asked von Aschenhausen.

"We were in the South Tyrol last year. I'd like to get back there just once more—" Frances' voice was honey-sweet—"just before the volcano erupts." The Englishmen smiled grimly. The German protested politely.

"What! With this peaceful England? There will be no war, no general war. Just look at everyone in this room. . . ." Unconsciously he straightened his back as he looked around the room. *And there's not a soldier among you* was the implication. He might just as well have said it. Michael flicked a piece of cigarette ash off his wounded arm. He spoke for the first time.

"There's a limit to everything, you know. Good-by, Frances. I must go now. Have a good time this summer."

The others had to go now, too, it seemed.

Von Aschenhausen remained. Frances shook herself free from her embarrassment. After all, he used to be amusing and gay. He had made many friends when he was up at Oxford; he had been invited around a good deal. She wondered how he was getting along in the New Germany; he used to laugh off any political discussions by protesting he wasn't interested in politics. She racked her brains for something tactful to say. It was difficult in this summer of 1939. You were so conscious of nationality now. She was relieved when von Aschenhausen spoke.

"I am afraid that young man did not like me particularly," he said. "Is it because I am a German, or is it his usual manner? I have noticed that a cripple is usually more bitter than the ordinary man."

"Cripple?" Frances' eyes widened; she was at a loss for words.

"Of course, there is a change in the attitude here towards me," he continued. "Six years ago I had many friends. Today—well—" he smiled sadly —"it would be better if I came as an exile."

"I wondered at first if you were, and then I thought not."

"How did you know?" He looked at her amusedly.

"By your clothes." She looked pointedly at his Savile Row suit. He hadn't liked that; his smile was still there but it was less amused. Good. Cripple, indeed!

"It is really very sad for a German to find how misjudged and abused his country is. Of course, our enemies control the press in foreign countries, and they have been very busy. They have clever tongues."

"Have they? It is strange, isn't it, how criticism of Germany has grown even in countries which were once really very close to her. I wonder how it could have happened." He looked as if he didn't know quite how he should take that. She gazed at him steadily with wide blue eyes.

He smiled sadly. "You see, even you have changed. It is depressing to return to Oxford, which I loved, and to find myself surrounded by glaciers." Was the man being really sincere, wondered Frances, or was it just another of those poor-mouth stories?

"Perhaps it is the change in you which has changed us."

He looked surprised. "Oh, come now, Mrs. Myles. I haven't changed so very much. I am still interested in literature and music. I haven't become a barbarian, you know. Politically—well, I have progressed. Everyone does, unless he is a cow. I am more realistic than I once was, less sentimental. I've seen the stupidities committed in the name of idealism and abstract thinking. People are made to be led. They need leadership, and with strong leadership they can achieve anything. At first they must take the bad with the good; in the end they will forget the bad, because the ultimate good will be so great for them." He spoke with mounting enthusiasm.

"You believe you have not changed. And yet, under the leadership which you praise so much, you may only read certain books, listen to certain music, look at certain pictures, make friends with certain people. Isn't that limiting yourself?"

"Oh, well, limiting oneself to the good, eliminating the bad—all that is better in the end."

"But *who* is to say what is good for you, or bad for you? Is it to be your own judgment, educated at Heidelberg, Oxford and Harvard, or is it to be some self-appointed leader who can't even speak grammatical German?" Von Aschenhausen didn't like that either. He obviously had no answer ready for that one.

Frances kept her voice gentle. "You see, you have changed. Do you remember the Rhodes scholar who preceded you here? Intelligent man, quiet, and very kind. What's his name? Rotha, wasn't it? You liked him then. But where is he now? Oranienburg, I heard."

Von Aschenhausen made an impatient gesture. "That is all very sentimental, Mrs. Myles. It is time that the British really saw the things which matter. Discipline and strong measures are needed in today's Europe. It is a more dangerous and forbidding place than it was six or seven years ago."

"That is just our point," said Frances. "What made Europe more dangerous and forbidding?"

He laughed, but it didn't sound jovial.

"You are a very prejudiced person, I can see. I suppose you will now lecture me gravely on the wickedness of Germany's claims to natural *Lebensraum*. It is easy to talk when you have a large Empire."

"On the contrary, Herr von Aschenhausen, I like to think of all people having their *Lebensraum*, whether they are Germans or Jews or Czechs or Poles."

His voice grated. He was really angry. "It is just such thoughts as these which have weakened Britain. In the last twenty-five years, she could have established herself as ruler of the world. Instead, she makes a Commonwealth out of an Empire, and they won't even fight to help her when she has to fight. She leaves the riches of India untapped; she urges a representative government on Indians who were about to refuse it. She alienates

Italy with sanctions. She weakens herself all the time, and she thinks it is an improvement."

"Hello, you are being very serious in this corner." It was Richard.

"I've been having lessons in statecraft," said Frances, conscious of Richard's eyes on the two pink spots on her cheeks. I shouldn't let myself get angry, she thought, and listened to von Aschenhausen, once more smiling and plausible. She had the feeling that he was trying to cover up, as if he were annoyed with the impression he had given her. He was very polite as they said good-by. He bowed low, his composure completely regained.

"I hope we meet again," he said. "And don't worry, Mrs. Myles. You will see that England will not be at war. You are all good pacifists, here. Enjoy yourselves abroad."

Richard said, "I hope so," and smiled. He took his wife's arm and piloted her skillfully to the door. Frame waved a sherry bottle from two groups away.

"Lovely party," Frances called over to him, but the noise of voices around her drowned her words. Frame's answer was also unheard. They exchanged smiles of understanding, a wave of the hand, and then Frances and Richard were outside the room into quietness and fresh air.

Richard lowered his voice. "I got to you as quickly as I could when I saw an argument had developed. I thought you had sense enough by this time not to waste your breath arguing with a Nazi. He is, isn't he?"

"Yes. I think he didn't mean to show it, but I made him angry."

"What interests me is what he said to anger *you*."

"Was it obvious?" Frances was dismayed.

"To me, yes. No one else would notice. What was it anyway?"

"Britain."

"Anything else?"

Frances shook her head.

"All right; let's drop it. I hope you weren't too intelligent, though. Peter wants us to be the unworldly don with his dim wife."

Frances stared. "But we needn't start that business until we are on the boat train."

"Probably not: still, you didn't notice Peter taking any chances, did you?"

"I must say I thought he was a little—theatrical. He was very unlike himself."

Richard shook his head slowly. "No to both of these. He was too worried to be theatrical. By the way, he didn't turn up at the party."

"Perhaps he changed his mind," said Frances.

"Perhaps. Or perhaps he was just being very sure that he wouldn't meet us again. That's probably nearer it." Richard's voice was gloomy.

Frances pressed his arm to her side. "Cheer up, Richard, or you'll have me worried in case I spoil your fun. It's one of the troubles of having a wife, you know. You just can't get rid of her." She was rewarded with almost a smile.

But the sun had gone, and with it the bronze in the leaves overhead. The playing fields were empty. Over the gray walls and the sharply pointed rooftops the sound of bells followed them as they walked slowly home.

CHAPTER 3   FAREWELL TO SAFETY

The rest of the week passed quickly. Frances was busy with the closing of their house. She also made a hectic dash to London for some clothes she "simply must have." Richard finished the odds and ends of work which face a tutor towards the end of term—but from Peter Galt they heard nothing.

"Which means we are to go ahead," said Richard at breakfast on Wednesday.

That morning, he bought their tickets to Paris and interviewed the bank about a supply of travelers' cheques and some French money. The expense of their unknown journeys had worried him, but his bank manager, who had always been tactful about overdrafts, met him with a discreet smile. The bank had been authorized to give Mr. Myles a letter of credit. Richard did not ask who had authorized it. The bank manager treated it all as something merely routine.

In the evening, Richard hunted through his bookshelves and picked out the Baedekers and maps. He had a fair collection of these, for since his first year at Oxford he had spent part of each summer walking and scrambling his way across mountains into villages. He spread them out around him as he sat on the floor of the study, and lit his pipe. He wondered which he could omit: surely the Pyrenees and Majorca would be unnecessary. Peter had hinted in the direction of Central Europe. Still, it was better to be safe; he knew his way about these maps, and they ought to go along, all of them. He would take less clothes, if his suitcase got too crowded.

Frances came in, her hair brushed loosely to her shoulders.

"Don't overwork, darling," she said with mock concern. "I begin to feel exhausted. I came in to ask you to sharpen my pencil." She held out a miserable stub.

"What on earth do you do with your pencils?" asked Richard. "Gnaw them?"

Frances disregarded this with the adroitness of four years' marriage. She looked at the notebook in her hand, and checked off the items she had written there. Richard watched her as she bit her lip and counted. He felt that wave of emotion which came to him when he looked at Frances in her unguarded moments; and he had the bleak horror which always attacked him then when he thought how easy it might have been never to have met her.

Frances straightened her legs. "That's that," she said. "Just my own things to pack tomorrow after Anni departs. Richard, that is going to be a difficult moment. Other summers, it was different. She always knew she would be coming back in time for October. She seems to feel she will never be back here. I found her packing in floods of tears this evening. I've sent her out now to say good-by to her friends. So there goes the best cook we shall ever have. It was really rather painful this evening. I've got just as much attached to her as she has to us. She wants her father's farm to have the honor of a visit from the *gnädige Frau* and the *Herr Professor*, if they should visit Innsbruck this summer."

Richard finished sharpening the pencil. "Her people were pro-Dolfuss, weren't they?"

"They were. . . . I have a feeling that they have changed. Anni has been very silent about them since she returned last year. One thing she did tell me. Her sister told her that if she came back to England and a war broke out, she would be stoned to death. That is what they said we did in 1914. Isn't it appalling?"

"Well, I suppose if a nation allows concentration camps, it will find it hard to believe that other people don't use similar methods. Cheer up, old girl, who cares what a lot of uncivilized people think anyway? It's only the opinion of the civilized that really matters."

"Yes, but it looks as if a lot of the civilized will be killed because they ignored the thoughts of the uncivilized. Ignoring doesn't abolish them, you know, Richard." She traced a pattern on the carpet with her pencil. "Sorry, darling. I'm tired, and depressed. We've all gone so political these days. I worry and worry inside me, and I think everyone else is doing the same; it is difficult to forget what we all went through last September."

Richard tapped the stem of his pipe against his teeth. "Yes, it's difficult," he said slowly. "I shan't forget helping to dig trenches in the parks, or the paper tape on all the windows, or the towels we were told to keep beside a bucket of water. All the time I was digging I kept wondering whether the trenches would be any good at all, and I knew they wouldn't be. I didn't think much of the towel idea either. But what else was there? And then bastards like von Aschenhausen come along all smiles and bows. And wonder why people are not enthusiastic about them. They blackmail us with bombers one year, and go back on the agreement they had extorted out of us, and then expect to be welcomed as friends. All within nine months. All that, Frances, makes one of the reasons why I listened to Peter. If I could put a spoke of even the most microscopic size in the smallest Nazi wheel, I'd think it a pretty good effort." He had risen, and was pacing up and down the study.

"I think this interruption is due. I see that proposition-look dawning in your eye. Don't try, don't you try to leave me at home. I'm coming."

"I was afraid you were."

"Richard, my dear, you know that whenever you imagine exciting things they always turn out duller than a wet day in Wigan. It's the parties you don't get excited about which turn out to be fun. Now here we are, both thinking of ourselves in terms of Sard Harker. What will happen? We'll go to Paris, and then find that the man does not turn up. I'll wear a red rose for three nights, and you'll spill Cointreau for three nights, until the whole café is gaping at us. And then we'll go on our holiday, wondering if Peter's sense of humor has become overdeveloped since Bucharest."

Richard laughed. "You sound almost convincing, Frances. But I know that you know what I know. This is no bloody picnic."

She rose from the floor, and went over to the window. It was wide open. She leaned forward to breathe in the dewy smell of the earth. The lilac trees at the end of the garden had silver leaves. Richard came to her, and slipped an arm round her waist. They stood there in silence watching a garden moonlit. Frances glanced at him. He was lost in thought.

"If you want to know," he said at last, reading her thoughts in the uncanny way two people living together learn to do, "I am thinking we should photograph this in our memory. We may need to remember it often for the next few years."

Frances nodded. Around them were the other gardens, the mixed perfume of flowers. The walls hung heavy with roses and honeysuckle, their colors whitened in the strong moonlight. The deep shadows of trees, blurring the outline of the other houses, were pierced here and there with the lights from uncurtained windows. The giant elms in the Magdalen deer park stood sentinels of peace.

She said suddenly, "Richard, let's go up the river; just for half an hour."

"The dew is heavy. You had better wrap up well."

"I shall. It won't take five minutes." She kissed him suddenly, and left him. He heard her running upstairs, the banging of the wardrobe door in their bedroom. So Frances had this feeling too, this feeling of wanting to say good-by.

She came downstairs in less than her five minutes, dressed in a sweater and trousers, and with one of his silk handkerchiefs round her neck. They walked the short distance to the boathouse in silence. They got out the canoe in a matter-of-fact way, as if they were defying the moonlight to weaken them. They paddled swiftly up the narrow river. White mists were rising from the fields on either side of them, encircling the roots of the willows which edged the banks.

"When I used to read my Virgil, this is what I thought the Styx might be like," said Frances. Then suddenly, "Richard, what are you planning to do in Paris?"

"Water carries sound," he reminded her. To prove his words, they heard low voices and the laugh of a girl, before they saw two punts drifting to meet them.

"You have your moments, don't you, Richard? By the way, I think you will like the hat I bought yesterday in London. A little white sailor with no crown to speak of, yards of black cloud floating down the back, and a saucy red rose perched over one eye." She heard Richard laugh behind her. "Practical, isn't it?"

"Very," he said, and laughed again. "Good Lord—trust a woman to think up something like that."

Frances was serious again. "Richard, do you think there will really be war this summer?"

"It's anyone's guess. The President was lunching yesterday with Halifax. He said—"

"Halifax?"

"Yes. He said no one in the Cabinet knew. It all depended on one man."

Frances was silent for a space. When she spoke, her voice trembled with its intensity.

"I resent this man. Why should the happiness of the whole civilized world depend on him? Why should I, an Englishwoman, have to look at my countryside, for instance, and even as I look have to remember that last September I had planned to help to take the Symons children in this canoe up this river, to hide them under the willows until the air raids had passed? I had blankets and towels and tinned food and chocolate all packed in a basket. A Hitler picnic indeed. There is not one of us who hasn't had fear and horror creep into all his associations. As I pass these willows I keep wondering just which one of them might have been sheltering the Symons children, and whether it would have done its job. And all because of one man. Think of it, Richard, there wasn't a farmer who didn't look at his land and the farmhouse his great-great-grandfather had built and wonder. There wasn't a townsman who didn't look at his business or his home and everything he had earned for himself and wonder. There wasn't a man or woman who did not look at the children and wonder. Richard, I resent this man and his kind of people."

"You aren't the only one." Richard pointed the nose of the canoe back down the river. "You aren't the only one. We have all had a year of brooding. And we have all come to the same decision. If anything does start, the man who starts it will be sorry he ever thought of himself as a kind of god. But take it easy, Frances. Promise me you will stop worrying while we are on this holiday. It may be the last—" he paused—"for a long time, anyway. There is nothing more that rational beings can do, anyway, except wait and watch. And when it comes, the Symons children will have better protection than the willows this September. And that's something."

"Yes, that's something." Frances' voice was quieter. "But when I meet some of those armchair critics who sit beside their radio in a part of the world which can't be bombed from Germany, and hear them tell me how England should have fought, I am liable to be very very rude. *And* I bet, if war does come, these same people will suddenly start talking about the greatness and glories of peace. Britain will then be just another of those belligerent countries. That is how we will be dismissed, as if neutrality implied a special sanctity. There now, Richard, I've got it all out of my system. I shan't mention it again."

"That's the girl. Remember this part of the river?"

Frances gave a shaky laugh. "Yes, darling. I was a sweet girl undergraduate, and you were in all the importance of your final year. Good bathes we had, too, in just this kind of moonlight. Look, there's some more of us." Some punts were moored under a bank, and the wet figures as they balanced to dive gave a moment's illusion of silver statues.

"I've found the difference between twenty and thirty," said Richard. "At twenty you never think of rheumatics or a chill in the bladder."

They guided the canoe back to the boathouse. They stood together on the landing place in silence, looking at the river and the white mist rising.

They walked slowly home. At the gate, they met Anni.

"*Guten Abend, gnädige Frau, Herr Professor.*" She was a tall girl, with a pleasant open face, and fair hair braided round her head.

"Good evening, Anni. Did you see your friends all right?"

Anni nodded. Her arms were full of small parcels. "We had cake, and tea, and then we sang. It was very *gemütlich.*" She looked down at the parcels. "They gave me these presents," she added. She spoke the careful English which Frances had taught her. "I've had so much pleasure."

"I'm glad, Anni. You should go to bed soon: you have a long journey tomorrow."

Anni nodded again. "I wish you good night, *gnädige Frau, Herr Professor. Angenehme Ruh'.*"

They walked round the garden after she had left them.

"It's funny, Richard. I really am tired, and there is a nice large bed waiting for me upstairs, and yet I keep staying out here looking at the stars."

"I hate to be unromantic, but I do think it is time we got some sleep. Tomorrow's a bad day. It always is: you have a genius for finding last-minute things to do." Frances smiled, and felt Richard's arm round her waist guide her to the house. On the steps, he stopped to kiss her.

"That's to break the enchantment," he said. His lips were smiling, but his eyes were the way Frances loved them most.

CHAPTER 4 · BEGINNING OF A JOURNEY

There was always a feeling of excitement after the unpleasantness of a Channel crossing, while the train waited patiently on the Dieppe siding for the last passengers. They emerged, in straggling groups, from the customs and passport sheds. Frances, already comfortably settled in her corner, watched them with interest. She glanced at Richard opposite her, leaning back with his eyes closed. He was a bad sailor, but he managed things like customs officials very well indeed. Thank heaven for Richard, she thought, watching other wives followed by harassed husbands whose tempers didn't improve under commiserating looks from unhurried bachelors. It was the stage in the journey when most people began to wonder if it all wasn't more trouble than it was worth.

The last nervous lady was helped into the train. The confusion along the corridors was subsiding. They were moving, very slowly, very carefully. Two young men had halted at their compartment.

"This will do," said one, after hardly seeming to glance in their direction. They swung their rucksacks on to the rack, and threw their Burberries after them. Undergraduates, thought Frances, as she looked at a magazine. Like Richard, they wore dark gray pin-stripe flannel suits, brown suède shoes well-worn, collars which pointed carelessly, and the hieroglyphic tie of a college society.

The train traveled gently along the street, like a glorified tramcar. The children with thin legs and cropped hair and faded blue overalls halted in their games to watch the engine. Their older sisters, leaning on their elbows at the tall narrow windows, looked critically at the people traveling to Paris. The women, standing in the doorways or in front of the small shops, hardly bothered to interrupt their gossip. It was only a train-load, and a full one too. All the better for their men, who worked on the piers: the arriving tourist tipped well. The old men, who sat reading the café newspapers at the marble-topped tables, looked peacefully bored. One of them pulled out a watch, looked at it, looked at the train, and shook his head. Frances smiled to herself. Things had been different when he worked in the sheds, no doubt.

She discarded her magazines. It was almost impossible to read on a foreign train. The differences in houses and people, in fields and gardens, fascinated her. She looked at Richard. He was staring gloomily at the fields, making up his mind to move. As he caught her glance, he roused himself.

"Come on Frances, tea or something. You've eaten nothing since breakfast and I haven't even that now." He rose, and steadied himself. "There's nothing like being back on solid ground, even if it does lurch at the moment."

They negotiated the two pairs of long legs, with the usual "Not at all" following them. In the corridor, Richard gave a grin, and squeezed her arm.

"Excited?" he teased. "I believe you are."

"I have two excitements inside me," said Frances, and smiled back. It was like being a child again, when a deep secret (*cross your lips and heart*) churned in your stomach, and the intoxication of knowing you were important, even if no one else thought you were, made your eyes shine. Frances controlled her exhilaration and tried to look bored. She remembered Richard's words last night. "Keep cool, don't worry. Don't talk about anything important, even when you think it's safe. Don't speak on impulse. Don't show any alarm even when you've just had an attack of woman's intuition. I can tell from your eyes when you are really worried. We can talk things over at night when we get to bed. We won't lose by being careful." *We won't lose!* She had chased away the exhilaration, and now she knew it had been guarding her against fear. *We won't lose.* The certainty of the words panicked her. She heard Richard order tea. *Won't lose, won't lose, won't lose,* mocked the wheels of the train. She suddenly knew that Richard and she had never been so alone before, in all their lives.

"That's better," said Richard as he lit a cigarette. "The compartment was much too crowded. Now what do you want to see in Paris?"

It was strange, she thought, how people seemed to change in a foreign train. More than half in this coach were English, but already they seemed so different. She became aware that Richard was watching her carefully. She smiled to him and calmed her imagination. Nice beginning, indeed, when every stout Swiss commercial traveler seemed to be a member of the Ogpu, or that pinched little governess looked like a German agent. I've seen too much Hitchcock lately, she thought; at this rate I'll be worse than useless.

Richard was talking continuously as if he had sensed her stage fright. She concentrated on listening to him; he had helped her this way before. Like the time she had climbed her first mountain, and had got badly stuck, so badly that she accepted the fact that she was going to be killed, actually accepted it with a peculiar kind of resignation—but Richard had talked so calmly, had compelled her attention so thoroughly, that she forgot she was already dead at the bottom of a precipice, and her feet followed his to safety. He was talking now about the French peasants. A French peasant, he was proving, would not be able to understand *The Grapes of Wrath.*

Frances, watching the farmhouses which seemed to grow from the earth as much as the little orchards which guarded them or the fields so carefully planned to the last inch, was inclined to agree. She thought of the despair of peasants similar to these during the last war, when they saw their fields shell-racked, torn with barbed wire, poisoned with gas, evil-smelling with death. . . . And yet, a few years later and these fields were again persuaded back into neat rows of earth, new trees were planted, new houses built.

"It is strange how little credit we give to the courage of quiet people," she said. "We sympathize most with those who find someone to champion their woes. We take all this for granted." She pointed to the farms. "We never think that this could be a wilderness. We look at it and think 'How pleasant to live here,' and yet to live here would mean back-breaking work and a continual struggle, if we wanted it to stay this way."

"There's nothing like self-pity for thoroughly dissipating a man. And when a nation indulges in that luxury it finds itself with a dictator. Wrongs and injustices come in at the door, and reason flies out the window. It's a solution which does not flatter the human race." He paused. "But what on earth brought this up?"

Frances nodded to the fields. "The earth itself."

People were now crowding into the restaurant car, looking reproachfully at their empty plates.

"Feeding time at the Zoo," said Richard. "Let's move." As he concentrated on the problem of francs and centimes, she caught sight of the gray-suited man and girl in a mirror. This was how we look to strangers, she thought. Richard had noticed the direction of her glance. His eyes were laughing.

"Beauty and the beast?" he suggested.

In their compartment, the two young men uncrossed their legs to let Frances and Richard pass. Frances had the feeling that they were interrupting a discussion. The dark-haired undergraduate seemed depressed and worried. She didn't look at the other, because she knew he was observing her in his detached way. She tried to concentrate on her magazines. She resisted the feeling of sleep which the train rhythm invited. . . . She never slept in the afternoon, but four hours' sleep last night could be an excuse. She looked at the field, she looked at the magazines, she looked at three pairs of brown suède shoes. When she awoke, they were in Paris. Richard was handing his rucksack and her hand case with voluble instructions to a blue-overalled porter.

He smiled down at her. "Time to powder your nose, my pet." Frances, in confusion, grabbed her handbag. She hated to arrive so disorganized.

The undergraduates were leaving. Frances' eyes were startled into looking at them over her compact mirror as she heard them say good-by to Richard, and then, more shyly, to her. She hid her surprise enough to smile, and bow, and say good-by to them in turn, before they disappeared.

Richard was still smiling. "Had a good sleep?"

"Marvelous. I've really got to admit I feel better. Did I make any peculiar noises?"

"No, you slept like a child. It quite won all our hearts."

A bulky shadow fell across the doorway. It belonged to a man with a neat black beard and a neat black suit, making his way slowly down the corridor. He was decidedly large, and he carried a suitcase in each hand, so that he had to walk crabwise. He gazed benevolently into their compartment over his pince-nez. Richard didn't seem aware of him.

He chose this moment to ask, "What about dinner at the Café Voltaire tonight?" Frances was enthusiastic. Her clear voice carried well down the corridor.

"Oh, yes; do. And we'll have decent Vouvray."

Their porter waited patiently. The platform was remarkably crowded, thought Richard, for this year of grace. His eyes searched for the two Englishmen. He saw them striding towards the main entrance, their felt hats in their hands. Behind them, at some distance, was a fat black figure, carrying two bags. . . . And then the crowd closed in again. He felt a sudden wave of relief. In the taxi, he avoided discussing anything except the streets and buildings.

Their hotel was one of the small ones on the Left Bank. They had stayed there on their first visit to Paris together, when they had little money to spend, and they always returned to it.

Inside their bedroom, Frances paused and said, as she always did, "It's just the same, even the wallpaper." Unconsciously, she always got the same note of surprise into her voice each year. Richard had come to the conclusion that she was surprised over anyone continuing to endure such wallpaper; she was probably right about that. It was hideously artistic. Frances was already in the bathroom, unpacking toothbrushes. He leaned against the door and watched her disapprovingly.

"Help me, darling," she said, throwing a sponge and talcum-powder tin at him.

"I'm damned if I am going to unpack now. I'm hungry."

"Richard, you know we'll be late tonight before we get back—we always are—and it will be too late to unpack then, and I hate going to sleep without washing or teeth brushing. I'll shake out my Paris clothes now, if you'll run my bath, like a darling." She went back into the bedroom, and he heard her moving about with her light step.

"It's just the thin edge of the wedge, if you ask me," he said. "First it is only a toothbrush, and then it's Paris clothes, and I bet you are starting on the whole suitcase by this time. You've too much damned energy, Frances. After last night, I thought you would never want to look at another piece of tissue paper for days."

"That sleep on the train made me all right." She slipped off her gray flannel suit. "Talking about the train, who were your young friends? The blond was just too beautiful for words, wasn't he? I felt sorry somehow for the dark ugly one: he was feeling grim about something."

Richard came back into the room, and stretched himself along the chaise longue which stood in front of the tall windows. He propped the rose-embroidered cushion under his head, and watched Frances unfasten her suspenders.

"If you want to know, you can come here. The bath can wait five minutes. It's too hot anyway. You'd only come out a rich lobster color."

Frances looked across the room at him, and smiled as she slipped the smooth silk of her dressing gown round her. She knew Richard, by this time. The bath would have to wait.

From the chaise longue they could watch the green leaves in the small courtyard outside the windows. The fears and uncertainty which had suddenly attacked Frances that afternoon seemed so remote now that they were almost silly. She lay feeling safe and warm and comfortable. Dangers and cruelty didn't exist; nor did lies and treachery, nor hatred and jealousy. It was fine just to lie like this, just to feel safe and warm and comfortable.

Richard watched the smile on her lips. "How do you feel, darling?" So he had been worried too about that attack of nerves this afternoon.

"Wonderful, Richard. Like a contented cow." He laughed. He knew now that everything was all right. When he got round to telling his story, there wasn't much to tell. The men had been undergraduates—Cambridge men. They had been vague about their holiday. The fair-haired man had said something about Czechoslovakia, but the dark one had shut him up rather abruptly, Richard had thought. What had actually started them talking was the man in the black suit. He had passed the compartment door twice, each time looking benevolently at Frances asleep in her corner seat.

"And that," said Richard, "aroused all our protective instincts. The dark-haired undergraduate muttered something about being haunted by black beards since Victoria. The other suggested it might only be a touch of Blackbeard's old bladder trouble again. That sort of broke the ice. I capped that suggestion, and then we just talked. Mostly the fair-haired glamour boy and myself. It turned out he was the brother of Thornley who was up at Oxford in my time. A friend of Peter's. As a matter of fact Peter visited them for a couple of days this week."

At the mention of Peter's name, Frances had stiffened. She didn't like it somehow, and for all Richard's calm voice, she knew he didn't either. She kept her voice low like his. "Complications?" she asked.

"You can't tell. I've been thinking about that. The dark-haired chap was certainly jumpy, but that doesn't prove anything. Probably they really are quite oblivious of anything except their own holiday, and our meeting them was just another of these coincidences. On the other hand, Peter might have roped them in just like us, or used them as decoys, and perhaps Blackbeard was trailing them. If so, then we had downright bad luck meeting them. All we can do is to disinterest anyone who might have become interested in us through them." Richard smiled wryly. "You see, young Thornley didn't mention his brother or Peter until we had reached the station. So there we were, talking for most of the journey, and anyone who passed the door of the compartment might have thought we were all together. The joke was on me."

Frances kissed him. "It probably is only a harmless incident. What about throwing off suspicion with dinner?"

Half an hour later, they left the hotel. The streets were quiet, the restaurants and cafés crowded. A worried Frenchman, hurrying past them, caught sight of a girl's laughing face under a pert white hat with a red rose, and turned to watch. English, he guessed, as he marked the cut of the man's suit and that peculiar stride which goes with such a suit. And without a care in the world, he thought. He hurried on, speculating on that peculiar people.

At that moment he was right. Frances and Richard had abandoned care. Their holiday had begun.

CHAPTER 5   PAWN TO KING'S FOURTH

June ended with their first week in Paris. They were very much on holiday. They rose late and breakfasted at their open window in the warm sunlight which then invaded the small courtyard. The insignificant little man who had watched them from the shadows of his room since their first morning at the hotel still sat far back from his window, but his interest was waning. He wasn't a romantic, and the appearance each morning of a pretty blonde girl in a dressing gown pouring coffee for a tall young man who lazily stretched himself on a couch at the open window was beginning to bore him. The leisurely manner in which they breakfasted and dressed annoyed him as much as the sound of their laughter and their English voices. He was wasting his time, he thought angrily, as he watched them leave their room after midday as they always did. The chambermaid could take care of them.

The second insignificant man who took over at this point was equally bored. His feet hurt, and he had never been interested in history anyway. He followed Frances and Richard from one church to another, from exhibition to exhibition, from palaces to slums. Towards the end of the week, he was beginning to wait for them in a café and let them visit the inside of the buildings themselves. For he too had become convinced he was wasting his time.

The third insignificant man, who joined Richard and Frances while they were having dinner, had slightly better luck. He liked theaters and night clubs. Even the two evenings which they spent more soberly, just sitting at a table in the Café de la Paix, were pleasant, because by that time he was convinced that the Englishman and his wife weren't going to complicate life for him. So he relaxed and enjoyed the thought that his expenses were paid. He was the only one of the insignificant men who was sorry to receive instructions at the end of the week to switch over to a newly arrived American. He had become so accustomed to their obvious approval of drinking their coffee and liqueur on the pavement in the French manner that he would not have been surprised to see them approach the Café de la Paix again, on Saturday night. He would have approved the fair-haired girl's black dress and the small white hat with its gay red rose perched over her right eye.

Frances was nervous, so she talked constantly as they walked up the Avenue de l'Opéra. "I've enjoyed this week, even if my feet feel two sizes bigger," was how she summed it up.

Richard nodded. "It hasn't been so bad. Life has been simpler than I thought it would be. I begin to feel I was oversuspicious of Blackbeard."

Frances stared. "I haven't seen him again; have you?"

"No, nor any possible relatives, either." Which would have pleased the insignificant men; no tribute to their ingenuities could have been handsomer. Richard piloted Frances carefully across the Boulevard des Capucines, and gave her an encouraging smile. "Cheer up, old girl. The first bathe is always the coldest."

They had arrived between the dinner and the after-theater crowds. There were a few vacant tables. Richard led the way to one on the left-hand side. As they sat down, a waiter appeared like the traditional white rabbit out of a hat.

"Coffee," said Richard, "and Cointreau for you as usual, Frances? I think I'll have one too. Yes, coffee and two Cointreaus."

Frances repressed a wifely smile. He always enjoyed ordering in French, even in moments like these. Poor old Richard, how he hated Cointreau.

They settled comfortably in their chairs, lit cigarettes, and looked at the traffic with the right amount of interest. The people at the other tables were the usual mixture of foreigners and Frenchmen. Two nights ago, the same kind of crowd had seemed gay and harmless. Tonight they seemed gay. Frances shook herself out of her imagination to admire the way in which the waiter poured the Cointreau.

"Penny for them," said Richard.

"I was thinking how people with guilty consciences develop persecution mania."

"Yes, they could, couldn't they? I felt the same." But what worried them most was how long they had to wait. Frances sipped her Cointreau. She noticed with amusement that Richard was restricting himself to coffee. As she listened to him, making conversation with one eye on his watch, she repeated to herself just what she had to say when the time came. She was the amateur actress taking one last look at her script as she waits in the wings. Her cue came sooner than she had expected.

A large, expensively draped woman was making her way with difficulty past their table. It seemed to Frances that it might have been the large lady who had brushed against the table, and sent the coffee swilling into the saucer. Yet Richard's Cointreau glass lay carefully pointed away from them, so that the liqueur trickled slowly over the other side of the table. Richard looked at it with some annoyance and resignation. The large lady continued oblivious on her way, trailing clouds of Matchabelli. The waiter staged his arrival from nowhere. He wiped and apologized with equal vigor.

Frances sat very still. She was conscious of the smile on her lips which had settled there and wouldn't come off, as if she were having her photograph taken. Richard's back was turned towards the man, and he hadn't noticed him yet. She let her eyes travel slowly back to their own table; she sensed, rather than saw, him making his way out of the restaurant. He was walking unhurriedly, and he would pass their table. Now he was almost behind the waiter, whose broad back blocked the narrow passage effectively as he bent to pick up the coffee cups. Richard was watching her. He was waiting.

"I was telling you about Mrs. Rose." As she spoke she flipped her cigarette case open. "Mrs. Rose told me we must see Le Lapin Agile. She said we would like it."

"Why?" Richard seemed more interested in ordering another drink.

That's just my sweet husband, she thought a trifle bitterly, and lighted her cigarette. She noticed the rug vendor with the turban who was silently offering his wares to another table.

"She was born in India," she said. Now let's see what Richard can make of that.

The waiter became aware of the man who was trying to edge impatiently past him. He stepped aside, but not in time. He must have knocked the man's elbow, for the cigarette fell from his hand onto their table. The man caught it as it rolled, and picked it up. There was just time for them to notice the peculiar way he wore the watch on his wrist, and the peculiar time it showed on its clearly marked face.

"India?" Richard was asking with a display of interest. "Oh, yes, she was a great rope climber in her day, wasn't she?"

The man had already reached the pavement; he paused for a moment as he lit his cigarette. He might be making up his mind how to spend the rest of his evening, and by the time Frances had replied gently but forcibly he had merged into the crowd.

"Did I ever tell you about my life among the Eskimos?" asked Richard, and shook his head in reply to the rug seller. He sipped the cognac which the waiter had brought, and added with approval, "Much more like it. Where were we? Oh, yes, with the Eskimos. . . ." He talked on. Frances was glad of the opportunity just to relax. She listened to Richard's inventions with a smile, and waited for him to finish the liqueur. Then they could get back to the hotel.

The dark-haired, sallow-faced chambermaid had just come out of their room. The towels over her arm were the obvious excuse. She smiled in her tired way.

"Good evening, Madame, Monsieur. You are back early tonight. Perhaps Madame is tired."

Frances agreed to that: she had just caught a glimpse of herself in the gilt-edged mirror on the wall. Perhaps it was the very large, very pink flowers on the wallpaper that made her feel so wilted. Richard said good night rather brusquely, and opened their door. The woman wasn't usually conversational, he thought, but she must have been surprised to see them. People generally talked too much when they were embarrassed. He locked the door behind them, and stood there, listening. Frances watched his face as she took off her hat. She liked him when he was worried: she liked the frown on his brow, the intent look in the thoughtful eyes. It had been his eyes which she had noticed when they had first met. She couldn't guess what lay behind their calm grayness; there was a hint of so many things. If that had been one of the reasons why she had married him, then she hadn't been disappointed.

Richard seemed satisfied. He had left the door, and started to undress.

"Bed," he said, and his eyes were smiling, now. "And don't, my love, clean each tooth for five minutes, tonight."

Frances laughed, and started to brush her hair, and then stopped with the hairbrush poised in midair. Her eyes were puzzled as they rested on her make-up box lying on the dressing table.

"I could *swear* that . . ." she began.

"I shouldn't," said Richard, his lips smiling, his eyes warning.

Frances bit her top lip. "I shan't be long now," she ended. Richard nodded approvingly. Good girl, he thought; she could take a hint without having it underlined.

Frances always lay on Richard's right side. It was hot and stuffy in the room, but Richard would open the windows before they went to sleep. He held her close to him. They could feel each other's breath coming in little warm waves as they talked, their low voices smothered in the pillow.

"What was wrong, Fran?"

"Someone has been meddling with my things. The cream jars were in the wrong order; you know how I always have them arranged in a certain way. They stand on a little tray, which you've got to lift up to get at the space underneath. Someone probably wanted to know what I kept there."

"What do you keep?"

"Just face tissues and cotton wool and odds and ends."

"Was anything missing?"

"My address book. You know the one, the little one I keep for addresses of hairdressers or hotels or cleaners in any place we have stayed abroad."

"That won't be much help to them."

"But who are they?"

"God knows. It might be friends of Blackbeard, or it might be someone who followed Peter more successfully than he thought. The maid is the obvious agent, anyway. I just couldn't place her when we met her in the corridor. And how did she know what time we usually returned to the hotel? She may have just been interested in how you get that complexion, or she may be yawning in that empty room next door, this very minute." He gripped Frances more tightly, and she let out a sudden squeal. Richard was nearer the truth than he would have cared to be. The dark-haired sallow woman, standing motionless in the empty room, her ear close to the wall, shrugged her shoulders: only murmurs and squeals in bed. A simple-minded race, the English. She moved silently to the door. She could go off duty now and report . . . Nothing, as usual.

Frances had asked, "You think we have been watched?"

"Only remotely. Our room has been searched, obviously, but there is nothing incriminating to find. And if they did follow us about Paris, then our movements have been innocent enough. The important thing will be whether anyone realized the meaning of tonight's incident, or whether we shall be watched tomorrow. They can follow us about, otherwise, until they are blue in the face."

"You sound confident." In the darkness, Richard smiled to himself. Confident? He had seldom felt worse in his life.

"The chap we met tonight seemed pretty calm and collected. He made everything look quite simple. Damned clever too. You got it, didn't you? One cigarette, and then, as neat emphasis, the watch which he wore the wrong way round so that we could see that it had stopped at one o'clock. I rather liked that touch."

"To be perfectly frank, I could hardly believe it was the clue. It was so easy."

"Well, it's all we've got to go on. Add one to one . . . and what do you get?"

Frances laughed. "It's too simple, really. And if at first you don't succeed . . ."

"Darling, why mention that when I'd like to get some sleep?"

"Sorry, Richard." She moved to kiss him and bumped her nose against his chin. "I'll pack tomorrow afternoon, and then we can leave anytime," she added sleepily. She stifled a yawn against his shoulder. "It's all this whispering," she said. "It makes me sleepy."

She was asleep by the time Richard had opened the windows and let the night air surge in with its welcome coolness. He looked at his wife's fair hair on the pillow, the curve of her cheek and the dark lashes. She slept like a child, with her hands resting above her head.

He remembered her voice, blurred with sleep. *We can leave anytime.* Leave, perhaps—but for where, and for what? He cursed Peter and himself. First instincts were often the right ones, when it was a matter of self-preservation. And keeping Frances safe was a matter of self-preservation for him. He should have stuck to his dislike of involving Frances. He ought to have come alone. But it had been easy to be persuaded, for the selfish reason, quite apart from the more practical one that this mission must seem a holiday as usual, that he would have been miserable without her. He lay and thought of the way in which two people, each with their own definite personality, could build up a third personality, a greater and more exciting one, to share between them. When two people succeeded in that, then they were complete. Without Frances, however definite his own personality might be, he was incomplete.

Sleep was impossible. He lay and watched the blackness of the courtyard bleach to gray, and felt the coldness of early morning strike his bare shoulders.

CHAPTER 6 THE AGILE RABBIT

A sudden coolness had come to the city. Frances shivered as she stepped out of the taxi. Above the roofs of the twisting narrow streets, she could see the illuminated dome of the Sacré Cœur. Behind her, withdrawing modestly into its shadows, was Le Lapin Agile. The doorman, like a nimble gnome in his red cap and tunic, darted down to meet them, and guided them through the narrow gate to the dark doorway.

Nothing had changed since they had last been here. It never did. The old grandfather, who had founded it, had died, but the rest of the family carried on in the way he had established. In the small entrance hall, Madame sat behind the counter with its shaded light gleaming on the trays of cherry brandy. The girl who sang so well to the guitar was leaning on the counter, talking to a young man in his shirt sleeves. She was dressed as usual in a skirt and blouse. There was a sound of a piano and of laughter from the narrow doorway at the end of the counter.

Frances and Richard waited until the applause told them that the Rabelaisian improvisor had finished. The girl nodded approvingly.

"I'll find you a place," she said, and led the way up the few stairs into the room. The long benches on either side of the monastery tables were well-filled, but the girl's eyes, accustomed to the dimness of the lighting, had found a bench where two more could sit. The shirt-sleeved man followed them, carrying two glasses of cherry brandy. You drank either cherry brandy or not at all.

The others at the table made room for Frances and Richard good-naturedly. They joked with the girl.

"Why don't you bring your guitar over here and sing to us?" asked one of the men. "It's only Marius here who is going to do a little recitation next. He is with poem, again. But we don't need to listen to it, we have been hearing it all evening." His round face creased with laughter. Everyone laughed, including Marius, a little self-consciously.

The girl smiled to Marius. "What is it tonight—a new one? Go on, do it now. I have time to listen, too."

Marius rose and hesitated. His thin, rather hard face relaxed. He might be a student, or an apprentice, thought Frances. He looked apologetically round the table and saw that Frances was watching him.

"I am not sure about the last couplet," he explained shyly to her. They were all looking at her, waiting for her to reply. She gulped, felt her cheeks afire, and decided to risk it.

"*Poète, prends ton luth!*" she declaimed with her best Alexandrine accent. Everyone laughed again. The fat jovial man was enjoying himself.

"The trouble with women," he said with mock seriousness, "is that they never finish quotations." He looked at his wife. "One of the troubles," he finished. Frances blushed again, and joined in the new chorus of laughter.

Richard was pleased. We couldn't have arranged it better, he thought, and looked sympathetically across the shadows of the room at a table where other foreigners had been grouped together. He leaned back against the stone wall, and filled his pipe. Marius had reached the ancient piano. He cleared his throat, and the conversations and arguments at the other tables politely diminished. He cleared his throat again, and, sweeping back the hair which fell over his eyes, began. Everyone was listening. Richard took the opportunity to look carefully round the room; his seat gave him a good view. He could observe without appearing to.

There was the usual crowd there. At first he couldn't see anyone remotely like their friend of the Café de la Paix. There might be the possibility of disguise of course. He looked at his watch. It was just after one o'clock: time enough. He looked at the large figure of Buddha at one end of the room, and his eye naturally traveled to the large figure of Christ on the Cross on the opposite wall . . . And then he saw the man. He couldn't be sure, but something about one of the men at the table at that end of the room seemed familiar. It might be . . . He gave all his attention to Marius, who was gathering himself to deliver the uncertain couplet. It was effective, judging by the applause. Marius, flushed with success, was returning.

The girl in the blouse and skirt rose to go.

"I have something new for you tonight," she explained.

"Sing, sing," they chanted.

"She has," explained the fat man, "a most charming voice, and she chooses her songs well. Or perhaps you know?"

"Yes, I know," said Frances.

"Aristide has set some of Villon's songs to music for her voice," the Frenchman continued. He nodded towards the man in shirt sleeves, who was now sitting down at the piano. He played softly to himself, as he waited for the girl to appear.

Marius and Richard had begun a discussion for two about the symbolist poets. Frances turned to the others. They were on to politics, now: one of the women had begun the argument.

"Don't spoil my evening," said the large man, almost savagely. "Politics, politics. There is no living, nowadays." He addressed himself suddenly to Frances. "I am sorry, but you will understand." Frances could think of several reasons. She wondered which of them was responsible. The Frenchman looked at her gloomily; the laugh-lines round his mouth straightened, giving it an unexpected bitterness. His brown eyes had become hard. He leaned over the table on his elbows and his hands marked each point as he spoke.

"Twice within seven months, I have had to look out my old uniform, close my business—I am a contractor—and make my good-bys. Twice. September 1938, April 1939." His wife beside him looked away quickly. His eyes, under the heavy brows, held Frances motionless. She could not even smile in sympathy. "There may be a third time. It will be too much. The third time will be just *two* too much."

Everyone sat silent for a minute, and then all began to talk at once.

"One war is enough for one lifetime," said his wife without lifting her eyes.

The girl in the blouse and skirt had entered again, carrying her guitar. The many voices of the crowded room faded into silence. Even the foreign visitors sat politely curious. The girl raised the guitar, its red ribbons falling over her arm. She smiled to the man at the piano.

"Aristide here has found music for the words of our François Villon. I shall sing two of his ballads."

Frances looked at the silent faces; she wondered how many of them hid the thoughts of uniforms waiting for the third time. It may have been the low sweet voice of the singer, or the simplicity of the music, or the poetry of the words. She felt her heart stifle. In it there were tears for the courage of ordinary people, hot rage against the disturbers of their lives. The Frenchman was right: it was too much. The singer's voice dimmed, sweetly lingering:—

> *Que ce reffrain ne vous remaine:*
> *Mais où sont les neiges d'antan!*

Richard's hand lay on her arm. "Steady," he said, "steady." There was something as well as gentleness in his voice. So he had seen the man, or hadn't he? She had no idea of the time. Perhaps they had failed. A moment of panic seized her. But Richard appeared calm. His eyes told her nothing was wrong, only to be prepared.

"I am afraid we must leave soon," he explained to the others. A chorus of genial protests rose.

"Then you must come back often. To this table," said the large Frenchman. "Let us drink to this." They lifted their glasses.

Frances suddenly said, "To all men of good will, who live and let live. And perdition to their enemies, breeders of hate and destruction." She was going to weep after all. Oh hell! . . . They drank. The good-bys were over. Richard led the way. The man from the Café de la Paix had just three minutes' start.

Others had begun to go too. A few late-comers were just entering. The little entrance hall was jammed. They made their way through with difficulty. Richard had got his hat, with the help of the man in shirt sleeves. He spoke for a moment to Madame. Still no one came. They left, as slowly as would seem natural, but the man had completely disappeared. They went down the steep steps. It had begun to rain, and the doorkeeper put up his enormous umbrella for them as they waited for a taxi. Richard swore softly. Frances knew then that something had gone wrong. He fished in his pocket for a tip for the doorkeeper, who was showing them his poems which he had printed on single sheets for sale.

And then the door behind them opened, and there was a path of light over the wet pavement. It was the man in shirt sleeves.

"Monsieur has left behind his book." He handed something to Richard. "Oh, yes," said Richard. He thought quickly. "Careless of me. Where did I drop it?" It was a small book and fitted into his pocket neatly. "In the hall when you spoke to Madame, and bought some cigarettes. The gentleman behind you saw it fall."

"Well, thank you very much," began Richard, but the man had given an easy wave of his hand and was already back in the shelter of the doorway. Again the street was in darkness; a taxicab had halted on the slope of cobblestones, and the red gnome was shutting the door. Richard leaned forward to give the taxi-driver their address. He noticed that more guests were leaving Le Lapin Agile. They stood grouped round the lighted doorway, and hesitated before the wet pavement. The man from the Café de la Paix was there among them. He might have been with the others, or he might have been alone. But one thing, anyway, thought Richard as the taxi skidded on the greasy streets: no one could say that he had been with the Myles'.

When they reached their room, Richard threw the book on the bed and went into the bathroom. Frances began to undress. She was determined she would wait for her cue. Inwardly, she was annoyed with herself. She had missed everything. She had been so interested in the people at their table that she had almost forgotten about the man, and she hadn't even seen him. She guessed that Richard was satisfied anyway, or he wouldn't be whistling. He undressed quickly, and sat on the edge of the bed as he set the small traveling clock's alarm for half-past six.

"We can always sleep in the train," he said philosophically, and picked up the book curiously. He hadn't even noticed that she had done his packing for him this afternoon when he made a tour of the chief Paris stations. (There were only three ways by which they would probably leave Paris: either by the north or by the south or by the east; and Richard had said it was just as well to know the early-morning express trains which left these stations.) But Frances had been mistaken. . . .

"Did you have a nice afternoon?" He nodded to the suitcases and grinned.

"Thank you, darling. Did you have a nice walk?" There was almost too much sweet solicitude in her voice.

Richard looked up quickly. "Come off it, Frances. You know I told you to leave my stuff."

"Someone had to . . ."

"My poor put-upon wife." He drew her down onto the bed and rolled her between the sheets. Frances began to laugh. It was no good harboring righteous indignation: not with Richard.

He picked up the book again. "Do you mind if I read in bed?"

"Not if you talk first; I'm too sleepy to wait until you've finished reading. I'm almost bursting with curiosity."

Richard was looking at the book in a puzzled way. "Yes, I may take quite a time to get through this." He held it out so that the title was towards her. Frances looked at it with a mixture of amazement and excitement. It was a guide to Southern Germany.

Richard kicked off his slippers and slid in beside Frances. His voice dropped naturally. "You didn't see him? He was there all right. Sorry to hurry you away, but if he didn't mean to get in touch with us inside the room, the only other alternative was for us to follow him out. He left on the dot of two. Then I lost him, or I thought I did. I had been expecting something unusual to happen. This book was the only thing that did. It's it—or nothing."

"And if you don't find any information there?"

"We are completely and beautifully stuck."

Frances adjusted herself comfortably for sleep. "Darling, you had better begin. It looks an all-night job." She yawned heartlessly and closed her eyes.

Richard settled the lamp beside the bed to suit him, and opened the book. It seemed a new edition. He began at the first blank pages, and examined each successive page carefully for any markings. His care was rewarded.

There was a small lightly penciled star opposite one of the sections in the contents list following the large map, title page and two introductions. It was the section on Nürnberg. There were still two other pencil markings on the list of contents; one was a small horizontal stroke, the other a vertical one. Star first, obviously, thought Richard and turned to the pages on Nürnberg.

The description of Nürnberg followed the usual thorough pattern. It led off with stations and hotels and other helps to tourists. Richard examined the small print carefully. There were so many helpful hints to tired travelers after each entry, so many abbreviations of map references and prices enclosed in neat brackets. It made finicky reading. A careful glance at a page wasn't enough. Richard groaned and started at the beginning of the page again. His eye-straining concentration was rewarded by the time he got to the section on tramways. Route 2 seemed interesting: from Gustav-Adolf-Strasse *via* Plärrer, Lorenzkirche, Marientor, Marienstrasse to Dutzendteich. A small horizontal line was neatly penciled before Marienstrasse. With so many brackets and hyphens and commas and colons mixed into the text, the line was scarcely noticeable. The marking connected with the pencil line in the list of contents. Nürnberg, Marienstrasse, horizontal line. He turned back to the contents page. The horizontal mark there lay beside Augsburg.

He studied Augsburg as he had done Nürnberg. Hotels, restaurants . . . He read on carefully, but it wasn't until he came to the historical details about the city that he made any further advance. There, among the early benefactors, was the name of one Anton Fugger (1495–1560). He liked the name of Anton Fugger, especially with that neat vertical line just in front of the A.–Nürnberg, Marienstrasse, Anton Fugger, vertical line. He turned quickly back to the contents' list. It was difficult to keep his excitement down. He forced himself not to be too confident. The vertical line marked Heidelberg.

This time, the information began with the air service and railway station. His eyes might have begun to tire with the strain, or perhaps he was too excited, or perhaps it was sleep. He knew he was jumping words. Frances slept comfortably beside him. He looked at the alarm, and checked it unbelievingly with his watch. It was nearly half-past five. There was no time to waste. He groaned again, and began to read, with his fist pressed hard against his chin. The discomfort checked that seductive idea of sleep.

He read on. Suddenly he sat up. It fitted in. God, it fitted in. He looked again: *Archæological Institute, free on*—yes, that was the penciled star all right—*free on Wednesday and Saturday*, 11 A.M.–1 P.M. So there it was, in its neat circle: Nürnberg, Marienstrasse, Anton Fugger, free on Wednesday and Saturday from eleven until one o'clock. A telephone book in Nürnberg would probably give the number of Fugger's house in Marienstrasse. But how to identify themselves when they met Herr Fugger? There must be some other clue. There had been no writing on the title page. What about a colophon? Failing anything there, he would have to examine the book right through perhaps in Nürnberg itself. But among the last blank pages he found two things. One was a red-rose petal, neatly pressed and pasted onto the paper. On the back of the page there were some music-notes, roughly jotted down in pencil after a treble clef. He whistled the notes to himself. The simple tune was vaguely familiar. All the notes were of the same value; it was this which had made the song seem vague at first. But it now was clearly recognizable. He relaxed back on his pillow and smiled amiably at the ceiling. He had forgotten about sleep. In any case, Frances would have to be wakened in less than fifteen minutes. What he needed now was a tub and a shave.

The sound of the running water drew Frances gradually out of sleep. Slowly and then suddenly she realized she was alone. She awoke fully with a panic of fear.

"Richard," she began, "Richard . . ." and then connected the sound of running water with a bath. She was calm again as Richard came out of the bathroom, the towel draped round him with one end slung over his shoulder. He had a crisp, curling beard of shaving soap.

"The elder Cato," he announced, "come to reprimand a slothful wife."

Frances looked at him sadly.

"No response? Is it as bad as that?"

"Go away, darling. I love you, but not at this hour." She settled drowsily on her pillow.

"Not on this morning, you don't, my love." He heartlessly pulled the sheet off the bed. Frances looked resigned. She lowered her voice.

"Where are we going?"

Richard sat down beside her. "Nürnberg."

"You've been there."

"Yes. Wake up, Frances."

"I haven't."

"No."

Frances roused herself. "What else did you find out?"

"You are like a red red rose."

"Oh. . . . I'm *what?*"

"My love. So the notes say."

"Richard, there is something peculiarly horrible about you this morning. God, how I hate men when they are secretly elated." She looked sadly at her husband, and then she began to laugh.

"Good. So you like Cato at last?"

"It's your beard, my sweet." She giggled weakly. "It pops."

"What?"

"The soap bubbles," she began, "listen . . ." She smothered her laughter.

"Anything to cheer a girl up. Are you really awake now? Well, listen, Frances. Get dressed. Get everything collected. Then we pay the bill and depart at once for the station. I got the train information yesterday, so everything is simple."

Frances sobered up. Richard was in earnest now. "All right. What actually did you find out last night?"

Richard was noncommittal. "A name and address in a town and the time we might visit it. Also that your hat will still be worn, and the first seven notes of a song."

"My love is like a red, red rose?"

Richard nodded. "Come on; rise and shine."

He obviously did not want to tell her any more than that, decided Frances as she bathed and dressed quickly, and packed away the final odds and ends. Richard was ready before she had put on her hat. He had finished writing the labels on the suitcases. Frances saw their name followed by the words *Passenger to Nice*. The room, stripped of their belongings, looked colorless in spite of the wallpaper. It was just another hotel bedroom.

The dark-haired, sallow chambermaid came in at half-past twelve. They were generally out by that time. The room looked empty. She had a sudden suspicion. Yes, she was right, they were not only out but gone. The boy who brought up the breakfast trays was whistling in the corridor. She ran to the door.

"Well, I see they have left. It is a bit sudden, isn't it? They must have been early."

"Yes. They didn't have breakfast. Pierre was downstairs on duty when they left."

"They are lucky, wandering about like that with no work to do. Did they go back to England?"

"Pierre said the labels were for Nice, and Michel drove them to the station."

"Nice? Well, some people have all the luck."

She waited for the boy to leave the corridor, and then she went downstairs. She searched for Michel before she slipped into the phone box. It was risky, if Madame saw her—but she couldn't wait until she was off duty. Fortunately this corner of the hall was dark, and she kept her voice low.

"Gone this morning. Gare de Lyon. For Nice. Nothing out of usual last night." Well, that was that nice little fee earned.

When they arrived at the Gare de Lyon, Richard paid the taxi-driver, Michel, as he directed the porter to the train for Nice. They were very early, the porter said. In that case, they would leave their bags at the left-luggage office while they had breakfast. Richard had the satisfaction of seeing the naïvely inquisitive Michel—it was part of his friendly interest —drive away. The porter was glad enough to have such a short trip. He departed with his tip, well-pleased. In ten minutes, Frances and Richard returned for their luggage with another porter. This time they drove to the Gare du Nord. Frances looked at Richard in the taxi, as he changed the labels on the suitcases. He was smiling broadly.

"I do believe you enjoy this," she said in amazement.

He laughed. "What about you?"

"I'm hungry."

"Well, we can have breakfast on the train. We'll travel luxuriously and get some sleep before Strasbourg."

As Richard had predicted, they breakfasted well. Frances watched him in the dining car with amusement.

"Every moment you look more and more like a cat before a dish of cream." Richard gave a laugh which degenerated into a yawn.

He said, "Well, I feel something is making sense. I'll tell you all about it as soon as we have finished our visit. Let's go back to the compartment."

"And sleep."

"I'll have a pipe, first."

Frances thought this strange. Richard didn't usually smoke a pipe until after lunch. However, back in the empty compartment she understood. Out of certain pages in the guidebook which he had studied last night he made very efficient lighters. When all that remained of them was curled fragments of charred paper, he threw the expurgated book out the window. It landed satisfactorily in a broad irrigation ditch. Richard watched it disappear, and then relaxed in his corner, stretching his legs. He gave Frances a satisfied smile.

"Everything all right with you?" he asked.

She nodded.

"Good. Everything's all right with me." His eyes closed. "Sorry," he added, his voice fading.

Frances looked at the trees and the fields and the sky. The express devoured the miles. Someone, she thought, ought to stay awake. But the journey was completely uneventful and, apart from an inner excitement at crossing the frontier, it was as dull as the scenery in the last stages of their travels. Once the minor thrills at Strasbourg had passed—when the engine had been changed for a (no doubt) superior German model, when the carriages had the last French dust swept from them efficiently and contemptuously by a squad of German cleaners, when their bags and money and passport had been thoroughly examined—there only remained the sagging feeling of relief. By the time they reached Nürnberg, Frances was cross and tired. She was resigned to a holiday in which the main excitement would merely be a succession of tensions. Richard was resigned to the fact that so far their luck had been almost too good to last.

CHAPTER 7   THE WALLED TOWN

It was very late when they did arrive in Nürnberg. Frances waited at the entrance to the Hauptbahnhof and stared across the warm darkness of the enormous square. Richard had told her that the old town lay beyond. Its lights were few. It seemed already asleep within its walls.

The porter had found them a taxi, at last. Richard gave the driver the name of the hotel. The driver looked at them. His face was large and round and expressionless.

"It isn't here, any more," he said.

The porter was listening. "The Königshof is near the same place. It is highly esteemed," he volunteered.

"All right, then," said Richard, "the Königshof."

They sat in silence during the short journey to the hotel.

"You could have walked," said the driver, as they got out of the taxi. He seemed as if he disapproved of their extravagance.

Richard made no reply.

"Did you know the Goldner Hahn well?" the driver asked suddenly. "I stayed there in '32. What happened to it?"
The man was silent.
"What happened to it?" Richard asked again.
The man hesitated. "Oh—they went away." His voice was as expressionless as his face. Richard noted Frances' speculative interest. He knew what she was thinking.
She was still silent when they reached their room. It was warm inside; the massive furniture made it feel still warmer. She opened a window and looked out into the Königstrasse. The houses had high steep roofs, some of them pitted with attic windows, while others turned their gable ends to the street. This was better, this was more like what she had imagined. She remained standing at the window, watching the moonlight on the roofs. When she moved at last, she found that Richard had unpacked some things for her. She smiled her thanks.
"Cheer up, old girl. You'll feel better in the morning," he said.
I hope, she added to herself.

But when Tuesday morning came and the constant hum of traffic outside their window awoke Frances, she did feel better. Richard was already dressed, and reading his Baedeker. They had breakfast in their room, and discussed their plans as they ate. Richard advocated the minimum of unpacking. No one noticed what you wore here, anyway.
While Frances had slept, he had decided to work in an opposite direction from their Paris experience. Instead of waiting the few days until Saturday came, they would call on Fugger tomorrow, and then they could spend three or four days playing the tourist in Nürnberg. But to Frances, he only remarked that today they could explore the old town, and leave the Castle and the Museum and the churches for the rest of the week.
"Unless I fry to death," Frances said. She looked out at the bright sunlight in the street, promising heat even at this early hour. Resignedly, she chose the thinnest town dress she had. Richard approved of the effect when she was at last ready, but he also looked at his wrist watch just slightly more pointedly than was necessary.
"Brute," said Frances, with her sweetest smile, and led the way out of the room.
There was that feeling of continual coming and going in the entrance hall which characterizes a busy town hotel. Just as well for us, thought Richard. Frances and he were only two more in the constant stream. The other guests were mostly German. They were serious-looking men and women, who walked quickly, as if they had important business to attend to. Perhaps they had. He noted the number of uniforms of one kind or another, and even—astounding thing—quick precise salutes and the violent two-worded greeting. It was astounding because it was so theatrical, so in-

congruous in a peaceful hotel lobby. He caught Frances' eye, and they both smiled gently. He imagined himself coming into a lecture hall at Oxford, surveying the rows of young faces before him, making a rigid salute and barking out "God save the King" in a parade-ground voice, before turning to his lecture on the metaphysical poets. He knew what his undergraduates would do. They would telephone anxiously for a doctor, two male nurses and a strait-jacket—and they would be right.

As they reached the front door, Frances paused to look at the roughly paved street and then at her shoes.

"I thought the heels were a mistake," said Richard.

Frances looked stubborn. "Well, if I change into my hiking shoes, I'll have to change my whole outfit. I'll manage."

A young man had come out of the hotel door; he halted as he heard Frances' voice, and looked at her, giving what Hollywood has perfected as the "double take." Then the pavement was crowded with the stamp of heavy boots. Frances was separated from Richard by a wall of brown shirts. She stepped backwards to the safety of the doorway, lost her balance and felt her heel sink cruelly into something soft. The young man winced, but stood his ground.

"I'm so sorry," Frances said and removed her heel. "*Verzeihung . . .*" That must have been a sore one, she thought.

"Pardon me," the young man said, lifting his hat and trying to walk away without limping.

Frances' handbag seemed to be infected with her embarrassment: it slipped from under her arm, and opened as it reached the pavement. The last uniform had passed, and in the temporary lull Richard bent down for the bag, and jammed the odds and ends back into place. The powder case rolled towards the man, who had turned as Frances had said "Damn." He picked it up, and handed it silently with a twist of a smile to Richard.

"Thank you," said Richard, and he meant it.

"You're welcome." He raised his hat again and walked quickly away, as if afraid of what Frances would do next. Richard looked down at her and shook his head.

"You surpassed yourself there, my sweet Dora. Now if you would really like to go somewhere, we can start on the old town. This way." He caught her arm as she moved off in the wrong direction.

"He was rather nice-looking. American, wasn't he? I liked his voice."

"Yes; yes; and rich baritone," Richard answered absent-mindedly. He was looking for a place to cross the street.

The exploration of the old town took care of the morning. Two o'clock found them exhausted in a beer restaurant, Richard having decided that the heat of the day called for a liquid lunch. Frances, atoning for the slow progress caused by her shoes—she *had* managed, but at a price—sat in sweet martyrdom as she talked and laughed. It was strange how the smell of beer clung to the room. The coffee did not taste very much like coffee, but she sipped it and kept her eyes off the beer mugs. She had never liked the stuff; from now on she would hate it. Even the table smelled of beer. Richard was asking her a question. How would she like a tram ride? Heavens, there was nothing she wanted less.

"Must we?" she asked as pathetically as possible.

Richard nodded. "I'm afraid so."

She lowered her voice. "Telephone book?"

"No good. I had a look at it when you were powdering your nose."

"Nothing there at all?"

"Nothing."

Frances resigned herself to the inevitable. "Well, let's go now, and get it over."

Richard finished his beer slowly. It was a good thing that one of them was having fun, thought Frances. Then she began to wonder. She had been in such a constant depression ever since they had arrived in Nürnberg. It was as if Gibbon's idea of the Middle Ages had interpreted itself here in the tortuous streets, the thick walls, the narrow crowding houses. A triumph of religion and barbarism.

"Well?" said Richard.

"I thought I liked Gothic."

"You like it spiritual and aspiring, my sweet."

"Perhaps it is that. Tell me, Richard, was Gibbon ever in Nürnberg?"

Richard laughed suddenly. Curious faces turned to look at them. They waited until the interest had subsided, and then they left.

"We must take a No. 2 tram, but God knows in which direction," said Richard.

"Going east or west?"

"Roughly east."

"Then it's this side."

A tramcar was approaching; there was no time for any argument. He followed Frances aboard with some misgivings, and then watched her trying to appear oblivious as the conductor agreed that they would be driven along the Marienstrasse.

"On a moor, or a hill or some place like that," said Richard, "but in a strange muddled-up town . . . It's quite beyond me how you know these things."

Frances relented. "I cannot tell a lie, darling. You saw the Lorenz Church?"

"Well, yes. We were just beside it."

"Well what way does a church point?"

"East, of course. . . . Upon my Sam." He grinned. "You know, Frances, just at the stage when a man thinks women have no brains, they confound him by some low cunning like that. Go on, have your laugh. You deserve it."

As they approached the Marientor, he pressed her hand.

"Keep your eyes open," was all he said. Frances remembered the name he had told her last night. They sat in silence, watching the shops and business houses, as the lumbering tramcar clanked its slow way along the Marienstrasse. They were now in the newer part of the town—the street was broader, and the names on the shops were less easy to see. Frances guessed that Richard had the idea that Fugger might be the name of some business; it was the one chance. For if there had been no Fugger of Marienstrasse in the telephone directory, then the only other way to find Mr. Fugger was either to make enquiries at the post office, which would be dangerously stupid, or to explore the Marienstrasse themselves. There must be a name to see, somewhere, or else no one could possibly get in touch with the retiring Mr. Fugger.

The tram had come to the end of the Marienstrasse. They had seen nothing which could help them.

"We'll have to walk. Sorry, Fran; you must be tired." They got off the car at the next stop, and started back towards their street.

"We'll try this side again," said Richard, and took Frances' arm. They walked slowly along, and covered two thirds of the street. Then Frances suddenly felt Richard's hand tighten. They stopped, as they had done at half a dozen other points in the street. It was a small bookseller's shop with a narrow window space and doorway, completely overshadowed by the larger, more prosperous buildings on either side. They looked at the books displayed in the window. They were mostly curiosities, with the title pages open to show the brown spots of age. There were also some music books. One, a collection of songs, was lying open.

"Very interesting," Richard said, and they walked on. He hoped Frances wouldn't look at the sign above the window. She didn't. It was of no help, anyway. It merely said BUCHHANDLUNG in faded letters; but above the door had been small, neat, white lettering: A. FUGGER.

CHAPTER **8** A. FUGGER

Next morning they left their hotel at half-past nine, and began their search through the bookshops of Nürnberg. Richard wanted a certain collection of early German lyrics. The two bookshops which they first tried were very modern; they specialized in books with streamlined printing and magnificent photographs, or in imposing editions of carefully selected authors. In the second shop, the assistant shook his head decisively. The only place they would be likely to find such a book might be in the smaller, secondhand dealers'. They thanked him, and walked towards the Marienstrasse. It was just eleven o'clock as they reached the small bookshop with the brown-spotted title pages displayed in the window. Richard noted that the books had been changed since yesterday, except for the collection of old songs, and that it had been moved to another corner of the window.

Inside the shop, there was the sleepy, dusty feeling which its outside had promised. The bookshelves ran ceiling height around the walls, and there were books overflowing onto the two large tables which crowded the narrow room.

At a corner of one table, a girl with glasses was working with scissors and paste. She had a white face, and dull blue eyes, and her hair was tightened back so ruthlessly that it hurt Frances to look at it. She looked up expectantly as the door creaked shut behind them. Frances had the feeling that the girl was disappointed. She left her work reluctantly, and came forward with no smile on her pale lips. No, she didn't think they had any such edition. She had never heard of it. As she made out that they were foreigners, she asserted her knowledge still more: she was sure, absolutely sure that such an edition did not exist. She neither offered to verify it from any catalogue, nor moved over to the poetry section to find anything else which might interest Richard. He exchanged glances with Frances, and then he searched in one of his pockets and brought out a small clipping. He handed it to the girl.

"The edition does exist," he said, as politely as he could. "Teubner printed it in Leipzig in 1836."

The girl took the sheet of paper, and held it without looking at it. The truth is, thought Frances, she doesn't want us here at all.

Richard raised his voice. "Is there anyone here, then, who *does* know about German lyric poetry?" The girl's face was still expressionless, but her eyes shifted for one moment to a door in the back wall of the shop.

"We haven't got it," she said.

"I'm sorry," said Richard. Frances knew by the cold edge in his voice that he was angry. She moved over to the pile of books on the nearest table, and lifted a volume. If it came to a test of endurance, she was determined to outlast the girl.

"Music, here," she said with charming surprise. She kept her voice as lighthearted as she could, and gave the silent girl a dazzling smile.

"You don't mind if I look through these? Thank you so much." Without waiting for an answer, Frances proceeded to blacken her white gloves on the dusty covers.

The door at the back of the shop opened. A short, stout man entered. He was in his shirt sleeves, and mopped his brow with a handkerchief.

He had shut the door behind him, but not before Richard had smelled something singeing, something burning. Paper, could it be?

The small man looked at the girl in some irritation as he said, "I thought I heard customers." He turned his back on her abruptly and listened to Richard's questions. The girl picked up her scissors again, and went on with her work, but Frances noticed that she made only a pretense of being busy.

The bookseller was interested. "That was a very fine collection," he said. "I had a copy at one time, but I believe it was bought. Over here I have some of the older editions of lyrics; I've so many books I sometimes forget what I have." He pointed to the farthest bookshelves. His eyes were fixed for a few moments on the red rose of Frances' hat.

She said, "I am very interested in some of these old song collections." She waved her hand towards the music table. The bookseller looked at her gloves in dismay.

"But the books are filthy," he cried. "Ottilie, where is the duster?" Ottilie mumbled something about the next room.

"Get it then," he said sharply. Ottilie went reluctantly towards the back door.

"Helpful creature," said Richard, more to himself than to the others. Frances had already picked up a large green volume, which she had noted particularly. Songs of All Nations read the fading gold letters. She turned quickly to the page which the index had numbered. She smiled to the bookseller.

"You are very kind," she said, and smoothed down the page with the back of her hand. She held the book flat on the table so that both men could see the song title clearly. The bookseller's eyes flickered as they read "My love is like a red, red rose" (*translated from the English*). And then he smiled gently, his round fat face creasing with genial puckers. He mopped his brow again, and Frances closed the book carefully. She had just replaced it exactly when Ottilie was with them again. She had come back very quickly indeed, for such a slow-moving person. She shook her head disapprovingly over the soiled gloves.

She actually spoke. "It would have been better to take off your gloves," she said.

"But my hands would have become dirty."

"It is easier to wash hands than gloves."

"But I couldn't put my gloves on again, over dirty hands," explained Frances gently. Ottilie shrugged her shoulders, and then suddenly became aware of the fact that the two men had gone to the far corner of the room. Frances hardheartedly pointed out a book to dust. It was a curiosity on early Church music.

"Do you like to sing?"

The girl said, "Sometimes." She looked as if she were going to follow the men.

"Do you like Mozart or do you prefer Wagner?" Frances continued relentlessly.

"Wagner." If eyes could poison, I am already writhing on the ground, thought Frances.

At that moment, the bookseller was shaking his head sadly. His voice was clearer. "No, I am afraid it's gone. Ottilie, do you remember a small book bound in red calf which I bought from Professor Wirt?" Ottilie shook her head too; she made a movement as if to go over to where the men stood.

"Have you got any editions of *Lieder* for a soprano voice?" cut in Frances with her disarming smile. Ottilie threw one last glance at the bookseller. The words "edition," "Leipzig," "difficulty" reached them. It sounded the usual business talk. Ottilie searched for the songs. Despite the foreigner's smile, there was a certain firmness in her tone of voice. Ottilie knew that type of customer. The quickest way to get rid of them was to find what they asked for; they knew what they wanted. If only she had recognized the type when they entered the shop, they would have been away by this time. But they had seemed easy to deal with, judging from their appearances. She found two editions, and watched Frances look through the contents with interest. Her last suspicion melted as the men came back to the table.

Richard addressed Frances. He spoke in English, carefully, noting the sudden gleam of concentration in Ottilie's eyes. He chose simple words, which would be understood by anyone who had had English at school.

"He cannot find the book. He must order it from Leipzig. Perhaps it may not be there. It may take time to find it elsewhere. It is a pity."

Frances recovered herself, and said gravely and just as clearly, "I am sorry. Perhaps we should go to another bookshop." She was enjoying herself immensely.

Richard returned to German. "My wife suggests another shop. Would you be so good as to advise us?" The bookseller smiled benignly. He dictated two addresses to Ottilie, who wrote them down, and Richard put the slip of paper in his pocket.

"If you cannot find it," the bookseller said, "then come and see us again. If I am not here, then Ottilie will take the order." He was looking speculatively over Frances' shoulder, out into the street. "Good day," he added suddenly, and walked with quick short steps to the back room.

The abrupt ending startled Richard. He saw a look of warning in his wife's eye. She had either noticed or felt something. As Ottilie wrapped one of the songbooks for Frances, they made their way to a bookcase near the door. Richard observed that the girl was glancing at her wrist watch, that she was taking little interest in tying up the parcel. As Richard handed her the money, she seemed as if she were not even counting it. . . . And then the front door swung open. It opened with such terrific violence that the hinges shrieked a protest which made Frances jump.

Three large men strode in, nearly upsetting Ottilie. Richard could have sworn that there was almost an approach to a smile on her face. She gestured quietly towards the back door. The three men strode on. Their boots hypnotized Frances. They moved as if they belonged to the same body. They drew their revolvers. The leader turned the handle of the door, and then kicked it open. But there were no shots, no voices. Frances found herself breathing again.

She looked with just sufficient amazement at the girl. "What's wrong?" she asked. "Burglars?" The girl gave her first real smile. Frances watched its contempt and was satisfied.

The men filed out of the back room. Their self-assurance was replaced by bad temper.

"Where is he?" the leader snapped. The girl's smile faded. Contempt gave way to fear.

"He went in there." She pointed to the back room. "There is no way out."

"There is a window, fool. Who are these?" He nodded towards Frances and Richard.

"Customers." The girl was sullen in her disappointment.

"What is your name? What do you want here?" He fired questions at Richard.

Richard looked surprised, and then let the right tone of slight annoyance creep into his voice as he answered. Frances registered appropriate amazement but she left everything to Richard. This was his show, and he was doing remarkably well as the innocent bystander. He was explaining at some length that they had tried two other bookshops and had failed in their search for this book; that they had been directed to the smaller secondhand dealers; that the book was still unfound; that the assistant in this shop had been good enough to write down the names of two other shops where . . . He at last found the slip of paper with Ottilie's sharply pointed script, and handed it to the leader of the men. Ottilie, on the verge of tears, verified the statement. It suddenly dawned on Frances that A. Fugger was gaining some very valuable minutes. It seemed to dawn on the leader too, or perhaps his first suspicions were fading. He impatiently interrupted Richard's description of the book.

"I shall leave this man with you to get further particulars. I have work to do." He stepped back, brought his heels sharply together, and raised his arm. He barked out his war cry. Now we're sunk, thought Frances. She saw Richard stiffen slightly, and then relax again as he gave an inclination of his head and said, "Good day."

The German trooper raised his voice. "I gave you our German greeting!"

"And I gave you our English one." Richard's voice was very quiet. "That is only politeness."

At the word *politeness*, the German looked searchingly at Richard, and

then at Frances. They held their expressions, and returned look for look.
There was a moment's tension, and then the two uniforms had marched
away, leaving the third to produce a notebook and pencil. It was a good
sign that they hadn't been taken to some kind of police station, thought
Frances, and touched the wooden table.

It was all over in ten minutes. The Nazi snapped his book shut. They all
made such businesslike gestures, thought Richard irritably. Did it really
prove greater efficiency to walk with a resounding tread, to open doors by
practically throwing them off their hinges, to shut an insignificant notebook with an imitation thunder clap? Probably not at all, but—and here
was the value of it—it made you look, and therefore feel, more efficient.
The appearance of efficiency could terrify others into thinking you were
dynamic and powerful. But strip you of all the melodrama of uniforms
and gestures, of detailed régime worked out to the nth degree, of supervision and parrot phrases and party clichés, and then real efficiency could
be properly judged. It would be judged by your self-discipline, your individual intelligence, your mental and emotional balance, your grasp of
the true essentials based on your breadth of mind and depth of thought.
Richard studied the young man opposite him. Viewed dispassionately, he
was tall and thin; he was already going bald; his chin was weak despite the
posed pout of the lips; but whatever strength his chin lacked, his eyes
with their intense stare sought to gain. It was a pity the effect was so like
that of a goldfish.

"That is all," the Nazi said. "We shall find you at the hotel if there is
anything else we need to know."

Frances leaned over the table and fixed him with wide-open, innocent
eyes. "Why?" she asked gently.

"Why?"

"Yes. Why? We are English visitors, we visit your bookshops, we buy a
book, and then you ask us questions and questions because the man who
owned this shop was a burglar."

"A burglar?"

"Well, don't tell me he was a *murderer!*" Frances was shocked. The
trooper looked perplexed.

"I mean," explained Frances as if to a child, "in England the police come
to arrest a man if he is suspected of a crime like theft or murder."

The man exchanged a look of amusement with Ottilie. Then he said
stiffly, "This is not England, thank God."

"Quite," said Richard.

Frances was keeping her jaw clenched; keep me from laughing out loud,
she prayed, especially when it comes. It came. The arm shot out, the heels
clicked, the magic words were invoked. The Myles' bowed and said "Good
day," gravely.

When they left A. Fugger's bookshop, Ottilie had again picked up her scissors and was bending over the table.

"Charming wench," said Richard. "One of the higher types, I suppose, of Nordic womanhood."

Frances had her own private joke. "No one told her to stop her work, and so she goes on. How long will it take before she realizes that she is already out of a job? Richard, if ever a sailor needed grog, that sailor's me."

They walked back to the old town at a medium pace. They didn't see anyone following them, but probably someone would. Richard, continuing his role of the wandering scholar, discovered another small bookshop with much secondhand material. The assistant, a pleasant young man with really gentle manners—Frances sat on a chair and watched him with a mixture of pleasure and relief—promised to make enquiries for the book, after Richard had spent half an hour in the poetry section. He bade them good morning like a human being. In fact, thought Frances, he is the first really obviously human being I've met since I arrived here.

When they got to their hotel, Frances went upstairs to change her gloves. Richard sat in the entrance hall and looked through a Nürnberg paper. It seemed as if the inhuman Poles and the wicked Jews were behaving with abominable, not-to-be-tolerated cruelty to the Germans who were living in Poland. The editorial worked itself up into a fine lather. It made crude reading. By the time Frances came downstairs, he was very bored. It was not only crude, it was an insult to intelligence.

He looked at Frances, and was instantly aware that something had happened. The look she gave him was too intense. She surprised him by suddenly standing on her toes and kissing him; but it brought her close enough to him so that he could hear the word "Searched," spoken with motionless lips. So they had taken advantage of their slow return to the hotel, as he had hoped they might. He returned her kiss and said, "Good."

Frances saw the American, whose foot she had mutilated yesterday morning, halt in amazement. On an impulse, she smiled to him. He reddened as he raised his hat and turned hastily away. Perhaps he didn't like to be found looking quite so amazed.

"Let's eat," she suggested. "I'm ravenous. Only, not a sausage place." She shuddered. Last night's dinner had been at one of the sausage showplaces, small and amusing, except that the whole menu was devoted to sausage. It was strange how her mind, as well as her stomach, rebelled when the choice was sausage or sausage or sausage.

"I'd like an omelet, and not one with apricot jam in it either, and fruit, and some hock, and coffee such as it is," she decided.

"I must say that for someone who comes from England you are pretty snooty about coffee."

"Well, it is even worse than ours, and that's something."

They found a restaurant near at hand, where they had their late lunch.

They ate it leisurely, and sat smoking their cigarettes long after Richard had paid the bill. The room had emptied, much to the annoyance of two uniformed men who were seated in one corner. As Richard said, it made things look a bit too obvious. The men may have come to the same conclusion. At any rate, they rose at last with bad grace, and on their way out clumped past the table where Frances and Richard sat. Richard had a Baedeker opened in front of him—lying between his elbows as he leaned forward to light his fifth cigarette. As the men passed, he looked up and spoke. Would they be so good as to help him? He and his wife were strangers, and wondered if it were possible to explore the charms of Dutzendteich this afternoon, or would it be better to make a day's excursion? The men were obviously at a loss for words. One said yes, the other said no, and then they both left the table.

"Well, it might be better to see the Burg this afternoon, after all," said Richard. Even if the men couldn't understand any English, at least the clearly spoken *Burg* would stick.

Frances watched their progress to the door. "They are phoning," she reported.

"Time to leave," said Richard, and tucked the Baedeker prominently under his arm. They walked quickly to the door, past the man at the public telephone and his worried companion. Frances gave him a sweet smile. She felt suddenly generous.

They entered a tramcar, at the Königstor, which carried them westwards and then northwards round the whole town. The heat was intense. Frances was glad of the open windows of the tram, which, as it moved, gave at least the impression of a breeze. They skirted the thick walls and their broad dry moat, and at last reached the Castle. There were a number of visitors to the Burg. Frances and Richard mixed casually with them and made a leisurely tour of the grounds. They didn't look back once. Richard said it would make whoever was following them in whatever uniform happier. It would have been discouraging for them really if Frances had insisted on carrying out her idea of looking back every hundred yards, smiling broadly and waving a cheery hand. . . . And Richard didn't really mind being followed in this way. They had nothing to hide . . . now. He added to himself, if A. Fugger made it, that is.

Richard had left the Five-Cornered tower to the last. He had a feeling that Frances might discover another allergy there. It was full of frightfulness, he remembered.

"Are you sure you really want to see this—It is rather monotonous, you know—" he asked as they reached the doorway. "There's no law compelling us to go in."

Frances looked surprised. "Why not? It's only an old prison tower with a torture chamber. I've been to the Tower of London, and the Conciergerie . . ."

Richard shook his head doubtfully. "This one could teach those places a thing or two." But he had only piqued her interest. Frances had already entered. Richard bought the tickets, and followed, with a shrug of his shoulders.

He had been right, after all, but Frances wouldn't admit it at first. Half-way through the tour of the long rooms, she began to move more quickly as the exhibits became more diabolic. Her eyes viewed unbelievingly the directions for extracting the greatest amount of pain which were hung on the wall above each instrument of torture. They were printed in black-letter for the most part, and were complete with diagrams, in case the minute detail of text wasn't sufficiently clear to ensure the fullest effects.

She suddenly spoke. "The cold-blooded beasts." Her voice was a mixture of incredulity and disgust. A tall young man, standing morosely before an intricate object of spiked iron, whose function had been to pierce and tear and burn all at the same time, turned as he heard her voice. There was an expression of fellow-feeling on his face, followed by a look of recognition. Frances, whose remarks had been for home consumption, stopped in embarrassment. The man looked as if he would speak, and then didn't. Frances felt he was leaving it to her.

"How's your foot?" she asked. "I'm really sorry, and I assure you it isn't a habit of mine."

"That's all right." His face relaxed, but he still didn't smile with any enthusiasm. "Enjoying this?" he added, with just the right note in his voice.

Richard grinned; he liked this man. "They made it quite an art, didn't they? The pages from the *Torturer's Handbook* are peculiarly thorough," he said, and won a smile from the American. Something caught the man's eye at the other end of the room, and a slight frown appeared; but it was gone so suddenly that Frances wondered if she was beginning to imagine things. She looked carelessly in the same direction. There were two uniformed men, who seemed to be interested in them rather than in the exhibits. She let her eyes pass through them, then over them, and then on to a German family who were arguing over one of the printed directions with naïve interest.

"Is there much more of this?" she asked.

The man said, "Piles of the stuff. I've just taken a look into the tower place and gotten a cold welcome from the Iron Maiden. There are several models of her."

"She would seem mild after these. At least she would kill you, and not turn you into a piece of gibbering flesh," said Frances. She turned to Richard. "You win. I thought I could manage historical objectivity. After all, I was brought up on Foxe's *Book of Martyrs* . . . But where's the way out?"

The American smiled. "It's past the tower dungeons. You can't escape them."

Frances looked at him. "You are in league with my husband. Our name is Myles, by the way. Would you come and have something to drink? I'm parched."

The American gravely acknowledged that he was parched too, and he knew of a good beer place just down the hill. They left the Five-Cornered Tower, to the amazement of the man on duty at the exit door, who pointed out to them that they had only seen half of the display. Outside, it was pleasant to feel the warm sunshine, and see the green trees and ordinary people looking neither efficient nor thorough. And then a detachment of troopers marched past them; actually, they were only a group of men going to some meeting, but they had chosen to march in military formation. Their faces were expressionless under their uniform caps. Frances felt her depression return. Men who marched like that, who dressed like that, whose faces held the blankness of concentration and dedication, were a menace, a menace all the more desperate because of the hidden threat.

"You are looking very solemn," said the American.

"I was thinking of icebergs. You know, one tenth above to impress you, and the rest beneath to terrify you."

"*If* you know the peculiarity of icebergs," said the American, with a quick glance at Frances. "There are still plenty of people who think there's very little of them under the water. But why did you come to Germany this year? I haven't met any English here so far. At first I thought you might be here to worship at the shrine, but you seem to have the wrong reactions for that."

Richard answered that. "Oh, the usual inquisitiveness. We wanted to see for ourselves. We haven't been in Germany proper since the new era got well under way. We thought this might be our last chance."

They had reached the Rathaus-Keller, and the American hadn't any opportunity for further questions until they were settled at a table, and beer was ordered for the men—Frances insisted on tea. She noted that her order gave the American some delight, although he really was very polite about trying to hide his amusement. I suppose I ought to play true to form, she thought, to keep up the national character. She had begun well with the big-footed note when she had trampled on him yesterday, and tea in the afternoon was another authentic touch; tonight, she really ought to ask him to dine with them, and wear a dinner dress. Only, Richard and she never traveled with dinner clothes; it would be such a pity to disappoint him. However, the American seemed less amused, and more convinced, when two hot cups of tea had produced more visible coolness than his two steins of beer. Frances caught his eye.

"There's method in our madness," she suggested, and noticed he looked a little disturbed, as if he had been found impolite. It was difficult talking to someone who didn't know you, especially when you both had a common language and thought that that made everything easy. There was always the chance that your words would be taken to mean too little, or too much. That was what made all the English-speaking peoples so damned touchy with each other. Someone who spoke a foreign language had more allowances made for him.

"By the way, we don't know your name, yet," Frances said. "We can't go on just calling you 'the American.'" The man smiled. Thank goodness, thought Frances, he gave up the idea that I was trying to reprimand him. He was searching in his pocketbook for a card.

"This makes it easier," he said. He was, they read, HENRY M. VAN CORTLANDT from High Tor, New York. He was, he said, a newspaperman, originally working in New York City, but now on an assignment in Europe looking for symptoms.

"War?" asked Richard.

"Well, perhaps that. What do you think?"

Frances looked at the well-cut features opposite her, and the well-brushed fair hair. The jaw was determined; the slightly drawn eyebrows gave a certain intensity. You would hardly notice the color of his eyes; it was as if the other features of his face overshadowed them. His skin was tanned—if it hadn't been tanned it might have seemed pale, even sallow. He had gone on talking without waiting for Richard's reply, and he talked well, with a fluency which showed he had either thought about his subject a lot or had already argued it into a neat pattern. As he talked, he smiled a good deal, showing very white, even teeth; but in repose, his mouth looked firm, even tight-lipped. Frances watched him as she listened to the well-tailored phrases. A very direct, a very controlled and a very impulsive young man.

"But surely you never took Munich seriously?" he was asking Richard.

And a rather disbelieving one, too, it seemed.

Frances spoke. "We were still at the stage of taking anything seriously or at the least hoping we could take it seriously, as long as the magic word of peace could be spoken. Until this spring. The march into Prague ended that coma."

Van Cortlandt shook his head. "Well, we never thought that in America."

"You mean you think we have been playing a kind of game? That we shall go on playing it, as long as we can keep ourselves out of war?"

"Well, if you put it so frankly, yes."

Frances leaned forward on her elbows. "Your President doesn't think so. I hear you've been calling him a warmonger because he really knows what's going on in Europe."

"Nice weather we've been having," suggested Richard. "Warm, though."

The American went on: "But Britain's policy for the last years . . ."

"I know," said Frances. "In America it is called isolationism, freedom from foreign entanglements, unwillingness to die on foreign fields. We've been trying all that. It hasn't worked. We admit it . . . we've come out of the ether . . ."

"And you're telling me that Britain is going to take off its nice clean coat and get its nose all bloodied up in defending Poland? What would you get out of it anyway?"

"A country fights for two main things, either for loot or for survival. We'll fight along with our friends for survival. The Axis is after loot. If Poland, or any other country, is attacked, then it is the signal for any nation who doesn't want to become a part of Germany to rouse itself. It may be the last chance."

Van Cortlandt smiled comfortingly. "Don't worry. I don't think you'll find your country at war. Your politicians will always see plenty of other chances."

"That's my main point. The politicians won't dare. The people are aroused now."

Van Cortlandt still looked unconvinced. "Well, that's a new one to me. We have some pretty swell news-hounds, and they nearly all scent out more appeasement."

"Their sense of smell has led them to the wrong lamp post this time. They will look very funny there, when the trouble starts."

"I tried the weather," said Richard, "and that wasn't much good. I think we'd be better talking about something else, for neither of you is convincing the other in the slightest, and we'll know soon enough which of you was nearer the truth. As Count Smorltork said to Mr. Pickwick, 'The word poltic surprises by himself.' Anyway, I have the unpleasant but increasing conviction that all of us who argue so much would be wiser if we learned to make aeroplanes or shoot a machine gun. That's only my academic point of view, of course. But that seems the only answer for certain people."

He nodded to a group of men in brown shirts at another table. "Now what about dinner?" he added.

Van Cortlandt rose. "Sorry, I've got to see a man."

Richard rose too. "We are sorry too. We shall see you again soon, sometime, I hope."

"Yes." The American's voice didn't seem overjoyed at the prospect. "Thanks for the beer. Good-by."

Frances looked after him sadly. "He really was so nice, you know, before he got caught up in his theories. I suppose if your country is three thousand or whatever it is miles away you can afford the luxury of pros and cons. I think you punctured him, someplace, Richard. He's probably saying we are one of the 'bloody English' at this moment."

"Nonsense. He handed criticism out. If you do that, you have also got to expect to take it. Anyway, hairsplittings are really becoming so very out of date. The time for theories is really past. But keep off politics, after this, Frances, even if you feel you have got something approaching an answer.

What do you say about something to eat, and then a movie, and then bed?"

Frances nodded her approval. There was much she wanted to know about A. Fugger. She stopped worrying about van Cortlandt and began thinking of the little man who had walked with quick short steps into that back room. Had he got away? Could it be that the Nazis were already picking out each agent in the chain, or was A. Fugger wanted on another charge? They would find out, one way or another, but it would be unpleasant waiting.

Richard had looked round the large room. At a discreet distance, the two men who had visited the Five-Cornered Tower that afternoon were sitting at a table. They had become hungry, it seemed, and had just ordered food. Richard waited until the steaming plates were put in front of them, until they had taken their first mouthful.

"Now's the time, Frances." She abandoned A. Fugger, and followed her husband quickly to the door. He seemed amused about something. As they left the room, he turned back to see the two men rising angrily to their feet.

"Would you mind, Frances, if we went to the flicks first of all, and then ate when we came out? I think that would be an idea." Frances saw the gleam in his eye. There was a joke somewhere.

So they went to a picture house. After fifteen minutes, Richard decided he couldn't see through the large woman in front of them, so they moved quietly to different seats, behind their original places. Richard's joke seemed to be getting better and better.

As he explained to Frances in bed that night, "They were hungry and when we landed in the cinema, they might have gone out in relays for their dinner. Then we moved our seats, and they didn't notice it at first. It was pretty dark, you know. We were just sitting down behind them when they noticed we were no longer in our first seats. That was really funny. It was easy for them to find us again, as the place was almost empty, but for five minutes they had quite a bad time of it. That probably decided them to stay together, standing at the back of the theater in case we changed our minds again. I could feel them getting hungrier."

"Why didn't we lose them when we had the chance?"

"And make them realize that we disliked being followed? They'd interpret that as a guilty conscience. Better pretend that it seems very harmless and amusing, the kind of silly adventure which you like to tell your friends about when you get home."

But about A. Fugger he wouldn't say anything.

"The less you know from now on, the better for you, my sweet." And that was that.

It was Frances who lay awake tonight. She thought of the bookseller; of the tall American who had either been offended, or bored; of the constant rhythm of marching boots. When she fell asleep her thoughts were still with her, and chased her through the Five-Cornered Tower. Richard was beside her, for she spoke to him and heard him answer, but she couldn't see him. A. Fugger was there trying to show her the way out, but he spoke in a strange language and she kept straining to understand it. The American was there too, observing everything, but contenting himself with a sad smile when she took the wrong turning. It must have been the wrong turning although it had seemed the only right one, because then there was no way out, and she was looking at the Iron Maiden, and the face was that of the girl Ottilie, and the hands were real. The fingernails were long and pointed, and they were colored blood-red.

CHAPTER **9** NÜRNBERG INCIDENT

Richard watched Frances closely, next morning. She had drunk several cups of tea and smoked three cigarettes. He kept silent about last night. Whatever had disturbed her sleep would gradually lose its detail and, if he didn't emphasize it by referring to it, it might lose its importance and merge into the vagueness of dreams that are past. He thought of something to do which would be interesting without being exciting. They would have to spend at least one more day in this place, perhaps even two or three if it seemed a good thing to do.

He made his voice as normal as possible. "What about the Germanic Museum today? It should be innocuous, and you'll like the costume section. If you ever do more designing in Oxford, you may find some good ideas there. Better take your notebook and pencil."

Frances nodded absently; she was wondering when they might leave Nürnberg and where they would have to go. . . . And there was always the thought whether A. Fugger had escaped. If he had been caught, there would be, no doubt, some ingenious way of trying to make him talk. And yet, did any trusted agent, such as he must have been, ever talk? Weren't they chosen for their capacity to keep silent even under the greatest persuasion? But then, they were human beings too. Somehow, her notebook and designs for Oxford dramatics seemed very remote this morning. Richard's voice had been light, but the slight emphasis with which he clipped his words proved that he was not as carefree as he would have her believe. She decided wisely not to pester him with questions about their plans. He was probably completing them now.

The silence in which they traveled to the Museum bolstered up this idea in Frances' mind. Their two watchdogs attached themselves at a reasonable distance. It seemed as if it didn't matter if they were noticeable. Frances thought this over. They had been so very obviously under watchful eyes, and their room had been so very obviously searched. She came to the conclusion that this might be especially subtle technique. Perhaps Richard and she were to feel persecuted, intimidated, very much in the power of a mighty secret police. The very cold-bloodedness of this cat-and-mouse game was to make them leave Germany if they really were only harmless tourists. If they were less innocent than they seemed, then they might be trapped into making a mistake. As for the mistake which they might make . . . Frances couldn't think of any agent trying to get in touch with one of his men at this stage. He would be liable to lie low, and he would most certainly try to lose the men who were trailing him. That might be it: if they were guilty, they might make clever efforts to free themselves from their two shadows. It was the natural reaction of any secret agent to outwit the other fellow. That indeed could be their mistake. She began to understand just how intelligent Richard had been last night, when he hadn't left the picture house.

But one thing still needed explaining. If the Nazis thought they were worth terrifying or trapping, they would surely not let them wander about for the next few days without some real shadow trailing them—someone, Frances began to believe, who would do his job very efficiently and secretly, someone who would keep on the job after the two men had been eluded. The more she thought of this, the more convincing she found it. It never paid to underestimate your opponents. Better credit them with too much than too little.

She looked at Richard. She became surer that he had guessed this too: yesterday he had taken such care not to lose the uniformed men. As they crossed the broad Sterntor, and found themselves momentarily isolated from people, Frances spoke for the first time.

She said, "They aren't the only ones." It was half a question.

Richard squeezed her arm affectionately. "Right you are. Too obvious." That confirmed her guess why they hadn't slipped out of the cinema last night, instead of innocently changing seats. One thing gave her some amusement: it looked as if the two stooges didn't know of a third man themselves. Otherwise they wouldn't have swollen their ankles, standing hungrily at the back of the picture house. They could have relaxed, depending on their accomplice, if they had known about him.

They were in the Museum until it closed at four o'clock. After that, all Frances asked was to be allowed to sit somewhere for a long long time, with something cool and liquid on the table before her—in the open air, if it could be managed. Richard arranged it, by taking her to a near-by restaurant where there was both a garden for Frances and beer for himself.

He looked thoughtfully at her as they sat in the coolness of the trees.

"I think the city heat is too much for you, Frances," he said at last. "It might be better for us to leave Nürnberg and go nearer the mountains. There's a nice little resort south of Munich on the Starnberger See. There's good bathing there. Or if you wanted some climbing, we could go farther south into the Bavarian Alps." He hadn't taken the trouble to lower his voice. Frances wondered which person at the surrounding tables would be interested in all this. No doubt their bodyguard were draping themselves behind some concealing tree, but she had ceased to worry about them.

"I've quite enjoyed it here." *Like hell I have,* she added under her breath. "But I should like to see some real country views for a change. I find the pavements very hot. And yet, you have simply got to walk if you want to see any of these too too lovely buildings." The saccharine dripped over her words. Richard was leaning back in his chair, smiling pleasantly at his wife. His eyes were applauding her; his mind was keenly aware that the handsome woman, who sat two tables away from them, was watching the foam in her beer glass with great intentness. Or perhaps she always studied beer in that way. If the woman had been interested in their conversation, he had at least this comfort: she could have heard every word of it.

They both thought it a good idea to return to the hotel and rest before dinner. Frances thought she would lie down for half an hour, and read. Richard thought he'd like a bath. He left the bathroom door open and, as he cooled off in the tepid water, he could hear a page being turned. Once she laughed. He was happier about Frances. The Museum had been a good idea; there was nothing like a Museum for calming one's emotions. This game was simple enough, he thought, and cursed the latherless soap. This game was simple enough if you could convince yourself that you really were on holiday; that as long as you carried no unexplainable documents and neither received nor sent any, as long as you were an apparently harmless tourist, nothing could really touch you. You could give yourself away, of course. If you became flustered or lost your nerve because of the continual feeling of threat which hung over you, you might do something which was either stupid or too clever. Either of these actions would be a dangerous weakness. It was no good trying to pretend that a threat didn't exist. It did, all the time. What you must do was to ignore it: acknowledge it and ignore it. The only real danger points were those of the actual contact with an agent. If you were discovered at that moment, nothing on earth could help you. Well, the danger point in Nürnberg was past. It had passed when Fugger had spoken so softly that he had had to strain to hear him. He had been looking down at the title page of a book, and the bookseller was searching through some other volumes.

"It is better in Innsbruck at this time of year. The Gasthof Bozen, Herzog-Friedrich-Strasse 37, is recommended. The owner is called Hans, and will help you. He likes music and red roses as we all do."

That had been neatly sandwiched in between their discussion on editions and editors. He had the satisfactory feeling that A. Fugger had escaped. He was too wily a bird not to have had all his preparations made for just such a day as yesterday. It wouldn't have taken him long to get through a window and lose himself in the labyrinth of passages and small streets which lay behind the shop. There were plenty of rooms there to have rented as a hide-out, or as a place to change your identity. Or perhaps A. Fugger already had another neatly established identity practically next door to his bookshop. There was no limit to the ingenuity of a foresighted man with sufficient time to arrange things.

Suddenly, there was a firm, businesslike knock on the bedroom door. He heard Frances say "Come in."

It *might* be a maid: some excuse, any old excuse. From the bathroom, he could only see the windows of the bedroom and the heavy green brocade curtains. But in his mind's eye he could see Frances, dressed in that pink frilly thing of hers and lying on their bed, raise an enquiring eyebrow from the novel she had been reading.

He heard her say, "Yes, it is warm, isn't it? Please leave the towels on that chair. My husband is having a bath. Thank you. Good day." It was only when he heard the bedroom door close sharply that he realized he was sitting bolt upright in the bath, his muscles tensed. Frances had remained where she was on the bed; nor did she call through to him. Thank heavens for that. She must have had a fright when that knock came; it hadn't sounded like a maid. He got out of the bath quickly and made some pretense of whistling as he dried himself.

When he entered the bedroom, Frances was lying on the bed with her eyes fixed on the bathroom door, waiting for him. The novel lay as it must have dropped when the maid had left the room. He felt her force her voice to say naturally, "Hello, darling. Cooler now?"

He lay down beside her, and with his head close to hers on the pillow, she whispered, "The knock . . . I thought he had been caught."

"Don't worry, Frances. I don't think he was. Please don't worry."

She was laughing softly, but it was a poor imitation of her laugh. It was becoming louder; her hands were cold.

"Snap out of it, Fran," he whispered. He slapped her jaw sharply. That helped. At least the laughing had stopped. He lay with his arm round her shoulders, quietening her with his firm grip.

"We'll leave here tomorrow," he said at last. "I'll get you to the mountains for some days."

Frances had recovered, and was looking rather ashamed of herself.

"Yes," she said, "I can always push someone over a precipice if there's any monkey business there."

Richard grinned. He was so unworried, so confident, thought Frances. It made her feel better just to look at him.

"That's the idea," he said.

After they had dressed, they went downstairs for dinner in the hotel. Frances had recovered completely. She had worn her smartest dress as a tonic, and the results were good. She was amusing and gay, even over a not particularly good dinner—German cooking was not at its best this summer. Many of the people in the restaurant turned their heads to watch the slender, fair-haired girl. She was easily the loveliest woman in the place, thought Richard with justifiable pride.

"That rest did you good, Frances," was what he said.

Frances only referred once to that afternoon. "You mustn't worry about me, Richard," she said. "I'll be all right now. I am like that, you know. At college I used to get quite panicky three weeks before the examinations were due. But once I had got my worry over, I was always perfectly cool when the examinations came. In fact, I used to enjoy them. Sort of legitimate showing-off, you know, with no one to reprimand you for being an exhibitionist. Well, I think it will be the same when whatever is going to happen happens. I was thinking about the war, particularly, Richard. The more I see of Germany, the more I know that a showdown *must* come, some day; and perhaps the sooner the better, before they are all turned into robots. When I think of the children leaving school each year, all of them carefully educated in the Nazi way, I honestly shudder to think what the rest of the world faces in ten years' time, if it waits. So don't worry about me, or start regretting that you brought me. I'm just in the process of adjusting myself between two very different ways of life, between peace and war. Coming here was a good idea after all: it reconciles you to the adjustment."

Richard knew Frances was right in her self-analysis—she was like that—but his job right now was to see that her nerve didn't crack before she had reached the cool, calm and collected stage. That would probably come before the end of this journey; at least, he hoped so. Her handicap was imagination. It was more difficult to face unpleasantness when you had imagination. But, as she had said, coming here helped to reconcile the adjustment. It also hastened it, thank heaven.

"I know," he said, and began some amusing suggestions about what they could possibly be drinking.

"It's really only habit which makes me order coffee. A few more days and I'll probably lose it," Frances said.

"It's extraordinary what people can swallow for the sake of their beliefs. I heard of a practising surrealist who spent many months eating his wardrobe."

"That sounds a good story," said a man's voice. Both Richard and Frances looked up in surprise.

"Hello, van Cortlandt. Glad to see you."

"May I come over here, for a while? I wanted to tell your wife . . ."

"I know," said Frances quickly. "I'm sorry I got so hot and bothered yesterday in that discussion. You know, it isn't easy for us to look at these things disinterestedly."

"And I came over here because I began to feel I might have seemed too darned callous. You see, I'm trying to look at things disinterestedly, and I'm finding that isn't easy, either."

"Well," said Richard, "now that we have all kissed and made friends, what will you have?" They all laughed, and van Cortlandt said he would have beer. Frances had a feeling that he disapproved of them somehow because they were English, and yet was surprised into liking them when they caught him off his guard.

"As a matter of fact," he was explaining, "I watched you being the only real human beings in a roomful of stuffed dummies, and I thought we were fools it we didn't get together. We may be a lot different, but we aren't just like—" He nodded over his shoulder in the direction of those concentrating on the mastication of specially chosen vitamins to build a specially chosen race.

"Zombies is, I believe, the technical term," suggested Richard. "Now would you really like to hear the story about the wardrobe?"

They talked for an hour, and then decided to have a moonlight walk. The bodyguard joined them outside the hotel, Richard noted. As Frances explained that they were probably leaving tomorrow for the mountains, he wondered just who had been watching them inside the hotel dining room. Not that it mattered, not now.

They didn't choose any particular way, but just followed any twisting street which would lead them to the banks of the Pegnitz. Away from the bigger streets, the lights were economically dim, but it seemed safe enough —even with the two men marching behind them at a discreet distance. In the narrower streets where there were so few people, the men were ludicrously obvious. Richard wondered if they never felt the ridiculousness of the whole thing. The American, after his first glance back at them, had ignored the two pairs of feet keeping time with such perfect precision. Later, Richard wondered why he never then questioned the American's lack of interest. Perhaps he was relieved that van Cortlandt appeared to think that this was only normal; it would have been difficult to pretend that they hadn't noticed a thing. At the time, he only felt grateful for van Cortlandt's tact. It was a little surprising in such a forthright, I'm-just-a-plain-man type of individual. Perhaps the American found that frankness could be a very useful front, just as many a Britisher found understatement a safe enough refuge.

Both van Cortlandt and Richard were in good form. They talked with a good deal of the fervour and conversational abandon which have an unexplained way of suddenly appearing between two strangers, as much to

their own surprise and enjoyment as to that of their audience. Frances
was very well content to be the audience. They had just cruelly dissected
Gothic art, and were proceeding to rhapsodize over Baroque, when Frances clutched their arms, and they moved closer to her.

From the quiet blackness of the little alley to the left of them came a
bitter cry, the high, self-strangling cry of fear or pain, or both. They looked
at each other.

"And just what is that?" asked Richard quietly. He made as if to move
into the alley. There was another cry. Frances felt her stomach turn, sick-
eningly. Van Cortlandt and Richard looked grimly at each other.

"You stay here with your wife. I'll investigate." The American had taken
a step along with Richard into the alley.

"Halt!"

The abrupt command came from behind them. The two men had increased their pace to a run, as they had seen the foreigners become curious.

"Halt!"

Van Cortlandt and Richard stopped; they looked belligerently at the
men. Frances came to the rescue.

"Something's wrong—a murder or something—down there."

The brown-shirted men exchanged looks.

"We advise you to take a walk," the older one said.

"But something is wrong," the American protested.

The trooper who was doing the speaking said, "We advise you to take a
walk. It is only a Jews' Alley."

So that was it. Frances thought for one moment that van Cortlandt was
going to jab his large, clenched fist right in the middle of that mock-pleas-
ant smile. There was a minute's silence, broken only by a faint moaning.
Frances turned abruptly and walked quickly away. The others followed,
and they heard the Germans laugh at something one of them said. They
were silent until they were almost at the hotel, and then van Cortlandt
spoke.

"That's it," he said savagely. "Just as you are enjoying yourself and are
thinking that life isn't so bad after all, you meet that. Blast them to hell."

"It's our last night here, thank heavens," Frances said.

"I've got to stay for two or three days more, and then I'll get the hell
out of here. Austria's next. I'm working towards Vienna. I have enough
material as it is, already, but I can't print half of it. The nice kind people
in the other world would think I was a liar, or another sensationalist; and
my boss would say I was sent out to report and not to do propaganda
which would harm his organization."

"Is that considered at this date?" asked Frances.

"From the strictly business point of view, yes." Frances began to understand why newspapermen were cynics.

They were silent again. All the charm of the night had been broken.

Hans Sachs had given way to the Iron Maiden. As they said good-by in the hotel lounge, van Cortlandt gave them his card, and wrote his New York business address on the back of it.

"That will always be able to tell you where I am supposed to be, anyway," he added, with the attractive smile which had quite won Frances yesterday. Yesterday, or was it weeks ago? They gave him their address in Oxford, and watched him write it down in his diary. Oxford, thought Frances, where the only scream in the dark came from the little Athenian screech owls. Firm handclasps—*they* were something friendly and honest, anyway.

"Tomorrow," Richard said firmly, as they went upstairs to their room, "tomorrow we leave."

CHAPTER 10   FRAU KÖPPLER RECOMMENDS

Early next morning they left for Munich. It was a town they had both known well in the old days. Richard expected that they might be still under some kind of supervision, although their uniformed bodyguard had been left behind the walls of Nürnberg. So he chose the simplest things to do. In the afternoon they walked through the central streets, and for once he had no objections to window-shopping. In the evening they visited the Hofbräuhaus.

Frances was pathetically eager to watch the people, the same people she had seen each day when she had been an art student here in 1932. She seemed as if she were trying to read a riddle. Eventually, she gave it up.

She shook her head sadly. "I don't understand it, quite truthfully. There is something in the German soul or mind which baffles other races; there must be. On the surface, all they have got out of it is a new grandiose building here or there where they can listen to more speeches, and I can't think of anything more boring. And they have also got a lot of uniforms, and high-signs, and a firm military tread. But to all appearances, the shops aren't any better, the restaurants aren't any better, the food is worse, so are the theaters and the books. The clothes of the people do not look any more prosperous; and the trains always ran on time here, anyway."

"They have also got Austria and Czechoslovakia and lots of promises," suggested Richard.

"And concentration camps, and universities which are travesties, not to mention the hatred of three quarters of the world at least."

Richard began to wish it had not been necessary to enter Germany. He thought of the pleasant holiday they might have been having in Switzerland, or in the French Alps, or in Ragusa. Some place where the things you saw didn't immediately start grim speculations . . . anywhere except this doomed country. That was what had depressed Frances so much, this feeling of doom which was apparent to the outside observer when he saw how blindly these people accepted their grand illusion. Richard felt as if he were watching passengers in a train whose engine crew were increasing speed, disregarding brakes, while the tracks in front were steep and twisting. Either the train would make the journey in record time, or they would end in horrible disaster. The strange thing, the terrifying thing, was to see the passengers accept the ominous swaying of the train along with the conductor's glib assurances; to watch them disregard the fate of the passengers who did raise some objections, even although they had once praised the intelligence of those they now abandoned so heartlessly. And the strangest thing about it all was the fact that all of these passengers—except the children, who were encouraged to stand at the window and cheer violently—all of them had been in a previous train wreck. No wonder Frances was depressed. She had always believed that men were intelligent animals.

If only the methods of hate and force had been resisted at the very beginning: not by other countries (for *that* would have been called the unwarranted interference of those who wanted to keep Germany weak), but by the people of Germany, themselves. But, of course, it had been more comfortable to concentrate on their own private lives instead of dying on barricades, if in the last extreme they had had to pit force against force. It was easier to turn a deaf ear to the cries from the concentration camps, to harden their hearts to the despair of the exiles, to soothe their conscience with praise of the Fatherland. And now, it had come to the stage where other peoples would have to do the dying, on barricades of shattered cities, to stop what should have been stopped seven years ago.

Frances spoke again. "I wonder where it will all end . . ."

"In the hall of the Gibichungs," Richard said bitterly, and with that he discarded the problem of the German mind.

On Sunday, the ninth of July, they arrived in Mittenwald. If Richard had been alone, he would have risked going straight on to Innsbruck, but with Frances beside him it was quite another matter. It was probably just as well that there was Frances, to keep him from taking chances which might lead to disaster. Some days in Mittenwald would help to smooth out any complications which might have begun in Nürnberg—and Frances needed the mountains. That was important to remember, with Innsbruck and whatever else lay ahead of them.

At first, Richard would only take her for a short ten-mile walk. "Your legs are out of training, and your feet need hardening," he insisted. The following day, they did fifteen miles. On the next, they included some climbing. By Thursday Frances could manage the Karwendel Peak without any trouble. It was on that day that Richard had begun to feel at ease again. The sense of being shadowed had gone, and Frances seemed as if she had successfully reached her past-worrying stage.

They had climbed steadily since eight o'clock, resting almost on top of the mountain to eat the sandwiches the hotel had provided that morning. They sat on the path, their legs hanging down over its edge as it dropped steeply away. Richard watched Frances open the thick hunks of bread, and extract the little grains of caraway from the slabs of soaplike cheese. She dropped them gravely one by one over the cliff, on whose edge she swung her tanned bare legs. Above the heavy-wool socks and the flat-heeled shoes, they looked like a schoolgirl's, thought Richard, with that attractive mixture of slenderness and strength. The light breeze ruffled her hair, which had curled round her brow with perspiration, and flapped her loose silk shirt. She had tied her cardigan round her neck by its sleeves. Her excavations for caraway over, she slapped the sandwich together, and took a lusty bite. Richard found himself smiling. There was something touchingly intent in her face as she looked at the Isar rolling rapidly far below them.

"It is lovely," she said quietly, "quite lovely. Look!" She pointed up the valley, with its green fields and winding ice-blue river. " 'God made the country, man made the town.' Pity man couldn't learn better."

"He is a messy imitator. He thinks complexity is a proof of progress."

They were silent, with their own reactions to the simplicity of the scene.

At last, when they had finished their lunch, Richard rose.

"Time to move," he said, and helped Frances to stand up on the narrow path. "Fifteen minutes to the top and then we shall see Austria."

"We have plenty of time," Frances said, looking at the sun. "It won't take long to come down."

Richard shook his head reproachfully. That was one thing he couldn't teach Frances; she couldn't resist coming down a mountain quickly. She would never make a real mountain climber. She was plucky enough, though. She was following him up the last difficult stretch to the top with no outward trouble, although inwardly she was probably cursing in despair. She hated going up a mountain just as much as she loved coming down.

As they regained their breath on the top of the peak, they faced the Austrian Alps, rising in rugged waves of gray stone, snow-streaked.

Richard pointed. "Over there lies Innsbruck. We'll go there tomorrow. We have been recommended by one of your school friends—Mary What-d'you-call-her—to stay at the Gasthof Bozen in Herzog-Friedrich-Strasse."

Frances nodded. "Mary Easton will do. She's now married to a man in Central Africa."

"That's remote enough," said Richard, and then changed the subject.

Frances took her cue from him, and they began the descent in high spirits which lasted until they came into the little hotel in Mittenwald. They had put up at the hotel where Richard had once stayed as an undergraduate on a reading party. In those peaceful days, there had been crowds of foreigners, mostly American or English. Tonight, as they sat in the half-empty restaurant, it was all so very different. The owner of the hotel, Frau Köppler, still sat in earnest conversation over a little table with her special friends. She still wore the long-skirted black day-dress which seemed to be part of her. On Richard's first visit there, that table had always been the subject of jokes by the people of Mittenwald who came in for their beer, or their game of *Skat*, or to dance and sing if there were an accordion or fiddle to accompany them. Richard looked towards the part of the restaurant which had been partitioned off for the local people. He remembered how shocked Frau Köppler had been when the undergraduates had preferred to drink their beer there, instead of in the room she had arranged for her guests. Then one of the jokes had been that she was pro-Nazi, and that she was plotting with her special friends at her exclusive table. The joke was increased for the laughing Bavarians because Frau Köppler was a Northerner and they said she was going to Prussianize them; and the word *verpreussen* had also come to have a coarser meaning in the South. Now it seemed as if the joke had become fact.

Richard wondered, as he watched Frances arrange the pieces on the chessboard, whether Frau Köppler was as happy as she thought she would be. The hotel certainly was less flourishing: the only other foreigners in the room were an Italian family who talked volubly and excitedly and tightened Frau Köppler's disapproving mouth. The prices for German guests were much lower, and those tourists who arrived in the middle of the day brought their own food with them. It was an extraordinary sight to watch them open their parcels of bread and sausages at the restaurant tables, ordering one glass of beer, clean plates and knives. Frances was particularly shocked when she found that not even a tip was left for the overworked waitresses.

Richard saw Frau Köppler look over to their table. He pretended to be absorbed in the game of chess. They were no longer shadowed, he felt, but it was noticeable that Frau Köppler had taken quite a lot of interest in their movements. It could very well be possible that such a strong Nazi as herself might be asked to mark anything suspicious about them. It was the kind of little job which she might enjoy doing; it would add to her feeling of authority. As he waited for Frances to attack with her knight, he wondered whether that look predicted anything, protected his bishop with a pawn, and waited. The music from the wireless set ceased. It was a pity, thought Richard, that the sounds of frying could not be eliminated instead of music with foreign or non-Aryan influences. A man's voice began to speak, peremptory as on a parade ground. As Frances ignored the pawn, and daringly took his bishop, Frau Köppler rose to her feet, and walked over to them.

Richard had risen to his feet too, taking the opportunity of offering Frau Köppler a chair to warn Frances with his eyes—and then the unseen voice ended its exhortations and the music of a very rich band filled the room. Even as the preliminary cymbals clashed they all knew what was coming. Frances remained as she had been, and lit a cigarette. Frau Köppler stood rigid beside the chair, looking straight ahead of her into the wall of the room. Poor old Richard, thought Frances, and watched him redden slightly. He couldn't sit down as long as Frau Pushface was standing, and she knew he wouldn't stand for that song. A hymn in glorification of a well-known pimp, he had called it. Frances smoked unconcernedly and watched the chessman fall from Richard's hand. It rolled under another table, and by the time he had retrieved it, the chorus of the Horst Wessel song had ended and the Munich time-signal tune was being played. Frau Köppler sat down, bowing as she did so. Richard sat down too, looking very polite and innocent.

"I hope I am not interrupting you," Frau Köppler began. "Are you enjoying your holiday?"

They said yes, they were, Mittenwald was a most delightful place. Frances let Richard handle the greater part of the conversation. She wasn't quite sure, to begin with, why they were being honored with a visit. It wasn't very much like Frau Köppler to unbend to any of her guests, particularly foreigners. She was a tall woman, but she held herself so erectly that she seemed taller than she was. Once she must have had some beauty. Her features were still excellent, but the yellow hair and blue eyes had faded, not in the soft and kindly way which gives a certain charm to age, but bleakly. Perhaps Frau Köppler would have thought such charm only a sign of weakness; she probably preferred the appearance of strength even to the point of hardness. She was, thought Frances, a grim-looking creature. She had the foundation for beauty, but the spirit was lacking. Even as she talked, she did not relax. She gave a funny twist to the phrase *Behave naturally*. Because Frau Pushface was behaving naturally, although she could never be natural.

She turned to Frances. "I am glad you are enjoying yourself. It is good for people to travel in the new Germany. There are many things we want to show them."

Frances looked quickly at Richard, and then back at Frau Köppler. She couldn't think of an answer that wasn't impolite. She smiled, which was always a solution, even if a weak one.

Frau Köppler hadn't expected an answer, for she went on, "You speak German very well, very well indeed. No doubt you have visited our country before? Did you come to Mittenwald by chance, or were you recommended to come here? I am always interested in what brings people here."

The question was out. What a bore it must have been for her to bother to make conversation in the hope of disguising her curiosity, thought Frances. It was a pity, after all her trouble, that she did not know Richard, and so couldn't interpret his smile. He always looked like that when the game was being played his way. He was ready with his answer.

"The mountains," he said. "I enjoyed them so much when I stayed here some years ago that I wanted my wife to see them."

"You stayed here before?"

"Yes; at this hotel. It must have been almost eight years ago. It was in the off-season, at the very end of September. We stayed until we returned to England to our University."

"Ah, yes. I remember now. There were nine students and two very young professors." She must have known all the time and verified his name from the visitors' record. It would have been better if she hadn't mentioned it at all. It only angered Richard. He had given her the benefit of the doubt, and had thought she was a simple-minded woman doing what she thought was her duty. Now she was a simple-minded woman who enjoyed setting traps and catching people in them. It shed a new light on her position as uncrowned queen of the village. She would wield her political power in rather a mean way.

"Yes," he said. "It was what we call a reading party."

Frau Köppler's voice was just slightly less assured.

"Well," she said, her tone on the defensive, "you see for yourselves that we are just the same, only so much happier." Her voice was polite; it would have been friendly if the smile on the lips had been less fixed. Richard looked straight into the faded blue eyes which didn't smile at all. He said nothing. She looked at the large picture of the unhappy-looking man with the ridiculous mustache, which hung prominently on the wall.

She tried again. "Thanks be to our Leader. Do you not admire all he has done for us?"

There was a difficult moment.

"The military roads are the best I've seen, and the buildings for speeches and political gatherings are very handsome," said Frances quietly.

Frau Köppler turned to her with some annoyance. "And a hundred other things. Look at our unemployment. We haven't any. Look at yours in England. It is so large."

"Yes, unfortunately it is," broke in Richard. He was damned if he was going to let this pass. "But we are very frank about our unemployment figures."

"What do you mean?"

"We count people as unemployed if they are being trained under Government schemes for new trades, or if they are casual or seasonal workers and just don't happen to be working on the day when the census is taken. So when you talk about England you ought to remember that."

"But that's madness . . . People trained by the Government unemployed?"

"Or facing facts. They can't plan to become settled members of the State unless they have a steady job, can they? Turning them into an army is not a solution, unless waging war is one of their country's plans."

Frau Köppler dismissed the point as negligible. . . . Her patience was wearing thin.

"How long will you stay here?" The directness of her question interested Frances. The velvet glove was off.

Richard was unperturbed. "I think we'll leave quite soon, now. We've done most of the walks and climbs which we intended to do . . . Actually, we have been just discussing tonight where we should go next. Perhaps you could advise us. We had thought of the Dolomites, but I believe it is difficult to visit there, this year."

Frau Köppler was silent; she didn't want to discuss the South Tyrol.

"I think it would be too tragic to go there this year," said Frances. "Last time we were there, only two years ago, in fact, the people were so sure that the end of Italian domination was in sight. They had a second Andreas Hofer, working secretly in Bozen, and they really believed that the heart of the Tyrol would bleed no more. And now they have been forced to leave their land or to remain and become Italians. I often wonder what they think about it all."

A faint pink color surged under Frau Köppler's pale skin.

"Then there's Bohemia," said Richard. "But I think it would be equally difficult to visit there, today."

"And of course there's Salzburg. But then the singers and conductors whom I used to admire so much aren't there any longer." Frances' voice had just the proper note of regret.

Frau Köppler looked first at her, and then at Richard. They were watching her politely, waiting for her to suggest something.

"You are very near Austria, here," she said.

"Yes, Austria is lovely," said Frances. "I remember the wonderful time I had in Vienna, three years ago. Everyone was so gay and charming. You think we should go to Vienna?" Richard watched Frau Köppler's rising embarrassment. Her theory that nothing was changed, unless for the better, was not standing up very well. She shrugged her shoulders.

"Vienna has no mountains, of course. I forgot you liked them. Perhaps the Austrian Tyrol . . . it always was popular with the English."

"Do you know of any particularly good place?"

Frau Köppler gave the advice they had wanted.

"The train from here goes direct to Innsbruck. It is the center of hundreds of excursions."

"That sounds a very good idea," said Richard. "We can go there tomorrow and then make our choice from that point. Thank you, Frau Köppler, you have been the greatest help." He rose as Frau Köppler stood up. "You seem to travel a good deal." It was almost a question. Frances smiled. "It is a necessary part of one's education, we think." Frau Köppler stood with her lips and arms folded. "Perhaps. But it is strange that so many English travel about, as if they were rushing away from their own country." Frances looked at her for a moment. "But the explanation is simple. It is only when the English travel in foreign lands that they learn to appreciate many things about their own country. Good night, Frau Köppler."

They turned again to the chessboard. Frances lit a cigarette with some enjoyment. When she came to think of it, the conversation had been rather like a game of chess, itself. From their point of view, it had been really quite satisfactory.

As Richard took her Queen, she thought of A. Fugger, and his neat, businesslike exit. It was just possible that the police or Gestapo or whatever they called themselves—there seemed to be so many organizations in this country, all with uniforms and high-sounding titles—it was just possible that they wanted to capture him for another matter altogether. He might have sold banned literature, or helped people to escape, or he could have distributed secret pamphlets. She remembered his first belated appearance, and the smell of burning paper which had come fiom tho back room in the shop.

She felt a sudden rise in confidence; it seemed as if these few days of wind and sun had benefited her mind as well as her body. The mental paralysis which had gripped her last week was gone. She knew now that no matter what happened, she must keep hold of this courage and hope. If she lost these, then all was lost. Tonight she could face a hundred Köpplers, even Nürnberg itself. It was such a relief to be nearing the last stages of this strange journey that even danger seemed welcome.

"Check," said Richard, "*and* mate, I think." He grinned self-consciously as he saw Frances smile. He could conceal his disappointment at losing a game better than his delight at winning. He bent down to pick up her handkerchief where it had fallen under the table. He tickled her under the knee.

"Sorry," he apologized with mock seriousness. Frances saw that Frau Köppler was looking at them.

As they rose, all conversation at Frau Köppler's table ended. The four men there were watching them intently, while Frau Köppler gave a queenly bow. There was the little white-bearded astrologer who was Herr Köppler, who typed all day in his room and came downstairs in the evening to sit by his wife. There was a fat, genial man; another fat man, not at all genial, who always wore uniform and his hair cut so short that it bristled; and the young schoolteacher, very conscious of his discipline and learning, acquired at a Party college. Baldur, the Almost Human, Richard had named him when he had first seen him. The group of men stared openly at Frances as she crossed the room. Richard returned Frau Köppler's bow, and Frances said good night, looking serenely oblivious of the gazes in her direction. She felt suddenly glad that she didn't live in this village. There were other reasons, apart from the fact that she was English and obviously stupid, why Frau Köppler disliked her. I'm too effeminate, she thought, and giggled as she took Richard's arm to go upstairs.

CHAPTER 11 AT THE GASTHOF BOZEN

On Friday they arrived in Innsbruck, and succumbed, as they always did, to its outward charm. They left their luggage at the station, and walked towards the Maria-Theresien-Strasse through busy streets bathed in the soft yellow light of the late afternoon sun. As Frances said to Richard, it was always difficult to tell who was on holiday or who was at work in Innsbruck. There were as many short leather trousers, green-feathered hats, and peasant-pinafored dresses among the young men and women at work as there were among the groups of holiday makers; but two changes became more and more evident. The holiday makers had the hard German accent of the North, and there was the Uniform.

The cafés were busy at this hour. The tourist shops, with their colorful peasant clothes, little wood carvings, flower charms and vermilion-tinted postcards looked gay to the passing glance. Frances knew from experience not to stop and look at them. Most of the articles were less imposing, were even crude, close at hand. They had a sort of Present-from-Brighton touch. It was pathetic, she thought, that "Tyrolean" clothes, bought in the smart shops of large cities far away from the Tyrol, should be better-looking then the originals they copied. It was the tragedy of city hands being more skillful in cutting better material, of colors more carefully blended with the sophisticated designer's eye.

And now they were approaching the Herzog-Friedrich-Strasse. Frances was looking at the people, at the way in which the towers and steeples around them were superimposed on the background of jagged mountains. One of the chief attractions of this country was its White-Horse-Inn quality. It could be felt even in a town with tramcars and tourist buses. If this region were to lose that, it would lose much. Frances wondered whether the people prized the asset of charm which lay in their country-

side, or would they ever be persuaded into thinking it was effete or sentimental or valueless, persuaded into an ill-fitting imitation of the hard
Northerner?

Richard's thoughts were already at the Gasthof Bozen. The best thing
to do on this job, he decided, was to have a general idea of what he was
going to do while he still kept his eyes open for any possible short-cuts. A
girl, carrying a basket filled with flowers, had paused before them to rest
for a moment. She was almost a child, and the flowers were simple garden
flowers, arranged into rough bunches. Richard stopped Frances. He returned the girl's smile.

"From our garden," she said, holding out a bunch.

"They are lovely," said Richard. "But I think I like this bunch better.
How much?" He lifted a bunch with some roses in it: two were red. They
paid the girl, and crossed over into the narrow Herzog-Friedrich-Strasse
with its arcades and balconies. As they approached No. 37, Richard took
Frances' arm. They entered the insignificant doorway with its worn sign.
On either side of the doorway were busy little shops with overcrowded
windows, as if everything they had for sale must be displayed. Still, they
had been comforting, thought Frances, as the heavy door swung behind
them shutting them off from the cheery babel of the busy arcade, and
left her gripping Richard with one hand and the bunch of flowers with
the other.

For it was dark in the entrance hall, dark and silent. It was narrow and
unfurnished; it contained only the staircase which lay in front of them. The
faint light which broke the darkness came from above, possibly from a
landing. It reminded Frances of some of the older houses in Oxford, except for the stuffy, sickly smell of stale beer and tobacco. She noticed that
Richard brightened. His dislike was the cafés with creamcakes. As he
moved towards the stairs, she broke off a red rose, and fastened it through
the lapel buttonhole of her flannel suit.

She wished she felt as confident as her heels sounded on the wooden
staircase. It twisted in an uneven curve to the left and they had reached
the landing, fairly broad and square in shape. This was where the light
came from. It hung over a desk which faced the staircase. There was a
man at the desk, watching them through his small half-closed eyes. Or
it might have been the largeness of his face which gave his eyes the appearance of smallness. Like two bullet holes in a lump of dough, thought
Frances. He was middle-aged, his figure had spread with his years, his
square-shaped head bristled with cropped gray hair.

At either end of the landing, which seemed to be the real entrance hall
to the hotel, were swing doors. They led to two rooms, one which must be
at the back, the other at the front, of the house. From the front room came
the surge of men's voices, whenever a waitress pushed open the swing doors.
The back room seemed to be the kitchen or the taproom, or perhaps both.

The two waitresses hurtied towards it with empty beer mugs, and returned to the restaurant with them filled again. The two women were so busy that they hardly glanced at Frances, as she waited for Richard to finish his arrangements with the square-headed man. As the swing doors were pushed open, she could see some of the nearest tables. The men round them were middle-aged, bulky, with faces red from arguing or laughing or drinking beer or all three. Blue tobacco haze coiled over bald heads. There were uniforms everywhere. Once a waitress swung the door wide open, and held it that way with her shoulder and hip, so that another woman could pass through with carefully held tankards of beer. Then Frances saw the flags and the outsize photograph. She looked at the desk where Richard was signing all the usual papers. It had a photograph, too, scowling benevolently down on a row of keys hanging on numbered hooks. They seemed to have landed in one of the Party's own particular haunts.

Richard had finished writing. He beckoned to Frances. Perhaps the man had looked for a moment at her buttonhole, but Frances couldn't be sure of that. His eyes had a way of wandering vaguely, as if he were ill or very tired . . . And then a green-aproned boy appeared, and she concentrated on filling in the details in the printed form. Now the signing was all finished, the man handed Richard a key, and abandoned them to the boy in his slow-moving, disinterested way. As they were led up the wooden stairs, irregular and creaking, he sank heavily back into his seat, and resumed his occupation of staring into the middle distance.

Frances glanced at Richard. He gave no sign of disappointment. He was talking to the boy, and was giving him the checks for their luggage at the station. The boy would collect it, Innsbruck fashion. Clever of Richard, she thought, to remember that. An arrival by taxi in this narrow street, with its mixture of medieval houses and small shops, would have been pretentious and stupidly conspicuous.

The way to their room led them up two flights of wooden stairs. Frances had the sudden alarming feeling of being suspended in midair. The only support of the stairs seemed to be the wall on her left. On her right was a large well sinking into the hall landing below. There were banisters of course, but they were thinly spaced and quivered to her touch. After that, she climbed the rest of the stairs well towards the wall side, and tried to ignore the way in which the steps sagged gently towards the well of the staircase. She wished she wouldn't imagine at such moments what a fire would be like. Probably one could make a spectacular, if undignified, exit by scrambling down the front of the house from balcony to oriel window . . . Probably.

The boy replied eagerly to Richard's questions. He seemed a friendly kind of person. Frances suddenly realized this was the first really friendly smile and voice they had met in two weeks. Except, of course, for the American. She thought of a London bus conductor or policeman, and felt a wave of homesickness strike her. This was the first time she had ever felt like this, abroad. Perhaps she was noticing too much this year, but then this year you couldn't be blamed for being coldly analytical. It would have been more comfortable to have visited Germany as a guest, to have been taken out and around by friends. Then you might not have the time to notice or compare policemen and bus conductors. Then you wouldn't take a late evening stroll past a Jews' Alley. But somehow, in spite of the grimness, Frances preferred this way; there was less chloroform, this way.

Their room faced the street and was pleasant in its simplicity. No massive furniture here, thank heavens, to smother you in bad taste. Clean poverty had its virtues. Frances went over to one of the windows. Along the street, the varied house fronts rose tall and narrow over the arcades where the shops hid. At the open windows, she could see women in their dirndl dresses looking down on the street. It was as if she were in a theater, one of those little opera theaters where white patches of faces look out of the boxes rising in tiers like those of a wedding cake. Guardi would have enjoyed detailing this scene.

Someone was standing behind her. She turned quickly. Richard was gone. It was the thin dark boy in the green apron. He held out a vase of water to her, and pointed to the flowers which she still carried in her arms.

"Thank you. That is very thoughtful."

He relaxed with a smile as he heard she could speak German.

"The gentleman has gone to the lavatory," he explained carefully

"Oh . . ." said Frances, suddenly stymied.

"Where would the lady like the flowers?"

"Could we move that small table near that mirror and place them there?" He approved of the decision, and watched her arrange the flowers.

"I think that is pretty," she said, to break the silence.

"Very pretty, gracious lady." His brown eyes were friendly. "I shall go for the luggage now, and I shall come back with it as quickly as possible." His smile was infectious. He might have been going to play a game of tennis instead of pushing a cart with luggage through busy streets.

"Thank you." Frances paused. "What is your name?"

"Johann, gracious lady."

"Thank you, Johann."

He paused at the door. "Is there anything the lady needs? The maid is having her supper. She will be here soon." Frances shook her head, but he still stood at the door, his eyes watching the corridor. Suddenly he turned with a smile.

"Here is the gentleman," he said. "Good evening, *gnädige Frau*."

"Good evening, Johann." So he had been staying with her until Richard came back, as a sort of watchdog. Was the hotel as peculiar as all that? She heard Richard's voice, and there was a smile on his face as he entered the room.

"Thank God for a friendly face and a kind word," he said.

"Yes, I like Johann."

"His name is Johann?" Richard's voice had changed: it was tighter, quicker. Frances raised her eyebrows, and watched Richard sit down on the bed, his eyes fixed on the scrap of rug at his feet. Johann—Hans— Johann. No; it probably wasn't . . . probably. He looked up to see Frances standing beside him, looking puzzled. He caught her arm, and pulled her down beside him.

"Anything wrong?"

"I don't think so." He lowered his voice, although the walls in this old house must have been thick enough for safety. "I was just thinking . . . What was Johann like? Chatty? I noticed he hovered about here, until I got back."

"Politeness, and really good manners. That's all. What people used to call a well-brought-up boy. You know, I had the funniest feeling that he didn't approve of this hotel, and wanted to . . . oh, it's silly. I am going all romantic."

Richard remained serious. He was still half-lost in his own thoughts.

"Frances, it's the rummiest place. I went to see where the bathroom was, and I took the chance of having a look round, in general. Most of the rooms on this floor seem empty, but I was almost run over by three expansive uniforms on their way downstairs to join the party. You noticed it, by the way?"

"Yes; it looked like an old boys' club."

"It probably is. All I've seen so far are middle-aged men, looking rather pleased with themselves. It may be one of those pubs where Nazi meetings were held secretly when Austria was still banning them. Either we've arrived in the middle of a reunion of some kind or they always are reuniting."

"That's cheery, I must say."

"I don't know if it is as bad as it looks for us. Our friends wouldn't quite expect us to come here if we had a guilty conscience, right into the spider's parlor, as it were. And then Johann told me that they used to have a lot of English and American tourists here, students who were having an inexpensive holiday; that some Americans turned up earlier this summer, but that so far we are the first Britishers. He noticed I had written Oxford University on that form at the desk downstairs, so we fit in, in a kind of a way. University people are generally thought to be odd."

Frances noted that he looked strained and tired.

"What about a spot of food, and some beer?" She smiled as she saw him brighten at the idea. She stood up and smoothed her skirt. "I'll wash first. Where's the bathroom?"

Richard grinned. "It's absolutely unique, Frances. You'll love it." She knew from his tone that she wouldn't.

"Where?" she asked philosophically.

"Straight along the corridor, past the staircase, to the back of the building. You'll find it on the balcony there. It's a square box to one side. You can wave to all the people sitting out on their balconies round the back courtyard. It's really very matey."

Frances said very slowly, "Richard, you are pulling my leg. I'll see for myself."

She walked quickly along the corridor. Apart from the additional local color of two pairs of large black boots outside one quiet room—Richard had been surprisingly discreet about that—everything was exactly as he had described it.

As they went downstairs, Richard was whistling softly to himself in a preoccupied way. Frances paid little attention; he often did that—but as they reached the desk, she suddenly realized that the last few bars had taken shape into something she knew. *My love indeed my love is like a red red red red rose.* Richard was laying their key on the desk, in front of the large, shapeless man. Without rising from his chair, he nodded his square head with its bristling hair, and grunted in reply to their good evening. He only looked for a moment at Frances' hat.

When they came in, he was still sitting there. He rose slowly and grudgingly to hand them their key. All his movements were those of a lethargic and not particularly amiable man.

This was all that happened for two days as they left or entered the hotel. The room which served as the restaurant was empty in the morning. The swing doors were propped open to air the place, the chairs were piled on the tables, and the two waitresses in old dresses were washing the floors. The tobacco smoke was gone, but the smell of beer still hung in the air. In the evening, the swing doors were closed, shutting in the dull hum of voices, except when the hurrying waitresses, now dressed in their bright dirndls, elbowed them open. Then the wave of voices rose and fell. They were always men's voices, thick and heavy. Frances wondered about the grass widows, deserted for the excitements of politics.

On Sunday morning, the silent man startled them by asking if they were comfortable in their room. They said they were, and waited. But he only hooked their key onto the board behind him, moving so slowly, with his back turned to them, that they knew the conversation was over. They didn't need to look back at the desk, as they took the first steps downstairs. He would be lowering himself slowly into his chair, folding his hands across his massive paunch, and settling his eyes on his favorite spot on the wall above their heads.

As they returned that evening, climbing slowly up the stairs to the rhythm of Frances' high heels, they braced themselves to face the desk, but no one was there. Just as Richard was wondering if he should risk getting their room key without arousing the owner's displeasure, Johann appeared. Herr Kronsteiner had just gone to have his supper, he explained, and moved round behind the desk. He had taken off his apron, and had become a very dignified Johann. Well, anyway, thought Frances, that disposed of Richard's theory that Herr Bristleneck did all his eating and sleeping at the desk. But Richard seemed in no way dismayed at having his theories confounded: on the contrary, he was in remarkably good humor as they climbed the rest of the stairs. He was whistling to himself again, softly, and absent-mindedly it seemed. But the wink he gave Frances as they walked down the corridor to their room was not at all absent-minded. Just as they reached the door, the whistling had slid into a recognizable tune. Richard opened the door quickly. He was not disappointed. Inside, standing at the window, looking at the street, was Herr Kronsteiner.

He stood just far enough behind the white curtain to see without being seen. He turned slowly round to face them as the door closed. Richard's whistling only stopped then.

Richard said quietly, "Good evening." Frances noticed that Herr Kronsteiner also kept his voice low as he answered. He was smiling politely, his eyes fixed vaguely on the wall behind them.

"I came to leave your account in your room, and then I thought I heard you coming upstairs. So I took the opportunity of waiting, so that I could explain any details which might seem doubtful. Many of our foreign visitors find German figures puzzling. I shall be away tomorrow on a short journey, and I may not return before you leave." For a man of Herr Kronsteiner's loquacity, it was quite a speech.

Richard's expression was unchanged. "Of course. It is just as well to be quite sure and to have all the details perfectly clear."

Frances glanced at him. There was just a shade of emphasis, a slowness in the phrasing of the words, which gave them a double meaning to anyone who looked for it; but if Herr Kronsteiner perceived it, he gave no sign. He held two envelopes in his hand; he chose one of them carefully and handed it to Richard. He waited. Richard ripped the envelope open, and extracted a sheet of paper. Frances, still watching him, saw a shade of disappointment pass over his face. The envelope had contained a bill, just an ordinary hotel bill. The name of the hotel headed the piece of paper, followed by the name of the proprietor. It was RUDOLF KRONSTEINER. He saw Fugger's head against the row of dusty books, saw the scarcely moving lips . . . "The owner is called Hans . . . He will help you . . ."

"Thank you. I think everything is quite clear." Richard spoke abstractedly. Would he risk it? It was now or never, he felt. On what he said or did depended everything, everything, including Frances' safety. At least the man had come to their room, with a very elaborate excuse. That had been the first step, either for or against them. The next step was his. He was amazed at the calmness of his own voice. "Except, of course, one silly idea I had. I thought you were the proprietor."

"I am," the man answered gravely, but his interest seemed aroused for the first time.

"Really? Then it's my mistake completely. I thought the owner's name was Hans, not Rudolf."

Herr Kronsteiner smiled. "Everyone knows that it is Rudolf." He looked at the envelope which he still held in his hand.

"God in heaven, how could I have made such a mistake? I gave you the wrong bill. My apologies, Herr Professor." His calm smile belied the amazement of his words.

To Frances, sitting on the edge of the bed, her hat with its red rose lying beside her, it seemed as if here were not only a maddening man, but also one who either enjoyed his own mystery, or—and that was a disturbing thought—believed in precaution even within those thick walls. Thank heavens, Richard and she had made only general conversation here, except when they had lain close together in bed. Could their low voices, deadened by the soft feather pillow, have possibly been heard, even if this room was wired for sound? Richard's precaution, which from the very beginning she had been inclined to deplore secretly, now lost all its theatrical appearance and began to look like wisdom.

Richard was smiling too, as he read the second bill very carefully. He was memorizing something.

"Everything is quite clear now," he said, "Would you like the bill paid this evening, or will tomorrow do?"

"That does not matter very much, but we have a rule in this hotel that all accounts must be paid each Monday. Tonight or tomorrow, it does not matter. One more thing I must trouble you about. All the rooms in the hotel have been reserved for a political conference this week. It begins on Wednesday."

"Oh, we intended in any case to leave Innsbruck either tomorrow or Tuesday." Did we indeed? thought Frances. The reply had pleased Kronsteiner. He had given his warning, and Richard had taken it. He positively beamed, although his voice was as impersonal as ever.

"In that case, I am glad I saw you this evening, for I may be away when you leave. I hope you have enjoyed your visit here."

"Very much indeed." It was Frances now who spoke. It seemed to her that it was time she said something. Herr Kronsteiner bowed, and moved with unexpected quickness to the door. He paused before he opened it, slowly, cautiously. Without looking back, he suddenly slipped out. They couldn't hear his footsteps in the corridor. For a large, heavy man he could walk with surprising lightness.

Frances felt that someone ought to say something. "Was the bill high?"

"No, it was rather reasonable. Now what shoes did you want to wear?"

Frances looked at the bed . . . But if Richard wanted to go out again, there would be a reason. Any suggestion he made had its purpose. She knew that by this time. She changed her shoes and washed her hands and face in cold water. She felt the better for fresh powder and lipstick. She wound a white chiffon scarf as a turban round her head; she was beginning to hate the sight of the red rose, anyway. As she finished tucking the ends of the scarf in place, she saw Richard watching her in the mirror. He was smoking his pipe, and in the ashtray beside him were the crumbled ashes of the paper which he had used as a lighter. His Baedeker was open on his knees.

"Ready?"

Frances nodded. She picked up a clean pair of white gloves and a fresh handkerchief. Richard had risen and replaced the guidebook in its drawer. He emptied his pipe into the ashtray, and stirred the ashes with his pen-knife until he was satisfied that no piece of charred gray paper could be seen. The bill which had been handed to him first by Kronsteiner he left lying on the little table beside the flowers.

Downstairs, Johann was still at the desk. He interrupted his conversation with two men, whom Richard recognized as belonging to the uniforms which had practically marched over him on the evening of their arrival, to wish them much enjoyment. He could recommend the film at the cinema in the Maria-Theresien-Strasse. His friendly brown eyes followed Frances downstairs, along with the open, noncommittal stare of his companion. One of them said something, the other laughed. Frances took Richard's arm, and pressed it. Her quietening touch, she called it. They heard Johann's voice raised in their defense.

"But the English are a truly German race."

"Which is probably the highest praise one could have from a German," said Richard bitterly, as they closed the heavy front door. "I wish," he added, "that we could afford the luxury of a scene. Just once."

Perhaps Richard had been infected by Herr Kronsteiner's supercaution. Anyway, he had varied his technique tonight. As they crossed the square towards the Maria-Theresien-Strasse, he chose the moments of isolation to tell Frances they would leave tomorrow for Pertisau am Achensee.

"It looks a decent sort of place on the map," he said with some pleasure.

"Are we near the end?"

"We'll know when we meet him."

"Then what?"

"We'll go to Ragusa, and post back the letter of credit."

"And if we don't find him this time? We haven't many days left, have we?"

"We'll have to try again, and perhaps again. After that, if there are no results, I'll wire Geneva, and we'll get back to London. We were given a month. It's now the sixteenth of July. I think we'll manage it in time."

"Then you have a suspicion this may be the last stop?"

Richard only smiled as an answer. They had reached the pavement and, surrounded once more by Sunday-evening crowds, they walked in silence towards the cinema. Outside its doors, Frances paused to look at the stills.

"I think I'd rather have a drink," she said.

"You've got sense," an American voice said behind them. They both turned in amazement. Yes it was, it was Henry van Cortlandt, sardonic grin and all. He shook their hands as if he really were pleased to see them.

"It was your wife's hat sort of thing which caught my eye. It's pretty smooth; not the kind of headgear a good *Hausfrau* wears. I've just been in there, and I came out halfway through. I've been wondering what to do until it's time to go to bed. And now you are here in answer to my prayers. The drinks are on me. We'll catch up on local color. I know a place where we'll get plenty."

As they walked towards the restaurant, there were explanations. Van Cortlandt had finished his assignment in Germany, and was now heading through the Tyrol to Vienna. He tactfully did not ask them where they had been, or where they were going. Frances filled in the gaps with what she always called girlish gossip. Tonight it served its purpose well enough.

As they sat at a table in the beerhouse, they all relaxed and prepared to enjoy themselves. Both Richard and van Cortlandt had stories to tell, and there was no need to worry about the conversation. It was pleasant, thought Frances, to lean on a table, to watch the curling cigarette smoke, to listen to laughter and voices raised in friendly argument. There was one thing about living under this kind of government—every moment of enjoyment was treasured. You appreciated any moments without fear or restrictions, and when they came your way, you made the most of them. There was a pathetic kind of determination to have a good time in the faces around her. It had touched even her. When they had sat down at this table tonight, she had made up her mind that she was going to enjoy herself. She was going to forget everything except that they were on holiday.

The men ordered their second large steins of beer. Frances left the conversation to watch the people around them. She noticed a young man, sitting alone at a small table, making the best of his splendid isolation. He was vaguely familiar. He looked suddenly towards them, and his eyes met hers. He hesitated. Frances felt that he knew her, that he was waiting for her to smile. When she didn't, he looked away quickly, and became absorbed in a large family party in front of him. Richard became aware of her look of concentration. He stopped what he was saying to van Cortlandt to ask, "Anything wrong, Frances?"

"I'm just thinking, darling."

"It looks rather painful." Both men regarded her with some amusement.

"I've got it . . . the young man in the train."

Richard didn't look any the wiser.

"The *beautiful* young man in the train to Paris. Your friend's brother, Richard, you know the one. He's here."

"Young Thornley. Good Lord. Where?"

"Over there."

Richard looked. "You're quite right, Frances. It is."

"He looks rather lonely."

"Well, we're not nursemaids." Richard was annoyed.

Van Cortlandt laughed at Richard's expression.

"Why do the English abroad avoid the English abroad?" he asked.

"Well, you know what we call a holiday . . . a change. But actually, he may not want to join us, and might only do it out of politeness."

Van Cortlandt looked surprised. He wasn't convinced. "Now who would think up that reason?" They all laughed.

"He might be waiting for someone, but I think he looks too bored for that. He is not annoyed; he is just bored." It was Frances again.

The young man decided everything by looking towards their table, and smiling wholeheartedly in his embarrassment at finding three pairs of eyes focused on him. Richard gave a wave of his hand, and the young man rose and came towards them.

"I hope you don't mind my butting in," he said, "but I have got very tired of laughing by myself." The American looked at Thornley just the same way he had looked at Richard and Frances when he had met them in the Five-Cornered Tower. It was a quiet summing-up, disconcerting in its frankness, but Thornley, like the Myles', pretended to be unaware of it. He sat down beside them, and started to talk. He was amusing, and seemingly lighthearted. Frances watched van Cortlandt make up his mind; after he had had half an hour of Thornley, she felt the judgment was mainly favorable. She sighed with relief; she felt responsible for Thornley. Van Cortlandt had decided, she could guess, that Thornley was a nice, amusing individual with a lot of charm—and not much else. It would depend on how much he got to know Thornley before he could revise that estimate. Frances guessed also that van Cortlandt hadn't thought any revision would be necessary.

"Where's your friend?" asked Richard, when the rush of conversation offered its first pause.

"Tony? Oh, he should be here any day, I hope. That's why I'm hanging about Innsbruck. We went to Prague, you know, and didn't find ourselves made welcome by the—authorities. Things were a little difficult, really. It seemed easier if we split up, and if I came here to let him get his job done."

The mention of Prague had interested van Cortlandt.

"Did you run into trouble?" he asked.

Thornley nodded. "A little." He saw that they were all waiting for him to explain. He could hardly ignore the interest in all their eyes.

"Is Tony in danger?" asked Frances. At least, that would give him the chance to say no, and to turn the conversation.

"Actually, he is looking for a girl."

Van Cortlandt and Richard exchanged glances.

"What's wrong with that?" asked the American with a smile.

"Nice healthy pursuit," agreed Richard.

"Usually," said Thornley. "But in this case she is the daughter of a professor who wasn't exactly popular with the new régime."

"Don't tell us, unless you want to," said Frances suddenly.

"Probably I'd be better confiding in someone. You've no idea how miserable you begin to feel inside when you can't talk to anyone. I've been waiting here just like that for two weeks. . . . The story is simple and innocent enough, Heaven knows. Tony began worrying about this girl when he heard her father had been removed. He had met her in England last summer, and since May he has become determined to get to Prague to see if she were all right. He had the idea of marrying her and getting her out of the country as a British citizen. Well, we got to Prague. It wasn't particularly pleasant for us, being English." He paused reflectively. "It became obvious that I was inclined to get involved in things, and there was no sign of Tony's girl. In the end, he thought it was better for him to do the job alone. He can control his temper better than I can. So I came on here, and I'm waiting for Tony and his girl to arrive. I said I would wait until the end of July."

"What happens if he doesn't turn up before the end of the month?" asked van Cortlandt.

"That would be a nuisance. I'd have to go back to Prague."

"I'd like to join you."

"Would you?" Thornley was pleased. "It's mostly strain, I warn you. Not very pleasant, really. The Czechs are suspicious, the Germans are intolerable. I can't say I blame the Czechs, at all. It is just like that all the time, you see, and then you start to be haunted by the girl, too. Tony's infected me."

"Did you know her?"

"I've seen photographs. And Tony would say something, now and again. She seemed a winner."

"Perhaps she is in hiding with her father," suggested Frances.

Thornley looked at her. His gray eyes were colder, brighter. "He is definitely dead," he said gently. It was the kind of gentleness which shocked them all into silence. Frances noted, as she lit another cigarette, that van Cortlandt was looking at Thornley in a different way. The revision process had no doubt begun.

Richard ordered more beer and coffee for Frances.

"We are leaving tomorrow," he intimated, "for Pertisau."

Frances blinked her eyes, and tried to look unconcerned. It was hardly the change in conversation which she had expected.

"I envy you," said Thornley. "Good place. Mountains and lake, and plenty of atmosphere. At least, it was, four years ago. I suppose it is still:

the small villages keep to their own ways longer than the towns, and mountains and forests don't change."

"I envy you, too," agreed van Cortlandt. "Sidewalks in summer become just one café table after another for me. Climbing isn't up my alley, though. I've never understood why people go up, when all they can do is come down again. But I'd like some real swimming. I haven't had much chance of it, this summer."

"Then why don't you both take a few days off, and come along?"

Both van Cortlandt and Thornley looked surprised.

"You both look as if you could do with some time off," said Richard, and left it at that.

Thornley and van Cortlandt eyed each other speculatively. Each was probably wondering if the idea would be as attractive tomorrow as it seemed tonight.

"It sounds all right to me," said the American.

"It certainly seems a good idea," said Thornley.

"I've some business to do here. It depends on that," qualified van Cortlandt.

"And I'd hate to butt in," finished Thornley.

They both looked at Frances. She sipped her coffee, and regained her composure.

"Richard never makes a suggestion out of mere politeness," she said. "If he actually invited anyone, then that means he really would like them to accept." She smiled to the two men, and added, "I think it would be fun."

"Yes," agreed Thornley.

"Well, I've had a grand evening," said van Cortlandt. "It would be a pity to miss any others we could have. If I can arrange the business on hand, I'll take you up on that suggestion."

Richard finished the debate. "We'll be there for about a week, and if we leave before you arrive, we shall phone you and let you know. If you can make it, then turn up anytime you feel like it. We'll leave it at that. I don't know where we shall stay, yet. Let's say the Hotel Post; there's always a Post in Austria. If you can't manage it, then we'll see you in London, we hope."

They rose, and straggled to the door. The restaurant was nearly empty; it must have been later than any of them had imagined. They parted with a good deal of warmth. Frances, who had been drinking coffee, wondered how much the beer had to do with it all. She watched the American and the Englishman walk away together, still talking their heads off.

"I'd like to see them again," she said and took Richard's arm. "I wonder if they'll come. You know, Richard, you did give me a shock when you suggested it. Won't it complicate matters?"

Richard shook his head. "Beer or no beer, I liked them. It's strange, how you can meet some people, and you might as well have been spending the evening looking at a fishmonger's window. And then again, you meet others, and a small flag waves, and you are a fool if you ignore it."

"Especially nowadays," said Frances. "I'm all for gathering the rosebuds while we may."

The street was almost empty. The light tap of Frances' heels alone broke the silence. She waited until they had reached a part of it where they were sure of being quite safe. She lowered her voice.

"Did the second bill tell you whom we are to see?"

"He's a chess collector, this one. Welcomes any fellow-enthusiast to view his collection. It should be easy getting in touch with him."

That was all Richard would tell, then. When Frances spoke again, it was about van Cortlandt and Thornley; she was still worrying about endangering them.

"They can take very good care of themselves, these two. If they come. What's more, we were told to behave completely normally. So I did."

Frances added nothing to that. For one thing, they were approaching the hotel. For another, she had the dawning suspicion that Richard was going to leave her under the young men's protection while he was being a fellow-enthusiast. She would see about that.

CHAPTER 12 BACKGROUND FOR TERROR

Johann was charmingly regretful in his mild way, next morning, when he found them completing their packing. He advised Richard about the trains, and arranged to take their suitcases to the station. As he spoke, he watched Frances pack bottles and hairbrushes into her fitted hand case.

"How beautiful," he said involuntarily, and then reddened as Frances looked up in surprise. "That leather, how is it made? I have admired your shoes each day. The material is so good." He looked at their flannel suits. "I don't quite understand it," he went on. "Are English sheep and cattle and horses so very much better than other countries'?"

Frances kept her face serious. "No, Johann, I don't think they are. Perhaps it is because the English are a slow and careful sort of people. Sometimes slowness has results." She would like to have added that even if his country hadn't got materials like these, they had always plenty of tanks and aeroplanes, but she didn't. Johann's sense of humor didn't stretch to the irony of that.

"Yes, they are slow people, I have heard. Their thoroughness is different from ours; sometimes it seems strange that they should ever get results."

He hesitated. "May I ask the *Herr Professor* a question? Do you think there will be war?"

Richard paused in locking his suitcase. He chose his words carefully. "Well, that depends, Johann. It depends on Germany. If she makes war against Poland, then there will be war."

"But why should England go to war for Poland? The Poles are not worth it."

"They do not deserve to be obliterated."

"But you did not go to war for the Czechs."

"You agreed that the British are slow. It has taken time to change them from hopes of peace to a determination to fight, if it is necessary. If Poland is attacked, the British will see *that* as a sign that fighting is necessary. It is quite simple, Johann. If Germany does not want war, then she must not attack Poland."

"Another war would be a dreadful thing," said Johann.

"Do many of your friends feel that way?" asked Frances.

"Of course, *gnädige Frau*. We are human beings."

"It seems so strange then that Germany should have twice built up the most powerful army in the world, within thirty years. Armies cost a lot of money, Johann. And the money is wasted unless the armies are used, and pay for themselves by winning. It is a very dangerous thing to build up a huge army when the rest of the world is at peace."

Johann was searching for a reply; what was it he had heard so often?

"But," he said at last, "we have to prepare against attack."

"From whom?" asked Frances gently.

"From all our enemies. France for instance."

"Johann, do you really think that if France was prepared for attack she would ever have had to sign at Munich? Tell me, when you lived in what was called Austria, were you all afraid of being attacked by France? Did you feel then that you must have the biggest air force in the world?"

Richard signed to Frances to ease up. As he explained afterwards, it would only land the boy in trouble if he really started to think for himself.

Johann was indeed looking worried. "If only you could live in our country for some years, you would understand, *gnädige Frau*." Frances, in obedience to Richard's signal, contented herself with smiling.

Richard spoke. "The cases are ready, Johann; you can take them away whenever you like. Leave the checks for them downstairs at the desk, and we shall get them there."

"Yes, *Herr Professor*." Johann looked unhappy about something. Perhaps it was that he hadn't made any converts to his cause. Or perhaps, thought Frances, he had found a question which the answers he had learned did not fit.

"You have made our stay very comfortable," said Frances, and was glad to see him cheer up. "And when you have that hotel of your own in the

Tyrol, you must let us know, and we shall come and stay there one summer." Johann flushed with pleasure; he saw that she meant what she said.

"It would give me the greatest pleasure to have you at my hotel, *gnädige Frau*," Johann said with unexpected dignity.

"Good-by, Johann," said Richard. It was always he, it seemed, who had to close Frances' conversations. Johann bowed deeply, smiled for Frances again, and left them at last.

Frances walked over to a window, and looked silently down on the street.

"You would have made a good father confessor," said Richard, and lit the cigarette which she held between her lips. It was really extraordinary how people would talk to Frances; more extraordinary how she would listen.

"Don't let the tragedy of the human race get you down at this time of the morning. Come and have some breakfast, first." He drew her gently from the window. "An empty stomach only turns thought into worry."

Frances smiled and kissed him. "You keep worrying about me, Richard."

"Well, whenever you start a train of thought these days, it runs non-stop to the sorrows of the world."

"I'm sorry, Richard. I'll give up the habit."

"Do. It would be frightful if you ever began to enjoy it."

Frances laughed. "A kind of mental pervert, working herself into depths of depression to enjoy her secret thrills of pity? No, thank you, Richard. Instead, I'll become accustomed to the idea that man is born in pain, lives in struggle, dies in suffering."

"Well, that's a better defense against the new Middle Ages than the nice ideas you got from your liberal education."

Over a café table, they made their plans. Frances was suddenly demanding action. She wanted to get to Pertisau as soon as possible. By the time they had finished their late breakfast and had walked back to the hotel, the baggage checks awaited them, along with a final bill. Herr Kronsteiner had already left, it seemed, and Richard paid the grim woman who sat behind the desk. He left more than the usual tip for Johann, placing it inside an envelope along with his card on which he had written *Good luck with your hotel*, and a tip for their invisible chambermaid. Perhaps she had been this grim-faced, silent woman.

At the station, their luck still held. The train for Jenbach would leave in less than half an hour. From Jenbach they could hire a car to take them to Pertisau. . . . But it wasn't until they were in the train, with their suitcases settled safely above their heads in their compartment, and they were watching the pleasant valley of the Inn spreading out before them, that Richard really relaxed. He admitted to himself for the first time that he was surprised that they had got away so simply, that his distrust of Herr Kronsteiner had been unfounded. He had looked like a man who would

sell his own sister to the highest bidder. He must be a pretty useful kind
of agent to have; crooked men would trust him, because they thought they
could use him. Richard was still speculating about Herr Kronsteiner when
their short journey ended, and the train stopped briefly at Jenbach to leave
them and some other tourists on the sunlit platform. Richard lifted the
two suitcases and joined the largest group which had jammed round the
exit. Frances kept very close to him, slightly behind and slightly to one
side, so that the man who was taking the tickets would only notice her,
and no more. And then they were out into a broad roadway of hot white
dust. There were two decrepit buses and some cars. The tourists, once the
first burst of activity of leaving the station was over, had begun to straggle
as they made up their minds. That gave them the chance to hire one of
the cars. They had already left the station road, and were turning into the
outskirts of the little town, before the others had found seats which suited
them and places for their luggage.

Their car finished the steep twisting climb from Jenbach, and regained
its speed on the road leading round the western side of the long narrow
Achensee. Halfway up the lake, the road ended. And there was Pertisau,
smiling with the sun on its green meadows to welcome them.

It wasn't the usual village. It gave the appearance, as the road curved
into the bay in which it lay and they could see it for the first time, of being
a landscape architect's dream. At the edge of the shore, divided from it
by the last of the road, were the hotels and chalets. Behind these, in the
large sweep of meadows stretching back to the wooded mountains, lay the
peasant houses like a scattered flock of sheep. A very small, neat pleasure
boat was taking on passengers at the small neat pier. Everything was neat,
even the arrangement of flags fluttering from the bathing houses on their
own part of the shore, or the pattern of striped umbrellas shadowing the
tables in front of the hotels. It was, self-admittedly, an artificial tourist
center, but its smallness and neatness gave it much charm, and some dignity. The forests and mountains were very real, anyway. The valleys between the mountains converged on Pertisau like the lines of a sundial.
There would be good walking and pleasant climbing, thought Richard with
some satisfaction.

Frances was frankly delighted. She had watched some of the dull collections of houses as they had skirted the south end of the lake, and had
wondered dejectedly if any of them could be Pertisau. In her relief, she
was enthusiastic. Even the fact that the Hotel Post had no accommodation
to suit them could not dampen her high spirits. The manager of the hotel
was sorry, but there were no double rooms vacant. If the lady and gentleman would consider separate single rooms, or a room in one of the villas . . . There were some which catered to visitors when the hotels were
full . . . Most comfortable . . . Highly recommended. And of course they
would have their meals at the hotel.

So they left their luggage at the hotel, and followed the manager's assistant across the road and over a field to a house. It was called "Waldesruhe," although the woods were at least half a mile away. But it seemed both clean and comfortable. Frances liked the petunias in the window boxes and the balcony in front of their bedroom with its magnificent view of the lake. Richard liked the impersonal owner, who took everything for granted in her calm, disinterested way. This sad-faced woman would not add to their complications. But he hadn't counted on Frances.

When he returned from the hotel again, after making "arrangements" as the manager euphemistically said, and leaving notes for van Cortlandt and Thornley, he found the quiet landlady talking to Frances on their balcony.

"It really wasn't my fault," said Frances. "It was simply that she was delighted to see someone who didn't come from Germany. They are having a rather bad year, here. Most of the visitors are Germans. With special rates, of course; and they spend next to nothing. They crowd into the hotels, and all the other visitors are chased away. I expect it's the way they eat their soup. Remember?"

"I believe you, darling."

"Really, Richard, all I said was, as she stood and looked at me on the balcony, 'How lovely it all is.' It was said to myself. And then she began to talk."

"Darling, don't explain. You're too kind; you just won't hurt people's feelings. You'll let yourself in for a lot of boredom, some day."

"I rather liked her, Richard. And she kept looking at me, not rudely, not inquisitively, but just as if she wanted to. All the time she talked, she was looking at me, and the strange thing was that I didn't feel embarrassed. There was a sort of pathetic expression in her eyes. I just couldn't ignore it."

Richard laughed, and kissed his wife. "Darling," he said for the third time, "I love you. Now come and see Pertisau."

They went down the light-pine staircase into the square-shaped room with its small windows and fluttering starched curtains. Like their bedroom, the furniture was simple in comfortable peasant style. Frances noted the number of hand-embroidered or crocheted mats on every available surface in the room. Frau Schichtl must have a lot of spare time, she thought, and followed Richard through the doorway onto the coarse green grass which surrounded the house. They chose a narrow road which led them through flowering meadows away from the lakeside and its holiday loungers. Richard was thinking about something.

At last he said, "Where does Frau What's-her-name sleep? Do you know?"

"Not near us, my pet, if that is what has been worrying you. There is an empty room next us. It separates us from a Leipzig honeymoon couple, and these are all the rooms upstairs. And a bathroom of course. The name is Schichtl, anyway."

Richard looked admiringly at her. "Now don't tell me that you found all that information popping out of Frau Schichtl's cash register. . . . I must say, my Frances, you have a knack."

"Now," said Frances, "it's your turn to tell me something."

"What?"

"Don't be a brute, Richard. No one can possibly hear us." She looked at the houses across the fields, their wide overhanging roofs anchored with roped stones, their window boxes gay with rich-colored petunias. Under the broad eaves sheltered neat piles of logs.

"You take a long time to think up an answer, Richard."

"Well, darling, there's no need, is there, for you to know more than you do already?"

"Richard, will you stop doing a Pimpernel? I don't talk in my sleep and, anyway, I sleep only with you."

Richard watched two distant figures cutting the grass. Their scythes flashed rhythmically. "All right," he said. "This is all I know. We were to come to Pertisau. There is a Dr. Mespelbrunn who has a house here. He collects chessmen. We have to see him, and tell him we heard about his collection in Innsbruck. That is what makes me think that he may be the man we are looking for. None of the others knew where we came from. But here we have Dr. Mespelbrunn who knows about Innsbruck. He is also a musician, it seems, and likes to talk music as well as chess. His love is again a red rose. If he doesn't think we stink, he will unburden himself. And then we can have our holiday, and send old Peter his Geneva telegram ARRIVING FRIDAY. That's all."

"So that's all. . . . Now, Richard, just tell me what was written in Herr Kronsteiner's second bill."

"More or less as I've said."

"Well, what was that?"

"You're an exasperating creature, aren't you?"

Frances only smiled and waited.

Richard looked at her, and then recited: "*Innsbruck recommends you to Pertisau am Achensee. Dr. Mespelbrunn. Collector of chessmen, songs, flowers.*"

"Thank you, my sweet. I just wanted to be quite sure you weren't trying to do me out of some fun."

Richard was all injured innocence. "Now, really, Frances—"

"I mean, could you have possibly thought of Henry van Cortlandt and Robert Thornley as such nice swimming companions for Frances while you went—mountain climbing, for instance?"

Richard began to laugh. "Some day," he said, "I'll have to believe in woman's intuition, or is it just woman's suspicion?"

"Now that's all settled," said Frances, "let's look at the view."

Their road had led them clear of all the houses. The fields now lay behind them; in front lay scattered twisted trees on a stretch of green grass. It was here that the paths into the converging valleys began. They found a rough wooden seat under one of the small twisted trees beside a small stream. Only the gentle murmur of the running water broke the silence of the valleys. The mountains circled round the meadows, and the sky had arranged its high summer clouds in appropriate clusters to balance the juttings of the peaks into its clear blue.

"It's a neat job," said Richard, at last, "almost too neat to be natural."

"Yes, as if a stage designer had advised nature how to make a really Tyrolean set. I expect a chorus of villagers to enter at any moment."

"I've been wondering at that. It's not exactly a hive of activity, is it? There were a few men over there working with the hay, or long grass, or whatever it is. We've seen one woman scrubbing a table at her door, and another woman gathering in some washing. Now and again I heard the sound of trees being felled in the forest. Perhaps they find tourists more profitable than the land."

"Found," emended Frances. "Here are some children anyway."

Three large-haunched cows ambled slowly towards them, the bells at their throat sounding a gentle melancholy with each lazy step. Behind them were the children, four of them, their straight hair sun-bleached and their bare feet and legs stained nut-brown. The cows wandered past them, flicking the flies from their dun hides carelessly. Frances, looking at them, thought of some people she knew.

"Bored is the word, not contented. They have been bored so long that they don't know what to do about it. Numbed into contentment."

The children had halted. They were staring at Frances, at her suit and her silk stockings and her high-heeled shoes. When she spoke, they retreated, still staring stolidly, and then when they were at a safe distance they turned and ran, whooping with laughter, after the cows.

Richard was grinning with amusement.

"Nice to be young," said Frances. "Then you can laugh at the other fellow, and leave it at that. You never think that the things which make you laugh can also strike you cold with horror."

"Stop thinking about goose steps and a property mustache," advised Richard.

"Don't worry. I'm out of the dangerous stage of being mesmerized with fear. If I'm cold now, it's with anger."

"That's safer, anyway, when you are dealing with those birds," Richard said, and rose. He took her arm affectionately. "Nice little avenging fury you'd make."

They chose another road back to the shore of the lake. It led them towards a group of trees, sheltering houses more closely grouped together.

As they approached this small center, they noticed two or three little shops, and even some women and children, in the road which had almost become a village street. There was an inn and a beer garden, which looked as if the inhabitants of Pertisau might be able to enjoy themselves after all without any help from tourists in imitation dress.

"Signs of civilization," said Richard, but he surprised Frances by not entering the beer garden. A small shop which was part of a house seemed to attract him. They crossed the narrow street, and looked at its window filled with wood carvings. Most of them were of the Present-from-the-lovely-Tyrol variety, but on the back shelf were a few carvings of really good design and careful workmanship. The finest of these were two chessmen. Frances knew Richard was pleased.

"This may be as good a way as any," he said, and led Frances into the shop.

It had been the living room of the house. Now there was a table facing the door, on which more carvings were displayed. Behind this, under a window at the side of the room, was another table covered indiscriminately with shavings, chips, blocks of wood and instruments to cut and mold them. On the bench beside the table was a man. He rose slowly, coming towards them with a half-carved piece of wood still in his hand. He looked at them keenly, and then smiled.

"*Grüss Gott!*" he said.

"*Grüss Gott!* May we look at your carvings?"

"Of course. The lady and gentleman are welcome." He went back to his bench and started his work again. Now and again, he would look up to see what held their interest. He nodded as Frances admired some figures of the Three Kings. His best, most careful work was given to Biblical themes; to them and to the chessmen which Richard was now examining with interest.

"How much are these?" asked Richard. The man watched his face as he told the price. It was reasonable for the amount of work in the carvings.

"It takes much time," the man said, as if trying to excuse the charge. Frances wondered how often it had been rudely beaten down by people who had ignored the time, the skill and the love which had gone into such work.

"The price is not high for such craftsmanship," said Richard. "I'd like a set of these to take back to England."

"The gentleman collects chessmen?" The woodcarver was delighted. "Then you will see something. I have still better ones; some which I do not sell." He rose, quickly this time, and went to a heavy chest at the back of the room. He opened a drawer and took out a large box which he carried carefully to his work table.

"If the lady and gentleman would come over here . . ."

They went, and as they looked at the contents of the box, they found it not difficult to express their admiration.

"I do not sell these; they gave me too much pleasure when I made them," the man explained. Frances noted the large clumsy hands, knotted and gnarled with age, and wondered at their expertness, at the delicacy of their creations.

"Do you ever make copies of them, for anyone who wants to buy them?"

"Sometimes. But it takes a long time. A gentleman who lives here in the summer months has asked me to copy them for him during the winters. I have made him one set, and here is another which I am now carving for him."

They were suitably impressed.

"He must know a lot about chessmen," said Richard, hoping for the best. It came.

"Herr Doktor Mespelbrunn? Yes, indeed. He has a large collection. He lived in the South Tyrol before he came here, and he has some Grödnertal pieces."

"Really?" Richard hoped his admiration of the Grödnertal woodcarvers was emphatic enough.

"But why do the lady and gentleman not go to see Herr Doktor Mespelbrunn's collection? He shows them to people who really admire and understand."

Richard looked doubtful. "I should like to see them very much, but after all we are complete strangers to Dr. Mespelbrunn. I shouldn't like to disturb him, especially as I am only an amateur . . ." Richard's words were cut short by the old man's laughter.

"The lady and gentleman would not disturb the Herr Doktor. He doesn't work; he writes music." The woodcarver's joke lasted him quite a long time.

"Perhaps," said Richard, when he could, "perhaps I may have the honor of being introduced to the Doctor some day when I visit you again."

The woodcarver pursed his lips and shook his head.

"He doesn't come down into Pertisau much during July and August. He doesn't like tourists. But if you pass his house—it is the large house with the red shutters on the Pletzach—you should visit him. You can say that Anton advised you to go. It is a very beautiful collection."

"Perhaps we shall," said Richard, and dismissed Mespelbrunn from the conversation by placing an order. He insisted on paying Anton half the price in advance, the rest to be paid when the pieces arrived in Oxford.

"That seems fair enough," Richard said to Frances as they walked back to the lakeside. "By the time he can start work on them, summer will be over, and then he will know whether it is any use starting them at all. I've no doubt that he will be worried about the deposit, but he earned it."

They met groups of men returning from the woods, with their axes slung over their shoulders. They were lean, weather-tanned men, slow-moving and silent. They might have been a group of Scots shepherds, with the same strong bones and rugged faces. There was even the same upward lilt in their voices, as they gravely answered "*Grüss Gott.*" Some of the older men smiled in surprise as if they hadn't expected the old greeting from a present-day visitor. Children had finished their task of herding cows, and were playing outside the open doors of the houses. Their clothes made them look like miniature adults. Smoke was beginning to curl up from the stone-anchored roofs. There was the smell of cooking food in the air, and the high tight voices of women when they are hurried and tired.

Down at the lakeside, there were also preparations for supper. Here the women were changing one undistinguished dress for another, and no doubt fixing their hair as unbecomingly as possible. Those of them who had already succeeded in looking grim enough to satisfy the requirements of a superior race sat at the tables in front of the hotels, contemplating their husbands with housewifely virtue. The men talked and looked at each other. The women looked at the men. Behind them, the shadows of the mountains were mirrored in the still waters.

A gramophone played in the little café where the younger men were. There were not so many young men, Frances noticed, nor were there many young girls. Perhaps the new Germany had other plans for the holidays of its youth.

"A few more years of this, supposing that there was no war," said Frances, "and no one, who wasn't a German, could bear to come to the Tyrol."

"I always know you mean what you say when your sentences run away with themselves," teased Richard. And then he was serious again. "We had better not rush things at this stage. The ice gets thinner as we get farther out, you know, and the shore is less easy to reach. I've a feeling we ought to play doubly safe. Peter's man, the one he sent out before us, must have managed Nürnberg and Innsbruck; although to tell you the truth, I had begun to think when we were in Innsbruck that we had reached the snag. So we are going to be very innocent for a couple of days. We'll relax. What about climbing that blighter tomorrow? It's an easy one to begin with." He nodded to the Bärenjoch, black with the sun behind it.

Frances smothered a smile over her husband's idea of relaxation.

"All right, darling," she said.

They left the quiet road, and turned towards the Villa Waldesruhe. It was as peaceful as its name. There was no sign of the honeymoon couple or of Frau Schichtl. As Frances unpacked, she sang. Richard dropped his book on the balcony, and listened as he looked at the steep drop of the mountains on the other side of the darkening lake. He didn't know when Frances had stopped singing, or how long she had been watching him from the door. He rose hurriedly.

"One of those adequate five minutes," he said awkwardly. He looked at

Frances' hair and lips. "Darling, you are going to be thought most awfully decadent. The master race will disapprove."

"Too busy eating soup," said Frances. "Nothing, not even their principles, could ruin their appetites." She was right.

CHAPTER 13 REINFORCEMENTS

They did climb the Bärenjoch next day. As Richard had said, it was easy, and it was also useful. Richard spent a lot of time on the peak, studying with his map and pencil the lie of the valleys which met in the green plain of Pertisau. They could see the Pletzach, flowing at the base of the mountain opposite them like a very narrow, very loosely-tied white ribbon. If they were to follow the stream up round that jut of mountain into the valley which it sheltered, they should find Dr. Mespelbrunn with his chessmen and music books. Frances watched Richard. He was interested in the mountains, unsuspected from the lakeside, which stretched into the distance in rough-tongued waves. Two of the valleys led to paths which would take them over that sea of jagged stone.

"Looking for a quick way out?" asked Frances.

"It wouldn't do us much good in that direction," said Richard. "That's Germany. I wish to heaven that Pertisau had tucked itself near the border of a nice healthy place like Switzerland. Still, even if we have to make a dash for it, it is just as well to have a choice of directions. Yesterday I was worried because Pertisau was such a bottleneck."

"You seem to expect fireworks. It's difficult to think of any danger or evil lurking in this kind of place." Frances settled down on Richard's Burberry, and fished for a cigarette in one of its pockets. She lit it, and lay back to look at the sky.

"How are we going to do it?" she added.

Richard folded up his map carefully and put it into his pocket. He stretched down beside her and watched the clouds.

"I think Anton is our best bet. We'll just walk in, one of these days, and ask if we dare have the great honor and pleasure of seeing the chess collection. Anton's name will get us past any servant who's about the place. All other excuses are pretty obvious."

"Such as?"

"Well, you could need a drink of water, but unfortunately there's a nice mountain stream running down that valley. Or you could sprain your weak ankle, and need help to get back to the village. But that's rather a poor effort."

"I'm glad it is."

"So we shall just blow in, probably on Thursday or Friday, when Pertisau has looked us over and accepted us. There's no use risking everything by an enthusiastic dash. For if this Mespelbrunn is Peter's man, then an explanation for his silence would be the fact that he was under observation. And if he is under observation, then his visitors had better be very natural indeed."

"He must be able to speak German pretty well, if Anton and the others in the village accepted him."

"It's his job. The accent hereabouts, anyway, is so peculiar that he could easily pass himself off as a real Berliner. When he is in Berlin, he has a Viennese accent, no doubt."

"Well, I am looking forward to meeting him."

"Are you definite about that?"

"Quite. You aren't going to leave me out at this stage. You know, Richard, the man in Paris was very efficient. So were the others, but they seemed simpler, somehow."

"I should think the Paris man is second in importance to Mr. Smith himself. The beginning and the end, as it were. Fugger and Kronsteiner are just moveable pawns in the game."

"I keep worrying about poor old Fugger," said Frances. "I wonder if he did get away."

"If he hadn't, we wouldn't be here. Or, we would have been continuously followed until they could catch us with another agent. Don't worry about A. Fugger. He's a wily bird." Richard suddenly sat up and watched the mountainside.

"I thought I heard voices," he explained. He was right. Below them were two men.

Frances rose to her feet. The two figures paused and then waved their arms and shouted.

"It's Henry M. and Robert Thornley," Frances announced. "You know," she added in amazement, "I never thought they'd come."

Richard got up. He waved and halloed back. Van Cortlandt yelled something which they couldn't make out; but Thornley was laughing, and they laughed too. The American seemed to be in good spirits. He kept calling remarks to them which sounded funny although they couldn't hear them.

At last the two men came over the last piece of rock, and dropped on the ground beside Frances. The American regained his breath, and pointed to his face. It was crimson.

"Well," said Frances, "if you will climb at twice the normal pace and make wisecracks to go with it—"

"This," said van Cortlandt with as much pride as if he had been fishing for marlin, "is my first mountain."

"We are overcome," said Frances gravely, and handed him some sliced orange. "It was a most spectacular appearance."

Robert Thornley explained. "We motored from Innsbruck this morning, at the most ghastly speed you ever saw. We found the hotel, and then your house. A nice old thing—"

"Frau Schichtl," suggested Frances.

"—told us you were up here. It looked easy, so we came."

"All lies. Perfidious British lies," said van Cortlandt. "I drove Bob as gently as if he were in a wheelchair on the Boardwalk at Atlantic City. When we found you weren't there with flags of welcome, he dragged me away from a very nice little table beside a lot of water. And then he told me it was no climb at all. Just kid's play." He looked sadly at his shoes. "They'll never be the same again."

Frances laughed. "Remember to borrow some of our first-aid kit tonight."

"Do you mean to tell me I'll feel worse tonight than when I climbed this mountain?"

"Your feet will, in these shoes. Cheer up; it wasn't a bad climb for your first."

"Wasn't bad? It's darned fine if you ask me."

"Well, have a sandwich," said Richard. "We're glad to see you."

As they ate, they explained further. The pavements of Innsbruck had become hotter and harder after the idea of Pertisau had been put before them. Last night they had met and celebrated together, and had suddenly decided to get away from cafés and conducted tours for three days. Van Cortlandt felt he was due a vacation, anyway, and Thornley was becoming bored with being bored.

"It's the first real holiday I've had in two years," said van Cortlandt. "I'm always either going someplace or coming away from it, and I've always got an eye open and an ear listening. I'm going to forget all that for three days. I'll have to be back on Friday. Until then I am going to have some peace for a change."

Frances caught Richard's eye. "How do you like the view we arranged for you?" she said quickly.

Richard pointed out the different peaks. Over there was Germany. Down there were the Dolomites, and then Italy. Here the Danube would be flowing to Vienna. Back there would be the Alps of Switzerland.

"So this is what makes some people want to rush up to the top of every mountain they see," said van Cortlandt. He looked at Thornley pointedly, so that they all laughed, but in the end he was the last to leave the summit.

That night the promise of Innsbruck was kept. They enjoyed themselves.

By the time they had finished dinner, and had gone into the hotel lounge for coffee, most of the other guests had disappeared.

"They must get their beauty sleep," suggested Frances, and giggled. She was in rather good form tonight. She had been worrying during the last two days that if the two of them did come to Pertisau, perhaps the party would be a failure. But everything was going well. She looked at van Cortlandt, leaning forward to catch Thornley's words with a smile on his lips, a smile ready to break into a laugh when the point of the long story was reached. Richard was lighting his pipe contentedly, his eyes on Thornley who had now risen to his feet to give full justice to the climax. It was when they were all laughing that Frances noticed the man. He was watching them. He sat alone at a small table, a dark-haired man with bold black eyes, heavy eyebrows and a prominent jaw. He was probably about thirty, guessed Frances; and already his muscles were running to fat, but he was powerful enough. She noticed the tightness of his shirt over the expanse of his chest, and the collar which, already tight from the thickness of his neck, seemed all the tighter because of a black tie firmly knotted. It was a strange way of dressing for a summer evening. The jacket slung over a chair was a drab green, his only concession to the Tyrol, for he wore black breeches and boots. Just as a retired Navy man can be spotted by his taste in neat navy blue, so it was easy to guess how this man had spent much of his time. Take away the Tyrolese jacket, and add a black one, and a heavy black cap, and a holster at his belt, and a rubber club, and he was typed as accurately as in a Hollywood casting office.

His eyes had been fixed on Thornley. They suddenly swung round to Frances and became aware of her scrutiny. Frances let her eyes pass through and over him, fixing them on the deer's horns just above his head. She held them there until he had stopped looking at her, and had risen from his table. He threw some coins down with a careless gesture, ignoring two which fell on the floor. She was very busy lighting a cigarette, as he walked loudly out of the room. Van Cortlandt had noticed the last few moments, and was watching Frances with a smile of approval.

"You got out of that nicely," he said. "That's one of the boys in the back room. I'll lay you five to one."

"Big odds," said Thornley. "Don't tell me that the Gestapo finds its way to a place like this."

"They'll find their way to any place, even into countries which aren't under Germany—yet," van Cortlandt replied sourly. "They give me a bad taste in my mouth," he added. He began a story about them. Frances listened, but she watched Richard. Apart from a tightening of his lips, he did not seem disturbed by anything.

"Not one of the pleasanter types of humanity," summed up Thornley. They all agreed on that, and rose. An evening walk before they went to bed seemed a good idea. Van Cortlandt looked at his wrist watch, and raised his eyebrows.

"It's only a quarter of ten," he protested. "I haven't been to bed at this hour since I was in kindergarten."

"Don't you feel you'd like to be a dog, and just risk it once?" Frances asked gravely. He looked at her quickly, and then laughed.

"I'm learning something by living among the English. I now know when to risk a laugh."

Richard and Thornley had gone ahead. Frances slowed her pace. Van Cortlandt was trying to disguise a limp.

"Let's sit here, until the others come back," suggested Frances, as they passed some chairs tilted drunkenly against a table.

"Thanks . . . this foot is a nuisance."

"I'll give you some stuff to doctor it, tonight. Everyone has foot trouble on their first day in the hills."

He looked at her, and hesitated. He said suddenly, "You know, you're all right. I have to admit that I didn't think so much of you when we first met. Apart from being easy on the eyes, of course. I thought you were a hidebound Tory."

"You must have thought me rather suppurating." She smiled, and added, "Perhaps I am. But I'm no Tory."

"So I found out this afternoon. That was quite a talk we had, coming down that hill. I've been thinking it over since, and although I still stick to my own opinion, I begin to see why my remarks in Nürnberg made you so mad. You must have thought me—" he paused for the word.

"Smug?" suggested Frances gently.

"Now, that's pretty steep. Or did you?"

"Well, I must say I thought you inclined that way."

Van Cortlandt looked glum. "Well, that's a fine impression to hand out."

"I didn't do so well myself, did I?"

They both laughed, and then Frances was serious again. There was a sadness in her voice which she no longer tried to disguise.

"You see, if it comes to a showdown, it's the much criticized Britisher who'll have to foot a good part of a pretty bloody bill. We'll need words of encouragement from the sidelines, not jeers. And I wish you could believe me about appeasement. After all, you wouldn't call America a prohibition country today, although you lived with it for years."

"I see your viewpoint," said van Cortlandt. "It's another angle, certainly. But . . ." He shrugged his shoulders.

Frances was silent. The moon was on the water of the lake, and she could see van Cortlandt's face, white in the blue light. He looked even less convinced than his words. A thwarted idealist he had said, this afternoon.

Cynic would have been the same thing. She shrugged her shoulders too and tried to smile. Van Cortlandt was watching her.

"Do you know you were being followed in Nürnberg?" he asked suddenly.

"Yes."

"In a jam?"

"Not so far."

"Sorry if I seem inquisitive, but I just wondered when I saw that bird circling us tonight."

"I don't think that meant much. Sort of incidental music."

The American looked embarrassed. "Look, I know you would have told me about it, if you had wanted to. But all I'm trying to get at is this: if you are in a jam, you can always let me know."

"I can't tell you about it, Henry. Not because I don't want you to know, but because there's no use complicating things for you. I'll tell you all about everything later—in England, if you'll come and visit us there."

"You needn't worry about me. Mrs. van Cortlandt's little boy can take care of himself."

"But you are not so sure about us?"

"Oh well. I mean, you're not the kind of people to handle trouble; you're not tough enough. I wish I could put it better. I mean—"

Frances nodded and laid her hand on his arm.

"You're all right, too," she said.

There were footsteps on the road, and they could hear Thornley's voice, and then Richard's in a fluting falsetto.

"What the . . ." began van Cortlandt.

" 'Merchant of Venice.' Last act, I think, at the beginning." She began to laugh. "We can manage the midday sun, but not moonlight. Meet it is you set it down in your tables, Henry. You know, that chapter on the peculiarities of the British."

"Now when did I tell you I was doing that?"

"All books on European travel or politics have one. Why, no foreigner would believe he was looking at an Englishman unless he was funny-peculiar or funny-ha-ha."

"And what does the Englishman think about that?"

"He doesn't really care what people think about him, as long as he knows himself."

Richard and Thornley had timed their duet well. Richard managed to get the last line in, just as they reached Frances and van Cortlandt. He grasped Thornley's arm in a fair imitation of maidenly flurry.

"But, hark, I hear the footing of a man," he ended, and looked wildly round.

"You'd be safe enough if you looked like that," said Frances.

"Limping, anyway," added van Cortlandt, "so you're safe twice over."

"That role doesn't really do my powers justice," said Richard. "You should see me as the second witch in 'Macbeth.' Now that's something."

"Not tonight," said Frances hastily. "Let's all limp home to bed."

The four of them linked arms, and limped in unison towards the hotel. As Frances and Richard said good night, van Cortlandt looked as if he wanted to say something, but he didn't. He seemed worried again.

They crossed the road to the Villa Waldesruhe. Frances was silent as they went upstairs, and silent as she removed her earrings and brushed her hair. And then she remembered about van Cortlandt's limp. She searched quickly for the methylated spirits and boracic and lint. Richard made a good-humored grimace, and started putting on his shoes again. She heard his footsteps echo on the empty road outside, and began to undress. When he returned, she was already in bed.

"That fellow was back again, talking to the manager."

She blinked sleepily. That fellow—"Oh, Beetlebrows?"

"Yes. He must think we are lunatics, chasing about at this hour with first-aid."

"All the better," said Frances, "or isn't it?"

"Does no harm. Only next time, my sweet wife, do remember such things before I get my shoes off."

"Yes, darling." She yawned prodigiously. ". . . doing tomorrow?"

Richard folded his trousers before replying. When he did, Frances gave no answer; she was, like the rest of Pertisau, asleep.

CHAPTER 14   THE SINGING OF A SONG

Friday came quickly for Thornley and van Cortlandt, slowly for Frances and Richard. They had enjoyed the bathing and climbing, the strange conversations which had a habit of cropping up, as much as the other two, but, as Frances said, Friday was like taking medicine: she wanted to get it over as quickly as possible.

On Friday, the mists were on the mountains, and the waters of the lake looked gray and uninviting. It takes salt water to make a bathe, when the sun isn't shining. Van Cortlandt was disappointed, for this was his last day. On Saturday he had to meet a radio man in Innsbruck, who wanted some impressions from him for a broadcast to America next week. Thornley thought it would be better if he motored into Innsbruck with van Cortlandt. He had begun to worry again about Tony and his Czechoslovakian girl. He wanted to make sure that his Innsbruck hotel hadn't mixed up his Pertisau address.

Over their eleven-o'clock beer, the arrangements were made. And then came the suggestion from Thornley that once the Innsbruck business was finished, he and van Cortlandt should return to Pertisau for a couple of days. At this, Richard looked slightly taken aback. By Sunday, God knows what would have happened. The two men noticed his slight hesitation, the vagueness of his reply. There was what Frances called a pregnant pause. She felt miserable, trying to explain to them with her eyes and her smile that it was no lack of enthusiasm for them which had caused Richard's embarrassment. Van Cortlandt suddenly saw daylight.

"Of course, your movements are indefinite, we know," he said and looked hard at Thornley. Frances had the feeling that he had told Thornley about their being followed in Nürnberg. The feeling was confirmed when she heard Thornley make a good follow-up.

"We can phone from Innsbruck, and find if you are still here. That is, if you don't mind."

"That would be fine," said Richard, obviously sincere, and the difficult moment had passed.

"It's a pity you must leave today," said Frances. "There's a dance this evening." The men looked bored at the idea.

"No, not in one of the hotels," she went on, reading their thoughts. "It's the real thing, held in one of the inns back near the woods. They build a platform outside the inn, and everyone comes from miles around to dance in their best clothes. Some of the costumes are really perfect, and it's fun to see people really enjoying themselves."

"When does it begin?" asked van Cortlandt.

"Nineish."

He shook his head. "Too late for me; we'll have to leave about six. But say, if you go, tell me about it, will you?"

"How on earth did you find out about the dance? There's no notice up anywhere that I could see," Thornley said in amazement.

"Oh, I have my agents," said Frances, and then blushed as Richard looked amused. "Actually, it was Frau Schichtl. She told me about it this morning, and said very pointedly that we would be welcomed."

"That's rather strange, don't you think, considering their German cousins are all over the place? You would think that they would be the ones who were welcome, and that we outsiders would be avoided like the plague."

"Lower voice," suggested Richard quietly.

Frances followed the suggestion. "No, it was quite the opposite. Frau Schichtl was eager for us to go and meet the real Austrians. She offered me the Sunday dirndl dress her daughter used to wear. Very lovely it was too."

"She really is awfully decent, you know," Thornley said. "She waylaid us yesterday when we came round to beat you up."

Van Cortlandt stared. "Bob, what the—"

"To beat you up or to hound you out or to collect you," Thornley explained as an aside. "Anyway, while we waited in that downstairs room, Frau Schichtl was baking in the kitchen. It was a damned good smell, too. So we looked in and made some jokes in terrible German, and we had to taste the cake just out of the oven. Haven't done that for years."

"I seem rather left out of all this," said Richard.

Frances laughed. "No, you aren't. Frau Schichtl said you were very well brought up and *so* polite. And she loves your imitations of the Bavarian accent."

Richard reddened. "Oh, come!" he said, and the others laughed.

But van Cortlandt had sensed a story.

"Where's the daughter?" he asked Frances. She studied her hands and said nothing.

"I won't use it for copy, if that is what you are thinking," he added with a wry smile.

Frances hesitated, but the others' curiosity had been wakened.

"She is dead. Some years ago, she went to Vienna to study singing. Frau Schichtl had saved a little money, and the girl was eager. She must have had some talent to get her way like that. But instead of becoming a great singer, she fell in love and got married. He was an active Social Democrat. They were planning to come here to visit Frau Schichtl; they hadn't much money, so they had to plan it carefully. And then the Nazis arrived. The husband's name must have been on their blacklist. They said he committed suicide. Nothing more has been heard of the girl." She paused. "Frau Schichtl says that I look very much like her, when she left for Vienna."

Van Cortlandt said, "She may not be dead."

"Frau Schichtl hopes she is."

There was a silence.

Then van Cortlandt said again, "Just another. That's what gets me down. It isn't just an isolated case. Wherever you go beneath the surface in this damned Nazi setup, there's tragedy, or something twisted. Nothing but complications, and fears, and threats. Even those who think they've jumped on the bandwagon are still standing on one leg. Only the dumbest of them can forget they are on the edge of a volcano. A nice crop of neurotics they'll be after whatever is going to happen has happened."

"Or corpses," said Thornley unexpectedly. "They'd make a fine row of corpses." He looked speculatively at the froth rims in his beer glass. The story of Frau Schichtl's daughter had started him thinking again about Czechoslovakia, thought Frances. She watched them finish their beer, each man with his own thoughts. The truth was that there was no peace of mind left for anyone—for anyone with a heart.

Richard had risen, and changed the subject. "Now about this afternoon.

Frances and I thought we'd take a walk, and let you pack and make your arrangements. We'll be back to give you a send-off about six. That's the time you thought of, isn't it?" It was more of an intimation than a suggestion. Thornley caught van Cortlandt's eye, and the two men exchanged smiles.

"That suits us," the American said, and then added almost too casually, "and if you can't be good, you know what."

Frances and Richard left Waldesruhe at three o'clock. Richard had calculated that the distance from Pertisau to the red-shuttered house was about two miles. Yesterday, as they had climbed a hill with a view of the Pletzach, Thornley had pointed the house out to them—standing isolated in a high meadow above the little river. It was a good sort of place to have for the summer, he had observed. He was one of those who got a simple kind of pleasure in choosing sites for houses which he would never be able to own. There were already three places on the surrounding hillsides which he had selected as admirable for a summer chalet.

As they passed the Hotel Post, Thornley waved to them from the doorway, but he made no move to talk to them. As they entered the road which would lead them up the Pletzach, Frances glanced involuntarily over her shoulder. He was still standing at the hotel door, his hands in his pockets, and she had the feeling that he was making a very good pretense of not watching them. So his appearance at the door had been no accident. That gave her a comforting feeling. At least someone who knew them could vouch that they had left Pertisau quite normally. The deceased when last seen appeared to be in good health and normal spirits.

"He's a good person to have around in a crisis."

"Who is?" asked Richard.

"Bob Thornley. He tries to avoid discussing anything he feels very deeply about. It's as if he were afraid to let himself get emotional. He covers up with a funny story or one of these jokes against himself. And yet he notices quite a lot that is going on around him."

"He's no fool. Neither is Henry, but in another way. Did you know that Bob was an amateur golf champion of Belgium and Germany? Henry unearthed that. He would, of course. Now there's another who is afraid of his emotions, but he takes refuge in being so damned critical that he becomes a sort of perpetual Doubting Thomas. Yet underneath, he has plenty of the right reactions. His heart is in the right place even if he has trained his mind to respond with a firstly, secondly, thirdly. When he forgets about that, then you feel he's made of very real flesh and blood. I bet his life is a conflict between what he thinks is the clever thing to do, and what he wants to do."

"And which wins?"

"I said he had the right reactions."

"He certainly had them this morning. I liked him when he lost his temper. He summed up everything I feel very neatly. It's strange how well Bob and Henry seem to hit it off; they have so many differences. I suppose it is a case of accepting them, and resisting the urge to reform the other fellow."

"They've both got sense," said Richard, and taking advantage of the fact that they had passed the houses at this side of the village, and that they were the only people on the quiet, narrow road, began to discuss their plans for the last time. He had chosen to approach the house quite openly and directly, so that if it were being watched, their reason for the visit would be believed. If they were to approach it in any roundabout way, it would be difficult to explain such caution. Frances could see the sense in that, although it seemed almost too simple to her just to walk up to the house and ask for Dr. Mespelbrunn. In spite of her determination to keep cool, there was already a feeling of excitement prickling her spine.

It was just half-past three when the road, now scarcely broader or more definite than a cart track, curved round the foot of the hill which buttressed the mountain range on their right. Only then could anyone from the road see the house. It was planted neatly in the middle of a broad green meadow on the sheltered side of the hill, the side which had been hidden from them as they approached from Pertisau. It lay peacefully isolated. There was no sign of any life in the wooded valley which it commanded, or on the mountains which walled in the valley.

Behind them, the jutting arm of the hill had so completely cut off the road by which they had come that Pertisau seemed blotted from the map. The mists had risen from the mountains, and the wind had dropped; the branches of the trees were motionless, the leaves were still. There wasn't even the sound of a woodman's ax. Even the Pletzach had subdued its chatter; it slipped, smooth and shallow, over its gravel bed.

"This is where we branch off," said Richard, as they reached a low wooden bridge over the stream. Across it was a path leading up to the fringe of trees which grouped themselves round the meadow. Behind the house, they thickened into a small forest which covered the slope of the hill like a neatly clipped beard, and spread onto the mountainside, which lay behind. When they reached the first of the trees, they saw that a track separated from the path to take them across to the front entrance of the house.

Richard looked at Frances. "Smile for the dicky bird," he said, and forced one out of her. They left the shelter of the trees to climb up the gently sloping grass. Frances wished she felt as cool as Richard looked. His small talk on the beauties of nature was faultless. For once, she could not think of a thing to say.

It was a small house, sturdily built, with the usual overhanging eaves, a balcony encircling the upper story, and shutters with the conventional heart-shaped decorations. The large window boxes at the edge of the balcony were filled with petunias. Perhaps there were more windows than a peasant would have thought necessary, but otherwise it was the kind of house which someone who had lived in, and loved, the Tyrol might build as a summer escape from his town life. Someone who had indulged his taste for an additional romantic touch in the red of the shutters. They made a convincing and yet inconspicuous landmark.

The heavy front door was closed. Richard knocked, and as they waited, they looked at the stretching valley below them. Thornley had been right; it was a perfect place to build a house. The rain clouds of the morning had disappeared, and the sun warmed the stillness all around them. They heard the door open behind them, and they turned to face a woman. She was past middle age, large-boned, with the impassive face of a peasant. Her graying hair was tightly knotted at the back of her head; her large-knuckled hands kept smoothing her apron.

"Good day," Richard said.

The woman nodded, but did not speak.

"Is Dr. Mespelbrunn at home?" At the name Mespelbrunn her eyes moved quickly from Richard to Frances, and then back again.

Richard tried again. "I am interested in chess collections, and I have been advised by Anton in the village to visit Dr. Mespelbrunn, who has some very fine pieces, I believe. If Dr. Mespelbrunn were at home, perhaps he would have the great kindness to let me see his collection."

The woman was still silent. She was not altogether stupid, thought Richard, remembering the quickness of her glance. Could it be that she was afraid? Then the woman suddenly looked behind her, and drew quickly away from the door. Yes, it was fear, all right. A man came out of the shadows. He must have been listening quite quietly all this time.

"Dr. Mespelbrunn?" he asked. His voice had a hoarseness which coarsened his accent. He had pushed the gray-haired woman to one side, and stood in the sunlight with a smile on his dark face. It was the man who had watched them in the Hotel Post three nights ago.

He was as swaggering as ever as he held the door wide open and bowed them politely into the house. Frances felt her legs prepare to run back down the hill as she looked at that welcoming smile; but Richard was waiting for her to enter. They found themselves in the large room, a mixture of a sitting room, a lounge, and a study.

"She's just a dumb peasant," said the man with a still broader smile. Richard ignored the remark. He repeated the sentences he had addressed to the woman.

"But of course." The hoarse voice was being genial, but the effect was far from pleasant. "If you wait here, I'll get Dr. Mespelbrunn. He is reading in the summerhouse."

The man left them abruptly, his heavy heels sounding on the hardwood floor with a precision which grated on Frances' nerves. She exchanged looks with Richard, but neither spoke. She had hated this man at first sight. Still, they must see Mespelbrunn before they passed any judgments. The man might be only a very clever touch of realistic color. She remembered the grim Kronsteiner and his hotel. There was no doubt that Peter's friend had a peculiar sense of humor. This might only be another example.

She drew her cardigan more closely round her shoulders, and lit a cigarette. She walked slowly round the room, feeling it like a cat. It was a pleasant room, a man's room, smelling of pine logs and tobacco. She noted the walls of natural wood, the leather armchairs, more comfortable than elegant, the functional disorder of books on every table and music on the piano. A low table stood in front of the deep couch before the open fireplace. An open fireplace—perhaps an Englishman lived here after all. Yes, in the interior of the room there was a certain touch. An Englishman lived here. She turned to Richard. He was standing before the piano, his hands deep in his pockets, his lips pursed. He nodded silently to a piece of music displayed prominently on the stand. It was their old friend. He shook his head disapprovingly. Rather obvious, was what he thought. He moved away from the piano towards the fireplace and lit another cigarette. They heard footsteps outside; a man's voice spoke as if to a dog. It was only a short command, but the words were English. She sat down in the nearest chair and tried to look as calm as she didn't feel. Richard's calm gray eyes held her own for a moment, and then she started to count the steps in the staircase at the end of the room. She had reached the ninth stair when the front door opened.

They both stared in amazement. The tall man who had entered was equally taken aback. He recovered himself before they did.

"Well, really," he said in perfect English, "this is a pleasure."

Richard smiled; his eyes were calm again. "How extraordinary to meet you here," was all he said.

The Freiherr Sigurd von Aschenhausen moved quickly over to Frances and bowed low over her hand. She smiled, but inside she was angry. An Englishman, indeed, with that acute Oxford accent so carefully cultivated in his years of free scholarship. Would Mr. Rhodes have enjoyed this joke as little as she did? Probably less . . .

"We came to see a Dr. Mespelbrunn, or rather his chess collection. We were told in the village that it was the thing to do." Richard looked at von Aschenhausen blandly.

The German smiled. "Well, you've found him, you know."

"Are you— But why on earth—" began Frances, and hoped that the laugh she gave was sufficiently amused. "How really very funny. But why take such a wretched name as that and give up your own perfectly good one?" Help me to talk gaily, dear Heaven, she prayed, to talk nonsense like a sweet little fool.

"It's perfectly simple," said von Aschenhausen. "When I live here I have to be very careful; it would be impossible to use my own name." He paused but the Myles' only looked at him with polite surprise.

"It would be too dangerous for me," he added, lowering his voice. But they still looked at him politely, as if they expected him to go on.

"Cigarette?" he asked Frances, and flicked open his gold cigarette case. As he lit her cigarette, she noticed the bracelet on his left wrist. The bracelet was of fine gold, too.

She pretended she thought he had meant to change the subject. "You are looking very well," she said. One up, she thought, as she noticed the flicker of disappointment in his eyes. "You have a charming place here," she rushed on, before he could reply. "I think all of Pertisau is delightful."

"Yes; it is beautiful," von Aschenhausen said, emphasizing the stronger adjective. Someone ought to tell him, thought Frances, that he ought to have said "Do you think so? I'm so glad" and left it to his guests to do the praising, if he really wanted to perfect his imitation.

"You look very thoughtful," he remarked.

Frances came back to the room with a jolt. "Oh, I was thinking about forms of politeness."

"Now you have made me feel I must be very careful. I wasn't very polite according to your standards, I am afraid, when we met at that Oxford party. Why didn't you tell me then that you were coming here?"

Richard entered the conversation. "Well, first of all, we thought you were in Berlin. And, secondly, it was pure chance that we did come here. We were at Mittenwald, you know, and then one evening someone or other started to talk about the beauties of the Tyrol. You know the sort of thing: you discuss some place, and then you feel you'd like to go there, and then you go."

"Charmingly quixotic," said von Aschenhausen.

"And the most quixotic thing of all is that you should be Dr. Mespelbrunn," Frances said. She felt his interest quicken. "I had imagined someone quite different, you know." The tension was growing. "You see, I once read a book about Pertisau. It was called *The Constant Nymph*. So when we were buying some things in Anton's shop, and he said that *the* chess connoisseur of the district was a Dr. Mespelbrunn, who just adored visiting chessmen, as it were, I suddenly thought 'Another Pertisau eccentric; how amusing.' He gave you a terrific build-up, you know, until I became quite intrigued. It was really I who am responsible for the visit, because Richard went all sort of diffident. Didn't want to trouble you, and all that sort of thing. But I expected to find a house filled with a remarkable family of chess experts and unrecognized geniuses, and here you are, a very comfortable bachelor. You've really let me down, rather. I shan't be able to romanticize again without Richard . . . well, just look at him. He is enjoying his joke, isn't he?"

Richard was indeed looking amused.

"I'd still like to see the collection, if I may," he said.

"I'm afraid it isn't here at the moment. It's being exhibited at Innsbruck." Von Aschenhausen looked as if he really were disappointed too. Or perhaps it was genuine: at the beginning of Frances' little speech, he had hoped for something, something more than he had got by the end of it. He tried again.

"I think you have been mistaken about me. I've already apologized for our Oxford conversation. Can't you see there's no other course for me? Some types of work—" he paused effectively on that word—"need strong aliases."

His meaning, accompanied by that shrug of the shoulder, that pained eyebrow, that so straight, so direct look into Frances' eyes, couldn't have been plainer. In another minute, thought Frances, he will start telling us anti-Nazi jokes, just to show us how mistaken we have been about him. She looked as if she believed him; Richard nodded sympathetically; but neither of them spoke.

Von Aschenhausen waited. And then he began to ask about Oxford. His visit this summer had lasted only for a day; he had had little time to find out all about his old friends. Frances could see where this line would lead him. So he was interested in Peter Galt, was he? She left it to Richard to handle the conversation this time. She suddenly wanted to leave, but they couldn't do that until von Aschenhausen was satisfied. She looked out of the window. Her thoughts turned to Mespelbrunn. Where was he? Probably dead. Perhaps dead and buried on the mountainside opposite her. She watched the sunlight strike on the dark rich green of the fir trees, and the shadows lengthening on the hill. The afternoon was ending. She turned impatiently to the two men.

Richard, by some feat, had switched the conversation over to the women's colleges in Oxford, and there it had stuck, imbedded in the higher education of women. He refused to abandon his advantage; he had got the conversation to a nice impersonal subject, and he was going to keep it there. He was politely defending the new freedom of women. Women had learned to compromise successfully between developing their mental powers and retaining their charm. The aggressive unfemininity of the original blue-stocking was already disappearing. It was only a matter of time and adjustment to a freer aspect of life.

Von Aschenhausen smiled his disbelief. "They are too emotional. They are limited in reasoning power. They are weaker, both physically and mentally. They can never be equal to men. Compromise, adjustment, matter of time. . . . You couldn't be more English, Richard." The use of Richard's first name carried all three of them back, back to a time when suspicion and hatred had only brooded in the hearts of a few vengeful men.

In the silence that followed, they looked at each other. There was no need to translate their thoughts into words; they were clear in their eyes.

The German spoke first. "You need not reproach me. What Mrs. Myles said at that sherry party was true. Our countries have gone different ways. And I have my work to do. But I think, as I said already, that you have been mistaken about me. It is a compliment, I suppose, to my powers of acting. I never knew they were so good as that." He shrugged his shoulders again and gave a rueful smile. You are not making a bad job of it, right now, thought Richard. Von Aschenhausen had been well cast for the part he had to play. To anyone who did not know that he was German, he would appear to be the authentic Mespelbrunn. Now, he was making the best of a very bad piece of luck: here were two people who could know that he was no Englishman. His hints at anti-Nazi feeling were just enough to win their sympathy, disarm their suspicions. He didn't protest too much, either; he had to pretend that their visit was innocent, in case it really was. He couldn't make any declarations; he had to give them confidence, and perhaps they would show their hand once that was established. His difficulty was that they might very well be only interested in chessmen. Considering everything which was at stake, he was not making a bad job of it at all, thought Richard again.

Von Aschenhausen suddenly rose, and walked over to the small table which was used as a bar. His voice was charmingly ingenuous.

"You used to play well. Why don't you now, while I mix some drinks?" As he measured out the whisky, Frances was aware that he was watching Richard move to the piano with more than friendly interest.

"Hello," Richard said casually, "what's this you've got? Do you sing?"

"Only for myself. You go ahead."

Richard noted the soprano setting of the song, and smiled gently.

"It's a good song, but not my cup of tea. What about 'The Two Grenadiers' or something with hair on its chest? I'll need the music, though. I'm very bad at playing things by ear." He turned to a pile of music and started to look through it.

Frances rose and went over to the piano.

"You are both so modest. I'll sing for you instead." She saw Richard stiffen slightly, and give her a blank look. Von Aschenhausen was watching her now. She returned his smile sweetly and sat down on the piano stool. Richard cursed silently to himself; surely Frances had not been duped by an earnest pair of blue eyes. Surely she couldn't . . . He cursed to himself. If he could only reach that little table and upset it by accident before she started to sing . . . But as he moved, the first notes sounded through the room, and the words of the song gathered strength as her voice grew more confident. Richard looked at von Aschenhausen. His politeness had vanished. The dueling scars on his face were very noticeable.

Frances finished the last melancholy chords. She stood up and faced von Aschenhausen. She spoke directly to him.

"It is called 'The Slaughter of the Innocents'—one of the old Coventry Carols. Do you know it?" Her voice still held the sadness of the song, but there was a challenge in her eyes.

"Sentimentalizing history, isn't it?" His accent was less English.

"Maybe. But it's only when you think of history as blood and tears that you can ever learn from it." She saw he understood the meaning underlying her words just as he had understood the application of the song. The cap fitted. Let it, she thought savagely.

There was a sudden crash upstairs, and then the thuds of hollow blows. The noises ceased as startlingly as they had begun. Von Aschenhausen saw the surprise on their faces. He was suddenly casual and polite again; he smiled easily.

"Don't worry," he said. "That's the dog. We keep him out of the way when we have visitors. He's very savage with strangers. He is just about due for his exercise, and he always lets me know very forcibly when it's time to take him out for a walk."

"Oh, we mustn't keep you, then," Frances said. "I am sure we have stayed too long, in any case."

"I am sorry I had to disappoint you about the chessmen. They may be back by Sunday. Come and see them, then."

Richard, still listening for further sounds, said they would be delighted to come, perhaps at the beginning of next week. He was thinking about the dog. It was strange to keep an animal locked up inside a room upstairs; that would hardly improve its temper. But of one thing he was certain: von Aschenhausen was determined to get them out of the house, as quickly as possible.

Frances had already reached the door. As von Aschenhausen opened it for them, they heard two other sounds from upstairs. Weaker sounds, much weaker. But they ignored them, and said their good-bys as if nothing had happened. And they equally ignored the dark man with the hoarse voice, who stood astride outside the front door, his thumbs tucked inside his belt. At a nod directed upstairs from von Aschenhausen, he sprang quickly past them, mounting the steps three at a time. Von Aschenhausen had regained his usual composure, but his smile was too fixed. He stood at the door and watched them until they had reached the trees. Frances hated the feeling of his eyes on her back; she forced herself to walk naturally, as if she were strolling down Holywell. Only now would she admit to herself what she had first known at a sherry party in Oxford. The man who had once been numbered among their friends had long since become an enemy. It was a painful admission.

When they gained the road, Frances took a deep breath.

"Well, I've made another step in my education," she said. Richard did not answer. He was lost in thought.

"What's wrong? You haven't forgotten the Geneva address, have you? Or what?"

Richard shook his head. He seemed to be paying little attention; rather, he was watching the road as if he were trying to remember something.

"It's just about here, I think," he said as if to himself. He saw Frances looking at him curiously. "Just about here, that the shoulder of the hill stopped hiding the house. We'll give it another twenty yards."

The road twisted farther behind the jutting hill; and as it passed through a fringe of trees, Richard suddenly pulled Frances up the short steep bank into the shelter of the branches. It was all so quick that Frances did not have time to say anything; her surprise held her silent. Richard looked back over his shoulder, and then relaxed his grip on her arm.

"The shoulder hid us, and they couldn't follow us yet. Not with the road so open as it is."

"What's wrong?" Frances asked again.

"Something. Haven't quite made up my mind."

He advanced into the small wood, and Frances followed; the feeling of confidence which had come to her as they left the path and reached the road quickly evaporated. Von Aschenhausen had discovered nothing, except that they didn't like the politics of his country—and that couldn't have surprised him, even if it angered him. What worried Richard? He had reached a large tree, which had sheltered the ground from the morning rain. There they regained their breath. It had only taken them two minutes to reach here from the road.

The wood had grown over a large mound, and from this elevation they had a clear view of one part of the road, neatly focused for them by the way in which the trees grew. They could see without being seen. Richard moved slightly to the left to get a better sight of the one visible patch of road. From this point, it could be seen even if they sat down. He seemed satisfied—but not with Frances' dress. He pulled off the red silk handkerchief which she wore tucked into the neckline of her white shirt.

"Put on your cardigan properly," he advised, "and button it right up to cover that white collar. I don't like the red socks: they shine up miles away. Here—" He reached for a handful of earth mold, and covered the red wool with an efficient layer of clinging brown earth.

"Here yourself," said Frances with a good touch of annoyance.

"My pet, you aren't in this for the benefit of your color schemes." He kept his voice low, but there was enough sharpness in it to tell her he was worried.

"Well, I'm glad that the cardigan is green, or I'd be rolling in the mud at this moment, I suppose . . . What's *wrong?*"

Richard put one arm round her shoulders, and kept his eyes fixed on the road.

"Frances, what did you think when you heard the noises upstairs?"

So that was the trouble. She looked at him in surprise.

"Well, it could have been a dog," she said.

"Forget about that dog. What were the noises like? As you heard them, and not as they were explained away?"

Frances studied her muddied socks for some moments. She had been standing beside the piano; the drinks they hadn't touched had gleamed amber in a ray of sunlight.

"Well, candidly, the first sound seemed a crash, as if something heavy, like a piece of furniture, something solid, had fallen. And then came some thumps."

"Well?"

"They might have been a fist, but I don't think any fist could have hammered loudly enough for us to hear, even allowing for wooden floors and ceilings. No, I don't think those thumping sounds came from a fist. They were too powerful for that. I thought afterwards that it *could* have been a dog leaping against a heavy door. A big dog."

"But those thuds were clear-cut. They were sharply defined. There were no scrabbling noises, which generally end a dog's jump against a door. Even when we were leaving, and we were standing at the foot of the staircase, there were no whines, no pawing sounds. Peculiar kind of dog it must have been."

Frances looked at Richard, who kept his eyes fixed on the road. She was beginning to see the reason for his worry.

"Yes," she agreed. "There were only clear-cut thuds. Sort of staccato thuds."

"And the last two, which we heard at the bottom of the stairs, and which should have sounded clearer to us if anything, were actually weaker."

"Yes." Something haunted her memory. "Wait," she added. If only she could think what it was that had that kind of sound. Something she had heard that afternoon . . . in that room.

"Richard—" her voice was excited now, and Richard laid a finger on his lips warningly—"Richard, if a dog jumped at the door as we are supposed to believe, the thud on the door would have a different sound from a thud on the floor, wouldn't it? Well, do you remember when that bull-necked man left us to go and tell Mespelbrunn that we had arrived? He swaggered across the floor and his heels made that same flat sound. The thumping was not against a door, it was on the ground. And I don't believe it was made by anything so soft as a hand or a dog's paw. You were perfectly right, Richard."

"You are more right, still. Good for you, Fran. Now for a spot of reconstruction. We heard a crash, as if a piece of furniture or something solid had hit the ground. What about a chair? And what about someone tied to the chair? That would make the crash quite as heavy as we heard it. Then there were the thumpings, harder and stronger than the blows from a fist. What about two legs tied together? Then they would have to be brought slowly up and allowed to fall on the floor. That would give the kind of noise we heard, all right; for with the legs or ankles tied the heels would strike the ground together. It also accounts for the fact that the blows got weaker. It's pretty difficult and tiring to attract anyone's attention that way."

"But everything was so quiet in that house until those last five minutes."

"Yes, until after you had finished your song."

"Whoever it was recognized it?"

Richard nodded. "Yes. . . . He couldn't have made out our voices when we were talking. And there would have been no hope for him if he had heard a German song sung by a German voice. But there was hope enough to try to attract our attention when he heard an English voice and a song which practically only an Englishman would recognize."

"So he may be our man? What on earth can we do, Richard? We've found him and we haven't found him." This was something which Peter Galt had not thought of; they should have either met an Englishman, or found he was dead. Something nice and straightforward, and not a hopeless complication like this.

"What's our next step?" she asked dismally.

Richard drew a slab of chocolate from his pocket. "Eat some of this," he suggested. He looked at his watch. "It's well after five now. We had better wait a bit. If any chance comes, we'll seize it. If no chance comes, I'll take you back to Frau Schichtl's, and come back here myself tonight. I'd like to look around."

"You've no gun," said Frances in a very low voice; her fears stifled her. "Perhaps he isn't our man after all," she added persuadingly.

"It's some man, anyway. I'd still like to look around. Henry may carry a gun. If so, I'll borrow it. If not, then I've always got my stick." He patted the *makhila* which lay beside them. Frances looked at the Basque stick of rough wood, with its round leather handle and its sharply pointed ferrule. It didn't look much protection; the iron point on the end was only good for helping you up a steep hill. Richard noticed her expression. He unscrewed the handle with a suspicion of a smile.

"I never showed you this. It's rather gruesome." The head of the stick and part of the top of it slipped off, and a wicked eight inches of pointed steel emerged. It was firmly fixed to the rest of the stick, and transformed it into an ominous weapon.

"I'm not really bloodthirsty," he added. "I bought it on that Pyrenees trip, when I was an undergraduate, because I liked the way the Basques swung these sticks with the leather thong of the handle fixed round their wrists, when they were returning from market. Going to the town, they kept the cattle in order with the steel point. Coming from the town, they screwed the handle back in place and slipped the thong over their wrist, and swung it jauntily—with their jacket over one shoulder, and money in their pocket, and a smile for all the girls. I liked the contrast."

Frances looked at him incredulously. "And I've looked at that stick for years, and I never . . . When you told me it was used for goading cattle, I thought it was the ferrule at the end of the stick which you meant." She began to giggle; any joke seemed doubly good at this moment.

Richard's smile broadened. "Really, Frances, you're wonderful. Have you ever seen Basque oxen?" He laughed quietly, and then kissed her. "I wouldn't part with you for all the gold in America," he said.

Frances recovered her seriousness. "Now that I've supplied the comic relief, how long are we going to stay here, and what shall we do, if and when and where?"

"First of all, I was curious to see if we would be followed. We weren't, it seems. Von Aschenhausen perhaps was quite convinced that we were harmless fools. I shouldn't be surprised, though, if he checks up on our travels. You know the Teutonic thoroughness. That may have been the reason why he had that afterthought of inviting us to come back and see the chess collection: just so that he can know more about our movements when he meets us again. Probably, too, someone will be sent to keep a watchful eye on us until we leave Pertisau. That's very probable. That leads to my second idea. I've been hoping that Beetlebrows might make one of his evening calls on Pertisau. If he does, then we'll improvise."

"And I'll be quite useless," said Frances bitterly. "What you need is another man with you. And then we might be able to do something."

Richard didn't answer that.

"If we could get to the house in a roundabout way, or something—" Frances went on—"but then we'd have to face two men, armed, as well as the dog—if there is one. It would be madness. What you need is darkness, and someone like Henry or Bob, or both. And at least one gun. It's hopeless."

"Let me do the worrying, Frances. I'll try nothing unless one of them leaves. I can manage one of them alone, easily, if I can get to the house unseen. There is no telephone, and that will be useful for us: I'm depending on Beetlebrows, and his visits to Pertisau." He looked at his watch again. "It's getting near his usual time."

Frances wondered why Richard was so confident that there were only two men to worry about . . . But his eyes were fixed on the road. She sat beside him and waited in silence. She felt she had made enough wifely objections to last for the next few hours. After all, she had insisted on coming. Richard had been against it. Wifely objections would only be doubly irritating. So she sat and finished the job of converting her red socks into a rich chestnut-brown.

CHAPTER **15** THE MOUNTAIN

It could only have been about ten minutes later when Richard's arm tightened round Frances, and pushed her quickly flat on the ground. She felt a stone dig into the small of her back, but Richard's grasp was firm. She lay still and watched him. He was lying flat on his stomach, his head only raised enough to let him see that free patch of road. It was the black-haired man, cycling towards Pertisau, with a wolf-hound at his heels . . . And then he was out of sight: the other trees hid him from Richard's straining eye.

Richard relaxed his grip, and Frances sat up and rubbed her back. The stone had become a boulder.

"So that leaves only von Aschenhausen," said Richard with some satisfaction.

Frances forgot her good resolutions. "How are you so sure?" she asked.

"If there were others, then the noises upstairs would have been silenced more quickly. And von Aschenhausen had to signal to that man to stop guarding the front door. It was only then that he was free to go upstairs and attend to the noises. If there had been others to stop us from getting away—supposing it had come to that—then he would not have stuck outside until he got the signal."

"But why only two of them?"

"It's a small house, and if a group of men had arrived to live there, the villagers would have started to talk. Then any prospective visitors might have had suspicions aroused. I expect that black-haired fellow poses as Mespelbrunn's new servant." Richard looked at his watch, and then added, "We had better let him get halfway to Pertisau, and then he can look round as much as he likes and it won't trouble us."

"They haven't anything definite against us, have they?" asked Frances.

"Nothing except the fact that we were found in a suspected shop in Nürnberg, and that we presented ourselves to an obviously suspected Dr. Mespelbrunn with a highly suspect form of introduction. They may dislike the coincidence. Perhaps von Aschenhausen has started to check up on us already. There isn't any phone, but he has some kind of radio transmitter and receiver, I'm sure. Perhaps Beetlebrows is going down to Pertisau to keep an eye on us. Perhaps all that. And again, von Aschenhausen may be congratulating himself on getting rid of a pair of unwelcome visitors, and Beetlebrows is cycling down to Pertisau to see a girl, or have his beer, or to keep his figure. I think myself that it's safer to overestimate your enemies than underestimate them, so I'm prepared to believe that they don't like us one bit."

"Von Aschenhausen certainly didn't like me," Frances said, and laughed gently.

"I could have strangled you, myself, when you played that trick at the piano. You had me as jittery as he was. For a moment I thought you were going to play that damned music."

"Was it as good as that? Darling, you've made me very happy."

"It was too dangerous, Frances. Never give in to your impulse for the artistic, not in a situation like that."

"Oh, it was safe enough. He thinks women have no brains. Even at the very end, he only thought I was parroting some phrases I had heard you say."

Richard smiled in spite of himself. . . . And then he looked at his watch impatiently, and then he looked at the warm glow of the evening sun.

"I wish it were darker, but we can't wait. Come on, Frances."

They made their way back to the road, and paused at the edge of the trees. There was no one in sight. They crossed quickly into the rough field which stretched towards the stream, skirting the foot of the hill. They covered the uneven ground quickly but carefully.

"No twisted ankles at this point," said Richard. Frances nodded. She was concentrating on the varying firmness of the treacherous clumps underneath her feet. The stream was shallow, fortunately. They crossed by choosing stones either jutting up or only lightly covered by the racing water. Frances congratulated herself on having her shoes only wet, and not swamped entirely. And now they began to climb the hill itself, aiming for a point in its shoulder which would bring them just above and behind the house. This side of the hill was dangerously open; there were no trees, only grass and shrubs which ultimately gave way to the rocky spine. Again Frances had the feeling that the hill which they were climbing was the buttress, and the mountain behind it was the cathedral. It was like a finger pointing out of the mountain's clenched hand. The climb was more difficult than it looked from the road, for there was no path to lead them over the easiest ground.

Two thirds of the climb found the undergrowth thinning out quickly. They paused for breath, while Richard scanned the ground above them. He shook his head as he noticed the increasing number of small screes. It was madness to try to scramble over their treacherous surface; the stones now under their feet were as knife-sharp as when they had been splintered from smashing boulders. The ridge of the hill was of rock, and, at this distance, there was a dangerous look to the last fifty feet. It would be slow work getting over that. He looked along its side to the place where the hill joined the mountain. Just at that point there seemed to be a slight hollow. It was the bed of a mountain stream, now dry, but no doubt forming a gleaming cascade of water in the spring.

"Our best bet is to strike for the stream," he said. "It will take us farther away from the house, but the dry bed of a torrent is easier than a miniature precipice." He pointed to the crest of the hill. Frances needed no convincing. They began to climb obliquely up towards the bed of the stream, avoiding any falls of loose gravel, and choosing ground where some persistent green still showed. That at least gave them some guarantee of safety.

It was slow work, until they suddenly met, to Frances' joy, a small track which had the same idea as Richard. It must have begun at the road, near the place where the shoulder of the hill had formed a jutting curve, and had traced its modest way parallel to the shoulder's crest.

"We could have followed this all the way," said Frances, with some exasperation, following their own course up the hill with a bitter eye.

"No, it began too close to the house. The road at that point might have been watched by Herr Von-und-zu strolling in his nice soft meadow."

Frances was standing very still. "Well, we only postponed it," she said so quietly that Richard stopped and turned to see her face.

"Down there," she added. Richard followed the direction of her eyes. The valley beneath them was no longer empty. Along the road which led from Pertisau a man was riding a bicycle.

"Like the hammers of hell," Richard said, and swore gently but wholeheartedly. "Don't move. Keep just the way you are."

"He looks like an ant," said Frances.

"Louse, you mean." Richard was worried. "I wonder now . . . what did he learn at Pertisau to send him back at this rate? No one there knew when we were returning, except Henry or Bob; and he can't have been talking to them."

"I wonder if he saw us. Do you think he would take me for another piece of greenery? There are at least two pieces of scrub near me." She looked fearfully at her socks, but the loam had been reinforced by some mud which she had blundered into on the soft bank of the stream. Richard watched the cyclist as he reached the curve in the road.

"He hasn't slackened pace yet; it looks as if he might not have noticed us. If he had, I should think he would have slowed up, just to make sure. God, that dog can keep up a terrific clip."

"What shall we do?"

"There's still daylight for some time," Richard said thoughtfully. "Once we are up there, we ought to have a wonderful view of the back of the house. Damn it all, if only I had left you in Pertisau, and come by myself."

"Then you wouldn't have had either an old English song, or these noises. Let's go on, Richard. I don't like the idea of going down the way we came up. And once we get up—we are very nearly there anyway—we might find a decent path on the mountain itself to lead us back to Pertisau. There's no law against us trying to climb our way back towards the village and if anyone wants to know why we took so long, well then, we got lost. That's all." But the truth was, she added to herself, that Richard would have gone on if he had been alone or with another man—and that settled it.

Richard still looked doubtful, but he was wavering.

"Well, we can watch from the top for half an hour, and if it all seems hopeless, then I'll get you back to the road before it's dark."

"All right. Let's move, Richard."

They started to climb the last stretch of hill.

The path was apologetic. At best, it was little more than a foot broad; at its worst, it effaced itself altogether under slides of stones. As they crossed these slowly, Frances held her breath. One slip here, and she would go rumplin' tumplin' down the Tankersha' brae. She kept her eyes fixed on the next step ahead, and avoided looking down to her right. For there the hill now fell steeply away, carved out by erosion into an adequate quarry. If this path had lain across a field, you could run along it, she argued. So there was no reason why she couldn't walk along it here, provided she didn't know how far she had to fall. And then the green scrub was again growing thickly, and they had reached the bushes and dwarf trees which edged the bed of the stream. The sides of the dry torrent, and even the bed itself, were piled with large rocks. They formed a staircase. A giant's staircase, thought Frances, but at least if she slipped here she would always have a boulder behind her, to block her fall.

They were both breathing heavily with the effort of hoisting themselves over the rocks which would form the bank of the torrent when the snows melted in the spring. But the worst of the climb was already past. The boulders in the bleached bed of the stream were thinning out, and the ground was leveling. They were approaching the saddle between the hill and the mountain. As it opened out before them they saw that it was broad and gently sloping. They left the stream which was turning towards the mountain itself, and walked quickly over the grass towards some scattered rocks on the saddle's crest. From there they could see the valley with the red-shuttered house. When they reached the rocks only half of their expectations was realized. All they could see of the house was some blue smoke which curled up lazily over the tops of the farthest trees.

Richard smiled wryly. "Anticlimax department, I'm afraid. It seems I dragged you up here to admire the view, Frances. I'm sorry."

Frances let her muscles relax. She pushed her damp hair away from her brow to feel the full coolness of the evening breeze.

"You can always study the paths," she said.

Richard was already doing that. The saddle seemed the meeting place of the paths on the hill and the mountain. If he could get Frances back to Pertisau as quickly as possible, and if the moon was as clear as it had been last night, then he could use the mountain paths to bring him right up behind the house. He could see both of them clearly from here; neither was difficult. Eastwards towards Pertisau stretched the first path he would use, which would bring him easily onto this saddle; and then, from here, there was a westward path, cutting across the mountain where it formed a background for the house. He could see at least one track descending from it into the trees which encircled the back of the house. Then he might try some stalking right up to the outskirts of the house itself. Thornley would be a good man to have along; he knew his way about a mountain. It was just as well that he had come up here after all. He looked at the mountain paths, and photographed what he saw in his memory.

Frances, lying beside him, her chin cupped in her hands, had been staring at the forest beneath them. Her eyes followed the well-marked path, which led from the saddle down through the trees towards the house. This was probably the path which began at the bridge in the valley. She looked at the trees, as if by sheer will-power she might see through them, through the walls of the house itself into that room upstairs. She was comparing her reactions as she had left that house to those of Richard, and the result did not flatter her. She had taken it for granted that their job was over, that there was nothing left to do except send a telegram and then go away and enjoy themselves. She had believed the story about the dog because she had wanted to believe it; it was a subconscious desire to be rid of complications, to avoid any further trouble. Now she knew that she wouldn't have been able to enjoy any holiday. She would have had to face the fact ultimately that it hadn't been a dog, and she would have remembered it just as long as she would remember the cry in a Jews' Alley in Nürnberg.

She suddenly stiffened.

"What was that? Richard, I saw something down there."

"Where?" He turned to look down the hill towards the house. The path, beginning near where they lay, twisted its way towards the forest. Beyond the last trees, the smoke curled from the chimney.

"Down there. Look. The twist in the path hid it . . . near the trees. Richard, it's a dog."

Richard grasped her wrist and the strength of his hand calmed her.

"So he did see us," he said.

The dog, bounding up the path towards them, had stopped and was looking backwards. When the two men came in sight, he again bounded on.

It was von Aschenhausen and the black-haired man. The path was broad enough to let them walk abreast. They carried no sticks, but their hands were deep in their jacket pockets. Their eyes searched the hill around them. Once they stopped, while the man looked towards the westward path on the mountain, but it had only been some animal which had attracted his attention. He had quick eyes all right, thought Richard.

"Keep cool, Frances. They haven't seen us yet."

Again the men stopped, and this time they separated. Von Aschenhausen left the path, and began to climb directly up the shoulder. His pace had slowed down, but even from that distance it was evident that he could climb. When von Aschenhausen reached the top, he would be just about the place which they had first attempted to reach. Richard reflected with some pleasure that the east side of the shoulder, which the German would then have to descend, would cramp his style a little. His plan was to encircle them, obviously. The black-haired man was plodding steadily up the path to the saddle where they lay; the dog bounded ahead.

As they backed cautiously from the sheltering rocks, and raced back over the gently sloping ground, Richard was thinking quickly but nonetheless clearly. Von Aschenhausen had taken the much more difficult way because his companion was probably a less expert climber. So much the better for Frances and himself. He would rather face brawn than brain, any day. You could outwit the former. They must make for the bed of the stream; that was their only hope for cover. Once they were hidden by the boulders and the bushes which twisted round them on the torrent's banks, they could follow the bed until they had reached the fields and the woods round the Pletzach—and then they would be safe enough. The incriminating thing for them would be to stay on the shoulder overlooking the house. If von Aschenhausen didn't find them on the hill, they could find an explanation for their late return to Pertisau. And he would have to accept it, because he wouldn't be able to disprove it. But it all made tonight's plans almost impossible. They would be closely watched from now on.

If Frances had been thankful for grass under her feet when she had first reached the saddle on the way up, she now almost wept with relief. She could run swiftly on this surface and, what was just as important, run silently. She had the feeling of desperate effort which she used to have as a child when she played Cowboys-and-Indians and she was one of the chased. It was no longer a game, but the old terrifying feeling of strained muscles bogging her down, of feet sticking to the ground, was still there. She must go faster and faster, but her body refused even as her mind urged her on. She sagged, her heart pounding and a strange thundering in her ears so that she couldn't swallow. But Richard's hand, which had not loosened its grasp on her wrist from the moment when they had first seen the dog, pulled her up and on. They had reached the stream.

Their run had slowed down to a scramble, but the first large rocks were near them. Richard had let go of her wrist now; they needed the use of their hands to steady themselves through the boulders. It would have been quicker work if they hadn't had to avoid any clatter of stones. Richard was thankful for what he had been cursing only half an hour ago, for the fact that they had worn rubber-soled shoes today to go visiting, rather than their nail-studded climbing boots.

The man could not have reached the top of the path yet; nor could von Aschenhausen have reached the crest of the shoulder. As the stream bed plunged deeply in between the crags, Richard looked over his shoulder. They were hidden now, thank God, from both the shoulder and the saddle of the hill. There was no man in sight. But there was the dog. It had marked them from the saddle, and instead of waiting there for the dark-haired man, had followed them. It hadn't barked. There was something uncanny in the silent way it calculated its powerful leaps over the rough stones, to alight on smooth rock. Its speed was checked by its twists and turns, by the way in which its thick haunches would brake suddenly on the steep side of a boulder. But its direction was unerring.

Richard hurried Frances on. They had passed the point where the track on the side of the hill had met the stream, and they were on strange ground now. The bed plunged still deeper, the banks were rockier, and more thickly screened by small wiry mountain trees. Their speed increased again, for the bed was less cluttered with boulders. The stones under their feet were sharp and uneven; those stones would hold up the dog, anyway. And then the stream curved round a mass of rock, and they saw that the narrow gorge before them suddenly ended. In front of them was nothing but space, and the precipice over which the torrents would pour in the spring, falling in a series of cataracts to the valley beneath.

They looked at each other, trying to hide the dismay in their hearts. To their left was the open mountain rising steeply; to their right, over the high bank with its crags and bushes, lay the landslide which Frances had called a quarry. They were neatly trapped.

Frances backed away from the edge of the precipice instinctively. Richard stood, his eyes turned towards the mountain, looking for some short-cut up to that eastward-bound path which would lead them to Pertisau. The ground was open, and there was little cover, but if the man had followed the dog into the bed of the stream, his view of the mountainside would be blocked by the height of the banks long enough to let them reach that point in the path where there were some trees and scrub. Anyway, there was no other choice.

And then, behind them, they heard the panting of the dog. It had followed the boulders on the banks of the stream, and now it was poised above them, eyes gleaming, teeth showing wickedly. Even as they had turned, it gathered its muscles to spring. Frances was the nearer. She heard Richard's voice behind her, low, urgent.

"Down! On your face!"

She was hypnotized as the animal, now more wolf than dog, hurled its huge weight down at her. She heard the snarl, saw the teeth ready to tear. Her eyes closed involuntarily as the slavering jaws aimed at the level of her throat, and she dropped on the ground. She felt it pass above her body, striking something beyond. Richard . . . Richard . . . That sound, what was that sound? She raised herself on an elbow, afraid to turn her head, afraid to see. Just behind her, so that she could have touched it with her foot, lay the dog. Its throat was spitted on the steel goad of Richard's stick. Richard rose, his face white, his hands still braced on the stick's shaft. The force of the dog's leap had knocked him backwards. He tried to shake the animal's body free from the stick, but the eight inches of steel were firmly embedded. With a grimace of disgust, he put his foot on the dog's chest, and pulled the stick as if it were a bayonet. It came out slowly.

From farther up the bed of the stream had come the rattle of stones, as if a heavy man had slipped badly. Richard pointed to the bank on the mountain side of the gorge. Frances rose, and moved with difficulty towards the protection of its rocks. The man would not see them until he had got well round the bend, and then he would see the dog first. There was no time to hide it, even if they could have brought themselves to touch its dead body. Richard followed her, the stick still blood-covered. He should have wiped it on the dog's coat, he knew; but he couldn't. He felt sicker than he liked to admit.

"Through there," he whispered, pointing between two boulders. Frances obeyed, keeping her head and shoulders low. By using the uneven rocks and the thick bushes for cover, they managed to clear the stream's high bank. The man in the stream bed would not see them, because of the twist in its course. Von Aschenhausen, now probably over the shoulder, might be on the difficult track which had led them to the stream. It had taken them a good fifteen minutes. It would take him as long; there was no easy way.

They paused for a moment. Behind them lay the bank; in front of them was the mountainside, its slope covered with scrub which would hardly reach their knees. They heard the man's steps now, in the bed of the stream. He would just be coming round the bend now. The footsteps paused, and then quickened. So he had seen the dog. They heard his oaths. Richard still hesitated, wondering if they should stay quietly where they were, hidden by the boulders. . . . And then he remembered. The bloodstains. They had laid a pretty track.

"Go on," he whispered to Frances.

She looked at him despairingly. "I can't lead. You must. I'll go over the side." She pointed to the steep drop down to her right. The landslide which had created the quarry and the cataract behind them had done its work here too. The shoulder met the mountain with a spectacular precipice. Their only hope was to keep away from the treacherous edge and work up towards the mountain path as quickly as possible.

Richard had already moved ahead. There were no more blood drops from the stick. If they reached the shelter of that boulder ahead before the man could follow their trail through the rocks on the bank, they could take cover there. If he didn't see them, it was possible that he wouldn't start to search this nasty piece of mountainside by himself. He might even think this way impassable and that they had doubled on their tracks upstream again. Judging from the noise the man had made as he had come down the bed, he was not much accustomed to climbing. That was something to be thankful for.

Richard moved quickly and carefully, conscious that the ground sloped on his right towards the precipice. The boulder he had picked out as a refuge lay farther up the hill, farther away from the edge. That would cheer up Frances. And then it was that he became aware that her footsteps were not following; or was it possible that anyone could walk so quietly as that? He turned slowly, carefully balancing his weight. Frances stood almost where he had left her. She had moved up the hill slightly, back towards the rocks. She was standing quite still, her body pressed against one of them. That damned precipice, he thought, and stʌrted despairingly back towards her. But she shook her head and waved him towards the shelter of the boulder. She had heard the man climbing laboriously, the leather soles of his boots slipping on the stony surface. She moved slowly up behind the rock to which she had been clinging, avoiding the large stones which were loose to her touch. The fear, which had paralyzed her legs so that she couldn't follow Richard, suddenly left her. All she felt now was anxiety for him. She pointed frantically towards the boulder; but he didn't or wouldn't understand. He was coming back to her.

The man was almost over the bank. Like them, he had chosen to keep in cover. Perhaps he thought they were armed, and was taking no chance of silhouetting himself against the sky. He would come out down there, just where they had emerged from the bank, for it was the easiest way through, but although she had followed his progress with her ears, it was a shock suddenly to see him there, only ten feet away. He hadn't looked up towards where she remained motionless behind the rock. If he had seen her, he ignored her; his eyes were fixed on Richard. He pulled out his revolver. It was a large, efficient-looking black one. Then, as he saw clearly that Richard was unarmed, he stepped forward out of cover. If he had expected Richard to throw himself on the ground, or to turn and run, he was disappointed. The two men stood scarcely twenty yards apart, looking at each other. There was a smile on the man's face. He was like a cat playing with a mouse. He lifted the revolver slowly, slowly. Frances raised the heavy stone which she had gathered in her two hands and threw it with all her strength from above her head.

It caught him between the shoulder blades, and sent him staggering forward. Frances saw him make a frenzied effort to regain his balance, half-turning towards her as he fell. Even then, he would have been safe if he had braked with his elbows and dug in his feet. But he had only one idea; he twisted quickly round to shoot. The sudden movement cost him his one chance. She saw the rock splinter beside her, and then heard the crash of the revolver. It was then that he realized his own danger. Frances, crouching at the side of the rock, saw the expression of hate on the man's face give way to fear. She saw him drop the Lüger, his hands claw the ground, too late. There was nothing on the sloping edge to grasp except loose stones. He was clutching one in each hand as he slipped over the precipice. His scream fell with his body.

It was Richard who stood beside her, trying to loosen her grip on the rock. He put his arm round her waist and helped her up the sloping ground, back towards the stream. They had followed the sheltering bank almost to the flat ground of the saddle before Frances realized they had retraced their path.

"Richard," she said, "I'm going to be awfully sick."

"Darling, try not to. Not now. There's von Aschenhausen still. He should be almost at the stream by this time. He must have heard the shot and the scream."

She passed a hand wearily over her white face. Her voice was flat. "I forgot about him. Do you think he has seen us?"

"I hope not. We've kept under the shelter of the bank all the way up, and we are on the mountain side of the stream, while he is, or was, on the shoulder side. Anyway, he will have plenty to occupy his attention down there. It will be quite a job looking for his boy friend. He will probably think we headed for the path on the mountain. It isn't likely that he would guess we are going to use his own path down to his house."

"Richard!"

"Yes, we are. It's quite the safest way down. I don't like the idea of the mountain path now that the sun is almost gone." It was true: the mountain was hazier, and the light had turned a cold-gray. Ahead of them was the only glow in the sky, where the setting sun colored the clouds.

"Keep low," Richard warned, "as we go across the saddle. And watch the sky line." They broke into a crouching run as they crossed the grass, and when they approached the top of the saddle, they used the boulders to black-out their outlines to any watcher beneath them. They crossed the top by lying flat on the ground and edging their bodies carefully over. When they had reached the western side of the rocks, behind which they had lain this afternoon and looked down into the valley, Richard stood up and helped Frances to her feet. Normally, he thought, she would have giggled at the ludicrous figures they must have made in the last ten minutes. She would have had some joke to make about the rips on her clothes, the bruises and scratches on her legs. But she said nothing, only faced him with her large eyes still larger. He felt her hands; they were cold, like marble. He pulled out his flask of brandy.

"It's safe enough on this path," he said. "Take a good swig, Frances."

She took it obediently, and handed the flask back in surprise.

"Not even a cough or a splutter," she said in amazement. Richard's anxiety lessened. It was a good thing if she had started noticing her reactions.

"Got your wind?"

She nodded. "I'm all right." The brandy had warmed her, and the sickness was gone.

"Well, I'll let you do what you've always wanted to do. I'll let you run down a hill."

She was almost smiling. He caught her in his arms and hugged her.

And then they were running, carefully but steadily, down the broad path. Richard kept to the outside, holding her right hand as they ran. Their speed increased when they reached the darkening wood, for the path had broadened and was softened with pine needles. It twisted through the trees in zigzag curves, and these they shortened by slipping and sliding down the dry earth of the banks. The wood was already asleep. There were no sounds except the muffled pad of their feet, the occasional snap of a dry twig, the heaviness of their breathing. The trees were thinning, there was a little more light, and they were passing the edge of the meadow and the track which led to the house. Down there, in front of them, were the bridge and the road itself.

Then Richard caught Frances tightly. Through the quickly falling dusk they could see a car on the roadway, and the men talking beside it.

"O God," said Richard.

Frances looked at him in surprise.

"What's wrong, Richard? Don't you see who they are? It's an American car."

She was right. They started forward again. The two men looked as if they were getting into the car.

"Hoy!" Richard called softly. The men halted, and turned round in amazement. And then they ran over the bridge to meet them.

"Well, I'll be—" began van Cortlandt, and then stopped as he looked at them. Richard pushed Frances into his arms.

"Get her into the car, and look after her. Park off the road, and not where it can be seen from the house. Keep the lights off. Be ready to start at a moment's notice. Need your help, Bob. Are you game?"

Thornley took his eyes off Frances' face and the cut on her shoulder where her ripped cardigan and blouse showed blood.

He nodded. "I'm ready," he said, and moved off after Richard.

Van Cortlandt watched them go towards the dark house.

"Now just what's this all about?" he said. Frances tried to smile.

"I sang and we heard noises and they said it was a dog." Her voice was low and tired. He caught her as she stumbled forward, and carried her to the car.

He moved the car as Richard had said, and then turned to look at the girl beside him. She hadn't fainted; she had just collapsed . . . Pretty thoroughly, too. There were tears running down her cheeks.

"I haven't got a hankie. I lost it," she said in a muffled voice.

He looked at her torn clothes. "I'm not surprised," he said, and handed her the neatly folded one he kept in his breast pocket. "Try this."

Frances saw his concern. "I'm all right, really. All I need is a good cry."

"Well, go ahead," he said. "I've another handkerchief in my hip pocket. They are all yours." He was rewarded with a weak smile.

"I can talk, now," she said at last. "I don't suppose you have anything I could eat? I'm sort of empty inside."

"Only candy. I could give you a drink, though."

"I've had one. Candy will do, beautifully."

He watched her curiously as she ate the bar of chocolate.

"You can tell me as much or as little as you like," van Cortlandt said. "I'll not use it."

Frances looked at his firm mouth and worried eyebrows.

"I know, Henry. I suppose it's only fair to let you know what's happening, seeing that you are partly mixed up with it now, anyway. Do you mind if I eat while I talk?" Van Cortlandt restrained his grin. These people, really . . . There, he was catching it from them. *Lost it,* she had said apologetically, when she looked as if she had almost lost everything else, including her life. *Eat while I talk, do you mind?*

"Remember, not a word of this to anyone. Not until we are all safely out of this country. It's—" She hesitated for the right word.

"Dynamite?"

She gave her first real smile. "Yes, dynamite."

She tried to get the things she would say into the right order. Her story was slow and halting. She began with the visit that afternoon to the Englishman who was no Englishman. Van Cortlandt listened attentively and patiently, his eyes trying to see her face in the darkness. He didn't miss the pauses, when she would struggle for words and the story would take a leap forward. She was near the end of it now. There was a note in her voice which held him silent through the long hesitations between the phrases.

". . . and missed . . . and fell . . . over a precipice. We climbed back on our tracks and crawled and ran and then we saw you."

"And what about the German whom you knew?"

"I suppose he would try to trace the other. He must have heard the shot, and the scream." She stopped suddenly, and there was another pause. "There were signs of the fall, you know, where the stones slipped."

Van Cortlandt whistled. "Well," he said, "that was quite an afternoon you had yourselves."

Frances said nothing to that. She tried to see out of the car, but it was almost dark. "I wonder why they are so long?" she said.

"Don't worry; they can take care of themselves," but his face was less confident than his words.

"I could kick myself," he added. "I'm the big mouth who gave you away."

Frances looked at him in amazement. "You know, I haven't asked you how on earth you got here. You should be in Innsbruck, and Bob, too. I was so glad to see you, I forgot to ask."

"Well, it was like this. Bob saw you start off, and when you didn't get back before six as you had promised, he got worried. My guess was that you had forgotten: you were sort of vague about it. But he just shook his head gloomily and said he was going to wait. So we hung about, and then that black-haired guy arrived on his bicycle. I was standing at the hotel door—Bob was somewhere inside—and he had a look at our suitcases and the car. Just then the hotel man came out, and stopped to speak to me. He said we were late. I said yes. He said was there anything wrong? And I said you hadn't got back yet. At that, the black-haired chap got onto his bicycle and went over to Frau Schichtl's. I didn't like that. And I liked it less when he must have found out you weren't there, because he shot past us and went right back in the direction he had come from, with the dog just behind him."

"I had the sense to ask who he was. The hotel man shrugged his shoulders and said something about the house with the red shutters. And then Bob came out, and he and I had some beer, and we talked it over. And the later it became, the worse we liked it. We went to see Frau Schichtl, and we worried her too. But anyway she could tell us the quickest way to get to the house. That worried Bob still more, because it was the road you had taken that afternoon. Then we thought we would go see for ourselves. Bob said you hadn't been prepared for a long walk or climb when you left the village; he had noticed you weren't wearing your boots, and that clinched the argument. We thought we would ask at the house and find out if anyone had seen you; we were both hoping that perhaps you had tried a short-cut home and had sprained an ankle or something.

"Well, we got to the house, and we knocked loudly enough, but we got no answer. Silent as the tomb. We were talking about what we should do next, and we were just about to leave, when we heard Richard."

"Thank Heaven for that," said Frances quietly.

They were both silent.

"I'm tired," said Frances suddenly, and he saw her eyes close. He reached for the rug and wrapped it round her, and pillowed her head more comfortably against the back of the seat. She was already asleep.

He strained his eyes through the darkness, but he could only see the outlines of the bushes and trees. He could hear nothing, except the gentle breathing of the girl beside him. Poor kid, he thought. What was that Gilbert and Sullivan thing? "Here's a how d'you do . . ." It was all that, and more. Expect the worst, and you won't be disappointed, he told himself. He slipped some gum into his mouth, and settled down to wait, with his gloomy speculations for company. What interested him most in Frances' story was the omissions.

CHAPTER **16** FRAU SCHICHTL INTERVENES

As Richard and Bob Thornley moved towards the house, Richard gave a concise and abbreviated version of what had happened. Like Frances, he was careful to be vague about Mespelbrunn, but his account of the way she had saved him on the mountainside was included.

Thornley listened in silence, and then as Richard finished speaking in the low voice which was almost a whisper, said, "Pity you didn't get the other blighter, too."

The house was just as van Cortlandt had described it to Frances. Silent as the tomb. They tried the front door and windows. As they expected, they were locked. The back door was locked, too.

"Goes to bed early," whispered Richard.

"Who?"

"The maid. Or else she was packed off home."

"Can't risk breaking a window, then?"

"No, she may be asleep in her room," Richard said. He pointed to a window. "That may be our room. Can you climb?"

Thornley looked at the balcony at the side of the house. He grinned.

"Easy meat," he said softly. He swung himself up easily from a window-sill. He had a professional way of feeling for a hold and using his feet. Richard wondered if he were one of the Cambridge roof climbers. In that case, it *was* easy meat. Thornley had hold of the balcony now; he pulled the rest of his body up slowly until he could swing a leg over the railing. The whole thing looked so simple that one would hardly have guessed the strain on his arms and shoulders. He disappeared silently over the edge of the balcony.

Richard kept close to the shadow of the house. Above him, he heard a shutter being tried. Then there was a shadow on the balcony, and a whisper. "Barred and bolted. Hopeless. I'll try another room." The shadow vanished.

Richard waited. The minutes seemed like hours. He thought he had heard a shutter being forced open. . . . And that sound might be a window. He began to blame himself for not having tried to climb up himself, even with his stiff shoulder and torn knees. What the devil was keeping Bob? Just as he was trying to think of the easiest way to get up, he heard Thornley's voice in a whisper above him.

"Here. Lend us a hand." He was supporting another man. Richard watched Thornley help the man over the railing, and then lower him, holding on to the man's wrists. Richard braced himself to take the man's weight as he dropped.

"Right," he whispered. Thornley, half over the railing, grunted, and let go of the man's wrists. Richard caught him by the thighs as he fell, and they rolled over together on the grass. Thornley swung himself lightly down beside them, and helped them to their feet.

"Winded?" he asked the man.

"All right, thanks. Neat job." He stood up shakily, and looked from Thornley to Richard.

"Who was here this afternoon?" he asked.

"I was," Richard said.

The man turned to Thornley. "There's a summerhouse at the edge of the wood, beside two tall trees hiding a mast." Thornley looked towards where the man pointed, and nodded. The man went on, "There's a wireless set there, and a motor bicycle. Can you put them out of action?"

"We'll start for the car," said Richard, as Thornley grinned and turned to sprint for the summerhouse. He put the man's arm round his shoulder, and held him at the waist; together they walked slowly towards the path. The man might have been thirty or fifty; he was one of those bird-faced Englishmen whose age it was difficult to guess. He was of medium height and thin. His hair was mouse-colored; his eyes were nondescript. His voice had no marked accent.

"Why were you here this afternoon?"

"We were directed to Mespelbrunn from Innsbruck."

"And you found him?"

"Not the one we were looking for."

"Who are the 'we'?"

"My wife and myself."

"You look as if you had met trouble."

"Complications. I left my wife in the car."

"You've a car? Good."

"And an American: a reporter."

"Not so good."

"He's a decent sort. We can trust him."

The man shook his head and cracked a smile. "Trust no newspaperman; they've an itch for a story. If he asks questions, I'm Smith, who helped escapes from concentration camps. That's true, anyway. Who's the other, our blond Tarzan?"

"I know his brother."

"I'll be Smith for him too."

They had reached the fringe of trees. There was no sound of running footsteps from the wood above them. There was still some safety, yet, thought Richard. He wished Thornley would come. The man's weight was tiring him.

"How are you feeling?" he asked.

"Shaky and stiff. But better every moment. Good to be free again."

"How did they get you?"

"The man who posed as Mespelbrunn was supposed to be in sympathy with the underground movement. He even helped some escapes. Got at me through them. How were Nürnberg and Innsbruck, by the way?"

"Nürnberg had to make a run for it. Innsbruck was getting suspicious about something."

They paused while Richard changed his hold on the man; the steepness of the path was a strain.

"And just what happened to my two bodyguards?"

"They chased us on the hills. Von Aschenhausen is probably coming back now. The other fell over a cliff."

"Too bad," Smith said, and looked at some burns on the palms of his hands. "And the dog?"

"Very dead."

Smith's face relaxed slightly. "You've been busy."

When they had reached the bridge, Thornley overtook them.

"There was also the bicycle, itself," he reported. "I buckled its wheels. Strangely enough, it took the longest time."

Richard looked up towards the darkness which was the forest and the hill; they were both now indistinguishable. They were probably safe— probably.

"Could you run, if we both helped?" he asked Smith.

"I can try."

They linked arms round him, and half ran, half swept him along the road.

Van Cortlandt had heard them. He had the engine running, and the back door of the car open for them, by the time they reached him. They thrust Smith into the car, and stumbled after him. Richard heard the man draw his breath in sharply when his body was thrown into the corner of the car as it jerked onto the road, and began the rough journey back to Pertisau. But even if he was hurt, he was safe.

Richard leaned over to look at Frances. She was still asleep.

"How was she?" he asked. The American answered without turning his head.

"Surprising. She'll be all right when she wakens. Best thing for her."

Richard relaxed, and leaned back against the seat, taking care not to jolt against Smith.

Thornley suddenly gave a laugh. "I haven't had so much fun for a long time," he said.

"I'm glad someone enjoyed himself," Richard said. "What happened upstairs, by the way?"

"The window you pointed out was barred and bolted like nothing I ever saw in a private house. So I tried the next room, and the shutter there was only latched in the usual way. I used my knife, and got it, and then the window, open. The light was pretty bad; I just could see dimly. A sort of man's bedroom it was, with a desk at the window. There was a lot of stuff on top of it. I was hoping I might find some keys, but there weren't any. But I found this."

He held up something in the darkness of the car.

"Electric torch. Damned useful, too. It was black as pitch in the corridor outside, and in the room where I found your friend. They had tied him up again."

"And very welcome you were," said Smith. He was rubbing his wrists and ankles with his knuckles. He didn't use the palms of his hands.

"Were you always tied up?" asked Richard.

"Always when any visitor was seen approaching the house. And then, I was gagged too, like this afternoon. During the nights, I was handcuffed to the bed. In the daytime there was always one of them on guard. They also had fixed bars onto the window. On the door they had put safety chains. They used to leave it just a chink open that way through the day, so that I'd feel someone was always watching me."

"It made things quicker for us," Thornley explained. "The lock on the door was the usual type; after that there were just a couple of those chains and a heavy bolt. They didn't expect you to be reached from the outside."

"I'm glad you were still alive," Richard said.

"They just didn't want me alone. There was a lot of information they thought I could give them. I couldn't give it if I were dead."

"Judging from the time they kept you, they didn't get very much."

Smith gave a bitter smile. "Nothing of any use. Every now and again I'd pretend I was weakening; that encouraged them to keep me alive for just another few days. And then, they'd like to confront me with anyone who had come looking for me, and had been trapped. They like drama, these chaps, you know. Faked confessions and all that. They got a man from London, and two poor devils from Germany. Von Aschenhausen did the talking, and his man did the persuasion. He's good riddance."

"What about the maid?"

"Oh, old Trudi . . . She was terrified. When they took over, she just had to go on serving them as if nothing had happened. Threats against her family. You know. They locked her up in her room at night, which was quite needless of them. She was much too frightened to have done a thing for me. It is extraordinary the amount of power you can get over certain types of people if you just terrify them enough."

They were coming to the village. Smith leaned forward.

"Keep to the dark roads, and away from that inn where they are dancing. Keep well over to your left. Just grass, anyway."

They saw the lights round the platform outside the inn. Through the trees came the sound of a polkalike tune. They bumped over grass, as Smith had said, and then they were on a narrow graveled road which led towards the scattered lights at the shore. Smith directed van Cortlandt again, and the car swung south, running silently and smoothly along a track which would take them behind the string of hotels on the lakeside.

Smith had taken charge; his voice was still as cool and impersonal as when Richard had first met him.

"What were your last actions when you left here?"

"Van Cortlandt and Thornley were leaving by car; my wife and I were going for a walk."

Smith spoke to the American. "You've paid your bill, got your luggage, and actually left?"

"All here, Captain," van Cortlandt said.

"Good. You can stay out of the picture, then."

He turned to Richard. "You and your wife had better leave the car at a safe distance from your hotel. Or perhaps it would be better if *you* went alone. Can you remember the things she'll need? Don't forget her make-up box, especially the mascara. Bring something for me, too. And money. Is there more than one entrance to the hotel, so that you could slip out without being seen?"

"We are staying in a house. I think we could both go. Quicker if there were two of us."

Smith nodded. "Much. If you think you could slip away without being spotted. With ordinary luck, we have got about an hour's start. We'll take the car to the south end of the shore road. There are some trees and a good stretch of grass just off the road near the last hotel. We'll wait there. The moon won't be up for a while."

Richard had been shaking Frances gently. She sat up and looked round her in a bewildered way.

"So am I," said van Cortlandt good-humoredly. "You go with Richard. We'll wait for you. Good luck to both of you."

"Thanks," said Richard. "We'll need it." The car was slowing down. Henry was no fool, thought Richard. He had halted the car behind that chalet which hadn't been rented, standing dark and silent with its shutters tightly fastened.

He slipped out of the car into the blackness. Van Cortlandt helped Frances into his hands. He put his arm around her, and walked her over the grass. Behind them, they heard the car move smoothly away.

Waldesruhe lay just ahead. There was a light at the back of it. That would be the kitchen. The hotels around it were silent. There were lights in the bedrooms, as if most of the visitors were going to bed. Those who were going to the dance must have already set out, for the road was empty.

There was the usual weak light in the downstairs sitting room of the house. It lighted the bottom steps of the staircase. Farther up, Frances stumbled in the half darkness, and they halted, but they heard no movement from either above or below them, and they went on to their room.

It was Richard who shut the windows, drew the curtains, and lit the two candles. He didn't risk a brighter light. From the outside, this room would still seem to be in darkness. Frances looked wearily towards the bed; she had never appreciated how soft and white it was. On its counterpane was spread a very charming dirndl. Richard had seen it too, and paused at the wash basin as he poured the drinking water into a glass.

"Take a long one," he advised, when he brought the glass over to Frances. "What's that for?" He nodded to the bed.

"Frau Schichtl wanted me to wear it to the dance." Frances peeled off the mud-caked socks with a grimace. Richard brought over a damp sponge smelling of pink geranium.

"Do your face and shoulder," he commanded. He poured water into a basin and carried it over to where she was sitting. He helped her pull off the tattered cardigan and blouse. As she cleaned the cut on her shoulder, he bathed her feet and legs gently.

There was a knock at the door. Frau Schichtl's voice said, "May I come in?" They looked at each other in dismay. Again there was the same timid knock.

Richard was about to say Get to hell out of here, but he checked himself in time. That would only add to their troubles. If they kept silent, perhaps the woman would think she was mistaken and go away. Instead, the door opened. He rose to his feet.

Frau Schichtl paused in dismay. "Oh, excuse me. I am so sorry." She was just about to turn in embarrassment, when she noticed Richard's leg . . . And then she looked back again at Frances, holding the towel over her shoulder, and she saw the basin lying at her feet. Richard still held a dripping sponge.

Frau Schichtl came in, closing the door quickly and quietly behind her. Her kindly face was clouded with worry and fear. She came over to Richard and took the sponge gently out of his hand, and knelt down beside the basin.

"You must bathe your own leg, Herr Myles. It is cut very badly. I should get you some hot water."

"Please don't; there isn't any time," said Frances, and then bit her lip as she looked at Richard. It was so easy to make a slip when you were tired and miserable.

Frau Schichtl looked quickly up at her face. She compressed her lips, but she said nothing. She dried Frances' legs very gently.

"Have you iodine?" she asked.

Richard handed it to her, and she put it onto Frances' knees very lightly.

"Now some talcum powder on top of these scratches and they won't show."

Frances smiled gratefully, and then grimaced as she covered the cut on her shoulder with iodine.

"We got lost on the hills," she explained.

Frau Schichtl cleared away the towels and the basin of water, keeping her back carefully turned to Richard, who had started calmly to undress.

"I knew something must have happened," Frau Schichtl said. "Your friends were worried. They left hours ago. And now you can't go to the dance. You would have looked so pretty in that dress. It would have made me very happy to see you in it."

"I should like to wear it, all the same," said Frances, looking at Richard. That dirndl would be just what she needed. "We may go to the dance."

"But you must go to bed."

Frances shook her head. Frau Schichtl looked quickly from Richard, dressed in clean shirt and shorts, to Frances, fumbling in the chest of drawers for some underclothes.

"I think you are in trouble," she said slowly, at last.

Richard said nothing. He was distributing his money and Baedeker, letter of credit, passport, into the pockets of his tweed jacket. He was trying to think how they could leave the house . . . Unless they were to tie and gag Frau Schichtl and lock her in this room, and the idea sickened him. Still, what else?

"I thought that when I came in here, first. You were so quiet going up the stairs. So quiet in the room."

Frances had slipped into the dress; she combed her hair, and creamed and powdered the bruise on her forehead, before she turned to face Frau Schichtl. She smoothed the apron.

"It is so very pretty, Frau Schichtl. Perhaps I may spoil it . . . perhaps I shouldn't wear it?"

Frau Schichtl shook her head slowly. "It is your dress now. I have no more use for it." Her voice had a quiet sadness; she was lost in thought.

Richard smiled to himself as he watched the transparent relief in Frances' eyes. A man wouldn't have had any scruples, not at a moment like this. He folded a suit to take to Smith, along with socks and shirt and tie.

"You are going?" said Frau Schichtl.

"We are going," Frances said. Frau Schichtl moved to the door before she spoke. Richard watched her tensely. But the sad smile on her face was honest and friendly.

"You will need food for the journey," she said. "Is it these Nazis?"

Frances nodded.

"I knew it. Ever since that rough fellow came here so rudely this evening. . . . Will there never be an end to all this hunting of people? They must not catch you . . . not as they caught my daughter. Where can you go?"

"If we hurry, we shall be safe," said Richard quietly. He hadn't rested since he had reached the room. He was now helping Frances to get her make-up things into her bag. Mascara and all. They were ready, almost.

Frau Schichtl spoke again. "When you leave, go out through the kitchen and the back door. I shall hand you bread and cheese. I wish you a good journey to a safer land."

"We cannot thank you enough," Richard said.

"It is a small thing. Perhaps I am repaying my daughter's debt to someone who helped her."

"For your own safety, Frau Schichtl, remember that you haven't seen us. You heard us come in and go out again. You thought we had gone to the dance. Can this dress be traced to you?"

"No. There are many like it, and it is a long time since my daughter was here. I have forgotten I ever had these clothes. I shall see you in two minutes, at the back door."

The bedroom door closed gently.

Frances looked as if she might cry. She tied the scarf which lay on the bed beside the hand-knitted jacket round her head, and knotted it under her chin. She buttoned on the white-wool jacket. By the time she stared at herself in the glass, she had recovered control of herself. She looked at herself critically in the mirror.

"I'll do," she said.

Richard nodded, and tucked the bundled clothes under his arm. He picked up his one decent hat. They looked round the room; Frances' eyes flickered for a moment as they rested on the fitted suitcase which Johann had admired so much in Innsbruck. Richard had given her that when they were married. As they went downstairs she wished that she did not get so much attached to certain things. She hoped Frau Schichtl would be allowed to keep it—not some little tart of a local *Gauleiter*.

The light was still on in the sitting room, but the curtains had been drawn, so that they could cross the room safely to the kitchen. It was in darkness, and the back door was open so that they could see the stars in the sky beyond. In the shadow of the opened door, Frau Schichtl handed them a large package silently. They didn't speak, but their hands caught hers and held them tightly for a long moment . . . And then they were gone.

They walked quickly over the grass, keeping as much in the shadow of trees, even houses, as was possible. The moon had risen, and the meadows of Pertisau were silvered and treacherous. From the distance came the music of a fiddle and a concertina, and an echoing *"Juch-hé."*

They had reached the last hotel. It stood far back from the road, with large gardens carefully cultivated. They skirted these, thankful for the shrubs and bushes which would make it difficult for them to be seen clearly. . . . And now they were on the road, walking as softly as they could. Smith had said something about trees, Richard remembered. There were some just beyond that patch of grass. It meant that they would have no cover at all until they reached the trees, and they might be the wrong ones. He had a strange empty feeling inside him as they covered the white stretch of road, with the silvered grass on one side of them, and the lake rippling with maddening calmness on the other. Probably hunger, he thought. He resisted the impulse to run, to cover the open ground as quickly as possible. And then he heard the car warming up. It backed out onto the road from the shadow of the trees, just as they reached them. The doors were open, and they were pulled in by eager hands. The car shot forward, and they heard Thornley say, "Good work!"

It was lighter in the car now, because of the moonlight. Smith nodded his approval to Frances.

"You've made good use of your time," he said, and began to examine the clothes they had brought him. "Mascara?" he added.

"And food," Frances said. She opened the parcel of food and shared it out.

The atmosphere in the car had changed. Van Cortlandt, without taking his eyes off the road in front of him, joked with Frances as they ate. Thornley had produced the torch again at Smith's request. He held it ready to shade it, when Smith needed it. Richard helped Smith rip off his clothes. He exchanged looks with Thornley as the shirt came away and they saw the cruel weals on Smith's back. But Smith took no notice of their stare. He was whistling to himself as he drew on the new clothes. With Richard's help he managed not at all badly, although there was a difficult moment as he tried to pull on Richard's shirt. It was only by the stiffness of one arm that they noticed it was bruised at the shoulder into a purple jelly. The clothes were loose for him, but the effect was passable.

He began on his face, now. Thornley held the shaded torch, and Richard tried to steady the small mirror from Frances' bag. Smith creamed and powdered the ugly bruises which showed. He darkened his eyebrows skilfully, altering their shape, and with the same pencil shaded in the lines on his face. Then he found the small pair of scissors in the bag, and looked at them thoughtfully.

"We'll have to stop to get rid of these anyway," he said, kicking the rags on the floor which had been his clothes. "Better draw up for a moment; this is as good a place as any." It was the beginning of the hill down into Jenbach. On their right was a steep ravine, thickly wooded. They could only hear the water of the stream. It was impossible to see it, at this point, for the undergrowth. Thornley slipped out of the car with the old clothes, and disappeared down the steep bank. When he came back, he reported that he had found a nice thick bush, not very far down. It had been too risky to go any farther.

"Not a place for picnicking, or a roll in the hay," he said. "They should rot there peacefully."

Smith had finished emphasizing a widow's peak with the scissors.

"All right," he said, and van Cortlandt drove on.

Smith took the mascara cream and rubbed it on the back of his hands. Then he tried to smooth it on to his hair like brilliantine, but it was too difficult.

"Let me try this," suggested Richard. He remembered what he had seen of Smith's palms. "I tucked a pair of chamois gloves into that jacket pocket," he said as casually as he could. "I find them useful for traveling."

Smith shot a quick glance at him. "Thanks. I'll need them." He looked at his hair in the mirror. "That's about enough; don't need much of that stuff. Thanks. I'll comb it through now."

As Richard wiped his hands, he watched Smith carefully combing the black cream through his hair, finishing by making a neat center parting. The finishing touch was a slight dab of face powder onto the hair above the ears. The transformation was complete.

"Not bad," said Thornley with a grin. "They'll never recognize you, unless they see your back."

Smith gave his first real smile. He had cleaned the back of his hands of the mascara, and was rubbing some cream into the burns on his palms and wrists. Frances had looked round, and remained staring, so that van Cortlandt took his eyes off the road for a moment to look too. He grinned widely.

"All you need is a monocle and you'd be a natural for a Budapest café," he suggested. Smith looked pleased, but he didn't volunteer any information.

Richard suddenly remembered the label on the inside pocket of the jacket. Smith ripped it out and read it with interest.

"Nice to know your name," he said. "But it would have taken some explaining. Thanks. What about the hat?"

"It's all right. You'd better take my stick, too. But don't unscrew it until you are in a safe place and can wash it. It's rather messy. What about a passport?"

"That can be got. By the way, I think you should go right away to this address in Innsbruck. They'll see about a passport for you." He scribbled some words on a page from Thornley's diary, and handed it to Richard.

"What about some cash?" asked van Cortlandt.

Smith patted the jacket pocket. "It's already here. That's about everything I think." He looked at Richard, and there was a kindly look in his eye.

"Richard." Frances' voice was urgent. "I've just remembered . . . what about our bill?"

The men all laughed, even Smith.

"It's all right, Fran. I've left enough to cover it inside my suitcase. It will be searched, you know."

Van Cortlandt seemed to be enjoying a rich joke.

The car was entering the village of Jenbach, running down through the steep street with its motor silent. There were few people out at this time. Jenbach was mostly asleep, it seemed. Smith was watching the street carefully.

"Just at that corner," he said to van Cortlandt, 'beside the road with the trees. The station is just to the left." He turned to Richard. "I seem to have caused you a lot of trouble. But perhaps you'll find some consolation in the fact that I really happen to have discovered something which will be extremely valuable. Quite apart from my own comfort, you really have been most useful." He leaned over to Frances. "And thank you for your song. Good-by."

The car slowed down. It paused for a moment, and they saw his shadow mix with that of the trees. He was walking, leaning heavily on Richard's stick, Richard's hat tilted over his eyes, towards the station, as the car swung to the right for the Innsbruck road.

CHAPTER 17 INNSBRUCK REVISITED

They would reach Innsbruck in half an hour, or even less. Richard leaned back into the corner, and closed his eyes. It was little enough time to decide on their own plans; but at least they had done the most they could for Smith.

The road was smooth and made driving easy. On their right were continuous mountains; on their left was the broad Inn valley and the railway line. Van Cortlandt pointed out the lights of a train moving towards Jenbach.

"That takes care of your friend. We've only you to worry about now," he said. Richard nodded. He wondered if Smith would really take that train, or whether there had been some little house near the station where he might have a friend. He had better stop thinking about Smith. He roused himself to reply to the American, who had looked round at him curiously.

"I've been thinking about that, Henry. I think we should follow his example and rid you of ourselves as soon as we get to the outskirts of Innsbruck. Then you can arrive as if nothing had happened, with the excuse if it's necessary of motor trouble and slow driving. You know the sort of thing. I think that's the only way."

Thornley said, "It's not a very good way for you."

"We'll manage, somehow—if we get that passport."

"And some money," said van Cortlandt. "You'll not go far without plenty of loose dough. Your travelers' cheques or your letter of credit will raise hell at any bank in Greater Germany. That chap just about cleaned you out, didn't he? He was a cool customer, all right."

"He has to be. I expect he has done more than that for others when they were in a jam." What was it Frau Schichtl had said in that sad slow voice of hers? Repaying a debt to someone who had helped her daughter . . . only the way she had said it was better than that.

"Help each other, or God help you?" asked van Cortlandt, half-seriously. "Have you any cash, Bob?" He threw his wallet into the back seat. Thornley caught it, and added his share. He counted it carefully.

"It will just about pay for the passport. I expect it will cost quite a lot. You'll need more than this. I can cash a cheque at the bank tomorrow, but how can I get the money to you?"

"Look," said Richard, "you dump us somewhere just outside Innsbruck. We can walk to that address Smith gave us. I think it's this side of the town. Have you that light, Bob? I'll just make sure." He studied his Baedeker. "Yes, we can reach it all right. In this costume, we'll look like any other couple returning from a moonlight walk. Your story is that we left you this afternoon to walk over the mountain towards Hinterriss. When we didn't return, you thought we must have gone right on to Hinterriss and stayed the night there. So when it reached eight o'clock, you left. You had a business appointment to keep. You were delayed in getting to Innsbruck by motor trouble. Henry, try to see your man tonight when you arrive; have a couple of drinks with him in some well-known restaurant."

"I'll need them," van Cortlandt said with a grin.

"Remember you never saw a house with red shutters. You never saw us after we set out for our walk. That's your story and stick to it."

"That's our story and we're stuck with it." Van Cortlandt was still grinning. "But what's your angle?"

"We'll get to that house, and arrange about a passport. They may take us in for the night, or send us to a safe place. And Bob will get the money, as he suggested. Tomorrow one of us will meet you some place about eleven o'clock. It may be Frances; she is better disguised than I am. The station is no good; it will be watched. A restaurant is dangerous . . . too many waitresses with an eye for their customers." He paused for a moment or two. "Try the Franciscan Church. It will have plenty of sightseers on a Saturday morning. You can potter about the Emperor Maximilian's monument; carry a catalogue, or a newspaper, and have the money in an envelope. Slip the envelope inside the catalogue. When you see Frances, go and sit down in the church itself. Choose a nice dark side. When you finish your meditations, leave the catalogue behind you. Frances will then slip into the seat you've just left. Would you mind doing that for us?"

Thornley repeated the directions rapidly. "I think I've got it all," he said.

Van Cortlandt said, "I must say for a couple of amateurs you two are showing high form."

"We go to the movies," said Frances gravely. He looked at her serious face, and then decided to risk a laugh.

"It's that dead-pan look you English have when you have your little joke which makes us think you've no sense of humor. You don't look as if you expected anyone to laugh."

Frances was smiling now. "Well, that doubles the joke for us. Our pleasures are really very simple."

"You mean that if I hadn't laughed just now, you would have been laughing because I didn't laugh because you didn't laugh."

"I would have had my giggle inside," admitted Frances. "Don't you think it's funny, too?"

Van Cortlandt just shook his head sadly. "About as funny as *Punch*. And much more dangerous. It makes people underestimate you."

"But that can be funny, too."

"It's dangerous."

"What's dangerous?" Thornley asked. He was shading the torch again to let Richard study a map.

"Being underestimated," said Frances.

"Oh, *that!*" he said, and went back to the map.

Richard explained. "After we have the cash, and the passport, we'll make for the border. The nearest one is the Brenner."

"That's guarded heavily," warned van Cortlandt. "The Italians are keeping an eye on the South Tyrol."

"Well, it will depend on our disguise whether we risk the train or try the mountains. If it's guarded heavily, then the Swiss frontier will be thought to be likelier. And the Brenner is probably more strongly guarded on the Italian side than on the Austrian. That suits us."

"And after that?"

"We'll make for Paris."

"When do you think you'll be there?"

"With luck, we'll leave Innsbruck by Sunday at latest. Say next week end in Paris. We'll leave word for you there with the Consul. We'll celebrate together. The evening's on us."

"I wish I could," said van Cortlandt, "but I'm a working man. I'll see you later in England on my way home. I have your address. There's one reward I would like, and that's the whole story."

"I promise you it," Frances said. "And please come to see us. Any time." She said it so warmly and earnestly that van Cortlandt reddened, but he looked pleased.

"I hate to be the skeleton at the feast," he said, "but what if you run into difficulties in Innsbruck?"

"We'll let you know; we can phone you. If we can't phone then it's too dangerous for you to help us. You've been dragged into quite enough trouble, as it is."

"I'll have finished my business there by midday tomorrow. I can be free for the next two days, if you need me. Leave a message at the hotel for me, if I'm not there. Say that the *Times* has an assignment for me. That will pass all right, and it's phoney enough for me to know it comes from you. I'll let Bob know, unless he's mixed up with his Czechs."

"There is one very important thing, Henry. Send this message to Geneva early tomorrow. Please don't forget. RESERVATIONS UNCANCELLED. ARRIVING FRIDAY. And memorize this address." He repeated it carefully. "Got it? Good. It's really important."

The lights of the town gleamed in front of them across the Inn. Frances turned to Richard, and smiled.

Van Cortlandt said quietly, "I hate to spoil the party, but there's a couple of cars on our tail. I've seen their headlights for some time now, but they are still far enough away, if it should be your friends. I'll slow up round the first bend. Get ready."

Frances and Richard looked at each other. Frances remembered how van Cortlandt had increased his speed just when he had asked about difficulties in Innsbruck.

"We'll say our thank-yous in Paris or Oxford," said Richard. "Good-by, meanwhile. And don't forget to turn up. And remember the telegram." He was holding the door open in readiness. They were reaching a bend in the road.

The car slowed up. They slipped quickly out.

"We'll see you," Frances said quietly, and then without looking back, she raced with Richard for the cover of some bushes. Safely hidden from the road, they watched the taillights of van Cortlandt's car streak along towards the town. They waited for some minutes, and then they heard the roar of a powerful engine. A large black car, followed closely by another, flashed past them. Richard watched them disappear after van Cortlandt.

"Henry was right, I think. Two cars together look as if they had urgent business. I hope they stick to that story."

"They will," said Frances. "I can see Bob looking rather sleepy and bored, and Henry looking very righteously indignant, calling on his rights as an American citizen. They'll play it up beautifully between them. I wish I could see it."

"You're better here. How are the legs?"

"Not so bad. My arm is stiff, though." She shivered.

Richard put his arm round her shoulders, and drew her beside him. They waited in silence. One other car passed along the road; its moderate pace reassured them.

Richard watched the clouds in the sky. He chose the time when one of them, thick and white, began to cross over the face of the moon; and they were back on the road. They reached the first houses without any trouble. It seemed they were in an open residential quarter, with scattered houses and gardens, or what might be called parks, surrounding them. Richard remembered they were either in or near the district for the large garden restaurants and family excursions . . . All the better.

It was also a district for late-evening strollers, making their way slowly back to the town. Ahead of them were a young man and his girl, with their arms linked round each other. The man talked, and the girl would laugh as she looked up at him.

"Watch the technique," said Richard, and measured his step so that they kept a short distance between them and the couple. He clipped his arm round Frances' waist, and she giggled in spite of herself.

"Perfect," he said, and won another laugh.

Perfect, he repeated to himself, as they followed the man and girl towards the bridge over the River Inn. In front of the bridge was a broad, open stretch of ground, where other roads met the one they were on. From the other roads came some more men and girls, forming a slow and scattered trail back to Innsbruck. And there were some cars. These were being stopped by two efficient-looking men in uniform, as they approached the bridge.

Richard looked down at Frances, and said some words to her in German. Just in front of them were the couple they had followed. The two uniformed men gave the group of four a brief look, and then turned back to the driver they were questioning.

Once they were over the bridge, they left the man and girl. He was still talking; she still looked up into his face and laughed. They would never have noticed who had walked behind them or who had passed them. Richard had taken a street which turned away from the river. After the bright lights at the bridge, it seemed dark and safe. But the journey to the house was like a nightmare for Frances. Richard had kept their pace unhurried, so that they appeared just two more walkers going home with the usual reluctance. The slowness of their steps increased her fatigue. She was painfully conscious of each muscle she had to use, of the hardness of the pavement which hurt her back with each step, of the cracks in the stones which caught her dragging feet. The ill-lighted streets heightened the dark houses; their silence sharpened every sound. It was less than a mile to the address which Smith had given them, but to Frances it seemed more like five.

Richard had knocked as Smith had marked it down on the piece of paper: a spondee followed by a dactyl. In his pocket, he fingered the part of the instructions which he had kept, the part with the curious little design marked on it. The rest of the paper had been torn up and dropped piece by piece from the car. As they stood in the darkness of the doorway and looked anxiously up and down the dingy, badly-lighted street with its empty pavements and sleeping houses, he had begun to wonder if he had got mixed up with the address. They were taking a hell of a long time to answer. He visualized the piece of paper as he had seen it in the car. The name, the address, and then *Knock––, –⌄*. Then the words *Destroy at once*; and then *Keep,* and a lightly drawn arrow to the foot of the page where the design had been sketched. He remembered everything, even to the jagged line at the top where the page had been torn from Thornley's diary. He felt Frances sag against him. He knocked again.

The door opened so quickly that he knew someone had stood behind it waiting for the knock to sound again. It was only slightly open, and in any case it was too dark to see anything; but the someone waited.

Richard's voice was hardly above a whisper. "Herr Schulz?"

The door opened wider and a woman's voice answered "In!" They heard the door close behind them gently; a heavy lock was quietly turned. The hall was unlit, but light came from a room at the back of the house. The woman who had let them inside led the way towards the lighted doorway. She turned to them as she reached it, and motioned them to enter. Frances saw that she was quite young. Her face was what Richard would call just medium: it was neither pretty nor plain. It was quite expressionless.

Richard had looked past the woman into the bare, poorly furnished room. A man laid his newspaper aside, and watched them keenly from where he sat. He said nothing, just sat and looked. Richard spoke, slurring his words as he had heard the Bavarians do. The man still sat; his eyes were impassive. He picked up his newspaper again.

"But my name is not Schulz," he said, as Richard paused.

Richard's eyes met those staring down at him from the large flag-draped photograph on the wall. For a moment, doubt halted the beat of his heart. He felt the sweat break in his palms. . . . And then he was aware that he was still clutching onto the piece of paper in his jacket pocket. He pulled it out, and handed it to the man, still watching inscrutably.

The man glanced at it and threw it on the table.

"Who gave you this?"

"A man from Pertisau."

"Was his name Gerold?"

"No. Mespelbrunn."

"Where do you come from?"

So that explained Smith's aside as he had handed him the paper in the car.

"From over the mountains," Richard said.

The man looked at him again, and then at Frances who had slumped into a chair. He nodded to the woman. She closed the door, and stood there, leaning against it.

"Sit down," the man said to Richard. His voice was warm, almost friendly. His eyes were now alive, kindly. "Relax. Relax. No need to look so cold. Are you hungry?"

Richard nodded. The woman moved from the door where she had been standing and went into another room. It was probably the kitchen. Richard heard the sound of a pot being placed on a stove.

"Relax," the man said again. "And how is our friend from Pertisau?"

"He is now well."

"So, he was—ill? We thought so . . . we have not heard from him for a long time. Well, that's good news. Good news. What about you? You said you wanted a room. Is there anything else?"

"The usual."

"You are leaving our happy Fatherland?" The man's voice was filled with heavy sarcasm as he looked up at the picture on the wall. "Well, it can be arranged. How are you traveling?"

"To Italy. Probably by train. And as quickly as we can."

"Of course; that is understood," Schulz said, and smiled. "You might go as Americans or English. You look very like them. Do you know the language at all?"

Richard shook his head.

"You'll have to go as Germans, then. How would an engineer do? Or a schoolteacher? I'll get you the right clothes. That will cost you extra, of course, but you'll find it worth every pfennig. Every pfennig."

"How much will it cost?"

"How much have you?"

Richard restrained a smile. After all, Schulz had been right that his help would be worth every pfennig.

"Only three hundred marks," said Richard. "We can get extra tomorrow to cover the railway fares."

Schulz seemed pleased with the directness of the answer. "Good," he said. "Good. Three hundred marks will do."

He rose from his chair and went over to Frances. He walked with a marked limp, but he held himself erect. Richard placed his age as about forty. He was almost bald. His face and body had thickened with middle age. Frances, white and silent, looked up and saw the shrewd eyes behind the thick glasses, the kindly smile on the broad mouth.

His voice was gentler. "You look afraid of me. You must lose that afraid look. Sometimes people stay here for almost a week, until they lose it. You must look very happy and proud when you cross the frontier. You are the wife of an engineer, who is taking you for a holiday to Florence. But we must change your hair; it is too pretty. Lisa!"

The woman came back from the kitchen. She carried two bowls of steaming soup.

"Lisa, what color would you make this hair? Black?"

"Not with these blue eyes. Brown is less noticeable."

"Good. Make it brown, mouse-brown. We can begin tonight. That and the photographs. Then tomorrow we can get the clothes, and the papers. And you will be all ready to leave tomorrow night. Is that quick enough for you? Now, eat up. Eat up."

The warm bowl of soup brought life back to Frances' hands. She held her fingers round it, and felt the warmth steal into them. It was almost as good as eating. She felt warm, warm and safe. She looked at the clock on the table. It was almost midnight. She felt warm and safe, safe for the first time in six hours.

The man was watching her curiously. "Eat up," he said gently. "That's good, isn't it?" It was the most wonderful soup she had ever tasted.

The man was speaking to Richard. "You've had a difficult time; you've come far, today?"

"Yes, we've come far."

"You will be able to travel tomorrow?" Schulz was looking doubtful.

Richard, remembering Frances' resilience, smiled. "Oh yes, we shall be all right. We recover quickly. We can keep going until we reach Italy. And then . . . well, it won't matter then anyway."

"When you first spoke of Italy, I thought I might advise you to try the mountains. They would be safer. But—" he looked at Frances doubtfully —"I think you will have to stick to your plan about the train. We shall do our best to make the train safe for you. Ready, Lisa? Good. Good."

Richard had finished eating, and the man began to cut his hair. On the table, the woman had arranged basins and some bottles and a saucer. Frances felt her eyes begin to close. Schulz waved his scissors towards her.

"If we can get her into that chair at the table before she falls asleep, Lisa can manage," he said. "We'll soon have her upstairs in bed."

Frances was helped into the other chair. I'm being very silly, she thought, but the trouble is that my eyelids are too heavy. She stretched her head back against the neck rest on the chair. It was hideously uncomfortable, but the eyelids won the struggle. She had dim sensations of the woman's fingers working with her hair, of water trickling across her face.

When she was awakened, she saw Lisa looking at her with almost a smile. It was enough to warn Frances of what she might see in the hand mirror which was held out to her. That look which only one woman can give another, that look of pity and amusement combined, roused Frances as no dash of cold water could have done. She took the mirror. Her hair was as bad as she had suspected; dull brown, lifeless, with the thickness at the back pinned tightly into a mean little knot. Frances stared in a kind of horrid fascination. Of course it would have had to be her hair, she thought, just because it had been her secret pride.

Richard was grinning at her. Then she saw that he was including himself in that grin. His hair had been clipped until it bristled. There was a funny look at the back of his neck. She began to laugh. She had the pleasure of seeing the half smile on Lisa's face give way to a look of surprise.

The man looked up from arranging a large box camera on some books on the table. He smiled encouragingly.

"That's better," he said. "Pretty ones find it harder to escape. Now, if you'll sit over here, we'll soon be finished, and you can go to a real bed."

The woman was clearing the table of its litter of basins and towels and hand dryer. She seemed to accept all this madness as a natural way of spending one's night.

Richard was being photographed now. He bulged his eyes, tilted his chin truculently, and looked on the point of uttering a loud "*Heil!*"

"Good," said Schulz, "good."

It was Frances' turn. She remembered to stare stolidly in front of her and part her lips slightly. We are all quite mad, she thought, or perhaps I am really asleep and dreaming. Sleep . . . sleep . . . it had a pleasant sound.

Schulz nodded approvingly. "That's what we want," he said. "That's what we want."

They followed the woman up a dark staircase to a room which was cold and shadowy in the meager candlelight. Frances felt Richard draw off her clothes: she awakened slightly as she heard him swear when his fingers stuck with some fastening on the strange dress. Then the cool rough sheets slid round her.

She could not have risen if six storm-troopers had come thundering up the stairs.

CHAPTER **18**   FRANCES IS FRANCES

Frances awoke with a feeling of compulsion. She had something to do. She lay in the strange bed and looked round the room for the first time. Slowly she began to remember what had happened last night. Her hand went to her hair; it felt dry and coarse. So it hadn't been a dream . . . And there was Richard, with his hair cropped like that of a child who has had fever. He was still asleep; his arms were thrown above his head; his face was relaxed. She looked at the cracked ceiling, at the limp curtains drawn over the window. Why had she awakened, what was it that had to be done?

Frances felt herself slipping into sleep again, and caught herself just in time. There was something she had to do. Her eyes fell on her handbag which Richard must have brought upstairs last night and thrown onto the rickety little table under the fly-spotted mirror. That was it, of course. The money. A sudden fear that she was already too late to meet Bob Thornley urged her quickly from the warmth of her bed. After the first dizziness—she had probably moved too suddenly—she felt all right. Her body had recovered surprisingly from yesterday's punishment; even the shoulder was healing nicely.

Richard's watch told her she had ample time. She washed and dressed quietly. She searched in her handbag, and powdered her face and lips so that her natural color was hidden. Then she removed all traces of powder with her handkerchief. With the dull-brown hair and the subdued face there was quite a difference. She could do nothing about her eyes, though. They were larger and bluer than ever. However, unless she met someone who really knew her, there was little chance of her being identified with the fair-headed English girl whose description was no doubt being circulated. She combed her hair with a center parting, pinning the ends tightly into a knot at the back as the woman had done last night. Before she left the room, she found Richard's Baedeker in his jacket pocket, and verified from its Innsbruck map the best way to reach the Franciscan Church. At the door of the room, she stopped. Some small change might be useful. With a suspicion of a smile she searched Richard's pockets, and took half of what was left. It would be just enough to pay for a ride in a tramcar and the admission to the Church, if there was one. She kissed

Richard lightly again. He didn't even stir. She closed the door gently and went quietly downstairs.

Lisa was in the sitting room. She seemed surprised.

"I thought you would sleep all morning."

"I must go out."

The woman shook her head disapprovingly.

"I must get money for the journey."

The woman accepted that. "You had better have some coffee, first," she said. "I've just had a cup. I'll get one for you." She went into the kitchen.

Frances waited, and looked at the little room, and the corner of the badly-kept garden at the back of the house, which she could just see from her seat at the table. Lisa was not unkind, but there was a certain businesslike attitude which paralyzed any conversation. Frances was glad of that; she was somewhat self-conscious about her Bavarian accent. She drank the coffee, and looked at the patch of garden. She felt a kind of excitement inside her. She would have liked to have given a war whoop— but Lisa was there. Her matter-of-fact kind of sanity smothered Frances' impulse, and she contented herself with looking at the garden and having another cup of coffee. She rose to leave.

"Not that way," said the woman. "Go out by this door: across the yard. Keep near the wall, under the trellis, and it will shelter you. Enter the door at the other end of the path. Walk through that house, and you'll find yourself in a shoemaker's shop. Just say as you pass that Lisa sent you. You'll be all right."

"Would you tell my husband that I'll be back about twelve?"

The woman nodded, and threw a *loden* cape lightly round Frances' shoulders. "Leave this in the shop," she said. She didn't wait for Frances to thank her. She was already carrying the coffee cups into the kitchen. As she turned to push the door open with her hip bone, she smiled—a friendly, encouraging smile. And then the kitchen door closed behind her. Frances turned toward the door in the living room which she had thought was a cupboard door. It led on to a narrow paved path beside a high wall, from which a coarse green climbing plant stretched greedily over the trellis above her head. In front of her were the backs of the houses on the next street.

Everything happened as Lisa had said it would. The cobbler in the front shop scarcely paused in his work as Frances slid the cape onto the counter. He didn't seem to hear her words. Outside in the street, there was the usual activity of a respectable working-class neighborhood. Housewives carried shopping bags made of knotted string. Children were grouped round doorways. Boys cycled wildly. Some of them wore a kind of uniform, others the usual short leather breeches and white stockings. She walked with increasing confidence to the end of the street. If she followed the tramlines from there, she would reach Museumstrasse, and then it would be easy to find the Church. It was the long, but the safe, way and she had plenty of time.

The walk was not unpleasant. In the busier streets, she felt still safer. She was just another girl dressed in another dirndl. At the corner of the narrow street which led to the square on which the Church stood, the traffic was heavy. Frances tried to avoid two women whose breadth filled the narrow pavement. She was swept against the window of a shop. Climbing boots, sports things, she noticed, and then, with her eyes still fixed on the window, she collided with a girl coming out of the shop's doorway. She was a tall, blonde girl, her arms filled with parcels.

Frances halted in amazement, and then stepped aside with an apology. The girl remained standing, her eyes on Frances' face, but Frances hurried on. It was Anni, looking just as she had looked in their garden at Oxford on her last night there.

"I looked at her too directly. She half-recognized my eyes, or perhaps she saw that I knew her," Frances thought. She glanced at her reflection in another window. She couldn't see much resemblance to herself, but she would have to watch her eyes, and her way of walking too. It was much too smooth. She would have to set her heels more firmly on the ground, in a kind of jaunty march. As she turned the corner to enter the Church, she looked back over her shoulder. Anni was still there, and, as Frances looked, she made up her mind and started towards the Church. Frances already regretted that afterlook. What a fool she was. She quickened her pace and hurried up the steps of the building.

Inside, there was the usual crowd of Saturday-morning visitors. She paid the admission to a man with heavily pouched eyes and a drooping mustache. At least that would prevent Anni from following her inside the Church: she had never spent a penny more than she could help in Oxford. Perhaps Anni was already thinking she had been mistaken.

In the nave where the Maximilian monument was she saw Thornley. He was standing, appropriately enough, in front of King Arthur's statue, with a catalogue in his hands. It was good to see him again, looking so untroubled, so completely unconscious of everything. She wandered round the statues as the other visitors did. She didn't look at him as she rudely passed in front of him to reach Theodoric the Terrific, King of the Ostrogoths. When she had admired sufficiently, she walked slowly towards the little chapel. Thornley was seated in the shadows. As she moved slowly towards him, he rose, and they passed each other without a glance.

The catalogue had been left on a chair. She sat down beside it, her wide skirt spreading over it. She waited while the other visitors came and went. Some sat down, some tiptoed about talking in penetrating whispers, others knelt. After long minutes she dared to move her fingers under cover of her skirt and feel for the small fat envelope inside the catalogue.

Slowly, without any visible movement, her hand pulled it out and folded it into her palm. It was done. It was over.

She reached the street, and slipped the scarf off her head. As she tied it round her shoulders, she slipped the envelope into the bodice of her dress. Under the fringe of scarf, it wouldn't be noticed—and it felt safe. There was no sign of Bob. But there was Anni. She had got rid of her parcels, and had been sitting in the little square of trees opposite the Church. She had seen Frances; she was almost running across the street. Frances bit her lip. There were two storm-troopers standing in front of the Church steps. If she avoided Anni, their attention would be attracted. There wasn't any time, anyway. The men had already noticed Anni's haste and were watching her with casual interest.

Frances made her voice enthusiastic. "Anni! I haven't seen you for weeks! How are you?"

Anni looked at her in amazement; she was speechless. It was the accent which had dumbfounded her. It was no longer the carefully spoken German which she had heard in Oxford. Frances was glad of the silence. She began to walk along the pavement, her hand on Anni's arm warning her with some pressure. They were passing the two troopers, whose interest had become more anatomical.

"How are your Mother and Father?"

"Quite well, *gnä* " The pressure on Anni's arm stopped her politeness.

"And your brothers?"

"Also well."

"And your sister?"

"The same."

They had passed the two men safely. Frances relaxed.

"Cheer up, Anni. You look so worried."

Anni suddenly led her across the street towards the garden in the square. In the quietness there, she faced Frances.

"O *gnädige Frau!*" She looked as if she were going to cry.

"Cheer up, Anni. It's all right. But don't call me that."

Anni said, "I knew something was wrong. I have been so worried about you."

"How?"

They were both talking in undertones, pacing slowly under the trees. Anni blinked back her tears.

"I knew you were here in Innsbruck, about a week ago. One of my brothers has a friend. He is the houseman in the hotel where you stayed. He knew I had lived in Oxford, of course, and he told me about the two English guests who came from there. That was how I found out that you were here."

"That was Johann, wasn't it?"

Anni's cheeks colored. "Yes. When he learned I had lived with you, I made him promise not to tell my family that you were here."

Frances was surprised. "Why, Anni?"

Anni looked confused.

"My sister always disbelieved me about England. When I told them about your house and clothes, she would only laugh. If she had learned you were staying in that place, she would have made fun of me to everyone."

"We stayed in *that* place because we like the old town, Anni," Frances said gently. That was true. They had chosen to live in the old town when they had last visited Innsbruck, although the hotel then had been an innocent place compared with their choice this time.

Anni looked relieved that Frau Myles was still smiling.

"Yes," she said, "that's what Johann told the police today."

Frances almost stopped walking.

"Anni, tell me all you know."

"I saw Johann this morning. We usually meet when I cycle into the town." Anni blushed again, and hesitated, but Frances waited in silence. "Early this morning, the Gestapo came to the hotel, and searched and questioned. They asked very particularly about you and the *Herr Professor*. Johann only knew that you came from Oxford and that you were on holiday."

"What about the owner of the hotel?"

"He left the hotel just after a telephone call came for him very late last night. No one has seen him since. So Johann was in charge when the police came. They seemed very angry."

Frances said nothing. Mr. Smith seemed to think of everything, she thought, even of the fact that their travels in Germany and Austria would be retraced. She would have liked to know how he had got that telephone call through to Kronsteiner without giving himself away. Possibly it had come through another agent . . . But if there had been a ghost of a chance left for their simple-traveler story, it had vanished along with Kronsteiner. His disappearance would confirm all the suspicions against them. Anni's face grew more worried as she watched Frances walk so silently beside her.

At last Frances asked, "Do the police know that you were with us in Oxford?"

Anni shook her head. "Johann never said anything about that. He didn't want to mention my name."

"I am sorry that we met today, Anni. I had better leave you now; it is too dangerous for you."

"But, *gnädige Frau*, I must help. What is wrong?"

"We must leave Austria at once."

Anni was silent. Then at last she said, "Johann could lead you over the mountains."

"Into Germany? That's worse still."

"He also knows the South Tyrol. He was born there. He escaped over the mountains when the Italians were conscripting the Austrians for the war in Abyssinia."

"That border is now heavily guarded." What was it that Schulz had said last night when she was half-asleep? . . . something about advising the mountains rather than the train, if she hadn't been so exhausted . . . But she was all right now; Herr Schulz wouldn't hesitate to advise them to go by the mountains if he saw her today. She disliked the idea of the train, for in a train you were trapped in a box.

Anni was speaking again. "But there is a way, if you know the mountains. Johann knows."

Frances was tempted. But she said, "No, Anni. Besides, Johann must not risk anything for us."

"He would do it if I asked him."

"No, Anni. Better not. Don't tell anyone that you have seen me; not even Johann."

Anni was still searching for some plan. "I can't ask you to come to our house. My sister hates the English, although she has never known any. My brothers would not help. They are afraid like my parents."

"Thank you a thousand times, Anni. But you must not help."

Anni began to cry. Frances watched her tears with distress.

"Please don't, Anni . . . we shall be all right."

"Where is the *Herr Professor?*"

"He is waiting for me. I must go now, or he will be worried."

"Please tell me the address. Then when I have thought out some plan I can come to you this afternoon and tell you about it."

Frances had an idea. "You said Johann knew a way over the mountains? If he could draw a map of it would you—" no good saying *post it*; perhaps Schulz was known by another name altogether. Frances paused. How on earth were they to get hold of the map?

"I'll bring it to you," Anni said eagerly.

"Then you must come when it's dark. Can you get away this evening without making anyone suspicious?"

"On Saturday, yes. I look after my brother's shop then, and I am often late before I reach home."

"And don't tell Johann that the map is for us. Please, Anni. It would be safer for everyone. Can you think of some excuse for him?"

Anni said she could manage Johann. She repeated the address which Frances told her. Tonight she would slip the map under the door of that house; and then she would forget the address forever. She promised. She was smiling again, as Frances said good-by. She seemed happier now that she could be of some use after all.

Frances recrossed the street. She felt she had every right to be pleased with herself. Such a map would be most useful, if, for instance, the train seemed too risky. There was no doubt that the search was on. She thought of Kronsteiner. Trains would be watched, perhaps searched. As for giving Anni the address—well, Anni would keep her promise. The secret would be safe. Anni was under no suspicion. She would not be followed, as Henry or Bob would be . . . And Anni did not know the importance of the house. It would seem just a rooming house to her. There were plenty of such houses in that district.

Everything began to look easy; and that was probably her undoing. If Henry could drive them almost to the frontier, they could follow the path over the mountains, and then meet Henry somewhere on the other side. He could take along their Schulz clothes, pack them somewhere in his suitcase, and they could change in his car once they had finished the climb. It was all so simple. She imagined Richard's look of surprise and amusement when she would present him with the idea. It wasn't at all bad, she admitted with some pleasure to herself. In her excitement, it was understandable that she forgot. She forgot that if you are playing a part you must live it, and forget your own identity. She should have been Mitzi Schmidt going to meet Fritzi Müller; but at the moment she was very much enjoying being Frances Myles.

She walked quickly with her light smooth step. If she hurried she would not be late for Richard. The man in the restaurant, who had chosen a window table next to where a young American and Englishman had sat, saw the Austrian girl who walked in that familiar way. He was suddenly alert. The color of her hair and of her face were different, but there was something equally familiar in that hint of a smile and the tilt of the nose, the shape of the eyes. She passed. He recognized the set of the shoulders, the shape of her legs. Yesterday he had watched them in a green meadow, from a doorway. He didn't need to verify his guess from the table next him, where the restless Englishman and the talkative American had suddenly become still and silent.

Van Cortlandt and Thornley looked at each other.

"He's gone," said Thornley needlessly. "God, he's recognized her."

"Are you sure it's that man?"

"Richard described him. Fits in. Cheek slashes, fair hair, gold-chain bracelet."

"He thinks it important enough to leave us alone, anyway," van Cortlandt said gloomily.

Thornley rose abruptly. "I'll follow and phone you at the hotel, if I can find where he has taken her. I'll phone you anyway. You had better stick to the hotel and wait for a call from Richard. He's bound to give you a ring when Frances doesn't turn up."

Van Cortlandt began to object, but Thornley had already left. The American paid the bill gloomily. He was just to go back to the hotel and wait. He was just to wait for phone calls. That was fine; that was just fine. There were times when playing the neutral tried even a neutral's temper.

Thornley saw the tall German and the girl in the Austrian dress ahead of him. The German had made no attempt to catch up with her. He was walking at some distance behind her. That way she would lead him to Richard.

Thornley crossed the street as a precaution, but either the German had not expected to be followed, or he didn't care. Nothing these English could do at this stage would prevent the drama from drawing to its close. . . . But he had not reckoned with the inspiration of the amateur.

Thornley saw several bicycles parked outside a café. He calmly swung himself onto one of them, and raced after Frances. His improvising was more successful than he had hoped. Three angry young men rushed out of the café and mounted bicycles too. Their yells were enough to make everyone in the street look round. And Frances had looked. And she had seen, too, for her step slackened and then she turned abruptly into an alley. The German broke into a run, and a slow-moving motor car suddenly ignored all rules of traffic to cross over to him. Thornley cursed himself for ever imagining that the German would be alone. A short command had been given, and the car speeded into the next street. Thornley guessed that it probably led round to the other entrance of the alley. He hesitated, wondering desperately what his next move should be. And then the three angry young men caught up with him. They were in uniform.

"I am very sorry," he said. "I was going to bring the bicycle back. I thought I saw a girl I must speak to, and she was far away. There was no time to ask your permission." One of the boys looked amused, but the owner of the bicycle was less amenable, until he noticed the money in Thornley's hand.

"To pay for the wear on the tires," said Thornley tactfully.

"Where is she now?" asked the one who had smiled.

"She went up that small alley."

"But it has another entrance! There's a short-cut! Come on. There's still time if we hurry."

Thornley found himself cycling furiously with the three young men grouped round him. The romantic one was enjoying himself. The other two were obviously intending to find out if the story about the girl was true. They followed a very narrow side street, which brought them suddenly onto the road which the car had taken . . . And there it was just ahead of them, standing at the end of the alley, ready to drive off. The back of the car was towards them, and the only one whose face they could see was the German with the scars. He was just getting into the front seat beside the driver. Behind was Frances, wedged in between two uniforms.

Thornley screened himself behind the young men as they dismounted.

They had stopped as soon as they had seen the open Mercedes. They were looking at him strangely.

"Was that your girl?" the romantic one demanded. His tone had changed completely. Thornley, his eyes fixed on the disappearing number plate of the car, shook his head. He was all disappointment.

"No. But from the distance their figures and legs were the same, though."

This proved a mild joke. The kindliest of the three relaxed again.

"Just as well she wasn't your girl," he said comfortingly. "She won't enjoy herself at Dreikir—"

"You talk too much, Fritz," interrupted the one who had taken the money. The third young man had stopped laughing. There was an uncomfortable pause.

"What about some beer?" Thornley suggested. They were stiffly sorry. There were meetings this afternoon, and processions. There was much to arrange before it began. They had all suddenly become very important. They straightened their shoulders and gave him a co-ordinated farewell. Thornley gave them a careless wave of his hand and thanked them again, solemnly. They swung onto their bicycles, but he noticed that the one he disliked looked carefully over his shoulder to watch him enter the restaurant which he had suggested. He stayed there for a few minutes, long enough to let the cyclists leave the street, long enough to write down the curious number of the black car and to find the telephone with its directory. But there was nothing under Dreikir—

He left the restaurant. Perhaps he might try the post office. He could have a letter to send, and he had forgotten the address. . . . And then he remembered Prague. No, the post office wouldn't do. It might be dangerous; too risky. It was obviously quite useless trying to trace the car. That would rouse instant suspicion. He remembered the guarded look on the young men's faces when they had first seen the car, the way in which they had dismounted so quickly at a safe distance. One thing he did know: the young man who had talked almost too much had recognized von Aschenhausen. That had been obvious.

He left the street as quickly as he could, in case the suspicious young man had changed his mind and returned, and walked quickly towards van Cortlandt's hotel. The shops were crowding round him once more. He noticed a tourist office and halted. Inside, he found a number of people booking their seats for that afternoon's excursions. They crowded round the various tables, each with its clearly-marked notice of a special tour. Beside the one labeled Brenner, a quiet man stood. He was watching: watching and listening. It was the only advertised excursion for anywhere near a frontier. Thornley noted the size of the group round that table— the Brenner was popular, it seemed—and decided to risk it.

He approached the desk marked Information at the other end of the large room. Behind it, a girl was handing out timetables and a few kind words to two men. Thornley, with his fair hair, his shorts and light gray tweed jacket, his almost white stockings and nail-studded shoes, felt safe enough beside them. The men were satisfied, at last, and left. He purposely chose the same place they had been asking about. That would take less time for the girl; and it might muddle her, later, if she were questioned.

The girl smiled at his request. "Kitzbühl? It is very popular today. You will find all information in this." She handed him one of the brightly illustrated folders which she still held in her hand. He opened it as the others had done, and studied its pages.

He looked up with a smile. "This is excellent." The girl seemed pleased. "Now, would you be good enough to tell me where the post office is? I have just arrived in Innsbruck."

"In the Maximilianstrasse."

"Is that far from here? I am late for an engagement already."

"It is quite a little way."

"It concerns a letter I want to post at once, and I have mislaid the address. I remember it began with Drei. Dreikir—like that."

"Ah—Dreikirchen. We used to have buses which visited it. But not now." She was looking at him curiously. "Do you know someone there?"

Thornley took his cue. "I was given the address two years ago. But my friend will still be there. I never heard that he had gone."

"Did he belong to the Church?" The girl had lowered her voice.

"He was studying." That seemed to be the correct answer.

"It's all changed now."

"Well, they will redirect the letter . . . I'll post it at once. Now would you advise today or Monday for Kitzbühl?"

A man and a woman had come up behind him.

"Today will be more crowded."

"And the bus will leave outside this office?"

"Just across the street. I hope you will enjoy yourself at Kitzbühl. Everyone does." She was a nice girl, the kind who really liked to please the customers.

Thornley thanked her, and studied the folder as he made his way out of the office. The queue at the Brenner table was still large. The man beside it was listening intently to each excursionist's request.

On the pavement, Thornley drew a deep breath. He stuffed the folder into his pocket. It would make a nice little souvenir along with the electric torch. The policeman's helmet hanging above his mantelpiece at Cambridge began to seem a poor effort.

All he could do now was to go to van Cortlandt's hotel. He hoped to high heaven that Richard was already worried about Frances, and that

he had phoned. At least they knew the name óf the place. . . . That was
something.

CHAPTER **19** DOUBLE CHECK

Richard woke about eleven o'clock, and his worries began with the
empty bed beside him. He ought to have wakened in time to see Frances
and talk to her. In fact, he ought to have gone himself, even if Frances
had been more adequately disguised. He dressed quickly, cursing at his
slight stiffness, his lateness, his difficulty in shaving with cold water.

When he got downstairs, the woman had reheated the coffee. It was
black and bitter, but it cleared his head. Twelve o'clock, the woman had
said. He drank more coffee in spite of its taste, and read the newspaper.
There was no mention of the Pertisau incident. So they were keeping it
quiet, meanwhile. Von Aschenhausen might be making desperate efforts
to turn his failure into success, before anything was made public. If he had
kept Smith on his own responsibility, in the hope of presenting his chiefs
with a large and very complete haul, then he would be in a dangerous
position himself, if he had failed. He had tried for too much; he had been
too ambitious. That would make their own escape twice as difficult. Von
Aschenhausen would have to catch them or face very unpleasant consequences. . . . And then, there was the matter of his pride, and revenge.
Vindictiveness was one of the strongest German traits. Richard sat and
looked at the patch of garden as Frances had done. But his feelings were
very different.

Twelve o'clock had long passed. The woman was sympathetic, but calm:
there was no need to worry. Innsbruck's streets were very difficult for
strangers, and she assured him for the second time that his wife's appearance was safe enough.

But by one o'clock, the woman was anxious too. She was obviously afraid
for Schulz and herself. Richard did not blame her.

"Can I phone safely from some place near here?" he asked. She nodded,
and pointed across the back yard to a house in the next street. And then
the doorbell rang. They looked at each other, with hope and fear allied in
their eyes. Richard moved behind the sitting-room door, where he could
see through the chink into the hall. He saw her open the front door
slightly. Someone handed her an envelope, and he heard a familiar voice.

"May I see the *Herr Professor?*"

Richard was startled. It couldn't be, it couldn't . . . But the door had opened farther, and there was no doubt.

"Anni!" he almost shouted. "Come in!"

The woman was so taken aback that Anni and her broad smile were already inside the house. Richard seized her arm and pulled her into the sitting room.

"Anni," he said again. "How on earth did you get here?"

Anni was delighted with his amazement, just in the same way as when she used to produce a triumph of a cake for a birthday surprise in Oxford. For her answer, she took the envelope back from the woman and handed it proudly to him. Frances, he thought; it must be a message from Frances. What had happened? Was she waiting somewhere for him? He ripped the envelope roughly open. All it contained was a small diagram, a sheet of paper with a map and no names.

"There's the Brenner," said Anni, pointing to a small penciled circle. "I thought it was better not to write in the names; instead, you will memorize them. That is why I had to see you."

Richard looked quickly from the map to Anni. "How did you know we needed this? How did you know you would find me here?"

"The *gnädige Frau* . . . didn't she tell you?"

"When did you see her?"

"After she came out of the Church."

"At what hour was that?"

Anni looked worried. "About a quarter to twelve. I reached my brother's shop just after twelve, and that was the time Johann comes to see me on Saturdays. You see, that is the afternoon my brother goes to the mountains —he's a guide on Saturdays and Sundays—and I look after the shop for him, then. So when Johann came, I got him to draw this, and I brought it to you at once. The *gnädige Frau* said tonight, but that was only because she was afraid for me. I thought you might want it now, so that you could leave at once. I didn't tell Johann about you. I promised I would tell him later, and it will be all right because he liked both you and the *gnädige Frau*."

Richard sat down for a moment. Anni saw the look in his face.

"The *gnädige Frau* told you nothing of our plans? What is wrong, *Herr Professor*? Is she not here?"

"No," said the woman gravely, "she has not come back yet."

"But she said she must hurry. She said you would be worried if she didn't . . . Oh, *Herr Professor!*" Anni was so upset that Richard rose and took her hand. So his fears had been real. While he had waited and worried, something had happened to Frances. Something must have happened. If he could only stop feeling so damned sick with worry. This was no damned good, standing here patting Anni's hand like a blasted idiot.

Something had to be thought of, something had to be planned. They had lost an hour already.

"Tell me, Anni, how did you recognize Mrs. Myles?"

"I looked right into her eyes, and they recognized me. And then there was something in the way she walked, the shape of her legs. It was because I know her so well that I could recognize her."

"Then someone else who knew her well might have recog—" He couldn't finish. He left Anni, and walked to the window. He stood with his back to them, looking out into the garden. He thought of van Cortlandt and Thornley. He must get in touch with them, and at once . . . But what then? What then? He must stop this. He had to keep calm, had even to forget that Frances was his; he had to think of all this mess in the way he had thought of Smith, as a kind of problem. And he needed all his wits about him to find a solution. Emotion would only hinder; worry might lose her forever.

He turned back to the room. "Anni, could you go back to the shop and wait there until an American and an Englishman come to buy climbing boots?"

Anni heard his calm voice with amazement, but it lessened her fears. If the *Herr Professor* saw some hope, then there was hope. She listened to his descriptions of the two men who would come to buy climbing boots. She memorized their names carefully, and the message she had to give them. The Hungerburg at four o'clock. Anni was not enthusiastic about that message. The Hungerburg was so big that they might miss each other. It was safe enough for them there, she agreed, but they might be late before they met each other. She didn't like to take the responsibility of the message. If anything went wrong, then she would blame herself.

"It would be better to meet them in the shop, and see them yourself. It would save time," she suggested. "There is a storeroom at the back of the shop with its own entrance. You could wait there until your friends arrived. My brother has left already, and Johann must go back to the hotel as soon as I get back to the shop— I left him in charge so that I could come here. There will be no one there except me." She laughed at any danger to herself. If the worst came, he would be an unknown customer; and there was the back entrance losing itself in courtyards and alleys, so that even if everything went wrong there was at least a chance to escape. Richard agreed with her in his heart. It would be the simplest solution, and the quickest one. That was the chief thing. Now that the suggestion had come from Anni herself, he accepted it gladly.

Anni had left by the back door, with a *loden* cape thrown round her shoulders. He waited for two or three minutes until she would be safely out of the other house, hoping against hope that Frances might suddenly appear. The woman was obviously worried, but she was unexpectedly sympathetic. Herr Schulz would be home any minute now; she had the dinner table all ready for him. And he would be able to advise them. Meanwhile, she offered him a bowl of thin brown soup with dumplings submerged in it. He must eat. Richard declined as politely as his revolving stomach would permit; worry churned him up inside like a Channel crossing. He had his eyes on his watch. Three minutes, he had thought, would be time enough for Anni. In any case, he couldn't wait any longer. He suddenly left the room.

"Say Lisa sent you," the woman called after him.

The formula worked. The cobbler obligingly made the call for him, and then left him alone with the telephone. He heard van Cortlandt's voice, and such a wave of relief swept over him that he realized he had been afraid of getting no answer.

"Hello!" said van Cortlandt, and waited. "Hello, there!"

"Van Cortlandt?"

"Speaking."

It was easier to talk now; the words which had deserted him came rushing out.

Van Cortlandt said, "Oh, yes, the *Times*. I'm sorry I'm late with that article. Glad you called. I thought you would because of this delay."

"Serious?" So van Cortlandt knew already; that saved explanations.

"At the moment, yes."

"Well, there's another article to write. Beauties of the Tyrol. Have you any climbing equipment?"

"Just my own two feet."

"Well, better add something to that. If you haven't boots, get them this afternoon. This is a rush assignment. Go to any good sports dealer, and he will advise you. There's Schmidt, or Spiegelberger, or Rudi Wachter. He is particularly good. You'll find him on the Burggraben near the Museumstrasse."

"Good. I'll go there at once. Hope to see you soon."

"I'll see you soon. Get a move on with the article, won't you? No delay for this one."

"Sure; you can depend on me. Love and kisses to Geoffrey Dawson."

"And mine to Luce." Richard heard a sudden laugh at the end of the phone, and then silence.

In the sitting room, Richard found Schulz sitting at the table, his head well down to his bowl of soup. Of Lisa, there was no sign. Schulz, busy with a dumpling, motioned him to a chair and pointed to the soup pot. Richard poured himself some coffee, and gulped it down. He thought of the brandy in his flask, but they might need that later on.

"I must go at once," he said. "My wife—"

"I know." Schulz wiped his lips, and swallowed some water. "I know. Lisa told me. There are all your papers and clothes." He nodded to a large envelope and a neat brown-paper parcel on a side table. Richard rose, and brought the envelope over to the dinner table. The document looked convincing; the photographs had just the right moronic look.

"Were we quick enough for you? That's everything, I think; everything. You've paid me. Have you any money left?"

"I'll meet some friends," Richard said.

"Well, good luck."

Richard's words came haltingly. "My wife may have been arrested. They may trace her movements to this house."

Schulz swallowed some more soup noisily. "Don't worry about that. I had already decided to change my address. I saw your friend Kronsteiner early this morning, at my place of—business. He had a message last night from our friend who used to be at Pertisau. So we are on the move again. Lisa is packing now." He smiled as he saw the relief on Richard's face. Richard prepared to go. They shook hands silently.

Then Schulz suddenly spoke. "Courage!" he said. "Courage! It's the only real weapon we've got. A man can win when he still has his courage."

Richard nodded. "I'm sorry if we have upset your plans."

"They are always being upset, but we go on. And don't worry about Kronsteiner. He's all right. He's much changed since his visit to me this morning." Schulz threw back his head and laughed. Kronsteiner's change seemed to amuse him . . . And then he went back to his soup. "It would be a pity to leave it," he explained, his voice once more matter-of-fact.

Lisa met Richard at the doorway. "This was all you left upstairs," she said, and held out his small razor case, and Frances' bag. He nodded his thanks, and watched her slip them safely into the brown-paper parcel.

"We'll give you five minutes, and then we leave," called Schulz, in the middle of the last dumpling. "Good-by, young man, and courage."

Lisa gave him her first and last smile.

He closed the door softly, and walked unhurriedly down the street. The brown-paper parcel attracted no attention. It was almost two o'clock.

CHAPTER **20** RALLYING GROUND

All Innsbruck seemed to be marching that Saturday. There had been two parades already, complete with bands, banners and uniforms. The on-lookers crowded into the principal streets, through which the processions passed, and even after they had gone the people waited. Perhaps there were still other processions to come. By avoiding the main thoroughfares,

Richard walked quickly through the deserted little side streets, and he arrived at the back entrance of the Wachter shop in record time. There was no one in sight, as he opened the back door and walked quietly into the small room which Anni had described as a storeroom. This was it, all right. He moved carefully and slowly between the neat stacks of boxes to a crate under the small, high window. No one would be able to look in through that window, unless he brought a stepladder along with him. He sat down on the edge of the crate, and waited. He could hear a murmur of voices, and once Anni laughed. The sounds were distant enough to assure him that a room lay between the storeroom and the front shop itself, where Anni was serving a customer. No one had seen him, no one had heard him enter; so far, so good. If anyone were to look into the room, the rows of boxes would hide him. He began to feel better.

The two doors worried him, all the same. He rose suddenly, and examined the lock of the door by which he had entered. It worked easily, so he locked it. Better that, than to risk some unknown visitor using this street door at an awkward moment. It would be a simple matter to unlock the door and escape by the alley, if any complication arrived. There was that other door, the one which must lead into that middle room; but he couldn't do anything about it until Anni appeared.

The voices were silent now. The customer must be going, for he heard the accustomed formula, and Anni's dutiful echo. There was a sound of a bell. Of course, that would be the door closing. Anni must have brought back one of those doorbells as a present for her brother after all. She had said she would. He smiled in spite of himself. It was rather odd to hear the familiar Oxford sound right here in Innsbruck. It made him think of a dark little shop, with the smell of rich tobaccos in the air, and neat white jars on its shelves; and the polished brass scales, on which the light and dark tobaccos were weighed before they were mixed and then carefully emptied into your pouch; and the darkened oak counter, with its rubber mat for your coins, and the change which came to you from the old wooden till; and then the gentle note of the bell as you opened and shut the door.

The bell was silent again, and he heard Anni's footsteps approaching. The door into the middle room opened, and she stood straining her eyes into the dim light. He stepped out from behind the boxes.

"God be thanked," she said.

"Did you hear me at all?"

She shook her head. "No. I've been coming through here between visits from customers, just to make sure. Have you locked that door? Good. I'll lock this one too. The room next you is a dressing room, where customers try on sports clothes if they want to. If anyone should go in there, just keep quite still. But if anyone with a loud voice tries this door, and rattles it, and asks me angrily for the key, then leave at once."

The front doorbell rang.

"It has been very useful, that bell," said Anni in a whisper. She turned to go, but Richard caught her arm as he heard a cheery voice call: "Anyone here?" from the front shop. That must be Thornley. It was.

"That was a darned lucky break, if you ask me," said van Cortlandt in English. Their voices sounded as if they brought good news.

Anni looked at Richard inquiringly. He nodded, and she went through to meet them.

He heard the men ask about climbing boots, but Anni's voice was too low for him to know what she had answered. He heard them suddenly quieten, and follow her quickly towards the storeroom.

She locked the door behind them, and they were left alone in the room, standing there looking at each other.

"God, and aren't we glad to see you," said van Cortlandt.

"Frances?" Richard asked.

Thornley spoke. "They got her. Just the rottenest luck. It was the fair-haired blighter with the bracelet who saw her, and recognized something. They've taken her to Dreikirchen. That's all I could find out. That and the number and identification marks of the car." He groped in his pocket for the sheet from his diary where he had scribbled the signs down in that restaurant, just after the boys had left him.

The door was unlocked, and Anni entered the room with Tyrolese jackets over her arm. She handed them to van Cortlandt and Thornley.

"Where is Dreikirchen, Anni? Is it a village or a house? Have you ever heard of it?"

"If the doorbell rings, get back into the dressing room, and try these on, in front of the mirror," she said to the American. "Lock this door behind you, and put the key up on that high shelf, there." She turned to Richard. "Now that we've made things safe, *Herr Professor*, there is only one Dreikirchen near here. It's just two hours' walk from here—to the south of Innsbruck. If you follow the Brennerstrasse, you will reach the Berg Isel, and Dreikirchen is to the right of that. I will show you on the map; you have one?"

Richard had already taken his Baedeker out of his pocket, and was searching for the Berg Isel. Anni looked over his arm, and pointed with her finger.

"There's the road. You see that small line on its right? That is the side road which takes you to Dreikirchen. There it is—these black squares grouped together."

"Is it a village, and why isn't it named?"

"It isn't a village. It is too small—just a few small houses and the monastery and three little chapels. Monks used to live there."

"Who lives there now?"

Anni seemed embarrassed. She wasn't sure. She had heard her brothers talk, of course, but they had never explained. One of their friends had been sent there.

"Is it a concentration camp?" asked van Cortlandt.

Anni was shocked. Oh, no. Nothing like that. There were boys at Dreikirchen, who were being educated. Specially chosen boys and young men. She admitted there were rumors. Of course, there always were rumors, but people didn't try to find out about rumors, not if they were wise.

"Has it any connection with the Gestapo?" asked van Cortlandt again.

Anni looked frightened. There were rumors, she said . . . And once Johann had made a joke about that in front of one of her brothers, and that was the only time they had quarreled. Richard thanked her; that was all she knew or wanted to know.

As she left them, Thornley stopped her. "If you were to see a large black car with these numbers on it, what would you think?" He held out the page from his diary.

"Special car," she said.

"Secret police?"

Anni nodded. "I must go back into the shop," she said, and left them.

"Were you followed?"

"We were at first," said van Cortlandt. "And then we had a break. The whole place is jammed with people. So we got mixed up with two processions, and here we are without our tail. We are probably safe for another ten minutes, until he reports to headquarters and they give him a list of our shopping places. They no doubt listened in to our talk on the phone today. So now let's get busy."

Richard said, "Thanks for all you've done. It would have been hopeless without you."

"Say, we're in on this too," said van Cortlandt. He turned to Thornley. "Imagine that . . . he thought he was going to get rid of us at this stage. It will take three of us to find Frances. And she's got to be found."

"We'll find her," Thornley said quietly.

Richard didn't waste any more time. He spread the map before them. "We'll meet here," he said, pointing to a part of the road as it touched the Berg Isel. "Bring a car, and all your things packed. And take this parcel and pack the things in it into your case. It's our stuff for Italy."

"I've arranged about the car," said van Cortlandt. "That radio man agreed to an exchange. He'll keep his mouth shut. He's going to Vienna this afternoon, and is traveling the Jenbach road. I've already told the hotel I'm going back to Pertisau to look for my friends. It all fits in nicely."

Richard looked at the American with respect. "That's a pretty good effort, Henry. Well, that's about all. Meet me at that place any time after four o'clock. That will let me get out there safely. And bring some chocolate and cigarettes."

"Say half-past four," said van Cortlandt. They shook hands.

"We'll be seeing you," he added, and followed Thornley back into the shop.

Richard waited for Anni. She hurried into the storeroom, and unlocked the back door.

"Good-by, *Herr Professor*, and give the *gnädige Frau* my . . ." She bit her lip. "Please let me know when she is safe. Please."

"Yes, Anni."

"Please hurry, *Herr Professor*."

"Yes, Anni." What could he say to thank her enough for what she had done? Anni seemed to sense his difficulty. She smiled sadly.

"I am only repaying your kindness in Oxford. The *gnädige Frau* was always so good to me." She opened the door and motioned him out.

"*Auf Wiedersehen*, Anni." He gripped her hand and held it.

"*Auf Wiedersehen*." Her smile was quivering. And then the door closed behind him, and already his steps had taken him far enough away to keep Anni safe.

Here was the street corner, and the crowds. He loitered with them until he saw Thornley and van Cortlandt leave the shop. They were carrying two or three parcels. He watched them until they were lost in the crowd.

He felt suddenly hungry, but he had just enough money to take him to the Berg Isel by tramcar. That would save his legs for tonight's climb. He and Thornley could get Frances over the frontier, and van Cortlandt could take their clothes by car, and meet them in Italy. On the Berg Isel, as he waited for the others, he would memorize that map which Anni had given him, and compare it with his own. He felt safe enough, partly because of the number of people on the streets, partly because von Aschenhausen would be the only person in Innsbruck who could recognize him—and von Aschenhausen was with Frances. The German was playing a deep and subtle game. If he had taken Frances to Dreikirchen, it was because her arrest must be unofficial until he had got the information from her which would help him to retrieve his failure. Frances knew enough to compensate him for the escape of Smith, and even that might be made temporary, if Frances could be persuaded. If Frances could be persuaded.

The journey to the Berg Isel, although dull and safe enough, was one which Richard would never forget.

CHAPTER 21 APPROACH TO DREIKIRCHEN

Van Cortlandt and Thornley made their way as quickly as they could through the crowd. They stopped twice: once to buy some biscuits and chocolate, and once to buy oranges. Van Cortlandt already had some brandy. In this matter-of-fact way, they quietly discussed their plans as they walked along to van Cortlandt's hotel. Thornley, with unexpected pessimism, had not unpacked his bag and in any case he always traveled lightly. Van Cortlandt, although most of his belongings always remained in his trunk or suitcases, had a lot of odds and ends to clear up in his room. So it was Thornley who would have the job of phoning van Cortlandt's broadcasting friend and of telling him the time they would meet him. He already knew the place where they were to exchange cars. Van Cortlandt had thought that out, this morning. Thornley was also to telephone Cook's agent, and have him collect van Cortlandt's heavier luggage, with the directions that it was to be sent on to Geneva.

Van Cortlandt was quite philosophic about it all.

"It was coming," he said. "I've got to the stage when I can't write at all. I've developed a sort of censorphobia. Every word I get down begins to look as if it won't get through anyway. And it's about time I changed my beat. If there are any surprises coming in the world's history, it won't be from this direction. They are all set for Poland. I'd do better to go there, myself. See it from the other angle."

"I had a letter this morning," Thornley said unexpectedly, and his tone made van Cortlandt look at him. "I'll tell you about it later. It was from Tony, on his way home."

"The girl?"

Thornley shook his head. "Alone."

Van Cortlandt was startled. He had never imagined that Thornley's face could have such an ugly look.

"Pretty bad?" he asked.

Thornley only nodded.

They finished the journey in silence. When he left van Cortlandt, Thornley's voice was normal again.

"I'll see you at four," he said.

It was four o'clock exactly when Thornley arrived at the garage. Van Cortlandt was already there, examining his car. The mechanic had lost interest, and was busy with some other work. He had overhauled the car

this morning and had found nothing seriously wrong although they seemed
to have had a lot of trouble last night. These Americans, if only they'd
take the trouble to learn about the insides of a machine, they would save
themselves a lot of money . . . But then they were all millionaires, and
that ruined them. Now, it was said, they were all starving in the streets.
What people had to suffer in other countries! Anyway, the car was perfect
now; and he had been paid; and he had other work to do, plenty of it
what with all the others at the parade. He had advised the American not
to miss the processions: that was something to see. That was something
to impress anyone. But the American had only smiled and nodded. Perhaps
he couldn't understand German. And now the American was pottering
around his car, pretending he knew all about the engine, looking for anything that had been left undone. Let him: there was plenty of more important work to be done. The money had been paid. The job was over.

Van Cortlandt motioned Thornley into the automobile, but he himself
didn't enter. He kept his eyes fixed on the entrance of the garage. When
a boy appeared, carrying two suitcases, van Cortlandt had the money
ready in his hand. The boy was gone as suddenly as he had arrived, the
suitcases were in the car, and they were driving smoothly out of the door.

"Quick work," said Thornley approvingly. "That was rather a brain wave
of yours."

Van Cortlandt grinned as he guided the car expertly through the traffic.
"How did you manage?"

"It was easy enough," Thornley said. "You know what a rabbit warren
my hotel was—no lift, just staircases and passages. Well, I paid the bill,
said I was leaving for Pertisau roundabout five, and apparently went back
to my room. I came down another staircase and took one of the back exits.
I wasn't even followed."

"If I was, I lost him in the crowds. Processions have their uses. Helluva
lot of uniforms today. They seem to crawl out from under every stone.
Wonder what's it all about?"

"Just any old excuse. It depresses me."

"That was the Myles' reaction."

"Aren't you? It looks as if we shall all just have to learn to march too.
No one can stop that spirit with arguments or good deeds."

"Well, I must say I think it *needs* stopping. But I don't think there's
a democracy left with the guts to do it. We are all tied to our mothers'
apronstrings—and big business keeps bleating about peace and prosperity.
Between the apronstrings and the bleating, we'll all hesitate until it's too
late. That is what depresses me."

Thornley said nothing to that. There were things stronger than apronstrings and bleatings, he felt. But it was no good talking about courage:
you could not prove it by talking about it. It was like a pudding: the
proof was in the eating. He contented himself with watching the way in

which van Cortlandt drove. The timing at the corners of the streets was perfect. If any car were following them, it would be jammed by the traffic from the cross streets. Van Cortlandt had forgotten his depression, and was enjoying himself. He seemed particularly pleased when they crossed the bridge and turned west towards the Jenbach road. The two uniformed men on the bridgehead had noticed the car; this amused van Cortlandt particularly. By the time they had reached the beer garden, the traffic had thinned out and they could see clearly that no car was following them.

Van Cortlandt's eyes searched the few cars parked beyond the entrance to the garden. They widened suddenly.

"Good man," he said with some satisfaction. "Space for us, and all." He drove neatly in beside a dark-blue car. Its subdued color made it almost invisible beside van Cortlandt's. Its doors were unlocked, and Thornley slipped into the back seat. He found himself calmly handing out the suitcase he found there to van Cortlandt, who gave him their cases in exchange. The easiness of the whole business took his breath away.

A thin man in an American suit and hat was walking leisurely towards them. He threw his cigarette away as he reached his new car, and gave van Cortlandt a sardonic grin as he opened its door.

Van Cortlandt got into the blue car. "Drive like hell," he said to the steering wheel.

"Sure," the man said to himself. He backed the car smoothly in a half circle, so that it faced in the direction of Jenbach. Thornley looked after the speeding car, and watched it disappearing round the trees. Anyone who might have been watching would have difficulty in knowing just what had happened. The only way in which he could see what man had got into what car would have been to walk past them. And no one had.

Van Cortlandt watched his car until it was out of sight, and then he swung back on the road by which they had just come.

"He's all right," he said, reading Thornley's mind. "We are just two Americans who traded cars. So what? If there is anything phoney about that, then we just act dumb. He doesn't know much about our game. He was a newspaperman himself, once, and he guessed I was on to a story. And he hates the Nazis' guts. What's more, he got a bargain in cars. We're all happy."

Thornley guessed that van Cortlandt was putting a very good face on the whole business. He had been proud of that car. He was a strange mixture, thought Thornley: just as strange and unpredictable as he himself found the British. That would surprise him. Thornley smiled. Van Cortlandt saw it in the mirror.

"What's the joke?" he asked. "I could do with one myself."

"The Nazis' guts. It is funny that it should be one thing on which most Americans and Britishers can agree wholeheartedly, without any reservations. The average Frenchman hates the Nazi, too; but half, or at least part, of it is due to the fact he is a dangerous neighbor. Now you and I don't hate the Nazis because they are German. We hate the Germans because they are Nazi. And if you didn't, you wouldn't be driving a strange car to God-knows-where into God-knows-what, this afternoon. You'd be standing at a street corner shouting *"Heil!"* with the rest, and feeling all uplifted and mystic. You like the Myles', I know, but if the Nazis didn't curdle you up inside, you wouldn't be doing all this. In fact, we've got to the stage where anyone who opposes the Nazis is worth helping. Isn't that it?"

Van Cortlandt grinned. "About. I didn't tell you how I felt when I arrived here? I was going to be the complete neutral observer. My stories were going to be a model of detachment. Can you imagine that? My angle was that the Germans had had a tough time of it. If they only had gotten a square deal . . . All that hash. It only took me a few weeks to find out that every deal was square if it benefited Germany, and to hell with the rest. Now I don't mind them looking out for their own rights; we all do. But what got me down is the way no one else has any rights, unless they say so. That's the rub. They are always in the right, and the rest of us just misunderstand them. Criticism is just another stab in the back from Jews and Communists. They've kidded other people so long now that they've started kidding themselves."

"Perhaps it is because they've developed two standards," suggested Thornley, "one for Germany, one for the others. They really believe that anything which is good for them can't be evil. That is how they can lie and commit all kinds of treachery. If it is for the benefit of the Fatherland, then it doesn't seem a lie or a piece of treachery to them: it makes everything moral."

"But then, there are the exceptions."

"Yes, and they should be thanking God for the exceptions instead of driving them into exile or putting them into concentration camps. If it weren't for them, after the next war Germany might be blotted from the map."

Van Cortlandt shook his head. "You can't destroy a whole nation."

"Can't you? Just wait to see how Germany will try it with some of her neighbors. She will give the rest of us a few tips. And it worked with Carthage, too. Don't look so worried, Henry, the exceptions will get Germany her second chance. Or is it a third?"

Van Cortlandt shook his head. "God knows," he said wearily.

They had circled round Innsbruck to the west. That avoided the main streets, which were crowding up once more. They passed several formations of uniformed young men. It seemed as if they were all marching their way to some meeting place. Neither the American nor the Englishman said anything but as they passed one set of exhibitionists in goose-stepping precision their eyes met in the mirror above van Cortlandt's head.

On the road which led to the Berg Isel (the road which led to the Brenner Pass eventually, as van Cortlandt carefully pointed out) three large black cars passed them in quick succession. They were filled with young men sitting uncomfortably erect, their faces white blurs under the uniform caps. Van Cortlandt heard a quick movement behind him, and turned to see Thornley looking through the back window of the car. He was repeating something to himself.

"Yes?" asked van Cortlandt. Thornley was clearly excited.

"One of these cars, that's it, one of them."

Van Cortlandt smiled. "Your grammar does your feelings proud," he said. "What about it, anyway?"

"One of these cars is the same one I saw this afternoon with Frances in it. Don't you see, Henry, if they have left Dreikirchen, it will be all the better for us?"

Van Cortlandt thought over this for some moments. "*If* they left Dreikirchen," he said. He was probably right, thought Thornley gloomily. And yet, pieces of luck, both good and bad, had the oddest way of turning up. Whichever way you added up your plans, you should always leave a margin on either side for luck.

"Any time now," said van Cortlandt. He had slackened the speed of the car as they approached the small railway halt; there were few passengers waiting on the toy platform. Richard had said he would be near here. Their eyes anxiously watched the road ahead and the paths which led into the surrounding woods, but it wasn't until they were round a bend in the road which hid them from the halt and its inn, and the car had stopped completely to let Thornley get out, that Richard stepped from behind some trees.

"I was beginning to think that we had missed you," van Cortlandt said, worry sharpening his voice, as the car moved on.

"Sorry," said Richard. "I forgot to ask you the color of the car, and I wasn't sure. Couldn't risk anything. Sorry. How did everything go?"

"According to plan."

"Good. Now, we've about five minutes more on this road, and then ten minutes more to the right. I did some map studying while I waited, and there seems to be a small road or track of some kind, just before we get to the Dreikirchen road. If we follow that track, then we can approach the place from the back. If it had been dark, we could have risked the Dreikirchen road itself. But we'd better not wait for darkness. We haven't time."

Thornley looked at Richard's white, set face. There was a gauntness about it which worried him.

"Had anything to eat?" he inquired casually. Richard shook his head, and then took the slab of chocolate which Thornley handed him. He ate it with his eyes fixed on his watch. He doesn't know or care what he's eating, thought Thornley; it might be linoleum for all he knows; he's all shot to pieces.

"Brandy?" he asked.

"We'll need it later," Richard said. He was still looking at his watch. Thornley began to guess the kind of time he had been having while he waited for them to arrive. Shouldn't have left him alone, thought Thornley.

"This is the track," Richard said, and the car turned from the Brenner road into a wood. Richard was still looking at his watch. He held up a hand to silence Thornley just as he was about to say something. . . . And then Thornley realized that Richard was timing the distance they had to drive.

"Now," he said, and the car swung off the track.

"I'll turn, while the going's good," van Cortlandt said, and maneuvered the car until it rested on the grass, hidden from the track by a clump of bushes, its bonnet pointed back towards the Brenner road. Van Cortlandt unscrewed his flask, and handed it to Richard.

"Bob's right," he said. "We all need it. I've plenty more."

"Rum ration," suggested Thornley.

"Any of you got a gun?" van Cortlandt asked.

They shook their heads. Thornley produced a strong-looking clasp knife and his souvenir torch. Richard had nothing. It might have been the shadow of a smile on the American's face, but his voice was serious enough.

"Well, I have, so if we get into a tight spot . . ." He didn't finish, but tapped his pocket thoughtfully. "Anything else, before we leave the car?"

They waited in the quietness of the trees, while van Cortlandt locked the car methodically. When he joined them, the three men looked at each other for some moments. Then Richard turned, and led the way up the wooded hillside.

It was a short climb. They paused on the crest, sheltered by the pines. Below them, the hill sloped gently to Dreikirchen. They could just see three spires above the last trees.

Thornley pulled out his knife, and motioned to them to wait. He disappeared back towards the road they had left, lopping off a thin branch from every third or fourth pine, as he passed. Van Cortlandt exchanged glances with Richard. The idea was good; the cuts on the trees were white and jagged. When Thornley returned, he seemed pleased. He must have found his way back in record time. As they followed Richard down through the trees, he used his knife continuously. It slowed up their pace, but now that they were so near their objective, there was little they could do but wait, until the clear afternoon light had given way to the dusk of the evening—except for spying out the lie of the land. So they went slowly, walking carefully in order to make no noise, while Thornley worked silently and unhurriedly. The spires had disappeared as they descended through the wood. Richard, who led the way, hoped that his sense of direction was as adequate as Thornley's trail blazing. He would soon know, for at last they were reaching the edge of the wood. A steep bank and a garden were all that separated them from Dreikirchen. Behind the cover of the trees overshading the bank they lay and watched.

The Fathers who had built the community had had an eye for balance and neatness. Into a curve of the wooded hillside, which had formed both a shelter and a background, they had built their miniature castle with its large chapel. Two smaller chapels flanked the main buildings on either side, standing at a respectful distance, and round these were grouped a few cottages. The effect was that of a semicircle which paralleled the curve in the hill, so that the small castle, as the center of the crescent, dominated everything.

From where they lay they could see the road which came from the south. Straight, broad and white, it approached the center of the curve of buildings in a dramatic sweep. That was something, Richard thought, which the founding Fathers had never even imagined. He remembered the map on which this road had been marked only as roughly as the track which they had followed. Anni had been right. Dreikirchen had changed.

In front of them was the garden which lay behind the right-hand chapel. It was the kitchen garden with its rows of neatly planted vegetables protected on one side by a hedge of red-currant bushes, which stretched from the bank almost to the chapel itself. On its other side, the side which adjoined the garden of the castle and the large chapel, there was a row of fruit trees. Pear trees, Richard thought. They were obviously intended as a screen, so that anyone walking in the castle's flower garden wouldn't have his eye offended by the patchwork quilt of vegetables. They served the purpose well enough, for it was difficult for the three men to see the flower garden. It would be better to move behind the castle itself, and from there they would be able to see not only the flower garden but whatever lay behind the third chapel. For the curve of the buildings now hid that completely.

"Mark this spot," whispered Richard. The others nodded, and looked at the shapes of the trees and bushes, at the outcrop of rock behind which they lay. It wasn't easy, but it had to be remembered. If they got safely away from the castle, and were in a hurry, as they probably would be, then they would have to depend on being able to find the blazed trail quickly. Without the trail they might miss the car. It was unpleasant to imagine what it would be like to be searching desperately for the car on an unknown road with pursuers behind them. The best thing to remember, thought Richard grimly, was the outcrop of rock which lay about twenty feet away from the red-currant bushes. If they could reach the red-currant bushes, he added to that thought.

Under the cover of the trees, they worked their way carefully along to the back of the castle. It gave them the view they had hoped for. It was easy to see that an approach would be more difficult through the castle garden, planted with rose trees and small flowering shrubs, than it would be through the kitchen garden. There was much less cover here. As for the ground behind the third chapel, it was quite hopeless. It consisted of tennis courts and a stretch of grass. There was no sign of life from the cottages on this side of the castle, either . . . no movement, no sounds of men's voices. If it hadn't been for the curl of smoke which came from the back of the castle, where a low, narrow building had been added as an afterthought, they might have been looking at a picture in a German calendar.

Richard motioned the others to go farther back into the wood. They reached some bushes, and sat down behind them. They talked in whispers.

"I can do the scouting," said Thornley. "I've done some deer-stalking. This should be easy." He drew his diary from a pocket, and began making a rough diagram of the buildings and gardens. Richard and Thornley exchanged glances. Thornley was obviously the best man for the job. Richard remembered the way he had climbed the balcony of the Pertisau house.

"All right," he said. "We'll watch from the top of the bank."

"This is how I'll go," Thornley said. He traced a line on the diagram with his pencil. He would use the red-currant bushes and reach the right-hand chapel. From there he would follow the path in the kitchen garden which seemed to enter a kind of shrubbery as it reached the line of pear trees. That would bring him to the right wing of the castle, to the back of it where the smoke came from. Then he could perhaps find out who was in that part of the building, or a possible back entrance to the place, or whatever was to be seen or heard.

"All right," Richard said again.

Thornley didn't waste any time. ᴴe was already moving quietly down through the trees, in a slantwise direction which would bring him out of the wood near the red-currant hedge.

Van Cortlandt abandoned the plans he had been making while they had watched the castle. He would have liked something with more action than this—one of them to have made some kind of distraction, while the other two rushed the place. The trouble was that they had no weapons worth a nickel, not compared with the arsenal they might expect to face. Still, there seemed to be no one there; perhaps just a cook in the kitchen where the smoke came from, and Frances in a locked room upstairs with someone left to guard her, while the others held their jamboree in Innsbruck or searched for Richard. All Thornley's caution would then be a waste of good time. He had the gloomy afterthought that Frances might not be there after all; that had been worrying him ever since they left

Innsbruck. In that case, they would have to imitate old Barney Finnigan. . . .

They had retraced their steps to the edge of the wood again, and had lain behind a fallen tree which would protect them from being seen. They themselves could see through its skeleton roots. As soon as Thornley reached the pear trees and followed the path towards the shrubbery at the side of the house, they could watch him. If anything went wrong before he reached the trees, then they would have to depend on their hearing. Richard raised himself to listen, but van Cortlandt shook his head. He was right; there was nothing.

They waited in the silence of the wood, and watched the tops of the trees moving gently against the background of the evening sky. The strain was beginning to tell on Richard. Again the fear came back to him that they might be on the wrong trail. Frances might be a hundred miles from here—injured, dead. He began to count the branches above him. Anything, anything to keep him from thinking.

CHAPTER **22** VIKING'S FUNERAL

Thornley felt a sudden wave of excitement as he neared the edge of the wood and saw the small chapel and the quiet little houses beside it. It was the kind of feeling he had when he'd stand patiently waiting for the birds to break cover; only this time he was one of the birds. It wasn't the excitement of fear or nervousness. It was the excitement of expectation. He had always lived in the country, and what might have been difficult for Richard or van Cortlandt seemed fairly simple to him.

He moved confidently and quickly, knowing that under cover of this string of bushes he could only be seen from the woods behind him. In that case, he would be seen even if he went slowly and carefully—and time was short: they could hardly wait until complete darkness, for he felt that the castle might not remain deserted so very much longer. This was what Henry called playing a hunch; well, he was going to play it as hard as he could.

He had almost reached the chapel. He flattened himself out under the last clump of bushes and waited. So far so good. He strained to hear any sound from the cottages or the chapel, but they were completely silent. What was more, the doors and windows of the cottages were shut. It would be strange for anyone inside them to sit that way on a warm summer's evening. He measured the short dash to the chapel with his eye, and timed it neatly. He stood flat against the wall, hidden from the main buildings. In two or three moments, he would slip round the corner of the chapel and reach the path. The fruit trees would shelter him from the castle gardens, the large shrubs growing along the path would shelter him from the castle's windows; the only danger lay in being seen from the other end of the path. As he waited, motionless, he became aware that the windows beside him were not the usual high, narrow windows of a church. They were square and broad, with ordinary glass. He edged to one and looked cautiously inside over his shoulder. The interior was very strange for a chapel indeed—it was a very complete gymnasium. He gained confidence; only now would he admit to himself that the responsibility of discovering Dreikirchen's existence had worried him. Now he was pretty sure of its purpose. It would be the natural place for Frances to be taken if von Aschenhausen hadn't turned her over to the regular police, and it wasn't likely that he had done that. This was more a case for secret police, with abduction, not arrest, as their weapon.

He left the security of the east wall of the chapel, and entered the kitchen garden. Fortunately, the path curved to suit the arc which the buildings formed. He was hidden from the end of the path where it probably skirted the castle. If he could reach the pear trees, then at least the path would be safer because of the shrubbery. At this point, it was rather unpleasant. There wasn't much shelter in a row of cabbages, or on the long north side of the chapel.

He had reached the pear trees. As he did so, he side-stepped into the shrubbery. The path itself was now too open. It curved straight to a door in the castle itself, a side door just where the low wing was joined to the main building. The smoke from the wing was curling up steadily. Kitchen, almost certainly, thought Thornley, and regained his breath in the shelter of the bushes. The door had been unexpected. In fact, it had given him a jolt, as he had come round the path and suddenly met it staring at him from the end of the path. It meant he would have to push his way carefully and slowly between the thick shrubs, sometimes almost through them. Not the pleasantest way of travel, he thought savagely. The earth here hadn't the clean wholesomeness of the earth in a wood. It seemed dank and stale, and a fine dust from the branches and leaves blackened his hands.

He had almost reached the castle wall. . . . And then he heard voices; at first distant, and then gradually getting louder. But they were far enough away to be indistinguishable. He must get almost to the end of the bushes before he would be near enough to hear them. The voices were clearer; two men were talking. Only two, he was sure of that. But he still couldn't hear any words. He knelt down on the moldering earth. He pushed down gently the branch in front of him. It let him see the side of the castle right up to the front corner. He saw that there was a broad path along this wall of the castle, which must meet the path from the kitchen garden in front of the side door.

Thornley moved his head to get a clearer view of the front corner of the castle. He dared not push the sheltering branch any more to the side. He judged that the men were walking in front of the castle, that any moment they would appear at the corner. The voices were coming nearer, and he could hear the heavy footsteps of men aware of their own authority. . . . And then there was a laugh, the belly laugh a man gives when he has just heard an unexpected end to a good story. The trooper who had laughed was still enjoying the joke when they reached the corner of the path. They were in their shirt sleeves, and capless, but they still wore revolvers at their side and the one who had laughed carried a loaded cane. He beheaded the large yellow daisies growing at the side of the path as he listened to his companion. They paused as they turned in their walk, and both looked up at the same window as if they had heard something. They were silent for a moment, listening. Then the one who had laughed said something to the other which made them both snicker, and they began their walk back along the front of the castle, and the corner of the building hid them.

Thornley wondered they had not heard his heartbeats. The man who had laughed and chopped off the flower heads was the one who had questioned him last night when he had returned to Innsbruck with van Cortlandt. Anyway, he had found out that there were two of them in front of the castle. They weren't on guard; they had lounged too much for that. But they were armed. It looked as if no one at the castle expected any uninvited guests. And why should they? This was one of their own strongholds, and once their prisoners disappeared from their homes the shock or the fear which petrified their friends ended all help for them. It took weeks, even months, for anyone who was mad enough to ask, to discover what had happened to those who had disappeared. So why worry about a foreign agent who had walked into an alley and had "vanished" at the other end? Her friends couldn't even make inquiries about her; they couldn't afford to. Thornley smiled grimly as he moved back towards the path from the kitchen garden. That was how these blighters worked it. Bribe enough men with a sense of power, reward them with luxury and grandeur, and they'd be loyal terrorizers. It was Faust all over again. Body and soul for sale to the man who could give them the things they had always wanted. And the greater the sale, the greater the rewards.

Thornley had reached the path. There, at the edge of the shrubbery, he could see clearly across the rose beds to the bank of the wooded hill. Would he go back now, or would he try to find out who was in the place he thought was the kitchen? The smoke was rising in greater volume. When he had first seen it, it had only been a trickle. He looked at the door. Could he risk stepping onto the path to reach the wall, and perhaps a window? The two men pacing in front of the castle would have nearly reached the other end of it. Then they would probably turn and come back. Now was the time to move. . . . And then the door opened, and as Thornley automatically drew back into the bushes, he heard a thin voice raised in its anger as high as a woman's.

The voice followed a man out into the path.

"Don't waste any time, either," it screeched. "I've had enough of you. Everyone else does the work while you stuff your belly. Go on, now."

The young man paused, his mouth stuffed with a large piece of cake.

"Shut your gub. If you're late, then get on with your work. What do you think you are anyway?" He came slowly down the path, grumbling to himself. "It's Hermann this and Hermann that. As if I hadn't my own job to do. As if I were a . . ." He didn't finish, but pitched forward suddenly on his face. Thornley pocketed the torch again, and dragged the man into the bushes. Quite a neat rabbit punch, he thought. Pity if it had broken the torch. He reached for one of the heavy stones which edged the pathway, and cracked the man over the head with it for good measure. He used his own handkerchief as a gag, and the man's belt and necktie to truss him neatly. The only place from which his attack could have been seen was from the woods. He hoped to God that Myles and van Cortlandt had been watching.

They had. They had seen him clearly as he had come out of the kitchen garden, had seen him hesitate as he left the cover of the pear trees, had seen him slip into the shrubbery. They waited for some minutes, wondering what on earth he had found interesting there. They hadn't heard the voices, but they began to understand when they heard a man's laugh. They strained their eyes, but they could see no one, not until a trooper walked slowly down the path, past the bushes, to drop suddenly like a stone. Then they saw Thornley again as he had pulled the body into the shrubbery. Van Cortlandt grinned: this was more like it. They waited impatiently. . . . But there was no further movement, no signal which they were hoping for.

Thornley waited. He was listening for the voices: the men should have reached this side of the castle again by this time. What was detaining them? Or was he misjudging the length of the minutes in his anxiety? And then he heard them. Almost there; pause; turn. They were walking away again. He relaxed, and looked at the man beside him. He was out cold—for a long, long time. He stepped back onto the path, and waved.

The others had seen him, thank heaven. He watched them scramble down the bank near the pear trees, and then it was difficult to see them. If they hurried, they would manage it. His anxious eyes saw them again for a moment. They were moving quickly and silently. They had reached the end of the trees, and like him they had noticed the door at the end of the path. Like him, they shied from it, and worked their way along towards him by way of the shrubbery.

They found him examining the man's revolver. He gave a satisfied nod, and slipped it into his pocket.

"Complications," Thornley whispered quietly. "Two thugs in front; one overworked cook in the kitchen; and this." He pointed with his foot.

"Cook next on the list?" Richard whispered back. Van Cortlandt was testing the knots; he seemed satisfied.

Thornley nodded. "Thugs due back any minute. Quietly . . ." He motioned them to follow him, and led them to the point where he had watched the two men. Their feet made no noise in the moldering soil, and the green branches could bend without breaking. And then they heard the voices, and were motionless. Richard and van Cortlandt looked carefully through the branches as Thornley had done. Van Cortlandt pursed his lips in a silent whistle as he saw one of the men. That was the guy all right, the one who had questioned him last night when they got back from Pertisau. So Thornley might have found the right track after all. He looked at the Englishman thoughtfully. Bob was looking at the watch on his wrist. Pause; turn; walk back—he would soon have this timed to a nicety.

They suddenly stiffened, and looked at each other. They heard a voice, excited, hurried. The heavy measured tread of the Nazis' boots broke into a run. The voice was giving directions; they could hear the tone, but not the exact words. Van Cortlandt looked inquiringly at Richard, who shook his head. No, that wasn't von Aschenhausen. So there was still another on the list. They waited, their bodies tense, their minds alert. The commands had been given. There was a loud *"Zu Befehl!"* That at least they could hear, that and the sound of running feet, clashing on the stones of a courtyard. And then the noise of motor bicycles ripped the silence.

"Two, I think," murmured van Cortlandt. They edged to the front of the bushes, and saw the roadway which approached the entrance of the castle. The two motor bicycles had already passed through the large gates, and were sweeping down the broad road. There was something peculiarly ominous in their speed.

"I don't like it," said van Cortlandt. "It's only a hunch, but I think we should get going."

The failing light helped them. They moved silently, one by one, from the shrubbery over to the castle wall and, keeping close to its shadow, edged towards the kitchen door. They heard a sound of movement inside, as Thornley's nail-studded shoe slipped on a stone at the side of the path. They stretched themselves more closely against the roughness of the wall. Thornley slid the gun out of his pocket and held it by the barrel. The kitchen door opened, and a broad beam of light streamed down the path to the kitchen garden. They could see the edge of a white apron, as the cook halted on the threshold.

"I heard you. You can come in. Where did you find the parsley? In the red-currant bushes, I bet." He stepped out of the doorway, peering towards the darkness of the garden. "Hermann. God in Heaven, I've always to do everything myself." His thin, high voice rose. "Hermann!" He sprawled forward as the revolver butt thudded dully against his square head.

He was a heavy man. It took the three of them to lift him back into the kitchen. Thornley locked the door, and then stood guard at the only other entrance—a door which led into a passage—while van Cortlandt helped Richard to gag the man, and tie his hands and feet. Then they thrust him unceremoniously into his own storeroom, and locked its heavy door. Richard pocketed the key, and nodded; they moved silently into the passage.

Thornley whispered, "There was a room which seemed to be interesting."

Richard looked sharply at him. Had he heard something while he had waited? A cry? His speed increased.

The passage led to the main entrance hall, a large, square, imposing place, with a broad stairway curving up the paneled walls. Richard had stopped, and looked again at Thornley. Where was the room? Thornley pointed above their heads to the first floor.

They mounted the staircase slowly, carefully, because of the nails in Thornley's shoes. Richard was thankful for the second time in two days that his shoes were soled with rubber. At any moment, he expected the door above them to open, and a volley of shots to pin them against the staircase wall . . . But the door didn't open. Its double panels remained shut. It was only when they had reached them that they could hear the voices from within. A man's voice, and then another man's voice. Again the first voice. Richard looked at the two men beside him and nodded. This time the voice was von Aschenhausen's.

He was speaking in German, his voice as angry as the other man's had been. They were not arguing with each other. They were talking to a third person; talking savagely. Von Aschenhausen had raised his pitch. Richard closed his eyes: he could see the two scars ridging the cheek. The words reached them in waves.

". . . regret your stupidity . . . advantage of my humanity. In two hours my young barbarians, as you called them, will return. I shall turn you over . . . If that fails . . . Gestapo . . . murderess and dangerous spy." The voice was clearer now, as if the man's anger were becoming cold and cruelly calculating.

"Your remaining days will not be pleasant. We shall catch Myles just as surely as we caught you. And your stupidity will be quite in vain." The voice altered again. This time it was speaking in English, rapidly, persuasively.

"You know how I have always regarded you. Otherwise I should not have brought you here: you would have been at the official Gestapo headquarters as soon as I had found you. Instead I bring you here, but do not mistake my feelings. I *will* find out. If you accept my offer, you will only remember these days as a bad dream. Otherwise any unpleasantness which you have suffered will be nothing, nothing to what is to come, and I am not being melodramatic." There was a pause. Von Aschenhausen spoke again. "You fool, you stupid little fool. Don't you see I *must*, I *will* find out? My patience is limited. Kurt, try some more of your persuasion. This is really tedious. You have only one . . ."

They had heard enough . . . two men in there. Richard saw the others were watching him, waiting. Van Cortlandt's mouth had an ugly look. Thornley was fingering the revolver thoughtfully, his eyes narrowing. Richard nodded his head towards the door. Van Cortlandt put his hand gently on the handle. He was feeling it; it was unlocked. He shoved both panels violently open. He and Richard entered as one man, with Thornley just behind them.

The surprise was complete.

In the flickering candlelight of the room, they saw von Aschenhausen sitting on the edge of a large desk. His eyes were fixed on the other man standing over the girl roped to a chair, as he himself paused in the lighting of a cigarette. The match was still burning as Richard's full weight knocked him backwards, pinning him against the desk. As he tried to throw Richard off, the grip on his throat tightened. He struggled but the increased pressure warned him. He lay still, choking. It was his only chance.

Frances felt the hand of iron release her aching shoulder. She tried to get her face away from the glare of the powerful lamp in front of her as she heard the rush of feet, but the light still pierced her eyelids with a dull-red burning. She heard the flat sound of a hard fist meeting solid flesh. She heard someone cursing loudly and exultantly with each blow. She knew the voice. . . . Van Cortlandt. Henry. She struggled weakly against the rope which held her. And then there was Bob's voice, too. Beside her. She heard the lamp fall, and the glaring circle of light had gone. The ropes had suddenly stopped cutting into her breast and thigh. Her body was falling forward, but an arm caught it before it slipped off the chair. The arm held her there gently. Bob's voice was telling her to move slowly, to get the blood in circulation again. She was not to worry; everything was all right. Everything was all right. So Richard must be safe too. Richard must be safe.

In front of her she could hear the heavy breathing of the two men as they fought, the half groan, half gasp from the man Kurt as van Cortlandt landed his blows. She forced her eyes half-open. She could see Thornley's face as a white blur, gradually steadying, slowly shaping into lines she could recognize. He was watching the punishment which van Cortlandt was dealing with a look of admiration mixed with pleasure, watching the man as he staggered under the hard punches. The man was trying to gain a moment. A gun, thought Thornley, but before he could yell his warning the man had side-stepped a blow successfully and his hand reached into his hip pocket.

Van Cortlandt had seen the movement in time: his hand gripped the man's wrist and twisted. The bullet dug into the paneled wall, and then the revolver was wrung out of the man's hand. It fell at their feet. Thornley, watching the man's bleeding face, contorted with rage, slipped his free hand into his pocket; that type knew all the tricks, he thought grimly. It came as he expected. As van Cortlandt tried to knock the gun out of reach, the man kicked suddenly, viciously. Van Cortlandt doubled up with a groan, and the man's hand was over the gun. Thornley's revolver flashed first. There was no doubt about that bullet. The man lay as he had fallen.

Frances heard Thornley say something, but his voice was so low that the words eluded her. Then he was speaking to her, his voice once more calm and clear.

"Can you hold on now, Frances? I'll come back."

She nodded, and watched him as he helped van Cortlandt to sit up against the wall where he had fallen. She could see more clearly now; she could see van Cortlandt's face twisted with pain as he doubled over.

"Trusting fellow you are," Thornley said gently, and was glad to see the attempted smile on van Cortlandt's lips.

The American spoke, his words coming in spasms. "How's that son of a bitch over there?"

"Passed out a minute ago." It was Richard's voice. "Frances . . . all right?"

"Richard." She tried to rise from the chair.

"Easy now, Frances," said Thornley, and moved quickly back to her. She was glad of his firm grip. He had picked up the rope which had bound her and, coiling it loosely round his right hand, he threw it towards the desk.

"You'll need this," he said to Richard. "I'll be with you in a minute." He helped Frances back towards the chair. He looked over his shoulder at van Cortlandt. The American was all right. He had slowly and painfully stretched out his legs, and was leaning against the wall with his hands in his jacket pockets.

Richard looked at von Aschenhausen lying limply across the desk. He was unconscious, and his arms, with which he had tried to grip Richard, sprawled inert over the dark wood. One hand fell over the edge of the desk; the other pointed helplessly towards the glimmering candles in their heavy-silver base. Richard picked up the rope with one hand, still keeping a firm grip with the other on von Aschenhausen's throat, but one hand was not enough; he sensed his mistake even as he caught hold of the rope. The split-second warning was too short. Before he could use both hands again, von Aschenhausen had swept the branched candlestick in his face. As he stumbled back under the weight of the blow, rubbing the burning wax from his left eyelid and cheek, he saw von Aschenhausen's hand come up from the drawer with a gun, and he heard the shots.

Frances saw the long barrel point towards Thornley and herself. She was pushed violently aside even as the gun crashed twice. The echo of the shots stabbed her head. Or was it the echo? Von Aschenhausen stiffened and slid grotesquely from the desk. His revolver thudded dully on the thick carpet. Richard had risen from the floor beside the burning candles. Thornley was on his knees where he had dropped as he had thrust her aside. Van Cortlandt alone was smiling, and with a grim satisfaction, as he held his still smoking revolver pointed at the crumpled figure.

For a moment they looked at each other . . . All safe.

Frances heard van Cortlandt's voice saying "I'm a quick learner, Bob," and Thornley's not very successful laugh.

Richard had picked up the fallen gun, and was coming towards her, his hand to his face. She raised her arms, and then she felt the burning pain. The men saw the expression on her face change to one of amazement, like that of a child who has fallen and only realizes it is hurt when the blood begins to flow. So Frances looked as the searing pain showed her a neat groove in her left arm. Unbelievingly she watched the blood as it welled up and overflowed the wound in a slow-moving stream. And then she felt the real pain; with each heartbeat it seemed to throb farther down her arm and claw her shoulder.

Richard was beside her. She wondered if she looked as white as he did. He was looking at her arm, but he didn't speak.

It was Thornley who said, "On the inside, by God." Van Cortlandt rose slowly, and limped painfully over to them.

"*And* a Lüger," he added quietly. "How close was your arm to your body?"

Frances remembered how close. That must have been the hot wind on her left breast just before she had heard the crash of the gun.

"I'd like a . . ." she began, but the word *drink* evaded her. The men were going away from her, moving back towards the desk, down the lengthening room. It was like looking through the wrong end of binoculars, she thought, and felt the black darkness smooth round her with its velvet touch. Then it was light again, and the men were beside her, and Richard's flask was at her lips, forcing her to drink more than she could swallow.

Someone said, "She'll be all right. Better look at the arm."

Richard was kneeling beside her, fumbling for his handkerchief. Van

Cortlandt produced a very white one, and folded it methodically into a wad. Thornley went over to a table and came back with a decanter of whisky. She didn't need that, she thought; not now. The clammy sickness had gone, leaving her tired, tired. But she must tell them . . . she must tell them, now. If only she could remember things in the right order, the important things first. She gripped Richard's hands as Thornley poured whisky on the wound. She struggled to control her voice as she looked at van Cortlandt.

"They stopped your car at Jenbach, and found your friend in it. They brought him back to Innsbruck. They phoned about it, and . . . that man—" she looked at Kurt's body—"was told to go down and order the two troopers into Innsbruck. They were to trace your movements . . ."

Van Cortlandt nodded thoughtfully. "Yes, they knew me well by this time. That means the car we've got is dangerous." He dug his hands into his pockets, and walked slowly across the room to the desk.

"We'll have to find another car, that's all, or travel by train, or if the worst comes to the worst we'll have to climb over the pass together." He stopped suddenly, and ran a hand through his hair.

"Say, Richard, what's the thing these boys use when they want to sneak into a country without having their baggage examined?" He prodded von Aschenhausen's body with his foot contemptuously. Frances tried to remember desperately: there had been something which fitted into all this. Richard was saying that there wasn't much chance for them that way, but van Cortlandt could take a look in the desk and see what was there. Henry was already searching von Aschenhausen's pockets. He had found some keys.

"Do you smell burning, any of you?" van Cortlandt asked as he tried the drawers in the desk. One was locked; it needed two different keys to open it. Inside the drawer lay a folder containing papers, a neatly bound notebook, a seal and a rubber stamp.

Thornley, holding Frances' arm while Richard bandaged it, looked up and said, "Probably the candles on the rug." Van Cortlandt was too engrossed as he examined the documents in the folder. He whistled to himself, and then looked towards Thornley.

"As a newspaperman, I find this all very interesting." He waved a sheet of paper in the air. He was almost excited. He looked at the rug. "Yes," he replied to Thornley, "and a nice little fire is just about to start in the wastebasket. Just like the Reichstag. . . . Such ideas these boys put into your head . . ."

Frances heard the amusement in his voice, and opened her eyes. It was true. The wastepaper basket was smoldering, and even as she looked she saw the first sign of flame. It was fantastic. There was Henry, reading the papers he had found in the desk as calmly as if he had just made a remark about the weather. Then, on the desk, she saw the crumpled envelope, still lying where von Aschenhausen had thrown it contemptuously. Money wouldn't help them, he had said.

Richard was looking at her intently.

"The money," she said, "is on the desk. That's it. They—searched me," she finished lamely. Richard said nothing, but his mouth tightened. Frances thought again of the moment when the money had been discovered. Money wouldn't help them. Oh, if only she could think straight. Money wouldn't help them. What was it he had said then? He had twisted the envelope and thrown it on the desk.

"He said," she began slowly, her eyes closed—he had said so much, but there *was* something which could help van Cortlandt—"he said money wouldn't help, that it was no use trying to hide where you had gone." Her eyes opened, and the words were now faster as she remembered. "Even if you had got over the frontier, any frontier, you would be followed at once and brought back. It wasn't the first time that escapers had been caught in Italy or Switzerland. He had all the powers, and you had none. He held up some papers with one hand and hit them with his other hand, the back of his other hand, and all the time he was looking at me." Her voice altered again. "These were some of his reasons to persuade me to be reasonable. He said that Kronsteiner had been caught, that Henry and Bob had admitted everything in order to save themselves, that our movements had been traced completely."

Thornley wondered what other kinds of persuasion had been used, as he noticed Frances' wrists, the torn blouse showing the ugly marks on her shoulder, her right cheek which was swollen and red, the angry stripes already turning purple on her legs, her eyes. Again he thought of Tony's letter, of Maria. At least Frances was alive and her body would heal, at least they had saved her from becoming a second Maria. Tony's words ate into his heart like vitriol into flesh. He moved to the door. Better begin to leave, he thought.

"I'll scout round, and find the garage," he suggested. "Don't wait too long in here: there's the makings of a good going blaze."

Van Cortlandt looked up as the door closed. "Frances, did you see where he put those papers he was waving at your face?"

"He was at the desk. They must be there." Unless, she thought, they were a lie, like the other things he had said. He had mixed lie with truth so cunningly. She watched van Cortlandt search once more, and then relaxed as he suddenly smiled.

"Well, this might be twisted to suit us," he said. Frances had never heard his voice so optimistic . . . And then the telephone rang.

The three of them looked at it as if it were a cobra.

"I might have known," van Cortlandt said, and the optimistic voice was gone.

Richard left Frances, and walked quickly over to the phone. He lifted the receiver. Frances and van Cortlandt, motionless, scarcely breathing, watched him tensely. But the German which he spoke was that of von Aschenhausen. Van Cortlandt caught Frances' eye, and nodded slowly, approvingly, before he went on with his careful writing. The wastepaper basket was flaming nicely; the thick wool carpet smoldered where the fallen candles had burned three round black holes.

Again Frances had the same awareness of unreality which would sometimes grip her for a timeless moment in the middle of a dream, which would drag her back to waking and the hotness of a crumpled pillow. But this was no dream. The high, paneled room was now filled with a stronger light from the leaping flames in the basket beside the desk. The smoldering rug and the guttering candles, the two bodies lying so quietly on the floor, the rich draperies and carefully arranged flowers, were all as real as the burns on her wrists and the blood which had flowed down her arm like a stream of warm red lava. She looked at the American, working at the other end of the desk; at Richard as he spoke in that excellent, rather hard German. So far, he had said little: he was listening to some story.

And then he cut short the long explanation impatiently. He was giving his own instructions. The American was quite useless. The girl had talked, and he knew nothing at all. He was to be released after he had given them a description of his own car. They would be able to trace that to St. Anton, where the other American van Cortlandt and the Englishman Thornley had gone. That was the meeting place; Myles would reach it tomorrow. They then intended to cross into Switzerland. That frontier was to be carefully watched.

The man at the other end of the wire spoke again. Richard listened impatiently. The flames from the wicker basket lit up his face as he concentrated on the man's words.

"Yes," he said, "I'll allow them to stay longer. I shall remain here with Kurt until the investigation is completed. I shall arrive in St. Anton tomorrow morning. Get all three of them, alive if possible. I rely on you."

Richard replaced the receiver thoughtfully.

"That takes care of your friend, Henry," he said, "and gives us a breathing space. The apprentices have had a successful parade, and are now eating heartily before they attend a meeting. I very generously allowed them to stay for that. They will return here by ten o'clock. It's getting rather warm in here, don't you think?"

Van Cortlandt rose, and handed him the sheet of paper on which he had just finished applying von Aschenhausen's seal.

"Not warm enough, yet, but it should be satisfactory by ten o'clock —with a little help."

He moved to the other end of the desk, and kicked the flaming basket over the smoldering carpet. The desk itself was beginning to glow just where the basket had stood, and a small streak of flame rushed up its side as he heaped the papers from the drawer beside it.

Richard folded the document and put it carefully into his breast pocket. "Good piece of work, Henry," he said. The American, placing the other branched candlesticks under the long curtains as he opened the windows, only smiled. It had been easy enough: all he had had to do was to alter a very little to suit their purpose. That was the advantage of dealing with a very systematic and thorough enemy. They made the arrangements and you borrowed them. It had been almost as easy as this. He threw the last candle lightly onto the couch with its pile of cushions.

"Keep moving, fellas," he said, and picked up the two caps and the jackets from a chair.

They left the doors wide open. Richard, his arm round Frances, turned for one last look. The current of air between the windows and the wide door was serving its purpose.

"Regular Viking's funeral," van Cortlandt said. "Too damn good for them."

They walked in silence down the cool staircase. Behind them they heard the indrawn breath of the flames.

CHAPTER **23**   THE BRENNER PASS

Thornley was waiting for them in the darkness beside a large official-looking car.

"There was another in the garage, and some motor bikes. I've taken care of them," he reported.

Richard was putting Frances into the car.

"Darling, we've got to get the other car and the stuff inside it. I'll see you soon." He turned to Thornley. "We'll meet you five miles south of this road. Wait for us there." Thornley nodded, and handed him something. It was the electric torch.

Van Cortlandt threw the caps and jackets into the car. "Better wear those. We'll only keep you about twenty minutes."

The large car moved off, and the two men started towards the gardens. As they passed the kitchen door, they suddenly remembered the cook. Richard cursed and tried to enter the kitchen. But they had locked the door from the inside, and it was too heavy to break open. Richard swore again.

"If you must; but we're God-damned fools," van Cortlandt said, and raced back towards the front entrance of the castle. "God-damned fools," he repeated when he opened the door into the kitchen. Together they carried the unconscious man into the shrubbery.

"Not too near the other blighter," the American said. "Hell and damnation, that's at least five minutes gone."

They broke into a run across the garden and fields. The woods were dark and silent; it was too early for any moonlight. Richard shaded the torch with his hand, as they searched for the path, scrambling along the edge of the trees.

Van Cortlandt said, "Just about here, I think. There was a mound. Rock."

Richard nodded. He tried to measure the distance to the long dark shape which must be the red-currant bushes. . . . And then the torch showed them the outcrop of stone. The path should be here.

They looked at each other with undisguised relief when they found it. The white slashes on the branches were picked out by the light which Richard held. Their feet stumbled and slipped in the darkness of the ground, but they pressed on hurriedly. They had passed over the crest of the small hill, and they were running and sliding down towards the road, following the trail which Thornley had blazed. They reached the cart track, and the bushes. The car was still there.

"Ten minutes late, already," van Cortlandt said, but his voice was good-humored again. He gave a laugh. "And there I was, having a fine joke all to myself about Thornley being the good boy scout."

Richard found himself relaxing calmly as the car jerked dangerously over the rough track and then gathered speed on the smoothness of the Brenner road. What would have seemed suicidal only forty-eight hours ago now only appeared all in the day's work. Van Cortlandt's driving had results; it was only a matter of minutes before they sighted the large dark car tactfully drawn up at the side of the road.

The first stars were beginning to appear over the Brenner. The man lounging at the doorway of the customhouse was watching the other side of the white barrier with interest. He wondered what it was this time. All day, the Germans had been giving themselves double work. They had stopped the cars coming out of Germany as well as those going in. It was a nuisance, waiting here with your eyes on the headlights, not knowing how long they would be before they came up to you. Sometimes it would be only a matter of minutes. Sometimes, a car would be held up for half an hour. Again he wondered what it could be. These Germans never told you much unless it was unimportant. He shifted his weight onto his other leg, and glanced back into the brightly lighted office. The man at the desk looked up.

"Anything happening, Corradi?"

"Two still held over there."

The tall thin Italian at his desk gave a sardonic smile and went back to his writing. The other heaved a loud sigh, and walked slowly towards the barrier. The tension, on a day like this, always unsettled him. He heard the voices of the others as they came out of the café down the street. About time too, he thought moodily. He could do with some coffee himself.

At the doorway of the café, the two officials halted. They stood looking out into the empty village street with its meager lights. Only the doorway of the customhouse was bright. The younger man shivered, and looked bitterly at the scattered houses, the long wind-swept station, the towering dark shapes on either side of them.

"Godforsaken place," he said.

"Wait until you have been here for a winter," advised the other. "You can't grumble at overwork today, at least. Not with our good friends over the way doing all our work for us."

He looked at the younger man's smart uniform, and buttoned his own crumpled jacket. It was just like the young, he thought. They never knew when they were lucky. A few more pretty girls to admire the way he wore his cap, and his young friend would have no doubt found the place tolerable.

"We could have had another coffee," he suggested, but the young man had already stepped into the street and was waiting impatiently for him.

"When you've been here as long as I have," the older man grumbled, "you will know it is hardly worth our while, on a day like this. Our German cousins don't leave much to be confiscated."

The other tilted his hat contemptuously. Here as long as this fat fool, he thought in amusement, who would now be in a comfortable office in a decent town if he had had any brains at all. Even the way he would speak of the Germans, with that sly note in his voice which he thought was funny, showed he had no brains . . . But curiosity overcame the young man's contempt.

"Is this usual?" he asked, as they reached the customhouse.

"Whenever someone who shouldn't be leaving the beloved Fatherland is being ungrateful enough to try to leave."

"They are fools to try to pass this way."

"There is only this way, or the mountains, or the railway. The border patrols have been increased, and there is pandemonium on the trains. Have you seen *them* on the trains, today?"

"It is efficient organization," the young man said sharply. The fat fool had no brains, but he was crafty enough. He always chose his words so carefully that you couldn't even report him. The tall thin Italian, who had come out from the office, exchanged amused looks with the older man and ignored the remark. They were both getting a bit tired of the new broom.

They saw the headlights of the two small cars begin to move at last. Behind them a large car advanced authoritatively in the middle of the road. Corradi seemed excited about something.

"They didn't stop this one. Salutes for this one," he called across to them. "Better not keep this one waiting. They never like it."

The tall thin man nodded, and turned to the young one.

"You deal with it, and see some of the efficient organizers of efficient organization. Probably diplomatic pass. You know."

The young man nodded as casually as he could, and moved over to the large car. He didn't feel as casual inside. Corradi had been right. The Germans didn't like being kept waiting. An officer's sleeve waved a paper peremptorily to him. He heard a request for urgency, which was a command.

The Italian took the document. His German was not so adequate as he pretended, but he knew his salute had been just right. He looked as efficient as possible as he glanced quickly at the paper. The signature on it made him hold his breath. . . . Four people in the car. That was right. He felt the cold impassive stare of the German. Further curiosity would be an impertinence. He folded the paper with a businesslike gesture. Speed and courtesy: that would show them efficiency could be found here, too. He held his salute as the officer acknowledged it, and the large black car swept past the raised barrier.

He turned back to the others. Corradi, he noticed, had saluted too. But the other fools were too busy examining and stamping passports, were even wasting good breath making polite replies to three middle-aged Englishmen.

When the two insignificant cars crawled slowly away through the village street, the others joined him.

"Well, who was it? The Archduke von Ribbentrop himself?"

He ignored their smiles. He made his voice as casual as possible.

"Freiherr von Aschenhausen, and three others, authorized by . . ."

But the others had lost interest and gone back to the office.

The young man stood outside, and looked at the stars. He forgot the cold wind. There was a warm, comfortable feeling inside him.

CHAPTER **24** END OF A JOURNEY

The swift journey down the Brenner road was a nightmare to Frances. She was conscious of a stiffening arm, of the burns on her wrist nipped by the cool air. She was so tired that the muscles of her body refused to relax. Thornley, unexpectedly gentle, tried to protect her from the twists and turns of the mountain road. In front of them were Richard and van Cortlandt, both of them silent and grim under the peaked hats. Van Cortlandt's eyes never left the road. Richard had a map spread over his knees. Although the Brenner was safely passed, there was no relaxing of the strain. Thornley persuaded her to eat something. He was so obviously worried about her that to please him she tried. She was surprised to find that the sick feeling was no worse, that the coldness which had first gripped her as they waited for Richard and van Cortlandt on the Innsbruck-Brenner road began to disappear.

That had been the worst moment for her, she decided. Worse even than the frontier and the silly boy with the exaggerated cap and salute. She remembered again when she had waited tensely with Thornley at the side of the road, when she had begun to think that Richard and Henry had been caught. She remembered the sense of haste which had almost choked her as the suitcases were lifted into the Mercedes and they had waited again while Thornley had set the American car crashing down into a ravine. Each minute, each passing car, were full of danger. Already, behind them, there had been a tell-tale glow of fire. Bob had said simply, "Garage, too, by this time, I'd think." After that they had driven in silence towards the frontier, and she had felt sick and cold. When the Brenner was passed (if it were passed) she had told herself she could sleep. That would heal the throbbing of her eyes. But the Brenner lay behind them, and the sleep which she had resisted refused to return.

It was not until they had driven through Bolzano and all the villages in between that she felt the tension lessen. Bob even made some mild jokes about all these places called Believe Obey Fight, like the English stations called Ladies and Gentlemen. He got her to sip some more brandy, as she ate the dry biscuits. They tasted wonderfully. The others were eating, too. She watched them drowsily; she was warm at last, and her body relaxed. *Ladies and gentlemen, ladies and gentlemen lend me your ears I come to Dreikirchen with rings on her fingers and bells where who, where who, where . . .*

At first she thought it was von Aschenhausen holding her shoulder, bending over her, but the grip did not tighten and hurt. It was Richard. Richard trying to smile and making a failure of it.

"Fran," he said, and kissed her.

The car had stopped in the shadow of trees. The trees were a different shape, the night air seemed milder, the ink-blue sky was more beautiful. And Richard's arms were round her. She suddenly remembered Bob and Henry.

"Where are they?"

"Freshening up. There's a stream over there. We'll go when they've finished. We can change, too: Henry has brought our things along with him in his case."

Frances looked at the trees again, dark islands in a sea of moonlight.

"We are farther south," she said.

"Almost at Verona, darling. It's one o'clock and all's well."

"All's well," answered an American voice. "Well Frances, how's everything?"

She gave him her right hand.

"That's the ticket," he said. "I'll get your clothes, and Bob will guide you to the stream. Here's your towel." He handed her one of his white shirts. "And your purse." He handed Richard her bag.

They reached the stream, and they bathed their faces in the cool water. The bullet graze had bled a lot; it looked unsafe to disturb the bandage, so Richard hacked a piece off the shirt and bandaged on top of the blood-stained handkerchiefs. The clothes for her consisted of a nondescript belted gray coat, a gray beret, a shapeless dress and shoes and stockings. Richard had an *ersatz* tweed suit, a rough green-felt hat, and a tie of indescribable hideousness. Frances dressed her hair and disguised the bruises on her cheek as well as she could with her one hand. It would be almost impossible to get the dress on without starting more bleeding. Richard helped her into the coat, and even that was difficult enough. The shoes were too big, but fortunately they had straps. Richard and Frances looked at each other, and she actually smiled; and then they went back to the car, carrying the discarded clothes and the rejected dress.

"Go on, laugh," said Richard good-humoredly.

Thornley and van Cortlandt grinned.

"It's not bad, you know," Bob said tactfully. "I've seen hundreds like you traveling in Germany. Have a cigarette? How long is it since we could risk one?"

"One thing I must say for these blasted Nazis," said Henry, and paused to enjoy his effect. "They make you damned well appreciate the simple pleasures of a peaceful life."

Thornley drove them, this time. In the swaying car, they made their last plans They were brief. They were to travel on their German passports, complete with Italian entry stamps (Schulz had earned his money), towards Grenoble. If the station would accept their marks, they could catch an early morning train. If not, they would have to wait until the banks opened. Van Cortlandt and Thornley, cutting back on their tracks, would drive through Lombardy until daylight made the car too dangerous. They would then get rid of it, and make for the Swiss border, if they hadn't reached it by that time. Van Cortlandt was confident that they would. They divided the marks they had, and van Cortlandt emptied the smaller of his suitcases to carry the dress and two extra shirts and socks for Richard. They could think of no other main points; the details would depend on quick wits and luck. They would meet in Paris. Van Cortlandt gave them the address of a hotel he knew.

"It's run by an American, who stayed over from the last war. You'll feel safe enough there. Just lie low until we get there. And then we'll celebrate. Better catch up on your sleep before we arrive."

His confidence and high spirits were infectious. Frances found herself laughing. And then the tears were running down her cheeks; even the pain they caused in her eyes couldn't check them.

"Well," said van Cortlandt, "well, now."

Thornley switched on the wireless tactfully. The overture of "Aida," badly recorded, swelled scratchingly into the car. Thornley tuned it down.

"Goes well with the writing on the wall," he suggested, and nodded towards the house they were passing. The lights from the car pointed the lettering on its wall. "WHO TOUCHES THE DUCE TOUCHES DEATH. Dear me!"

"One up on the Victorians," said Richard. "They only hung banalities round the house. Now we get totalitarian mottoes in two-feet-high letters all over the gable ends."

Van Cortlandt, keeping his eyes away from Frances, tried to think of something to add to that, but he could only think of the silent way in which she wept. He peered out into the darkness.

"Houses are getting closer now," he said at last. "Better waste no time."

Frances had regained her control. She made a pretense of powdering her face.

"I'm ready," she said, "any time. We'll see you in Paris." She managed a smile. "I'm sorry. It was all my fault. I've ruined all your plans."

The American shook his head. "My plans were going to be ruined anyway, although I kept persuading myself that they wouldn't be. We all have our wishful thinking, but it's just as well to come out of it."

Thornley switched off the motor carefully, and turned to face Frances.

"I have no plans either, Frances. Don't worry about that. I had a letter from Tony this morning."

"Tony?"

"Yes. He's on his way home to enlist."

"And the girl in Czechoslovakia?" Frances could have bitten her tongue. Thornley examined the back of his hand.

"Suicide," he said, too coldly.

Frances saw the three men exchange glances. So they knew. Bob must have told them as she had slept. It must have been something which they thought would have sickened her, unnerved her. As if the man Kurt, when he had tried to break her silence, had not described in detail her possible future. As if she couldn't guess. . . . But knowing evil could be worse than guessing. When you guessed, you could always hope that evil things might not be so bad as your worst fears. But when you knew, then there was no hope left. Then you knew this and this, and the evil of it drove away all hope.

She said nothing, only remembering the look on Thornley's face when he had looked down at the man Kurt. He had spoken as if to himself, and the words had made no sense then. Now they took shape. One for Maria . . . the first one for Maria. Frances leaned forward and touched Thornley's shoulder with her right hand, and then van Cortlandt's.

Richard helped her to step out of the car. The savageness of his voice did not startle them.

"Yes. I'm all for international understanding: *real* understanding." He looked at the other two men, and voiced their thoughts. "This isn't the end for any of us. It's just the beginning."

They were all silent for some moments, and then Thornley switched on the engine, and the car moved into the night.

Richard picked up the suitcase, and gripped Frances' right arm. They walked softly through dark streets, guided by scattered lights. At last, they saw the station. Frances pressed his hand to her breast, and held it there.

Horizon

1945

We are but warriors for the working-day;
Our gayness and our gilt are all besmirch'd
With rainy marching in the painful field;
There's not a piece of feather in our host . . .
And time hath worn us into slovenry:
But, by the mass, our hearts are in the trim.
                              —*King Henry* V

CHAPTER 1

When you rested on one elbow the third strand of wire cut across the mountaintops. When you sat up and stared at the gray faces of the precipices, irregular and massive against the high blue sky, it was the top strand of wire which now spoiled their line. However you looked you were always forced to remember you were caught, caged like an animal. The only way to see the mountains and enjoy them was to walk right up to the ten-foot wall of barbed wire and look between two of its strands. Even then, although you weren't actually looking at the barbs, you could feel them, twisted and jagged, trying to draw your eyes away from the mountain peaks. And then a sentry would yell some fine Italian curses at you, and if you didn't move quickly enough out of the twenty-foot zone behind the wire a bullet would whistle towards you. It depended on the Italian's temper whether it whistled high above or unpleasantly near your shoulder.

Peter Lennox's set face—grim, hard, expressionless—turned away from the view of mountains. He felt his tense body might give his thoughts away; he leaned back on his elbow again. His fingers touched a solitary tuft of grass-blades, pitifully small and yet growing in spite of the heavy boots which paced over this ground. You have a view, Lennox was thinking, but you cannot enjoy it. You've fresh air, coming down from the freedom of the mountains, but all you can smell is the tannery which lies between them and you. The smell seemed always ripest at this late afternoon hour, just at the time when the prisoners were exercised. Perhaps that was why this period was chosen for their daily forty minutes of fresh air. (As a prisoner you had come to believe that anyway, whether it were true or not: it just fitted in naturally with all the pettiness of malicious restrictions and unnecessary domination which had become the background to your life.) Lennox began counting the short blades of grass. . . . Nine. One more than yesterday. He began remembering how it felt to walk over a whole stretch of soft, fine grass. Hundreds and hundreds of blades—thousands, millions, of blades of grass. And here he could touch nine. He began admiring their defiance and their determination. And somehow his confidence—which had seemed to desert him this morning—began to return.

He turned his head carefully to look at the walls of the prison behind him. You could tell from their appearance that they were thick and clammy, enclosing small dank rooms behind the boarded-up windows. Once the place had been called a castle—it was set proudly enough on the mountainside above the valley. Then it had become a nunnery, with its upper rooms walled into small cells. Later still it had become a hospital for the poor and the despairing. It had been a natural choice for housing prisoners of war, where men who had tried unsuccessful escapes from other camps could be taught that hope was abandoned by all those who entered here.

Dispassionately Lennox studied the walls; the scabby plaster, once white and now weathered into green and brown streaks; the eternally shuttered windows. Only the windows in the left wing of the castle were not boarded up. That was where the Italian commandant and his staff had their quarters. They, too, suffered from the perpetually sweating walls. But at least they had heating when they needed it, and furniture and rugs and other aids to comfort. Lennox smiled grimly as he wondered where the commandant's friends were this afternoon. The windows were empty: no one there to stare down at the men below as at some monstrous wild animals in a zoo. The adjutant's windows were empty too. No girls laughing up there today. No gramophone records being played. Even the guardroom windows were silent, staring blindly at the mountains rising on the other side of the valley.

Lennox shifted his weight to his other elbow. Something's wrong, he thought; something's wrong with the Italians. It seemed as if the other prisoners felt that too, for they were enjoying their forty minutes of fresh air with a good deal more zest and noise than usual. The stretch of grass outside the barbed wire was empty of the customary spectators. Generally some civilians from the town would choose this time of day for their late afternoon stroll past the camp. There, on the wide slope of grass at the prescribed (and safe) distance from the barbed wire, some would stand, some would stare, and some would laugh. "Eighth Army!" was the usual gibe, spat out with a good deal of venom as an arm was raised to point— in the silly way in which a mocking child points—at the ragged men crowded into the meager exercise ground.

But today there was no one there, no one except scattered sentries. And the prisoners—at least, those who were fit enough—were enjoying themselves. Some thirty of them had gathered round the goal post—the solitary tree which never blossomed, but in some strange way still stood erect in a patch of bald earth—and were playing a game of mock football. There wasn't enough room for a proper game: the men had to content themselves with taking odd shots at the goal. The ball was a wad of old newspapers tied into shape with knotted string. (Last week the leather ball which the Red Cross provided had been confiscated, after it had "accidentally" smashed the adjutant's bedroom window, scattering his squealing guests with the broken pane.) The men had slipped off their tunics and were playing either in shirt sleeves or vests. The deep bite of the North African sun was still on their skin. Their months of captivity, of work in the near-by tannery, of fresh air and exercise measured by minutes in the late afternoon, had only bleached the varieties of brick-red and walnut-brown into a sickly tan. Lennox looked down at his hand, with its bones and sinews now so prominent. A most sickly and unbecoming tan, he decided. His wound didn't improve the general appearance: it had healed in an angry white gash across the back of his hand. He began flexing his muscles, slowly and carefully. The wound had healed, but every month the hand seemed tighter. It might be merely worry or imagination which tightened it. Once he got out of here the hand would probably be strong once more.

About a hundred other men, less energetic than the players, lounged on the hard patch of earth. They were content to be spectators, content to catch the last rays of autumn sunshine before they were herded behind the thick walls for the long night. Besides, dysentery doesn't encourage a man to chase after a football, or to plod round and round a meager rectangle of restricted space as a few of the more determinedly hearty were now doing.

From the scrambling group of players there was a shout, "To me, lad, to me!" That was the sergeant major, square-set, broad-voiced, and as Yorkshire as his vowels. He was waiting impatiently for a pass from Miller, the New Zealander. And Miller, swerving aside from two of the walkers who doggedly kept their even pace in spite of footballers and bodies strewn over the ground, obliged. The sergeant major swung into position, and missed the goal by a foot. There was a laugh, and a mock cheer.

Miller had dropped out of the game. He was limping slightly, as if his wound was troubling him again. He picked up his shapeless jersey, wiped his brow with it, and pulled it over his cropped fair hair. He was walking slowly, at a tangent, stopping here and there to speak a word or reply to a question. Gradually he drew near the waiting Lennox. The sentries guarding the double wall of barbed wire would have thought there was only chance in the meeting of the two men. Lennox's tight mouth relaxed as he glanced over his shoulder once more and saw that the commandant's and adjutant's windows were still quite lifeless. He felt in his pocket for a cigarette, and expertly halved it.

"Thanks," Miller said. "I've a match." He bent down to light Lennox's half. "Mountain gazing as usual, I see."

Lennox half smiled as he pulled steadily at the mutilated cigarette. His gray eyes flickered over the New Zealander's face and then returned to the wire. The sentries were still bored. The bell, which would end this reprieve in the open air, would not ring for another six minutes. It looked as if Miller and he could talk before they were shut away into their separate sections of the prison. Miller was pretending to watch the game of football. They were two men drawn together by a cigarette and a match, with no other interest at the moment except the game and a row of mountains. They seemed to be as bored as their guards.

The New Zealander was speaking, quietly, lips scarcely moving, head unturned. "Johann has come through."

Lennox's lips tightened on his quickly burning cigarette. "No," he said at last.

"Yes. Told you he was all right."

"The buttons?"

"Complete set. German infantry, as you wanted."

When Lennox didn't answer, Miller said quickly, "Johann's all right. I've told you. He's Austrian. Tyrolese. Hates the Eyties. Hates the Germans, who abandoned him and his people to Mussolini."

"You are taking a steep chance," Lennox said. Seven months of planning, of alarms and subterfuge. Seven months of tedious preparation, of gathering a disguise together. Seven months of giving up most of his precious food packages to pay the more bribable guards, so that he could secure a piece of string or sewing thread or a small tube of glue. Seven months of worry and strain, of perpetual threat of discovery, of working out a map, of learning more German and enough Italian. And now the buttons, which would give the finishing touch to his old army coat, bleached and dyed so secretly and painstakingly, had materialized. They came too easily. After so much trouble and worry they came much too easily. He stared at the wire, and it seemed to tighten round his throat.

Miller was still talking about Johann. "I told him nothing about you. He thinks the buttons are for me. So if he's been planted here to trap us he will give the wrong information." He allowed himself to glance at Lennox for a moment. This will be his third attempt, he remembered: the first from this camp, but the third altogether. The other two had failed because of sheer bad luck. Miller himself had only tried once, but it hadn't been planned in the careful way Lennox worked out his escapes. When a man planned like Lennox it was unfair that he shouldn't succeed. He remembered now that in each case Lennox had been caught (once in sight of Jugoslavia, once in Southern Italy) by trusting to the good faith of smiling civilians. No wonder that the mention of Johann, the seventeen-year-old Tyrolese in the prison's post office, had stiffened Lennox like that. He scarcely trusted his own shadow now. And you couldn't blame him: not after two disappointments.

"I passed the buttons to Jock Stewart when he was scrubbing the post office floor today," Miller went on quietly. "He is hiding them in your mattress now."

Lennox stirred. That at least was a good plan. Stewart, the intransigent Scotsman, had been detailed to a week's fatigue duty for some minor infraction of the rules. This meant a good deal of scrubbing and cleaning and slop-carrying. It also meant no exercise in the yard, for the adjutant had so arranged the fatigue party's routine that they were emptying the slop pails from the rooms of the other prisoners at this moment. So Stewart, although he lived in a different part of the prison, would now be in Lennox's room. That was a good plan. In the event of an escape the men who were examined most carefully were always those occupying the same quarters as the man who had escaped. Suspicion fell naturally on them.

"Thanks," Lennox said. "Thank you, Dusty." He stared at a small white cloud, already tinged red round its soft edges. The sun would soon go down. The bell would ring any minute now. "What did it cost you to get them?"

"Nothing," Miller answered. "Johann doesn't take bribes."

Lennox's eyebrows went up. "A jailer who doesn't take bribes?" he asked mockingly.

Miller's good-natured face was frowning. "He's all right, I tell you," he said shortly. After all, he thought, I've been working in the post office for months now. I've seen Johann every day. I ought to know what he's like. "If it hadn't been for him and his information we'd never have known about the capture of Sicily or any of the recent news," he said. Then his frown cleared as he saw Lennox's eyes. Men got that way just before an attempt to escape: after they had perfected the main plan they would worry about the details unnecessarily. Miller pulled his sweater more closely round his neck. The first evening breeze from the mountains was shrewd. "Going to be damned cold here this winter," he said, looking down at his thin shorts. Like most of the men, he was still wearing the lightweight clothes in which he had fought in Africa. Warmer clothing had been promised, but then the commandant always promised. And now it was the beginning of September, and the cold autumn rains would soon lash the unheated prison. "If we are still here," he added, and half smiled as he glanced at Lennox's face for a moment. "Something's blowing up, judging from the calm all round us today. Reminds me of the Sunday when Musso resigned. Something's blowing up."

Lennox didn't seem to think the idea so very funny. "Yes," he said grimly. "Maybe peace will be signed and you'll all ride out of here while I'm still squirming through ditches."

"Oh, we'll stop and give you a lift in our borrowed Bugatti," Miller said generously. He was grinning openly now as he watched the game of football. He laughed more than necessary when the sergeant major missed another shot at goal. Then, suddenly, he was serious again.

"Don't worry, Pete. You'll make it. Good luck to you," he said as he rose. "This will be the last time I'll get a word with you, I suppose."

Peter Lennox said "Yes." It was the habit of those who were about to make an escape to avoid in the last few days the friends who had helped them. It averted suspicions and shortened the punishments for the men left behind. "Thanks, Dusty."

For a moment the two friends looked at each other. Then the New Zealander moved away as slowly, as desultorily as he had come. He was talking to Ferry, the South African, now: they were still chatting when the bell began its mournful peal. The sentries, usually nagging the men to march quickly inside, were less urgent today. Lennox picked himself up slowly and joined the tail end of the straggling crowd. He had his last look at the Dolomite ranges. Well, he thought, it wouldn't be long before he might look at them as a free man. With luck and care, it wouldn't be long.

Then he noticed that the two sentries outside the wire were no longer bored. They were staring at the road, some hundred yards across the grass from the outer wire. Lennox and the men beside him stared too. Three large army trucks were coming swiftly towards the camp from the direction of the town. And they were not Italian. They were German.

"Perhaps some boxes," a man beside Lennox suggested hopefully. "About time some more packages were arriving."

"The Germans don't act as the Italians' postmen," another said acidly. He muttered something under his breath about bloody optimists.

But speculation was silenced as Falcone, the least likeable of all the prison guards, appeared at the wide arch of doorway. He was a small, thin-faced man with a thick skin, which the Abyssinian campaign had stained into a permanent walnut color. Camp gossip said he suffered from flat feet, an unfaithful wife, stomach ulcers, and strong Fascist convictions. Today he seemed to be feeling the effect of all four ailments simultaneously. There was more than the usual violence in his voice. His mounting rage contrasted strangely with the lassitude of the five other guards.

The prisoners had to content themselves with an exchange of side glances, as they marched in obedience to Falcone's shouts through the stone cavern of a hall into the room where thin meals were doled out. Yet this was not the time for food. Usually at this hour of the afternoon those whose names had appeared on the day's letter list would be taken to the post office in the Administrative side of the building; those who were less fortunate would be marched to their rooms and locked into bare boredom to await their shift for the mess hall. And now they had been gathered together, jammed up against the long tables and fixed benches in a room which had never been built to contain so many at once. This break with routine stirred the men for a moment, but the sudden undercurrent of excitement ebbed away as the solid door, which separated this room from the hall, was closed decisively. There was coughing, shuffling of feet as men tried to keep their balance in the crowd. There was Falcone's vigilant eyes and sharp tongue calling "Attention!"

From the courtyard at the back of the castle came the sound of grinding brakes. The trucks had arrived. But speculation was already dying. The boarded windows blotted out sight of a sky stretching to freedom. Under the naked bulbs, with their wavering electric light, the prisoners' faces were still more haggard. The animation of the exercise yard had gone, and with it the moment's forgetfulness. Here they remembered again.

CHAPTER 2

The men waited, outwardly patient (so much they had learned during their captivity) even if their thoughts were unprintable, and chalked up another petty annoyance on the Italian score. There weren't any cases of open brutality at this camp. Not since the Swiss representative had two of the worst bullies removed from the guardroom. The rest of the jailers weren't so bad, considering how bad the deposed two had been; for the most part they were inoffensive creatures, with weak hearts and stout stomachs, determined to keep their jobs so pleasantly far from the battle-field, and not averse to stretching their own rations with a pilfered package or two. The prisoners had been quick to learn: a package, with a tin of meat or a slab of chocolate neatly filched out while it was being examined for contraband, meant a bribable jailer. Not that judicious bribing meant real kindness. But it did mean a cigarette from the town, or some little item which the camp commissary didn't have on sale, even if the price charged by the obliging jailer secured him a 600 per cent profit.

The minutes passed. The men were still held to attention. Then the uneasy silence was broken suddenly, and the men's thoughts switched from their own grievances over to the dulled sound of heavy boots shuffling through the hall outside. Peter Lennox's eyes left Falcone's savage little face and turned towards the door. Its solid thickness depressed him still more. What's going on? he wondered again. Whatever it was, he didn't like it. Any new developments in this camp meant complications in his escape. It was too near, he thought, it was too near. . . . The nagging worry of today and yesterday suddenly sharpened into anger.

"Hell!" Ferry said suddenly, and relaxed ostentatiously. That would mean another two weeks of "solitary" in a basement cell. Ferry had only recently completed such a turn. But his name had been on the letter list this morning, and he hadn't received any mail for over four months. "Hell!" he said again, and stared into Falcone's bulging eyes.

"And hell!" another voice said. Someone laughed, and the laughter increased. The Italian guards glanced uneasily at each other: here was another of these mad outbursts by the *Inglesi*. It began with nothing; just a laugh like this one now. And then it would spread into a chant—no violence, just chanting. You hadn't any justification for shooting at them. The most you could do, if you didn't want the Swiss to complain about the way this camp was run, was to choose the ringleaders (the basement cells being unfortunately inadequate in number for all the prisoners) and shut them up in darkness for a week or two. You could also cancel all privileges for the rest of the camp, and keep them confined to quarters. That was the most you could do: but the prisoners either couldn't or wouldn't learn.

Of all the guards Falcone enjoyed these outbursts least. He always seemed to think that they were an insult specially directed against his dignity. Now his dark face turned into a ripe pomegranate. The veins in his neck swelled. His hand was on his revolver. As the chorus of "Where are our letters? Where are our letters?" increased in volume his voice rose and was all the more ludicrous lost in the uproar. His eyes turned towards the doorway. He was worried as well as angry, almost nervous. Those who noticed that look paused for a moment, and then resumed their song with still greater enthusiasm. I'm a fool, Lennox was thinking: we'll be jugged for this, and the chances to escape will be more difficult. I'm a fool. . . . But the intoxication of this moment of small triumph, of seeing Falcone no longer assured and somehow shaken, couldn't be resisted. His voice joined the chorus even as he told himself just what size of a fool he was.

As the door half opened the men realized at last what had been worrying Falcone. The commandant himself had come, fat of face, sad-eyed, with his pouting lips ready to say so very gently "Such bad boys!" That was his usual phrase when he was about to order the meanest form of punishment he could give. But somehow, today the words weren't spoken. Lennox thought, he's worried too— What is wrong, anyway? The Italians hadn't lost so much composure since the day that Mussolini's fall was announced over the Rome radio, and the prisoners had all started a song with scurrilous additions about Humpty Dumpty. (It was after this unfortunately frank radio announcement that the wireless set in the prisoners' dining room suddenly went out of order and was never repaired. Since then the only news had come through Johann's asides to Miller, working beside him in the post office.) What was wrong, anyway? The other men near Lennox had sensed something too. They might still be the prisoners, and these Italians were their keepers, but in this minute it was the prisoners who were victorious. Their answer was given once more by the door. It opened fully, and the prisoners could see a line of uniformed men, slowly filing through the hall towards the staircase. There were some heavily armed guards. There was an officer, now standing in the doorway. He was German. So were the strange guards. But the men in the dining room staring into the hall at the slowly moving file there stopped their chanting.

"British," Miller was yelling. "Canadian."

"American," Ferry added to that. "Hi there, Yanks!"

"And officers," Lennox heard his own voice shouting. The men stared, each at his neighbor. "Officers? What's the bright idea?" "Officers? What are they doing here?"

The German captain looked savagely at the Italian commandant. "What discipline!" he said. "Keep those men quiet." He turned to Falcone. "Keep these men quiet. What's wrong?"

"They want their letters—"

"Give them their letters." And then the captain turned to the prisoners, now silenced by their curiosity. "Any more of this and we will consider it mutiny. We will shoot." To the Italian guards he said, "Keep your guns ready."

"But—" the commandant began.

"No time for 'buts.' Give them their letters. Send that man for them." He pointed to Falcone. "At once!"

Falcone, taking the short cut to the post office, moved quickly through the back door of the mess hall into the kitchen.

The German captain looked around the room, his eyes narrowed. He spoke once more to the commandant. "Keep them quiet." His tone was so savage that Lennox, Miller, Ferry, and a score of others exchanged glances. The rest of the prisoners were either content that they were to be given the letters, or were still speculating why any officers should be brought to this camp. But Ferry and Miller had a different look in their eyes, and there was a grin on their lips. They were guessing, and the guesses were very comforting.

"Shut up," Lennox said quietly to the clown next him, who could only think of raising a smile at this moment by his "Officers? What next? I'm going to complain to the management."

"Shut up." And then as the man looked at him with a blank expression, he said quickly, "They can't have enough guards. They've got to bribe us to keep quiet. They can't even detail guards to take us to the post office. So shut up. And get ready. Pass the word along."

The man still stared, but he obeyed, talking in the prison way, as Lennox had done, with his lips scarcely moving.

The German officer sensed a stirring in the mass of men in front of him, but their faces seemed quite expressionless. A rabble of common soldiers, he was thinking, and thank God for that; they would take orders, they knew nothing. He turned back to the entrance hall, leaving the commandant to hover hesitatingly in the doorway.

Lennox heard the German suddenly curse. "What's this now?" he was demanding of one of his own men. The commandant's curiosity moved his bulk through the doorway into the hall. Once more the prisoners who stood near the door could see the beginning of the staircase. The file of Allied officers was no longer ascending. The new arrivals were sitting on the steps, holding their bundles of possessions on their knees. They looked as if they were enjoying themselves immensely. Their innocence was too bland to be natural.

As the German captain stood hesitating, his eyes narrowed, his hands on his hips, a lazy American voice said to him mockingly, "Sorry, General, but there's a traffic jam."

One of the Englishmen said, "The rooms have not been cleared upstairs. We may as well sit down. We have a long journey ahead of us into Germany." He had raised his voice for the last sentence, and it carried clearly into the dining room. He smiled as he saw from the expression on the faces of the prisoners, who stood nearest to the door, that they had heard his words. And they had understood his meaning. These British and American officers were being shipped into Germany from Italy. Their appearance here was an emergency halt on that journey. They had been unexpected, and their arrival had thrown the camp into an uproar.

There was a burst of angry German commands. And then, in answer to them, a Scots voice shouted clearly downstairs, "We're doing the best we can. Tell your own ten chaps to do it if you're no' pleased." Now that look of quiet enjoyment on the officers' faces was explained, too. This delay in the clearing of some rooms for them was no accident. Jock Stewart and his fatigue party had been detailed by the Italians to throw the soldiers' possessions out, so as to make room for the new arrivals. And the officers had passed word upstairs to tell Stewart and his party to take as long as possible. And unless the Germans (*ten*, Stewart had obligingly reported) actually did the work themselves, Stewart would see to it that it would take as long as possible.

It was then that the commandant collected enough of his wits to close the door. The noises from the hall became muffled once more. All that could be heard was the shouting of the German guards, now subdued by the thick door into a blur of sound.

Ten of them, Lennox repeated to himself. Stewart had thought it important enough to say the exact number. There were five Italian guards in here; and there should be thirty-five other Italian guards around the camp, not to count the civilians who were employed either in the post office or in the commissary or in the kitchen. Yet, come to think of it, there hadn't been many Italians on view this afternoon. And when Falcone had left this room he had gone through the kitchen. And the kitchen was empty. Usually you could hear the Italians in there a mile off, as they wrangled over their share of the prisoners' supplies before they started cooking. But this afternoon there was only silence. This afternoon there had been fewer guards round the wire fences. No movements had come from the watch-tower overlooking the walls. No movement from the guardroom.

Lennox felt his throat close in his excitement. His humorous neighbor was being serious for once. "What's it all about?" he was asking.

Lennox stared at the heavy door which shut this room off from the hall. Behind there lay the answer. The officers knew; and Stewart and his party must have learned from them, for they knew. Here, one could only guess. But the door blocked contact. If the men in here and the men outside could act simultaneously there would be a chance to escape. Not for one, but for all of them.

"A chance," Lennox was saying, "a chance." He was now staring at the Italians' guns. Had Ferry guessed? Had Miller? If so there was indeed a chance. The humorist was looking at him. "What chance?" he kept repeating.

The kitchen door opened. But it wasn't Falcone who entered. It was the boy Johann, a small bundle of letters in his hand, a bright smile on his round face, now flushed with excitement. He was alone. He moved quickly towards the middle of the wall along which the guards stood, their guns held ready as the captain had commanded, and then turned to face the men. He spoke as quickly as he had moved, and, strangely enough, he spoke in the Italian which he had been forced to learn at school. Lennox suddenly realized that Johann was talking more for the benefit of the Italians than for the roomful of men, only a tenth of whom could understand his words.

"I brought the letters, for there was no one else to bring them." Johann's smile broadened, as he watched the Italians' faces. Miller was saying, "What's up? Johann, what's up?" Ferry was shouting, "Where's Falcone, where are the other guards?"

Johann was still watching the Italians. He said, "All are gone. One after another. Just slipping away. Like that." He moved his hand slowly in an arc, as if tracing the course of a sun which had risen, had stood high, and was now falling out of sight.

One of the Italians, with less will to believe than the others, said, "You lie." But his voice didn't sound too sure.

"Me?" Johann handed the small bundle of letters over to Miller, who didn't even begin to distribute them. The others had forgotten about the letters too. They were as silent as the Italians, but there was hope and expectancy in the prisoners' faces.

"Why," Johann was saying casually, "if you had been listening to the radio during the last half-hour, you would have heard the German announcement. It said just what I said when I came back from Bolzano this afternoon. Only some of you would believe me then. Now all, except you five dolts, believe me."

"We have capitulated?" one guard asked slowly.

"Unconditionally," Johann answered, with high good humor. "Unconditionally." He was obviously fond of that word.

There was the beginning of a shout from the prisoners. Those who hadn't understood the language fully had yet understood the meaning. There was little need for those who were translating so enthusiastically.

Johann pointed warningly towards the hall. "*Warten Sie noch!*" he said in his own language. Miller and Ferry silenced the impatient men. "Not yet, not yet!" Miller repeated.

Peter Lennox watched Johann uneasily. Was he with them, or against them? "Wait," he had said. But why wait? This chance might slip away. Now was the time. Why wait? Had this boy some plan which he had brought back from Bozen as well as the first news of the surrender? Or was he only enjoying this moment as any Tyrolese against the hated Italians?

One of the guards had tightened his grip on his gun. A hard, clever look came over his face as he kept the rifle pointed at the mass of men. He backed slowly towards the hall door. Three others wavered, and then followed his example. Peter Lennox cursed silently. The chance was slipping. The guards should have been rushed when the first shock of the news was upon them. Only, the prisoners had been too surprised themselves to be able to act then. Now there was only silence in the room.

"Fools!" Johann said quietly, looking at the hall door. "No help for you there. The Germans are calling the Italians traitors. They are killing Italians in Naples."

The guard, who had almost reached the hall door, paused.

"The Germans are killing Italians, and the Italians are killing Germans," Johann said very slowly. He was enjoying the idea so much that the Italians knew he spoke the truth. "Look," he went on, now urgent and serious, "I give you warning, more warning than you gave my friends when you seized them for your army in Albania and in Greece. I give you fair warning. The Germans are taking over Northern Italy. The Italians are leaving Bolzano. The South Tyrol is no longer Italian."

The guards were staring now at the boy's triumphant smile. For over twenty years the Italians had tried to make the South Tyrol a part of Italy. Now, if their authority were removed, the Tyrolese would have a long-remembered score to settle. So the guards were silent, as if numbed by the fear which must have tormented them for many weeks now. The fear had been too real, too well-earned, to let them have any doubts of the truth in Johann's words. First one, and then the others left the hall door, and backed slowly along the wall towards the kitchen entrance. Their guns were no longer truculent. They were no longer the jailers. These prisoners didn't matter now that war was over. There was only one purpose now, and that was to reach the Italy where Italians lived. The guards, admitting that, measured their own imminent danger. It grew with each hour of delay.

Lennox watched the strangely silent men, whose slow, uncertain movements were now beginning to take the shape of hurry.

As they reached the kitchen door Johann spoke softly. "Your guns will show you are deserters. Best leave them here, so that if you meet any Germans they will think you are only going off duty."

The Italians hesitated.

"All right. Don't believe me," Johann said. "Find out for yourselves. The only Italians who keep their guns are those who are going to fight the Germans. The Germans know that. But find it out for yourselves." He held out his hand for the weapons. The Yorkshire sergeant major, pushing his way through the mass of prisoners, pulled a rifle out of an unresisting hand and pointed with his thumb to the kitchen door.

"Go on," he said encouragingly. "We won't shoot you." The Italians hadn't understood his words, but they caught their meaning. They went, with a haste so precipitous that even the sergeant major looked somewhat amazed at the five rifles stacked in his arms.

Lennox felt an emotion which was almost pity. It isn't pleasant to see men realize that they are trapped and helpless, that now it's their turn to be kicked about. And then he was telling himself to keep his pity for those who deserved it. None of these guards had ever done a spontaneous, decent thing for any of the prisoners: their occasional kindnesses had been granted when the payment—in food from the prisoners' boxes—had been exorbitantly extracted. Humanity had been lowered to the level of barter and grab. Even now none of the guards had volunteered to fight along with the prisoners: now they were only thinking of how to save their own skins and property as they scrabbled their way through the kitchen door. Let him keep his pity for those who had practised pity.

There was a movement as if the prisoners had decided something too. The mass of men came to life. Even those who were ill, who had propped their bodies against the tables in the room, watched with eager eyes. They were waiting, ready.

Miller, talking urgently to Johann, had now started to tell the sergeant major the boy's suggestion. It had sufficient possibilities, because the sergeant major nodded and selected five men. Johann, it seemed, was to be entrusted with a gun; he and the five men were already leaving the room by the kitchen door. Lennox edged his way to where Miller stood.

"What's the idea?" he asked, more quietly than he felt. Fool, he was thinking, to sacrifice a gun to Johann. . . . What good would that do?

"They will reach the courtyard through one of the kitchen doors. There are three German lorries under guard in the courtyard."

It wasn't a very perfect explanation. Miller was too busy trying to persuade the sergeant major that he could use a rifle as well as the next man.

But the word "courtyard" caught Lennox's ear. In the courtyard was the guardhouse, where other weapons, including machine guns, could be found. The five men would march in good order across the courtyard, as if they had been detailed for some camp duty. If the Germans guarding their lorries were to turn their attention on the prisoners, then Johann, armed and in correct uniform, would give the authentic touch of control to the scene. The Germans were strangers here and ignorant of the camp's routine.

"What about the Italians in the guardroom?"

"Gone. So Johann said."

Lennox's mouth twisted. "So Johann said," he mimicked, but Miller had followed the others, who, realizing that the remaining guns could only arm four men, were now invading the deserted kitchen. Quickly they passed out to the mess hall any choppers, pans, ladles, rolling pins, they could find. Ferry was testing a carving knife thoughtfully; Miller had compromised on a meat mallet. Lennox refused a Chianti bottle and made his way into the kitchen to choose his own weapon. He came back into the dining room gripping in his left hand a length of iron chain which had once held a soup pot suspended over the kitchen fire. He knotted it loosely at the end, and a slow grin came over his tight mouth as he tested the chain's weight. He glanced at his taut wrist. His watch said it was now thirty-five minutes past six. Johann had brought the letters at six-twenty-six. Nine minutes had passed. Nine minutes against seven months. Seven months of worry and sweat to prepare for an escape. And here it was in nine minutes, flat.

The sergeant major held up his hand. He was standing at the hall door, ready to swing it open.

To the three sharpshooters he had chosen he said, "I take the captain. You, the man to his left. You, the man to his right. You, the German at the top of the stairs. After that, pick off the nearest. You others, start rushing when we stop shooting. When I give the signal everyone yell his bloody head off. Ready, boys?"

The men nodded, and tightened their grasp round their weapons. Those who had nothing but their bare hands gathered together in a solid mass behind the crudely armed spearhead.

The sergeant major held his hand raised. He's waiting, Lennox guessed, for the courtyard; the men who had marched towards the guardroom with Johann should have taken possession of the machine guns by this time. He glanced quickly at the tense, waiting faces around him, and then at his watch. Another minute and a half had gone. His muscles tautened, and he felt a drop of perspiration trickle over his upper lip. He stared at the door as the others did. Each slipping second could spell disaster.

From the courtyard there came the sharp, uneven rattle of a machine gun. The diversion had begun.

The sergeant major's arm dropped. Someone knocked the door's latch free, someone swung the heavy mass of oak wide open. The four sharp-shooters were already taking aim as they entered the hall. The men surged forward. They were shouting. The haggard faces were alive once more.

CHAPTER 3

In the hall the German captain had placed six of his men in a well-spaced line to flank the curve of stairway. Their guns were pointed towards the row of officers, still waiting patiently, expectantly. Two other German soldiers guarded the head of the staircase. Their guns pointed too, but their eyes kept glancing sideways along the upstairs corridor, in which the angry voices of the two remaining Germans were combined with the sounds of a rough-and-ready removal.

The captain, standing at the foot of the staircase, was obviously angry. His fury increased as his patience evaporated. He fingered his revolver. Another minute of this impudence and he would order his men upstairs to shoot. If only these damned Anglo-Saxons would make one move then his men's guns would have an answer for them. But they gave no appearance of mutiny, no excuse for shooting. They just sat and stared at him calmly. Impudence—that was it. Some of them were even smiling: that American up there was grinning broadly. Damn these Italians and their lax discipline. If only they had had their full quota of guards when his party had arrived here the rooms upstairs would have been ready by this time. And if only the damned Americans hadn't bombed the Brenner railway line yesterday the damned train carrying the prisoners wouldn't now be held up at Bozen until the damned line could be repaired. He glared at the Italian commandant. He'd tell this fat bucking jackass a thing or two, once they had the prisoners all safely locked up.

The commandant fingered the decorations on his tunic and cleared his throat. But the German's angry face silenced the beginning of an apology. The commandant even stopped fingering his decorations. This captain wouldn't let himself notice the row of medals. This captain hadn't even treated him as an officer of superior rank. The smothered apology turned sour in his mouth. With stilted dignity he walked over to the wall, and looked at the mass of foreigners with distaste. Two years ago everything had been so different. The tears filming his eyes as he thought of that change dried in alarm. He had suddenly remembered that he still had to explain to this German that the Italian guards, now away from the camp, were absent without leave. Deserters . . . he hadn't dared mention that word. He sighed wearily. He wished he were upstairs in his pleasant room, listening to his wireless set: he might have learned by this time if this afternoon's rumors were true or false. Then he would know what to do. He glared at the smiling Allied officers. His heart suddenly twisted as he thought of his country at the mercy of barbarians. His eyelids drooped. He held his weakening underlip rigid with his teeth. He studied the floor at his feet, as if he could read there why his Italy should suffer such unhappiness, such injustice.

There was the sudden rattle of a machine gun in the courtyard.

All heads turned sharply to the entrance door of the hall.

"Watch the prisoners!" the German captain shouted. "You there—anyone who moves will be shot. Meyer, Hofmann, with me!" He started smartly towards the courtyard. Probably only an Italian trying to desert, he thought, and his pace hesitated. The commandant's eyes lifted and met his, and the German saw the same thought in them. There was fear, too, and shame.

Perhaps there was more than one deserter, the German thought, perhaps that was why this fat fool had acted so strangely ever since the unexpected arrival of prisoners in this camp. Perhaps there was a lot of trouble here to be settled. He was staring with increasing suspicion at the Italian, and so he did not see the broad thick door of the mess hall as it opened. But he saw the Italian's eyes dilate. He heard the beginning of a shout, and turned, and fell. The Yorkshire sergeant major had aimed well.

The commandant stared at the German captain's body, lying so still and now forever humbled. The two soldiers who had followed the captain had crumpled on to the paved floor. Blood trickled slowly. The commandant stared incredulously. Other shots crashed through the hall, deafening, terrifying. He was scarcely aware that the staircase was a seething mass of officers, that the hall was filled with sweating, cursing, ragged men. He stared at two bodies falling from above, as if two sacks of flour had been thrown over the balustrade, and then remembered the two Germans who had guarded the head of the staircase. He could not hear the hard thud of their bodies on the stone floor so near his feet: the volume of noise in the hall was smashing into his ears, puckering his face with fear and pain. These yelling savages swarming towards him . . . these answering yells from upstairs, telling that the last Germans had been dealt with. . . .

Then, suddenly, out of the mass of noise and movement, he saw one of his prisoners run towards him. He felt naked in his helplessness, alone with savages. Savages. His muscles obeyed him at last. He ran from the prisoner, from the swinging piece of chain. He ran towards the entrance.

Out there in the courtyard the Germans would help him. They'd machine-gun these savages. They would cut them down like ripe hay.

The door opened as he reached it, and he saw men advancing towards him out of the courtyard. The light from the hall gleamed on a machine gun. A sob of relief rose from his tight throat. And then he recognized them. . . . They were *Inglesi*.

Another figure came running out of the darkness.

"Schichtl!" the commandant shouted. But as he saw the boy's face his sudden hope died.

Johann raised his arm and fired his gun. The commandant's face was blotted out. He hadn't even had time to wonder why such injustice should be happening to him.

Johann stepped over the commandant's body. "Come on," he said to the three Britishers. "Come on." His tone was even and urgent.

One of the men gave a low whistle of admiration. "Make up your mind quick, don't you?"

"Come on."

But inside the hall there was no need to set up the machine gun. All resistance had ceased. The irrepressible man gave another whistle. "Like Christmas night in the workhouse," he said cheerily.

No one else spoke. Some men were picking themselves up from the floor. Five—including the sergeant major—were wounded badly. Two were as motionless as the Germans. The rest just stood, and stared. After the uproar of the last two minutes the silence was like death itself. Then someone raised a cheer. It was a thin, pathetic effort. But the others joined in, and the cheer swelled almost to a shout. Then everyone was as suddenly silent again, looking sheepishly at one another, beginning to move round the hall. One of the American Air Force officers said, "We're a funny-looking bunch all right," and a laugh began. Men laughed for no reason at all.

But the American had spoken the truth. They were a strange collection. They had been civilians in countries as far distant from each other as they were from Italy. They had become soldiers. Craftsmen, workmen, businessmen, professional men, had learned how to march and shoot and drive a tank, how to handle artillery or a parachute or an airplane. They wore the faded, stained uniforms of the veteran. Their bodies were thin, their faces were gaunt. But the look of the prisoner—the desperate, self-tortured look of the forgotten man—had vanished. They were laughing for no reason at all, but they laughed like free men.

Peter Lennox didn't laugh. He was kneeling beside Miller when Johann came up to him.

The boy's excited face became grave too. He bent down and touched Miller's brow. He drew back his hand quickly, and his mouth became set.

He said nothing. He straightened his back and stood quietly there, looking down at the dead man's face. There was a band of white flesh at the edge of Miller's hair, where even the desert sun hadn't managed to reach the skin. You saw it clearly now, as he lay with his head thrown stiffly backward. The blue eyes stared up at the damp stone ceiling.

Lennox glanced at Johann Schichtl's broad-boned face, impassive and yet somehow all the more expressive. The boy kept his silence. Miller had been right, Lennox thought. Miller had liked and trusted this boy. And this boy had really liked Miller. Johann suddenly looked at him, and Lennox felt ashamed of his initial distrust, of his unreasoning dislike of the boy. He looked quickly down again at Miller, and tried to straighten his friend's body into a decent sleep.

"Who's this?" an officer was asking. His voice was hard, his hand was on Johann's shoulder.

CHAPTER 4

"Who's this fellow?" the officer repeated. His faded insignia showed he was a captain in the Tank Corps.

Lennox rose to his feet, and unconsciously stood beside Johann. Something in the officer's high-pitched voice, in his way of repeating the question so insistently, annoyed Lennox. What did he think Lennox was? A blasted idiot? Johann wouldn't have been alive if he had been an enemy. Lennox remembered Miller's words that afternoon. He repeated them now. "He's all right," he said, and then remembered to add "sir." Johann's anxious face was turned towards him. The boy's light blue eyes were worried as he listened to the English voices. The officer's hand left his shoulder, and the worried look eased.

"He's a friend, sir," the captain reported in his turn to a colonel who was watching the group curiously.

The colonel nodded. "Where are all the guards?" he asked Lennox.

"They left before the fight started, sir," Lennox answered. He looked bitterly at the officers' insignia. All that old stuff again, sirs and salutes and sirs. "Johann, here, scared the daylight out of them with the news."

"And what was that?" the colonel asked quickly.

"The South Tyrol is no longer Italian."

The colonel half smiled and glanced at Johann's face. "And Johann belongs to the South Tyrol?"

"Yes, sir."

"Any other news? We heard rumors of peace on our journey north."

"The Eyties have surrendered, sir."

The officers exchanged broad grins. "Better tell the others," the senior officer said. "And tell them there's no more fighting to be done here meanwhile. Seemingly the rest of the guards have upped and left us." He stood watching Johann. "I'd like to see you once we straighten things out here," he said in very precise German.

Johann looked worried. He answered quickly, and at some length.

"What the dickens is he talking about?" the colonel asked in amazement.

"I didn't catch all of it, sir, but I think he was saying that he wants to leave now. He says he has proved that we can trust him."

"Yes, but he's just the chap we need. Tell him to stay here meanwhile. Better keep beside him. You seem to understand his lingo."

"I've got accustomed to the accent, sir."

"Well, stay with him. We want to be sure we don't misunderstand him when we have time to question him."

Lennox said, "Yes, sir." He spoke without any enthusiasm. He had a uniform upstairs. He had a map and money. He had his plan. Now would be the time to use them. Darkness was coming, and he could have been far from here by daybreak. He would have managed it, too; this time he would have escaped. It was just his blasted luck, he thought; seven months of planning for nothing. And then, as he saw Miller lying at his feet, his lips tightened, and he stopped grousing about his luck.

The colonel had looked at Lennox keenly for a moment before he turned away to attend to the decisions which were being carried out. As senior officer, he had much to organize quickly.

The wounded were taken to be patched up in the camp hospital across the courtyard. The dead were carried out of the hall, and the Germans' weapons, uniforms, and papers were removed for future use. Extra men were sent out to join the two who had remained on guard over the captured lorries. A detail was dispatched to the kitchen and storerooms to forage for food. Officers were in the commandant's office, examining papers and maps. One of them was installed at the telephone: he had taught Romance languages at a university, and could cope with any sudden calls to the commandant from the town. Another, who had been an advertising artist, was making sketches of various sections of the enormous relief map which was cemented into one wall of the office. A party had gone down to the blackness of the detention cells, where they found the jailer had long left his basement post, and seventeen cold, filthy, and truculent Tommies were helped upstairs. Others searched the castle and outbuildings with care. The guardroom was emptied of weapons and ammunition. The commissary was ransacked for useful equipment. Armed sentries, in German coats, were posted round the camp. The searchlight at the gate was manned, ready to give its usual five-minute sweep, so that any Germans in the town would see its customary watchfulness.

The men and officers accomplished their jobs quickly and efficiently. But there was an underlying cheerfulness which would break out into a laugh, or a quip, or an exchange of good-natured libels. The younger officers were as excited as the men. Only the senior officer, and the two majors who stood talking to him, were grave. Only Lennox and Johann Schichtl, standing together in the hall, were silent. And both were equally impatient.

But when the colonel came over to them once more he didn't waste much time in finding out what he wanted to know. Johann, in spite of his obvious impatience, answered each question quickly and directly. Lennox translated, when necessary, with equal simplicity. The officers, grouped round the colonel, watched the boy's face as they listened to Lennox.

First of all, they were assured, they need have no fears about Falcone or the five guards who had been the last to desert from the camp, and who were the only Italians to see the revolt begin. For these men had been strong Fascists like the commandant. They would never reach the town. ("We've taken care of that," Johann said with a grin. "It is easier to kill them now than to have to search them out later.")

Those who had deserted earlier in the day had slipped away, one by one, each thinking he was the only man with foresight in the camp. And so each would believe that the camp was still guarded by those he had left behind.

None of the Germans in the courtyard had escaped to give warning.

No house was near the camp, and no one in the town could have heard the shots.

No one would come to the camp tonight. The first arrivals would be at six tomorrow morning, when the daily food supplies were brought to the camp.

The staffs of the kitchen, commissary, and post office, who were civilians recruited from the town, generally arrived at seven o'clock each morning.

So much for the camp's routine and personnel.

As to the town ("*Bozen,*" Johann said pointedly, as the colonel again made the tactical error of using the Italian form of Bolzano), only Italians had occupied the barracks until recently. After Mussolini's fall some Germans had been placed in command. That was what caused the trouble in the town this afternoon. The Italian soldiers had said the war was over. They had put down their guns and tried to walk out. The Germans had shot at them. And then the Italian officers, who until then were not sure what they should do, had ordered their men to shoot back. There were not many Germans in the barracks so they were all killed. A number of Italians were killed, too, and the rest had left the barracks. Some of them had taken rifles and ammunition, but many didn't. These had stripped off their uniforms, and had left their guns in the barracks. They were pretending now to be civilians.

The Nazis would probably take over the town, for they were already in firm control of the station and the railway to the Brenner Pass. They were playing a double game: they were backing the Fascist Italians, who were still working with the Nazis, and they were trying to win the support of the Tyrolese. Some of the Tyrolese listened to the Germans, believing that Hitler would free them from the Italians as his secret propaganda had promised for many years. But other men of the Tyrol only saw the Germans as new dictators to oppress them.

When Johann ended the colonel exchanged glances with the two majors. "At least," he said, with a wry smile, "we are probably safe enough here for the next few hours. We have time to eat and finish our plans."

One of the majors—he was an American wearing Rangers' insignia—said, "But it's a hell of a setup."

The other major nodded. "Absolutely." He looked at Johann again. "It seems we have three kinds of Italians to deal with. Those who won't fight at all; those who won't fight against the Germans; and those who want to fight Germans. And there are two kinds of Tyrolese: those who are pro-Nazi, mainly because they hate the Italians; and those who hate the Nazis and who want to get rid of the Italians by themselves. That gives us five different sets of people to handle, not to mention the Germans."

"Personally," the American said, "I'll be glad when we come up against the Germans. At least, you know what to shoot there."

The colonel was still watching Johann. Half to himself he said, "If we only knew more about politics here we might be better able to—" He turned to Lennox. "Do you know anything about the political quarrels in this district?"

"A little. But Johann could tell you much more, sir."

"If we had time . . . " the colonel said. "If I were sure of enough time . . . " He had started worrying again. "Pass out the food, anyway," he said to the majors. "Share round any weapons you've found. Make a division of the men into those who are fit to travel and fight, those who are not. Find out their special branch of the service and decide how we can best use them."

The officers hurried away. The colonel still watched Johann.

"Let me question him, sir," Lennox said suddenly, and his suggestion surprised himself as much as the colonel.

"Go ahead," the older man said. He watched Lennox with thoughtful eyes.

Lennox said quietly, "Johann, who told you to give the prisoners information? Who told you to spread the news among the guards so that they'd desert? Someone you met down in Bozen, when you were off duty today?"

A careful look spread over Johann's face, and wiped all the emotion out of it.

"Someone told you, didn't he, Johann?"

Johann didn't answer. I bet I'm right, Lennox was thinking. Johann was no fool; but there was a cleverer man than he would ever be behind all this.

"I must leave," Johann was saying. "I must go now. I have told you everything. I must go."

"To see this man?" tried Lennox.

Johann looked at him unhappily. "Our plans have changed. I must report," he admitted.

"Changed? You mean the Germans who arrived here and are now killed have altered the plans?"

Johann said nothing.

"But, Johann, they are dead. They won't inform. How can they alter any plans?"

Johann still said nothing.

Lennox looked at the officer. "Sorry, sir. That's as far as we get."

"You didn't do badly. At least you've discovered the boy is part of an organization. Pity he has suddenly shut up like this. Might have been helpful."

Jock Stewart appeared with a rough bandage round his head and a stack of thick sandwiches in his arm. "Best chuck we've had here yet," he said cheerfully, and handed out the slabs of bread with their generous slices of cheese. "Eyties' larder," he explained. "Soup is being heated now. Won't be long, sir." Then as Lennox took his allotted sandwiches, Stewart suddenly said, "Hey! I've got something for you. Didn't get time to hide them before the Jerries arrived. There in my pocket. No. The left one."

Lennox obeyed. He pulled out the German buttons which Miller had got for him. They gleamed in his soot-smeared palm.

"Not much good to you now," Stewart said, with his usual combination of the practical and the obvious.

Lennox's lips tightened as he looked at the buttons. And then he saw that both the colonel and Johann were staring at them too.

"When did you plan to leave?" the colonel was asking quietly, almost sympathetically.

"Tomorrow or the next day, sir. Before the moon grew too big." Lennox made an attempt to smile. Suddenly he handed the buttons to Johann. "Perhaps you'll find someone else who needs them."

"They were for you?"

"Yes."

"Not for Miller?"

"No."

"For you? You were planning to escape?"

"I was." Seven months of work, of planning, of worrying. Seven months of self-centered concentration. That's what these seven months had done to him. That's all they had produced.

Johann's face changed. "Then *you* are the one we want. Please come. The man you were asking about wants to see you. Let us go at once. We are late. Very late."

The colonel had understood part of these words. "He wants to see you?" He looked at the puzzled Lennox. "That means he wants to see the man who was determined enough to escape from this prison camp." He paused for a moment. And then, with a mental jump which seemed at first inconsequential, he said, "I believe any man sent here had a record of escapes from other camps. And the corporal told me that any who tried to escape from here were shot if they were found. Is that so?"

"Shot while resisting arrest," Lennox said bitterly. "Their bodies were sent back here to prove that to the others."

"But escaped prisoners are unarmed: weapons are the one thing that a guard can't be bribed to procure."

"They were unarmed, sir."

"I see." The colonel was silent. Then to Johann he said very carefully, "Why does this man in Bolzano—Bozen, I mean—want to see the prisoner who planned to escape? For what reason?"

Johann was undecided, hesitating, worried. And then, as if realizing that the quickest way to end all this questioning was to give direct answers once more, he said simply, "We need him. To go with us into the mountains. We need him. When your armies will be coming up to the Brenner Pass we need someone who can"—he fumbled for the right word—"connect us with you."

Lennox translated the boy's sentences quickly. "Liaison officer is what he means, I think," he concluded.

The boy nodded eagerly as he heard "liaison." "That's the word. We need liaison. We are working alone. We need someone to connect us with you, to tell you that we are patriots and to be trusted. To tell you what we have done and why we have done it. Or else the Allies would think when they came that we were only joining the winning side, that we hadn't earned the right to be masters in our own land."

Lennox translated again.

"So that's it!" the colonel said. Then, "Suppose we agreed to this, and gave you a liaison officer, would the man in Bozen help us now? When we leave here we will fight our way south to join our troops coming north. But we need more guns—many more. And we need help for the wounded who can't travel with us. Can your people help them?"

Johann considered these problems. "Perhaps. I don't know. He could tell you."

"Who is he?"

"The man in Bozen." And that was all Johann would say.

CHAPTER 5

The colonel began eating his sandwich. In between bites he was talking to Lennox. He seemed to have forgotten Johann. By the time he had finished his ration of food he had learned that Peter Lennox was an infantry man, enlisted in the Territorials in August 1939, who had seen service in North Africa, Greece, Crete, and then in North Africa again. He had been wounded and captured in the fall of Tobruk. He had been held in two other Italian prison camps. Because of attempted escapes he had been transferred to this one.

The colonel was thoughtful for a minute. Then he asked suddenly, "What were you in civilian life?"

Lennox hesitated, and then—steeling himself against the usual smile which his answer to that question always roused—he answered, "I used to paint."

But the colonel didn't smile. He looked at the shape of Lennox's hands. He noted the mocking scar on the right hand. "An artist?"

"Yes, sir."

"Know your way around, abroad?"

"Some places, sir."

"Know Austria?"

"Yes, but not this part of the Tyrol."

"You know the Northern Tyrol?"

"Yes, sir."

"Know it well? Where did you stay?"

Lennox repressed a smile, remembering how little his travels had to cost. "I stuck to out-of-the-way places, sir." Not Salzburg. Not Innsbruck. Not St. Anton. Not for me.

"Would you say that you would find the North and South Tyrol similar?"

Lennox stared. Whatever the reason for these questions he didn't at all like it.

"Yes, sir. At least, I've seen many a Johann Schichtl in the North. I think the most obvious difference is in the shapes of the mountains."

The colonel was still watching him carefully. He asked unexpectedly, "Didn't you try for a commission when you joined the army?"

"I prefer this way, sir."

The colonel smiled at that. He wasn't so very surprised. He had already decided that this young man with the shock of brown hair, hard gray eyes, and unsmiling mouth had his own ideas about what he wanted to do. Probably he had chosen to be a private in the infantry because he obviously thought you suffered most as a private in the infantry. Well, if this man thought service was measured by suffering he certainly had served well. The colonel wondered for a moment if Lennox had been a pacifist in the nineteen-thirties. Probably.

And then the American major returned. His information wasn't pleasant. There had been nine men in the hospital; three of them couldn't walk. Of the other prisoners, twenty-three were weakened by malaria. Of the five wounded in the hall tonight, only two could travel. They, like the malaria cases, would have to be considered passengers. They weren't fit for active combat.

The colonel's face was tight and grim once more. He was looking at Johann Schichtl, as if his eyes could gauge the Austrian's worth. When time was short you had to depend on your capacity to judge character by what you saw in a man's face. The difficulty with Johann was that he was still a boy, without any definite character written on his round red-cheeked face. His blue eyes were honest and eager. His mouth was capable of two expressions: a friendly curve and a rebellious line. At the moment it was the rebellious line which straightened his lips and gave his good natured chin an angry, disappointed set.

The colonel turned to Lennox, and spoke in halting French. "You knew him for some months. Did you feel you could trust him?"

"I didn't trust him then, sir."

"But you trusted him this afternoon."

"Only since Miller was killed, sir."

The colonel stared. "You don't seem very clear about it," he said sharply in English.

"Yes, sir," Lennox agreed. The trouble is, he was thinking, when you tell people the truth they won't believe you. If he had said he trusted Johann because he had helped them against a batch of lousy Fascists he would have lied. He hadn't trusted Johann then. This afternoon Johann's politics had run a parallel course with the prisoners' hopes. That was why he had fought with them. You couldn't trust a man whose only thought was politics: he was only your friend as long as it suited him. But there had been something in the way Johann had stood and looked at the dead Miller, something of real feeling and sadness which had jolted Lennox out of his cynicism. There was decent good will in this boy. He could be trusted.

The colonel looked gloomily at his watch. "The time is now almost eight-fifteen. By the boy's information, we still have some hours of safety here. We shall have to trust him—that's all. We need friends. We shan't find them by refusing to meet them halfway."

He turned to the American. "You and Major Cummins take charge. I'm going into this Bolzano, or Bozen, or whatever it's called. I'll see this man and get his help. If I don't return by ten o'clock leave here. Don't wait one minute after ten."

The American major was looking worried now, in his turn.

"The wounded?" he asked.

"If I get back there will be a plan for the wounded. This man in Bozen will have to take care of them. That's the price I'm going to ask for the man who is going up into the mountains as liaison officer."

"Why not send someone else in your place to Bozen?" the American suggested.

"Because I've to make the decision about leaving a man with these Tyrolese. It's my responsibility. Besides I want to know just what we might expect when our armies reach this part of the country." The colonel smiled faintly as he added, "I am not at all so necessary for leading a party to the south. You and Cummins can do that as well as I could. And if I go myself to this man in Bozen then we are showing we are in earnest. We'll get quickest results that way."

He turned to Johann and asked, "How soon can we reach this man?"

Johann's smile came slowly back. "Twenty minutes on foot. Five minutes with the lorry," he said happily. "It will be safe enough if we wear German coats. Perhaps there will be something you could bring back in the lorry."

The officers looked at each other. "What could we bring back?" the colonel asked.

"The barracks in Bozen had much equipment." Johann was grinning cheerfully, and the officers were smiling too; their guess had been right. The answer was guns.

"Come along," the colonel said to Lennox. "I shall need you. And I'll need a couple of other fellows. Pick out two of the toughest men here. Two who understand some German."

Lennox obeyed without any enthusiasm. Hell, he was thinking, nothing ever goes the way you plan it. He would be stuck here for the rest of the war. He could see it coming. If the colonel had his way—and who was to stop a blasted colonel?—he would be left here in those mountains while the others marched south. If only he had been stupid, talked foolishly, pretended to know nothing about Johann or his language. Too late now; he had been the bright little boy, and his seven months of planning had landed him among mountains.

"I'd like to—" began the American.

"Sorry, old man. You're needed here." The colonel signed to two junior officers. "Cover that up with these," he ordered, pointing first to their commando uniforms and then to the pile of German coats. He was no longer worried. Now that the decision had been made he looked even happy, as if he were going to enjoy himself. Blast him, Lennox thought bitterly, and picked up a German coat and cap as the two lieutenants had done.

The two men he chose were Ferry and Merriman. (Stewart had to be passed over: his bandaged head would have been too conspicuous.) They were as excited as the lieutenants, and they had already covered their bleached uniforms with the German coats. They were smiling all over their faces as they left the hall. Johann, as happy as anyone, waited at the door. The colonel, strangely formidable in the German captain's long military coat, turned at last from the two majors and walked towards Johann.

"Come on, there," he said quickly, over his shoulder. "Step lively."

"Yes, sir," Lennox said. He looked at Stewart, who was watching the departing men glumly. "You know where I've hidden my coat, Jock. There's a good map, and some money and other things behind the loose board—the one that's covered by that calendar I made. Perhaps you can use them."

Stewart gave him a sharp look. "I'll find a use for them," he said. He clapped Lennox on the shoulder as if he realized this was the last time they would see each other. "It's a damned shame," Stewart said. "It's . . ."

"Step lively!" the colonel yelled from the doorway.

Lennox nodded to Stewart, and then he was hurrying between the groups of men in the hall. He followed the colonel out into the night. Seven months, he was thinking bitterly. As he passed two German-like sentinels in the courtyard, and heard them wish him luck, he was wondering whether he would have managed to escape this time, or whether he would have made just another "shot-while-resisting" corpse. Third try was usually luck, it was said. But now he'd never know. He felt cheated. This thought was so busy rankling in his mind that he blundered in the darkness as he climbed onto the lorry, and the high mudguard struck sharply against his shin. He swore much more than was necessary, but at least he felt better. The colonel's taut wrist pulled him safely on board, down onto a hard wooden bench, as the lorry started impatiently forward. It swung through the gateway, past the watchtowers with their machine guns and the swinging searchlights, past the masses of ten-foot-high barbed wire. It jolted over the wooden bridge which spanned the deep, moatlike pit encircling the walls of wire.

"Do you smell that?" Ferry said in great awe.

"A tannery, I rather think," one of the lieutenants said.

"Maybe," Ferry said, and his voice was strained. He drew a long breath, as if to steady himself. "But it's free air to me."

The rest were silent. They huddled together as the lorry swung down the mountainside. The only sounds came from the wheels grinding over the loose stones on the surface of the road. The engine had been switched off. The lorry was running silently, depending on its brakes and Johann's skillful driving, down towards the town.

CHAPTER 6

Johann snapped his fingers to attract attention, and then pointed. The men's eyes followed the quick movement of the boy's outstretched arm, black against the dark-blue sky. The lorry was coming well down into the valley now. The road had twisted in long, serpentine loops as it descended through the vineyards. Houses had been few, and silent. All around were the dark silhouettes of heightening mountain peaks. Below them was the River Eisak, which the Italians had named Isarco, with its flat, narrow valley broadening as it reached the scattered lights of a town.

"Bolzano," the colonel said.

"Bozen," Johann insisted. Over his shoulder he said, "We shall halt the lorry soon, northeast of the town. The English officer and Lennox will come with me to see the man. That will only take ten minutes. The lorry will wait for us until we have seen him."

"And the barracks?" asked the colonel. Quick work, Lennox thought approvingly: the colonel was picking up Johann's way of speaking. He didn't need a translator now to help with the South Tyrol dialect twist in the words. Then why, Lennox demanded of the dark sky, why did he bring me down here? To reassure Johann? Or had Stewart's premonition been right? Lennox kept his gloomy silence, and listened to Johann's polite but adamant refusal to go near the barracks.

The lorry should be left on a side road on the outskirts of the town. It was just there that this man from Bozen was waiting for Johann. And the man would be able to tell them whether it was safe to try to reach the barracks. (For the barracks, seemingly, lay on the south side of the town at the river's edge. To reach it, they would have either to pass the station, which certainly had been in German control this afternoon, or to make a detour through the center of the town.) Perhaps, Johann suggested with a smile, the barracks had even already been emptied of its arms and ammunition. The man at Bozen would know.

The colonel said nothing. But when Johann stopped in the shadow of some trees just where a rough track, emerging darkly from a small wood, joined the road they had followed, Lennox could almost feel the colonel's unwillingness to leave the lorry guarded by the four other men. His plan, like most bright ideas, seemingly excellent at the moment of discovery, was beginning to tarnish with each minute of delay. The colonel had started worrying again. The barracks were his chief objective: he disliked having them made into secondary importance.

"If anyone starts asking questions just remember to keep talking German," he said to the men. "Your story is that the lorry has broken down on your way back to the station after delivering the officers to the prison camp. Don't shoot, unless you are desperate. Get rid of any curious stranger quietly." The colonel looked round him. The countryside was peaceful, the isolated houses were dark and seemingly asleep even at this early hour. The lights in Bozen itself were scattered and dim: there were no shots, no shouts, to break through the deep silence of the night. The lorry was swallowed up in the trees' shadows. Anyone passing along the road wouldn't even notice it. All was well, so far. And yet his worry grew.

The colonel looked at the faint green numbering on his watch. "We've taken exactly six minutes to reach this point from the prison courtyard," he said. "If Lennox and I aren't back at the lorry in fifteen minutes flat, return to the camp. Remember to signal with your headlights as you approach it so that our guards will recognize you at once. Lieutenant Simmins, check the time." The two officers compared their wrist watches. There was a tightening in the faces of the waiting men.

Johann moved impatiently, and the colonel slowly left the lorry's shadow. Lennox, at a sign, followed with equal reluctance. Johann was leading them into the wood by a well-marked path, so carefully cleared of trees and branches that Lennox realized it was as well used as it was marked. It was only the black blanket of night, smothering recognizable shapes and distorting them into ominous shadows, which made this small wood seem so mysterious and dangerous. In daylight it would probably seem a very simple and innocent place.

When they had traveled less than a hundred yards (at first slowly, then more surely as their eyes became accustomed to the depths of shadows around them) and found themselves in a clearing Lennox knew his guess had been accurate enough. The path had been merely the entrance to a beer garden. For in the clearing before him were wooden tables and benches, and beyond these lay a two-storied wooden house built in the Tyrolese manner with broad eaves overshadowing its side walls. An inn. That's what it would be: a nice, woodland place for a picnic or a family reunion.

A family reunion. Lennox's lips tightened, and he stared at the chalet, still and shuttered, lit only by the clear stars which shone so brightly above the clearing.

The colonel had halted too, but he was watching Johann. "Is this the place?" he asked.

Johann nodded. He was already walking over the stretch of soft, fine grass towards the house. He motioned impatiently with his hand for them to follow.

"Stay here," the colonel said quietly, grasping Lennox suddenly by the arm. "Keep in the shadows. I'll do the bargaining. I think I'm getting the hang of the boy's dialect now. If I need you I'll call you. If I meet trouble I'll fire a shot. Then you will get back to the lorry and tell them to make for the camp at once. All quite clear?"

"If you are expecting trouble, sir, then I'd better—"

"No. You get back to the lorry to warn them." The colonel's voice was gloomy. His thin face was white under the starlight, but there was a determined cheerfulness in the smile he gave Lennox. Somehow it depressed Lennox still more. But his resentment against the colonel was disappearing. He was beginning to understand the colonel. He was even beginning to feel sorry for him.

Lennox settled back into the shadow of a group of trees, watched the tall, thin figure hurry after Johann, and then stared at the wood around him. "Rather he than I," Lennox said to himself, as the officer followed Johann into the inn. He thought of the colonel's gaunt white face, lined with perpetual anxieties, tight-lipped and cold-eyed with worry. That's what responsibility did to a man. You could never make a decision without worrying whether it was the best one; you could never refuse a possibility without thinking of a lost opportunity. Whichever way you chose, you worried. Now the colonel was probably beginning to wish he hadn't started on this plan of Johann's. And yet, as Lennox waited, more nervously than he was willing to admit, he couldn't see what else the colonel should have done. For the men in the prison camp had little chance as matters stood now: they hadn't enough arms, they had wounded among them who couldn't travel or fight, they didn't know much about this countryside. The only alternative, as far as Lennox could see, would be for the band of prisoners to scatter and to look out each for himself. That would have been all right for Lennox or any who had been planning escape, but the others wouldn't have much of a chance. And if any were captured then there would be no chance at all for them. The dead Germans in the little castle, up there on the hill behind him, would decide that.

Lennox stared at the wood's shadows around him. He stared at the door of the silent chalet. He stared at the faintly glowing numbers on his wrist watch. He held the revolver in the German coat pocket so tightly that his weakened hand grew quite numb. Six minutes, eight minutes. He shifted his weight and tautened as a twig broke under his foot. Eleven minutes. The door opened at last. He raised the revolver slowly, supporting his hand with his left fist. The colonel was there all right. And Johann. And two other men—young men by their easy stride. As the group approached him he could see the strangers were wearing the usual dress of the South Tyrol—leather breeches, light-colored wool stockings, shapeless felt hats, tweed jackets.

Lennox could see by the way the men walked that much had been decided. It didn't need the colonel's quiet "Everything laid on" to tell him that it had been thoroughly decided.

As they left the clearing to plunge into the wood the colonel was saying, "These chaps have already moved all guns and ammunition from the barracks—they knew the Germans would occupy it as soon as the railway was secured. The guns have been hidden in this wood, and these men are going to help us load the lorry with what it can hold. They say they've enough ammunition, too. They will take care of our wounded, and shelter them until they are strong enough to follow us. They will give us guides to help us by-pass the German troops in this valley. After that we fight on our own to the south. If we move quickly enough we have a sporting chance to reach the Allied front before the Germans can reinforce the gaps which the Italians have left in their defense lines. God knows where our front will be before we reach it; it may be in Rome and moving northwards before the month is out if the Italians really rise up against the Germans. But wherever they are we'll make a stab at finding them. We can't go far wrong if we keep going south."

Lennox said nothing for a full minute. Everything was settled, then; as fully settled as it could be. The men up in the castle had now, at least, a fighting chance. Sporting was the word that the colonel had used. Fighting would be nearer the truth. After his years of experience with the Italians Lennox wasn't so sure that the Allies' path to Rome would be made easy for them. He was willing to bet that the colonel had not been fighting long in the Mediterranean theater. The colonel still believed in the milk of human kindness.

"What's the guarantee of good faith, sir?" he asked quietly. These Tyrolese had given too much without demanding something in return.

"You are. You are going up there with the boy, Johann." The colonel pointed northeast where the black mass of jagged peaks rose beyond the River Eisak. "There is a plateau up there which they call the Schlern. You will stay there, keeping your ears and eyes well open, until some of our men can be dropped in to join you."

Lennox stared through the darkness. The colonel must have felt his amazement, for he said quickly, "When we reach the Allied lines we'll get Intelligence onto the job. They'll send some of their men by parachute onto the Schlern to join you. We'll build up something there that will jolt the Huns."

Lennox thought of several observations to make on such optimism, but none seemed suitable to a superior officer. He said, more quietly than he felt, "Very good, sir."

The men round the lorry listened to the colonel's instructions. Below

them the lights in the town pinpricked the darkness. The three Tyrolese
stood quietly competent, eagerly ready. Everything was, as the colonel had
first said, everything was laid on.

The lorry had started back up the hill with its load of men and guns.
("Enough," the colonel had said, "enough for a starter, anyway. We'll collect more on our way south.")

Johann touched Lennox's arm. The Englishman was watching the crawling truck, already part of the night's blackness. Then he turned to follow
the boy. To the northeast the mountains were still as remote and fantastic
as they had seemed to Lennox staring at them through the barbed wire
of a prison camp. Then they had been remote and fantastic because they
had symbolized freedom. Now they themselves had become a prison,
from which there was no escape. And he was walking into that prison, if
not willingly then certainly without a revolver at his back.

"Why do you laugh?" Johann asked curiously. "It isn't wise to laugh yet.
We are too near these houses. Tomorrow, up on the Schlern, you can laugh
all you want to."

Lennox was suddenly serious. "Yes, I'll laugh then," he said grimly. He
followed the boy's sure steps, and wondered how many weeks it would take
his comrades to reach the Allied lines. But he didn't let himself think of
the feeling they would have when they could be back with their own
people again.

Johann's quiet voice held its own revolt. "I had other plans too, for tonight," he was saying, almost reprovingly. "My girl is down in Bozen, and
when I don't turn up to see her as I promised she will start worrying about
the stray bullets which were flying this afternoon. And I don't know
whether she is safe either. She is not the kind to stay at home and hide
under the bed. So," his voice sharpened, "let's start moving."

Lennox thought how easy it was to forget that other people had their
own private worries and disappointments. To appease this sudden twinge
of conscience, he said politely, "Is she from the Tyrol too?"

"Eva?" Johann asked quickly, and by that quickness and that pleased
note in his voice he showed that he wanted the other's friendship. "Yes,
she's from my village. Now she is living in Bozen with relatives." The boy
talked on, quietly, interminably—about his village, which had been called
Montefierro for the last twenty-four years, but which now reverted to the
name of Hinterwald that had suited it very well for over three hundred
years; about Eva Mussner.

Lennox followed him obediently, imitating his short plodding step up
the steep incline of hillside. But Lennox said nothing at all. He began to
regret his simple question. The friendly warmth in this boy's voice beat
against the cold wall which imprisonment had built round his emotions.
He had learned to live within himself. Miller's death tonight only proved

that affection and human liking brought deeper sorrow. The man who lived alone could laugh at life and tell it to do its damnedest. That way, a man was less vulnerable. What he wouldn't allow himself to enjoy, he couldn't be afraid of losing. Lennox stopped listening to Johann; his uneasiness turned to resentment. Hell, he thought irritably, what's this Hinterwald or Eva Mussner to me? He scarcely noticed when the boy's mumbling words grew farther spaced, and the sudden burst of confidence became a frozen block of silence.

Far to the south of them came a sudden burst of rifle fire. Lennox halted instinctively and looked back. It wasn't an attack on the prison camp, for the machine guns, now firing heavily, were down in the valley.

Johann pulled his arm impatiently. "It is only the Germans and some angry Italians shooting it out," he said. "And that will be good for your friends. The Germans have many worries tonight."

Lennox watched the distant flashes of light, the sudden flaring of some ammunition or petrol dump. It was not an unpleasant feeling to turn his back on the skirmishing, to walk away into the darkness and leave those who had killed and mutilated so many of his friends now tearing at one another like the traitors in Dante's hell.

CHAPTER 7

The Schlern is really the highest of a group of mountains in the Dolomite Alps, but its name has come also to mean the high plateau of rolling meadows and forests over which the steep face of this rocky mass rises like some enormous fortress.

The road up to the Schlern begins in the Eisak Valley, which leads southward to Italy and northward through the Brenner Pass to Austria. The road ascends steeply, by sudden twists and sharp turns. It cuts through cliffs of rock by narrow tunnels; it holds precariously to the precipice edge; it arrives at last—much to the relief of the traveler—on what seems to be the top of the world. But relief gives way to amazement, for up here lies still another world: one of villages and scattered farms and churches, of winding roads and streams and green meadows, of forests and mountain peaks challenging to still greater height. This is the Schlernland, an island of Alpine scenery pushed into the sky. It isn't a naked, jutting kind of island, for the deep valleys surrounding it have their rugged waves of mountains too. On every side the sea of precipices is unending.

Perhaps it was because this road up to the Schlern was so treacherous in winter, or because the Germans found they had enough to worry about in keeping open the supply route in the Eisak Valley, that the Schlern had had one of its most peaceful winters. The Italian policemen, postmasters, soldiers, schoolteachers, and hotel owners had gone. The skiers had not come this winter, just as the mountain climbers had been absent last summer. The larger chalets and villas, which the wealthy Italians from Rome and Milan had built to give their children pleasant holidays, were now as empty as the small cottages abandoned by those Tyrolese who had listened to Hitler in 1939, and had moved into Austria. The people of the Schlern who had clung to their heritage, who had refused to put their trust in politicians' promises, called themselves—with their own grim smile—the survivors.

The winter had been hard. High on the Schlern a thick frozen blanket of snow had covered the gray peaks and the green slopes. The small villages, the scattered houses of forester and farmer, had fallen into a seeming sleep among the white mountains. Down in the valley below the Schlern, where the gap in the Dolomite highlands led north to the Brenner Pass, there were snow and sleet and cruel winds to huddle the people into their houses. There were other reasons, too. The Germans had taken possession: their soldiers patrolled through alternating ice and slush, as they guarded the railway line and the flow of supplies to the German armies in Italy. German edicts, German puppets, controlled the towns on the railway line. Allied bombing planes attacked them. Far to the south, in Italy, there were driving rain and earth so sodden that the fighting fronts churned into delaying mud. The hope that October had brought had become as frozen as the earth from which the Dolomite Alps rose so steeply. The winter had been hard.

In the houses high on the Schlern it was whispered that the Allies couldn't approach the Brenner until autumn now. Perhaps not even then. This spring would come too quickly to be of any use to people who waited four hundred miles north of the Allied lines. But hope was like the earth: it was frozen, but it was not dead. The old men, the gaunt-cheeked women, the remaining young men (who had escaped from the recruiting interest of any German ski patrol by vanishing into the thick pine forests which fringed the mountains' base), didn't talk very much. But they had their own thoughts. They listened in to the forbidden Allied broadcasts, and they were making their decisions. Here was a third group of foreigners who would come to invade the Dolomites. Would they be like the Italians or the Germans, who, once they came to a country, claimed possession? Or were these foreigners, who called themselves "The Allies," different? Were they really fighting for other peoples' freedom as well as their own? After twenty-five years of Italian domination the people on the Schlern, like all the Tyrolese on the other Dolomite slopes, were waiting for the autumn of 1944. If it couldn't be this spring which would end this waiting then let it be the autumn. It was more than a hope; in many hearts it had become a prayer.

The people went about their daily tasks as if there were no war. But they measured their food carefully, they listened eagerly to the radio, they hid their men from the German patrols, they pretended ignorance in reply to all the regulations and proclamations of the newly named "Alpenvorland." They never forgot that in the village of Kastelruth at the edge of the Schlern, where the road from the valley below came to rest on a gentle green slope, there was a token German garrison. They never forgot that these armed foreigners were there, not to give them a feeling of "protection," as the Germans said in the best gangster fashion, but to police the Schlern plateau and keep it under informal observation.

The Germans didn't expect trouble. The people of the South Tyrol were Austrians, after all. And Austria was now a part of Greater Germany. So the garrison was small, and its periodic patrols were less thorough as the winter severity increased. And if the Tyrolese up on this plateau had shown no response to the February proclamation, that all men between eighteen and fifty-five years of age must report to the German Military Headquarters in Bozen, then the Germans at Kastelruth blamed that on the slow and stubborn nature of the highlander. They would deal with him, once the more accessible districts of the South Tyrol had been brought into line. The Germans were quite content to play a waiting game.

But the peace of the mountains is a deceiving thing: the impassive face of the highlander is equally baffling. Neither the mountains nor the people who live among them are as simple as they look.

CHAPTER **8**

Peter Lennox watched the pools of green grass appear through the melting slush. With the same impatience, he had watched the first blanket of snow on the Schlern. But now there was a bitter feeling of failure added to the impatience, turning its edge to knife-sharp disappointment. The inactivity of the long winter months frayed his nerves. The people who had sheltered him had been decent and kind. He would admit that. But their very quietness, their acceptance of the fact that no message had come from any Allied Command, only added to his sense of failure. He had helped no one. He had been of no use to anyone. And the colonel and Jock and Ferry and all the others—whose names were even beginning to fade from his memory (he could only remember those of his fellow prisoners whom he had either liked or disliked very much)—had been either captured or killed. For that must be the explanation of this silence. There could be no other reason: that damned colonel couldn't have meant him to sit up here all winter, watching the snow clouds bank against a string of rocky teeth. Or could he have? When they had parted eight months ago down on the roadway outside of Bozen the colonel had talked of action, of urgent necessity. Action . . . urgent necessity—sugar-coating on a bitter pill, so that his inflated pride would let him swallow his disappointment about being left up here among a lot of women and boys and old men.

And now it was May. The last blot of snow had soaked into the sodden fields. Lennox had made up his mind. As he dressed in the small room which had become so familiar—with its narrow window tucked under the broad overhanging roof, with its carved wooden bed and thick soft mattress, with its one small table and chair, and white scrubbed floor—he was rehearsing the speech he would make.

"Frau Schichtl!" he would say. "What's the use of staying here any longer? The plan, which your highly esteemed brother in Bozen made, has definitely not come off. The only sensible thing now—begging your esteemed brother's pardon, for he seems a most determined man—is for me to leave your house and end the worry you've had ever since Johann brought me here. I had a plan for escape, and I haven't forgotten it. I'll reach the Allied lines. And I'll tell the Whosits all about you here on the Schlern. I'll tell them about the man from Bozen whom I have never met, and about the hatchet-faced old boys, who come on a Saturday evening to drink your homemade wine around the kitchen table and talk and talk and talk. And the Whosits will send the right men up here. Men who will talk and talk and talk, and feel perfectly happy because they know what they are doing. They won't have guilt every time they look at the mattress on a most comfortable bed; and they'll have so many plans inside their specially trained brains that they won't mind sitting in a room all day and every day. They enjoy hiding. That's part of their job. And they'll be really helpful. They'll parachute all over this place." He paused while he crossed over to the window to shut out the cold morning air.

"You are getting soft," he told himself angrily. "Now, where were you?" He stared at himself truculently in the small square of mirror. He saw a white-faced young man with even features, and strong eyebrows now drawn together in a bad-tempered frown. His hair was too long, his chin needed a shave. The gray eyes were clear and direct, but their look was hard enough to jolt him away from the mirror. He didn't like his looks. He picked up the loose jacket of gray tweed and pulled it over his white shirt and black waistcoat as he started to descend the bare staircase. His heavy shoes, low-cut, ugly and strong, struck angrily on the white-scrubbed wood. He slowed up, and set his feet down more quietly. In the kitchen below was a bright wood fire in a neat stove, the smell of newly baked bread, the early sun streaming through the small windows, and Frau Schichtl.

She had poured out a cup of new milk as she heard him leave the room upstairs, and she was now measuring the careful spoonfuls of homemade jam onto his plate. The newly baked bread was wrapped in its white cloth on the dresser: on the table was a staler loaf. (New bread was too uneconomical: it sliced extravagantly and was eaten too quickly.) The rough linen cloth on the table was clean; the large white coarse cups were clean; the room was clean. Everything was neat and clean, from the well-scrubbed face and well-brushed hair of Frau Schichtl to the stiff little curtains of white lace above the precise row of ivy pots on the sill.

Lennox said a mild good-morning, and fingered his chin nervously as he slid into his chair at the table. He ought to have shaved after all, he thought, as he glanced up at Frau Schichtl's quiet face. She had the same wide-spaced blue eyes as her son, Johann. Now these eyes were watching him curiously. He wished she would sit down. She was almost his height, and that was tall for a woman. Now, as she stood there so impassively, her strong arms and capable hands flowing from her broad shoulders, her well-shaped head erect on the long, firm neck, he felt as young as Johann. He resented it. And that gave him courage.

"Frau Schichtl!" he began. "Frau Schichtl, what's the use of—"

But she had turned her back towards the door and was listening to something else. He watched the decided curve of jaw and the line of high cheekbone in profile.

"Anything wrong?" he asked.

"No. I only thought I heard Johann. He came home at dawn today. He's asleep now. He had a long journey this time." She moved suddenly to the entrance hall, which formed the sitting room of the house, and stood listening at the foot of the staircase. He could see her, the tall, strong figure in its severe black dress, intent on listening. The beams of light from the kitchen and sitting-room windows made a good angle against the soft background of darkened pine walls. The still darker furniture formed solid shapes, bright surfaced with polishing, so that they held the glancing light. Interior, he thought, interior in the Dutch manner. And then he glanced down at his right hand. Frau Schichtl, coming back into the kitchen with her slow, even step, saw the bitter smile on his lips. She forgot about Johann.

"What is it, Peter?" she asked quickly.

Lennox's right hand slid under the table. He lifted the heavy cup of milk with his left hand. He didn't want to test the right hand now, not with Frau Schichtl's sharp blue eyes watching him.

"What news does Johann bring?" he countered.

"A lot. About many things." She stopped watching him and moved suddenly over to the oven. She unwrapped the white cloth which lay on its side ledge. She picked up a loaf and cut a thick slice with its floury golden crust still warm.

"Try this," she said, and offered him the new bread.

Lennox stared at her in surprise. He took the bribe with almost a smile. But Frau Schichtl was now too preoccupied with her own thoughts even to notice it.

"Why don't you like us?" she asked suddenly, staring at the floor in front of his feet.

Lennox moved restlessly. "I do like you," he said very evenly. "You have been very kind."

"Yet you are not happy. If you really liked us then you would be happy."

"That doesn't follow."

She raised her eyes and studied his face with a puzzled look. "You want to leave," she said at last. "You think this is a prison." It was a statement, rather than a challenge, and she said it so sadly that Lennox found himself answering. He tried to keep the irritation out of his voice, but his words were tight and hard.

"That," he said, "is a fact about me, and not about you or about the people of those mountains out there." He nodded towards the window. "You've all been kind. You've given me as much food as you've had for yourself. Sometimes more. You've given me shelter. You've hidden me well. I understand why I can't leave this house through the day, why I've got to stay upstairs most of the time. I understand why the neighboring houses aren't even supposed to know I am here. I understand why no one sees me except you, and Johann, and the local Committee who come up to visit you once a week. Your brother who lives in Bozen has provided excellent identification papers proving I am your nephew from the North Tyrol. The story is plausible, I know: I came here this winter, after being discharged from the German army, and the wounds I got in North Africa keep me close to this house. You've done your best for me. I know all that. But I also know your risk is greater than mine. I'll lose one life if I am caught. But you'll lose everything—Johann's life, your friends' lives, this house, everything. So, Frau Schichtl, I know this isn't a prison. But I still feel a prisoner. That's a fact about me."

Frau Schichtl said slowly, "I don't understand." She passed a flat hand over the side of her brow, smoothing the soft curls at the temple into the heavy sleekness of her hair.

"I am not a prisoner of your friends," Lennox said gently, "I'm a prisoner of events."

"But so are we."

He shook his head impatiently. "My job for eight months has amounted to sitting here and doing nothing. That's a fine way, I must say, to fight a war."

"But that wasn't your fault. Or ours. We've been waiting, like you, for instructions. We could act, all of us, but we might do the wrong things. We might bring the Germans down on us like an avalanche, and then we never could do anything. Then, when we *were* needed, we would be unable to help. Don't you see, Peter, we've got to wait until we get the right orders?"

"But we may never get them. Something's gone wrong. The Allies don't even know we are waiting for one small sign from them."

"Surely—" Frau Schichtl began, and then stopped. The lines at the side of her mouth deepened. Her eyelids drooped as if to hide the hurt look in her eyes. Suddenly she came to life again. She shrugged her shoulders, and there was a difficult smile on her lips.

"I know," she said, in a low voice. "I've thought of all of that too." And as Lennox stared at her in amazement, she began to straighten the tablecloth, smoothing off the crumbs of bread into her cupped hand. Then she laid two plates neatly opposite each other, and two cups for milk. For a moment he wondered if she had waited to eat breakfast with Johann. And then he saw that she was lifting the kerchief and green cape which hung on one of the wooden pegs near the door. She was leaving, as she did each morning, for the small school down in the village of Hinterwald. Last autumn Frau Schichtl had volunteered to become a teacher again. The Italian teachers had gone, and Frau Schichtl had taken over the job of keeping the school open. That, as she had explained with one of her infrequent smiles, at least prevented a stranger from coming into the Hinterwald to teach—a stranger sent by the Germans. Now she was gathering together the textbooks she had studied last night and the notebook in which she had so carefully prepared today's lessons. Her pupils would have been amused at the homework which their new teacher had to do.

"Who has come here with Johann?" Lennox asked, looking pointedly at the two cups on the table.

Frau Schichtl's thoughts came back into the small room. She said quickly, "I meant to tell you. It's my brother. He has some special news for you, and for the others."

"The man from Bozen," Lennox said softly. "So he's here." He smiled, and then he began to laugh.

Frau Schichtl looked at him almost sadly. "That's the first time I've heard you laugh," she said, "and I don't know why you are laughing."

"I was thinking what a fine soldier I've become. I didn't even hear your brother or Johann arrive. I'd have done just as well if they had been a couple of Germans."

"In that case," Frau Schichtl said, "I would have found a way of wakening you." She didn't say, as she might well have done, "Please don't think that everything is perfectly normal and safe just because I try to give the appearance of being normal and unworried. Don't think that, young man."

Peter Lennox rose and went towards the door of the kitchen. "I'll get back to my room," he said. Rules of the house. When Frau Schichtl went out he had to stay upstairs with the bedroom door locked. Then he added, "I'm sorry. I've worried you. I never thought you did worry, because you always look so calm. If I had known your brother was here I would have kept my remarks for him." He touched her awkwardly on the shoulder. She smiled suddenly, and the lines of her mouth were no longer tired or unhappy.

She moved slowly towards the entrance door. "Perhaps I should have told you more this winter," she said, "and then you wouldn't have worried because you thought there was nothing to worry about."

Lennox had no answer to that. He began to climb the stairs. He was glad, unexpectedly, that he hadn't made the speech he had prepared. He ought to have remembered that women, no matter where they came from or what language they spoke, always had the last word. Never argue with a woman, he thought: it's a waste of good breath. When he reached the small square landing he heard the entrance door open and then shut. The heavy sounds seemed to tell him that the conversation in the kitchen—as far as Frau Schichtl was concerned—was equally closed. Even the way a woman shut a door could be her last word. He smiled in spite of himself.

CHAPTER **9**

He loitered in the darkness of the upper hall for some moments, wondering in which room Johann and his uncle were sleeping. This wooden house was solidly built: he could hear nothing. The silence oppressed him. He moved quickly into his own room, and, out of habit, twisted the clumsy key in its iron lock.

From the window, shielded by the white starched curtain from outside eyes, he could see Frau Schichtl making her way carefully round the pools of heavy mud. The road to Hinterwald was scarcely more than a cart track. It served as a link between Hinterwald and these outlying houses, and as a short cut over the wooded hillside to the next village. A better but longer road twisted through the meadows farther to the west. It was the "foreigners' road," Frau Schichtl had said. But whether that meant it was built by foreigners or used by foreigners, Lennox didn't know. At least, the Germans didn't use this cart track. The Schichtl house, and the Kasal farmhouse some fifty yards away, might have been a hundred miles from anywhere. Lennox could have counted on one hand the number of strangers whom he had watched passing in the last eight months.

The Kasals' eldest daughter was waiting at the doorway of the farm-house as usual. Her yellow hair gleamed in the early morning sunlight as she ran to join Frau Schichtl. The girl was laughing. Her bare feet and legs ploughed carelessly through the spring mud. Her shoes were held safely together in one hand, her school books were in the other. He envied her the freedom with which she could walk and laugh. He opened the window carefully, slowly. The fresh air brought the smell of grass and rain, of pine trees and free mountain winds into his small room. He had an impulse to lean out of the window and feel the touch of the early morning sun on his face. But he stayed dutifully behind the white screens, under the broad, overhanging eaves, and looked at the green alp sloping gently down towards the village.

The Kasal house was silent now. Smoke was trickling placidly from its wide stone chimney. Its broad roof was safely anchored against winter storms by large stones roped together. The bright blue shutters, whitened at the seams, needed their spring coat of paint. The pile of logs under the ground-floor windows had grown small. Soon the woodcutters would need to go to work in the forest. The window boxes on the carved wooden bal-cony, which ran across the front of the house, waited for their load of flowers. The five gaunt cows had been allowed into the highest field today and were guarded there by the Kasals' dog, so that they would not wander into the lower pastures, which were still waterlogged. From across the fields Lennox could hear Alois Kasal's voice giving encouragement and commands, and the sound of the harness bells on the plow horse as it obeyed him. Spring, Lennox thought, and hope was stirring everywhere. The dead sleep of winter was gone. Now he knew the reason for his mount-ing bitterness: when it was the time for hope, and you knew that there could be no hope, you became bitter. He hated everyone and everything in that moment. Most of all, he hated himself.

He looked at his watch. It was now eight o'clock in the morning. At two o'clock Frau Schichtl would be home and would start preparing dinner. At five o'clock they would have their one real meal of the day. At seven o'clock they would sit around the kitchen oven. Frau Schichtl would go over her work for school next day. Lennox would practice drawing with his stupid left hand, and wonder bitterly if ever it could be taught to obey his mind. At eight o'clock they would try to hear the news from Allied broadcasts. They would strain to catch a small piece of information through the con-stant background of interference. And then, if the weather were good and the moon was weak, Lennox would take a short walk towards the pine forest at the back of the house. Or more often, when the weather was so bad that it was dangerous to move outside, he would stand in the shadows of the opened back door with a darkened room behind him, and stare into the freezing, wind-swept night. He would lose his thoughts in the swaying mass of pine branches, in the hard resolute face of rocky peaks which rise behind the forest's crest. He would wait until the blood in his veins froze with the cold mountain air in spite of the green *loden* cape round his shoulders. He would wait until his hope was frozen, too. (No one was coming: this mission was useless. He was wasting his time, losing his energy, bringing danger on this house and its neighbors. And each month his maimed right hand became gradually and steadily more helpless, as if the old wound were now paying him out for the perfunctory treatment it had been given in a prison camp.) Then, before nine o'clock, Frau Schichtl would stand shivering behind him, prodding him on the spine until he turned back into the house and closed the door, barring it, shutting out another day of his life. At nine o'clock the lights were extinguished, the oven fire was carefully banked for the night, and he would lie in this lonely room, listening to the roof's strange groans and the uncanny noises of the wooden walls. At first he used to think they were the sounds of movement outside the house, and he would rise quickly to stand beside the cold window. But now his alarms had vanished with his hopes, and he no longer leaped out of bed in anxiety or expectation. Now he expected exactly nothing.

For a moment he hesitated, his eyes still on his watch. What should he do today? He could read the books he already knew by heart. He could straighten the bed and put things into order. He could practice some more left-handed writing on the few precious pieces of paper he had borrowed from Frau Schichtl's school notebook. He could do some physical exercises, which was the only way he kept his muscles firm. He could slump on the bed and memorize once more the things he had learned in the last months. Or he could slump on the bed and think of the old days. Or he could slump on the bed. After eight months these suggestions had lost all variety. He went over them nonchalantly, and was no longer amazed that his thinking was not done in English but in the Austrian dialect of the Tyrol. He had started this habit about Christmas, so that he would really learn the language. Now it seemed the natural way to express his thoughts. He wasn't laughing any more, either, at the strange place names of the Schlern. If only Dusty Miller had been here with him, or big Jock . . . someone to talk to. Someone who would not always be polite. Someone who'd argue with you. Someone who'd see the joke in everyday names. "Puflatsch, Bad Ratzes, Eggen-Tal," he said aloud, but he didn't even smile now. Miller could have woven half an hour's conversation out of them and raised a dozen laughs. Lennox could have done that too—once.

"Time I was getting out of here, and getting out pretty damn quick," he said emphatically. Now that the man from Bozen was here it would be easier to give his ultimatum. It hadn't been so easy with Frau Schichtl. Three times now, upstairs in this room, he had made the resolution that he was leaving. Three times, downstairs, his resolution had melted away. Somehow a woman always made you feel a swine if you insisted on doing something she didn't want you to do. Today, it was true, he had begun to say what was on his mind. He smiled, remembering the way in which the door had closed.

"Five minutes past eight," he said. He talked aloud quite a lot now. Well, he had certainly used up five minutes of this day. He looked down at the roadway, and wondered how slow it would be to travel through roads as mud-filled as that. The ground was thawing out now, and the water from the melting snow on the mountains streamed down onto the meadows. But Frau Schichtl had said it drained off quickly. She had said the higher fields and woods were already passable. If Johann would guide him by the secret paths known to those who had been brought up in this district the journey would be much simpler. And once he was out of this chain of mountains he could strike, alone, southeast across the plains. He could reach the Adriatic and Jugoslavia this time. His plans to reach them were still as fresh in his mind as they had been eight months ago.

He stiffened. He stood motionless, his eyes rigid. On the road, slipping heavily on the yellowish mud, were two figures. They were walking towards Hinterwald. They hesitated as they neared the house, halted beside a tree. The taller figure seemed to be urging the other on. They started again towards the house. The uncertain one was limping now. He was leaning heavily on his friend's shoulder.

Lennox moved quickly. He was out of his room, and he was knocking sharply on all the three doors on the landing before he had even got his thoughts straight. From one door came Johann's voice, and then a deeper voice asking, "What the devil?"

It was Johann who appeared. His sleepy eyes opened fully as Lennox pushed past him to confront the bearded man who was sitting up in bed.

"Two men are approaching this house," Lennox was saying. "American flyers, I think. One of you had better get downstairs and put out the Welcome mat."

"What the devil—" the bearded man began. He rubbed the back of his head and yawned widely. But he was reaching for his trousers lying over the rail at the foot of the bed. "I'll go," he grumbled. He glanced at his large silver watch on the chair beside him. "Three hours' sleep. Hand me those boots, damn you. Thanks. So you are Lennox? I'm Paul Mahlknecht. Johann, stand by. If I call come downstairs. Lennox, you stay up here."

Lennox nodded. Paul Mahlknecht was already hurrying out of the room, buttoning his trousers with one hand, slipping his broad bright-colored braces over his shoulders with the other. He lifted his waistcoat from the chair as he kicked the door open. He gave Lennox a rueful shake of his head as he left the room. "No rest these days," he said, with considerable enjoyment.

Downstairs the front door was opened. There was the sound of heavy, dragging footsteps.

"Anyone here?" a strange voice called. It repeated the question in English.

Lennox stood very still. Then he crossed over to the door and closed it quietly.

"Perhaps they are *your* friends," Johann said, with his broad, simple smile.

"Perhaps." Lennox was too tense. He walked over to the window. This time he was looking from the back of the house, over to the pine woods, up to the mountains. This was the view he had seen each night as he had waited for someone who had never come. Now they had come. He couldn't believe it.

"Perhaps," he said again, trying to fight down his emotion.

CHAPTER **10**

Johann was talking as he dressed. He was half grumbling, half pleased. "Another journey," he was saying. "I've just finished taking three Americans into Jugoslavia. God, can't they give a man some rest?"

Peter Lennox smiled at that. He turned from the window to look at the "man." The boy's face was hidden by a rough towel as he polished his red-apple cheeks.

"So that's what you've been doing in these last months," Lennox said. He realized now why Johann had kept silent about such a job. Lennox would have wanted to go along too.

"That's what I've been doing." Pride was in Johann's voice. "Personal escort service." He threw the towel at Lennox, and began pulling on his shirt.

"Meet any trouble?"

"It's getting more difficult," Johann acknowledged. "The first batches were easy. The Germans never guessed we would help any Allied flyers. But now the remains of several planes have been found in the South Tyrol, without a live American or Britisher to show for them. So the Germans are beginning to wonder. No grounded flyer could make his way alone out of these mountains unless he were an expert climber and had a mountaineering map. He would have to come down into the valleys and ask for help. Now the Germans are increasing their garrisons and patrols. They are in a nasty temper about that, too." The smile had left Johann's face. Watching him, Lennox suddenly realized that Johann was no longer a boy. But then, journeys over and around these Dolomite peaks in winter would age anyone. Death lay waiting at many a twisting corner in a mountain path.

"And how have you been?" Johann's politeness was formal. He was really listening for any possible call from downstairs. When Lennox gave no answer to that he went on cheerily, "Got to keep an ear cocked, you know." But his eyes were thoughtful and he was watching the Englishman.

"What you need is some exercise," Johann said suddenly. "Perhaps it wouldn't be a bad idea if you started some mountain climbing too, soon."

"Perhaps I shall," Lennox said grimly.

Johann was still watching him, as if he could read the meaning behind the short words. "I don't blame you," he said at last. "Being shut up in this house would drive me crazy. But you can't tell that to my mother, though." He laughed and then stopped short. He opened the door slightly. It was Mahlknecht, calling in very definite terms for both of them to hurry up and come downstairs.

"Both of us?" Lennox asked, and there was a first real note of gladness in his voice. His hope had grown to a certainty.

Johann pushed him good-naturedly out of the room towards the staircase. "Let Uncle Paul set the pace," he whispered, "Cousin Peter from the North Tyrol." He was grinning widely. Lennox was smiling too as they clattered down the wooden stairs.

In the sitting room there were mud-caked footsteps on the floor, and two pairs of heavy flying boots lying side by side. That must have been the point where Paul Mahlknecht had stopped the two strangers and made them take off their boots. Frau Schichtl's rules were observed even by the formidable brother from Bozen, it seemed.

Mahlknecht had chosen to remain standing. The two flyers were sitting on the hard wooden bench against the wall near the stove. They were huddling towards the heat of its wood fire. On that seat the light from the two kitchen windows fell sharply across their faces. Their eyes looked up as Johann and Lennox entered.

Mahlknecht said, "One of them speaks a little German. The other doesn't. They don't seem to understand me very well."

Lennox, conscious of the strangers' eyes watching Johann and him curiously, kept his face emotionless. But the tide of hope which had surged through his heart only a minute ago suddenly ebbed. These men hadn't come seeking him. They had obviously not even asked for him; and they couldn't even talk German properly. The men who would be sent must certainly be able to talk and understand the Austrian dialect of the Tyrol. And then Lennox was conscious of another thing: Mahlknecht, whose voice upstairs had held less accent than Johann's, was now using the coarsest form of dialect. Words were slurred, endings were altered, some consonants were eliminated, vowels were broadened to the point of caricature. Lennox had to strain to catch the meaning of these three sentences. And a signal seemed to have been given to Johann. He stopped lounging, drew his hands out of the pockets of his trousers, and decided not to sit at the table as he had intended. He strolled carelessly over to one of the windows, and leaned against the broad sill with his back to the light. Lennox chose a chair in the darkest corner of the kitchen, between Johann and the door. It was then that he wondered why Paul Mahlknecht should have called him downstairs along with Johann. Unless these men had been sent to make contact with him, it was dangerous and stupid to bring him down here. But the dark, bearded face of Mahlknecht with its broad brow, deep-set and thoughtful eyes gave no answer. And something in the rich, deep calmness of this man showed his strength and will and judgment. Peter Lennox sat back in his chair. He was watching the two strangers now. If he had been brought down here then there was some reason. He would have to find it.

"Does no one speak English?" the taller of the two strangers asked. He spoke slowly in German, looking anxiously at Johann and then at Lennox. He was a dark-haired, broad-shouldered man with irregular features. The other had a charming, pretty-boy look, with fair hair and a delicate cut to the bones of his face. His light gray eyes were quite blank of expression, as if he had come to the end of his resistance. He would be a tiger among the girls, Lennox thought, but this was definitely not one of his better moments.

Mahlknecht drew a deeply curved pipe from his pocket. He concentrated on lighting it. His eyes met Lennox's. There was a single urgent message in them. Then they fell to watching a briefly flaring strand of tobacco. He packed the smoking bowl more tightly with his thumb, and then took a long pull at the yellowed pipe. Lennox wanted to smile: this was the treatment with a vengeance. He had been given the same long silences, the same pauses between question and answer, when he had first come here. The only difference was that he had been offered something to smoke, something to eat and drink. The only difference. . . . Lennox sat motionless in the shadowy corner, withdrawing into the anonymity of its stillness. But his eyes were doubly watchful now, and his mind was worried.

Mahlknecht began to speak, telling Johann and Lennox that here were two American flyers who had crashed some miles away after yesterday's attack on the Brenner railway. They were the only survivors. They had walked through the night. They wanted help to take them out of these mountains.

The two flyers were watching Mahlknecht with intelligent concentration. They seemed reassured by his voice, for they leaned back against the wall as if the action was now taken out of their hands. The dark-haired man was beginning to feel warmer: he opened his lambskin-lined flying jacket, and pulled it off his shoulders. He wore a faded and worn American flyer's blouse, decorated with three medals and the insignia of captain. The fair-haired flyer followed his example. Again there was an American blouse, well-fitted and this time less worn. There were decorations along the left breast pocket, and a lieutenant's bar. Both men were lusty specimens: there was a natural glow of health on their skins, their eyes were clear and alert. The fair-haired one drew a crushed packet of American cigarettes out of his blouse pocket, and lit one with an efficient lighter. He was sitting more erect now, as if his initial exhaustion had passed. He listened in silence, his eyes watchful, while his companion spoke.

"Will you help us? We need a place to sleep, some food and drink, and a guide tonight to take us south through the mountain passes." The man's German was ungrammatical. It was slow and halting. But some vague disturbing emotion jangled an alarm in Peter Lennox's mind. The man's German was ungrammatical, but words he used were easy, colloquial words, and they were correctly pronounced. If you used such words so naturally why should there be such grammatical mistakes? Why the long pauses between fluent phrases? These things didn't match.

Lennox glanced at Johann and Paul Mahlknecht. They had noticed no inconsistency in the man's speech. Johann was still watching the flyers placidly, neither believing nor disbelieving. Paul Mahlknecht drew patiently at his pipe, one hand cupping its heavy bowl, the other tucked into his belt. His brown eyes were watchful under their heavy brows, but there had been no change in his expression during this last minute. I'm imagining things, Lennox thought angrily. He hated any proof of these months of loneliness: he had become too damned jumpy, too suspicious, too bloody-well sensitive. And yet the uneasiness in his mind wouldn't leave him. Johann and his uncle hadn't noticed the strange unbalance in this foreigner's speech, but then they had never had to learn to speak German as a foreigner. They had grown up with the language. And Lennox, remembering his own first struggles to talk German, thought of the stilted vocabulary and the mistakes in pronunciation which went with grammatical errors and stupid pauses.

"Why did you come here?" Mahlknecht was asking slowly. He was fussing with his pipe again. It seemed as if nothing was going to hurry him. The quiet room, the quiet fields and trees beyond the windows, gave emphasis to his deliberateness. The two flyers were beginning to be restless. The blond lieutenant fingered the decorations on his chest, as if to win the three peasants' trust and sympathy. The captain began replying. He was explaining that a house near the plane crash had sheltered them yesterday, that they had been told of men who lived under the Schlern Mountain who would be able to help them, that they had walked all night with the massive peak to guide them.

Lennox was only listening to the man's voice and the way he used it.

He didn't listen to the words. He was suddenly convinced that Paul Mahlknecht had called him down here to make a decision. He had been called down here to determine if these men were really American flyers. The responsibility of refusing help to possibly honest friends had been placed on him. He glanced quickly at Mahlknecht. The same short but insistent look which had been given him when he entered the room was his reply. Now he was indeed convinced: Mahlknecht needed his help; Mahlknecht was somehow doubtful; Mahlknecht depended on his being able to judge a real American when he saw one.

He could have laughed. He had known Americans. Some had been with him in the second Italian camp in which he had been imprisoned. One of them had actually made that attempted escape with him, and they had come to be pretty good friends. But how was that going to make him an expert on recognizing an American? If these two strangers had been British he couldn't have been an expert on them either. The Americans and British varied too much: it was only on the stage or screen that you found stock characteristics. If he could have talked in English he could have tried some operational slang on them. Then he might have learned something. Or he could have spoken about New York. His American friend used to talk a lot about food, about certain restaurants in New York, until Lennox almost believed that he had eaten there himself. But he couldn't speak in English. He was a peasant living near Hinterwald. He could have laughed in his frustration, but there wasn't any time for laughing. Desperately he tried to think of some way, some way to find out.

"But we know of no one who could help," Mahlknecht was saying. He was playing for time, waiting for Lennox's help. "My nephew here reports for service in Bozen this week. I myself know only the mountains which lie above us. My other nephew is ill as you can see. He was honourably discharged with wounds after having fought in Libya. There is no one here who can help you. And we know of no one who could."

It struck Lennox that, for a man who could speak little German, the captain was fairly quick at understanding dialect.

"There must be some one in this village who would help us," he said quickly. "We cannot enter the village in daylight. You could at least send your young nephew to the village for someone who will help us." The voice was pathetic in its urgency.

Lennox leaned forward. The palms of his hands were hot and damp. In German he asked, "What are these?" He pointed to the ribbons on the flyer's chest.

The captain frowned in annoyance. "Medals." He turned towards Mahlknecht again. "We are desperate. We need—"

"What for?" Lennox asked. His was obviously a one-track mind.

"For campaigns," the flyer answered impatiently. "Please help—"

"Where?"

The two flyers exchanged bitter glances.

The captain said, pointing, "This is for Egypt and Libya, this for Tunisia, this is a D.F.C. for battle."

"Libya," Lennox said reminiscently. "I was there too. And I was in Egypt. But I got no medals, only bullet holes. Where were you in Egypt?"

The captain took a deep breath. "Everywhere."

"But there weren't airfields everywhere," Lennox said slowly, with the obstinate logic of a simple man who lived among simple people. "Where was your field? I once was in an attack near a British airfield. There were Americans there, too. That's where I got this." He held up his scarred right hand. He smiled to show that there was no ill feeling. "Perhaps you or your friends gave it to me."

The captain smiled back uneasily. "Perhaps," he said.

"Where was your airfield? The one we attacked was at Beni Jara. Did you know it? About five miles south of a place they called Himeimat. That was a big one. We fought two weeks near there. That's where I got wounded." Lennox's palms were no longer sweating. He was beginning even to enjoy himself. South of Himeimat was the ugliest piece of salt marsh where no aircraft could ever have landed. And Beni Jara was a name that had just occurred to him. It sounded good enough, he thought. In fact, it sounded damn good.

"I was stationed nearer El Alamein," the captain said. He mentioned a well-known airfield. But it seemed to Lennox that the captain wasn't quite happy about something. With a consciously pleasant smile, the captain said quickly, "But of course we knew Beni Jara. In fact, I've refueled there. Why do you ask?" There was a touch of steel in his voice.

"It was a dangerous place. We attacked bravely. Perhaps you did win your medal."

"Of course I did." The captain was half indignant, half amused.

"I never won any medals," Lennox said. He looked at the scar on his hand.

The captain sensed an advantage. He pressed it hard. "The Germans treated the Austrians badly at Beni Jara," he said with sympathy. "Threw them against us in hopeless attacks. I remember my friends used to talk about that. Don't you see that is why you must help us? We are your friends. The Germans are enemies of both of us." He was looking at Mahlknecht as he ended. So was the lieutenant. It was the last appeal.

Lennox was looking too. And Mahlknecht's deep-set eyes, hardly flickering, caught that look. He saw the slow, careful movement of Lennox's head. He saw Lennox's tense left hand, the knuckles folded, the thumb pointing downward.

Mahlknecht cleared his throat. "I have already told you that you came to the wrong place. If there is such a house as you describe then I have never heard of it. We cannot help you. No one can. Please go."

The two flyers stared at him. Mahlknecht's face was still impassive, as if what he said now was exactly what he had been saying all along.

"Go," he repeated. "You came into this house uninvited. Go. Or I shall walk to the village and 'phone Kastelruth that you are here."

They rose to their feet, and struggled into their flying jackets. The captain's jaw was rigid. The fair-haired man's lips were white-edged. Mahlknecht's quiet, determined voice was final. They knew that now. They halted in the sitting room to pull on their cumbersome flying boots. The three men in the kitchen watched them in silence. In equal silence, the two flyers left the house. They didn't turn towards the village. They went back towards the pine woods from which they had come.

There was a drawn look on Paul Mahlknecht's face. He was knocking the ashes out of his pipe with solemn concentration.

"I hope to God that you were right," he said to Lennox.

CHAPTER 11

Frau Schichtl came home early that day. She brought a pile of textbooks and notebooks. The Kasal girl accompanied her to the door, helping her to carry the slipping load of books. The girl didn't follow Frau Schichtl indoors. She stood hesitating, speaking a few words in her quiet voice. And Frau Schichtl didn't invite her to come in. She wasn't even talking very much. All she said was, "Thank you, Katharina."

The girl spoke again, but her voice was too low for Lennox to catch the meaning of her words. All he could hear was the soft lilt of a girl's voice. It was the first girl's voice he had heard in two years. He moved to the window and watched her walking slowly towards the Kasal farm. She was older than he had thought, but perhaps that was because she was now walking gravely with her head slightly bowed. Before, he had always seen her hurrying, generally running. She was wearing her shoes, and didn't even seem to notice that the mud was ruining them. He didn't need to hear the clatter of the books, which Frau Schichtl let fall on the kitchen table, to realize something was wrong.

He turned from the window, and left the fair-haired girl with the strong young body walking over the green fields. Frau Schichtl's face was white: the bright color had gone, leaving two small pink daubs on her cheeks where the red veins were broken. Paul Mahlknecht put aside his pipe carefully.

"Well, Frieda?" he asked.

Frau Schichtl sat on the bench. She folded her hands tightly on her lap. Her lips were in a bitter line.

"No more school," she said, in a low voice.

"Yes?" Mahlknecht's quiet question urged her on.

Suddenly she was speaking quickly, angrily.

A man had been appointed teacher of the school. He was Heinrich Mussner, the same Mussner who had left for the North Tyrol in 1939. He had come back to Hinterwald last week. Last night Germans had come from Kastelruth. They had come to see that everyone was happy in Hinterwald. That was their story. They called a meeting to discuss how Hinterwald could be improved. The meeting became merely an intimation that as this district was now incorporated into the Reich, the school would have to be better managed. The woman volunteer must go: she had been a pupil-teacher in 1917, it was true, but that was too long ago. Someone with more recent experience must be chosen. A man must be chosen. Volunteers for the job were asked. And before the slow-moving, astounded villagers had begun to understand the meaning of this move Heinrich Mussner had volunteered. He had been accepted.

"And what teaching has he ever done?" Mahlknecht demanded.

"Seemingly he has been learning to teach in these last five years."

"Aye," her brother said grimly. "We can make a guess at what he has been learning to teach."

Frau Schichtl closed her eyes wearily. "Anyway, he's in. And I'm out. The Germans left after the meeting. But they are setting up a police station, too. German policemen are arriving tomorrow. And there is to be a German postmaster. And next week more people are returning from the North Tyrol. People like Mussner who left in 1939. They are going to run this village. I can see that."

"Mussner. . . . Well, at least we know now where he stands," Mahlknecht said. He picked up his pipe again, and studied the bowl thoughtfully. "We are supposed to be such fools that we really believe Mussner just happened to volunteer. We are supposed not to see that the whole meeting was an obvious German maneuver, so that Mussner wouldn't seem the German choice." He smiled grimly. "And so we would not distrust or hate him."

Frau Schichtl rose and went to the table. She began arranging her books on a shelf along the wall. "Where's Johann?" she asked.

"I sent him to the houses of the Committee with some information. He should be back soon."

"Anything wrong?" Frau Schichtl asked sharply. "Come, Paul, you don't have to pretend with me. Something *is* wrong." She turned to look at Lennox, and then at the kitchen, as if her answer might be found there. She noticed, for the first time, the dried mud on the sitting-room floor. She walked slowly towards it.

"Oh, Paul!" she said in dismay. "I scrubbed it only yesterday afternoon." Then all her postponed emotion broke. She began to cry.

"Now, Frieda," Mahlknecht was saying uncomfortably, "we'll scrub it for you today. I'll tell you what happened as soon as you are a sensible woman again. Perhaps this rest from school will be good for you. You've been doing too much."

"I have not." Frau Schichtl's tears were in control, but her temper was ragged. It was the first time that Lennox had seen her anything but calm and capable. Somehow she was all the more human. "I have not. None of us have. We've done too little. We let the Germans appoint this and that. We do nothing but plan for the future. What good is that to us now?"

"The Germans have the machine guns and we have not," her brother said patiently. "We are a small collection of people. We are farmers. We have no factories, no machines to help us. We can't make arms. We've stolen some from derailed trains, and from the Italians' barracks. But we haven't enough yet. If we use them now we'd be wiped out within a week. What good would we be then to the Allies or to ourselves? All we can do is to wait, to have our plans well made, to be ready. Then we can help in the fighting when the Allies are coming up towards the Brenner. There will be plenty of fighting and dying then, Frieda. But it will be useful fighting and useful dying. Ask Peter, here, if you don't believe me."

Frau Schichtl was silent. And then she said sadly, "I don't need to ask him. I just get so tired of waiting, that's all. And I get worried. Everything seems to be going wrong." She looked at Lennox. "He's unhappy: he wants to leave. And Johann is seeing too much of that girl. He went to see her yesterday before he came home, and that's why he arrived only half an hour before you did, this dawn. He should have been here yesterday. And now this school business. The children will be questioned about their families, and their minds will be poisoned. They will be told the wrong things."

"What girl are you talking about?" Mahlknecht asked.

"Eva Mussner. Mussner's niece. She was in Bozen for the last five years, Johann saw her there. Now she's come back to Hinterwald. She opened up her uncle's house. She's staying there."

"Eva Mussner," Paul Mahlknecht said thoughtfully. "A skinny little thing with straight hair, if I remember."

"She's hardly that now," Frau Schichtl answered tartly. "She met me in the village today. She was very upset about what happened. So she said."

There was a pause. Mahlknecht was lost in his thoughts.

"What was it you were going to tell me," Frau Schichtl asked at last, "about that mess of mud on my best sitting-room floor?"

"We had two visitors this morning. American flyers."

Frau Schichtl glanced at the ceiling. "They are sleeping now, I suppose."

"No. We sent them away." Mahlknecht began to light his pipe. "We don't think they were Americans, although they were dressed correctly. We think they are Germans."

"But, Paul, what if they aren't?" Frau Schichtl was roused once more. "How could you be so sure?"

"They said their plane had crashed many miles away, and that explained why they could arrive without us hearing their plane. But the houses are scattered so much over the Schlern that someone must have heard and seen the crash. And when flyers are dragged from their planes or are found wandering near them our rule is that someone accompanies them to the places where they can get a guide out of the mountains. They said a house had sheltered them near where they had crashed. But no one had been sent with them to prove to us that they had crashed. That made me wonder. The only men who would come as quietly and unannounced as they did would have been men who had parachuted on to the Schlern. That is what I thought they were when I went downstairs to meet them: but they didn't ask for Peter or for me, and they didn't give any of the right identifications. So I called Johann and Peter downstairs just to make sure that they were Americans. The slightest doubt, and we couldn't help them. Peter found a doubt." Mahlknecht began to laugh. He threw back his head as he had done when Lennox had first explained his trick, and his teeth were white against the dark beard. He was explaining it now, all over again. Frau Schichtl smiled too, and then a new worry appeared.

"If they were Germans, and you called Peter down here so that they could see him . . ." Frau Schichtl began. "Paul, how could you!"

"He didn't talk English, Frieda. In fact, he gave a good imitation of old Schroffenegger's style of conversation."

Lennox grinned self-consciously. He had often watched Josef Schroffenegger, one of the Committee men who came up to visit Frau Schichtl on Saturdays, with a good deal of amusement. Now that he considered it, he had given a sizable imitation of the old warrior.

"What else could I have done, Frieda?" Mahlknecht went on. "I had to know if these men were real Americans. It was logical to believe that Peter would know more about judging them than we do. He has fought and lived beside them. And our risk did work. He did find out."

"Then they will blame him."

"No. I took care to do all the deciding. It is I whom they will blame. Anyway, all they can report is that we refused to help American flyers."

Lennox said, "Won't the Germans expect us to report these flyers?"

Mahlknecht smiled. "That is a good idea," he said. "But perhaps it is too good. The Germans might begin to wonder why we were suddenly so helpful. The only informers they have found are people like Mussner, and the Germans know them all. From the rest of us, they may not expect actual trouble, but they have learned this winter not to expect help either.

They think we are a slow, pigheaded, selfish lot of peasants. They think we are inefficient and lazy. Unbiddable thickheads. No, we don't have to worry about reporting to the Germans. It would seem out of character." He smiled again, encouragingly, as he watched the younger man's face. "It was a good idea, well worth suggesting," Mahlknecht added. "We would have used it, if the Germans weren't so convinced that people fall into rigid classifications."

Frau Schichtl wasn't listening to this explanation. She was still worrying about two particular Germans. She asked impatiently, "So you sent Johann to warn the Committee? Do you think there will be more trouble?"

"We shall have to keep our eyes open. For if the Germans chose this house for their trick then they had some suspicion."

"Suspicion." The cold word set Frau Schichtl's face into a mask.

"Yes. Kasal's farm would have been a better place to find food or to hide. A farm has always more food than a cottage; it has outbuildings and barns. Yet they chose this house."

Frau Schichtl was silent. And then, looking at Lennox, she said, "What about Peter?"

Mahlknecht walked over to the window. "Roads are bad," he said, "but this part of the hillside always did trap most water. Can't judge by it. Most roads will be drying up by another week, and there are some parts of the woods that are passable even now. Schönau, for instance. I think Schroffenegger's lumber camp at Schönau will have to open early this spring. Schroffenegger has got his men all selected for it: we can trust each one of them. Peter will join them there. Ever cut down trees, Peter?"

Lennox shook his head.

"Good for you. Gives you exercise. Makes you fit."

They heard Johann's cheery whistle. He came in with high good humor. "Everything's all right," he said. "They must have been Germans. Didn't try any other houses. I saw all the local Committee, and they are keeping watch."

"You didn't see that Mussner girl, did you?" Frau Schichtl said.

Johann's smile faded. "What's she got to do with the two flyers?" he asked, defensively.

"Frieda, let me deal with this my way," Mahlknecht said, almost sharply. "Come on, Johann, lend us a hand with the scrubbing of this floor. You came just in time to help us clean it up. Your mother can start cooking dinner. We'll have it early, today. There's a lot of talking to be done tonight."

Frau Schichtl's hands went to her mouth. "I almost forgot," she said. "The Committee is coming up here this evening."

"And tomorrow at dawn there is the spring festival in Hinterwald." Mahlknecht looked thoughtfully at his sister. "I wonder if the Germans timed their interest in our village just to coincide with our feast day. They know the people from miles around will be coming to Hinterwald tomorrow."

"Rubbish," Frau Schichtl said. "It is just the Germans being Germans. They always were too officious. They like making regulations and rules." She was tying on her large white apron over the small silk one which was part of her dress. She began to measure a meager quantity of flour into the large mixing bowl for the soup's dumplings.

"Not so much rubbish," Mahlknecht said quietly. "You don't like the Germans, Frieda, but you don't know how they work. They've done things you couldn't believe just because you have lived among normal people most of your life. I am willing to wager that they chose our feast day for some reason. They know that everyone will be there. They will have us all gathered together like a flock of sheep."

"A feast day is a holy day," Frau Schichtl said. "Only heathens would cause trouble then." Her voice was indignant. Her hands kneaded the dough vigorously.

Mahlknecht shrugged his shoulders. "I can feel the screw going on," he said quietly. "That's all."

"I wonder just how much suspicion they have," Lennox said. "They may have discovered that there is active opposition here, even if it is hidden."

"Perhaps," admitted Mahlknecht. "And perhaps it is only the news which is worrying them."

"What news?" Lennox asked. For the last two nights it had been impossible to hear Allied broadcasts. There had been atmospherics and much interference. "What news?"

"The Brenner railway has been bombed. There has been a very thorough job. I left Bozen in flames two days ago. The German supply system has been wrecked. And the Allied push into Italy has begun."

Frau Schichtl stopped her work. She stared unbelievingly at her brother. It's begun, Lennox kept thinking; at last it has begun. He said, "And no one has yet come here. The colonel didn't get through."

"On the contrary, he did. He sent some men to see me in Bozen. We have our plans all made, don't worry about that."

"And what about the men who were coming here?"

"They are coming. Any day now. Why the devil did you think I came to Hinterwald? Why the devil did I nearly break my neck this morning getting down those stairs?" Mahlknecht halted, looked at his sister and Lennox. "What's wrong with both of you?" he demanded. "Jumpy as a couple of cats. Filled with worries. Don't you trust me or our Allies? What do you think we are, anyway? A bunch of newly born lambs?"

Lennox smiled at that. "We've stopped worrying," he said. "If things have really started moving then we've stopped worrying. We'll have plenty to do instead."

Frau Schichtl was smiling too. "It's begun," she said happily. And then the smile vanished. She brushed some flour off her forearm. "I am glad. I am glad and I'm sorry. Sorry for the men who will die." She looked as if she were going to cry again. She began pummeling the small handfuls of dough as if they were Germans. "Why couldn't they leave everyone alone? Why couldn't they stay in their Germany? What's wrong with them?" Her voice was angry now. She slapped the dumplings into the pot of thin soup. "And I've probably ruined these. I've probably put in salt twice over." She suddenly hurried out of the kitchen and climbed the stairs to her room.

Mahlknecht ignored all this, although his face was grave as he gave Lennox his answer.

"Plenty to do," he said briefly, and turned to look out of the window at the green fields.

CHAPTER **12**

Lennox woke to hear the first *"Juch-hé!"* coming down the mountainside. Today, he remembered, was Hinterwald's feast day. He lay under the thin padded quilt, feeling the cold morning air strike round his ears. Again a *"Juch-hé!"* sounded, and again. The last one was long-drawn-out, with the accent on the *"Juch,"* while the last syllable fell gradually away. The groups of men, women, and children, making their way towards Hinterwald, were silent once more. Now there was only the deep peace of the darkness before dawn.

"Damned fools," he said, but he was smiling. He tried it. There was something merry and high-spirited about the yodeled call. It meant nothing except that the man who called it, with his hands cupped round his lips, was feeling in good form. "You're a damned fool too," he told himself. And then he laughed. It was difficult this morning to work up his usual awakening gloom.

But then, last night had been a good night. The Committee had met— the hatchet-faced old men, the serious grim-eyed boys, talking of freedom. Freedom made good talk. Last night it had been especially good. For the news from Italy had wakened hope, and the winter plans were alive at last. Lennox, sitting quietly back in his usual corner, had watched with increasing interest the quickening faces around him. He had seen them before, never all at once but in various groups of two or three. Now the eleven men (three from this district, the others from more distant parts of the

Schlern) had come together. Openly, their reason was the feast of St. Johann, with its early mass in the morning, to which all the friends and relatives of the people of Hinterwald would come. Secretly, their purpose was a final meeting—with Paul Mahlknecht here from Bozen to give the latest report on anti-German organizations—before the men scattered into the forests and onto mountain alps for the summer.

And Mahlknecht had brought encouraging news. Contact with the Allies had been made; the Committee's plans had been accepted. The band of prisoners from the camp above Bozen had fought their way through to the Allied lines, and Colonel Wayne, who had talked with Mahlknecht last September, was one of those who were still alive. His report had interested Allied Headquarters, and they had sent three men secretly to Bozen. There, in February, they had met Mahlknecht and some of his friends. They had listened and they had questioned. Then they had left Bozen, to make their way back to the Allies. In April one of them returned with fuller instructions. He was working in Bozen, now, along with the Committee of that district. Besides his instructions, he had brought the news that as soon as the snows melted on the high meadows two men would arrive on the Schlern. They were coming to help to prepare the way for still more Allies to come.

The Tyrolese listened with scarcely a flicker of emotion over their wind-tanned, hard-boned faces. Lennox knew them well enough now not to be deceived by such calm. His respect for them grew as he watched.

For one thing, he had gradually become more convinced during this long waiting winter of the worth of Mahlknecht's plans. At first he had been cynical; now he believed that they contained the germ of real help. For when the Allied armies drew near the difficult mountains of the South Tyrol—mountains which made South Italian peaks look like molehills—they would find people who were not only willing but ready to help. There was a list of men and women who could be completely trusted, a list of those who were neutral, a shorter but definite list of those who were enemies. They would find guides who could lead them over little-known mountain paths in infiltration movements and surprise attacks on German set positions. They would find women who would shelter the wounded; people who had measured their food supplies so that there would be enough; villages which could be responsible for order; men who would fight dependably and teach the tricks of the mountains. Practical help like that was something the Allied soldier could appreciate. When civilians didn't malinger or cheat, a soldier could get ahead with his job of fighting. That was all a soldier wanted.

For another thing, there was a broader possibility to Mahlknecht's plans. Last night Lennox had suddenly seen it. In his excitement he forgot all about his old dislike of responsibility. Perhaps the incident with the two pseudo-airmen had proved that there was a difference between taking responsibility and mere self-assertion. Anyway, he had risen to his feet and made a speech.

"These ideas are good," he had begun. "Why don't you spread them across the Brenner Pass into the North Tyrol? The people there are of your blood; they could be organized as you are organizing yourselves. They would listen to you. If our troops are to make quick progress they must find a population that is willing to help. They must find order, no politics being played, no nuisance refugees, and no mean profiteering at their expense. An army doesn't want volunteer recruits who haven't been trained in its way. Its striking power depends on being a single trained unit. But it does need people who will really help, and make themselves as little of a worry as possible. It needs people who will be dependable guides, people who will give accurate information, people who will use the supplies we send them to sabotage the right place at the right moment. If the North Tyrol will agree to that then you will have won us a battle. Remember that the North Tyrol borders Bavaria. And Bavaria is the back door into Germany."

That, Lennox decided as he lay under the quilt's warmth and watched the sky lighten into a cold gray, had been quite a speech. It had sort of overpowered him at the end. He had begun with a plea for wider help and had ended with the key to Germany's back door. It had sounded all right last night. And the Committee's reaction had been flattering: already the men, who could travel into the North Tyrol in small groups of two or three, were being chosen to make contact with anti-Nazi groups there. As Mahlknecht had said, plans north and south of the Brenner Pass could be co-ordinated: the Tyrol would be united once again. But, Lennox wondered as he watched the long streaks of yellow light split up the gray sky outside, did it sound so well this morning? For a man who had been in revolt against authority for so many years of his life, he had certainly gone off the deep end. The Committee's plans were already broadening to suit his idea: and on whose authority had he spoken? On his own. "By God," he said, suddenly subdued.

And then he wondered just for how many weeks the idea had been simmering in a secret place of his mind. Last night it had boiled over.

Again the call of *"Juch-hé!"* sounded. This time it was near. A group of people must be coming down past this house. He rose quickly and went to the window. Day had fully broken. The birds were wide awake and chattering. The pine forest was a mass of black-pointed shapes with golden high lights. The five lean cows were walking, in leisurely single file, out from the Kasal barn. The thin notes of the bells round their dun-colored necks jangled in broken rhythm. The Kasal family, dressed in their very best clothes, were standing stiffly at the doorway of their house. They were looking towards the pine forest, waiting for those who were walking into the village.

Then Lennox saw them too. Eight women and three men, five young boys and four girls. Today the men had given up their leather breeches and white wool stockings for tight black trousers tucked into high leather boots. The high white plumes on their slouched hats were held proudly. The women wore wide black skirts and bright aprons. They had thrown heavy shawls over their white silk blouses as a protection against the morning air. Their hats were broad-brimmed, with the tight, rounded crown cut off flatly on top. Their hair was braided and twisted round their heads. Most of them were very fair. Lennox saw the gleam of pale gold under the black felt hats. They walked barefoot, with their white stockings and polished shoes carried carefully over the muddy paths. They would bathe their feet in some stream at the edge of the village, draw on their stockings and shoes, and then advance sedately towards the church. They would look as if they had just stepped out of their cottages, instead of having walked for ten miles through the night.

One of the boys let out a yodel as he saw the waiting Kasals. From across the fields came the *Juch-hé!* call from another group. Higher up on the hillside there was a further burst of calls. It was the peasant way of contact and answer over mountain spaces. It was infectious. Even the birds had started to sing in a sudden frenzy of excitement. Lennox was tempted to lean out of the window, cup his hands round his mouth, and join in.

But there was a knock, and he turned away from the window to open his bedroom door. Frau Schichtl, along with her brother and son, entered in full regalia. Lennox, in his gray flannel nightshirt, swept them a low bow. "Most elegant," he said.

Frau Schichtl's face colored, and she looked pleased. She smoothed her red silk embroidered apron over the wide black skirt, adjusted the fringed scarf crossed over her breast, pulled the edge of her black lace mittens more closely to her elbow, straightened the strange-crowned hat. She smiled self-consciously. Then suddenly she laughed and said, "If only you could see yourself, Peter."

Lennox looked down at his bare calves, and was inclined to agree. Then he looked at the elaborate costumes and thought that remark could cut both ways. He smiled blandly.

Johann said, "Pity you've got to stay here. After mass and the procession the fun begins. Pity you couldn't come down for the dance tonight." He spun his hat, with its soft white feather, round on his hand. His gay clothes had affected his spirits. His high boots beat out a brief sole and heel rhythm. His face had lost the angry look it had kept last night after his uncle had talked to him about the Mussner girl. He patted his black velvet waistcoat with its pattern of red embroidered flowers, and pretended to polish the silver buttons. "Not a bad fit, either," he admitted, proudly surveying his father's clothes. "Well, we had better start. Mass is at half past six. Time's shifting."

"You know where to find breakfast," Frau Schichtl said, "I left the table ready for you last night. I wish you could come." She looked at her brother.

Paul Mahlknecht shook his head. He had adopted a new character with the traditional clothes: he was no longer the man from Bozen. He was a man of the Tyrol, as quiet and imperturbable as the mountains which brooded over the meadows. In this costume he was keeping faith with his father and grandfather and the fathers before them. This was the symbol of his fight. This was the outward sign of his inner loyalties. The man who wore these clothes so confidently, so proudly, was a man who would never become either an Italian or a German.

Lennox was thankful he had resisted making that crack about fancy dress which had almost rolled off the tip of his tongue. He was now ashamed that he had even thought about it. He glanced nervously at Mahlknecht's somber face, and worried about mind reading.

But Mahlknecht was saying, "I'll return here before the evening begins. We can talk together then." Frau Schichtl and Johann were beginning to descend the stairs.

Lennox said quickly, "Do you think I could take a short walk this afternoon through the woods? Everyone will be down at the village. And if Germans watch this house—well, they already know that a disabled soldier lives here."

Mahlknecht nodded thoughtfully. He hadn't missed the urgency in Lennox's voice. "A walk would do you good," he said. "But don't go far away. I'd rather not spend this evening looking for a man lost on a mountainside. I'd rather finish our talk. I shall have to leave here soon, you know."

"And what about the men you are expecting?"

"They should have arrived yesterday or the day before. Weather permitting, they should have arrived then."

"Parachuting in?"

Mahlknecht nodded. "I'll give you instructions tonight about identifying them, in case they come when I am away from the Schlern."

"It would be better if you were here to welcome them yourself."

"They will see me later. Besides they will want to talk to you." Mahlknecht grinned suddenly. "Just to make sure that your colonel and I haven't brought them here on a wild goose chase. You can tell them just what you think of us."

"I wonder why they didn't send someone before this," Lennox said, half angrily. "Devil of a way they've kept us hanging on."

"There was no need to have anyone here in the winter in addition to you," Mahlknecht reminded him. "They did a much cleverer thing. They sent men to talk to me in Bozen. That was all that was needed while winter lasted."

Yes, that's right: I was good enough as an outpost up here in the winter months when nothing happened, Lennox thought. But as soon as action starts and some real fun begins, then out goes the poor bloody infantry and in comes the professional officer.

Frau Schichtl's voice called from downstairs, "We are all waiting, Paul."

"Coming." Mahlknecht descended the staircase. Halfway down he called softly, "You'll have your freedom soon, Peter. You can start your own plans again."

Then his light footsteps were crossing the sitting room, and the door closed softly. Lennox could imagine the smile on Mahlknecht's lips.

He closed his bedroom door, locking it automatically.

He deserved that last remark. He deserved the smile—if it had been there. He had wanted his freedom. He was getting it.

He walked back to the window. The group outside the Kasals' house had grown. They were waiting for Mahlknecht and his family. He watched the movement in the crowd—the white-plumed hats, the spreading black skirts, the tall men and women with their erect heads, the smooth golden hair of the laughing children. The older people walked first, the men leading the way. At the end of the procession he saw Johann. His hat was now jauntily set on his slicked hair. He was talking to Katharina Kasal, walking beside him with that long, effortless step which seemed natural to the women of this district. At the point in the winding road where it swerved behind a group of trees the Kasal girl halted. She turned and looked towards the Schichtl house. Then she went on.

Lennox drew back from the window. He had been leaning out, like a fool. He hadn't thought anyone would turn round to look this way. They were all so intent on their festival. He wondered if she had really seen him. What on earth had made her do that?

He peeled off the nightshirt and began the morning's usual stretch and bend. That was how he got exercise. Stretch and bend, and bend and stretch. Suddenly he remembered he was going to have real exercise today. Mahlknecht had given him the permission which Frau Schichtl had never been able to give. He could walk outside. He could taste free air. He wouldn't wait until this afternoon, either. He kicked the nightshirt aside, and poured the water out of the jug into the basin on his small bedroom table. The water held the night's cold air, but at least he hadn't to break the ice on it now before he could wash or shave.

He dressed quickly, remembering to take the gray woolen jacket which Frau Schichtl had found for him in her late husband's clothes' chest. It would be cold outside until the sun was really high. He ran downstairs, and stopped to pick up a slab of bread for his pocket. He opened the back door and looked at the high peaks with the sun rising up behind them. He took a deep breath of the cold, crisp air. It tasted differently down here. It couldn't be the same air which came into his room upstairs. It didn't seem the same air at all, with his feet free on this grass.

In the pine wood behind the house there was a narrow path hidden behind three tall trees clumped together. He had looked at it bitterly on every one of those rare nights in which he had walked to the edge of the wood. Now he stood hesitating, wondering if the path was still there, wondering if he had imagined it. He began walking slowly towards the three trees. He saw the beginning of the path. Suddenly, he started to run.

CHAPTER **13**

Lennox explored the wood thoroughly. He found that its boundaries were very simple. On its west was the road which led past the Schichtl and Kasal houses. On its east was a steep hillside and, above that, the series of precipices which formed the mountain's peak. From the north edge of the wood he could see sloping meadow-land, a twisting road, scattered houses, distant villages gathered round church spires, and a sea of mountains as background to all this. From the south edge, there was the road curving down to Hinterwald. But the village itself was hidden by trees. Only the church, with its onion-shaped spire, and a few chalets were to be seen. Beyond the trees of Hinterwald were falling and rising fields, and then more mountains. There were mountains everywhere.

On these four sides of the wood Lennox had rested and stared at the views. They were incredible. He had often admired rows of savage mountains, but in this country they were strangely combined with smiling meadows and wide stretches of wooded slopes. The scattered chalets, the small neat villages, gave a comforting feeling. Mountains alone dominated and threatened. But here, pleasant houses and a picturesque church and a comfortable inn would welcome you at the end of a lonely walk. This would be a country worth exploring. A man could find peace here.

Now it was almost midday, and he ate his piece of bread, and slowly drank a mouthful of water from a clear icy stream. He settled himself on a rock sheltered by the last fringe of trees on the high east side of this wood. The wood covered a steep incline from the mountain's stony base to the Schichtl house, so that he could sit here and watch the pines drop away in front of him and look at the far mountains to the west. Over there was the Brenner railway in its deep valley, and beyond it the western mountains, and beyond them the Swiss Alps. He thought, at this moment

I don't believe I have ever been happier in my life. He remembered suddenly that he should be amazed, and yet he wasn't. He looked at his scarred right hand. "Get well, blast you," he said. "You've got to paint. Now you've found something to paint." He was grinning like an idiot. "You're drunk," he told himself. "Drunk with this feeling of being free. Drunk with all this peace and beauty. You're drunk."

Certainly, he felt wonderful. Those two Germans neatly handled yesterday, the successful meeting last night, Mahlknecht's plans no longer hopeless but fitting nicely into the latest news from the Allied front in Italy—all these contributed to this sense of jubilation. And he could laugh at himself again. This view of mountains and unlimited space put everything into proper perspective.

He rose, somewhat stiffly, carrying his jacket jauntily over one shoulder, and began the descent to the house. He was hungry, and thought with pleasure of the remains of some cold meat in the larder. He would reheat some of Frau Schichtl's excellent soup. There was rich milk from the Kasal farm, and white bread baked only yesterday. He remembered the sour, stale food of the prison camps, and the meal he was going to prepare seemed an epicure's delight. Then, after a leisurely dinner with some of the German-published newspapers, which Mahlknecht had brought from Bozen, to provide amusement on the side, he would— He halted his thoughts with his stride. He stopped close to a tree. Standing quite still, he listened intently. He heard nothing. Yet he sensed movement. Someone was coming quietly towards him. He drew quickly behind the tree, and prayed that its cover was adequate.

Then he saw the wide-skirted black dress and its bright silk apron. Above the gay scarf, with its tapering ends crossed demurely over her breast, was the face of the Kasal girl. She was looking puzzled, as if she had heard him and was now wondering where he had gone. She hesitated, and then stopped. There was something so pathetic in her sudden dejection, in her hesitation as her eyes anxiously searched the path ahead of her, that Lennox stepped forward into the open. She flinched at that, and her hand went quickly to her heart. But she didn't cry out. And then she was smiling, and all the worry was gone from her eyes. They were very blue. Her hair, so smoothly parted and brushed back from the high forehead and with its long, thick plaits circling her head, was very fair. The color in her cheeks had been deepened by her haste. She came forward to where he stood, walking with that easy step of hers. She was broad-shouldered and tall, taller than he had imagined, and her body was well-shaped and strong. Good bones, he observed with a professional eye, and a face molded in excellent proportions. It was a calm face, and a strong face, and a face still so filled with hope and belief that Lennox felt sorry for her. She wouldn't look so trusting as that in ten years' time. She'd learn that the world wasn't so big and beautiful by then.

She said in her quiet voice, "Uncle Paul sent me." He stopped thinking about the girl. He was suddenly alert.

"Yes?" he asked.

"He will not be back here tonight. Two friends have arrived."

Peter Lennox watched her face: it was evident that she knew the message was important, but he was equally sure she didn't know the reason of its importance.

"Where is Johann?" he asked.

"He's with Uncle Paul. They want you to bring them their everyday clothes. You'll find them on the chairs in their room. Bundle them up tightly—everything you see there. I'll go to our house and change my dress. I can't travel quickly in this." She looked down at the silk apron, at the silver buttons on the black silk bodice, at the wide skirt banded at the hem with embroidery. She was smiling at the very idea. She suddenly noticed the look, half puzzled, half anxious on Lennox's face. "I shall lead you to Johann and Uncle Paul," she said. "They are only about three miles away from here. But they are a difficult three miles."

"What's happened?" Just when all the plans seemed ripe something had gone wrong. His good temper had vanished: he was worrying and heartsick once more.

"Nothing. Not yet. Some Germans have come to the village. They've opened a police station, and they've put up notices that all men must register there today. The Germans are watching the processions and the people. They are very quiet and friendly. But they have two trucks hidden half a mile from the village. Andreas Wenter saw them as he was taking a short cut to the village this morning. Paul Mahlknecht thinks the trucks have come for men to work in labor gangs on the Brenner railway. That's what some of us think, although many won't believe it. But the younger men believe it. They've listened to Paul Mahlknecht. They are all slipping out of the village before the dance begins this evening, for that's when the Germans would expect all the young people to be together."

She had already started to descend the path. He caught up with her, his mind still filled with questions.

"Why were *you* sent here?" he asked.

She answered, "I was sent home by my mother. I'm in disgrace." She wasn't smiling. She was very serious, and he restrained a laugh in time.

"What . . . ?" he began. But she shook her head. "Later," she said. "We must hurry now."

He was thinking partly that she was neither so young nor so helpless as he had first thought; and partly that the people of Hinterwald must be having a difficult time at their feast-day celebrations. What with Germans . . . two important strangers wandering in to join the fun . . . mothers sending daughters home in disgrace. . . . He wondered if the stolid faces were still as expressionless, if the processions and all the other formalities were still following the usual routine. The postponed laugh began to take shape, and couldn't be controlled this time.

"It isn't funny," the girl said reproachfully.

"No," he agreed, "it isn't funny." But he went on laughing to himself.

The sound of a motorcar checked him. The girl looked at him anxiously. They halted, listening, judging the distance by sound. The car stopped. It was near them; perhaps in front of the Schichtl house. Quickly, he grasped her arm and led her to the left. They must get off this path. The girl not only understood that, she was untying the too-bright apron from her waist, folding it up tightly to carry in her hand. If Lennox hadn't been so worried he would have been surprised. She understood, all right.

"Let's get to the edge of the wood. Let's see," he whispered. She nodded, following him obediently. He must see, he thought desperately. He had to know what was happening down on that road.

When they reached the edge of the wood it was the girl who led him to a point where the trees were thick enough for safety. From there they could watch the Schichtl house and the Kasal farm and the road in between. Lennox nodded, well-pleased.

He could see the car, drawn up at the left corner of the Schichtl house. German, of course. None of the people of this district owned a car. Two men were seated in the car, waiting. Civilian dress. Two others in black uniform were coming out of the Schichtl house. They halted at the car. Much talking. The two civilians got out of the car. The two uniforms got in. The car, slipping in the mud, was turned around and pointed back to the village. The two civilians walked towards the Kasal farm. They went into the house. They came out. Then they walked round to the barn at its side. One was offering the other a cigarette. They were settling down for a long watch. They were hidden now by the barn. They didn't reappear.

Lennox drew a deep breath. The girl was saying, her voice desolate, worry drawing her brows together, "We must leave now. Without food or proper clothes. We must leave."

Lennox was thinking. So they *were* Germans. We were right. They were Germans, and not American flyers. For the two civilians, who had so leisurely lighted cigarettes and had wandered so innocently towards the cover of the farm buildings, were of the same build and size and coloring as the two men who had come yesterday to the Schichtl house. Somehow he was suddenly glad of this moment which had proved yesterday's decision.

"Please." The girl was shaking his arm. "Please, we must go. We must get to Schönau and tell them. We must go." She was frightened now.

Lennox touched her shoulder encouragingly. "Don't worry," he said awkwardly. "They've only chosen your barn so that they can have a comfortable front view of the Schichtl house."

She nodded, and bit her lip. "We must tell Uncle Paul," she said. "Come." He realized then that she wasn't afraid for the Kasal house: her fear was for the Schichtls. They backed carefully away from the outside fringe of pines. And then, safely in the depth of the wood, they began to climb. Lennox didn't speak at first. He was trying to get his thoughts into order. These two Germans had come back to the Schichtl house because they could identify the men in it. But why had they come back? Why the openly official visit? Had they learned his true identity? They were waiting, certainly. For what? For him, or for Paul Mahlknecht, or for . . . He suddenly thought of the two "friends" whom the girl had mentioned in her first sentence. Had they been seen landing, and followed? Had their parachutes been discovered? Was the Schichtl house naturally suspected? Was the search on? He suddenly felt that he knew only half of this danger: Mahlknecht and Johann would know the other half. Together, they'd form a clearer picture. He forgot he was tired, forgot he was hungry. He only remembered the need to get to this Schönau, wherever it was. He followed the girl, watching the way she moved so easily, so capably. Mahlknecht had been right: the people who lived in this country made excellent guides. They knew the terrain: walking and climbing was a natural way for them to spend their free time. It was as natural for them to scale these mountains above, as it was for people at home to put on their best hats on Sunday afternoons for a stroll in the parks. He kept the girl's steady pace, content to let her choose the path.

CHAPTER **14**

They had come to the northeast corner of the wood. The lower mountain slope, with its mixture of grass and boulders and small shrubs, lay before them.

The girl spoke for the first time. "We cross this until we reach the valley, which leads up in between that group of mountains." She pointed to three towering peaks of rock. "Schönau is the name we give the alp in the middle of the high forest up there."

Lennox nodded. He could neither see any valley, nor any sign of a higher forest. All he could see were the bold precipices of the mountains and this lower slope falling to the wood where they now stood.

"Where's the path?" he asked.

"Here." She smiled. "You will get accustomed to seeing it. It is difficult for strangers' eyes at first."

Lennox said nothing. He still couldn't see any path. She sensed his annoyance, for she turned the conversation politely. "You knew where I lived. Do you know my name, too?"

"Katharina Kasal."

She laughed and said, "And I know who you are."

He pretended to smile. He said very quietly, "And who am I?"

"Peter Schichtl, of course."

His smile became easier. "How did you know I was Peter Schichtl?"

She hesitated, looking sideways at him, and then said with considerable embarrassment, "I saw you. I saw you sometimes taking a short walk to the wood at night. My bedroom window has a good view of this wood, you see. Then one day I asked your aunt who you were."

"And what did your father and mother say?" He tried to keep his voice amused, but he wasn't feeling quite so casual as his question. Alois Kasal was one of the men on Mahlknecht's doubtful list: Alois Kasal was a most annoying neutral. Suddenly the whole winter of secrecy and imprisonment seemed a complete farce.

The girl's quiet voice said, "I didn't tell my father or my mother. I was supposed to be asleep, not standing at a window looking at night on the mountains. You see," and she was smiling, "I am always doing wrong things."

"What did you do that was wrong today?"

She looked at him, and she was suddenly grave. "You shouldn't keep laughing at me," she said with Frau Schichtl-like dignity. "It was nothing very much, anyway. I gathered the school children and told them not to go back to the school until Frau Schichtl was again their teacher."

"You did what?" His voice was suddenly serious. "Who heard you?"

"The children. And then my mother and Eva Mussner arrived just as I was finishing my talk."

He looked at her so intently that she lost her smile. "You are just as bad as my mother or Eva Mussner," she said angrily. "Don't you see something has got to be done about the school? Now, hurry; I have got to take you to Schönau and then get back home before my mother or father returns. Don't you understand?"

"I didn't." He was abrupt and angry. He wasn't thinking about the need for hurry. He was still thinking about this girl's words in the village. And Eva Mussner had heard them. "I am only asking you questions to try to understand. You don't explain much, do you?"

She didn't answer, but turned her back to him. She was taking off her stockings and shoes. She faced him once more, her cheeks still more highly colored. "My mother would be angrier if I were to ruin these shoes," she said. She laid the shoes and stockings and the pink apron neatly together behind a large rock, placing a stone carefully over them as an anchor.

"It won't be comfortable walking that way," he said.

She shrugged her shoulders. "I've no choice. Now we'll hurry."

"May we talk? I'd like to hear what has been happening at the village." He had started worrying again. The name of Eva Mussner was a bad omen. He began to wonder how much she had actually learned from Johann. The boy had sworn last night that he had told her nothing, but some women didn't need to be told very much. They guessed too easily. And now she had heard Katharina inciting a revolt among school children. He didn't like this Eva Mussner. He didn't like her at all.

Katharina said, "Of course we can talk—if we have any breath left. But I've already told you all about today in the village." She started forward impatiently. She obviously thought that this Schichtl nephew wasn't very bright. And Lennox didn't argue. As a Tyrolese, he ought to have had a picture of today in the village quite clearly fixed in his mind's eye. He followed her in silence, noting that there was indeed a path, barely perceptible and narrow as a sheep track. It led them north, away from Hinterwald. Gradually it ascended the steep shoulder of the hillside. Above them, to their right, were the large teethlike ridges of dolomite rock. The sun was warm now. There was silence everywhere. There was no other living thing in sight.

When the roughest piece of climbing was over Lennox said determinedly, "Tell me everything that happened from the moment you left your house this morning."

Katharina threw a quick glance over her shoulder. Her face showed surprise, but her pace kept the same unbroken rhythm.

"Is it important?" she asked. "Really important?"

"Yes." He had to know. It might tell him why the Germans had come back to the Schichtl house. He had to know whether they were there to question, or there to arrest. He knew, when she began to talk, that she was trying to obey him fully. For she began with the moment when she had looked back at the Schichtl house. Sometimes she would pause and say, "Am I telling you too many things? Do you want all this?" And he would answer, "Go on. This is what I want to know." He began to feel as if he had been in Hinterwald himself that day. He became more sure of his judgment.

First there had been mass at the little church. Then there had been a procession. The holy image of St. Johann was carried through the village balanced on the shoulders of four young men. Behind them walked the older men, then the women, then the children. Late-comers in everyday clothes waited quietly at the side of the street. This year a larger crowd than ever had gathered to watch the festival. Many had come from distant villages. Some had come from other districts and valleys. It was a true gathering-day.

Among those dressed in ordinary peasant clothes were two men whom Katharina couldn't remember. But they must have been relatives or friends of Josef Schroffenegger, for they sat at his breakfast table in the Hotel Post's garden after the procession. Josef Schroffenegger had a large party round him that morning. There were two men from the Grödner-Tal and one from Seis, and one from the Tschamin-Tal. Paul Mahlknecht and other men of the Hinterwald had talked to the two strangers, too. So, although Katharina couldn't remember who they were, they were certainly recognized by Paul Mahlknecht and Josef Schroffenegger and their friends. Eva Mussner had asked who they were, and the owner of the Hotel Post had said, "Don't you remember them? Why, they are Ludwig Plank's boys, who used to live over in the Grödner-Tal." And then of course everyone remembered Ludwig Plank, and no one had asked anything more about his sons. Eva Mussner said of course they had changed, and Frau Schichtl had said, "Well, none of us get any younger."

After breakfast there was a second procession—this time with a band and gay music. It was then that the Germans appeared. They were dressed in police uniforms. They stood outside the Golden Roof Inn, and they were enjoying the music. But all round the village large notices had been posted while the people had eaten breakfast. The notices said that every man between the age of eighteen and fifty-five years was to register at the new police station today. No one paid much attention to all this, because no one was going to bother to register. They hadn't registered last February when that regulation had been made a law. They weren't going to register now. Six German policemen weren't going to make them. Then the man Wenter arrived.

He was very late. His wife had just given birth to twins, and he had hurried from his farm to tell the good news to his friends in Hinterwald. He came by short cuts over little-used paths. That was how he had seen the two German trucks, and German soldiers sitting on the grass beside them. The trucks were well-hidden, and they were scarcely a mile from the village. Wenter didn't let the Germans see him. He came to Hinterwald and told everyone about the twins. Then he had joined the procession, walking between Schroffenegger and Plank's sons. Before the time for resting came, when the women went visiting in the different houses and the men gathered round the tables in the inns, everyone who could be trusted knew about the German trucks. Only people like Mussner hadn't been told; everyone was avoiding them, anyway.

It was then that Katharina had gathered the older village children together and had told them to stay away from school. It was then that her mother had found her, and sent her home at once. People spoke to her as she left the village: no one knew why she was leaving, for her mother would tell no one the real reason. And among those who had spoken to her was Paul Mahlknecht. He gave her the message for the Schichtl house. If she didn't find Peter Schichtl at home she would find him walking in the wood. She must go quietly, she must not call to him, she must wait at the path until she saw him. She had done what she had been told.

The girl's voice, as regular as her step, now halted. Then, when he didn't speak, she said, "Now, have I told you enough?"

"Yes." He was still seeing, in his mind's eye, the crowd of gaily dressed farmers and foresters with their quiet wives and handsome daughters. He saw Schroffenegger's two strange "friends," merging into this natural background. After what he had been told he felt that the Germans were merely there to press-gang the stronger men for the army or for labor camps. The two strangers would never have been allowed to walk in the procession if the search had been for them: they would have been arrested in the first five minutes. And, as he thought still more about it, he felt that the Germans who had visited the Schichtl house today and the Germans who had watched the procession in the village had different purposes. The latter had wanted laborers. The former—well, that was something he still had to find out.

The girl said, "But you are still puzzled. What else can I tell you?"

"Nothing." He was surprised at the gentleness of his own voice. Its bitter edge had gone. "You've told me everything. That's what I wanted to hear."

They halted now that they had reached a spur of sloping rock. In the shelter of a large boulder they rested. The wood, and the road to Hinterwald past the Schichtl house, was far below them.

The girl watched him curiously as he looked at the long stretch of country sloping away from him. So much peace, he was thinking, and yet so much threat of danger. Peace and yet no peace.

"Whom do you hate most?" he asked suddenly.

She stared at him in surprise. "Once I would have said the Italians. Now I say anyone who comes into my country and says that it is his. I hate him, whoever he is."

"Someone once said, 'Let them hate, provided that they fear.'"

She frowned as she followed the meaning of his words. And then she smiled. "But what if we don't fear?"

He smiled too. "There is no answer to that," he said, with a good deal of feeling. He gripped both of her shoulders, and held them tightly. They stood there smiling—as Lennox suddenly thought—like a couple of imbeciles. His hands dropped to his side.

"Where's this valley of yours?" he asked quickly. "I don't believe it exists."

"But it does!" She took his hand, and walked beside him, pulling him gently on. "Look! There it is." She was watching him again, not curiously this time. Whatever he had said in these last minutes had been the right thing to say. It wasn't mere politeness now which kept her smiling. She liked him, without knowing why he was here and without the feeling that she ought to like him. She was a friend with no conditions attached. He kept smiling too: somehow he felt like a human being again.

CHAPTER **15**

The narrow valley, a gorge of rushing water deep down in the cleft of mountains, led them eastward. Lennox, looking upward at the jagged peaks above him on either side, felt as if he were buried in mountains. Ahead of him were mountains too, crest rising behind crest towards the eastern Alps. He was climbing with considerable effort along the narrow path which followed the turbulent rush of water, digging in with his feet, holding on with his hands. Katharina seemed as confident as the pine trees which grew so boldly on the steep banks. He had long since given up admiring the beauties of nature, and concentrated on following the girl.

Even when the path ended abruptly she didn't pause, but led him towards the source of the stream—a series of waterfalls cascading down the ledges of the mountain precipice. He stared at the lowest fall, where the arc of whitened water plunged into a turbulent pool before it raced down through the gorge. We are stuck, completely stymied, he thought; she's made a mistake—we have taken the wrong path. And his annoyance at having been outwalked and outclimbed vanished, and he felt sorry for the girl. She had tried so hard to help.

"Too bad," he said commiseratingly, but the noise of the falling water blotted out his words. Katharina smiled, said something which he couldn't hear either, and then laughed. He laughed too, just to cheer her up. Inwardly he was groaning at the idea of having to retrace his steps over that path. She had said Schönau was three miles from the Schichtl house. They must have traveled well over two miles. If they had found the right path they would have almost been at Schönau by this time. Inwardly he began cursing.

The girl was pointing to his shoes. He got the idea that she was telling him to remove them. At her instruction, he rolled up his white footless half-stockings almost to reach his leather breeches. "Legs wash and dry more quickly than wool," she shouted, and then laughed once more at the whisper of her words. She picked up her wide skirt and innumerable layers of starched petticoats, drawing them up to her knees. Lennox noted the shape of her legs with approval. And then he was jolted out of his admiration as she stepped onto the soft ground where the path ended, and he realized he was supposed to follow her. Her precautions were justified. By the time they reached the waterfall and were walking over rocks, smoothed by floods and weather, their legs were generously coated with the rich black earth which comes from centuries of dying trees. As the fine spray of falling water pinpricked his brow, Lennox looked at the girl in amusement.

"Do we just walk through it?" he shouted, and decided that sarcasm needed a quiet voice.

But she nodded seriously. She pointed, and he saw a rocky ledge which ran out from the bank to disappear under the waterfall.

He shook his head. "Not I," he said decidedly.

She laughed at that, and placing her mouth against his ear, said, "The water falls out from the mountain, not down it. There's a shallow cave hidden behind that sheet of water. Four men could walk abreast under the fall. Come."

She didn't wait for him to finish his headshaking. She started over the rocky bank of the torrent, along the ledge. She seemed to disappear into the fine spray. He was left alone on the bank, staring at the boiling pool. He cursed, and then called her name. There was only the roar of water for an answer. He cursed again and began to walk slowly over the ledge. The foothold was slippery, and the rock against which his hand balanced was too wet for any secure grasp. But strangely, the spray was less strong here than it had been on the bank. Soon it had ceased, and the ledge had broadened. It was as the girl had said. A shallow cave had been hollowed out of the mountain face, a place of cold shadow. The sun's rays were broken and trapped by a curtain of water. There was only a strange green light and a constant dull roar, like the continuous grinding of heavy wheels on cobbled stones. The world outside didn't exist.

He stood and stared at the sheet of water which fell in front of him. Now he began to see the texture of the torrent, like long close strands of gleaming silk. But the noise blotted out even his thoughts: he felt he couldn't even hear himself think. He left the broadened ledge, watching it narrow, feeling the spray sprinkle his face and hands and legs once more. And then he was out into a world of blinding yellow light, and he was groping carefully along the narrow foothold with his hand once more balancing him. The waterfall was behind him. The girl was waiting on the other bank. She had washed the mud from her legs and feet, and she was now carefully shaking down her skirt and petticoats.

"You can put on your shoes again," she advised. "We travel a short distance through pine trees now. No mud to worry about there."

He washed the mud away beside a small inlet of water at the bank, and drew on his shoes. He was still staring at the waterfall. And it still didn't look possible. He felt a fool, but anyway he had been a logical fool. It didn't look possible that anyone could walk under that sheet of water. From the bank, the ledge looked only a natural roughness in the face of rock.

The girl was examining a smear of green on the wide sleeve of her blouse. "That rock!" she said in disgust. "It's oozing slime. Now I *must* get home before my mother does, so that I can clean this." She began to hurry up through the pine wood which covered this part of the mountainside. Lennox chased after her. His legs were tiring now. He kept pace with her only with difficulty. He didn't talk, but the girl pretended not to notice.

"The lumber camp is just five minutes away now," she said. "There's a broad meadow up there. That's Schönau."

When he still didn't say anything she went on cheerfully, "The real road to Schönau lies along the north side of the valley. That's the way the foresters and their carts come. But this short cut along the south side is very useful. We keep a watch on the north road, and if we don't like who is coming then we take the south short cut back to the village. Johann once spent two hours in that cave under the waterfall while the Italians searched all around for him."

He nodded. He was saying to himself, "You damned superior fool to get angry because a girl had more sense than you had; because a girl can walk this way on bare feet and you've got to have shoes; because she's as fresh as a daisy and you're dead beat." And, having admitted his damned superior foolery, he was able to smile. The girl seemed to have understood, for she was smiling too. She pointed to the liberal green smears on his clothes, evidence that he had hugged the wall of the waterfall too closely. They both began to laugh.

Johann was standing behind a tree at the edge of the wood, watching this path so quietly that they hadn't noticed him.

"Thought you were never coming," he grumbled. He looked at them accusingly. "That path is supposed to be a short cut, you know. Come on. All the rest of us are here." He gave a short whistle as a warning signal to the others wherever they were.

"I had to walk in my best dress," Katharina explained. "We came as quickly as we could." It was a neat feminine excuse, all the neater because she didn't look at Lennox to place the blame on him.

Lennox didn't have to speak, because Johann had grasped his arm and was walking beside him, talking in that hoarse, confidential whisper of his. "One's an American. One's English. Both were dropped by parachute about six miles from here. They went to Schroffenegger's house. He brought them to us. They are all right. We are sure of them. They knew all the right questions and answers."

The wood thinned. At its edge there was a forester's hut. Before them was a broad stretch of fine green grass with isolated trees. A cart track wound down into the valley. That would be the usual road, which followed the valley back to Hinterwald as Katharina had described. The hut door was open, and Paul Mahlknecht was standing in its shadow. He looked pleased. At least, he was grinning widely. He put his arm round Lennox's shoulders and drew him into the hut.

"Your friends are here," he said.

Lennox looked over his shoulder, out at the green grass and the sunlight and the twisted oak trees. Johann was there, but Katharina had gone.

"Don't worry. We've two men out there watching the north road," Mahlknecht said, misinterpreting that look. "We are well protected."

"Where's the girl?" Lennox asked quickly.

"What? Missing her already?" said Mahlknecht, with mock concern, and he began to laugh. His head was thrown back, his teeth were white against the dark, bearded face. Johann and old Schroffenegger were laughing too. The two strangers smiled politely and looked at each other, as if the joke might be funny but not quite so funny as all that.

Lennox said angrily, "She shouldn't have gone back to her house. There are two Germans in her father's barn now."

The laughter ceased. Lennox explained quickly. The faces round him became more serious. He ended with the true reason why Katharina had been sent home from the village by her mother. The faces were thoughtful now.

"She went back just after I met them," Johann explained worriedly to his uncle. Then, as if to convince himself, "She'll be all right. Katharina will follow the wood almost to Hinterwald before coming down into the road. She won't walk straight out of the wood at our house. The Germans will only think she is coming back from the village."

"That is, if that Mussner girl doesn't tell them when Katharina was sent home from the village," Lennox said. "Or why," he added grimly.

Johann moved to the door. "I'll see if I can catch up with Katharina. What shall I do? Give her warning, or bring her back here? If she doesn't return home her mother will have a search party out for her. The whole village will be talking then."

Mahlknecht glanced worriedly at the two polite strangers. He had a habit of biting the corner of his lip when he was working out a problem. He must have solved it, for his lower lip suddenly covered his top one determinedly, and his chin was more aggressive than ever.

He said, "She can't come here, obviously. Tell her to go to her aunt's house and stay there today. Her aunt can let her mother know where she is."

Johann nodded. He saluted them all with a perky forefinger, and stepped outside.

Lennox moved quickly to the door. "She will have to pass the large boulder at the northeast corner of our wood. She left her shoes and apron there."

"Bet you I find her before she leaves the torrent," Johann said, and with a parting grin which split up his face into two wide curves, he began a steady, loping run. There was something very neat and compact and capable about his movements.

Lennox was thinking of the boy's cool confidence. It wasn't boasting. Johann would probably overtake Katharina before she had traveled very far. He began to share the boy's quiet assurance, and he realized that if ever anything were to come of Mahlknecht's plans then he and these two other strangers would have to learn to trust the people of the mountains. For they knew their own capabilities, and they didn't claim anything beyond what they could do. He remembered the incident at the waterfall: certainly he had been too quickly discouraged there. And as he turned to enter the foresters' hut and meet the men who had arrived on the Schlern Lennox was thinking that perhaps nothing was so difficult, or so easy, as it first seemed.

CHAPTER **16**

"Come and meet your friends," Mahlknecht was saying. Lennox came into the room slowly, his tired muscles jibing at him.

It was a simple place, divided for sleeping and for eating. One half of the room had a wooden table and benches, shelves—obviously for dishes —and a cupboard—probably for food. The other half had a row of rough wooden bunks along its walls. In the center of the wall opposite the door was a crude stone fireplace. The four windows were high-placed, small, and sheltered by the deep, jutting roof. They gave a feeling of snugness and security to the room.

The two strangers rose from the table. He suddenly realized that they were as wary of him as he was of them. They had given the right questions and answers; that was what Johann had said. But he still looked them over, as carefully as they were watching him. Leather trousers, embroidered braces, rough gray jackets not too new, collarless white shirts opened at the neck, battered felt hats with a jaunty feather, white stockings, heavy climbing boots with coarse leather laces. Their faces were tanned with sun and reddened by wind. Both were fair-haired, both were thin and yet tough-looking. One had snub features and gray eyes. The other had sharper features and blue eyes. Both sets of eyes were equally watchful. Both men could have been anything, pure Tyrolese for that matter. He couldn't even guess which was American, which was English. Their anonymity was striking: they had the kind of face which you forget easily and remember with difficulty.

Old Schroffenegger nodded approvingly. "Well, you'll all know each other again." He laughed. "They are all good Tyroler. Look, Paul: they don't move a muscle. Good Tyroler. Why, I remember when the Italians used to meet each other there would be embracing and kissing. They did more kissing than our women." His thin hands slapped the two nearest shoulders with surprising strength. "We can work with these dour faces, can't we, Paul? Eh?"

The two strangers and Lennox weakened enough to exchange a self-conscious grin. Their tension relaxed.

"Can't imagine us wasting kisses on each other," the blue-eyed man said. He spoke in English, and judging from his voice, he was an Englishman.

The gray-eyed man's smile broadened. "No darned fear." He turned back to the bench and sat down. "We were just making sure, that was all. You fit the colonel's description all right."

Lennox said, "But I have still to make sure. The colonel couldn't give me any description of you."

The Englishman looked at him appraisingly.

"Fair enough," he said at last. "Well, I am Roy Shaw, captain, Royal Sussex Regiment. This is William Thomson, captain, Signal Corps, United States Army. We were both sent here to follow up information given by Colonel Wayne after his escape from a prisoner-of-war camp outside of Bozen. Shall I have to go on describing the colonel's graying hair; or the wound on Private John Stewart's forehead and the dyed coat he was wearing—your coat once, I believe; or Corporal William Ferry's views about the most hated guard at the prison camp whose name was Falcone?"

So Jock and Bill Ferry had got through. . . . "Good old—" he began, and then halted. He felt a fool: he, the amateur, had challenged the professionals in what must have seemed a very naïve way. He gave Shaw a grudging good mark for his patience. He also remembered the word captain. He drew himself erect. "No, sir," he said. His face was too expressionless.

"Cut that out," Thomson said, grinning.

Shaw nodded his agreement. "We won't get very far, that way," he said. He sat down at the table. "Come on, Lennox, take a seat and tell us how you've been holding the fort. How did the winter go? How serious are these chaps?" He looked at Mahlknecht and Schroffenegger. "That's the first thing we want to know."

Mahlknecht had probably not understood the quickly spoken words, but he had interpreted Shaw's look correctly enough.

"We'll leave you here, and take a walk down to the woods to watch the south path for Johann," he suggested. He walked to the door. "One of us may have to go down later to the Kasal barn just to make sure there is no trouble." That was all he said, but Peter Lennox knew he was worried too.

The three foreigners watched the two men walk into the sunlight with their solid, heavy tread.

"It's tough on them," Thomson said. "Underground resistance is the toughest fight of all. It's the women that make it so tough. That girl you were worrying about, for instance. . . ."

"It's easier for us," Shaw agreed. "Our wives and children are safe at home. But here, a German can use them as blackmail." He looked at Lennox thoughtfully. "Do the men up here know what they are letting themselves in for?"

Lennox nodded. "We've talked about it this winter. They know that there can be no successful resistance unless the women are with them. If a wife starts weeping she'll hold her husband back. That's what old Schroffenegger said. But as far as I could make out, the women here do not go in for much weeping. They'll follow their men, and they'll take the risks."

His voice was grim, and he eyed the other two bitterly.

Shaw noticed that look. "I know," he said quietly, "our arrival spells trouble for many people. And yet if we hadn't been asked to come here then there would have been no spirit of resistance, no proof that these people weren't collaborationists. There's no easy way for an occupied country. They fight either on our side or on the other. Inaction and neutral thoughts fight for the other side. That's how you have to measure it. You count the facts and avoid imagination. That's what you've got to do."

His words made sense. But, Lennox thought, Shaw hadn't lived with those people for eight months. They were part of a military plan to these two men: they weren't Frau Schichtl and Johann and Katharina Kasal and old Schroffenegger. He said nothing. He watched the calm face and the cold eyes. The American, too, had lost his bitter emotion. He was equally matter-of-fact and objective.

Shaw's colorless voice went on, "We'll get down to the business on hand. Lennox, you've said the people here will accept the consequences. Do you mean they have all agreed to act?"

Lennox hesitated. It would have sounded better if he could have answered yes; but that wouldn't have been accurate. "Many of them have agreed. All those whom Mahlknecht can trust."

The American said, "Our information is that in the plebiscite of 1939 the Austrians of the South Tyrol were sharply divided. Some hundred and eight-five thousand voted to leave the South Tyrol to go to Austria. Up to date only about seventy per cent have been transshipped. The other eighty-two thousand voted to stay here and become Italian citizens. From your observations here this winter, can you add anything to these facts?"

Lennox said, "Statistics in this case don't tell us a thing. In the first place the people of the South Tyrol had that plebiscite forced on them by what they consider to be two foreign governments—the Italians and the Germans. The people just wanted to stay here and to be left alone. But they were forced either to leave their homes if they wanted to keep their own language or customs, or to become Italian citizens if they didn't want to leave their own land. Of those who chose to leave, only a few were pro-Nazi: most of them had only a hatred of Italian domination. Of those who stayed, none of them considered they had become Italians; they played out the farce, stuck to their homes, and hated the Nazis for having forced this plebiscite. They knew they had been put between the devil and the deep blue sea. Then the Germans sent many of the exiled South Tyrolese away from the North Tyrol where they had expected to settle. That isn't being forgotten, either by those who stayed here, or by those who left here and were then cheated. When the Germans took over all the South Tyrol last September, all the Austrians were glad the Italians had gone. But many of them consider the Germans are just another gang of tyrants. And these are the people whom Mahlknecht has organized."

"And what about those who haven't been organized by Mahlknecht?" Shaw asked. "A lot have been coming back from the north this winter."

"These can be divided into two groups. The larger one hasn't done any-thing to help us so far, but they haven't helped the Germans either. They are waiting and watching. They are just pro-themselves. The smaller group is pro-German, because they still believe the German promises to save them from the Italians. They've seen the Germans replace the old Austrian names and inscriptions and Austrian is again being taught in the schools. They therefore believe that atrocity stories from other countries are merely propaganda, and some of them—who have returned from Germany, where they were made teacher's pets—think they are going to become powerful in key positions. Mahlknecht told us last night about some of these boys who are already Nazi bosses down in the bigger towns. Peter Hofer, for instance, in Bozen. He was killed in December. Karl Tinzl is still alive, though. Mahlknecht has a list of them. They will be taken care of, either now as supposed air raid victims, or quite openly later when the need for secrecy is gone."

Thomson was smiling. "Peter Hofer was reported to have been killed in an air raid on Bozen," he said.

Shaw was thoughtful. "Mahlknecht and his friends have a difficult job. They haven't a clear-cut issue to put before their people: the Italian problem makes a mess of that. Did he tell you the Socialist underground paper, *Avanti*, has been having editorials showing that Italy must be given back the North Tyrol? It's Italy's historical function to protect the Brenner from the Germans."

"Swell job of protection they did when they got the chance," the Amer-ican said. He gave a short laugh.

"It's a serious matter, though," Shaw said at last. "It's enough to throw all the South Tyrol into cynical neutrality."

"Not Mahlknecht or old Schroffenegger or any of their chaps!" Lennox said determinedly. He halted in amazement at the warmth of his own voice.

"I believe you," Shaw said. "Our men who made contact with him in Bozen saw some of his work there."

"All the more credit to these guys like Mahlknecht who do see the issue even if it's all blotted over for them. A lot of men won't fight unless they see things pure black and pure white," Thomson said. "Now, what interests me is just how Mahlknecht proposes to use his organization. What about that?"

"Yes," Shaw said. "We've learned why. But how?"

Lennox hesitated. He was gathering the facts together. He was worried in case he would forget the most important angles. Or perhaps the things which he thought important would not be what these two men wanted. That would be a criminal blunder on his part. They were waiting expectantly. That made him feel all the more nervous.

He began speaking too quickly.

"Take it easy," Thomson advised with that slow smile of his. "I'm kind of dumb." Shaw was smiling at that, and Lennox's tension eased. His explanation began to take concise form.

First of all, there was the German defense of the Brenner Pass and the Eisak Valley to be considered. That was the road into Austria. German guns, placed high on the mountainsides, would hold up any advance there by Allied troops for months. There would be wholesale slaughter. But men who knew the mountains, who had been supplied with the right equipment, could do an efficient job of sabotage. Some highly trained men should be sent into the mountains to help Mahlknecht's organization. It was willing and eager to do the job. It only needed a few experts—and a lot of explosives.

In the second place, there was the Allied attack. Parachutists, even gliders with air-borne troops, could land on the broad high meadows. If they were given excellent guides these advance units could cut off the narrow valley entirely and trap the German armies retreating from Italy.

Thirdly, there were political possibilities to be considered. The North Tyrol, where there was already much feeling against the Nazis, could have its resistance linked to the South Tyrol. Ties of blood and family were strong between the two districts. In action against the Germans they could achieve the union they had wanted. And if the North Tyrol were to rise —well, the North Tyrol bordered Bavaria. It was the biggest back door to Germany.

When he had ended the other two sat for some moments without speaking.

Lennox began to wonder if he had seemed a fool. He watched them nervously. They were looking at each other now, and he thought he saw an amused glance pass between them. Or perhaps it was a pleased glance.

He hung on to that hope. Damn it all, what do they expect from a blasted amateur? he thought angrily.

Shaw said, "Ambitious, but exciting."

Thomson was grinning broadly. "At least, we won't be chasing our tail," he said. And Lennox suddenly realized that these two men had been as much afraid of being disappointed in his information as he had been afraid of their scorn.

The tension broke. The American rose, still smiling, and began pacing the floor. "Boy, it gives us some scope," he said at last. "I've got a couple of maps, but what about those guides you mentioned? One reliable guide is worth ten maps."

"Four members of the Committee are guides. That was their job in peacetime. And there are guides in every village. They know this country like the back of their hands."

"Have they much ammunition stored?" Shaw asked practically.

"No. They have small arms and a few machine guns which they swiped. They need more. And they need dynamite and grenades."

"What kind of man power?"

"They can't offer us quantity. They admit that. But they also say that you don't need numbers for fighting here. This is a place for infiltration, not massed attacks."

"Can they fight?"

"They are a fairly peaceful people. They are law-abiding and honest. But if they are roused they will fight. They are as hard as their mountains."

Shaw nodded thoughtfully, and then fell silent. He was thinking over what he had just heard. Thomson too was far away in a world of mountain contours and safe landing places.

Well, that's that, Lennox thought. He rose and walked to the doorway. He had given his report and his vote of confidence. His job was done. All he had to think of now was the road which would take him south into Italy. At last he could try that long-planned escape. Yet strangely, now that he could have it, he didn't want it. He glanced over his shoulder at the American and Englishman. He envied them.

He looked out over the grass—fine, thin grass, like the kind he used to see in a seedmonger's window display. There were small blue flowers close to the earth. A large flying beetle snapped its hard green wings at his feet. The small oaks, with their curiously gnarled trunks, were putting out their uneven leaves. The larch and spruce were tall and straight. They gave a blue cast to the depths of green in the woods. Soon the mountainside would be a stretch of bright color. The last snows on the tall gray mountain teeth would melt, and there would be peaches and vines ripening in the valleys under the high blue skies. "A poor country," Mahlknecht had said yesterday, but he had said it proudly. Now Lennox understood the simplicity of the people who lived here: they were content with little because they had so much.

He saw Mahlknecht leave Schroffenegger at the path into the wood, and start slowly towards the hut. He walked as a man who is worried and thoughtful.

Lennox turned quickly back into the hut. "There's still the problem of these two Jerries," he said quickly. "I had almost forgotten them."

Thomson and Shaw stopped their discussion.

"We can't get rid of them the easy way," Thomson said. "We can't have men with bullet- or knife-wounds lying about." Then thoughtfully: "We buried our parachutes according to the book. They might have heard our plane, might even—from some distance—have seen us drop. There's always that chance. But how did they connect all that with the Schichtl house?"

"They didn't connect it," Lennox suggested. "I don't believe they know you are here. You just timed your arrival for a rather delicate moment, that's all. They are looking for the men who guide Allied flyers out of these mountains. Johann disappears at certain periods and returns, exhausted but weather-beaten. Someone who knows Johann well enough to note his disappearance and reappearance has given them that information. They have found that these disappearances take place after the remains of an Allied plane have been discovered. They are just checking up on Johann. That's all."

"But who could give that information about Johann?"

Lennox said, "He has been seeing a girl. Last thing on leaving, first thing on return, no doubt. She's the niece of a collaborationist. Mussner is the name."

"Johann's a bloody fool," Shaw said. He was angry. Thomson didn't seem any too pleased either. They both looked as if they had begun to wonder how many fools they might find on this job.

"No," Lennox said. "He isn't a fool. He's just young. He thinks that if a girl kisses you she really means it." Lennox was silent for a moment. He was too busy remembering the past to notice the American's uplifted eyebrow. "Perhaps he *was* a bloody fool," he concluded with a bitter smile, forcing himself away from the memories which he had thought were long buried.

Mahlknecht entered the room. He looked quickly at the two officers. "Well?"

"Everything is all right," Shaw answered. His Tyrolese accent wasn't too bad, Lennox noted. It would be perfect in a week or two. He couldn't resist feeling pleased that his own accent was better.

"Good." Mahlknecht was relieved. His whole face smoothed out. But his eyes were still thoughtful. "There is an immediate problem," he said.

The three younger men exchanged glances and smiled. "We know,"

Thomson agreed. "We were just discussing at this moment how to silence the two Germans and the Mussner girl."

"That can be managed." Mahlknecht's voice was quiet and capable. He was doing his best to keep the two newcomers' confidence in his people. It had been bad luck that the Germans' sudden interest in the Schichtl house had happened just at this time. Mahlknecht's pride was hurt: he had worked carefully, and now there was this incident which a stranger might think was a proof of incompetence. It showed Lennox somehow how sincerely Mahlknecht wanted the help of the Allies. He wanted these men to stay, to trust him and his people.

Mahlknecht was biting the corner of his lip again. When he spoke there was a certain dignity in his words. There was no minimizing of his worry.

"We can take care of the Mussner girl in a civilized manner," he said. "We shall send Johann away, with one of the missions into the North Tyrol. She will not see him again, so she will have no more guesses to pass over to her German friends. We shall watch her closely, from now on."

"And the two Jerries in the barn?" Shaw spoke crisply. He wasn't the man to make excuses, and he didn't expect any. He was a hard case, Lennox thought. That was the kind of man Mahlknecht had wanted; he had certainly got it.

"It would be easy to lead them up a mountain. There's many a way of getting rid of a man on a mountainside. But even if these Germans seemed to die accidentally on a mountain the question of why they should have been climbing is still unanswered. And other Germans, with stronger suspicions, would come and take their place. So the problem is this: we must lead them away from the Schichtl house back to where their friends can see them. And either we must put an end to their suspicions, or—if necessary—kill them. But on no account must their death confirm the German suspicion."

Shaw and Thomson nodded. They were pleased with Mahlknecht's quiet analysis. They were relieved that they weren't dealing with a hot-head, filled with heroic plans which would only lead to disaster.

"You were right," Shaw said to Lennox. "Our friend Mahlknecht is a very careful fellow." Then he turned to Mahlknecht. "What is your explanation of these waiting Germans?"

"First, they had some suspicion about the Schichtl house giving help to Allied airmen who had crashed. We believe that their suspicion came from vague information supplied by Eva Mussner. It must have been vague, or else we in the Schichtl house should all have been arrested yesterday. . . . Secondly, they must have learned that two men dropped from a plane near here last night. But they can have no idea whether these two men were parachuting as agents, or simply bailing out of a plane which might later have crashed in the high mountains. Certainly they have no idea who you are, for today, in the village, you were accepted by them as men of the Schlern. And that makes me believe, although we cannot be sure, that they are looking for two airmen rather than agents. . . . Thirdly, they went back to the Schichtl house, to see if the parachutists had gone there for help. The two Germans who are now dressed as civilians came along with the S.S. men because these civilians had seen us yesterday and so could identify any newcomers today."

"And that," Thomson said, "sounds as near the truth as we shall ever know. We'll have to work, as we've often done, by guess and by God. But the first problem is, they are still waiting."

Lennox said, "Yes. And why? They must have some real suspicion now about the Schichtl house." He kept worrying about the sure way in which the two Germans had walked to the Kasal barn. They had been settling down to watch and to wait. Of that he felt sure. "They found no strangers in the house. Why should they wait?"

"Perhaps," Mahlknecht said slowly, "perhaps they are waiting for you."

Lennox was silent. It was true: he hadn't been seen in the village, and so he should have been at the house. The Germans would think it interesting if he were to be found neither near the house nor in the village. He realized suddenly that this was the thought at the back of his mind which had been worrying him all afternoon. He realized that now as he listened to Mahlknecht's words. He knew what he had to do, what they expected him to do.

He moved over to the door so that he could see the grass and the trees and the mountains. He was wondering how you fought Germans with bare hands and quick wits. This was the civilian way of resisting; this was something new for a soldier to learn. A tommy gun would have seemed very comforting at this moment.

"I suppose I ought to move back to the house, then," he said. "The longer I stay away, the more questions they will begin to ask."

The others didn't answer. They were thinking of their other problems, balancing them against this one. They probably had a dozen worries to solve at this moment.

His voice became more assured. "Look, you have other things to think about. I'll shut up those two Jerries somehow. Johann will help me. Anyway, this looks like our particular headache."

The others accepted this solution.

"I'm glad you volunteered," Shaw said. "You'll manage it all right."

"If there's any questioning then act dumb," Thomson advised.

Lennox smiled grimly. "I shall be dumb, all right," he said. He was still wondering how to fight Germans with bare hands. And then it didn't seem so difficult: anyone who had been a prisoner of war had learned to fight with his wits.

Mahlknecht said, "Use your own judgment." And as Lennox looked at him sharply, he added, "—whether they stay alive or not."

Lennox nodded. He moved slowly over the clearing, and then as he saw Johann standing talking to old Schroffenegger at the path his pace quickened. Johann had won his bet. Katharina had been warned. Lennox was smiling as he said to the boy, "We have a little job to do."

The three men in the hut returned to the table.

Thomson straightened the map thoughtfully and picked up his pencil. "Pity we hadn't time to give them a helping hand."

The Englishman's silence showed he agreed.

Mahlknecht said slowly, "I am sorry, gentlemen, that this incident had to happen at this time." He was embarrassed as if he blamed himself for this complication.

The American laughed. "Don't let that worry you. Something always happens at the wrong time. Doesn't it, Roy?"

The Englishman nodded, absent-mindedly. "You know," he said, "that man Lennox might not be a bad chap to have around. Useful, perhaps."

"Yes." Thomson was thoughtful too. "Remember the colonel's report on him? Intelligent man, but undisciplined. Either Lennox has learned the hard way or the colonel was making a snap decision. I don't know of any greater discipline than being able to take your own orders."

"He's learned." Shaw paused, pretending to examine the map. "Now we had better get on with our own job. We'll have to trust Lennox to do his."

Mahlknecht sat astride a wooden bench, and began to advise. His own worry about Johann and Lennox began to recede: he began to believe, even as these two foreigners had assumed, that the Germans would have their problems too.

CHAPTER **17**

The journey to the Schichtl house was swift. Johann's pace was steady and unbroken. He moved over the more difficult ground quickly, without slackening speed, as if he expected Lennox to follow easily. And because it was expected of him, Lennox managed it. Either the brief rest at Schönau, or the stimulus of the two Allied officers' arrival, or the sense of necessity which surrounded him had chased away the fatigue of his muscles. Or perhaps they had never really forgotten the long months of training in the desert. They were obeying him, anyway. His mind was clear. He had a feeling of growing confidence. He was sure now that the job which he and Johann had to do could be done, if only they were quick enough at improvising. Improvise, he told himself—that's your best chance.

As he followed Johann's easy stride, imitating its changes in rhythm, matching footholds down difficult terrain, he could let his mind think about the simplest plan on which improvisation could be worked. He kept remembering Mahlknecht's implication. The Germans were first to be satisfied that he was alone at the house, that he didn't expect anyone. Then they were to be led away from the house. They were to be led away. And after that he was to use his own judgment.

The sunlight was deepening in color. A cool breeze was blowing up from the meadows. From the direction of the village he could hear the gay, distant music of a band, ebbing and flowing like a tide as the wind dropped or strengthened. The late afternoon had brought high clouds, tight and withdrawn into the soft blue of the sky. The rock of the mountain precipices had lost its hard gray look: the yellow sun was drawing out the warmth from its veins. The dark fir trees grew more secret with the coming of evening; the thick stretches of woods, like twisting bands of rich green velvet, separated the bright new grass in the meadows from the giant teeth of rock. Lennox thought of the men and women gathered together in the village, of their gay costumes and bright music and friendly laughter disguising nagging worries. He thought of the Germans in the village and the hidden trucks, quietly waiting. He thought of the two Germans in the Kasal barn, impatient, speculating. He thought of the three men in the forester's hut on the Schönau; of old Schroffenegger guarding the south path while his two sons kept watch on the northern road to the lumber camp. He thought of Johann and himself moving on their grim errand across the wide mountainside. The background of space and height gave the feeling of peace. It was a most noble illusion, he decided bitterly.

At the wood behind the Schichtl house they avoided the path, and made their way carefully and indirectly down between the thicker trees. Halfway Lennox stopped to give his quiet instructions. Johann nodded; he was listening intently. His young face was strangely blank. But the plan seemed to please him, for he nodded again and clapped Lennox's shoulder as much as to say, "We'll give the blighters a run for their money." Then he cut swiftly off to his left to reach the edge of the wood where Katharina and Lennox had watched the German car on the road. Lennox walked on to the house.

The untouched breakfast table reminded him that he was hungry. The fire in the stove was almost out. The house was forlorn and cheerless, as if it remembered the disordered bedroom upstairs, the neglect downstairs, and resented such unusual treatment.

He decided to attend to the fire first. It was something of a job to get it lit if he once let it die out completely. He raked the ashes gently, threw on some small dried twigs, and then decided to go out for more wood. The logs were piled outside under the windows. Here was the chance for anyone watching this house to see him being thoroughly domestic. He felt self-conscious about the way he wouldn't let himself look at the Kasal barn. And then he wondered suddenly whether the Germans were still there. He'd feel a fool if they weren't, pretending so hard to be so damned natural. He brought back two logs into the house, carrying them in his left arm. He hoped his right arm would look weak to any observer. He made a second journey, and a third, using only his left arm for the carrying.

After that he felt he deserved an outsized sandwich. He ate it, standing at the side of the neat window with its crisp curtains, keeping his body well out of sight of the road. He was wondering just what the two Germans were planning now; they must have identified him from the Kasal barn, and yet they themselves couldn't come over here to question him. It gave him some pleasure to think that life was complicated for them too. If anything he had the advantage over them: the Germans were watching him, but they didn't know that they themselves were being just as carefully watched. His vigil at the window was rewarded. He saw one of the men leave the Kasal barn, moving quickly round its side so that he could no longer be seen from the Schichtl house or the road. He didn't appear again: he must have gone down into the low-lying field where his movements would be hidden. Lennox heard the Kasal dog bark. The German must be walking past the lean cows at pasture. Well, that was one way of reaching Hinterwald quietly and making a report. The other must still be waiting in the barn. How both of them must have cursed the simplicity of life in these mountains: a telephone in the Kasal farmhouse would have been a useful gadget at this moment. Anyway, Lennox thought as he turned away from the window, he had ruined a fine May afternoon for them. He hoped they had run out of cigarettes, too.

He poured some milk, cut another slice of bread and another chunk of cold meat, and sat down at the table with a feeling of satisfaction. The next move was the Germans', and he guessed it wouldn't take long. He had made the opening gambit. This whole business was, the more he thought of it, rather like a game of chess. It was a damned queer way to fight a war. Yet this was the way it was being fought by a lot of people. He wondered how many women and men in Europe were at this moment waiting for a German to come and question them.

He had finished his second glass of milk, and was making a third sandwich, when he heard the approaching car. So the German, slinking across the fields, had reached Hinterwald and recruited strength. And now the test. He imagined Johann at this moment, alert, watchful. Probably sweating it out. Lennox wasn't exactly cool and collected himself. But he would have to be. . . . Lack of confidence was an expensive luxury when you paid with your life. Prison camp had taught him to be an actor, a dissembler. He had faced questioning before; all he had to do, he knew, was to stick to his story.

He began eating the sandwich. He sat down once more, sprawling with his feet resting on a second chair. He unbuttoned his waistcoat, and propped the German-published *Bozener Tageblatt* against the earthenware crock of milk at his elbow. The haggled loaf spread its coarse crumbs on the tablecloth. The remains of meat looked as if it had been enjoyed. Lennox studied the effect and was satisfied. The observant German eyes, which would mark every detail, would see a picture of a bucolic bachelor enjoying the simple pleasures of home.

The car halted outside the house. Peter Lennox looked up from his newspaper as the front door was pushed open.

The two Germans, in the black uniform of special police, whom he had already seen today, were standing in the doorway.

Lennox stopped chewing, and surveyed them gravely.

"This the road to Seis?" one of them asked.

Lennox nodded with deliberation. "Yes," he said. "Yes, it's one of the roads to Seis." He ignored the prying eyes. He went on eating. "There's a better road down on the meadows."

"Have you been here all day?"

"Mostly."

"Did you see two men following this road?"

Lennox shook his head.

"Are you sure?" While the one man questioned the other looked round the kitchen intently. He didn't learn anything there, for he moved back into the living room. It seemed to Lennox that he was staring at the steps leading up to the bedroom.

"I didn't notice anyone while I was here," Lennox said with determination through a well-filled mouth. He chewed reflectively.

"You were down at the village?"

"No. I was out for a walk this afternoon. Went to get a breath of air."

"Did you see a car?"

"I heard a car just after I left the house. Couldn't see it, though."

"Were you away from this house for long?"

"Not so very long. An hour or two. Perhaps three. Time passes quickly."

"Three hours looking at the view?" The German's voice was losing any patience it had adopted initially.

"I fell asleep." Lennox's voice was friendly and confiding. "There's a good place under a pine tree. The sun was warm. And the view was good."

"Enjoying life, aren't you?" There was no humor in the hard eyes.

Lennox finished the sandwich and then looked up at the German. "There were no mountains to look at in Africa," he said. "There wasn't much sleep either."

The other German was standing at the entrance to the house. His head was bent as if he were studying the gleam on his well-polished boots.

"So you're an old soldier. Got your papers?" the cross-examining German asked. Lennox produced them. The German read them with interest.

"From the Zillertal, eh? You're quite a way from home."

"I've no home there any more. I came here because my aunt could give me one until I got well again."

The German didn't answer. He was now studying Peter Schichtl's discharge papers. He glanced quickly at Lennox's right hand. The scar reassured him, for he went on reading with less interest. Severe wound in right hand, shrapnel fragments in right forearm, bullet wound close to left lung and possible weakness of lung.

The German threw the papers on the table. "Report with these at the police station," he said. "All men are to register there."

Lennox stared stupidly.

The German said impatiently, "The police station in Hinterwald."

As Lennox still said nothing, still sat staring, the German said with rising anger, "Report at police headquarters. At the Golden Roof Inn. To-day. Understand?"

Lennox gathered up his papers slowly, put them carefully away, rose, and searched for his hat, and nodded.

The German, who was waiting at the door, said, "Nothing here. Come on." He moved out into the sunlight.

The German who had done the talking followed him. They didn't speak within Lennox's hearing. He heard the car start, and saw it follow ostensibly the track to Seis. He was quite prepared to wager that it would swing west on the first crossroads it met, and circle round by the "foreigners' road" towards Hinterwald again. The Germans were concentrating on Hinterwald today.

He cleared the table so that the littered kitchen wouldn't upset Frau Schichtl on her return. The stove was burning slowly with the new wood. The logs he hadn't used were drying on the whitewashed stone hearth. Before he left the house he paused as the curious German had done, and looked at the staircase. The steps were perfectly normal, practical wooden steps scrubbed white. But as he looked he had a sudden doubt. The four bottom steps were less white, as if a dust film were over them. He bent down and drew a finger along the surface of the lowest step. There was a whitish powder on his forefinger. He walked up the four steps and then walked down again. The dust had clung to his shoes, and there was the faint but clear outline of their soles. He crossed over to the front door. The same fine powder had been scattered over the threshold, for the impression of the Germans' boots was there. Not strong, but definite enough if you were looking for it. At the back door, he found the marks of many footsteps, but it was plain they came from the one pair of shoes—his shoes. Anyone coming into this house, carefully, cleverly, to avoid the Germans would have still been caught; anyone hidden in a secret place upstairs which the Germans hadn't been able to discover in their search, anyone venturing downstairs when he thought the house was empty, would have been discovered.

Lennox was not exactly cheerful as he left the house and started to walk towards the village. He was too angry with himself for having taken so long to notice the German trick, a petty trick, a silly trick. But still a trick which might have come off. He reflected that when he had been a prisoner of war he had been sharp-witted enough to notice that kind of thing, or at least to have suspected something like it. He had learned the old lesson once more this afternoon: expect nothing, trust nothing. Fortunately the Schichtls and Mahlknecht hadn't been so simple-minded as the Germans had thought. There had been no strangers as secret guests in the house.

He passed the Kasal barn, and then the farmhouse. Johann, from his vantage point in the woods, must have seen him on this stretch of road; and he would know that all was well so far. And Johann would now be keeping a steady pace on the higher mountain path to Hinterwald, so that he would reach there before Lennox did, and would be standing at the doorway of the Hotel Post to welcome his "cousin." They had chosen the Post as their meeting place, for it lay at the beginning of the village, and Lennox would see it very easily. Besides, the owner of the hotel was a trusted friend of Mahlknecht.

The Kasals' dog barked. But there was no other noise or movement from the farm buildings. As he followed the twisting road, and knew that he was now hidden from view from the Kasal barn, Lennox began to walk more briskly. His movements felt natural once more, now that no German eyes were watching him.

The first stage was over: he had made his claim that he had been near the house all day, and that he had been alone. There was no evidence, yet, to disprove that. The second stage was now beginning: the Germans were to be drawn away from the Schichtl house. The solitary German, now left in the barn, must have seen Lennox take the road to Hinterwald. There were two things the German could do. Either he could keep right on sitting in the barn, and much good that would do him watching an empty house, or he could set out to follow his suspect to Hinterwald. "Don't look now, but . . ." Lennox told himself. He began to whistle one of Frau Schichtl's favorite songs.

His spirits mounted as he thought of the three men—the German, Johann, and himself—all traveling to Hinterwald by parallel routes:

Johann up on the hillside, he on the cart track, the German no doubt using the short cut across the fields. It amused him still more that the Germans were under a pretty delusion: they didn't know that within this last hour their whole function had changed. They had become just as much the hunted as they had been the hunters.

CHAPTER **18**

The road began to wind downhill like a snake basking in sunshine. Evening was drawing near. The cool breeze on the hillside gave way to the still air of the valley. Sounds were magnified. The music was stronger now: Lennox could hear the clear notes of a trumpet and the deeper tones of a trombone. The drum beat out the first pulse in a gay three-to-the-bar tune.

He passed four large summer villas, shuttered and abandoned, hiding their loneliness among scattered trees. Then there was a small meadow, falling in a gentle curve towards the village. A small church, no longer than forty feet, had been built on top of the meadow. The wooden spire, rising from the square tower, was onion-shaped. The plaster walls had been colored, and they had weathered into a faded pink. There were wide-spaced paintings of saints, which decorated without concealing the walls' surface. Lennox noted that the balance of the design was good. He slowed his pace, and then suddenly climbed the short slope of grass towards the church. He began walking round its outside walls.

Some of the murals showed definite training and talent, some were more primitive. Those on the south wall had almost disappeared under sun and rain. There were cracks in the wall too, now that he examined it closely. This church was poor: little money had been spent on it in recent years. Above the door was the figure of Christ on the Cross. The loincloth was painted white, and the flesh tone was dark brown. The artist had captured a strangely pitying look in the large, gentle eyes. Lennox's interest quickened.

He hesitated on the worn stone step. The inside of the church was in shadow, for the windows were high-placed on the walls. There was a pyramid of candles burning with a clear, steady flame on the small altar. Behind it was an elaborately carved wooden triptych. Lennox took a step forward. It was as if the last five years of his life had vanished in as many minutes.

There was the rustle of silk and the light sound of narrow heels. A woman came out of the church. She pulled back the embroidered scarf which had covered her smooth dark hair, and let it fall around her shoulders as a shawl. She was young. Her low-necked black dress was of rich silk banded with velvet. The wide sleeves of her blouse, very white above the black lace which covered her forearms, were transparent and crisp. Her flower-embroidered apron was of a curiously clear blue. It matched the color of her eyes.

She looked at him in surprise for a moment. But she recovered first. "*Grüss Gott!*" she said.

"*Grüss Gott!*" he answered slowly. He was watching her, with the background of gleaming candles behind the dark head, with the faded pink walls framing the slender figure in its elaborate costume.

"There is no one in the church. Father Sturm had to leave—he was needed at Seis. Frau Kaufmann is dying."

"In that case," Lennox began awkwardly, and moved away from the church door. He didn't finish his sentence. He remembered that Hinterwald shared its old Austrian priest with several other small villages. The Tyrolese were deeply Catholic, but they had never attended the larger church which the Italians had built to the south of Hinterwald, even if it were in good repair and had a priest who lived beside it. For the Italian functionaries and their families and the summer visitors had worshiped there. And as long as the name of Hinterwald had been struck off the map to give way to the alien Montefierro, as long as the children at school were forced to speak in a foreign language, as long as a man could be arrested for whistling a Tyrolese song in public, these Austrians of the South Tyrol had avoided the well-provided church at the other end of the village. That, reflected Lennox, was something for the future peacemakers and map drawers to remember about human beings.

The girl had been speaking. Lennox said, "Please?" politely. He noticed, with approval, the high cheekbones and the almost classical line of nose and chin. The texture of her skin was smooth, its color was vivid and alive. Beauty, when it is natural, is overpowering.

"Are you going to the village?" she asked for the second time. She was smiling now.

"Yes."

"Then we can walk together." She wasn't smiling any more. In repose, there was a certain sadness, almost a tenseness, in her face. She looked sideways at him as he fell into step beside her.

"I didn't see you there this morning." Her voice was polite.

"No. I have only just arrived."

"You are a stranger?"

"I'm Frau Schichtl's nephew. Peter Schichtl. Before the war I lived in the Zillertal."

"Then you are Johann's cousin." The warmth of her voice should have warned him, but he was still watching that line of throat and chin.

"Yes."

"Why did you come to the South Tyrol?"

"I've no home left up north. My mother died while I was in the Army." He thought grimly of the double meaning to his words. His people had indeed died while he was in the Army—a land mine in Chiswick had blotted out everything that had formed his home.

"Your brothers and sisters?"

"Scattered. I don't know where they are." Again it was bitterly true. The war had altered a lot of things.

"Are you here on leave from the Army?"

"Discharged." And that would probably be true, too. The murals on the church wall had reminded him of his hand. If he couldn't hold a pencil he couldn't hold a gun. He'd be discharged, all right. The bitterness in his voice reached the girl, for she was silent.

"You are sorry you are no longer in the Army?" she asked after a pause.

"Yes," he replied shortly. He noticed a shade of disappointment pass over her face. She looked at him coldly, almost accusingly. And he remembered, as he felt the first blight of disapproval, that she had been referring to the German Army.

After that she fell silent. They were walking on the road now, and on either side were scattered houses built among the trees which encircled Hinterwald. Then suddenly the road became a village street. There was a fountain, with the gaily colored wooden figure of a child holding an emptying pitcher out of which the water fell in a thin arc. There was a row of white houses winding downhill, with their carved wooden balconies and broad gable ends turned towards the street. Other houses were scattered in depth behind those on the street. None were in a straight row— the broad, flat roofs angled in every direction. There was a feeling of independence in the disarray of houses which were, in themselves, so well-designed and neat.

Lennox heard the voices of children, and their laughter. Ahead of him was the band, and people listening to the music. He halted. The girl stopped walking too, and watched him curiously. It was difficult for him to pretend to be as placid as these groups of oldish men who talked so quietly together, their weather-beaten faces impassive under the white-plumed hats. It had been nearly three years since he had seen a crowd of people enjoying themselves, since he had seen so many women gathered together.

The young girls stood like a cluster of blond statues, tall and broad-shouldered. Their hands were folded in front of the wide, deep layers of their skirts, as they gravely watched the red-faced musicians. Their restraint, their quietness, emphasized the strength of their bodies. Some older women stood behind the girls and watched them carefully, proudly. The children, with fair hair bleached silver, darted about among the spreading skirts and bright silk aprons, pursuing mysterious games, laughing for no obvious reason at all. He had forgotten how children could laugh. Over nothing.

Lennox's throat tightened, and there was a pinpricking behind his eyes. Bloody hell, he thought, and looked quickly away from the people to the inanimate houses. This girl beside him wasn't going to see him turn sentimental. He stared fixedly at the wall of the nearest house. And there, under a coat of white paint he could see the dimmed outlines of giant black lettering which had once greeted those arriving in the village. It was the Fascist slogan: *Crédere—Obbedire—Combattere*. Believe, obey, fight. Lennox's eyes hardened. He was in complete control again. It took more than a coat of paint, he was thinking, to obliterate that memory.

The girl said quietly, "We left it still showing. It's our monument to remind us of what the Fascists did to our village." She was watching his expression, and she became more friendly. "If you didn't come down to see the procession this morning why do you come down now? You shouldn't have come. See, there are few young men here now."

"I was sent down here. Two Germans came to the house and told me to come. I have to register at the police station."

"So here you are—just like that!" She stared at him in scorn and amazement. And then she was alarmed. "They came to the *Schichtl* house?"

He looked at her in some surprise. "Yes."

"What did they want?"

"I don't know. They asked questions, and then they went away. I don't know."

The girl looked at him as if he were a complete fool. He had to admit he had tried to give that impression. And then he saw she was angry because she was afraid.

"Was Johann with you?"

"No. He's in the village."

"He isn't. He hasn't been here all afternoon." The lovely face was tense with worry. "Can I trust you?" she asked suddenly, pathetically. "Johann is in danger. These two Germans came to question him. He's in danger, and it is my fault."

Lennox was looking at her so uncomprehendingly that she began an urgent, rambling explanation. Her voice was low as if she were afraid that a passer-by might overhear; it was hurried as if she knew there was little time. She had trusted her uncle. She had not seen him for a long time except for his two visits to Bozen at Christmas and Easter, for when their house in Hinterwald had been closed he had gone to live in the North Tyrol. She had preferred to stay in Bozen with her cousins. When he visited them it seemed natural that he should ask news about their old village, about the people she was meeting in Bozen. And she had, without thinking, answered his questions about Johann Schichtl.

When she finished Lennox was staring at her.

She misinterpreted his expression. "Do you understand what I mean? You must warn Johann. He avoided me today. You will tell him?"

Lennox smiled slowly, "You are mistaken," he said. "Johann isn't in danger. He has done nothing to put himself in danger. What danger is there?"

The blue eyes looked at him in anger. "You are a fool," she said.

He avoided her gaze. "Yes?" he asked quietly. He was looking down the village street again. At the door of the Hotel Post he saw Johann. And beyond, at a safe distance, he saw two men lounging against a wall. They were listening to the band which was now marching determinedly, if somewhat exhaustedly, towards the Hotel Post's garden. Their heads had turned away from him, but he knew that they had seen him. They were dressed in ordinary clothes, of the color and shape which he had seen entering the Kasal barn this afternoon. So he had brought them back to the village, and away from the Schichtl house. At least, he had managed the second stage of the job.

He looked once more at the girl, and smiled generously. He was thinking of all the German tricks. He couldn't have played a safer game than to look a fool. Her report to her uncle and his Nazi friends would give him a lot of comfort.

He was surprised to see her anger give way to tears. She said again, with difficulty, "Please tell Johann."

"Tell him yourself. He's over there," Lennox nodded to the door of the Hotel Post.

She looked, and she was obviously surprised. And then she shook her head. "He will avoid me if I go over, as all the others have been avoiding me." She turned towards him and said bitterly, "Why do you think I was in the church this afternoon? I'll tell you. I was running away from eyes in the street. Eyes which dislike me. That's why I was in the church." Her voice changed again. It was almost lifeless now. "Once I had friends here. When I came back here from Bozen I thought I would be happy. But I found today that I was mistaken. I've been mistaken in many things, it seems. My uncle— Won't you believe me? Have you never known someone you loved and trusted, someone who was separated from you for five years whom you still loved and trusted? And then you found that, although he looked the same, spoke the same, seemed the same, he had changed here"—she placed her clenched fist over her heart—"and here?" Her hand went to her brow.

Lennox was quite motionless. His voice was cold and hard. "It doesn't take five years. Six months is long enough with some women."

The girl was watching him. She was neither curious nor angry any more. She touched his arm gently for a moment.

"I'm sorry," she said, so quietly that he could hardly hear her words.

"You do know, then, that I speak the truth." She wondered what woman had changed in six months to hurt this man so deeply. Perhaps when he was away at the war. It would hurt most then.

He left her suddenly, as if he had read her thoughts.

She would have run after him, even if the whole village had laughed at her. But her uncle, sober-faced, soberly dressed in ordinary town clothes, was coming towards her. She waited, wondering what he would have to say now.

Johann took his hands out of his tight pockets, and removed the weight of his shoulder from the inn door. But he did not look at Lennox. His eyes looked beyond, to the street. "That was Eva Mussner," he said.

Lennox nodded.

Johann was still watching. "Her uncle has reached her," he reported. "They are talking. . . . She is walking with him. . . . They are going towards the Mussner house. And our two German snoopers are moving towards it too, and they've reached it, and they've gone inside. The Mussners have now reached the house also. . . . They've entered it. . . ." His voice was bitter. In his heart he had defended Eva Mussner, even if he had accepted his family's judgment for security's sake. In his heart he had hoped he could find proof that his family was wrong. And here was proof of another kind. The girl and her uncle had followed the two Germans into the Mussner house, as if by some prearranged plan. No doubt the Germans had thought of it, and given Mussner his instructions when they had seen the Schichtls' cousin talking so seriously with the girl.

Johann said roughly, "Come on. My mother and Frau Kasal are waiting for us. Come on."

Lennox still had nothing to say. He had resisted the momentary temptation to turn and look at the Mussner house. For all he knew, the Germans might be now watching from its windows to see how interested Johann and he were. Well, they weren't interested. Johann and he were now entering the inn.

Johann led the way. In the dark, wood-paneled, flag-stoned hall he said, "What's wrong with you? Did you tell Eva Mussner too much?" He smiled derisively. "She's easy to talk to, isn't she?"

"She learned nothing."

Lennox pretended to look at the carved design on the nearest panel. It represented a harvesting scene, with thick stacks of rye ready for the miller and rich vines heavy with grapes for the wine press. The artist had dated his work 1771. Lennox kept looking at the date. He was seeing it, but he wasn't even thinking about it: it was just something to fix his eyes on, to avoid looking at Johann.

"Tell me, Johann," he said very quietly, "do you think she is with her uncle in this?"

Johann said gruffly, "She's certainly with him at this moment."

Lennox stopped looking at the carved panel. The two men eyed each other carefully. But they said nothing more.

In the little wine room some of the older men and women were resting. Tired children sat obediently beside their grandparents. Their small, fair heads leaned back against the paneled walls, and their short legs stuck out numbly from the broad high benches. Above them the wooden panels were carved out into elaborate hunting scenes, but the children were too weary even to look at the stags and the chamois. Their bodies drooped with temporary exhaustion. For once they were silent, and only asked questions with their eyes.

Frau Schichtl had chosen one of the long tables, and beside her—talking worriedly, seriously—was a thin-faced woman who was evidently Frau Kasal. There were others at the table too, but they had grouped round Frau Schichtl and they were talking so continuously that they scarcely noticed the two young men beyond a polite phrase of greeting and a dignified bow. Usually a stranger would have excited interest. But today the people of the village were too occupied in hiding their worries by argument among themselves. They had too many questions of their own, still unanswered. Young Schichtl and his cousin seated themselves at the unoccupied end of the table. They seemed, outwardly, to belong to this party of peasants; actually, they were as isolated as if they had had a small table of their own. And they were less noticeable this way. Johann's next words confirmed that. With his elbow on the table, and his chin cupped in his hand so that the movement of his lips was scarcely noticeable, he said, "We can talk here."

"Give me five minutes," Lennox answered. Johann nodded, and became absorbed in ordering some wine.

Peter Lennox slumped on the hard bench as completely as the children. He would rest for five minutes and let his body relax completely. Then he would start shaping the plan which had begun to exist in his mind. For he must have a solid, simple plan; he must have a basis on which he could improvise, as he had been told to do. That was his job.

Around him was the constant rise and fall of voices. He watched the black flies circling aimlessly above the wooden table, and listened to their steady humming. Frau Schichtl and her friends were talking, but he heard nothing. He tried to think about nothing, too. But he kept thinking of Eva Mussner. She knew all the tricks, he decided bitterly. And then he was conscious that Johann was refilling his glass with wine, that Johann was waiting with eager impatience. Lennox pushed aside his glass, and rested his elbows on the table. He didn't look at Johann. He was watching the others, as if what they were discussing interested him. Johann was studying the jerky progress of a thirsty fly, as it scouted round the edge of some spilled wine.

Lennox began to talk, speaking in the old prison-camp way, his voice low, his lips scarcely moving.

CHAPTER **19**

The band had finished drinking its beer in the garden of the Hotel Post, and had begun to play once more. It seemed as if these people couldn't have enough of their simple, lighthearted music. But then, this was the first village festival for twenty-five years at which the old Tyrolese songs were allowed to be played in public without threat of fine or imprisonment. The wine room had emptied. The children went out holding their grandmothers' hands, and the old men followed to sit in the garden and listen to their music.

Frau Schichtl had gone too. As she left the table she had come round to where her son and Peter Lennox were sitting, and she had paused long enough to say in a low voice, "Take good care of each other." She placed her hand for a moment on their shoulders. Lennox realized, as she had already done, that he might never see her again.

The empty room gathered its shadows. From the darkening garden came the lilt of a light-stepping air. No one was dancing yet, as if the people were trying to postpone it.

When darkness came, Lennox thought, there would have to be plenty of dancing. The older men and women would pretend it was quite normal that the younger men were no longer there. And the girls would dance with each other, as if they were enjoying themselves, as if it didn't matter that there were no young men to dance with. And those who were determined not to believe any wild rumors about German trucks would blame the suspicious young men for having ruined the festival. All of those people were facing an evening which their stubborn highland pride would not let them abandon. Some of them hoped to cover the absence of the younger men, to give them enough time to reach the huts scattered high over the mountains. Others were going to stay to prove that the hotheads were wrong with this whispered talk of danger. But none of them had a real sense of disaster: tonight was only a repeating pattern to the people of Hinterwald. Once the Italians had come hunting young men too, and when there were no young men to be found the Italians had gone away. The village had been fined. That was all. These people had not yet learned that the Germans are more persevering, more thorough, and more ruthless than the Italians.

When darkness came, Lennox thought, Johann and he must be ready. He had already explained his plan to the boy beside him, and the main points—the timing and place of their action—had been decided. Only one problem remained. The room had remained empty, and the hotelkeeper —he could be trusted—had stationed himself in the hall. When darkness came, Lennox thought once more, he and Johann would be moving quietly to the road which led away from this village to Kastelruth. For although the Tyrolese might think that the trucks would roll away empty if there were no younger men to fill them, Lennox wasn't so sure about that. He knew the Germans better than these people did: he had seen what they could do when all disguises were down.

Johann was trying to find a solution to that last problem. He was biting his lip in a beardless imitation of Mahlknecht.

"No telephone wire anywhere?" Lennox asked again. "Surely somewhere, Johann."

"We should have to strip the telephone poles. No time. What about rope?"

"Not strong enough." Lennox was worried. It showed in his eyes, and the impatient tapping of his fingers on the table. The last detail was a small one, but unless it were perfect, his whole plan would be useless.

"Or a tree across the road would block them. That would give those in the trucks a chance to escape. If you could find a gun we could divert the soldiers' attention. They would think it was an ambush," Lennox said. He was thinking out loud now, but even as he spoke he knew that this alternative suggestion was no good.

Up on Schönau Mahlknecht had said that for the moment there must be no obvious evidence of violence. And the two officers had agreed; for German retaliation and restrictions would make their work twice as difficult, twice as slow. At this stage of the organizing of resistance it would be better that no action were taken by Johann and Lennox if that action meant open trouble for Shaw's and Thomson's plans now being made at Schönau. Lennox suddenly realized that they had given him a pretty big responsibility: it was up to him entirely to keep a balance—to do neither too much nor too little.

Johann said, "I don't see why it isn't strong enough. It is strong enough, certainly, not to be sawed through by the edge of rock."

Lennox stared. "Mountaineering rope, you mean?"

"Of course. What else? We've plenty of it in the village. It has wire woven through its center."

Wire through the center? That might do. Lennox said, "What about its color? It is almost white, isn't it? Can you get any dark paint or stain?"

"This is the season for painting shutters and window boxes, isn't it?" Johann was smiling now. Their plan was beginning to look simple once more. "I'll attend to it right away, eh? It won't take long. I'll meet you at the trees just southwest of the church, beside St. Johann's shrine. In half an hour—as soon as the dance starts."

"How long will it take us to reach the part of the road you've chosen for the accident?"

"By short cuts, about fifteen or twenty minutes. Maybe less. By the road itself, it would take us three times as long as that. The road winds to avoid hilly ground." Johann's hand traced the road's curves through the air as he spoke.

"Good. You are sure that part of the road is suitable?"

"Sure? It is what you described, isn't it?" Johann was beginning to get impatient. Lennox decided not to say, "Perhaps we shouldn't take any of this action. It is on our own authority. Perhaps we have done enough already. Perhaps the trucks will return empty to Kastelruth, after all." For Johann would have been too disappointed. He would have thought that Lennox did not really want action, or even that a doubtful plan was not worth preparing. No; better let Johann keep his excitement and his energy. Any qualification on the plan at this moment would only dampen the boy's enthusiasm. It would only lead to disappointment and resentment.

"In half an hour," Lennox said.

The hotelkeeper straightened his shoulders, moved away from the door, and had a short attack of coughing. Someone must have entered the hall from the street. Lennox and Johann exchanged glances. Johann's hand traveled to his waist, where he kept his sheathed knife. Lennox was calculating the distance to the kitchen entrance to the room; there would be a back exit through there. Even if the inn had been surrounded the number of people gathered in its garden would make escape possible. You could lose yourself in a crowd.

But the person who entered was a woman. She stood very still at the threshold of the room, as if she were trying to identify them in the dusk. She seemed satisfied, and came forward into the room.

"Why don't you turn on the light?" she asked. "I nearly missed you." It was Eva Mussner.

Johann rose abruptly. The wooden bench scraped angrily on the floor as he pushed it aside, and he walked past the girl without even looking at her.

"You see," she said to Lennox, "I have lost my friends."

He rose too. He walked towards the hall. Johann had already vanished. In half an hour he would be waiting. In half an hour Lennox would have to decide what Mahlknecht and his two visitors would want him to do.

Eva Mussner caught his arm as he passed her.

"Please," she said. "Please."

She had dropped her voice, until it was almost a whisper. "I have something to tell you. Not here. This isn't a good place: no one could talk of secret things here. Let us go outside, and pretend to be watching the alpine glow. Please."

She was walking beside him. He pretended to agree. He was planning to lose her in the crowd, quietly, effectively: that was the best treatment.

She said, "They sent me to talk to you. They want to know more about you."

He halted for a moment, looking down at her.

"You are all wasting a lot of breath," he said brutally. But he had changed his mind about losing this girl in the crowd. He wanted to hear what she had been told to tell him. And he wanted her to repeat to "them" what he wanted them to believe.

The street was still more crowded. People were coming out of the houses, out of the other inns. They were walking slowly towards the Hotel Post. Soon the dance would begin.

The girl drew close to his side, and guided him towards the house at the beginning of the street where the obliterated Fascist slogan stood. It was less crowded here, as if the people disliked this end of the street. The girl walked slowly now, and she began to speak, quickly, quietly. Both of them seemed to be watching the sun's last rays reflecting on the high mountain walls. The sun was almost set, and the air had lost all its light, but the peaks of gray rock came to life. They glowed with the rich fire of rubies. The sun disappeared, even as Lennox watched, and the village became a place of deep twilight with white ghostlike houses. The mountain walls had turned to opals. In the dark sky they glowed with the sunlight they had trapped and still held. They shone with the changing, blending shades of gold and purple and rose. There was stillness over the village as everyone, standing in the first darkness of night, turned to watch the alpine glow.

The girl was watching too. She was speaking, and her voice was unsteady as if she had been tortured at the sight of the glowing mountains.

"The Germans have trucks outside the village. And soldiers. They have been waiting all day for the signal when everyone is gathered together."

He said nothing. He hoped she would think his face, if she could see it clearly, was registering doubt. But he was thinking that she couldn't have chosen a more clever opening. She was establishing confidence by news which was no news.

When he didn't answer she said quickly, "They've decided the dance will be the best time. They need volunteers. Men."

"Do they?"

She ignored his sarcasm. "They are angry. A police station was set up here today. Notices were posted. But no one has registered. Only my uncle has been, what they call, polite. And they began to notice, in this last hour, that the young men have left the village. They are angry and worried. They are beginning to ask questions. They asked me about you."

"And you said?" The mountain colors were infused with streaks of indigo, turning the rose color to a violet-red. The sky above, the forests below, were almost black.

"That you were a stupid country bumpkin, and that you hadn't become any less stupid in the Army."

In spite of himself, he was annoyed. "Thank you for the compliment."

"I also said I had known you for a long time, that you came to Bozen on leave."

He didn't reply at once to that. He was too busy thinking he couldn't blame Johann for having trusted this girl. There was a sincerity in her voice which was disarming.

"And why did you say that?" he asked coldly.

"Oh, please!" The girl was almost in tears now. "No man can be so stupid that he doesn't see the dangers staring him in the face."

Lennox kept silent. Blindness doesn't only attack fools, he thought grimly.

She said, "Listen, you've got to believe me. Listen. They have been ordered to treat us with velvet gloves so that we'll collaborate easily. They don't want to stir up any more trouble at the moment. The news has just come that Cassino has fallen, that the German Army is withdrawing. Rome will fall too."

Lennox was standing very still now. But he wasn't looking any longer at the glowing mountains suspended in darkness. She sensed she had won some reaction, for she was speaking still more urgently. "But what if they find no one who will collaborate with them except men like my uncle? They have begun talking, up at my uncle's house, about how firm they can allow themselves to be. They have decided that if they can find no men to volunteer they will take women and children and hold them as hostages at Kastelruth, until the young men come down from their hiding places in the mountains to volunteer."

"And when is this to happen?"

"At eight o'clock."

Eight o'clock. That was earlier than he had thought the Germans would act. They must be worried. He asked, more casually than he felt, "And what am I supposed to do?"

"You could tell Frau Schichtl—Johann—anyone who could pass the word round. You could warn the village, let everyone know, let everyone go away."

"And what about the people who live in this village? What are they to do? Will your uncle defend them against reprisals?"

She ignored that jibe. "If we could save some, and then plan together to take action—I don't know—just something. Some kind of action—not just waiting around to be driven like a flock of sheep. Something—you're a man. You ought to know what to do. I know something must be done, but I'm a woman, and I don't know what to plan."

Lennox turned to watch the violet, rose-veined mountains. "Protests don't do any good," he said at last.

"I'm not asking you to make protests. I'm asking you to do something, even if it is just to warn people, to tell them."

"And how?"

She stamped her foot like an angry child.

"Look, before nine o'clock the trucks will be moving out of the village. They'll have their 'volunteers' whether it's men or women and children. And along with the trucks will be that car with the two men who watched the Schichtl house today. You didn't know, did you, that two men were watching you all afternoon while the police were paying you a visit? These two men have talked about you. And they were talking about some airfield in Egypt. They were worried about that airfield—and they were talking about it when they were discussing you, so it has something to do with you."

"What airfield?" This time he was startled. The Germans had been holding a post-mortem on their failure as American airmen yesterday. And they weren't satisfied with it. Perhaps he had been too clever about that Beni Jara.

"One of them said they could find out about it from von Haller in Kastelruth."

"And who in creation is von Haller?"

"An expert on airfields. He arrives on the Schlern in the next few days. He is to plan something up here. That's all I know."

It was enough. It was news of several kinds. Lennox stared at the girl's white face, with all its color and subtle shadows blotted out by the darkness. And then his lips tightened as he saw everything very clearly. It was a clever trick. She had been told enough to win his confidence. She was to appear as the girl, betrayed by her uncle, who wanted action against the Germans. And if he were to say, "But there is action being planned. Come along, we need women like you to help us,"—well, then, the Germans would have very quick, very final proof. It wouldn't only be Lennox who would be arrested and questioned. It would be Frau Schichtl who had sheltered him this winter, it would be the neighboring Kasals. It would be Mahlknecht and all his friends.

"Who else was talking about these things?"

"Only my uncle and these two men. They were asking him about you. You see, my uncle spent part of his time in the Zillertal when he was in the North Tyrol. He has friends there."

He stared at the darkened mountains. The alpine glow had ended. The peaks were now black shadows in a night sky. Torches were being lit around the garden of the Hotel Post. The dancing would soon begin now.

Eva Mussner seemed to sense the direction of his thoughts, for she gripped his arm. "What can we do?" she asked. "What can we do?"

"What *can* we do?" he repeated. "Don't be a fool asking unanswerable questions. You are only putting us all in danger."

She drew back quickly from him. "Then why did you let me talk? Why did you let me go on hoping that here was someone who would listen to me?"

"Look, I never let you go on hoping. Don't start inventing things." Additional things, he added to himself. "Besides, what can anyone do? We've no guns. Nothing. Bare hands against revolvers and machine guns, eh? And nothing would be solved. Violence would bring reprisal."

"You've no guns? Not one of you here has a gun? You've all handed them over to the Germans like a batch of ninnies?"

He smiled and said, "We've no guns." Not handed over but hidden, and well-hidden for the day on which they would be needed.

"Why, even my uncle had more sense than that," she said. "He has a gun."

"Doesn't he trust his new friends? Or is he afraid of his old ones?" Lennox asked derisively. He began walking towards the garden of the Hotel Post.

Eva Mussner didn't follow him. He looked round in some surprise. He hadn't expected to be able to shake her off as suddenly as this. She was running towards the alley which led to the Mussner house. She was running home to her uncle, to tell him and his German friends that it was useless to try to find out anything from this Peter Schichtl, for there was obviously nothing to be found out.

Lennox should have been congratulating himself: he should have felt delighted. But somehow the feeling of satisfaction was tempered with bitterness. He had almost believed her. Somehow he was angry that anyone as lovely and intelligent as Eva Mussner had joined the Judas gang.

CHAPTER **20**

The dancing was about to begin.

Lennox, on the fringe of the crowd, saw that no Germans had yet appeared. Eight o'clock that girl had said. That gave about fifteen minutes of grace. Before then he would be meeting Johann near the church. (It was just as well he hadn't complicated Johann's emotions about a plan which might not be used. Now the plan would have to be used.) And then he realized that he was preparing to act on what the Mussner girl had said, and his anger about her turned against himself. Bloody fool, he said to himself. Bloody fool. He knew she was a collaborationist of the worst kind—the kind that tries to trip up his own countrymen—and yet he had been thinking in terms of "eight o'clock," and of a German car with two potentially dangerous spies in it, racing to Kastelruth and the expert on airfields. He wished desperately that he could talk to the men at Schönau about this. They would know what to do. But the responsibility was his. He looked round at the people beside him. They felt some of the danger. They didn't know it all. The responsibility was all his.

The musicians, their energy restored by a hasty supper, were grouping together under a flowering chestnut tree. The red-faced man who was involved with the tuba tried a few muted blasts. There was a stirring among the people. Some of the younger women had taken off their hats. Lennox noted that their partners were only very young boys or fatherly men. They formed up in a long queue, with the first couple ready to climb up the three wooden steps to the dance platform and lead off the first measure. Lighted torches had been fixed in sockets on the wooden poles at each corner of the platform. The last curious child was pulled firmly down from his perch on the surrounding railing. The drummer was anxiously eying the concertina player.

Something wasn't quite in order. There was a stirring, a rustling, a murmur among the waiting pairs of dancers. They parted, either as if they were pushed aside or were avoiding someone. And then that someone was climbing the three steep steps, was standing alone on the wooden platform. It was Eva Mussner.

She gripped the railing's balustrade with one hand as if to steady herself. Her other hand was hidden under her apron. She said, with her clear voice carrying across the crowded garden out into the street where Lennox stood, "Go home at once. Leave here—now. The Germans are coming in a few minutes to gather men into their trucks. If they cannot find men they will take boys and women as hostages. Go. Show them that you are unwilling. Show them that if they do this to us then we know that they are worse than the Italians. Show them that if it is trouble they are seeking then they'll get it."

Lennox stood unmoving, rigid. Only his mind was active as his eyes watched.

Somewhere a man shouted. Shouted in anger. The crowd was silent. Their distrust of this girl left them doubting, hesitating. The man shouted again. It was Mussner himself, pushing his way to the platform. Two Germans in black uniform followed him. There was a stirring among the people, as if by the anger in these three men's faces they began to hesitate in their doubt. As Mussner leaped up the stairs and gripped his niece's shoulder they began to believe her words. Eva Mussner struggled against the strength of her uncle.

Lennox raised his voice and yelled. "Quick. Scatter into the darkness. Quick."

The Nazi policemen halted and turned to look in his direction. But the crowd was moving at last as if the authority of his shout at that moment had decided them. "Quick. Scatter," other voices were calling. "Quick; into the darkness."

The crowd increased its speed. It was pouring out of every side of the garden. Men and women and children hurried past Lennox as he stood jammed against the shadow of the inn wall. They were half running now, but there was no panic. For instance, a child stumbled and one of the fair-haired girls stooped to pick him up and then hurried on. The men were helping the older women. The first waves of people were already disappearing into the dark side roads which would lead them up into the woods. From the distance came the sound of trucks in low gear, pulling their way into the village.

"Here they come. Quick," Lennox yelled. The last doubtful stragglers broke into a run. The two Nazi policemen, unable to move in the surge of people, had grasped the man nearest them. Lennox saw the tuba player swing the large brass instrument, as if it were a battering ram, and knock the Germans sideways. And then the tuba player and the man he had freed were running towards him. Lennox himself started out of the safety of the shadows. He was halfway to the platform and Eva Mussner when the first shot rang out. It came from the platform. Eva Mussner had fired it.

Lennox saw Mussner crumple and fall, and he knew he could not help the girl now. The Nazi policemen were too quick to answer; their revolvers were drawn and they had fired at the platform. The last fringes of the crowd, now reaching the roadway, turned to stare back at the garden. They saw Eva Mussner falling to lie beside her uncle. One of the policemen fired again at the girl. But her body lay still. The last of the people at Hinterwald's feast day moved quickly away among the dark houses.

Lennox began running too. Behind him there were the shouts of the two Germans in civilian dress, of the other Nazi policemen. He caught up with the tuba player. Together, they raced out of the garden. The tuba player was cursing the Germans, over and over again. As they separated Lennox could still hear him, stumbling through the darkness, cursing the Germans.

Lennox, as he raced up a side path, saw the two trucks arriving in the village street behind him. But the street was already emptied as the garden had been. The German soldiers were left to stare at the German policemen and the torches on the platform, at a tuba and scattered hats and a dropped shawl lying on the grass.

Lennox halted at the edge of a small belt of trees, and regained his sense of direction. He heard movements near him, but they weren't Germans. The officer in command had given no order for pursuit: he probably realized it was useless, with his men blundering about over strange ground in this darkness. Perhaps he even saw the ridiculousness of such pursuit. Its little chance of success only made the Germans more of a laughingstock. Lennox listened until he was almost certain he was right in his guess. That was the most he could allow himself. He couldn't go back to see. He had to reach Johann. They had a job to do. Now the job was more urgent than ever. If Eva Mussner's death was to be justified the job had to be done and done well.

As he made his way quickly towards the church Lennox kept thinking of the last moments in the hotel garden. At this moment he seemed to see it all more clearly than he had seen it then. It had happened so quickly that his eyes hadn't believed. Eva Mussner had suddenly freed herself from her uncle's grasp, just as the two German spies had appeared. That was the moment she had chosen. Of that Lennox was convinced. She had waited until most of the people were gone, until the Germans could see her plainly. And she had uncovered her right hand, which she had held stubbornly under her apron. She had a revolver, and she had fired it at Mussner. The Germans had taken no chances then. The man who fired that Lüger had been near enough to kill.

Lennox stared into the dark masses of shadows to the southwest of the church. The shrine of St. Johann was over there, but he couldn't see it. His eyes seemed still blinded by the flaring torches lighting an emptied garden and German faces turning towards the platform as they forgot the fleeing people. He still saw the heavy bulk of Mussner falling at the girl's feet, the sort of useless way she then held the revolver. He still saw the way she had fallen too as the German bullet retaliated. Flaring torches, an emptied square, and one collaborationist less to be killed. And a girl willing to die to prove to the Germans that she alone was guilty, to prove to her people that she was innocent.

"Here! Here!" The urgent whisper was Johann's. "What's wrong? What happened?"

Lennox regained his breath. "The people got away. Scattered. An alarm was given, but our plans stand. We have still a job to do." He was beginning to see more clearly now in the shadow of the tree under which Johann had waited. "Where's the rope?"

"Sent it on ahead—special delivery. I felt we might have to make a quick dash. Besides, that rope's heavy. Too much like work carrying it." Johann started to move away from the village, traveling westward, following trees as far as they would shelter them.

"Whom did you send?" Lennox's voice was worried.

Johann grinned widely. "Don't worry, cousin. They can be trusted. They will arrive with the rope just about the time we reach the place."

They had better, Lennox thought grimly. He didn't even answer Johann's question about the shots from the village. "Later," he said impatiently. "Later—when we've finished our job." He forced himself to keep up with Johann's quick pace. If you didn't admit you were exhausted then you weren't exhausted. He had failed Eva Mussner once: he wasn't going to fail her a second time.

CHAPTER **21**

There was nothing to do now but wait.

Lennox sat wearily beside the tree. Across the road from him Johann was sitting equally well hidden. He was worrying too, Lennox realized, although that cheery grin was still probably in place. For every now and again there would be a flick of movement to the darkened rope which stretched between them.

Lennox gave up wondering if the rope was strong enough, if windshield height would be the most effective, if the trees were well chosen to bear the strain. He looked at the dark road, twisting and curving down the hillside. At night, with no moon yet strong enough to light the rise and fall of ground, he could not be sure that this was the best place. He had to rely on Johann for this choice. He tried to reassure himself by looking at the bridge on his right. He could hear the strong fall of the torrent under it, and the noise of the rushing waters gave him at least an assurance of depths.

The steep hillside, falling away from the scattered trees on Johann's side of the road into a short precipice, had seemed abrupt and dangerous enough to him in the darkness. Yet, standing over there, looking down into sharp crags hidden by the night's blackness, he had wished he could have seen this part of the road by daylight. Or even by moonlight. Then he would know whether the rope, strung across this road obliquely—with Johann's tree in advance of his chosen one—would be a real weapon or just a simple-minded booby trap. Behind him was the hillside down which he and Johann had slithered. Up there, to his left, were the two boys who had brought the rope to this place. They were keeping watch on the long curve of road descending from Hinterwald along this hillside towards Kastelruth. The boys were to let them know when the first headlights were approaching. They were to let them know whether it was a car's headlights or a truck's. Lennox had no interest any more in the trucks.

It was strange that when this plan had first formed in his head, as he had climbed down from Schönau this afternoon, he had been thinking of merely stopping a truck. Just something to halt it to give those inside a chance to scatter over the hillside. Some might have escaped. It had struck him as funny, at that time, that he should have first come up to these mountains by planning his own escape, and that he should now be leaving them by planning escape for others. But now those others had escaped, not through him, but through a girl. She had been right in sensing that her people should be warned publicly and forced to make an open choice. Now those of them who had thought they could stay neutral, and still keep their independence, knew that there was no choice. After tonight and that girl's death there could be only those who were either anti-German or pro-German. She had forced the issue before the Germans could bewilder her people with smiles and false promises. She had been right, and he had been wrong. She was dead, and he was alive.

From the hillside above him he heard the noise of a dislodged stone. He was ready by the time the boy reached him. The hoarse, excited whisper said, "Headlights. Car first, traveling fast. Two trucks a mile behind, moving slowly."

"Right." Lennox flapped the rope sharply three times and felt an answering tug from Johann. They lifted the rope carefully, pulling it even and taut, and secured it tightly round their trees. Perhaps because of the wire woven into it, it did not feel as if it were sagging. Lennox was wondering whether the blotched coloring of the rope would show—patches of the stain had come off on the boys' hands and clothes as they carried it here—and then decided that perhaps these shadings would be better than a rope forming too much of a black line. Certainly, it didn't form a white line, and it wasn't obvious to his eye at the moment. But headlights might pick it up, even if its oblique stretch would lessen that danger. All he could do now was to trust the curving road which made the headlights less effective. They ought to swing out over the ravine as the car came round that corner, and before they were focusing on the road properly the rope would be struck.

He hoped to God that Johann had moved away from the tree to his piece of chosen cover. If the car skidded it was likely to fall in his direction. This rope would only have halted a slow-moving truck. But a quickly moving car by its own speed would have more damage done to it. That was what they hoped for, anyway. Johann had insisted on taking that side of the road. He could, so he had solemnly sworn, hang on to a mountainside by his eyelashes if necessary.

The noise of rushing water had obliterated the sound of the car's approach. Lennox heard it just before he saw the headlights' yellow glare probing into the darkness. He had only time to flatten himself behind the tree. The grim sequence of noise was too confused, too quick, to be analyzed. The rope snapped, and whipped dangerously over his head back around the tree. We have failed, he thought desperately; failed, God damn us to everlasting hell. And then he heard only the sound of rushing water. He raised his head.

The car had swung around and was hanging on the edge of the road, its front wheels on the last foot of ground. The rope had shattered its windshield, and had been cut by the frame. The driver had lost control, and the road was torn where the wheels had skidded deeply into its surface.

Lennox couldn't be sure that the four men in the car were dead. They seemed lifeless—two, at least, were unpleasant to look at—but they might only be stunned and injured. For a moment he stood looking at the two men in civilian clothes who had watched from the Kasal barn, the two men who had made such amiable Allied airmen. The others in the car were the two policemen who had questioned him in the Schichtl house that afternoon. Well, here was a combination that would work no more together. Whatever they knew would never be written down as a report.

"Let's give it a push," Johann said urgently. "There's a good drop into the torrent."

Lennox was already reaching into the car, feeling for the reverse. Then it only needed a very short push indeed. The torrent was silenced as the car's wild plunge ended. Lennox backed slowly away from the edge of the precipice, his ears still shocked by the sudden smash after the tense moment of waiting. The torrent's voice lifted once more.

"Now your rope," Johann's practical voice said. He had already uncoiled the length from his tree. "We have less than two minutes."

The boy who had brought the warning of the car's approach was already unwinding the rope from the tree beside which Lennox had lain. The other boy had come down from his vantage point to see what had happened. He helped, too. The rope was uncoiled and laboriously unknotted. The two boys, carrying its folds between them, started over the hill.

"They know what to do with it. And with themselves. Come on, we had better not be found near here either." Johann's advice was good. Lennox followed him wearily, imitating Johann's bent shoulders and half-running pace. He would have liked to stay to see the trucks arrive, but it was safer to leave curiosity unsatisfied. The drivers must have heard the noise. They were probably traveling still more slowly, for they would now be expecting some kind of trouble. Then their lights would pick out the skid-marks on the road, for the surface had been badly torn. But even if they guessed that some accident had happened—a tire suddenly blown out or a turn too sharp and too quick—they could see little over that precipice edge. It was too steep, too deep, and the night was too dark. Later, when the moon came up, they would be able to see something. But there could be no salvage party until daylight.

Once they were over the spine of the hill Johann's pace slackened, and he walked upright. But even being able to move more naturally didn't lessen Lennox's exhaustion.

"I'm tired. I'm damned tired," he said to Johann. "I'm out of training, remember."

"Maybe," Johann said, without much conviction. "What happened in the village?"

"I'll tell you when we see your uncle. I need my breath for climbing. I suppose we are heading in his direction now?"

"Yes. We've got to report."

"At Schönau?"

"Yes. Good job you know how to cross the waterfall. It's tricky at night." Lennox groaned. He had forgotten the waterfall.

"You'll manage it," Johann said cheerily. "After tonight we could manage anything, couldn't we?"

Lennox wasn't so inclined to agree with that.

Anyway, he thought, there was one thing they had managed to do. The reports and suspicions which that car had been carrying to Kastelruth had been blotted out. Other reports would be made, other suspicions might grow, but these particular ones would do no more damage. That was one thing they had managed to do. They and Eva Mussner.

CHAPTER 22

Schönau—the beautiful high meadow—was earning its name. The sun was strong today, so Lennox had taken off his jacket and opened the collarless neck of his shirt. He stretched his body contentedly on the carpet of fine green grass. There were more flowers spreading their miniature petals close to the ground. The scent of pine and new-leaved trees from the surrounding woods was stronger. Each day there was a little more of the promise of summer.

Lennox stopped looking at the blue sky with its soft white clouds, high and unmoving over the line of mountaintops, and turned to watch the foresters' hut. No one had come out yet. Either they were giving him plenty of time to make up his mind, or they were discussing some new points. Not that he could imagine them finding a new point: since he and

Johann had arrived here last night, there had been enough careful discussion to fill a millpond.

It was the American who came out at last from the hut and walked casually towards Lennox. Nothing in his leisurely step—he was a loose-limbed sort of chap with easy movements—nothing in his placid face showed he was coming here with a purpose.

Lennox rose to his feet. . . . Private Lennox, sir, reporting. . . .

"Cut that out," Thomson said, with his good-natured smile. He dropped into the grass, and motioned Lennox to sit beside him. "You'd better be careful," he warned, "or we'll commission you temporarily on the field."

"I'd prefer to remain as I am," Lennox said.

"Determined guy, aren't you? But you've certainly been more co-operative than we expected."

"Thank you," Lennox said. He half smiled, and he suddenly thought of the colonel. Not co-operative . . . was that the colonel's description of him? Anyone seemed not co-operative when he was asked to do what he didn't want to do. Especially if his mind had been quite made up otherwise. "I suppose I was a sort of resentful blighter," he added, his smile broadening.

"You probably only needed a rest up here in these mountains. They'd cure anyone."

Lennox nodded. "I didn't know I was cured either. That's the funny thing. I didn't know it, until the two Jerries dressed as American airmen walked into the Schichtl kitchen. I had been telling myself all winter that I was a useless crock—" Lennox halted in embarrassment. He was saying too much. The American was so easy to talk to. He just sat there, with his arms around his knees and a friendly grin on his face. Not too much of a grin, either, but just enough to make you go on talking. Lennox went on. "There didn't seem anything I could do up here. You fellows were coming, and I was only a stopgap. There didn't even seem much for me to do if I ever managed that escape to the south. The Army would probably discharge me. This hand has been getting worse all winter. A prison camp wasn't the best place to cure it properly."

"Tough luck," Thomson agreed. "But I've heard of left-handers who were crack shots. Don't see why you couldn't learn. Besides, this war won't last forever. You'll be thinking of going back to your old job then, and it won't matter a damn whether you can shoot a gun or not."

Lennox was silent.

"Will it?" the American asked sympathetically.

"No. I don't suppose it will." His voice had changed, and the American watched him curiously. If the American had lost eight years of his life, Lennox thought, he wouldn't be so puzzled. Eight years learning to paint, scraping up money for tuition, living from hand to mouth so that he could get abroad where the light was warm and the colors were bright. There had been trouble with his people because he wouldn't settle down to a profession. There had been a lot of private trouble and disappointments because he had insisted on going on with his painting. And then, after eight years, there had been the beginning of some success. That was the summer of 1939. Eight years . . . eight years, hell! He wasn't the only chap who was now finding that after this war he would have to start all over again.

"Have you made your decision?" Thomson asked. "Do you take your long-promised trip south, or do you go into the North Tyrol with Johann?"

"It's a long walk either way." Lennox's voice was quite normal now. "I'll travel north with Johann."

"Fine." Thomson was genuinely pleased, perhaps even relieved. He rose. "Come on. They're waiting for us in the hut."

As they walked slowly over the broad meadow the American said, "Lennox, I should be keeping my mouth shut, but I won't. If you traveled south there might be still hope for your hand. If you go north—well, you could get no specialist's treatment there. You realize that?"

"Yes. I'll just have to make my left hand useful," Lennox said. And if I lose that one, he thought, I'm damned if I don't learn to paint with my toes. He began to smile.

"We are about ready to push off," Thomson said. "We've been given two of those guides you were talking about. You and Johann will leave tonight. Schroffenegger's son is going along with you."

Lennox nodded. "Is Johann still asleep?"

"Yes, he's earned it."

And that was true. For last night Johann had gone back to the village to scout carefully around. He had returned at dawn with a variety of news. The people had left the hillside, some to reach their distant houses, others to return to the village. They knew grimly that there had only been a respite and no material gain for them. Even now the Germans would be planning a change of policy towards their Austrian "cousins." But there had been a moral victory for Eva Mussner. It was the girl's death which had shocked the people most of all. They had been angered by the fact that the Germans had chosen their feast day in order to gather a rich haul of what they would call volunteers. But it was the girl's death they were talking about. Mussner's treachery and the danger to the village, coming from all such treachery, had been clearly shown in that last scene in the garden. Those who had witnessed it were describing it in detail to those who had already fled. They told how the girl had stood with her uncle's revolver, no longer pointing, no longer threatening. Yet the Germans had killed her. And she had not shot her uncle as a murderess would have killed, out of envy or greed or evil. Yet the Germans had killed her. Without a trial. From now on, Johann had reported, there were no more neutrals in this district. Mahlknecht's list of those who were doubtful friends of the Allied cause, because they were neutral, could now be scrapped.

"He's earned it," repeated Thomson. "By the way, we got some more news when you were asleep this morning. The Fifth is rolling up the Krauts like a red carpet. The Eighth is slugging right up the middle of Italy. I'll lay you five to one we'll be in Rome within the month."

Lennox shared the American's wide smile for a moment. "No takers," he said. "I'm on your side." He turned to stare at the mountain peaks to the south. He had stopped walking.

"Wish you were with them?" Thomson asked. "So do I. And yet we are, in a kind of a way. We're an advance unit. That's us."

When Lennox didn't answer he asked quietly, "What made you choose to go into the North Tyrol with Johann? You'll be useful there. We need you. But why did you choose it?"

The American would never have got his answer if he hadn't been so easy to talk to. If Shaw had asked that question Lennox would have said, "It's a nice climate, I hear." But to Thomson he said, "I'm trying to show someone I'm not just the selfish fool she thought I was."

"Hope she appreciates that some day," Thomson said. He looked as if he wanted to ask more, but he didn't. It was just as well. Lennox couldn't have answered that one. He couldn't have answered, "She is dead. She was shot by the Germans."

In embarrassment he said quickly, "I'll do more damage to Jerry up there than I could from a hospital behind our lines."

Thomson was satisfied. Lennox suddenly felt satisfied too.

In the hut there were Mahlknecht and Shaw and young Josef Schroffenegger. Johann was snoring steadily on one of the straw mattresses. He could sleep until dusk came. And then he and Lennox and young Josef would set out together. They would climb to the mountain hut near the top of the first peak on their journey. They should reach there before midnight, and sleep there, and leave there—to tackle the difficult part of crossing a mountain—in the good light of early morning.

On the bunk next to the one where Johann lay there was the equipment they would need, and the small packages of food which they could carry. Schroffenegger's son had brought these necessary supplies this morning. He would be useful on this trip. Both he and Johann had climbed through that sea of mountains once before. Then it had been to avoid Italian recruitment for the Albanian campaign. Now it was to win recruits for the fight against Germany.

"He's going," Thomson said to Shaw, and they both looked satisfied.

Mahlknecht too was in good spirits. The plans were well made. They had purpose, careful arrangement, and more than a chance of success. The months of worry were over: action lay ahead. He laid his hand on Lennox's shoulder. "I didn't kidnap you this time, did I?" he asked jokingly.

And yet he was anxious, too, as if he wanted reassurance that Lennox no longer thought of him as a whipcracker.

Lennox said, "So it was you who insisted on giving me time to decide?" His voice and his smile showed that resentment was dead.

Mahlknecht laughed. "Last time I had no choice. It was you, or nothing. And it did some good, didn't it?" He nodded towards Thomson and Shaw. "They wouldn't be here unless you had come up onto the Schlern."

"Oh, perhaps they would," Lennox said, but he was pleased that Mahlknecht had spoken that way.

A birdcall came from the path which Schroffenegger's second son guarded.

"It's a friend," Mahlknecht said, in answer to the three foreigners' tension. "That's the signal for a friend."

"Better keep him out of here even if he is a friend," Shaw said crisply.

Mahlknecht nodded and stepped outside.

After a few minutes he returned with a bundle. "More food," he said. "It's Katharina. She wants to see you, Peter."

"Was it wise of her to come here?" Shaw asked sharply. Thomson too was looking worried.

"My sister sent her. Katharina says no one followed her. There are only four policemen at the Golden Roof Inn now, and they've stayed there all day. Perhaps they are waiting for instructions, or perhaps they feel they need reinforcements. The village is in an ugly mood. My sister thought it was safe, and I think we can trust her. She has sent a specially marked map which her husband made when he was a guide, and some more food, and some brandy."

"All right," Shaw said. "But send the girl away quickly." He offered no further objections.

"She has a message for you, Peter," Mahlknecht repeated.

Lennox walked to the door, very conscious of the look in both the officers' eyes.

"Business and pleasure mixed?" Thomson was saying with a laugh. "We could learn a tip or two from him, Roy." But in the joke there was a neatly conveyed piece of advice.

Katharina was waiting down near the path into the wood. She held a neat package in her clasped hands. Her cheeks were flushed, her eyes smiled as she watched him approach.

"Frau Schichtl sent me with this. She said you needed it." She held out the small package with the same directness in her movement as in her words.

It contained a small pad of paper, something which he could slip into his jacket pocket easily. And his two favorite pencils. And some of the sheets of paper which had lain in his bedroom: the first attempts to sketch with his left hand were there, along with the drawings he had made last week. Frau Schichtl was telling him that if he could make so much progress he could make still more. He had thought she had never paid much attention to his scribbling, but in her quiet undemonstrative way she had known all the time.

Katharina looked at the contents of the package with disappointment. "Is that all?" she asked. And then she noticed Lennox's face. Something had pleased him. Something had made him happy. So she smiled too.

"Frau Schichtl tells me that you are going into the mountains for the summer, like all the younger men." She nodded in the direction of the Schlern peaks.

"Yes," he answered. Obviously the girl knew nothing about the mission into the North Tyrol. And he was not leaving for just this summer, either. The job he had to do now would last through the autumn, perhaps even into the winter as well. It might be spring before he saw Hinterwald again. With luck. . . .

She gave him her hand and said, "I wish you a safe journey, and a quick return."

"Thank you." He was equally grave.

She turned to go back along the path which would take her to the waterfall. And then she halted and said in dismay, "I nearly forgot. . . . Frau Schichtl gave me a message for you. After the war is over the church walls will need a man who can paint."

When he didn't reply Katharina said, "That was the message. It sounds silly, I know. But that was what she said."

"It isn't at all silly. It makes a lot of sense." He smiled and added, "I shan't forget that invitation. Tell Frau Schichtl that."

He stood watching the girl as she walked away with that long, even stride. She looked back and waved as she reached the curve in the path. She hesitated for a moment, and he knew how she would be smiling. Then the gold-braided head was hidden by the green trees.

Lennox moved towards the hut. He walked with a lighter step. In the spring, he thought once more, and then he laughed. For he knew he was indeed cured. He had stopped brooding about the past: the long, bitter, wasted months and years had lost their power to nag him. And now they didn't even seem so wasted; he might find that they had taught him something if only he were willing to learn. Anyway, he was cured. He could think of the future.

Back in the hut Thomson and Shaw were showing signs of impatience. Mahlknecht and young Schroffenegger were talking quietly together. "Is this the way you always work?" Shaw said with a slightly raised eyebrow, and an acid smile.

"She's on the young side, if you ask me," was Thomson's milder reproof.

Lennox laughed. "Don't be bloody fools," he said, and he didn't even remember their rank. "Now, what are these final instructions?"

His whole manner was so different, so confident and alert and interested, that the two officers exchanged glances. Their annoyance left them. Shaw, who had been on the point of deciding that Lennox might be too erratic and undecided a man for this North Tyrol job, was thankful he had kept his mouth shut. Plans depended on the men who carried them out. It was better to have a plan incomplete and a man who was sure of himself, than to have an excellent plan and a man who was unsettled.

"Good," he said, most emphatically, and motioned Lennox to sit down at the rough wooden table and look at the outspread map as they talked.

*   *   *

When Johann woke the hut was in darkness, and the Englishman and the American had already gone. Young Josef Schroffenegger was sitting with Paul Mahlknecht, and they were talking together in the quiet, slurred drawl of men discussing important things. Johann stretched and yawned. "That was good," he said with satisfaction. "I could travel for days now. Where's Peter?"

"Outside. He's waiting for you to wake up. He's getting impatient." There was a pleased note in his uncle's voice which wakened Johann still more.

"So?" he said, and went out-of-doors. Some cold water from the spring at the side of the hut would freshen him up. He was fully awake by the time he had dashed the icy water over his face and neck. He couldn't see Lennox at first, and then he noticed—as his quick eye scanned the trees which encircled the meadow—that the Britisher was sitting on the ground as motionless as the log lying beside him.

Johann crossed over towards him. Lennox was watching the alpine glow.

"All set?" Johann asked.

"All set," Lennox said, but he didn't take his eyes from the living mountains.

"Pretty, eh?" Johann said, with the inadequacy of well-concealed pride. "Haven't you got accustomed to these fireworks by this time?"

Lennox laughed, and rose to his feet.

"Where do we go, Johann?" he asked.

Johann pointed towards a wall of gold and ruby and amethyst. "Up over there," he said, "that's the way. It's easier than it looks. We'll manage it."

"I'll make a damned good try, anyway."

"We'll manage it," Johann's voice was hard. They began walking towards the hut. "We'll beat them. They asked for it. They'll get it." At the door of the hut he said, "I've been thinking. I've been wondering just how many girls they have murdered in all these years?" Lennox didn't answer: no one knew the answer to that.

The table was lighted by one small piece of candle. The windows were shuttered, the door was carefully closed. Mahlknecht and young Schroffenegger were examining the equipment and clothes for the journey. The food and brandy which Katharina had brought were laid out on the table. Everything was arranged: everything had been taken care of. All that the three younger men had to do now was to remember their very complete directions. There were two addresses in the North Tyrol which were reliable—Thomson and Shaw had vouched for that—and they could make these their headquarters. For at these addresses they would find men who had radio contact with London. Shaw's last instructions had been, "If you want to send news here then send it to London. They will see that Thomson gets it. Our news to you will travel the same way."

Lennox pulled on an extra pair of heavy woolen socks, with their heels well soaped. He laced his climbing boots carefully: they must give support without being tight. Johann was packing what they needed for the journey into a rucksack. Each of them carried a sheathed knife, and each had been given a revolver.

"Well," Mahlknecht said, standing beside Lennox and watching him tie the last lace into a firm double knot, "well, you will be back here by next spring at the latest. Perhaps sooner, but . . ." He shrugged his shoulders. Nothing was certain in war. Time drags out longer than one expects.

Lennox rose and tested the comfort of his boots and the thick layer of socks by tramping on the earth floor. He picked up the light *loden* cape which would protect him from wind and rain, and slung it over his shoulders. He followed Johann and young Josef, who were moving towards the door. Johann gave his uncle the usual forefinger salute, but tonight his lips were solemn and his eyes were grave.

Lennox looked back at Paul Mahlknecht, standing alone in the empty room.

"I'll be here next spring," he replied. "Perhaps a lot of us will be here before then," he said.

Paul Mahlknecht must have been thinking along these same lines, for there was a sudden smile in the dark, thoughtful eyes.

"Perhaps," Mahlknecht said. His voice was very quiet as he added, "We shall be waiting."

Peter Lennox closed the door. He followed the others into the dark night.

Assignment in Brittany
1942

FOR G.

CHAPTER 1 LEAP INTO DARKNESS

It was almost daylight. Ahead of them, the cold darkness of the early morning sky waited for the first pale fingers of light.

It should be almost time, now. Hearne glanced again at the watch on his wrist, and fingered his kit. Everything was ready. Underneath his flying suit, in the inside pocket of the torn, shabby jacket, were the tattered letters and photograph and the identification papers. He felt for them once again, and caught a sympathetic smile from the gunner who had moved up close beside him. So he was to be helped safely off the premises. . . . He grinned back to the boy, and nodded reassuringly. He wouldn't need much helping, not after the last three weeks and the practising he had been through. What had worried him most had been the thought of interception by enemy aircraft, or of being spotted after he had left the plane. That wouldn't be at all pleasant, dangling between heaven and earth with some blighter grinning as he got you fair and square in his gun sight.

But the twenty-two-minute journey was almost over: only one more minute to go. The engine was suddenly silent, and the pilot waved a bulky glove.

"That is when you get ready," he had told Hearne cheerily, over their last cup of hot chocolate. "Second time I wave is good-by and good luck."

Hearne rose and stood as he had learned during the past three weeks. The boy at his elbow steadied him for a moment. Hearne cursed his own clumsiness. These fellows seemed to move about as easily as if they were in their messroom. The gunner's fingers tapped sharply on his forearm. "All set?" they spelled quickly in Morse.

Hearne nodded again. His eyes hadn't left the pilot, silhouetted black and shapeless against the lightening eastern sky. How long, Hearne was wondering, how long did it take to glide from twenty thousand feet to six? He was answered by the movement of the padded arm. Good-by and good luck. Well, here it was at last. The gunner had enough sense to stand clear, thank heavens: he could choose his own split second.

"Good luck, yourselves!" Hearne called over his shoulder. He saw the gunner begin to crack that warm grin of his, and the thumb go up. And then he was diving through bleak gray air. He started to count.

"Not too soon, not too late," he reminded himself. "Take it easy and don't think about what happens if the damned thing doesn't work." But what if it didn't? His sudden fear was as cold as the air through which he hurtled. However much he practised, he never got rid of these moments of panic. He restrained himself in time from pulling the rip cord. Not yet: the longer he fell, the quicker, the safer. Perhaps. He pulled the cord. It wasn't going to work. It wasn't going to— Then the sudden jolt to his plunging body, the feeling of being pulled up backward into the sky again, the abrupt change from the hurtling drop to slow-motion floating contradicted him. He took his first breath since he had left the plane.

Drifting down to the colorless, formless land, he strained his eyes towards the sky. In the east, the heavy black curtain was slowly rising to show a steadily broadening river of light. Its edge which touched the darkness flowed grayish-green; and even as he watched, a streak of flame lined the horizon, and the earth and clouds took shape. Then, from the west, he heard the sound of the plane's motors. They must have glided round to get well over in that direction before they had started climbing again. They had given him every chance, anyway.

He looked down at the fields, swaying gently beneath him. They were no longer formless. Dimly, he could see the triangular outline of a wood on a small ridge just to the south. That was what he had hoped for, that was what they had aimed at. Cheery lot of coots, he thought gratefully, remembering the gunner's grin. Pity they couldn't be here to see how neatly they had landed him almost on the doorstep.

He pulled on the ropes, so that he would keep clear of the trees. And then the last few feet suddenly shortened, and the ground seemed to rise up to meet him. It was unexpectedly rough: from above it had looked so smooth and simple. As he landed, his right arm reached high above his head to grasp the control rope, and the clip on his belt automatically released the parachute as it pulled him forward. He was thoroughly jarred. That was all.

From above, he had thought at one moment that he was on top of the trees, but actually he had landed almost a hundred yards from them. He must have pulled on the ropes too much. Still, you couldn't expect everything to be perfect, and a hundred yards was better than being noosed up in high branches. Around him were fields which were half moorland. No house was in sight. He looked up again at the eastern sky. It was a uniform pale gray, bleaching slowly but dangerously. Now there was light enough to see: very soon there would be light enough to be seen.

Hearne rose to his feet from where he had fallen, and started to pull the parachute's folds loose from the clump of gorse bushes against which they had blown. It was slow work, and seemed all the slower because every minute was precious. He must reach the trees before the light strengthened, and he couldn't leave the parachute billowing here as a landmark. He pulled savagely, gathering the flapping silk into a rough, cumbersome bundle. Holding it in front of him, his arms filled with its softness, he half-ran, half-stumbled towards the wood. The ground was rough but not treacherous, and the gorse bushes in their sparse clumps were now useful. He ducked down behind them, gathering the parachute more tightly as its folds slipped from his arms, cursing its maliciousness. It seemed to take a pleasure in thwarting him. Its weight had doubled.

He finished the last twenty yards in a despairing spurt. . . . The trees closed in around him, and he fell grotesquely on top of his burden. He buried his face in its folds to smother the gasps which shook his body, and then, as he felt himself stifle, he rolled stiffly over onto his back. Burning liquid welled up suddenly in his dry throat. And then at last he could breathe normally again, and the cold air was drying the sweat on his face. He lay, waiting for the heavy heartbeats to quieten, watching the leaves above him suddenly waken at the touch of the morning breeze. In the world outside, a lark was singing.

CHAPTER 2   GONE TO GROUND

Hearne waited until the pounding of his blood had stopped. Then, gathering the parachute once more in his arms, he dragged it further into the wood. He moved quietly and capably, like a man who had so often imagined this moment that his movements were almost mechanical. When the undergrowth was thick enough to please him, he halted and eyed the ground round the bush he had chosen. He went to work with his clasp knife, cutting the turf into neat squares, stacking them methodically at his side. The loam under them he scooped out with his hands. It took time, but in the end he was satisfied. He had packed the parachute into the hole he had scraped, thrusting it tightly down under the thin straggling roots of the bush. On top of the parachute lay his flying suit and helmet, and over them all were spread the thick rich soil and the sods, fitted together as neatly as the bulging earth would allow. He had worked lying uncomfortably flat on his stomach. Now he crawled out from the thickness of the bush to find some twigs and leaves and, with luck, some stones. These he scattered over the parachute's grave, covering the gaping cuts between the sods. After two such journeys, he had finished. The evidence was well-buried.

He looked at the unfamiliar watch on his wrist. Three hours ago he had joked with the redhaired pilot over a last cup of hot chocolate. Three hours ago he had stood on English earth. Three hours ago he had been Martin Hearne with twenty-seven years of his own life behind him. Now he was Bertrand Corlay, with twenty-six years of another man's life reduced to headings and subheadings in his memory. He looked down at the faded uniform which had been Corlay's, felt once more for the papers in the inside pocket.

"All set?" the gunner had asked.

Well, that would be the last time he would listen to English for some weeks. All set. . . . He patted the pocket of the tunic with his earth-stained hand, and smiled grimly. From now on, he would not only have to speak, but think, in French.

He moved slowly westwards along the wood, keeping parallel to the open stretch of fields, so that he would not wander too far into the maze of trees. He still moved carefully and quietly, but he was less worried. He had plenty of time, now that he had got rid of the parachute and fly-ing suit. Once he got far enough away from where he had buried them, he would find some place to lie hidden until night came again. Fourteen hours ahead of him for thought; for sleep, if he felt safe enough. Yes, there was plenty of time, and plenty to think about. He would review all the details he had learned by heart, all the movements and expressions he had memorized. Nothing which he had discovered in the past three weeks must be neglected.

At last he found his hiding place under a small, unimportant-looking tree, with a tangle of bramble bushes behind him and a screen of bracken in front. When he lay stretched out under the tall curling fronds of the fern, he felt safe. Barring accidents, such as a rabbit-hunting farmer and his dog, there would be little chance of anyone stumbling across him. And a farmer wouldn't be surprised to find a disheveled *poilu* waiting for the daylight to fade. There were many of them, this summer of 1940.

It was cold and damp, but the discomfort sharpened his mind. He thought of Corlay in his white hospital bed in England, and smiled wryly as he felt the heavy dew soak efficiently through his clothes, as he watched the black bugs clinging to the underleaves of the bracken. Well, if Corlay's hipbone hadn't been shattered on the way out of Dunkirk, he might have been doing this job himself. And if Matthews hadn't been examin-ing a boatload of French and Belgian wounded after it had arrived at Folkestone; if he hadn't seen the unconscious Corlay, believed he was Hearne, and then notified Military Intelligence that one of their men had just got back in an uncomfortably original way, then this scheme would never have been born in Matthews' fertile brain. That was like Matthews. He must have mulled it all over in his mind for a couple of days, and out of his sardonic amusement had grown the germ of an idea.

"Well, I'm damned," he would say. "Well, I'm damned." And then he'd begin to think of a use for such an extraordinary likeness, especially when

he learned more about the Frenchman and where he came from. That was
like Matthews. He never wasted an opportunity. Two days after he had
seen Corlay, he had not only the idea shaping nicely, but also the go-
ahead signal from his own department.

Strange bird, Matthews, thought Hearne, and rolled over on his side to
ease a hipbone. He took some deep breaths, tautened his muscles to warm
himself. His clothes would dry when the sun really got into this glade.
He'd be warm enough, then. Strange bird, Matthews; he sort of sensed
things coming. He'd cook up some plan, keep it simmering until the right
moment arrived, and then dish it up piping hot. The right moment in
this case had been a week before the French-German armistice. It was
then that he sent for Hearne.

"Glad you got back in time," he had begun, and smiled quietly. Hearne
knew that smile. He waited, wondering what was coming this time.

"How would you like to spend a summer in France?"

That meant he was going to spend a summer in France. He allowed
himself one objection—not that Matthews would show that he had ever
noticed it.

"But I've just come back from there." Thirty-six hours ago, Hearne
added under his breath.

"Brittany, this time." Matthews gave his imitation of a benevolent Santa
Claus. "That should interest you, Hearne."

It did, in spite of the fact that for the last month he hadn't slept in a
clean bed, or seen anything which might be remotely called a bathroom.
Hearne saw his leave and the quiet comfort of his flat evaporating as
quickly as August rain on a hot London pavement.

"When do I go?" he asked. Brittany . . . well, that was something.

"In about two or three weeks. That is, if things go the way they are
shaping. Looks bad, at the moment. If there's a separate armistice, then
we shall use you, because every Frenchman who can get back to his home
will then make a beeline for it. A lot of them won't get back; and there
will be some with the guts to fight on. But you are to be one of the Frenchmen who do get back, and stay there."

"Home?" Hearne was incredulous. Home meant relatives, and complications. He had never tackled anything so domestic as that.

And then Matthews explained about Corlay.

"Here's all the official knowledge about him," he ended, pushing a folder
across his desk to Hearne. "All checked and amplified by a French Intelligence chap—Fournier, he's called—who will be one of those who fight on,
so there's no danger of the wrong people learning about our interest in
Corlay. You'll find that Fournier has done a pretty good job. He included
a detailed map and description of the district. St. Déodat is the name of
the village. Know it?"

Hearne shook his head. He had no idea where it was. He searched his memory in annoyance. Hell, he thought, Brittany is supposed to be my pidgin.

"North or South Brittany?" he asked at last.

"North. Just southwest of the town of Dol. Within walking distance of the railway line from Rennes to St. Malo. Near enough Dinan to admire the canal. Close enough to the main north road from Rennes." Matthews was speaking slowly, underlining the importance of the towns with the inflection of his voice. "And also," he added, "not so very far from Mont St. Michel, and our old friends Duclos and Pléhec, if you must send us news about your health."

Hearne smothered a smile. Matthews was at his old trick again of coating the pill lavishly with sugar. He liked to make his assignments sound like a Cook's tour.

"Duclos is still there?" Hearne asked.

"Yes, and very useful he will be from now on. I am rather afraid his archeological researches are going to be disturbed. Then, for emergency use only, you will find another friend outside St. Malo. Fournier guarantees him. You'd better talk to him about this man of his before you leave."

Hearne nodded. "And I've to take moonlight strolls round the railway line and road and canal?" he asked.

There was almost a smile on Matthews' face. "You are being sent to this farm so that, within a patch of about two hundred square miles, you can find information which will fit neatly into the reports which we hope to get from all the other patches of two hundred square miles. Then, when all the pieces of the crossword puzzle are fitted together, we will have a working idea of German intentions. Now, here are the particular pieces of information which we need. First, we want to know if North Brittany is being fortified and garrisoned for defense; or is it being prepared as a base for an attack on the British Isles? If so, then just in what way are the Germans preparing to attack? If airfields are being constructed then they are aiming for our southern ports and our shipping lanes. If huge masses of troops and boats are being prepared, then our southwest flank is in danger." Matthews stabbed at the map on the desk in front of him. "The Devon Coast, the Bristol Channel, Southern Ireland. Brittany is just the right position to try for these places. So look for airfields, troop movements, types of supplies being sent by road and rail and canal, new construction works, underground dumps, gun installations. You may not see much sense in what you observe, but your report will fit neatly into the other reports we'll receive. When we fit them together, they will make a pretty pattern. So don't even let the little things escape you. Work at night. I think you'll find plenty of material for your usual precise reports. Anything you pick up will probably be useful."

There was a note in Matthews' voice which raised Hearne's eyes from the map to the older man's face. *Anything you pick up* . . . Was that inflection on the *you* intended? If it were, then that was high praise.

Matthews was speaking again. "I don't think you'll find this a difficult job." Again, there was that hint of emphasis on the *you*. "I think," he was saying, "I think we can depend on you only to follow your instructions, and not to suffer from any attacks of misplaced brilliance."

Hearne's elation faded, and then he saw the gleam in Matthews' eye, and the repressed smile. He breathed again. So Matthews wasn't displeased over his last attack of "misplaced brilliance," after all. Hearne suddenly thought, perhaps he's giving me this job just because I find it hard to be orthodox in my methods. Perhaps he isn't so much against them as he always pretends to be.

Matthews seemed to guess Hearne's thoughts. "Seriously," he said, "you did a good job at Bordeaux. But I'd like you to restrain yourself on this trip. No good getting lost to us." And then, as if he felt he had been too expansive, he added, "Not after all the trouble I've had in training you."

"Yes, sir," Hearne said.

Matthews' voice was matter-of-fact once more. "I suggest you memorize the contents of that folder. You'll find all the necessary data in it, including observations on Corlay by one of his officers and by a man who had known him as a student. After you've got all that information memorized, you can start on Corlay himself. You'll visit him each day in hospital, for two or three weeks. He can talk now. Find out everything you can to fill in the gaps. Study his voice, his expressions, all that sort of thing."

"What if he won't talk? The Bretons can be very reticent, you know."

"I think he will. There is a certain amount of questioning which all strangers in Britain must go through at this time. We've never had so many aliens dumped so unexpectedly on our shores, and at rather a dangerous moment for us, too. There are rumors, even among the wounded, of what's now called the Fifth Column. Fournier has seen Corlay, and dropped him that hint. He will talk, just to identify himself."

"Well, that sounds more hopeful. . . . You say he looks like me?"

"Looks? My dear Hearne, he's the dead spit of you. If he could mislead me, you can mislead anyone who knows him."

"But his mother and father?"

"Father killed in 1917. Mother bedridden. You'll find it all in that folder. I investigated that sort of thing before I called you in. Now, if there had been a wife . . ." Matthews smiled, and shook his head slowly. When he spoke again, his voice was crisp and businesslike. "I think you're in luck, this time, Hearne. You'll learn more about your Celtic peoples in a month at St. Déodat than you did that year at Rennes University." There was the sugar coating being spread on again. "What made you interested in the Bretons, anyway? Was it because you are a Cornishman, yourself?"

Hearne nodded. "That, and the fact that I like them, and that my father spent all his time in between his sermons writing about the early British saints. A lot of them ended up in Brittany, you know."

"Déodat being one? Well, that makes one of these nice coincidences."

"I can't think of any Déodat except Saint Augustine's son," Hearne said with a smile.

"Saint Augustine?" Matthews looked startled. "Didn't know he was married."

"He wasn't," Hearne said, enjoying the shocked look on Matthews' face. He added, "That was probably during Augustine's 'O God, *make me pure, but not yet'* period." For a strong Scots Presbyterian, Matthews was reacting in a very High Church manner. Hearne grinned amiably.

"Well, I'll be damned," said Matthews. "Well, I'll be—"

"That's about all, then?" Hearne asked tactfully.

"Yes," said Matthews. "Yes. I'll see you again before you leave."

"How do I go?"

It was Matthews' turn to smile. "Just drop in," he said.

The sun had come out, and with it a swarm of flies, fat black flies, inquisitive, persistent. But, at least, Hearne was beginning to feel dry and warm. He took the map out of his pocket to verify his position again. It was a detailed French map of Brittany, with well-worn creases, stains and a jagged tear over the Atlantic corner for good measure. If he were questioned, he was to say that this map had been given him at Brest, after he had arrived there by fishing boat from Dunkirk. Better allow himself a slight case of shell shock to account for the period between Dunkirk and the armistice. Shell shock might be useful later: it could explain any strangeness, any lapse of memory. So, with this map, he had found his way home to the North of Brittany. The food in his pocket could be explained away, too . . . friendly peasantry department. *Could be explained away.* He smiled grimly at the phrase. He would just have to take especial care tonight in his short journey to St. Déodat, and then no explanations would be necessary to any curious patrol.

He examined the map for the last time. He must be able to remember the details of the district to the north and west of this wood, to reach the toy railway which trailed the main road from Rennes to St. Malo. It would guide him part of the way. The rest would depend on his knowledge of these thin and thick red lines and winding black ones. He had looked at them so often in the past few days that they were etched on his memory as well as on this map. At last he admitted that he could do no more, that he must depend now on a combination of intelligence and intuition. There would be no moon tonight, but if the sky stayed clear the stars would be enough. Failing them, it would have to be by guess and by God.

He settled himself more comfortably in his bracken bed. The sweet smell of fern and grass, the warmth of the sun, the increasing hum of the innumerable insects, drowsed him pleasantly. He felt himself slipping into light sleep. Tomorrow, he was thinking, tomorrow Bertrand Corlay would be home.

CHAPTER **3** NIGHT JOURNEY

A cool breeze awakened him. The bright green of the bracken and trees was no longer bathed in sunlight. The glade had darkened, as if a shade had been pulled down over a window. The gentle hum of insects had gone, the birds had become silent. There was only the uneasy stirring of branches overhead, the anxious rustling of the leaves. Not a pleasant sound, Hearne thought, especially when a man was hungry and cold. As the dusk deepened, he made an effort to get up. He was much stiffer than he had even thought. He sat with his back against a tree, and ate half of his rations, such as they were. The other half he replaced stoically in his pocket. If he bungled tonight, there would be another day to provide for.

At last the darkness had thickened enough to let him reach the edge of the trees. He walked slowly, even painfully at first, but by the time the first stars began to show, he was ready.

He looked at the North Star, and got his bearings. The fields ahead seemed horribly naked. In a way, he thought as he left the trees, this was something like taking a dive from a plane, except that he didn't have to worry this time about the parachute opening.

The ground, becoming more tamed as it descended, sloped gently into a broad shallow valley. The clumps of gorse grew more sparsely, much to Hearne's relief. It hadn't been so easy to avoid them at first. By the time he had reached the first cultivated patch of land, he was moving more confidently. His stiffness was forgotten, and his eyes had become accustomed to the shapes and shadows within the darkness.

He passed a house, hidden unexpectedly behind some trees. A dog barked, and he saw a dull yellow light fill one of the windows as a lamp was lit. He felt an extraordinary compulsion to stay and watch. The glow from the small square window reached out into the coldness of the night and held him there, standing irresolute. Then the dog barked again, and the spell was broken. He moved swiftly away. Behind him the light still shone, but there was no sound of men's voices or of following feet. Then other trees and a twist in the path blocked out the house, and he was alone in a field of straggling corn, hedged with gnarled fruit trees.

It was strange how you could be trapped by a moment like that, when your control over your movements was suspended, when nothing seemed to matter anyway. Strange, and dangerous. He couldn't allow himself any off-guard moments, he reminded himself grimly. He thought again of that light. No footsteps, no men's voices. When the dog had barked, the light had appeared so quickly, as if someone were lying awake, listening, waiting. A woman, perhaps, hoping against hope. This summer, there would be plenty of women, waiting and hoping. And he couldn't allow himself any sentiment, either: that was another luxury he couldn't afford this trip. He concentrated on the fields.

The faintly luminous hands on Corlay's watch told him it was fully an hour since he had stepped out of the woods. He was late. Either he had gone too carefully, or he had missed his direction. The discouraging idea that he had landed in another part of the Breton countryside, after all, began to take root. One minute he was calling himself a damned fool; and then the next, he was imagining what he'd use for transit if he found himself on the steep banks of the River Rance. It should be well behind him. If it weren't, he'd have a nice cold swim ahead of him. He remembered Matthews' old consolation: blessed is he who expects the worst, for he shall not be disappointed. He walked gloomily on. If he came to a village, he could scout out its name. Of course the villages hereabouts would all have gold-plated neon signs and—and at that moment, he almost tripped over the miniature railway line. Not that it was noticeable, wandering so light-heartedly through the grass and flowers, along the hedgerows, and across the winding country roads without so much as a by-your-leave. He advanced cautiously along it, moving quietly through the shadows. The new moon was not yet born. Only the stars lighted the clear sky.

He passed occasional farmhouses, darkened and asleep in the curves of their fields. Now and again there would be a village to avoid. Once he came to an unexpected road and a small wooden shed which was probably a station—nameless, in the best railway traditions. Twenty yards away was a hidden village, a dozen little stone houses round the inevitable church. German notices were posted here on the wall beside which he sheltered. But no one stirred. Reassured, he crossed the treacherous road, his eyes searching the sleeping village. "Café de France et de Chateaubriand," he noted. That cheered him up, somehow, in spite of a large white proclamation with giant black letters shouting after him *Bekanntmachung!*

He had reached the protection of some trees. And then a shadow moved —just there, about fifty yards ahead, in that unfortunate patch of open ground. He drew back against a tree. Another shadow moved, close behind the first one. His eyes followed their careful progress as his mind raced quickly from one plan to another. If he kept behind these two men, they would slow up his pace. He must circle to his left (for to the right lay the main roadway to the coast, and he had better keep well clear of that), increasing his speed, so that he would pass the two men and come back to the railway line well ahead of them.

And then the noise of heavy trucks rumbled across the quiet fields. When they were about a quarter of a mile distant, Hearne glanced at the watch on his wrist. It pointed to 10:58. The trucks were traveling slowly, probably half-blacked-out. About fifteen miles an hour, he guessed. He strained his eyes, but the trees which were spaced along the roadway broke his line of vision. Here and there, where the edge of the road was clear, he could see black lumbering shapes, like a herd of elephants stringing out towards a water hole. Yes, fifteen miles an hour was about right. He listened patiently, his eye on his watch. When the last of the column had reached about a quarter of a mile away, and the hum of engines was fading towards the coast, the time on the watch was 11:01. They had taken three minutes to pass through half a mile, roughly, at about fifteen miles an hour. That would give him almost a quarter of a mile of trucks. And many of them had been carrying oil: there was no mistaking the noise of the chains trailing on the paved roadway, clattering above the hum of the powerful engines.

Ahead of Hearne, the two men had fallen flat on the ground. When the sound of motors had died away, they moved quickly towards the nearest cover. They didn't want to attract any German interest, either. But even if they wanted to avoid the Nazis, that didn't mean he wanted to meet them. He moved quickly to his left up the sloping hill, working round the edge of the patch of open ground in front of him. He set off impatiently: he was losing time having to make this detour to avoid these two blighters. But his temper improved with the easiness of the ground. He could no longer see the men, but he would allow himself half a mile before he turned back towards the toy railway again. He made it in good enough time, for he found plenty of cover. He blessed the Breton habit of never clearing their fields completely of trees. He had often wondered why the farmers should have taken the trouble, year after year, to plow and reap all round every small tree. Now he felt grateful to them.

The half-mile was covered. Time now, he told himself, to swerve to his right, down through that small wood. Beyond it, he would find the railway line again. It was strange, he thought, to slip so quietly and cautiously through this peaceful countryside, past the small stone houses with their black windows staring at him like sightless eyes, past the sleeping people and the brooding church towers, while down in the valley the Nazi trucks lumbered along with their death-bringing loads.

He had entered the wood, and, for the second time that night, almost fell over the narrow tracks of the railway.

"What the hell—" he thought, and then cursed silently as he realized that he must have been working his way gradually down towards the railway all the time he had thought he was keeping parallel.

And then suddenly, a weight hit his knees, two arms were tightly locked round his legs, and he pitched forward onto his face with a grunt as the wind was knocked out of him. When he got back his breath, he found he was pinned to the ground. The larger of the two men was sitting astride him with a firm grasp on the back of his neck, with a strong knee-hold on his arms.

"He's French." The boy who was squatting in front of him, watching him gravely, pronounced the verdict in a low whisper. "At least," the whispered voice went on, "he's wearing a French uniform. But he may be a Jerry. Never can tell, these days."

"You should have let me fetch him one, lad," whispered back the weight across Hearne's shoulders. The slow drawl and flat overtones were unmistakably Yorkshire.

Hearne thought quickly: maintain he was French and speak with a bogus English accent, and he'd still lose time in explanations; or he could just speak French, and they'd still argue whether he was friend or foe. He decided to risk it.

"You tackle too high," he said in English to the big Yorkshireman. The weight on his back shifted.

"Eh, what's that?"

"You tackle too high. And for Jesus' sake, don't raise that voice of yours. Do you want to bring a pack of Nazis down on us, you bloody fool?"

The Yorkshireman dropped his voice again, but there was an angry vehemence in his whisper. "I never tackled high in my whole life."

"Well, that's no reason to flatten me now, you blithering idiot."

"Sounds as if he might be English," the boy remarked. He was feeling Hearne's pockets gently. He removed the revolver and slipped it into his own pocket. "Get off, Sam," he said then.

"Not me," said Sam, and settled his weight more squarely. "I'm fine as I am."

Hearne addressed himself to the thin-faced, anxious boy. "Go on, pick up his moosket for him, Wellington. Do you want us all to be caught?"

"What's your regiment?" the boy asked suddenly.

"Liaison officer," parried Hearne. "Ninth French Army. Sedan and points west, ever since."

"Where did you get these clothes?"

"Where did you get yours?" Hearne grinned as he looked at their blue peasant blouses, ill-fitting jackets and ragged corduroy trousers. "Look here, I could talk much better with Sam off my back, and it's about time we were moving on. I'm in a hurry, if you aren't. And you might remember that I'd have used my revolver at once, if I had been a Jerry."

"One wrong move from you, me lad, and I'll flatten you proper," Sam said placidly, and rose to his feet. He thrust one large red fist under Hearne's nose for emphasis. "See?"

"I see," Hearne said with a smile. "And even if it was high, it was a damned good tackle." Sam only grunted in reply, but an answering grin spread slowly over his large face. Strange couple, thought Hearne: the serious, fair-haired boy, thin and haggard, who spoke such precise clipped English, and the plain Yorkshireman with his broad back and vowels.

"Which way are you heading?" the boy asked. He might have been twenty, but he looked more like seventeen.

"North."

"Then we can go on together." His tone was very definite. That would have been his answer if Hearne had said "South."

"I don't want to lose that gun," Hearne said.

The boy smiled. "I'll look after it very well." He nodded to Sam, who took his place behind Hearne, and set off without another word.

They covered the next three miles in Indian-file, first the boy, then Hearne, with the Yorkshireman bringing up the rear. The pace was surprisingly good. They only had to slow down twice: once when they circumvented a village, once when they struck a broad stretch of completely open ground. Then the choice was either a wide detour up a hillside, or a ten-minute wait for the cotton-wool clouds to spread themselves over the hard, bright stars. The boy, to Hearne's surprise, chose to wait. It amused Hearne to see how calmly the younger man had taken the command from the start; and he had taken it well. This was the first time that Hearne disagreed with him. And then he remembered that compared to these two men he was fresh and rested. He could only make a guess at how far they had traveled and under what conditions. Even then, like all guesses, his would be short: guesses didn't tell the half of it. He noticed that the boy's jacket was too thin: he was shuddering in spite of himself. Sam had noticed that shivering, too. He looked up at the sky and the slow clouds.

"Blast you and blast you and blast you," he muttered with surprising venom.

Then the light dimmed at last, and they had a few minutes' grace to cross the open ground. They ran silently with a grim desperation. Ahead of them were some trees, beautiful trees, lovely trees, gracious trees, noble trees. Hearne sank breathless beside Sam on the cool, shadowed ground.

"I'm a tree lover for life," he said, but the others weren't listening to him. The boy, standing so rigid, suddenly groaned and moved away.

"He's ill," said Hearne in alarm, although his voice was no higher than a whisper.

"Don't let him hear you say that. He'll be all right." But Sam was anxiously watching the trees behind which his friend had staggered. Hearne started to move, but Sam's hand stopped him. "He wouldn't have you near him. Sort of worries him for anyone to hang about him. He has these attacks regular as the clock every hour. Ate something which turns him inside out, even when he hasn't anything left inside him to turn out."

They lay and waited. "Pretty bad attack," Hearne whispered.

"Aye." Sam was more worried than he had pretended. "Plucky lad, all right. Come all the way from a prison camp across the Rhine." He was talking now for the sake of talking. Hearne welcomed that too.

"Were you with him?"

"No. Met him halfway. I was in Belgium."

"How the devil did you get as far south as this?"

"There was some of us got lost, and we thought we'd fight our way back to the French. Funny, come to think of it. We landed in a French part of the line, all right, and there we were, moving back and moving back, just moving back without ever a stand. It was right discouraging, I can tell you. Then they told us the fight was off, and there we were slap in t' middle of France. An officer said we were to get a train to where the last English were getting off in boats. But the blasted engine-driver just spat and said the war was over. Then one of the Poles—"

"Poles?"

"Aye. Poles and Belgians and some Czechs and us. A proper tower of Babel, I can tell you. Well, this Pole, he had been an engine-driver, and we threw the Parley-voo off his cab—we were all raving mad, that we were, what with fighting our way south and then being left high and dry—and we started the train." He paused and listened. "If you don't mind, I'll go and see how his nibs is, now." He slipped noiselessly into the further darkness of the trees.

Hearne grinned to himself. And what had happened to the train, he wondered. It hadn't got very far, obviously. He saw the two dim shapes returning to his tree. Sam barked his shin on a stump, and grunted.

"Black as the Earl of Hell's waistcoat," he said angrily.

"Sorry." It was the boy. He sat down weakly beside Hearne. "Sorry. Tummy all skew-wiff." He was wiping the sweat off his brow with his sleeve. Hearne nodded. Cold sweat it would be, and the twisting pains would still be clutching at his stomach and bowels. What he needed was a rest for a couple of days and a starchy diet to cement him up.

"Do you know where you are going?" Hearne asked.

The boy nodded. "Got a man's name at Dinan. He will take us in his boat down that river towards the coast."

"Down the Rance? That sounds O.K. But can you depend on him?"

"Others have, and managed it. Well, I'm all right now for a while. Let's move."

And then once more came the roar of a huge fleet of trucks. Hearne motioned silence, and kept his eyes fixed on his watch. When he had finished, he noted that the boy was looking at him curiously.

"Let's move," he said again, and his tone was friendlier. "Can you lend us a map, by any chance? I lost mine while I was having a spot of trouble with a river, and I'm doing this sort of out of my head. We are fairly near Dinan now, aren't we?"

Hearne hesitated for a moment. "I'll put you on the road for Dinan. You'll reach it by dawn," he said. "And I can give you some stodgy food." He fished in his pocket and handed over what was left of his rations. "Rest up for a couple of days when you get there," he added. "Keep warm. Don't let them feed you shellfish, or cheese, or butter, or heated wine. The Bretons believe in a wine toddy. It cures a lot of things, but not your trouble. Herbal tea is good, and plain unseasoned macaroni or potatoes. It all tastes rotten, though."

"Yes, doctor."

"And you'd better listen to me. You've a long sail ahead of you. Now, come on."

This time, Hearne led the way.

There were still more roads to cross now, little straggling roads which twisted and turned from village to village. And there was a German patrol to be avoided. They managed that by throwing themselves flat into a ditch beside the road which they had been on the point of crossing. It was unpleasant but effective. The motorcycles swept past them, and they could breathe again in spite of the mud. When they crawled out of their hiding place, Hearne looked anxiously at the boy. But the haggard young face gave an attempt at a smile.

"All right for another half hour, I think," he said. "Come on, Sam; breakfast in bed tomorrow." Sam only gave that slow grin of his. And then they were moving silently again: walking, slipping, crouching, crawling, but always moving forward.

They had passed the village Hearne had been expecting. There was no mistaking that church tower. Norman-Gothic, English influence, interesting, the guidebooks would say. It was interesting, all right. This was where they'd branch off, and he could make up for the time he had lost. Matthews would have been apoplectic if he could have seen him in these last two hours. "Well, I'm damned," he would say. "Of all the infernal stupidity . . ."

Hearne halted. He pointed to a line of trees. "There's your road," he said. "When you reach it, turn left and that will take you west to Dinan in six miles or so. I'll leave you here, now that we are getting towards the towns. Three's a crowd in this game, too."

They saw reason in that. "By the way, what would have happened if I had put up a real fight or tried to dodge you?" he asked, as they parted.

"Our suspicions would have been aroused," the boy said. He handed over the revolver to Hearne. He was beginning to shiver again. His eyes were looking towards the line of trees.

"In plain English, I'd 've twisted your damned neck with my two bare hands," Sam said amiably, and then he noticed the shivering too. "Time to be off, lad," he added, and taking the boy's arm pulled him quickly away. Hearne watched them go—two shadows as he had first seen them, merging cautiously into the blackness of the trees.

"With my two bare hands," he repeated to himself. Then, "See, Matthews?" as if to the stars overhead.

I wonder, he was thinking, just what did happen to that train. Well, he wouldn't know now. Good chap, that Sam. Hearne remembered how carefully he had listened to his advice about the diet for the boy. Sam would see that that young man did rest up. Yes, they were a strange couple, all right, each of them thinking he was responsible for the other. That way, even with the odds against them, they might have a chance. For a minute, Hearne envied them. The worst of his job was that he was always so completely alone. But, he reminded himself, that could also be the best thing about it, too. He looked at his watch, and smiled to himself as he noted he now called it "his" quite naturally. He had about four hours left and twelve miles or so to go. If the ground was easy and patrols not too frequent, the distance could be lessened. He should manage it all right.

As he turned eastwards, he felt more confident. In these last two hours, he had felt all the old tricks and instincts coming back to him. He was covering the ground more quickly now, decisions were easier, movements were surer. The footling pessimism and nervousness which had attacked him at the beginning of this night were gone. When dawn came, he would be home.

CHAPTER **4**   THE SLEEPING VILLAGE

The last obstinate stars were fading in the sky when Hearne came to St. Déodat. His arrival at this hour solved some minor problems for him, for even the early rising villagers would not yet be stirring. He paused on the path which had brought him so quickly round the curves of these last gentle hills, past the endless slate-roofed farmhouses, past the orchards and well-tilled fields. And right there, just below where he stood, lay St. Déodat: fifty, or less, stone houses clustered near the church and its soaring towers. Nothing moved. There was no sound. It seemed a deserted village, asleep in its sheltered hollow.

Hearne repressed his excitement. He had better see how far wrong he had been in his idea of the place, before he started congratulating himself. He had two choices: either he could keep to this path on the hill, rising to the west of the village, until he reached the Corlay farm, or he could cut down to the road and enter the village at the north end. He chose the second course. It was safe enough with the village still asleep. Even if some early bird did see him, it would be noted that he came from the north, which fitted in very nicely with his story of walking from the coast. Also, he would feel surer of reaching the Corlay farm if he followed the road through the village, for there were many small farms all remarkably alike scattered over the hillside. It would take some explaining if he were to approach the wrong house and claim it as his. Slight shell shock would hardly be an adequate excuse. Finally—and this was the chief reason, he admitted to himself quite cheerfully—he just wanted to see St. Déodat. He had thought of it constantly in the last three weeks; he had examined drawings, memorized descriptions, made his own sketches. He knew it forwards, backwards, sideways—on paper. Now he had the chance to walk quietly, slowly, through St. Déodat, and in the graying light he would see it as it really stood.

It was a compact little village. First, there had been the church, built in the tenth or eleventh century: the two Romanesque towers bore testimony to that. Then, gradually, houses had grouped themselves round it; and a narrow road found its way up between the little hills, from the flat plains of the northeast. By the fourteenth century, St. Déodat was a flourishing community. It had a proud castle on the western hill, and feudal overlords to bring it reliques from the Holy Land. In the market place which had formed itself opposite the church, the country people from miles around came to buy and sell. That was when the Gothic part of the church had been added by the prosperous, and grateful, villagers.

Nothing changes had been the proud motto of the castle. St. Déodat kept faith with it, although the castle now lay in ruins since its last overlord had abandoned the village for the richer graces of Versailles. Hearne wondered if he had still said "Nothing changes" when he had mounted to the guillotine. If he were a true Breton, he probably did, just to spite the howling mob. Even as the blade descended, and the unchanging Comte had change thrust upon him, his village asserted itself for the last time in its history. Its people joined the desperate Vendée revolt against the Revolution, and were rewarded by the despoiling of their castle, the burning of their houses, the slaughter of their young men in the market place. Yet their church, although bruised and crippled, still stood.

The people took courage from it, and when they came back from their hiding places they rebuilt enough of the destroyed houses to suit their diminished numbers. The market place once more heard weekly gossip. But after that bloody 1793, the inhabitants of St. Déodat avoided trouble by strictly minding their own business. And they had succeeded, at the price of becoming a forgotten village.

Hearne stopped thinking of St. Déodat's past as he reached the narrow road which entered the village. Now he was concentrating on its present.

He passed fourteen houses, five of them empty (not only a forgotten village, he emended then, but a dying one; and a deserted one, in years to come, unless something were to happen to rouse St. Déodat from self-destruction), and he named them as he went. He could no longer repress his excitement. There was no doubt about it: he could recognize this village.

That was the house of Trouin, carpenter and candlestick-maker. And that belonged to Guézennec, the retired schoolmaster. One small school, Hearne remembered parenthetically, tucked away behind the trees beyond the houses round the market place, despised because it was the usurper of the education which the Church should have been allowed to continue. It hadn't been so bad when Guézennec had been appointed, for he was one of them, and he had been half a priest before he became schoolteacher. But now, there was a young foreigner in the school, a man from Lorient in South Brittany who had studied in Paris. Kerénor was his name. He limped badly. He lived in the little hotel on the market square.

Hearne reached the church. On the far side of the market place facing it were grouped the grain dealer and baker, Guérin; the butcher and veterinary surgeon (kill or cure), Picrel; and Picrel's mother, the widow who kept the very small, very general store. On the north side of the square was the Town Hall. On the south was the hotel, where the new schoolteacher, Kerénor, lodged. It really was a glorified pub, Hearne decided, with a few rooms to let upstairs for occasional commercial travelers and stray summer visitors. It was called quite logically the Hotel Perro: Madame Perro owned it. She came from somewhere in the east of France, had married a St. Déodat man stationed in Lyons during the last war. But her late husband and her twenty-one years' residence in the village were extenuating circumstances. Now she was only half a foreigner.

Beyond the church, the road passed the curé's house. Hearne heard the sound of running water. That would be the stream from the western hillside, flowing under this road into the curé's garden (and there, on either side of the road ahead of him, were the two short stretches of stone wall to prove his guess and give the effect of a bridge). But he wouldn't have time now to explore the meadows below the church, with their little lake in which the stream ended. The sky was changing to a greenish-gray. He increased his pace to pass the last row of houses. Another Trouin lived there; and there, another Picrel; and some "negligibles." The word had been Corlay's. Seemingly the Corlays didn't know the "negligibles." And then he was across the piece of road which formed the bridge, and he had reached the path which led west from the road to the Corlay farm.

He paused there for a moment to look back. So that was St. Déodat, or at least the main part of it. There were also the small farms scattered around the village. He had a feeling that he would know the fields better than the village before the end of his stay. It was through them that his business lay.

The path led him up through a thin wood. And then he was walking over Pinot's land. He could see the blue, slate roof of its farmhouse glinting in the first rays of the morning sun. He hurried. He was glad of the soft white mist which was rising from the grass.

When the Pinot farm had been safely passed, he let himself admit that he hadn't been exactly enthusiastic about crossing these fields. He looked back over his shoulder. Only the last edge of the farmhouse roof was visible. And under that was Anne Pinot. . . . Anne Pinot: just another of the minor headaches on this job. "And, by heaven, I'll keep her minor," he said savagely to himself. After all, it wasn't the first time that a man had come back from a war, and had seemed changed. It would be better to seem cold rather than to assume affection that was false; it would be kinder in the long run, for when the war was over the real Corlay would return. Not that Corlay had displayed marked sentiment when he had mentioned her name. "Arranged," he had said. "Practical and suitable. The farm is next to ours. If they were joined, they would form the biggest farm in St. Déodat, and my mother and old Pinot would stop quarreling about the dovecote."

The farm is next to . . . Why, of course, he must be now on Corlay ground. To prove it, he saw the dovecote rising out of the mist on his right, a round tower of gray stone with a pointed cap of blue slate, marking the border of the two farms. He should soon see the Corlay house. He couldn't miss it, not on this path. "Stop it, you fool," he told himself. "You're too anxious again. That won't do." He could look tired, ill, unkempt—and he probably did—but not anxious. He, Bertrand Corlay, was reaching home at last, weary and bitter, impatient of foolish questions and futile answers. He only wanted to be left in peace, to brood in his room, to take solitary walks over the fields. It would only be natural if he couldn't bear the sight of a German. And all that could be convincingly managed, if he didn't start worrying; if, he grimly reminded himself, he managed to get through the next half hour. He could almost hear Matthews saying, "Worry before, and you'll be prepared. Worry afterwards, and you'll keep your feet on the ground. But don't worry during action; that's fatal." Well, he had worried plenty in the last three weeks over the smallest detail. Even Matthews would have been almost satisfied with his preparations. And he might have some memories, before he finished this job, which would worry him afterwards. But now . . . well, now the Corlay farmhouse was just fifty paces away. Hearne braced himself.

There was a short path of rough stones, patched together in the rich black earth. On one side of the two-storied house were apple trees; on the other, a hayfield almost ripe for cutting. The narrow windows were tightly shut and screened. But smoke was thickening above the chimney, as if someone had just thrown more wood on the night embers. He skirted the corner of the building, following the path into the back courtyard of the farm. The door ahead of him lay open.

CHAPTER **5** THE FARM

The woman, stooping in front of the enormous stone fireplace, half-turned as she heard the footsteps on the path. The man halted in the doorway and leaned against its heavy wooden post. His black hair was disheveled, falling over his high forehead to shadow the melancholy brown eyes. His high cheekbones added to the gauntness of his face, gray in the cold early morning light. A heavy growth of short black hair shaded the outline of his jaw. His blue jacket was faded and torn. His heavy boots were so encrusted with mud that his feet looked swollen.

The woman rose to her feet, clutching the black shawl more closely round her thin shoulders. Her lips remained half-open, as if she were frozen into silence. The bright color drained from her cheeks, leaving only a network of thin red veins.

She was frightened, Hearne realized. Perhaps he looked more like a ghost than he had thought. He advanced slowly into the large room, his feet suddenly dragging on the hard earth floor. She stood motionless, her eyes fixed on his face, her voice still silent. He would have to speak first, after all. He tried to smile that controlled smile which had been Corlay's.

"Well, Albertine, I've got home." His voice was the voice which had haunted him for three weeks, day and even night. The familiarity of its accent startled him. As he heard it, so strangely translated to this room, he could smell the antiseptic cleanliness of the hospital, he could see the black hair against the white pillowcase. And then Albertine moved, and as she came slowly forward she spoke.

"My God," she was saying, "my God. It's himself."

"Yes, it's me." Hearne sat down heavily on the wooden bench at the side of the long narrow table in the middle of the room. He felt suddenly tired, very tired.

Albertine was standing over him, her rough voice hurrying in its emotion, her gnarled hand smoothing the hair tightened under her starched white cap.

"I thought you were a ghost. You were just like one, standing there with the light behind your back, saying never a word."

Hearne smiled and checked his jaws from yawning. The warmth of the kitchen was having its effect. Albertine touched him suddenly, lightly, on the shoulder, as if she were reassuring herself.

"I'm alive, Albertine. I'm tired and I'm hungry, but I'm alive."

"You've been ill." Her eyes on his face embarrassed him. He leaned his elbows wearily on the table and rested his forehead on his hands so that they partly covered his face.

"Yes," he said, with the listlessness of someone who is too tired to think, far less talk. He added, "How is my mother?"

"Just so-so." Albertine's voice was normal once more. It was a plain voice, unemotional and heavy. "When she wakens, I'll tell her. Then you can go upstairs. But first I shall give you something to eat, and then you must clean yourself. Where were you?"

It was as if she were speaking to a small boy. It seemed as if she not only kept the house and the farm in order, but Madame Corlay and her son as well. There was a curious blend of familiarity and deference, a kind of proprietary interest mixed with critical pride. Albertine had turned away as she asked the question. She was now stirring the contents of the large black iron pot suspended from an iron hook over the burning end of the log. It was more a young tree than a log; the shriveled brown leaves still clung to the end lying over the stone hearth, waiting to be fed onto the flames in its turn. Albertine tasted the soup, and spooned it generously into a thick earthenware bowl.

"Where were you?" she repeated. Hearne started slightly and brought his gaze away from the dancing flames.

"You're tired," she said. "You're half-asleep. Eat this and then you'll feel better. But where have you been?"

"Belgium. Dunkirk," he said mechanically and warmed his hands round the bowl of soup. "I got to Brest in a French boat. I was ill. When I recovered there was the armistice, and I began to walk home."

Albertine had cut him a thick slab of coarse white bread, and watched him critically as he swallowed the soup.

"You're hungry," she said, and moved suddenly into another room, with the quick sure movement of a practical woman who has not time to waste over decisions. She came back with a small piece of cold pork, a still smaller piece of sausage, and a glass of milk. It was good milk, with the yellow cream still there.

"The Germans haven't been here," he said suddenly.

Albertine looked at him in astonishment, her almost invisible eyebrows raised. "They came and they went. Just six men on motor bicycles. Why should they stay here? There is nothing for them here."

Hearne smiled as he shook his head, and wiped the thick cream off his upper lip. He remembered the truck convoys he had seen last night.

"Have the others in the village got home?" he asked tactfully.

"Picrel's son. The Picrels always look out for themselves, you may be sure of that. Trouin's son was killed, and Jean-Marie Guérin has been a prisoner for four months in Germany." Her voice droned on monotonously. Apart from the family tragedies in the village, all due to the war, life in St. Déodat was very much the same as usual. There were the weekly markets, smaller now certainly, but then most of the young men had been away. Even with smaller markets, there had been enough food last winter, and enough fuel, and enough wool. Enough was all St. Déodat had ever wanted. Monsieur le Curé had been ill with rheumatism again, and some of the children had had a fever. But that of course was what happened when children were all shut up together in a schoolhouse. That young man Kerénor had . . . And then the church bells rang, and Hearne never learned what had or hadn't happened to Kerénor.

Albertine looked at him blankly. "I was forgetting," she began incredulously. Her forehead wrinkled into deep lines so that Hearne knew the colorless eyebrows must again be raised. He looked at the prominent bones of the thin face, the bald brow with the hair combed so severely under the high cap.

"But of course you must go," he said. "Don't wait at home for me." Albertine looked relieved. There might have also been surprise on her face, as she moved towards one of the three beds which lay along the wall, opposite the fireplace. From a chest of richly carved wood, arranged as a kind of step in front of the high bed, she lifted a rosary and another black shawl.

She was at the door now. "Don't waken Madame," she said briskly. "Henri is with the animals." She nodded towards the wooden wall beside the door he had entered. He remembered the outbuilding which joined this corner of the house at right angles and sheltered both the entrance and the small courtyard from the north wind. So through that wooden wall was the cow shed. That accounted for the warm, farm smell, not unpleasant, which had filled this room.

"Henri?" he remembered to say in surprise. Henri wasn't the name he had expected.

"Yes. He came to help me, but he is too old."

"And Jean?" Jean was Albertine's nephew who had lived on the farm and done the harder work.

"Missing." Her face was expressionless, a mask of tightly drawn skin over rugged, strong bones. Then she was gone, pulling the second shawl round her shoulders. Hearne listened to her sabots clattering down the flagged path.

"I'm accepted," he thought. "I've been left in possession."

Now he would have about three quarters of an hour before Albertine returned, while Henri was with the cattle and Madame Corlay slept upstairs. He finished the last crumbs of his meal and drained the drops which had gathered at the bottom of the soup bowl. He was feeling better, already.

From Corlay, he had gathered only rough details about this house. There were three rooms downstairs: this large room, the smaller room from which Albertine had brought the food, and a front room which was a kind of entrance-hall parlor with its own front door, seldom used. The staircase to the three rooms upstairs led from that entrance-hall place. Overhead was Madame Corlay's large bedroom, stretching across the full side-length of the house, as this kitchen did. Above the entrance hall was his room, and behind it, over the room where the food seemed to be kept, was another room for storage. Definitely utilitarian architecture, he thought. And then there was that outhouse tacked onto the end of the kitchen, separated from it by a wooden partition. There had been openings along that partition at one time, like so many booking-office windows in a railway station, but now they were shuttered and blocked. Under them, there still lay a thick tree trunk, shaped into a shallow trough. Hearne had a sudden vision of five cows shoving their heads through the five openings, their jaws working steadily, their scanty eyelashes unmoved as they watched their master and his large family grouped round the table, eating their meal with similar concentration.

And there must have been a large family at one time, judging from the size of the table with its two long benches and from the three double beds arranged sideways along the wall opposite the fireplace. Each bed had its encircling drapery, suspended from the wooden ceiling above, so that the men and women and children could sleep in the same room without offending *les convenances*. There were a chair and a chest before each bed: they were so high with piled mattresses that otherwise it would be difficult to climb into them. At either end of the row of beds were two wardrobes, broad and deep. Like the chests, they were of age-stained wood, beautifully fashioned and carved. The two doors flanking them occupied the last available corners of space on that long, well-filled wall. The one beside the back-door entrance was the one which Albertine had used: downstairs storeroom it must be. He moved across to it quickly, and glanced briefly inside. A bicycle, a bowl of milk, some wine bottles, a cider keg, some twisted rope, large iron cooking utensils, a few small barrels, a few large earthenware bowls neatly covered, all standing on the stone floor. There were two windows, both of them small and high in the wall and tightly shut. 'Ellish dark and smells o' cheese, Hearne thought. Now for the upstairs part of the house.

He took one last look at the kitchen. He would have to know it backwards. The windows here were also small. Two lay at the other end of the room with a dresser and its rows of dishes between them, while two higher windows flanked the fireplace. Under one of these was another dresser, and more dishes, under the other was a small table. Between them stood the enormous stone fireplace, with proportions and simplicity worthy of a castle hall. From the dark wood rafters overhead were suspended two hams and a long shelf containing a wooden rack. In the rack were numerous thin circular disks.

"Now, what the hell—" began Hearne. Disks . . . Probably edible; they certainly weren't ornamental. He strained his eyes, and then something clicked in his memory. Rennes, and a small inn outside the city, and a cheap student meal, and pancakes. That was it. Pancakes.

Then he became aware that someone had entered the room, that someone was standing behind him. There had been no footsteps on the flagged path outside; he was sure of that. He turned, slowly, casually he hoped. A man was standing in the corner of the kitchen, against the wooden partition which was the dividing line between the animals and the family. Behind him, a narrow door was open, a door whose edges fitted so neatly into the wall that Hearne had been unaware of its existence. Blind oaf, he said to himself in annoyance. He ought to have realized an opening would be there. There were plenty of dirty wet nights in the winter, and what peasant was going to leave the warmth of his kitchen to visit his animals by way of a cold dark farmyard? Certainly not a peasant who had arranged his eating and sleeping so practically.

The man stood silently, impassively, a small thin figure in a faded blue blouse hanging loosely over worn corduroy trousers. Behind him, there was only a black smudge, and silence. The animals must have already been turned out into the fields. There was no mistaking the warm smell of straw and cows which filled the kitchen. Cosy little joint, thought Hearne; for those who liked it that way, he added hastily, as the smell strengthened. Well, now, what should he say or shouldn't he say to Grandpa? He watched three white hens negotiate the old man's wooden shoes, and jerk their way hesitatingly into the kitchen, picking spasmodically at non-existent crumbs with a kind of I-really-don't-have-to-do-this air. But he still hadn't thought of anything to say. It was the old man who spoke first, as he closed the door carefully behind him and came slowly past the end of the trough into the kitchen.

"She's gone?" His French was heavy and slow, as if it were almost a foreign language.

Hearne nodded, and said "Yes." That seemed to be all that was expected of him.

The old man moved more quickly. He picked up a bowl from the small table beside the fireplace and helped himself to some soup. He seated himself at the large table and began eating. He had seemingly identified Hearne in his mind, and, having accepted him, was now concentrating on his breakfast. Hearne stood, feeling rather futile, and watched the soup disappear. The old boy had quite a capacity, considering his dimensions. Then Hearne suddenly realized that he was the master of this house. He'd better stop acting like an unwanted week-end guest. He turned abruptly towards the doorway which he had not yet explored. Henri stopped chewing and watched him.

"I'm going to sleep. I'm tired," Hearne said.

"Aye, it'll be wet tomorrow," Henri replied slowly and amiably. His face was as weathered and as wrinkled as a dried russet apple. He nodded sagely as he spoke. His smile showed no teeth, but the eyes were as blue as his smock. They looked up at Hearne with their strange mixture of ingenuousness and shrewdness. Hearne smiled in turn, and nodded vigorously. As he was shutting the door, he looked back towards the table. Henri was scouring round the emptied bowl with his last crust of bread. Under the table, at his feet, the three white hens had abandoned their condescension and were competing openly for the few crumbs which had escaped.

It was just as well that he was not really a hero returning from the wars, Hearne thought, or he'd be feeling as flat as a punctured tire after that welcome.

It was cold in this entrance hall, as well as dark, for it lay in the southwest corner of the house. It would be a cheerless place even when the sun did get round to it: no one used this room. It was just a square-shaped box with more heavy carved furniture, a flagged stone floor, a wooden staircase hidden in the shadows of the central wall, and a front door which was as obviously unused as it was imposing.

He mounted the staircase warily. It was really only a glorified ladder. He could see the stone floor beneath him, between the treads. He began to guess why Madame Corlay kept to her room. This was hardly the kind of staircase for arthritic joints. The landing at the top of the stairs was scarcely bigger than a cupboard. There were two doors. That one on his left would be the large bedroom above the kitchen, so this one must be his. He touched the latch gently and pushed the door slowly open. Inside it was dark, save for a faint blot of light where the window lay on the west wall. There was the same damp smell which he had noticed in the hall downstairs. He walked cautiously across the uneven wooden floor. His feet were beginning to feel the weight of his muddy boots. He pulled back the curtains clumsily and opened the window. There were the clean smell of trees and the nervous twitterings of wakening birds. He leaned heavily on the broad sill, formed by the thickness of the house walls. The fresh air should make him feel less tired. He stretched up his arm to touch the steep, fluting roof which flared out just above his head. Below him was the orchard, with Henri's pigs already rooting in the grass. Beyond the apple trees was a small field of grain, and then other small fields, all banked on the gentle slope of the hill. Then the fields ended, and there was a line of trees overtopped by the proud square tower of what had once been the castle of St. Déodat. So this is my home, he thought, and somehow the idea no longer felt strange.

He turned away from the window. Albertine would soon be back, and he ought to finish his inspection. There was still the third room on this floor. The door beside the carved wooden bed must lead to it. He started wearily towards the door. He ought to finish his inspection. He ought to . . . and then, somehow, it didn't seem so important. Three mattresses, he counted slowly. Three. Somehow, it didn't seem so important.

He stepped heavily onto the chest lying at the side of the bed, and slumped onto the sheet which had protected the mattresses from dust. He just had time to think, as his filthy boots on the white sheet faded from his view, Albertine will give me hell for this, I bet; and then he was suddenly, beautifully, wonderfully asleep.

CHAPTER **6** ANNE

When he awakened, the sun had crossed over to the western side of the house. He lay looking at the warm pool of light on the white scrubbed floor, letting himself drift slowly and pleasantly into consciousness. He could feel he had slept his fill: his eyes had lost that glued-up feeling which came with exhaustion. His mind, too, seemed to be wide-open. He felt warm and clean and comfortable. Clean? He looked at his hands in amazement. Yes, he had been scrubbed clean. And he was no longer lying on top of a dust sheet. He was between coarse linen sheets, with a broad pillow propping up his shoulders. A quilted mat, its blue pattern bleached with many washings, covered him. He was wearing a loose white shirt, and the filthy rags which had been his clothes had disappeared. He raised himself quickly on one elbow, but the contents of his pockets had been laid neatly on the small writing table near the window. Papers, clasp knife, gun. Yes, they were there all right. He relaxed back on his pillow and looked at his clean hands. Albertine had certainly been busy. He found himself grinning in embarrassment. Well, what of it? She had been midwife to Madame Corlay. It wasn't the first time she had washed young Bertrand. But it was lucky about that birthmark. He had thought Matthews was being just a touch too realistic there, when he got that chemist fellow to imitate the red splotch on Corlay's back. Strange that it should have been the first of his faked credentials to stand a real test.

It was warm in the room. Albertine had closed the windows again. He sat up in bed, swinging his legs onto the chest. He rubbed the back of his head, stretched himself and gave a long satisfied yawn. And then he smothered a laugh. Not one of his better moments, he decided, looking at the dangling legs under the short shirt. He crossed to a mirror, framed in carved wood, which hung against the white wall. The view there pleased him just as little. The tired lines under his eyes had faded but not departed, and he had never admired Corlay's haircut anyway. Still, he did look less like himself and more like the Frenchman. He gave a wide grin to himself and saw the gap at the side of his teeth. Another of Matthews' bright ideas. "If," he had said, "if you were to smile broadly or to laugh, the gap would be seen. You must have a gap." So he now had a gap. He felt the still tender gum with his tongue. Yes, he had a gap, all right. But what Matthews expected him to laugh at on this trip was beyond him.

He opened the window. Now the fields and trees were bathed in the amber light of early evening. All the smells of grass and leaves and hay and clover and ripening wheat, distilled by the day's warmth into one sweetness, hung in the air around him. Time seemed suspended in the silence of these fields. "Why should they stay here?" Albertine had asked in answer to his question about any visiting Germans. Living here, one could become as simple as that: one could believe the delusion that peace was self-perpetuating.

There were footsteps in the room below. They were climbing the staircase, slowly and heavily. He closed the window quickly, and moved silently back to the bed. He was seemingly asleep, when the door opened and Albertine entered. There were footsteps following her: heavy decided footsteps. Hearne stiffened.

"He has been like that since yesterday morning," Albertine was saying. Not this morning then; yesterday morning.

The man grunted in reply, and Hearne heard something being set down heavily on the wooden chest beside him. For a moment he felt danger. Albertine had seen through the deception. He was caught not only helpless in bed, but ludicrous in a nightshirt. If he could get the man off-guard, if he could reach the gun on the table . . . and then four cold fingers were laid gently on his wrist and stopped the wild plans. Albertine had only brought a doctor. He wondered where she had found him, for there was no doctor in St. Déodat. Doctors practised by districts, not by villages, in this part of the world. It would be just as well to stop feigning sleep. Doctors were doctors. He groaned slightly and twisted his body as his eyes opened. The doctor was shaking his white head and saying, "Very fast." Considering the emotions he had caused, it would have been difficult to have found a normal pulse, Hearne thought.

"He is awake," Albertine said, announcing the obvious.

The doctor grunted again. "How do you feel?"

"Tired." Hearne's voice was low.

"He's been ill," Albertine said.

"Wounded?" The doctor was looking at him fixedly.

"I forget things sometimes . . . It was the guns . . ."

The old man nodded his head sagely. "Ah!" he said. "Shell shock. And do you remember things now?"

"Sometimes. And sometimes I forget." He let his voice trail away in dejection.

"He needs rest, rest and quiet. No one is to worry him. If he has any more attacks, then he must rest here until he recovers. Just rest and quiet." The doctor was examining his chest, feeling his brow, looking at his tongue. Hearne wondered what all this had to do with loss of memory, and then he noticed Albertine. She was watching every movement intently. She seemed satisfied when the doctor had gone through all the motions: without them, she would have felt cheated, and the old man had known that. For good measure, he produced a box of pills. Albertine nodded sagely as he gave her full directions.

His last words were, "Don't worry if you find it sometimes hard to remember. Don't worry, and you'll be completely cured. Just rest and quiet." He shook his head sadly, lifted the heavy bag from the chest, and followed Albertine out of the room. He was still talking of rest and quiet as they went slowly downstairs.

When she returned, Albertine found him staring at the window.

"I'd like it open," he said.

"But you will catch a cold."

"I'd like it open. I am far too warm. I haven't slept indoors for almost two months."

Albertine stared unbelievingly, and then the doctor's advice must have prompted her. The advice had cost money: it must be good. *Humor him when he seems strange. Rest and quiet.* Her thin lips closed disapprovingly, she shrugged her shoulders impatiently, but she crossed the room and opened the window.

"Where are my clothes, Albertine?"

"You are to stay in bed." She might give in to this madness of opening a window, but as for clothes— Her lips formed a straight line. Her voice was harsh as if she were tired of all this nonsense. And then she was probably angry because he was ill. He didn't blame her: she had work enough to do without a sick man to add to it.

"But I am not ill, Albertine." He was reasoning gently as with a child. "My body is well. It is only my mind that is sick. I have slept enough. I need to stretch my legs before I can sleep again."

Albertine seemed incapable of grasping the fact that the sickness of body and mind could be different. They were all one to her.

"You are to stay in bed." She was quite decided. Her tone nettled him, unexpectedly. So he was to stay in bed in a short nightshirt, day after day, with a bowl of soup grudgingly but loyally brought upstairs to him. Perhaps you don't know it, he thought as he stared back at her, but I've work to do, and a hell of a lot of it too, my sweet Albertine.

He sat up in bed and swung his bare legs over its tall side. Most women would have retreated, but Albertine stood her ground.

"You'll catch cold," she said, with her masterly grasp of the obvious. Hearne looked at her incredulously and then he began to laugh, softly at first and then gradually more loudly until he was rocking on the edge of the bed. He suddenly remembered the gap in his teeth, and checked himself in the middle of a laugh. Blast Matthews: that man was always right.

Albertine's eyes were round circles. "He's mad," she said, backing to the door. "He's mad."

"I'm *not* mad." His voice rose. He got off the bed and advanced towards her. "I only want my trousers. Steal a man's trousers, would you?"

Then the door opened. A white-haired woman stood there, watching him silently.

"He's mad, Madame. He's mad."

"She's taken my trousers," Hearne said angrily. He was suddenly aware that his voice was loud, too loud. "She's taken my clothes. I'm not a child," he ended lamely.

Madame Corlay, leaning on her stick, looked at him dispassionately. "So you're back," she said coldly. And then to Albertine, "Give him his clothes." And then she was gone, leaving them staring at each other. So that was his mother, Hearne was thinking. Well, it certainly had been the strangest of meetings; hardly what he had been steeling himself against. Once more he had the feeling of anticlimax. That coldness, that hardly concealed look of bitterness . . . What kind of mother was this, anyway? What kind of son was he supposed to be? So *you're back*. Not, *so you're home*. So you're back, with the implication that because there had been a scene, then he must be back. Yes, there was a lot to that little word *so*. . . . Corlay had talked willingly, almost diffusely, about his everyday life: about his education, about the farm, about the village and the people who lived and worked there. It seemed as if he were eager to identify himself. He had said, "So you want to know about me? Why? Do you think I am *not* Bertrand Corlay of St. Déodat?" They had both laughed at that, and certainly Corlay had proved his identity by the completeness of his descriptions. But about his personal life and emotions he had been vague, even bored. He had given a very good impression of a life which was so simple that it was dull and uninteresting. Corlay had been far from cheery: he had been unhappy and moody. But Hearne had thought that could be attributed to the obvious boredom of his past life, to the constant depression about the future of his country. It was enough to depress any man. Staring at the door which Madame Corlay had closed so definitely behind her, Hearne felt the first twinges of a new worry.

Albertine was watching him. He suddenly realized that it wasn't the fact that his voice had been raised in anger which had seemed so strange to her. It was the fact that he wanted open windows, that he wanted to dress when he should stay in bed. It wasn't the loud voice which had been mad: the loud voice was something which she thought normal. He sat down on the bed again, but his emotions were less calm than his words.

"Albertine, you know what the doctor said. You know what my mother said. All I want is to be left in peace, and to have my clothes. There is nothing mad about that. You needn't worry—I'm not going away. I'm going to stay here. Now, where are my trousers?"

"They are washed."

"Well, what about other ones?"

"I've got them all packed away with your things." She looked towards the door which he had meant to investigate, before the three mattresses had seduced him.

"Good. Shall I get them, or will you?"

She moved so quickly towards the storeroom that he was surprised. Her polite grumbling echoed back into his room.

". . . you'll just make a mess of everything," she was saying.

He waited patiently, reflecting on the charms of home life, as Albertine made her silent journeys between the two rooms bringing with her each time a newspaper bundle smelling of some strange herb. She had obviously decided to be the complete martyr and unpack everything at once. It was just as well, Hearne thought. That made it easier for him to find his way about another man's strange wardrobe. He snapped the thin string on the parcels of yellowed paper, and began to shake out the clothes, and then paused as his eyes read the heavy black print. The clothes must have been packed away in September. *French successfully attack Siegfried Line. English allies arrive with full equipment. Miracle of the Machine in Modern Warfare.* His eyes traveled down the columns of close print. There was a glowing report on the miracle of the Maginot Line, on the modern conveniences which made life so much more pleasant for the troops. As a sour joke, someone had printed a photograph in the very next column showing the English digging in. Or perhaps he never realized it would be sour, or a joke. Only our very best crack troops, thought Hearne, standing waist-deep in mud, digging and draining a French field into a prepared line. No, it was much more pleasant to read of electric light and red wine, of underground movies and chapels, of hot and cold water and heating systems. So much more pleasant, more comfortable—so impregnable.

Albertine had finished and was standing silently watching him. He kicked the papers aside, and turned to the clothes which were laid on the bed. They weren't country clothes. They had been bought in some town. Perhaps in Rennes . . . yes, that was what the labels said. Corlay must have had quite a taste for suits—not that it had been particularly good taste. But there were certainly more clothes than Hearne had expected.

The chief thing was that they looked as if they might fit him. He groaned at the thought of having to put on such underwear. Yards and yards of the stuff, he thought despairingly. But if he didn't wear any of it, then Albertine would really think he was mad, and he couldn't afford to have her become permanently worried about him. The doctor had prepared her for a certain mild strangeness, but there must be nothing beyond that really to alarm her.

She was down on her knees, now, smoothing out the newspapers, folding them neatly. She wound up each little piece of string separately and slipped the knotted rolls into her pocket, one by one. Nothing escaped her careful, thrifty fingers. And then she solved the problem of what clothes he would wear. She left them on the bed, while she hung up the others inside the wardrobe or folded them neatly into the chest in front of the bed. But it was the inside of the wardrobe which interested Hearne. More than half of it was filled with books and papers. He stopped Albertine as she lifted the first armload of these, with the same look of resignation on her face which had haunted it for the last fifteen minutes.

"Don't worry about that stuff, Albertine," he said. "I can arrange it myself, later. You know you've plenty to do, as it is."

She softened unexpectedly, but her eyes also held surprise. It was the same look which he had noticed, this—no, yesterday morning, when he had had no objections about her going to early Mass and leaving him unattended at breakfast.

He pretended to be shaking out the trousers and pullover he was going to wear. "Tell me, Albertine, why is my mother so annoyed with me? She has seen me angry before now. What is wrong?"

It was now Albertine's turn to pretend to arrange her apron. "Your mother is upset about the war."

"Yes, I know. But she wasn't even pleased to see me home safe."

Albertine's voice was gentler. "You must remember your father died in 1917. And your grandfather died in the siege of Paris. So Madame is very upset about this war. Myself, I think we should thank the good God who has looked after us and let us keep what we have."

"So my mother is angry because we lost this time, because I am home safe?"

"She is angry with all the young men. She says that if a German comes near this farm she will kill him with our ham knife. She says—" Albertine stopped and shrugged her shoulders. "Myself, I think we should thank the good God who has left St. Déodat in peace."

"What else does my mother say?"

"She says that now the young men, who talked too much, have done too little; that they have sold France by all their politics."

"And what of the old men?"

"They will be punished by dying in unhappiness, for they will never

live to see France free again. But they will soon be out of this life, while
the young men will have to live in misery. They will suffer more than if
they had died in war. Yes, she is very upset."

"Seemingly." Hearne was thinking quickly. There had been still more
to Madame Corlay's bitterness than even that: as if there had been a deep
conflict between herself and her son, as if what had happened to Madame
Corlay's France was only the culmination of such a conflict.

"And what did my mother say about me?" he added.

Albertine looked restless. She was now smoothing the stiff white cap,
tucking away imaginary stray wisps of hair. But when her answer did come,
it was as direct as it was harsh.

"She did not want to see you again."

There was a pause. Hearne swallowed, and said, "Well, now . . ." He
couldn't think of anything to add. There was something too final about
Madame Corlay's words. He picked up his clothes.

"I'll dress now, Albertine, or else I will catch that cold of yours. And
then I'll walk in the fields for half an hour. And then I'll come in for
supper. And then I'll go back to bed."

Albertine seemed to find this reasonable if unnecessary. She seemed
relieved by the quietness of his voice. It seemed to restore her confidence.
As she left the room, she walked over to the window and closed it.

Hearne waited until the heavy footsteps on the wooden stairs had faded
into the kitchen, and then opened the window. He was thinking about
that strange meeting with Madame Corlay. He saw her once more framed
in the darkness of the doorway, dressed in black with the long gold chain
gathered tightly into the small round brooch at her throat. The white
hair was carefully combed, the white face with its faded color in the lips
and cheeks was set in a proud, disdainful mold. It was the face of a woman
of character, who had been continuously disappointed in life. She was not
the negative personality he had expected. She was a self-effacing invalid
only in the sense that she no longer interested herself in the management
of the house and farm. But upstairs in her room, Madame Corlay was indeed a very definite personality.

It was good for his purpose, in one way, that she should have been so
unnatural in her welcome. A gentle mother, full of sympathy and tears,
would have worried him. And yet, in another way, Madame Corlay's attitude made things more strange and difficult. For there was the hint of
dark currents in Bertrand Corlay's life, which weren't covered by the data
he had learned by heart. He had studied Corlay, questioned him skillfully,
memorized all the details which he and Matthews and that French Intelligence man, Fournier, had gathered. Not that he had expected Bertrand
Corlay to be so simple as a string of dates and facts. Human beings weren't
like that. He had only learned to know the skeleton, as it were. Now he
must fill in the flesh. It might be a stranger job than he had imagined.

This evening, after supper, he would unpack the books and papers from the wardrobe and place them back in the empty bookcase. He would find out a lot about Corlay, that way: books were half a man.

He went downstairs, passing through the kitchen where Albertine was working in front of the fire. The air was cool, the fields were empty. The cows had no doubt been safely locked in for the night by Henri. He walked slowly up the hill to the west side of the farm until he had reached the last field and the beginnings of the castle's woods. He halted and looked down towards the farm, towards the apple trees outside the window of his room.

It wasn't a big farm at all. It consisted of this large field divided into three for various crops, of scattered groupings of trees, of the orchard which stretched from the house up this western hill, of the meadow and hayfield edging the path to the Pinot farm. If only there had been a man to manage and work it, instead of poor old Albertine and one of her relatives, the farm might have produced more than mere subsistence. For it was good soil, and centuries of careful nursing had left the grass smooth, the branches heavy with ripening fruit. The wheat in one part of the field was standing strong and upright. The breeze whipped over its yellowing greenness and the whiskered heads of grain rustled gently like silk skirts in a ballroom.

Beyond the farmhouse, down through the fields to the east, lay the road which passed through the village. From here, he could see its church soaring over the tops of the trees which fringed St: Déodat. Still farther to the east lay the busy plain, with its highway and railway, its villages and towns. But here, on this gentle hill, touched with gold in the rich evening light, such things might be a hundred miles away. He could hear the stillness around him. Its peace made him a part of itself, holding him immobile, suspended in time like a figure on a painted canvas.

The bells from the church swung him out of his inertia. Below him the road would now have its black-shawled, white-capped women, walking with their heads already bent. He saw Albertine leave the kitchen door, and set off quickly down the path. Poor old Albertine, he thought again: her rewards were so few.

And then he saw a girl on the path, her hair gleaming in the low rays of the setting sun. She didn't turn towards the kitchen door as he expected. Instead, she had begun the climb up through the sloping fields towards where he stood. She had seen him. She waved, not excitedly, not full-heartedly. It was more of a gesture than a greeting. Nor did she quicken her steps, but walked towards him at the same steady pace. The silver-gold of her hair was unmistakable. This must be Anne Pinot. As she came nearer, and the white blur of her face resolved itself into a short nose and rounded chin, level eyebrows above grave eyes, he knew he had been right in his guess. She looked exactly like the expressionless photograph which Corlay had shown him. "Very fair hair," Corlay had said in a disinterested voice. "That's about all."

And that was about all, thought Hearne, until he noticed the eyes more blue than gray, and the sprinkling of freckles over the short, charming nose. She had possibilities, but she either ignored or despised them. Even the black dress with its bodice tightly buttoned up to the neck, with its long sleeves covering her wrists, seemed to have been chosen to constrict and hide her strong young body. Her stockings were black, and they weren't silk ones, either. Her shoes were of plain black leather, low-heeled. He found himself thinking again of Corlay's disinterested voice which had jarred on him at the time.

"Anne," he said, and smiled.

"I met Albertine." Her voice was clear and soft. She spoke French carefully, with no Breton accent and only the hint of an intonation. "She said you had gone up the hill. I wanted to see you." Her eyes were fixed on the ground at her feet. Hearne suddenly remembered that he had made no move to touch her. He took her hand awkwardly.

"You look just the same, Anne," he said gently. "Just what I hoped to see when I got back."

She took her hand away quickly, and raised her eyes.

"Bertrand," she said in that clear childlike voice which matched the simplicity of her face. "I want to tell you at once . . . Yesterday afternoon I learned that you had come back. I didn't sleep all last night. So I must tell you now. I—" The resolution was fading with her voice.

"Tell me what, Anne?" It was strange how gently he spoke to this girl, as if he were addressing a child. They stared at each other. "Tell me what, Anne?" Hearne smiled into the serious eyes.

"I do not want to—" She stopped once more. Whatever she was trying to say was too difficult for her.

"Anne, what's wrong?" He was thinking that she reminded him of a startled fawn. He found he was smiling naturally and easily at last.

She looked at him disbelievingly. He could hear the short sharp breath. She bit her lip. And then she turned suddenly, and was running down the hill.

"Anne!" There was real concern in his voice. He started after her, and cursed silently at his stiff muscles. It was as if he were running on stilts. He forced himself to greater speed, but even at that he was gaining only slightly. Had she guessed? Had she found out? His thoughts urged him on. He drew level with her almost at the bottom of the field. He caught her arm sharply, so that she stumbled and exclaimed, but his voice mastered hers.

"Anne, what is wrong? You must tell me."

She was trembling. He let go her arm, suddenly and painfully aware of the madness of his emotions in the last two minutes. He felt strange and foolish. Chase a girl, he thought savagely, and you feel like some primeval Pan. Hell, he thought, think of Matthews and cold blue eyes and a matter-of-fact voice, think of a job to be done, a dirty rotten job which might bear some good, some good for others but nothing but hell for yourself.

She was looking at him, wide-eyed, the startled fawn again. She was nursing her arm; but she was still there, looking at him.

"Anne," he said. Nothing but Anne. He kept saying Anne. What else did you say to a girl to whom you had been conveniently betrothed?

"Anne," he said again. "I'm sorry. I didn't mean to hurt you. But tell me what is wrong, what is wrong."

He was tired, he thought, or else all movement had gone into slow motion. No one could have looked so long at him as this. And then her clear simple voice cut in on his emotions. *Frère Jacques,* he was thinking, either *Frère Jacques* or *Sur le pont d'Avignon.* It was that kind of voice, made to sing the simplest melodies.

"My father died two months ago."

"Your father died . . . Oh, I am sorry. I didn't know." But still he couldn't fathom her meaning. He looked at her and waited.

"I am now my own mistress." She was becoming more confident.

"Yes, of course." Just what, he wondered, was she trying to say with so much difficulty and hedging? When it came, even he was surprised. He had imagined a number of things, but not this.

"So I shall not have to marry."

Hearne remained completely motionless. The blank expressionless look which he had often found useful when suddenly confronted with a strange twist in events slipped over his face. He said nothing. He was wondering just how Corlay would have really felt. Surprised, and hurt: incredulous, probably even angry. Most men would be at such a reception as this. He, himself, felt an immense load lifted from him: thank God, he wouldn't have to pretend a lot of nonsense, anyway. He felt like smiling when he remembered his elaborate plan to keep his betrothed at full arm's distance. Just another set of bright ideas he needn't have bothered thinking up, just another set for the wastepaper basket. If all the plans which he worked out and never had to use could be kept in files, how many sides of a room would they cover? Probably they would make too depressing a room: they were better scrapped and forgotten.

Anne was watching strangely. Let her, he thought. She ought to know Corlay's reactions better than he did. If he were to keep silent, with his brows down and his lips tightly drawn, she would probably read into his expression the emotions he ought to be feeling. She was losing her confidence again. Serve her right, Hearne thought. What a fine welcome Corlay was getting after having walked the length of Brittany to reach these people. Just the sort of welcome to cheer a chap up after his country had been slapped down. First of all he would have had all his ideas smashing round his head; and now he was having all his personal emotions added to the general rubble heap. He suddenly started to walk down the path towards the house.

Anne tried to match her pace to his. She was looking vaguely unhappy, he was glad to see. Poor old Corlay . . . what a welcome.

It was she who had to speak first. "Please don't pretend, Bertrand."

"Pretend?" Hearne's tone was unexpectedly savage.

"Yes, *that* is more like you. Once your pride has recovered, you will be really very glad. You didn't love me." It wasn't a challenge; it was a quiet statement of fact.

"I agreed to marry you."

"That was before—" She stopped. "You see, Bertrand," she continued, "I knew all the time. I knew." Her tone puzzled him, but his face was cold and expressionless. "I haven't told your mother, yet," she finished lamely.

"Which means you think I shall tell her? That will be slightly difficult, considering the fact that my mother doesn't want to see me." He could imagine Madame Corlay's delight when she found that her son had failed her again. The Corlay and the Pinot farms would never be joined. The old quarrel about that dovecote on the boundary line would never be solved. "I think you had better finish what you've begun," he ended quietly.

It was with considerable relief that he saw Albertine approaching them, her black shawl tightly drawn round her thin shoulders, her precarious white cap soaring so securely from the tightly bound hair. It was strange that anything so fantastic was neither shaken nor blown from her head as she walked, that she could turn so quickly from Anne to him and then back to Anne without even seeming to be aware of balancing a starched cylinder on top of her crown. She greeted them with a sparse remark about supper. It was a command rather than a suggestion. He was glad to follow her into the kitchen, glad that Anne had refused to eat with them. It was only after he had entered the room that he wondered if he ought to have taken her back across the fields to her farm. But the strange thing had been that Anne didn't seem to expect that: she had moved so quickly away by herself. And stranger still was the fact that Albertine, who obviously still regarded them as engaged to be married, had most certainly not expected it.

Albertine served him a supper which was identical with his breakfast, except that a piece of cheese was substituted for the pork, and there was a small glass of cider. Henri was tactfully nonexistent, and he noted that Albertine had only set one place at the table. They must eat after he had gone. It was rather a formal arrangement for such an informally managed farm. For the third time that day he found himself wondering just what kind of chap this Corlay had really been. Of one thing he was certain: there was much more in Corlay than he had ever imagined. I don't believe I am going to like him at all, he thought suddenly.

He finished his supper quickly. Upstairs he imagined himself examining and arranging that stack of books and papers. He might find something there to solve these peculiar questions in his mind.

But when he went upstairs, the dusk had thickened in the room, and Albertine had conveniently forgotten to fill the lamp with oil. There were no candles in the candlestick on the small table beside the empty bookcase. In spite of his annoyance, he had to laugh. Albertine certainly had her little ways. He undressed quickly, alternately admiring the low cunning of women and wondering where he was supposed to wash. A small ugly-looking cabinet pulled open at last and showed a basin with a pail concealed underneath, and a tap which turned on water from a container hidden above. It was the sort of thing which small yachts and steamers like to produce to comfort their passengers for the lack of running water. It was no doubt one of Corlay's innovations, for he could think of no one else here who would have bothered about it. Anyway, it meant he could wash. In the growing darkness of the room, he miscalculated the swill of the water and felt it drip over the floor. Albertine, he thought, would—oh, damn Albertine. Of all the people he had met so far she was perhaps the kindest, certainly the most self-sacrificing; and yet she worried him the most. Partly because he realized that if Albertine were to become suspicious, then his difficulties would be enormous; it would be dangerous trying to explain things to her, trying to make her understand without giving too much information. And partly, he had to admit, because of the natural fear in every man that he is liable to be bossed by a woman. He opened the window defiantly before he climbed into the bed.

Tomorrow he would examine these books and that room next door, and then when darkness came he would have his first long walk through these green fields down towards the plain and the main railway line. Tomorrow and tomorrow, the nights after that, the next weeks . . . In the middle of forming his plans, he halted abruptly. He suddenly knew that long-term planning wasn't necessary on this job. If he could manage to improvise from night to night, he would do very nicely. Now, he would be very much wiser to get what sleep he could. Later, he might not be so lucky.

He didn't waken until the sun had risen and the faint sound of the five-o'clock bells swung over the fields into his room.

CHAPTER 7 STRANGER ON THE HILLSIDE

But next morning, the books were not rescued from the wardrobe and placed on their shelves. Instead, the Germans came back to St. Déodat.

The news arrived with Henri, who suddenly and unaccountably appeared at the kitchen door when Hearne was having breakfast. He stood there, breathing heavily, and then said simply, "The Boches are here."

Hearne, his elbows resting on the wooden table, looked up at the thin little man in the doorway, and set down his bowl of soup slowly. Albertine, bending over the heavy iron disk which was hung over the fire, hesitated as she turned over the paper-thin pancake baking there, and then moved so suddenly that the half-finished pancake was jolted into the flames. She clutched the wooden spade which she had been using as if it were now a weapon. There was silence in the long room, except for the sizzling of the dough as it spread over the glowing log. Afterwards, Hearne remembered that moment by the smell of burning which filled the room: that and Albertine's eyes, and the toothless grin of Henri with the morning sun behind him.

"They are here? Outside?" Hearne asked the old man. Henri shook his head slowly.

"No. Going into the village," he said.

There was an almost audible slackening of tension. Henri's capacity for holding only one idea at a time had certainly had its effect. He now slipped off his muddy sabots, and walked slowly towards one of the beds. From the chest in front of it, he took out a knotted sock and a gun. The sock contained coins. Hearne heard them jangle as Henri stowed it away carefully inside his loose blouse. The gun was an old one, probably only good for shooting rabbits.

"That's no use," began Hearne gently. "They'd only shoot you in turn."

But Henri wasn't listening. He was absorbed as he began to take the rifle apart, slowly and yet methodically. Then he rummaged in the wooden chest once more, and taking a large piece of cloth which had served to bundle his clothes he tore it into strips and wound them carefully, almost lovingly, round the parts of his gun. When that was done, he carried them towards the door. Hearne rose quickly from the table.

"I'll help you," he said.

The old man was shoving his feet into his sabots. "Eh?"

"I said I'll help you."

They left Albertine, still holding the wooden spade raised in her hand, still standing beside the tub of dough. It looked as if the week's baking of *crêpes* was going to be a failure for the first time in Albertine's life. Hearne paused at the door and caught her eye.

"Better hide that ham knife, Albertine," he said with a grin, "or my mother will get us all strung up." Albertine looked at him in surprise, and then there was the beginning of a smile in spite of herself.

"God knows what Madame will say," she answered and looked at the black lava-like crust of dough on the log. She shook her head at the appalling waste. "These Boches," she said.

Hearne reached Henri at the seventh row of trees in the orchard. The old man was kneeling down under the third tree in that row, fumbling away at the turf. It had already been neatly cut. After that, the digging didn't take long. The linen-covered rifle and the knotted sock were laid side by side, and covered with the rich black earth. Henri, himself, replaced the jigsaw puzzle of turf. Watching the gnarled hands fitting each diamond of grass into its proper place, Hearne knew that Henri had been expecting the Germans. So had Madame Corlay. Only Albertine, the most practical and efficient of them all, had been caught surprised. The Germans were at Rennes, they were at Combourg and Dol and Dinan, they had long ago reached St. Malo and the coast, they had flooded the whole of Brittany to the very western islands like some powerful turbulent tide pouring over broken dikes into a flat plain-land. Nothing could stop them once the dikes were down. Yet Albertine had had her own reasons, her own brand of wishful thinking. In Rennes and Dol? But of course: these were important towns. In St. Malo? Of course: the ships were there. In the villages down on the plain? Why, that could be understood: the farms there were rich, and there were a lot of things to be bought. Bought? Well, paid for anyway, even if the money was foreign-looking. But up here in St. Déodat, the farms only kept the people of the district. Kept them comfortably? Well, no one starved, certainly. But then no one was idle. Everyone worked, and worked hard for what they had, and that was only enough for the people of St. Déodat. There was nothing left over for anyone else. They were all peaceful, hard-working people on this hillside, owing no man anything. Why should they be disturbed?

When Hearne got back to the kitchen, Albertine was placing the last thin disk of baked dough into a division of the long wooden rack which had so puzzled him on the morning of his arrival.

"I've sent Henri to the village," he said.

"He's got to dig the west field." The way she handled the rack told him she was annoyed. She was resentful over the wasted pancake, and she was more scared than she would allow by Henri's news. The rising note in her voice showed just how she was going to get rid of her anger.

He cut her short. "Henri can dig for potatoes another day. This morning he is in the village, and he is going to find out for us if the Germans are going to stay there, or if they are just passing through. If the potatoes worry you, I'll dig them for you. And now you'd better tell my mother about everything. And tell her to keep calm: worrying won't help us at this stage." He turned on his heel, and left the kitchen. That certainly stopped the argument he could feel brewing. But what on earth was she staring at?

As he walked up to the field, he was still wondering.

Henri had left the spade stuck into a ridge of earth. There was another implement, too. Probably a hoe, or a mattock, Hearne decided. Not that it mattered much: there was no one here to see his raw technique. He smiled grimly. Once, he had done this sort of thing for Saturday pennies in a kitchen-garden behind a Cornish rectory. Now he was doing it partly to keep Albertine quiet, partly to be out in the open with a good view of the path from the village.

He worked for three hours. Twice Albertine had come to the kitchen door and looked up the hill. He gave her a cheery wave, before he bent over a neat row of potatoes once more. The second time she gave a small wave back.

It was hot now, for the sun was directly above him. Soon it would be time for dinner, and Henri's return. The old man never missed a meal. But there was still no sign of anyone on the path. The sun's rays seemed to be concentrating on this patch of ground. The heat gathered in the earth round him and then struck backwards at him. This was the time when a farmer should have a mug of cider under the coolness of these trees over there, and let himself enjoy a satisfied conscience. He couldn't have the cider, but he stuck the spade in the earth and walked over to the green shade. It was good to lean his back against the trunk of a tree, to stretch out his legs in the soft cool grass. He yawned, and wiped the sweat from his brow. Still no sign of Henri, blast him. He should have been back an hour ago. And he ought to have told Henri to get him some cigarettes in the village—if there were any. He himself couldn't risk a visit to the village merely for a cigarette. But a smoke was what he wanted, right now. He looked at the farm and its orchard and fields, and thought, This would be a good way to live if there wasn't a war, if the Jerries weren't sitting on your front doorstep. Just to have a ten minutes' rest with a cigarette and a mug of cool cider; with this view of your land and your house looking as if it had grown from the earth, so natural was its shape and color; with Albertine cooking a thumping dinner for you in that enormous kitchen. No, someone younger and prettier and gentler than Albertine, he decided. That would be a good way to live. In the evening, you could have books, a radio, a gramophone; you could read, and listen, and think. Corlay could have had all that; and yet he hadn't known his luck. "I'm not interested in the farm," he had said. "My mother inherited it from her uncle. I only went to live there when I could find no suitable teaching job. I'm interested in writing." And again that unemotional voice, "Very fair hair. That's about all."

Hearne listened to the drone of bees and yawned once more. And then he was on his feet, his mind and body alert. Something had moved in that tangle of bushes beside the windbreak of trees. It might have been some animal. It might have been. Five steps, and he was past the bushes. Then he stood staring at the man sitting there. The man returned his stare, and then shook his head slowly as he grinned.

"I thought you had gone," he said. "I watched you working and then I must have fallen asleep. When I awoke just now, I thought you had gone." The words were fluent enough, but he wasn't a Frenchman.

"Why were you watching me?" Hearne spoke calmly, and his voice seemed to reassure the man.

He looked at Hearne for a minute, and then said, "To see what you were like. I don't go near farms, now, until I see what the people are like. It's difficult to tell nowadays who's a friend or an enemy."

"Who's your enemy?" Hearne asked.

"What do you think?"

"It's difficult to tell nowadays."

The man laughed silently. His teeth showed very white, and they were all the whiter against his skin, which had been tanned with exposure. His hair would be quite fair once the dust and grime were washed out of it. Determined jaw, noted Hearne, and eyebrows slightly drawn. He smiled a good deal as he talked, but his mouth was firm enough in repose. You would hardly notice the color of his eyes; it was as if the other features of his face overshadowed them. He was no fool, this man. He was waiting for Hearne to speak again.

"You want food?"

"Yes." He wasn't smiling any more.

Hearne looked at the man's torn tweed suit. It was filthy now, but once it had been good. No cheap tailor had made that shoulder line. His eyes traveled to the man's shoes, still holding to his feet by some miracle. Shoes were a good test. Just as in peacetime, you could generally tell the real down-and-out by the shoes. Fakers generally arranged to have their feet comfortable, at least. The man was watching his survey, but he didn't speak. He's exhausted, thought Hearne: he's so exhausted that he can't make any further effort to talk: he's holding tight onto himself at this moment.

"Wait here," Hearne said. "I'll come back."

Albertine was standing over the soup pot like a guardian angel. "Dinner's long ready," she began indignantly. "I went to the door to call you, but you had disappeared."

"I was behind the trees. There's a man there, and he's starving. Get that soup into a bowl and tie a cloth round it, Albertine. And bread, too."

"But there's only enough for us, and scarcely that."

"Well, he can have mine." Albertine didn't move. He picked up a bowl and ladled the hot soup into it.

"Who is it?" she demanded. "Some beggar? You can't give to all of them." He took a large hunk of bread, and cut a thick slice of ham. He could hear Albertine flinch.

"Someone trying to reach the coast. He's either British or American. He's all in." Hearne pulled the small checked cloth off the end of the table, and folded it to tie round and over the bowl.

"But the Germans—"

"To hell with them." He finished the last knot carefully. "Don't worry, Albertine. I'll throw food to him behind some bushes as if he were a dog. I won't touch him, so I won't get leprosy. I won't give him a bed, or a wash, or any clothes, so that everyone in this house can go on living peacefully and happily." The savage bitterness in his voice struck Albertine like a bucket of cold water. She was still half-worried, half-angry, but for once she didn't have an answer, not even as much as a gesture, ready. He left her just standing there.

The man had been keeping watch for him. Hearne noted the expression on his face.

"Did you expect me to bring back a gun and a dog?" he asked.

The man smiled wryly. "It has happened, once or twice," he said. He seized the bowl which Hearne had unwrapped for him. "Hot!" He was incredulous. "Hot! The first hot food in days."

Hearne sat down beside the man and waited. When the food was eaten to the last crumb and the last shred of vegetable, he said, "What are you? English?"

"American."

Hearne imitated Corlay's English accent. "I speak English."

"You do?" It was an American voice all right, deep and comfortable. And the man was probably genuine, too. The more Hearne looked at those feet, the surer he was. It had taken a lot of walking to produce feet like that. And there had been a kind of heartfelt relief in the upsurge of his voice as he had said, "You do?"

"A little."

"You're the first farmer I've met who did."

"I'm not a farmer. I live here with my mother when I can't find a job as a schoolteacher."

"I thought you looked queer on that potato patch."

Hearne smiled sourly. "It's probably my job from now on."

"You speak English well."

"Thank you. I studied English once." Hearne looked sidewise at the man, and then added, "I used to see a lot of American movies. That gave me some idiotisms."

"Idioms," corrected the American. "Something quite different."

"Oh yes. Idioms. That's the word," Hearne acknowledged gravely. " 'Honey,' and 'nuts,' and 'sugar,' and 'you can't do this to me.' You know the sort of idioms. At first it was very difficult."

The American was smiling. "I guess it was. *You can't do this to me.* Doesn't mean much now, does it?" He looked at his torn feet. Hearne looked at the potato patch.

"Nothing at all." Hearne paused. He had given the man enough time to become accustomed to him. Perhaps he could risk a roundabout question.

"But why do you have to hide if you are an American? Your country isn't at war."

There was a short laugh. "But I am. I'd just as soon not meet a German or start any questioning. Just as soon."

Hearne said nothing, but he looked interested. If this man felt like talking, he'd talk. If he didn't want to, then nothing that Hearne could say would change his mind. So Hearne was silent, but just kept on looking interested. If this man felt like talking, he'd begin in another minute. He did.

"Do you know Paris?"

"Once I was there," Hearne said.

"Do you know the Ritz?"

Hearne shook his head.

"Well, that's where I began all this." The American pointed to his clothes and shoes. Hearne smiled politely, incredulously.

"It's the truth. There I was in the Ritz Bar about five o'clock in the evening, and in came a friend of mine. He was an ambulance driver. I'm a newspaper man, myself. Well, in he came, and he said, 'We're leaving.' I said, 'You are?' and I finished my drink and I went round to the depot where his bus was stationed and got hold of him before he left. I wasn't going to ask him questions in front of the crowd of newspaper men at the bar. He didn't know what had happened, or if anything was going to happen, but they had been ordered to stand by. And when he left that night I jumped a ride with him. For two months I had been waiting for something to happen. Now it was happening. And I was going to find out for myself all about it. Well, I found plenty. Plenty. In fact, so much happened that we got sore. There we were with a Red Cross plastered all over us and some bandages and a stretcher and a portable typewriter. And there were the Stukas diving at us and hedge-hoppers spraying us with bullets as if we were an armored train. We covered over the Red Cross, and that way we managed to reach the front, or whatever you could call it. We loaded up with wounded, and by that time we were worse than sore. The man I was with didn't like the responsibility of carrying back wounded without a Red Cross sign, so like Goddamned fools, we uncovered it. We never got further than six kilometers. The whole bus went up in flames. It just went up like a torch as we were racing round to the door. Couldn't do a thing for them inside. So then we found a machine gun, and I played around with it. By this time, this was my war, too. The fellow with me kept worrying about his badge and some oath he had taken, but being an angel of mercy didn't make much sense at that time. I left him trying to patch up some refugees, swearing his heart out, and I never saw him again. Thought I wouldn't make his conscience feel too bad about me. I was doing all right, too, when I was taken prisoner. Then I cooled down when they were checking up on me. I remembered a lot of unfinished business left over from an Austrian incident in the summer of 1939. I had a hunch that the Nazis would be gladder to see me than I was to see them. So when it got dark, I walked out on them before they finished checking up. I just waited for my chance and then beat it. I've been beating it ever since."

"So I see," Hearne said, and looked pointedly at the American's feet.

"They were a nice pair of shoes, once." He paused and then added, "You know, it's strange. Whenever I met someone friendly, someone who gave me food or shelter, they always piled on the questions until I was as tight-lipped as any Englishman. You're the first who hasn't asked questions—only what nationality I was, and that's fair enough—and look at the last five minutes."

"I didn't ask questions because I get tired answering them, myself. I've been walking like you, but not so far. I got home this week."

There was a silence, which Hearne felt compelled to end. He went on, "You are probably wondering why we are sitting here. Actually, it is as safe as any place in the district. The Germans arrived this morning in the village. I've sent old Henri down to see what's happened, and I am waiting here until he returns."

"I see. I was wondering why you were watching that path. But why didn't you go to the village yourself? After all, there's an armistice, a big beautiful armistice."

Hearne exchanged a sour smile with the American. "If the Boches see young men without work to do, they will find work for them," he said. "If they see me digging potatoes, they may let me go on digging potatoes so that they can get them."

"There's someone on the path, now," the American interrupted.

But it was Albertine, walking quickly up the hill towards them. She stood before them, regaining her breath for a moment. The annoyed look had left her face. Her voice was almost friendly. "Your mother says that if the man is ill he is to come down to the house." She gathered up the bowl and cloth. "Now; at once," she added over her shoulder, and marched off downhill, her white cap bobbing with each decided step.

Hearne was unexpectedly moved by the look of hope in the American's eyes. "I didn't ask you before," he began awkwardly, "because my mother is—" He hesitated. "How do you say it? Difficult? She's very upset by the armistice. She thinks I didn't fight very well."

The American nodded understandingly. "It's her farm, isn't it?" he said. "But do you think we can risk it?"

"It seems quiet enough, just now, and the sooner we get your feet attended to, the better for them, I think. Anyway, orders are orders."

The American rose stumblingly. Hearne steadied him, and then, as he felt the man's weight slump so heavily on his shoulder, helped him towards the house. Their pace was surprisingly quick: the American must have been making a terrific effort.

"I am Bertrand Corlay. Corlay," said Hearne slowly, as they neared the kitchen door.

"And I'm—" The American hesitated as if for a breathing space. "My name is Myles."

"Tell my mother the story you told me. She may adopt you."

The American smiled, and stepped heavily across the doorway.

But, as it turned out, that piece of advice, unlike most pieces of advice in the world, had good results.

CHAPTER 8 ELISE

Madame Corlay wished to see them. That was the command which Albertine had been instructed to give. Hearne exchanged looks with the American and shrugged his shoulders. The American who called himself Myles looked at the staircase and shook his head.

"You've got to," Hearne said in French.

Albertine nodded vigorously. Together they helped the fumbling man up the treacherous stairs.

"I'll never get down, not this trip," he said when they stuck halfway, which was something of a prophecy.

Madame Corlay was sitting with her back to a window. The door was open, and she was sitting there waiting for them to appear in the doorway, her hands resting on the stick which she held in front of her. She said nothing, but Hearne had the idea that her glance softened as the slow procession halted inside the room. She wasn't so angry with him as she had been, he realized suddenly. He must have done something to please her at last.

He was very formal, responding unconsciously to the erect figure, to the composed hands. "This is my mother, Madame Corlay. Monsieur Myles, an American who is escaping."

Madame Corlay bowed. The complete duchess, Hearne thought, and glanced casually round the room. Similar in size and shape to the kitchen downstairs: more windows, though. Here the east wall had no cow shed behind it. It was an end wall, up here. Two beds, draped; three chests; dresser; desk; two small tables; two chairs; and, strange among these heavy carved furnishings, a ramshackle upright piano. That would be a relic from Rennes, where Madame Corlay had taught elementary music to the tradespeople's children in order to give her son a good education. That was when her uncle had lived here and she had refused his charity, still bitter over his quarrel with her husband. Even after her husband had been killed in 1917 and she had been left alone in Rennes, even after the uncle had forgotten his anger, she had refused any reconciliation. And only when the old man had died did she come back to the farm where she had lived as a girl. But by that time, she was half-crippled and unable to enjoy it. By that time, the son for whom she had worked was the qualified schoolmaster she had wanted him to be, but a schoolmaster without any pupils to teach. It would have been better for them all, even for the short years of peace which had been theirs before this war began, reflected Hearne as he walked slowly over to the east window, if Madame Corlay had swallowed pride and ambition and taught her son to be a farmer.

Behind him, Madame Corlay was being dignified and polite. In front of him, the roof of the outbuilding came just below the window. Useful, he decided, really very useful. He went on admiring the view.

Madame Corlay had finished her gracious speech of welcome. The American had begun to reply. Then there was a crash, and Hearne turned quickly to see Myles sprawling across the rug at Madame Corlay's feet. What else could she expect, Hearne wondered savagely, as he bruised himself against a heavy table and almost upset a chair in his quick journey towards the American. But then Madame Corlay and Albertine had never been hounded over open country for three weeks.

"What did you propose to do?" he asked Madame Corlay after he had unloosened the American's belt, and had sent Albertine running for water.

"The man is really filthy," Madame Corlay said, shaking her head incredulously.

"What did you propose to do?"

"We must feed him, and let him rest here today. Tonight he can continue his journey to the coast." To the coast . . . So Albertine must have reported the argument he had had with her in the kitchen, and something

which he had said to Albertine must have pleased Madame Corlay enough
to thaw some of the icicles in her eyes.

"He couldn't go on tonight," Hearne said. "He will have to stay here."

"Stay here?"

"Stay *here?*" echoed Albertine, reappearing in the doorway. "But the
Boches—"

That word was sufficient for Madame Corlay.

"He stays here," she said, rapping her stick defiantly on the ground.
She was watching Hearne thoughtfully. "War seems to have improved
you, Bertrand," she observed with a peculiar smile. Hearne shrugged his
shoulders and went on with his job. Myles was recovering.

"He may be here for a day or two," Hearne said at last. This was, he
had decided, a diversion rather than a complication. The stranger had
already pushed Hearne into second place as far as the women's interest
was concerned. And he was an intelligent man: if he were a newspaper
man, then he was also a practised observer. It would be nice to know
just what he had seen as he had traveled through that very interesting
piece of countryside in the last few weeks. If he would talk, it would be
useful. If he would talk.

Albertine said, "He can hide in the straw in the shed."

"That's the first place the Germans would look." Hearne had helped
Myles onto the nearest chest and was now trying to ease the shoes off
the American's feet. It was slow work. He added, as Albertine stood un-
believing, "Any place with livestock is a sure place for them to look."

Albertine didn't like that idea: it troubled her.

"Well, then, in the storeroom upstairs?" she suggested with an effort.

"Storerooms are equally dangerous. Food may be kept there."

"Then where?" Albertine was alarmed. Good, thought Hearne: it was
only alarm which forced Albertine's type of humanity out of its neat,
orderly groove. Fear ended complacency; fear spurred on the imaginatively
lazy.

"Here."

"What?" Both Madame Corlay and Albertine had raised their voices in
shocked protest.

Hearne pointed to the draped beds. "There's nothing wrong with the
idea. It's a good old Breton custom. And this is one place where the
Germans will not look unless they are really suspicious, and in that case
no place would be safe for him at all. This is the bedroom of Madame
Corlay, who is an invalid. That's the safest place for this man."

"He couldn't stay here *all* the time."

"No." Hearne repressed a smile. "Not all the time. He can use my room
or the storeroom all day. But if anyone strange appears, or at the first
sign of a German, then he'd better slip into that spare bed."

"And at night?" Madame Corlay's voice was cold.

"Here," Hearne said decidedly. It had to be here: his plans for these night journeys must not be interfered with. He looked earnestly at Madame Corlay; his voice didn't weaken. "Then we won't be caught unawares if someone awakens us in a hurry. And if the Germans seem suspicious and demand to search your room, then he can escape by that window over there. This is the safest place in the house for him." His tone was final.

The second shoe was at last removed. Myles had screwed up his face, but he wasn't letting any sound escape. Albertine was watching in dismay.

"It's all right, Albertine. They've stopped bleeding now. The floor won't be marked." And then as he saw her expression change, he added more gently, "Better get a bath ready for him." She nodded and left the room.

"He'll look much better when we clean him up," Hearne said cheerfully. "The trouble will be clothes. He's taller than I am."

Madame Corlay looked at Hearne, as if surprised. "Yes, he is tall," she said thoughtfully.

"And he's killed a lot of Germans. You must get him to tell you the story tomorrow."

"Tomorrow?" The questioning eyebrows were her last protest.

"Or the next day."

Madame Corlay was looking at him speculatively. Hearne wondered just what that look meant: it was kind enough, but he didn't like it somehow. She might be almost about to smile. Blast Corlay, he thought, for refusing at the last moment to give a letter or a message for his mother. As soon as they had told him of the proposed impersonation, he had shut up as tight as an oyster. Fortunately for their plans, they hadn't told him until the last day, and by that time all the information they needed was already gathered and tabulated. If Corlay hadn't been so unwilling at the last minute, then Hearne wouldn't now be going through this miming act. It would have made things easier, all round. And it would have made things pleasanter, too.

Madame Corlay reached suddenly towards the table beside her. She fumbled, and then lifted a pair of spectacles. At that moment, Hearne bent over to help Myles to his feet.

"Better get that bath," he said, his face turned away from Madame Corlay. "I'll bring him back later to you. His story will interest you."

He helped Myles towards the landing, and closed the door of Madame Corlay's room in relief. That last minute had been really embarrassing. Blast Corlay, he thought again.

But two things he had found out. Madame Corlay didn't like to wear glasses: and without these glasses, Madame Corlay didn't see so well as she pretended.

That afternoon, Hearne worked in the field. The American, washed and fed, rested in the house. He had asked for paper and pencil, and had settled himself in the one comfortable chair in Hearne's room. "To get my thoughts licked into shape while the memory is still hot," he explained with a smile which had become broader and easier.

"They will make interesting reading," Hearne said politely.

"That's the idea."

"Sit near the open window. I'll give a whistle if any Nazis arrive. You know where to go?"

"If it isn't going to worry your mother."

"The war hasn't finished for her. This is one of the few ways she has of fighting on. And tell her that story of yours."

"I gather she has no love for the Nazis."

"She hates them passionately."

The two men exchanged smiles. Then Hearne had gone out to the field.

He worked where he could have a clear view of the path which led from the farm past the round-towered *pigeonnier*, past the Pinot lands, down to the belt of trees hiding St. Déodat. But no Germans appeared, and no Henri. Once he thought he saw Anne's smooth fair hair; once an old, slow-moving peasant woman crossed the fields to the east, and then disappeared in the direction of the Pinot farm. Behind him, the trees surrounding the ruined castle seemed silent and safe enough. On his first job, he used to imagine an enemy behind every bush, but now he was past that stage. There weren't enough Germans to surround and spy on every lonely little farm throughout occupied France. Danger would come only when suspicions were aroused. At present, he was just another peasant working in his field.

By five o'clock he was no longer annoyed with Henri: he was worried. He carried the spade and the two other tools carefully down to the house. Albertine was working in the small vegetable and herb garden.

"Henri?" he asked.

Albertine was worried, too. "I'll go and find him, the old fool," she said slowly.

Hearne thought about that. "No," he said, "you stay here. You've plenty to do. I'll go before it's dark, if he isn't back by that time." The Germans might be patrolling after dark: then the fields, and not the road to the village, would be the safer place. And he couldn't tell Albertine the kind of thing he wanted to know. He would have a better chance of finding out just what had happened to Henri—not that he could help the old boy if he were in trouble. That would be a dangerous complication. But he had to know what was going on in the village, and to discover, if it were possible, whether the Germans intended to stay. Perhaps they weren't even there now; perhaps Henri's report that morning had been only a temporary alarm. He had to know.

He walked quickly down to the village. It was strange to think how long the path had seemed on that morning when he arrived. Now he was rested, and no longer hungry, and the way was quite short. Almost too short if the Germans were going to leave some men in the village.

At the bridge on the road, a young man sat on the low wall, staring at the shallow water beneath. He looked up as Hearne's footsteps neared him.

"Well," he said, "so you're back." Light-haired, freckled, a nose which wasn't quite straight, high cheekbones, blue eyes, a twisted smile.

Hearne said, "Yes," and walked moodily on.

The young man slid off the wall and hurried after him. He limped badly. So this was Kerénor, Jean-Christophe Kerénor, the "foreign" school-teacher from Lorient.

"How's the writing?" he asked with the same twisted smile.

"I'm looking for Henri," Hearne said briefly.

"He's at the hotel. He's had a busy day." There was only the inflection of a Breton accent in the man's speech, but the voice held the same mocking quality as the smile. Hearne said nothing. He turned into the market place. On his left was the long, low hotel. And in front of it were two large cars. He saw the Nazi flags, the soldiers on guard, and halted involuntarily.

"We have guests," smiled Kerénor, watching Hearne from the corner of his eyes. "Not so very many, but seemingly · important." His arm swept to the large black-letter notices pasted along the blankness of the hotel wall.

"Henri?" asked Hearne. Kerénor had said Henri was in the hotel. And it was obvious that the hotel was the chosen headquarters for the visiting Germans.

"He's all right. He's in the bar."

There were other people in the market place. Some grouped under the trees and talked. Others walked slowly, their heads bent. All looked subdued and anxious. The fact that other men were on the street decided Hearne. He was one of them—just another beaten Frenchman.

He started towards the hotel. Kerénor limped along beside him. At first, Hearne wondered; for Kerénor had obviously never liked Bertrand Corlay. And then he remembered. Kerénor lived here, lodging in the hotel which the other "foreigner," Madame Perro, owned.

The Nazis standing so proudly on guard didn't even seem to glance at them. There were so few of them, Hearne thought; so few, and yet so sure of their own safety. And why not, if you knew planes were only fifteen minutes' flying time away, planes which could level this village to a pile of rubble in even less time than that; why not, if you knew that the people in this village knew it too? Blackmail with planes . . . only the Germans had thought of that and planned accordingly. Here was a community of perhaps some four hundred people in all, and it was occupied and controlled by a handful of self-assured men. Four hundred would do what twenty, or less, would tell them.

Kerénor followed him into the bar. As he limped, he put his hand on his right thigh as if by leaning on it he could keep up with Hearne's stride.

"Elise will be delighted," he said suddenly.

"Elise?" Hearne stared at the bitter smile. He was strangely uncomfortable at the naked look in the other man's eyes.

"Elise." Kerénor lingered over the name. He was hurting himself purposely, thought Hearne. His eyes showed it: they didn't smile, but the twist on his lips seemed to have frozen there. "Yes, Elise. She's back too." And then he was gone.

Who the devil was Elise, Hearne was wondering. Better get Henri. Better get out of this place before any other riddles were put to him. He looked round the room with its small stone-topped tables. In the large alcove at the curtained window there was a group of men. Old men. They sat staring at the glasses before them. Henri, his chin sunk in his gnarled fists, was motionless. No one talked. No one moved, as Hearne went over to the table.

He's drunk, solidly drunk, Hearne thought. He said quietly, "Henri. Come."

Henri raised his eyes slowly, and looked at Hearne from under his lowered brows.

"*Ni zo Bretoned, tud kaled,*" he said.

"Yes," Hearne answered, remembering the little of Breton which he had once known. "Yes. But Albertine wants you."

The old man rose slowly and left the table. None of the others spoke. Henri didn't look at them; he was walking with a visible effort towards the door, unnaturally erect, looking neither to right nor to left. Hearne followed. At least, he was congratulating himself, the old chap looked as if he could make it under his own steam. One thing he must remember about these Bretons: they were powerful drinkers. In one way, it was funny to think how worried he had been all this afternoon when Henri was missing, and all the time Henri had been just drowning his sorrows. It was so funny that Hearne didn't even feel angry. It was funny, and pathetic. *Ni zo Bretoned,* Henri had quoted: *We are the Bretons, a hard race. . . .* There they were, not one of them under seventy, just sitting and drinking and thinking of the national songs, as if to cling onto some pride, as if to keep themselves from drowning in a sea of Celtic despair. Hearne looked back at the group of men. They hadn't moved. Henri had already passed through the doorway with its tightly gathered yellow curtains. He was literally walking straight home.

And then, as Hearne reached the yellow curtains, the door behind him, which led from the bar into the restaurant of the hotel, swung open. He turned at the grating noise of the hinges. He could see a tablecloth in the background, and an officer's cap lying on its whiteness. But his eyes came back to the girl standing in the open doorway.

"God!" he said to himself.

And then she came forward. Only a girl with the face of an angel could move like that. He suddenly realized that the lips were parted in a breathless smile, that the large eyes were fixed on his.

"Bertrand!" And then she had caught both his hands in hers. Cool hands, soft hands.

"Bertrand." The dark eyelashes flickered. She shook her head slowly, unbelievingly. "I've just come back. No one told me you were back until Kerénor came two minutes ago. . . ." Hearne felt the blood high in his face.

"Most touching," said Kerénor. He was standing at the counter of the bar, watching them with that same look in his eyes which had embarrassed Hearne before. Elise turned her face towards Kerénor.

"Go away, Jean," she said, but the laugh in her voice took the sting out of the words; the long look from her eyes softened the frown. Hearne watched her profile incredulously.

Kerénor bowed, and wheeling abruptly on his heel, he limped out of the door. Masochist, thought Hearne, and then as the girl in the clinging flowered dress turned her face once more towards him, he forgot Kerénor.

"You look as if you could scarcely believe your eyes," she teased in her low voice.

"I—I didn't know—"

"Of course not. I was in Paris after Strasbourg was evacuated. Now it is more—well, suitable"—her eyes emphasized the word—"that I should come back here."

Hearne stood without speaking. Who on earth was this girl? Corlay had told him of Anne, of Albertine, of his mother; of everything, it now seemed, except a goddess with green eyes and a warm smile, with smooth white skin and sculptured bones.

She interpreted his silence in her own way. "You were worried about me? And I was for you. I thought you were either dead or taken by the English and I wouldn't see you perhaps ever again. But now we needn't worry any more. I may be here for a month, two months." She paused. "When can we meet? Tonight? The usual place?"

Hearne was taken aback. He hesitated.

"What's wrong?" the girl asked.

"Would it be safe?" he hedged.

"Why not?" The large eyes were still larger. "I've so much to tell you. I must see you." It was a command.

"Of course," Hearne said. "Of course."

"Is that all you can say?" There was a frown shadowing the smooth brow.

"You are so beautiful."

She laughed, as if to herself. "That is better. . . . So you still love me?"

"Yes, I love you."

"More than ever?"

Then the grating of the restaurant door interrupted them. A large woman, tightly encased in black silk, her hair flagrantly dyed and tortured into rigid waves, had entered the barroom.

"Elise," she said, and motioned with her head towards the restaurant.

"Yes, Aunt Marie. Coming."

"Be quick then." The large woman nodded again. She looked at Hearne and pursed her lips; and then the door screeched once more.

Hearne stiffened. "Who are your friends in there?"

"Bertrand!" The girl was delighted. "I've told you before you mustn't be jealous. Business is merely business." She looked contemptuously round the empty room, at the desolate tables, at the small group of men sitting so silently in the window alcove. "We have still a lot of work to do," she added. "You will be needed more than ever. I'll tell you when I see you. Tonight . . ." She hesitated and glanced towards the restaurant door. "Well, perhaps tomorrow night would be better. Tomorrow night at ten o'clock?"

"Yes," said Hearne. There was nothing else he could say. "Tomorrow night at ten. At the—?"

"Yes, at the usual place." She gave him a last long look, a warm smile, a pressure of her cool slender hand. The protesting door was held open long enough for a glance over her shoulder and a last smile; for his eyes to see the tables beyond, empty except for one where three uniformed men had risen to their feet.

Hearne took a deep breath. He needed it.

He had left the Hotel Perro and the market place behind him before his thoughts began to take shape. He felt like a man who had been caught in a strong river current and had managed, somehow, to pull himself out onto the bank. He passed some men, but he kept his eyes fixed moodily on the road. Someone said in a strong Breton voice, "It's Corlay." But Hearne only raised a hand in greeting, and kept his eyes lowered. He had had just about enough for one night; just about. And then he remembered that tonight he'd have to try a first journey. He'd have to test that front door. Sometime before supper, he'd have to examine that lock, perhaps grease it. Sometime when Albertine was feeding the hens or even looking after the cows, for Henri wouldn't be much use this evening.

He quickened his pace. The fields were empty, the woods were silent. In the autumn, when the late evening sun rested on the rich brown leaves, the trees would match that girl's hair. But he wouldn't be here to see.

By the beginning of September, his job would—must be finished. No, he wouldn't be here to see. "All right, then," he said to himself savagely. "You won't be here in September. You'll be lucky if you are anywhere in September."

In the farmhouse kitchen, he found Henri sitting at the smaller table, his elbows on the hard wood, his eyes firmly closed. There was the sound of a piano.

Albertine's face was like a thundercloud. "He came in without a word and sat down and went to sleep," she said. "Not a word out of his head, not a word. And after me worrying myself to death over him, and all the work left undone." She stopped abruptly. "What's wrong?" she asked, her voice unexpectedly softening.

"Nothing. Not many Germans so far. Just some flags and some large notices plastered on the walls. Where's the American?"

Albertine smiled and pointed to the ceiling above her head. Hearne listened more intently. It wasn't well played, and it was softly played, but there was no doubt about the tune. It was "I can't give you anything but love, baby."

CHAPTER **9** PAGES FROM THE LIFE OF
BERTRAND CORLAY

When Hearne awoke next morning, his legs stiff, his arm cramped in the deepness of sleep into which his exhaustion had plunged him, he noticed first his muddied boots lying drunkenly on the floor, then his clothes abandoned in a heap beside them, and last of all the half-open door leading to the storeroom. A chair scraped; something moved. Hearne, suddenly very much awake, pulled on the nightshirt lying at the bottom of the bed and crossed quickly to the door.

It was the American, sitting on an uncomfortable chair in front of the open window. On his crossed legs, he balanced a book and some sheets of paper. He saluted Hearne with his pencil.

"Sorry if I woke you," he said. "But I had to get up to stretch my legs."

"Very difficult," Hearne answered, looking at the mass of objects which were hoarded in the room. "This place looks like a furniture shop. We never throw anything away."

"Some people would pay a lot of money for much of this stuff."

"But they seldom do."

The American grinned. "I guess not. We are all bargain-hunters."

"How is your writing getting on?"

"Not so hot. But I am getting the stuff onto paper: that's the main thing."

"It must be very interesting."

"It'll sell, anyway."

"Won't it be dangerous to take notes along with you?"

"I'll abandon them if need be. Meanwhile I get everything in order, and I'll remember the facts better when I see them written down. That's the way my memory works."

"Are you comfortable? Did you sleep well?" Hearne was being the polite host.

Myles laughed. "After three weeks of straw, if I was lucky?"

Hearne smiled wholeheartedly. Then Myles wouldn't have heard him last night. Not that he had made much noise: the door had worked smoothly enough after proper coaxing. He had left the house at ten when everyone seemed asleep, and he had returned before dawn. Myles hadn't made any joke, either, about the clothes on the bedroom floor. Perhaps the curtained window had blocked enough light so that the American had only noticed a crumpled heap instead of mud. And dampness couldn't be seen; it wasn't likely that anyone moving quickly through another man's bedroom was going to stop to touch things. Hearne waited for a stray allusion; if Myles had noticed anything, now would be the time for one of his cracks. But Myles was smiling placidly, trying without much success to ignore Hearne's nightshirt. *Chapter nineteen,* thought Hearne: *The Bretons at Home.* He looked down at his knees, wondering how they'd appear in print.

"I'd better get dressed. I seem to have slept very late," Hearne said.

"It's almost ten o'clock. I suppose that's almost the day over in this country."

"Almost. I've been ill, so Albertine lets me sleep half the day. Now I've got some work to do. I write, too."

"What's your line?" The American was interested.

"Oh, only small things." Hearne was charmingly modest.

"I'd like to see some of them."

"Thank you. We must compare our different styles." Hearne smiled and nodded towards the pages of notes on the American's knee. "Now, if you will excuse me . . ." He bowed as gallantly as he could in the short shirt.

"Of course." Myles was being equally gallant. He saluted again with the pencil. He was trying valiantly to hide a private joke. Hearne kept his face straight with difficulty. This was a moment when he would have liked to discard this French-intoned English for his own voice to say, "Go on, old man, have your laugh. It's on me." He bowed again.

"Hope I'm not disturbing you," Myles called after him. "This was Albertine's idea. She wouldn't have me downstairs in case anyone looked through a window. Which reminds me—did you see many Germans yesterday?"

Hearne came back to the door. He had pulled on his crumpled trousers and the harsh wool sweater. "Not many, so far," he said. "There were some officers in the hotel, and a handful of soldiers. But not enough to patrol the farms. Not yet, anyway. I think you'll be safe."

"As long as I keep away from the main road and that railway. That's how I found myself on your farm. Two nights ago I was down in the valley. It wasn't so healthy, so I came up onto the hillside."

"I wonder what the Boches want down there?"

"It's a main line from Northeastern France to the coast. I'm telling you I saw enough stuff being rolled over these tracks to set up whole airfields."

"But couldn't they fly planes? Why do they send them by train?"

The American was very patient. He was, decided Hearne, a decent sort of chap. And he liked to explain. "You fly planes, certainly. But then there are the spare parts, and the oil, and a hundred other things to fix up an airport."

"But we had some aerodromes near here, I think."

"If they weren't destroyed completely, they are only being fixed for decoys. The Germans are building others. And this part of the country is good. It can't be shelled from the English coast, but it'll make a good springboard against Southampton and Plymouth. These airports are springing up everywhere. I'm telling you I saw them with my two eyes. I could name ten places I've come through, all of them with new camouflaged airfields. They are so well hidden—netting and leaves over the planes, lying well-spread-out beside clumps of innocent trees, with little runways to hayfields which are the real taking-off point—that I almost got caught at one of them. I had been coming through a thicket of trees, and there was a path ahead. At one end of the path was a plane all in fancy dress; at the other end, there was a hayfield. I had been avoiding a big hangar and a fine airfield about three miles away to my left. It must have been a dummy. I guess the idea is that the British will probably find out there's an air base beside village X. They will come over and bomb X, and will naturally aim for the flying field. The Germans at point X, but just a mile or two from danger, will smile and rub their hands and go on bombing Britain."

"It would be very important then for the British to find out—" Hearne halted and shrugged his shoulders. "But it would be too difficult."

"It would be important. And not too difficult. I, myself, could tell them of several places which would interest them. And I'm willing to bet the British have ways of their own for finding out."

Hearne shrugged his shoulders again. "It seems so hopeless," he said.

The American smiled. "The British don't know what that word means. They can drive an American nuts with their slowness and self-complacency. But they never think anything's hopeless."

There was a pause.

"How are the feet?" Hearne asked politely.

Myles looked at them in their white linen wrappings. "Doing nicely, I think. This was Albertine's idea, too. She covered them with some kind of paste which her grandmother used. It certainly looked moldy enough, but it's working miracles. They don't even hurt now when I stand on them."

"Good," Hearne said, and turned towards his room. "I must work now, if you'll excuse me." He bowed gravely. The American saluted again with the pencil; his eyes weren't at all grave.

It didn't take Hearne very long to jot down in his private shorthand all the particulars he had noted last night. He considered that journey merely as a kind of introduction to the countryside round the railway. Tomorrow, he would explore westwards and watch the roadway from Rennes to St. Malo on the coast. Once he got accustomed to short cuts and patches of good cover, he would travel more quickly. But even judging from what he had seen tonight, his job might be quite useful. That idea cheered him; he wrote quickly and continuously. When the time came to get a report sent out from Mont St. Michel he could choose the most urgent of these points. Meanwhile, like the American, he was noting everything down.

Myles's remarks had only confirmed his own observations. There was some terrific construction work going on up there to the north of St. Déodat. He remembered that the railway ran through the old town of Dol before it swerved northwest to the coast. And northwards above Dol, the land was a flat plain, miles and miles of plain, most of which had been reclaimed from the sea. The more he thought of Dol, the more interesting he found it. First, there was the railway direct from the east to Dol. Secondly, Dol was connected to Dinan by a good road, and Dinan was at the end of the canal from Rennes. Thirdly, there was a main highway from the east which ended at St. Malo on the coast, and that highway cut across the road from Dinan to Dol. So Dol could be served three ways if the traffic were heavy towards that town. And Dol, lying back from the seacoast, commanded a long stretch of plain. Yes, this job he had to do might be quite useful.

He finished his last entry, and looked round the room for some place to keep these notes safely. The empty bookshelves yawned at him from the corner. "Stop gaping at me," he told them. "I'll soon have you filled up." His words gave him the idea: the safest place for his sheet of paper, and the sheets which would be added, was the inside of a book. He looked at the rest of the furniture: this table on which he had written, with its one unlocked drawer kept obviously for writing material; the chest beside the bed; the wardrobe; the concealed washbasin affair. None of these was practicable: Albertine had access to everything. The only thing which wouldn't interest her would be the contents of the bookcase. He rose and walked over to the bed, pulling the cover aside. He felt the mattresses: straw, feather, wool, in that order. No, he decided: they'd only ooze if he slit them, and their depths could lose anything they were hiding. It would have to be the bookcase.

Unlike the rest of the furniture, it was a rough, amateur piece of work. Whoever had made it had been impatient. The shelves hadn't been sandpapered sufficiently before the first undercoat of stain, and the varnish had been scantily applied. The top and sides had been finished well enough; viewed that way, it wasn't a bad job at all. But the man who had made it hadn't bothered about the rest of it. He had probably thought it didn't matter because the books themselves would hide his unfinished work. At the moment, standing empty as it was, the bookcase looked as hideous as a child with ringworm.

By dinnertime, the task of sorting the books was only half-done. Albertine, bringing some food to the American in the storeroom, halted in amazement at the litter surrounding Hearne on the floor. He followed her obediently downstairs, and ate his meal in silence. His thoughts would have increased Albertine's amazement. After some attempts to talk about the potatoes which he had bruised yesterday in his digging, she was left to concentrate on the fire and the soup pot. "Back to your old ways," she had said sourly, and the remark only added to Hearne's thoughtfulness. He finished the food hastily, hardly concealing his impatience to be back in his room. As he mounted the stairs, he found his excitement growing. Albertine was calling after him something about pictures on his wall. He paused on the top step to shout down "Later! Later!" and then he was once more among the piles of books.

But he wasn't alone. The American had hobbled to the connecting door as he heard him return.

"Hello," he said in a mixture of surprise and pleasure as he looked at the books on the floor. "Can I help?"

"No. It's all right. It will be bad for your feet; you must rest."

"As you like," Myles said stiffly. "Thought I could lend a hand, that's all."

Hearne relented. He lifted the small pile of fairly recent novels which he had discarded as being of no interest to him, and carried them into the storeroom. "Here's something to read," he said. "You shouldn't try to walk about so much."

"To be perfectly frank, that was all I wanted . . . just something to read. Thanks." He looked at the novels. "If," he added, "if my French will take me that far."

"It will be good for you to read French. You've still a journey to make."

"Yes, I wanted to ask you about that."

Hearne looked at his watch. "I'll be finished in one hour, or perhaps two hours at the most. I shall come and talk with you then. O.K.?"

Myles laughed unexpectedly. "O.K.," he echoed, and laughed again.

Hearne closed the connecting door firmly behind him. "Now," he said to himself with considerable satisfaction, and sat cross-legged on the floor.

The books were indeed a strange collection. As he had pulled them out of the wardrobe that morning, Hearne had noticed two things. One part of this small library was formed of old books, badly printed in eye-straining type. Their bindings ripped at a touch, the paper was yellowing not so much with age as with cheapness. But the other part, and by far the greater part, had been bought within the last two years. Handsome volumes they were, with binding and paper and type to shame the older books. The first thought that struck Hearne was that Corlay must have been making money then with his teaching. The older books, obviously second- or third-hand, were a monument to the days when Madame Corlay had pinched and scraped to let her son stay at the University. Then, when he had a job, he had begun to buy himself some new books. It was just after this solution that Hearne saw the signature on each flyleaf, together with the date when Corlay had added each book to his bookshelves. The solution crumbled away. Hearne examined all the new books methodically; his mind was a strange mixture of excitement, dawning suspicion and dismay.

The earliest date on any of these newer books was January 20th, 1938. By that time, Corlay had been out of his temporary teaching job for over six months. For six months he had been living on the farm, dependent on Albertine's work for his food, on his mother's generosity for his pocket money. Hearne had seen enough of the life on this farm to know that there was little pocket money for anyone. Madame Corlay's dress had been of the ageless variety, of a cut and color which a careful woman would wear for years. Her one piece of jewelry, the gold chain and brooch, had obviously been inherited like the house and furniture. The piano was a relic of the hard years in Rennes. There was no wireless set, the usual consolation for an invalid.

Hearne rose on impulse, and went over to the wardrobe again. He counted the jackets and suits thoughtfully: more than he would expect for a man in Corlay's position. He fingered the materials; they felt as new as they looked. Cheap clothes, imitation smart clothes, none of them any older than two years. Hearne was thinking, I don't like this at all. Perhaps Corlay had saved enough money, somehow; perhaps there had been a legacy; perhaps he had won a lottery. Perhaps any of these. Perhaps. Hearne shook his head slowly, and walked back to the books.

The second thing which had startled Hearne that morning was that

Corlay had rarely finished reading a book. Or else the man was a genius and could read through uncut pages. In the whole collection, there were only about ten books with the pages entirely cut. The rest had pages cut for the first chapters, and occasionally some pages cut at the end. But not one of these books had been read right through.

Hearne found himself looking at the bookcase. I bet he made that, he thought; made it, and then lost interest in it before he had it properly finished. The wood was sound, and the design was an attempt at a piece of modern furniture. Corlay must have seen some pictures of Swedish modern. That was what he had copied. Grand ideas he liked. Grand ideas . . . The phrase haunted Hearne. He shook himself free of speculation and went back once more to the books. The beginning of the riddle would be solved with them, he felt.

He would begin with the earliest volumes, and here Corlay's passion for inscribing his name and the date would prove invaluable. Hearne laid the books in rough groupings, according to the dates on their flyleaves. Each heap of books on the floor represented a year of Corlay's intellectual life.

The first book belonged to 1928: a school prize for ancient history. Next came 1930: a school prize for medieval history, and three textbooks on French history, with the sections on Brittany closely underlined and annotated. By 1932, Corlay was at the University of Rennes; and for the next four years, the books were texts on either French literature or history, or potted biographies of famous Bretons such as Jacques Cartier, Surcouf, Mahé de La Bourdonnais, or abridged cheap editions of Chateaubriand, Lamennais, Brizeux, Renan, Villiers de l'Isle Adam, Abélard. And these were all Bretons, too, reflected Hearne.

It was just at this point that Albertine had appeared with food for the American, and had reminded him sharply that dinner had been ready for half an hour. If only, he had thought, as he followed Albertine downstairs, if only people would stop being well-meaning, if only they'd leave him alone.

But now, at last, both Albertine and the American had been settled. "Now," he said to the books with considerable satisfaction. "Now . . ."

CHAPTER **10** POEMS FOR E.

Hearne adjusted himself comfortably on crossed legs, and reached for the 1937 pile of books. There were magazines, too, in this lot, but the subject was uniform. It was politics.

Corlay had definitely been interested in Breton nationalism. That was hardly surprising after his earlier choice in history and literature. But he had also now branched into Royalist ideas. Perhaps he had thought that Brittany's cause could be best served by a restoration of a King in France. And then, in the summer of 1937, he had ended his subscriptions to Royalist publications as if he had had a sudden revulsion. After that summer, there were no books or magazines on the Royalist side. In fact, from the summer of 1937 until January 20th, 1938, there were no books bought at all. That was when he was unemployed. Then, in January of 1938, began the new series of books—first editions, modern, well-bound, well-printed. But, Hearne reminded himself, Corlay was then still unemployed. He sat and looked at these recent additions to the library, the witnesses of Corlay's unexpected prosperity. As a last excuse, he thought that a friend might have sent them to Corlay. A friend . . . but a peculiar kind of friend. For these books dealt with the decadence of democracy, the future for men of action, the new order in economy and politics.

"Well," said Hearne, "well, now."

He felt he could do with a cigarette, or a drink. He rose and went to the window. The air was heavy with the smell of the fruit trees after rain. But at least it was clean. He looked at the pile of Fascist literature on the floor: at least the air was clean.

There still remained one heap of books to be examined. They looked like copybooks. Hearne picked them up one by one, glancing quickly but methodically through their pages. Corlay's writing was flamboyant, but in spite of the excesses of sweeps and curls the pen-marked pages were easy to read. Most of the notebooks belonged to his university days. At first, he had been a prolific note taker and underliner, but the lecture notes tailed off as his classes progressed. By the end of a year, they were short and uninterested, and the margins were filled with the variations of the Bertrand Corlay signature.

But two notebooks really attracted Hearne. The first was a desultory diary, or, rather, a series of condensed complaints. Corlay had been an unhappy young man: little, if anything, had pleased him. He hadn't liked his schoolteaching job—the pupils were uniformly stupid, his fellow teachers were nincompoops. But when he lost that job, then his scorn switched to the unfairness of a government which preferred a Paris to a Rennes degree. There was a hint of "victimization," of persecution for his nationalist beliefs. And yet, when he came back to live on this Breton farm, it was strange that he seemed still unhappier. This time he railed at the stupidities of the Breton peasant, the banalities of country life with its mixture of coarseness and superstition. Occasionally there would be a page concentrated on the Corlay family. He went to some length to identify his ancestors: all of them seemed either very noble or very brave or very artistic, or all three. His last entry, dated January 7th, 1938, stated flatly: "It is intolerable that we should have been forced to live like animals.

Once our name was famous, but now we must be content to eat and sleep our way to death. I will not be content." That was the end of the diary.

It was nice that he could eat, anyway, Hearne thought grimly. That was more than some families were able to do.

He carried the second notebook over to the window. He felt he needed some more fresh air to help him finish this job. So Corlay would not be content. . . .

The second book contained Corlay's own writings. They amounted to exactly eleven pages—the sum total of his work from August 1937, when he had come to live on his mother's farm, until January 1938. January 1938. The date haunted Hearne. Something pretty powerful had struck Corlay's life in that month. January 1938. Hearne roused himself to look at the eleven pages of poems and epigrams. It was just as he feared: Corlay would probably have made a good farmer. His curse was his desire to live in the Ritz, to be a Breton without living in Brittany, to be the best poet explorer cinema-star orator artist statesman tennis-champion scientist of his time. He was mentally aged fourteen, except that that slandered most fourteen-year-olds.

The joke is on me, Hearne thought savagely, and went back to the books. Corlay's possibilities were more than either he or Matthews had bargained for. He began to jam the books into the bookcase. Automatically he chose the heaviest volumes for the two lowest shelves, but the books he had tried to thrust into the second bottom shelf wouldn't fit. They overlapped the edge by two inches. Hearne struck at them impatiently with his fist. *The Myth of the Twentieth Century* . . . *The Myth of the* . . . "Damn you all to hell," he said, and gave a blow with the side of his wrist to their bold titles. His wrist hurt, but the books didn't move. They couldn't, for the shelf was not wide enough for their breadth: the shelf could only hold the smaller octavo-size books. Whoever heard of anyone making a bookcase with the small books on the second bottom shelf? And Corlay had taken some trouble about that. The back of that second bottom shelf had been blocked in to hold the smaller volumes securely. Blocked in . . . Hearne's fingers lightly tapped the back of the shelf. It was of lighter wood, possibly a thin plywood. Between it and the real back of solid wood there must be a space. But how to get into that space was another question. Corlay must have been a cleverer carpenter than Hearne had imagined.

But he needn't have credited Corlay with too much skill. As he pushed and shoved and pressed the false back with the palm of his hand, it suddenly slid along grooves in the two shelves which it had separated. The end of the plywood panel came out of the side of the bookcase and stuck there incongruously, quivering with the force of Hearne's effort. It was as easy as that. He pushed the panel back into position, and looked at the side of the bookcase. Simple, but neat enough, he decided. An imitation join going up the whole length of the bookcase, like the stripe on a Guardsman's trouser leg, had disguised Corlay's subterfuge.

"Cunning chap I'm supposed to be," Hearne said. Cunning: still another aspect of the simple Corlay, the misunderstood genius. Hearne grinned. "I really begin to think I'm a bit of a stinker," he added. He pushed the panel sideways once more, slowly, carefully this time, so that the plywood board wouldn't crack up. This secret compartment might have its uses. It had, as he found out when the panel was slipped aside to its full length. There, in front of his hand, lay two notebooks and some sheets of paper fastened together with an elastic band. As he removed his discovery, he replaced his own notes in the neat recess. And before he closed the false shelfback once more, he retrieved his revolver and map from the unlocked table drawer. They would be safer inside that bookcase, if any stray Germans had the inspiration to search for weapons. Then he stacked about twenty of the narrower volumes along that shelf. They would be a safeguard if the American got tired of vicarious passion in high places, and abandoned the overcomplicated emotions of the novels for a walk, perhaps a talk, in this room. Hearne filled the other shelves, too, for good measure. The room looked neat once more; that should keep Albertine happy.

He carried the treasure-trove over to the table. Now he might find something really solid. He might as well admit his excitement.

First, he examined the papers. Two sheets were joined together with a rusted clip: one, a map of Northern Brittany with neat, red-ink numbers over certain villages and towns; the other, a typed list of names and street addresses, with red-ink numbers in the margin opposite each name. He would study this combination later; perhaps, and this was the likeliest guess, these were the names and districts of trusted Breton nationalists. Strange that Corlay should have taken so much trouble to hide them, for Breton nationalists hadn't been proscribed, even if they weren't exactly loved, by the French government. Perhaps Corlay had been hiding the list from his mother: she certainly didn't agree with any separatist ideas. She believed that the Bretons were the flower of the French Republic, and flowers wither when they are cut from their stalks.

Next came three sheets of paper, this time pinned together, listing dates and names of cafés. The dates ranged on a monthly average from January 1938, until the end of August 1939. These sheets were all typewritten, too, which meant that this stuff had been given to Corlay, for Corlay had no typewriter. Meeting places and meeting times: that was the best guess Hearne could make, but the information on these sheets would need more careful examination when he was less pressed for time. He slipped the rubber band round the papers, and placed them between the double sheet of worn blotting paper which lay inside the table drawer.

He closed the drawer thoughtfully, and abstractedly picked up the two notebooks.

They were of a nobler brand than the copybooks which he had found in the wardrobe along with the books. They even had mock-leather covers. He had the sudden premonition that they belonged to Corlay's period of unexpected prosperity. When he opened them, he saw he was right. One was a diary; its first entry was under the heading January 18th, 1938. The other contained Corlay's poems, each neatly dated at the foot of its page. The first of these poems had been written on January 25th, 1938. January 1938 . . . January 1938 . . .

"Well," said Hearne, "what a peculiar thing." His sarcasm left a smile on his lips until he began to read the poems. They were highly emotional, increasingly passionate, but obviously sincere. Poor devil, he thought, she twisted him around all right, whoever she was. And then he came to twenty lines of verse written in October. They described Corlay's love with great detail. I don't know about the hips and breasts, but there's no mistaking the eyes and hair, Hearne thought. He re-read the description of the hair—autumn leaves caught in the warmth of the late evening sun. He remembered his walk yesterday, on his way home from the village. "Damn," he said aloud, "damn it all." He was suddenly annoyed, almost angry. And then he laughed. "Fool!" he said to himself. Matthews, no doubt, would have put it more strongly. It only proved, anyway, that Corlay wasn't a good poet.

Towards the end of the poems—there were fourteen in all—it was obvious that Corlay had achieved quite a lot. The last effusions were almost hysterical with joy. It embarrassed Hearne to read them. "All right," he said irritably, "I get the idea. All right." And then one line held his attention. *In the shadows of the dovecote, fortress of our love and of our secrets* . . . Dovecote. Could that be the place which Elise had meant when she had asked him to meet her? If so, then he hadn't the excuse that he didn't know what she was talking about. And he had been hanging onto that excuse. It had been going to preserve his detachment tonight when ten o'clock came, and he was securely and respectably in bed. But now, it was entirely his own choice whether he met Elise at the dovecote or not. The choice was his own, and he didn't want to make it. The girl was dangerous; and it wasn't the belief that she was a Breton nationalist which made her seem dangerous, either. He wouldn't go, he decided; he'd read that diary in bed.

And yet, the line of poetry haunted him . . . *fortress of our love and of our secrets.* . . . What secrets? Secrets of love, secrets of Breton autonomy, what secrets? He paced the room, his head bent as if his eyes could read the riddle in the unevenness of the floor. Business before pleasure was one of Matthews' original remarks. No, he wouldn't go, he repeated, and thought of Matthews' cold blue eyes. Business before pleasure. And then the idea came to him that he was thinking of Elise solely in terms of pleasure. Could it be possible that she might be part of his business, too?

It was almost time for supper. He placed the two notebooks inside the table drawer and resumed his restless walking round the room, his hands in his pockets, his eyes still fixed on the lines of the scrubbed white floor. He was wasting time, he thought in sudden depression: he should be concentrating on railways and canals and roads. And yet, as long as he didn't understand Corlay he would feel in danger, and therefore be in danger. For there was something which worried him about Corlay, something indefinite as yet, something increased by today's discoveries. He had thought the examination of these books and papers would have settled his mind. But it hadn't. January 1938, he thought again . . . *of our love and of our secrets*. Secrets. Probably the word meant little: just a poet's addition to perfect a meter or complete a line.

He halted at the window. He could always read some of the diary before ten o'clock. Then, he could decide whether he was imagining possibilities, or whether he was just trying to find any old excuse to see her again. He turned from the window as he heard Myles's footsteps crossing the storeroom. It would depend on the diary, then, he determined, and faced the opening door.

"Pardon me. Am I disturbing you? I thought I heard voices, and that you had finished your work."

"Voices? Oh, that was me. I've a bad habit of talking aloud."

"You do?" The American looked both amused and relieved. "I knew a man from Texas once, who used to talk to himself. He used to be alone out on the range for long stretches at a time. That's how he started the habit."

Hearne said quickly, "How's the reading?"

"Not too good. I slept some of the time, I must say. My French can't be as good as my French friends pretended. By the way, do you understand everything I say?"

"Enough."

"You speak quite good English. Your accent is your own, but you have the grammar all right."

Hearne tried to smile calmly. "Oh, I had plenty of grammar at school. I even took a degree in English at Rennes University."

Myles looked as if he believed that. There was no reason why he shouldn't.

"And I had some English friends at the University," Hearne went on glibly. "One in particular used to talk a lot to me in English. That was after I got to know him of course."

"Of course." There was a reminiscent look in Myles's eyes. "Last summer—" But Albertine entered, and the story of last summer ended before it was begun.

"Food!" said the American, and this time the look in his eyes was much more understandable. Albertine was actually smiling. Her nod was approving as she looked round the room and saw the neatly arranged books.

And then, downstairs, someone knocked.

"The front door," said Albertine needlessly. The three of them looked at each other. "It must be Monsieur le Curé; he always uses the front door."

Again there was that knocking. "Very powerful man, Monsieur le Curé," Hearne observed, and saw a sudden fear on Albertine's face.

"It doesn't sound like him," she said slowly, her cheeks paling.

Hearne took command. "Go downstairs slowly, call you are coming, and don't be afraid. Give me that food." To Myles he said, "Into bed with you."

As he opened Madame Corlay's door, he saw Albertine was indeed going slowly. He planked the food down on the table beside Madame Corlay, covering the eyeglasses heavily with the bowl of soup. There was a snap as the bowl tilted over its victim.

Madame Corlay's amazement at their sudden entry gave way to partial understanding as Hearne put his finger to his lips, pointed downstairs, and sat down in a chair at some distance. She tightened her lips as she heard Albertine's voice, and then a man's voice, firm and assured. He was speaking careful French, loudly, coldly, with that unmistakable authority. The white draperies were pulled roughly back into place, swayed, and then hung rigid in their heavy folds. Madame Corlay looked as if she were about to explode.

"The Boches," she said.

"Gently, gently," warned Hearne. He was listening to the footsteps on the stairs.

Albertine had come up with more speed than she had gone down. "They've come. To see if we have room. For soldiers."

"I'll see them," said Hearne, and rose quickly.

But there was no need. A German officer stood in the doorway. Behind him was a soldier.

CHAPTER **11** VISIT OF INSPECTION

"You are the owner of this property?"

The German's voice was as coldly assured as his face. Under the exaggerated peak of his cap, the straight features pointed expressionlessly towards Hearne. His eyes and skin and hair were colorless: it was as if the uniform blotted them out. All you noticed was the regularity of the outlines of his face, the assertive confidence of his body.

Hearne shook his head wearily, and gestured towards Madame Corlay. "You are the owner of this property?"

Madame Corlay, her eyes still dilated from the effect of the German's salute, nodded abruptly.

"How many rooms do you have in this house?"

There was a silence.

"Six," Albertine said.

"How many rooms?" the German repeated, his eyes fixed on Madame Corlay. She sat quite still, her hands clasped tightly on her stick. Her knuckles were white.

"How many?"

"My servant has told you." Madame Corlay's voice had tightened, but it was still under control. Hearne watched her not without admiration.

"Is this the only servant?" The German pointed towards Albertine.

"There is Henri, who works on the farm."

"And this man?" The German indicated Hearne, slouching on his chair.

"My—" there was the slightest hesitation, perhaps a catch in Madame Corlay's breath—"son." Her eyes met Hearne's. He had stiffened involuntarily. She smiled gently, and he relaxed. She knew, he was thinking, she knew; or did she? If she had known, what had prevented her from saying "A man who pretends to be my son"?

The officer crossed over to the fireplace, and examined the view from the windows on that side of the room. "Quite good," he said, as if to himself. Then he walked quickly over to the window which overlooked the farmyard, passing the bed with the white draperies gathered round it so innocently. Madame Corlay, Albertine, Hearne, were as motionless as the soldier at the door. The officer opened the window, and they could hear German voices in the yard. The voices suddenly were silenced, as the men saw the captain at the window. He beckoned once, sharply, silently, and turned back into the room. Behind him, the breeze from the opened window fluttered the white curtains and the draperies on the bed.

Albertine hastened to close the window. "Madame is ill," she said reprovingly. "She will catch pneumonia."

But the German wasn't listening to her. He was standing impatiently at one of the tables, his fingers tracing the carving round its edge, his eyes on the doorway where the soldier still held his pose. They heard quiet, quick footsteps on the stairs, and then a little man slipped into the room. A thin little man with spectacles and opened notebook and poised pencil. Apart from the uniform weighing so incongruously upon him, there was little about him which seemed military. An auctioneer's clerk, thought

Hearne; that was what he was, an auctioneer's clerk dressed up as an officer.

"Captain Deichgräber?" His voice was as quick and light as his step. The tall officer left the table. He spoke rapidly in German. "This isn't bad. It is the best I've seen. It will have to do. The colonel will be furious, but you will have to explain to him that the only castle is in ruins, that this is the best house we can find near the village. You can make it comfortable for him. Have a look at the other rooms on this floor."

"Very good, Captain Deichgräber." The quick footsteps pattered into Hearne's room. When he at last came back, the notebook was closed. The reedy voice went on, "Two other rooms, Captain Deichgräber. Four officers could sleep there once we cleared all the rubbish out."

"Good."

"Then, Captain Deichgräber, there's the hall downstairs for a dining room, and also downstairs there is accommodation for four soldiers."

"Good." The officer called Deichgräber felt in his pocket for a cigarette case. "You can tell them of the arrangements," he added, and motioned with his cigarette to the owner of the house as he sauntered to the door.

"You will be requested to leave here by tomorrow. These rooms are urgently required." The little man's French was excellent.

"Tomorrow?" Hearne spoke for the women. Albertine looked as if she had turned into a pillar of salt. Madame Corlay's nostrils showed a strange rim of white, as if they had been molded from wax.

"I said tomorrow. No doubt you will be able to stay with friends until you come back here. It will only be a matter of weeks, September at latest, before you return. You will be recompensed for any damage, of course. And one more thing: leave such things as these"—he swept his arm towards the china and crystal displayed on the dresser—"and your linen and blankets. We can make the decision what we need of them. You will be adequately recompensed for any damage, you may be sure. I shall be back here tomorrow morning before you leave." The tone was so polite, so correct, so insufferable.

I'd like to kick these shiny teeth down your scrawny throat, thought Hearne. He said, "But my mother is an invalid."

There was a blank stare.

Captain Deichgräber had turned at the door. He hadn't liked Hearne's interruption. "Your mother can stay with friends. If necessary, she may have a permit to travel to a relative." Hearne thought, now isn't that generous of him? But he kept silent. Seemingly Captain Deichgräber hadn't liked Hearne's restraint, either.

"You, yourself, need employment," the German went on. "We don't tolerate unemployment. There will be a job for you."

"I am a farmer," Hearne said quietly. "I don't need a job."

"You will not be needed on this farm for the next few weeks." Both the officers were smiling now, but there was no hint of amiability in these smiles. "All the harvesting necessary can be done very quickly when it is efficiently done. We shall see to that. You will be back in time to dig for next year's crops."

"And this year's?" It was Albertine now. "We live on that: that's all we've got."

"You will be paid for anything we need."

Hearne looked at the two men. Using just what for money? he thought savagely.

Perhaps Deichgräber hadn't liked the look in his eyes. Perhaps Deichgräber didn't like him at all. Anyway, his voice had hardened, his careful accent lost its Frenchness.

"Your name?"

"Bertrand Corlay."

"Tomorrow you report for work at the Hotel Perro in St. Déodat. Tomorrow. You understand?" He turned to his auctioneer's clerk. "Make a note of his name, Traube."

Traube was looking suddenly thoughtful. "Bertrand Corlay," he said slowly. "One moment, please, Captain Deichgräber." He reached into his breast pocket and produced another notebook, a small insignificant one. But what his quick fingers found on the second page did not seem at all insignificant. He glanced sidelong at Hearne, and then back to the book again. "Bertrand Corlay," he said softly. Hearne stood looking at the little man, hoping he didn't seem as alarmed as he felt. What had they against Bertrand Corlay? Perhaps he wouldn't even be given that twenty-four hours' grace until tomorrow, to make his escape. Perhaps, within the next ten minutes he would be marched right into the village, between that deaf-mute soldier and his comrades downstairs.

Deichgräber had noticed the change in Traube's expression. He threw his cigarette on the floor. Together they walked towards the window beside the fireplace and stood there, with their backs to the room. Traube was talking quickly. Deichgräber was holding the small notebook. When they at last turned round to face Hearne, the German's expression was masked, but it was a thin mask hardly covering his anger.

"There has been a mistake. This house will be hardly suitable for us." He looked at Hearne. "Corlay, you have wasted my valuable time. Why did you not tell me your name?"

Hearne reddened. He avoided the look which Madame Corlay was giving him. Even Albertine was watching him curiously. "I'm sorry," he said stiffly. "I gave it to you as soon as you asked me." No, Deichgräber didn't like him, quite decidedly no. I must, thought Hearne, have an unfortunate way of answering him, or perhaps he feels he has lost face.

It was Traube who broke the tension in the room. He moved quickly to the door and waited there for Deichgräber. The two officers were once more correct, even to the precision of their parting salute. But as they reached the bottom of the stairs, Deichgräber's anger broke loose. Traube, it would seem, was trying to restrain him. Hearne tried to catch the words, but the voices were pitched too low. All he could learn from some of the German words which floated upstairs was that Deichgräber was furious at having been made to look a fool, while Traube was being philosophic about it all. He had obviously been more accustomed to rebuffs in his past life than the very assured Deichgräber.

The front door had closed noisily. There came an angry command, heavy footsteps running round the house to the front entrance, the shuffling of boots, the clank of gun butts on the paved pathway, the steady rhythm of precision marching. Hearne moved over to the window and cautiously looked out. Only four soldiers and two officers. He watched them march away until they reached the Pinot land. After that, the path to the village was hidden by trees.

"Such a beautiful right wheel," he said, as he turned back into the room. "They came more quietly than they left, didn't they?" He picked up the burning cigarette. The two women didn't answer. They watched him in silence. "Albertine," he said, "go all through the house and see if we are really alone. Ask Henri how many soldiers there were down in the back yard." Albertine was still watching him; her mind was fumbling for an answer to all this. She took the cigarette end which he presented her with a slight bow and stood there, holding it.

"Go, Albertine," Madame Corlay said. Albertine came back to earth. She looked at the offending cigarette, picked up the bowl of cold soup, and moved slowly to the door.

"Tell us quickly, Albertine," Hearne said urgently, and the tone of his voice arrested her attention. He pointed towards the bed which had concealed the American. Albertine's eyes widened, a hand went up towards her opened mouth, and she scurried from the room.

"I believe she forgot all about him for a moment," Hearne said smilingly, but Madame Corlay wasn't thinking of Albertine, or of Myles.

She was picking up the pieces of glass from her broken spectacles on the table. She shook her head sadly. "You did not need to do that," she said. She raised her eyes to his. So she had guessed.

When she spoke again, her voice had hardened, and her lips were twisted bitterly. "Bertrand seems to have had powerful friends," she began, and then she was weeping quietly. All the pride had left her face. She was an old woman mourning her son.

Hearne walked over to the window. It would be easier for her if she would really let herself cry, he thought. Behind him there was only silence. He looked down on the fields, but all he could see was the slow tears falling so quietly over the bloodless cheeks.

Albertine had returned. "All gone," she announced triumphantly from

the doorway. "Tell the young American I've brought him some hot soup."
She carried the steaming bowl into Hearne's room.

"All clear," said Hearne and walked towards the bed. "All clear," he
repeated, and pulled the white folds aside.

The American stepped out slowly. "Just wanted to make perfectly sure,"
he grinned. "Got rid of them all right?"

"I hope so."

"Smooth bit of work." Myles was looking at him curiously. You're not
the only one who's puzzled, not by a long chalk, thought Hearne. Only
Madame Corlay in that room had seemed to understand just what had
happened. Only Madame Corlay and the peering Traube. Even that other
officer, called the Ditch-digger, had been out of his depths.

Hearne steered Myles towards the door. "Supper," he said, "is served."

"You think it's wise? Not that I'm an anxious man, but I don't trust
those bastards a square inch."

"It's safe enough at the moment. But we may have to hurry you away
from here. I'll talk to you about that later. Now you must eat, and I
have things to discuss here." He nodded over his shoulder to Madame
Corlay. Then to Albertine, waiting outside on the small landing, he said,
"Lock all the doors, and bar them. If we have any more visitors, they'll
come announced. See that Monsieur Myles has enough to eat. And you
can open that last bottle of wine. If we don't drink it, others may." He
smiled pleasantly as he re-entered Madame Corlay's room. One thing,
anyway, he was thinking—Albertine has had enough shocks today to complete her education.

He said to Madame Corlay, "I'd like to talk a little with you, if I may."
He drew a chair towards the old woman, again sitting erectly with her
hands clasped on the walking stick. The knuckles no longer showed white.

"Yes?"

"First of all, when did you guess?" That could apply to either Corlay's
"powerful friends" or to himself. If she really knew about him, that was
. . . He might have jumped too quickly to conclusions in this last half
hour. He would soon learn, anyway.

She returned his look calmly. Her voice was gentle. "About you?"

He now knew, anyway. He smiled halfheartedly. Damn, he was thinking, you couldn't have been so good after all.

"I wish you hadn't broken my glasses," Madame Corlay said with some
asperity, and narrowed her eyes as she looked at his face. "Yes, as far as
I can see, the likeness is remarkable. Are you Breton, too?"

"I am a Celt," admitted Hearne truthfully.

"Yes, you look like Bertrand: you even talk and move like him. At first,
I thought you were my son. And then the little things were different."

"What?"

"Albertine talks with me a good deal. You see, we've been a long time together. She came to this farm when she was a girl, and she has stayed here ever since, except for two visits to Rennes when I needed her. One was when Bertrand was born: the other was when I was very ill. She was waiting here to welcome me when I came back after my uncle's death. So, you see, we talk a good deal."

Hearne smothered his impatience. "Yes?"

"Although I sit up here, I know what's going on downstairs. When Albertine told me how much easier it was to live with you nowadays, I thought that perhaps war had made you gentler, more sympathetic. Suffering can do that to men. You didn't grumble about the food, you didn't grumble about Albertine going to Mass, you didn't grumble at having to eat in the kitchen. Apart from the time when you lost your temper with Albertine in your bedroom—when I first saw you—you did seem changed by the war. I was beginning to hope that perhaps some good comes of war even in little things, that perhaps you had stopped being so self-centered and opinionated. Then you offered to work in the fields, you helped the American and even admitted, at that time, that clothes for him would be a difficult problem as he was so tall. Taller than you. Bertrand would never have admitted that. Then you went down to the village to find Henri. And today, Bertrand would have gone down to welcome the Germans himself. He might even have offered them wine. He would certainly have not risked hiding the American."

"That's incredible," burst out Hearne, and then lowered his voice. "Why?"

"I don't know why. All I know is that he would have. He never thought of anyone except himself since he was a small boy. You see, that's how I guessed. You had the one quality which Bertrand lacked. Even Anne, when she came to see me that evening you went to find Henri, even she thought the war had changed and improved you. I found in you, and Anne did too, just what I always had looked for in my son."

Hearne's eyes were fixed on his hands. He cleared his throat, but he didn't speak. Whatever was coming was going to embarrass him. He knew that from Madame Corlay's voice.

"And that was," continued Madame Corlay, "just ordinary human kindness. That was something Bertrand couldn't even understand."

There was a pause.

"You called the Germans his friends," began Hearne, and then stopped. This was far from pleasant. He felt he was probing an open wound.

But Madame Corlay's strength of character was equal to the strain. She didn't try to dodge the unspoken question. Her voice was hard, as if she was determined to force herself to speak. "I don't know exactly," she was saying. "I don't *know*. . . . He had strange friends, strange ideas, and he had some strange money too, in recent years. I made that remark about his 'friends,' because I was so angry at having the Boches give favors to my son."

"Yes, it looked like a favor. On the other hand, it may be their way of winning over Breton nationalists. Your son was a nationalist, wasn't he?"

"Certainly. That I do know. But then he has also been a Royalist, and at one time he was a Communist. That was after his revulsion from the Church."

"He had many enthusiasms."

"But only one at a time." Madame Corlay paused. "You may think I have driven him to these—enthusiasms. I assure you, I made excuses for him every time, until last year when this terrible war began. You may think I am a bitter old woman, but my bitterness only began then."

Too late, thought Hearne pityingly: too late. If less excuses had been made ten years, even five years, ago for Bertrand Corlay, there might have been no bitterness today. There were some types of men whose willfulness thrived on the excuses that were made for them. And they were the kind of people who never knew when they had gone far enough in their selfishness, who never knew when to stop. The more allowances that were made for them, the more they presumed.

"Perhaps we are doing your son an injustice," he said out of his pity for the tortured old woman. "Perhaps he is a true Breton loyalist."

Madame Corlay said wearily, "The true Bretons are not paid."

"He showed you money?"

"No. But he didn't bother to hide the fact from me that he could buy clothes, and books, and drinks at the hotel. Once, I asked him. He said his writing was successful."

"Perhaps it was."

Madame Corlay smiled sadly. "You are too kind."

"No, I'm not. Both of us have definite suspicions, and I won't deny that they are strong ones. And yet, the only conclusive proof would be if we could really know where that money came from. It might, as I said, have come from newspaper articles, or reviews, or short stories." Certainly not from poems, Hearne added to himself. "Now, one last thing. Was there anything else which you noticed about me? You see, I wouldn't like the Boches, or any friends of theirs, to get suspicious."

"You need not worry. Any people like that would not notice the quality which my son lacked. It is only someone like Anne, or myself, who wanted to love him, only someone who wanted more kindness in his heart, who would . . ." She halted. And then, wearily, she added, "No, you have nothing to fear."

"Your son is now in good hands, Madame Corlay. He was wounded, but he is recovering. And he may be thinking over things. Many men do when they are ill, when they have ceased to be the very self-efficient creatures they thought they were. Perhaps when he comes back, you will find the war *has* changed him. Mental and physical suffering are good purges, you know."

There was a silence, and then Madame Corlay spoke again. "Perhaps. Now, I have answered your questions. In return, I shall ask you only one. Why are you here?"

"Because I am an enemy of the Germans. For me, the war has not yet ended. That is why I was sent here."

Madame Corlay sat more upright. Her voice was clearer. "That is enough for me."

She was about to say more, when Albertine entered. "I've opened the wine, Madame. But the American won't take any until you have had the first glass."

Madame Corlay was smiling. Watching the pleasure in her eyes, Hearne wondered how he could have been so mistaken when he had first seen her. An honest laugh, a kind word, a friendly idea: they didn't cost much. The more he thought of it all, the more Corlay seemed just a bloated fool.

"Ask Monsieur Myles if he will be so good as to join us," Madame Corlay said. "And over in that dresser, you will find four glasses."

"Your best crystal?" Albertine was shocked.

"Four glasses, Albertine."

When Myles came, there was an uncertainty in the way he halted at the threshold of the room, there was a hesitation in his usually cheery smile. He thinks we are going to turf him out right away, guessed Hearne, and gave him a reassuring grin. But Hearne's guess was only half the explanation, as he knew when he caught the American's wary eyes fixed on him. Myles was doing a little thinking about the Germans' hasty departure.

Albertine had filled the four crystal glasses. In her nervousness, the bottle neck struck lightly against the rim of one of them, and a thin clear note shimmered through the still room. The light was fading. The massive furniture stood like black shadows against the white walls.

Here we are, thought Hearne: two old Breton women, an American who'll probably go through worse before he's better, and an Englishman who spends his nights hiding in ditches. What would they drink to?

It was Madame Corlay who gave the toast, leaning on her cane as she rose slowly and painfully to her feet.

"To our war," she said; and no one smiled.

The Corlay farm was asleep. The only light left burning was in Hearne's room. He sat at the table, his watch in front of him, the diary propped against some books. He had opened it in excitement, but long since the excitement had given way to disappointment, and then the disappointment had given way to exasperation. He turned over another page. Just the same old thing, he thought, just the same old thing.

> *May 15.* Met E.
> *May 20.* Met E.
> *May 21.* Talked with H.
> *May 25.* Met E. Visit to Paris planned.
> *May 29.* Talked with H. Meeting at Rennes.
> *June 12.* Met E.
> Met E. . . .   Met E. . . .   Met E. . . .

All the consciously fine writing of the earlier diary had disappeared. Since January 1938 everything had become concise, objective. E. was obviously the beautiful Elise. H. . . . that was something which Hearne could not yet understand. And nothing which he read helped to explain H. Perhaps, thought Hearne flippantly, H. was a brunette, just to complete the circle: Corlay had a redhead in Elise, a blonde in Anne.

Only once did anything longer than these brief memoranda appear. That was in December 1938, when Corlay had made his first speech. Then he had written: "The audience was small, necessarily, but appreciative. It was a terrific experience to feel them respond. When I admired, they admired. When I hated, they hated. Today, they could be counted in tens, but tomorrow they may number hundreds, even thousands." There had been some other speeches recorded after that, but Corlay had managed to curb his self-approbation. It must have been quite a strain. Once he had noted that he was tired and depressed, but that E. was encouraging. It was shortly afterwards that the trip to Paris had taken place. E. had been there too. There were no more entries about tiredness or depression after that visit to Paris.

But not all the notes were devoted to meetings with E. or H. Occasionally there would only be a number within a neat circle. Hearne remembered the loose sheets of paper held together with the elastic band, and the numbered map. Something made hard sense somewhere. Even this diary might become interesting if he only knew exactly what Corlay had been doing. His guesses weren't enough: he had to know. He had to know what Corlay's game had been. Then either he could stuff the diary and papers back into their hiding place and forget about them, or—and Hearne drew a deep breath—they might prove to be something much more than interesting.

Anyway, he consoled himself, he had spent just as useful a day as he would have done lying on his bed or digging in a field. For one thing, he couldn't have handled that conversation with Madame Corlay if he hadn't found out more about her son than he had memorized in an English hospital. So nuts and double nuts to Matthews. The trouble with people with cold blue eyes was that they kept floating in front of you with a reprimanding look.

He strapped the watch onto his wrist thoughtfully. Twenty minutes to ten. Nuts again to Matthews. He wasn't going to leave this self-imposed job half-finished. He had to find out Corlay's game, and Elise was his last chance for that. With a suspicion of a smile, he lifted his pencil and copied Corlay's writing as carefully as he could. *"July 9, 1940. Met E."* He closed the diary and placed it in the drawer.

And then he unlaced his boots.

*   *   *

Outside, the stars were dimmed by broken clouds. The young moon was shrouded. There was a smell of rain in the air. Hearne knelt under an apple tree, and pulled on his boots.

He approached the dovecote with a care which would have seemed exaggerated to most people. But Hearne had learned that no care was ever exaggerated: not in this kind of work. When he was satisfied that the surrounding fields were really as deserted as they looked, he advanced through blocks of shadows to the dovecote walls. There he paused, leaning against the curved side of the tower. He regained his breath, his eyes and ears alert. No windows. No sound of any movement. He edged carefully towards the door. It lay open, a black gaping hole in the rough wall. There was still no sound. Either she was late, or he had credited that line of poetry with too much sense. The half-light of the moon faded behind the thickness of a cloud. He moved quickly into the darkness of the tower.

The door hadn't been opened: it lay, torn off its hinges and abandoned, in the middle of the uneven earth floor. He tripped over it in the darkness, as his eyes looked up to the broken roof with its slits of night sky. He regained his balance, and cursed under his breath. And then something moved behind him.

He turned quickly, and instinctively reached for the shadow which had separated from the blackness of the wall. Then, as his mind caught up with his instinct, he softened his grip. What would have been a stranglehold became an embrace. He heard her gasp, and then there was a low laugh, and her arms were round his neck. Her cheeks were soft and warm. She was wearing the perfume he had noticed yesterday.

"Bertrand," she said when she paused for breath.

"Elise," he said for lack of anything better to say. From now on, he remembered to think, it was a case of follow-my-leader. He waited for her next move, his face pressed against the fine silk of her hair. He was thankful for the darkness. Even as his eyes became accustomed to its depths, he could only distinguish outlines. That made him feel safer, more assured.

The tenseness of her body suddenly relaxed. She drew away from him. "Come," she said, "we have little time. You were late."

"It was difficult, tonight. My mother was ill and restless. We had visitors this afternoon and they upset her."

"Visitors?"

"Two officers. They wanted to commandeer our house for some colonel."

Elise had moved towards a mound of earth banked against the wall; she still held his hand. "How ridiculous. . . . Where is your coat? Don't tell me you've forgotten it." Her voice was half-laughing, but only half. The iron hand in the velvet glove, thought Hearne. What was he supposed to have a coat for, anyway?

"They packed away all my clothes," he answered. "I've had the devil of a time finding things since I got back." Then, as he saw her hesitating before the mound, he guessed her thoughts.

"Here's my jacket. That will do." He spread it on the earth at her feet.

"Yes, that will do." She caught his hand again, and pulled him down beside her. She was wearing a thin silk dress and little else under her opened coat. Poor Anne, Hearne suddenly thought: she never had had a chance with Corlay, not one solitary chance against this. "I shall keep you warm," Elise said. Her voice had lost its edge and was once more good-humored.

Warm was an understatement, Hearne thought. He said, "You're still as beautiful."

She laughed that slow breath-caught laugh of hers. "But tonight we have little time for your poetry, Bertrand. When I come back from Paris, you can tell me how much you love me. But tonight it is business."

"Paris?" Hearne hoped his voice was sufficiently dismayed.

"Yes, tomorrow. That was why I had to see you tonight. That was why I was annoyed when you were late. I must be back at the hotel by eleven. A lot is happening, Bertrand." There was an excitement breaking through her voice.

Hearne waited for her to speak again. She rested her head against his shoulder, and looked up towards the patches of cloud and stars above them. He was conscious of the coldness of the night, the warmth of her body, the line of her throat as she watched the night sky through the gaping roof, the perfume in her hair, the emotion in her voice. His mind was as alert as his senses. He waited.

"Yes, a lot is happening. And you managed to get back at the right time. Oh Bertrand, how could you have been so stupid as to get into real fighting?"

He gave a short laugh. "I couldn't very well avoid it, could I?"

"Well, why didn't you get captured, right at the beginning?"

"That doesn't always work: there's often a chap on the other side who shoots first and then questions afterwards."

That made her laugh again. "You must tell me what happened. After I get back from Paris. Now—" Her voice was serious, assured, almost commanding. She gives the orders, Hearne judged, and the curve of her waist inside his arm didn't soften the thought. "Now, listen. They are moving into St. Déodat. The hotel is already taken over." She paused for dramatic emphasis.

"So I noticed yesterday. But what trouble do they expect here? The place has been half-dead for years."

The interruption annoyed her. "There will be no trouble here, silly. That is why they've chosen here. Think of St. Déodat's position. It's central. It's a control point for the whole district. And it's safe. It's as safe as—as—"

"The Bank of France."

"This isn't the time for jokes, Bertrand, not even bad ones."

Hearne listened to the sharp edge in her voice, and decided it certainly wasn't the time. And yet it was difficult to restrain his own particular brand of humor when a young woman took herself so seriously; still more difficult, when the young woman was so beautiful as this one. He mumbled what might have been an apology or an endearment, and kissed her hair.

"From St. Déodat," Elise went on, "the hundreds of surrounding farms and all the villages scattered over this area can be controlled, just as they were by the Church centuries ago."

Hardly for the same ends, Hearne thought, as he answered, "But St. Déodat may have been central once: now it's isolated."

"Not with a well-made road, and that will be easy for them. It will only be a short detour, really, from the main road in the valley."

She was excited: she was making it all sound so very important. Granted St. Déodat's one-time dominance over the district, he could still think of other places which the Nazis would be more likely to pick. Then he realized what she had meant by saying it was safe. St. Déodat *was* safe; for he wouldn't be the only one to believe it was negligible. That was its safety.

"The valley?" he echoed, picking up the emphasis she had used on that word.

"Yes." The excitement in her voice increased. "The valley—or Dol, to be precise. You don't believe me? Well, wait until you see the airfields that are being built now all round there. Wait until you see what happens in August, what the results will be by September!"

"By September?" He kept his voice casual.

"Yes!" The nonchalance in Hearne's voice sharpened her tone. "Yes, Bertrand. By August 15th the Germans will be leaving us here. Britain will be under attack. By the middle of September, Great Britain will be finished."

Hearne kept silent.

"What are you thinking?" she asked impatiently.

Hearne said, "I'm thinking that the time is short. I haven't seen many Germans about St. Déodat, so far."

"I don't think you need worry about their efficiency. The plans are all ready, the preparations have begun. In fact—" Elise's voice was a mixture of amusement and sarcasm—"in fact, Monsieur Corlay, the army is arriving the day after tomorrow."

The army . . . the army . . . And she didn't mean masses of soldiers by that, either. She meant the army as opposed to the other branches of the invasion horde. The military element was still to come: the day after tomorrow, she had said. The hotel was already taken over, by a handful of soldiers and some officers responsible for the billeting of the troops who were still to come. He suddenly wondered if there were any other types of Nazi at the hotel: Gestapo or Military Intelligence, for instance.

"Just who are in the hotel now?" he asked casually, and the answer this time stiffened him.

"We are." She could no longer hide her sense of triumph. "We are." She tightened her hands on his wrists until they were numbed. She raised her head from his shoulder and tried to see his expression through the darkness. "What's wrong?" she asked suddenly. He kissed her, and his thoughts were cold and bitter and completely realistic at last. Corlay was no Breton nationalist, or if he had been one, he had been sidetracked by a very beautiful body. He wondered what the correct answer should be. What would Corlay have said? The kiss ended.

"What about me?" he asked.

She regained her breath and her hands went up to her hair to arrange it. "That was what I am coming to. . . . At present, you are to ignore the hotel. You've got to concentrate on your meetings: we are in no danger now, of course, but for the sake of results it will be wise to keep them secret from the Bretons. I'll send you a list of future dates and places, where you can discuss your progress with the men from the other districts. Then, you will also have nationalist meetings, which you are to pretend to keep secret from the Germans. In that way, you'll get more response from the Bretons. The idea is that Brittany will be separated from France, and we've got to get the people to accept it. That is why you must keep our real meetings secret, so that our connection with Germany won't be recognized, and then the nationalist meetings, which we shall encourage, will have some chance of success. If we work it properly, we'll have them accepting this Breton National State as the thing they have always wanted. There will be a German Governor, of course. I hear that Weyer will probably be chosen. And there will also be a Breton National Committee. And you, of course, will be the delegate from this district."

She laughed, and struggled free from his grip. "I thought you'd be pleased. Don't hold me so tightly, Bertrand, you'll bruise me. I'll be able to tell you more when I get back from Paris."

"Wish I were going with you again," Hearne said, and mentally thanked the diary.

"Not this time, my love. Later, perhaps. We'll see. And now I must get back to the hotel. Hans is arriving tonight."

"Hans?"

"Now, don't start all that silly jealousy again. Hans has been a good friend—to both of us. Who do you think was responsible for getting you into this new National Committee?"

"How long is he staying here?"

"The hotel is his headquarters for the next few weeks, until we get everything nicely organized and co-operative. He's got to go to Paris too, of course." Her voice was too casual, but the kiss she gave him was meant to soothe any doubts. "And one more thing, my sweet, have you still got those lists?"

Hearne remembered the map, and the list of names and addresses, and the connecting numbers. He said, "They are safe."

"Good. I'll leave a note for you at the hotel tomorrow with my aunt. I'll give you the corrections to that list. Most of our men are still intact, but one or two of them were stupid enough to get killed."

"Perhaps they surrendered to men who shot first, and asked questions afterwards."

She laughed and lifted his wrist to see the illuminated face of his watch.

"You know," she said, "I do believe carrying a gun has made your hands bigger."

"All the better to hold you with." Hearne hoped the strain in his voice would pass for emotion.

"Five minutes more," she announced. "Bertrand, do you love me as much as ever?" Her emotions were like a bathroom fixture: hot, cold, to be turned on at will.

"As much as ever I did."

"Am I still as beautiful? You haven't forgotten all your pretty speeches, have you?"

"You are the most beautiful woman I have ever seen." That at any rate was true. There was a pause. She was waiting. "Your eyes," he began, "are like the crystal depths of a sunlit pool. Your hair . . ." He remembered

enough of the verses he had read in Corlay's notebook: that helped him
to improvise for the rest of her anatomy. One hour ago, he would scarcely
have imagined such cold objectivity possible. He felt a sudden relief as
he realized he was safe from Elise; and it was she, herself, who had saved
him. The iron hand in the velvet glove, he thought again. She could flutter
those black eyelashes, turn that profile, lift those breasts: it would all
be an interesting and aesthetically satisfying performance. But the hand
was iron, and the velvet glove was wearing thin. Her mind was carefully
calculating. Her heart was self-possessed. She might have just as well admitted that she was an incurable leper, with festering flesh concealed
under the skillful drapery of her silk dress.

He looked at the shadow of upturned face. "You beautiful bitch," he
said to himself, and helped her to rise to her feet. The stipulated five
minutes of love was over.

They halted at the doorway. The arc of moon was fitful, but the light
was stronger than it had been inside the dovecote. Once again, Hearne
was glad that the inside of the tower had been so dark.

"Don't come over the fields with me," she said. "It will be better for
our plans if you seem to have no contact at all with anyone living at the
hotel. It is only for a week or two. This Breton National Council and sep-
aration from France will probably be an historical fact by the end of July.
That's our aim." She added a smile to sweeten her command.

Hearne looked disappointed. "But there's no one to see."

"You know this place. It's all eyes and tongues. Guess who followed
me part of the way, here? Kerénor."

"Kerénor?" Hearne remembered the limping man's animosity. A lot of
things were being explained away tonight.

"Yes, the stupid fool that he is. We have nothing to fear from him now.
We can deal with him, if he doesn't behave." She paused, and then mimicked Kerénor's voice: " 'What are we fighting for? Comrades, do not be
deluded by an imperialist war.' Yes, his days of usefulness are over. Either
he now co-operates, or—" She changed her voice again. "Good night,
darling. It has been lovely to see you again." Hadn't it just, he thought. He
let go both of her hands slowly.

"I'll think of you all the time you are away. Let me know at once when
you get back."

"Don't forget the note which I shall leave at the hotel."

"I won't forget," he said, and watched her. She had drawn her coat more
tightly round her. Her hair suddenly gleamed into life as the moon freed
itself from a cloud. The green of her eyes had darkened. She turned her
profile to look up at the sky. Hearne wondered who had first told her
how lovely she looked that way. Once more he was thankful that it had
been so dark and cold inside the tower. If he had been able to see that
profile as clearly as this, it would have been more difficult to judge Elise

correctly, before she had condemned herself with her own words. He might have been too late for his realism: he might have been caught off guard. But now, he didn't envy Corlay any more. He pitied him. How long would she consider him "useful"? And then, like Kerénor, he could be "dealt with."

"You'd better start working on your speeches, Bertrand. They are going to be important. I'll be back here in ten days' time, and we can have our first meeting with our group then. That will give us time to have some progress to report on our work with the Bretons. Use any means in dealing with them. Hans said you could have a very free hand, but try persuasion first. Co-operation makes things much easier for us than suspicion and hate, so have patience at first. You know the line: the British are treacherous cowards, the Americans are selfish cowards, the rest of France are bloodsuckers as well as cowards. A separate Brittany, friendly to Germany, can be secure and happy. You know the sort of stuff. Pile it on, but keep dangling autonomy like a big juicy carrot in front of their noses. God knows they've wanted a separate Brittany for years, but trust a Breton to stop wanting it once he gets it. At the meeting on my return, we can discuss how well we have succeeded in our various districts. These are the orders."

She gave him a last kiss, and then, freeing herself from his arms with that smile which promised so much and meant so little, she turned towards the path. She didn't look back. She wasn't the kind who did.

He stood in the cold blackness of the doorway until she had disappeared into the half-shadows of the night. Far below him, the church tower was outlined above the trees which hid the houses of St. Déodat. He suddenly remembered his emotion when he had first seen the village. Peace, he had thought, lived here. Peace? He smiled sardonically: romanticism always ended in such bathos. Life liked its little jokes: and the more bitter they were, the funnier. He must remember to laugh, some day.

A fine rain drizzled over the fields. He turned up the collar of his jacket and abandoned the idea of bed. Day after tomorrow, she had said. In that case, Myles must be on his way by tomorrow night. And that meant the job which he had set for himself tomorrow night must be done now.

He began his steady pace up the hill towards the ruins of the castle. Once over the crest of that wooded hill and he would reach the road from Rennes to St. Malo. It was strange to think that what he had learned in this last hour might be as important, in its own way, as anything he could discover in the next few weeks. He hoped, as he felt the rain settling on his shoulders and his feet settling into the soft earth, that the St. Malo road would be as interesting as the railway line he had watched last night.

It was.

CHAPTER 13 WARNING FOR ST. DÉODAT

There was no time for sleep. Hearne looked at his gray face in the gray light of the mirror, and shook his head wearily. He yawned, and felt his chin with his hand. No time for shaving, either: his fingers were too cold to make a quick job with Corlay's cutthroat razor. He splashed his face with the three inches of water, and combed his hair. At least, he had done a good night's work. Behind him on the table lay two pages of compact notes. On the floor were his soaked clothes. He would feel warmer once he had some hot soup inside him. There might be even some of that wine left: yesterday Albertine had carefully corked the bottle after their toast. Corked wine was better than none when you felt as cold as this.

The papers were at last hidden, the bed was appropriately rumpled, the sogging clothes and filthy boots were picked up from the floor. He stood at the door, and gave a last careful look. The room looked innocent enough to please him. As he went downstairs, he looked at the boots: they'd have to be scraped and dried as much as possible. He grinned as he remembered Elise and her half-joke about his hands being bigger. It was lucky she hadn't remembered the size of Corlay's feet: none of the shoes in Corlay's wardrobe would fit him.

Albertine had heard him coming, and had already served his breakfast. She wasn't talking, this morning. In fact, she seemed to be ignoring him. So she had been thinking about the Germans' visit, yesterday. Hearne smiled to himself as he swallowed the hot soup hungrily. Even Albertine who only wanted to be left in peace didn't like the taste that German favors left in her mouth.

At first, she paid no attention to the clothes which he had thrown on the stone hearth, but her curiosity at last prompted her to pick them up. She said something to herself, and then waited for him to explain. Hearne finished his bowl of soup, and then helped himself to some more. Albertine, standing with the wet clothes held far out from her white apron, was still waiting.

It was she who, after all, had to speak first.

"Where have you been?"

"Couldn't sleep much. Went out for a walk."

"In that rain?"

"Dry these boots, will you, Albertine? I've got to go to the village this afternoon."

"Where are your other pairs of shoes?" She was looking disapprovingly at his stockinged feet.

"Upstairs. But I don't like them: they are not strong enough for this weather."

"I told you that when you bought them." The hint of self-satisfaction in her voice was a good sign. The storm was dispersing.

"You were right and I was wrong, Albertine." He rose and clapped her shoulder. "You are always right, Albertine."

As he left the kitchen, she was already scraping the thick yellow mud off the boots and laying them down on their sides not too near the fire.

Upstairs, the American had already been installed in the storeroom. He was less talkative, today. His "Good morning" had been no more than polite. Hearne leaned his shoulder against the doorpost and watched him as he pretended to go back to his writing.

"Busy?" Hearne asked.

"Fairly."

"Too busy?"

Myles looked up from the pad of paper balanced on his knee. He kept rolling his pencil between his thumb and forefinger.

"Sorry," continued Hearne, "but there are some things we must discuss."

"Yes?"

Hearne looked at the American. His jaw was noticeably stubborn; there was a wary look in his eyes. All the friendliness had gone from them. So he, too, hadn't liked German favors in retrospect.

"I think," said Hearne, "that this is hardly the moment for you to begin distrusting me."

"Well—" said the American, and then stopped.

"Well?"

"Well, I am thinking that I'm more trouble to you than you bargained for."

It was at that moment that Hearne noticed Myles was wearing boots.

"Your feet are better?"

Myles's face was expressionless. "Yes."

"Where on earth did you get those boots?" Hearne kept his voice friendly, even amused.

"Your mother gave them to me. They belonged to her uncle. I'm to get some of his clothes, too."

Hearne's voice was less amused. "And you were just waiting for them to arrive before you slipped away, preferably when I wasn't about the house to see where you had gone?"

Myles stiffened at the barely concealed anger in Hearne's tone. "Here," he said, "that's a bit harsh. After all, I'm only a nuisance here. I don't like putting anyone in danger the way I've been putting you all."

"And you'd have ruined everything, including your own chances to escape." Hearne's voice was calm once more. That was the trouble with a sleepless night: it made you bad-tempered whenever you felt yourself thwarted next day.

"I'll look after my own escape." It was the American who was angry now.

"Don't be such a damned fool. If you do arrive at the coast, what will you do then? Go round asking fishermen if they'll take you across the Channel? You may ask the wrong fisherman, you know."

"I'll manage," Myles said stubbornly. "I've managed before."

"You'd manage much better if you would listen to me. Tonight you'll leave here. There is a man in a small fishing village on the river, just before you reach St. Malo. He will take you across the Channel. And he doesn't do it for money, either. Every able-bodied man he saves is another for the Boches to face later."

Myles said nothing at first. He was staring at Hearne, as if he were trying to read his thoughts. At last he said slowly, "I don't follow this. I'm willing to bet that you aren't doing this for the sake of my bright blue eyes."

"You'd win that bet."

That startled even Myles. He smiled in spite of himself.

"Well, why then?" He wasn't angry now, but he was still watchful.

"In the last three weeks, you've stored a lot of details inside that brain of yours. As a newspaper man, you are a trained observer. The things you would automatically notice during your journey here would be interesting and perhaps useful to the right people."

There was a pause, and then Myles answered, "I guess they would. But who are your 'right people'?"

"The ones who'll meet the fishing boat when it crosses the Channel."

The American's eyes were examining the toes of his boots.

"So you've taken all this trouble with me so that I can spill what I know to the 'right people.' . . . Why bother? I know what to do with the information I've gathered."

"But you might not be able to do it quickly enough. You might take two or three weeks to reach England. *If* you go my way, you'll be in England by the fifteenth of July at the latest."

"*If* . . ." Myles repeated Hearne's emphasis on the word. "Then the choice is up to me? This isn't an ultimatum?"

"The choice is yours."

The American relaxed slightly. "You are the funniest farmer I've ever met," he said, and his voice was almost friendly once more.

"I *am* the funniest farmer."

Myles shot a sudden glance at Hearne's face. It was grimly serious.

"It doesn't make sense," Myles said, and then shut his lips into that tight line.

"What doesn't?"

"Your touching farewell with these Jerries yesterday evening, and the way you've taken so much trouble to hide me here. Why didn't you give me up, then and there? You seemed to be a friend of theirs."

"Shall we say, they *think* I am a friend of theirs?" Hearne's quiet voice had no hint of mockery. He returned the American's direct look with equal steadiness.

Myles said, "You are taking a big chance on me. What if I didn't turn my information over to the proper quarters? What if I never went near your man outside St. Malo?"

"I shall see you do. I shan't leave you until you are on that boat, and then I'll get a message over to the other side to expect you and your information. They'll meet you all right."

"Well," said Myles, and gave a short laugh. "You've got it all arranged pat, I must say. You weren't a newspaper man, yourself, at one time? No? I didn't expect any company on this journey to the coast. I won't weary, anyway, I can see."

"No. I don't think either of us will weary."

The American's interest quickened. "Will it be tough going?"

"Possibly. But we'll manage. And we'll only manage if we trust each other. I am trusting you, even if your name isn't Myles."

The American was silent; his face seemed unchanged, but he had stopped playing with the pencil.

"I get it," he said at last.

"Fine. Now, today, go on remembering every detail you've seen, shaping them into order. Eat plenty, and get some sleep. You can use my bed."

"There's only one answer I'd like to know," the American said.

Hearne turned at the door. "And what's that?"

"I'll ask you when you get me onto that boat. We'll skip it now."

"O.K."

The American laughed. Hearne looked puzzled. "Kind of cute how all foreigners think they have to say 'O.K.' to an American," Myles explained.

"Or perhaps it is the way we say it?" Hearne suggested. With the smile still on his lips, he said, "And you should also rest your feet today. Better take the boots off now."

Myles tightened his lips, but he did bend down to unlace the boots.

"Yes," he said, "that will rest my feet. It will also prevent me from running away without you. Here, take the damned things." He threw them, each in turn, over to Hearne, with the beginning of a grin. "What was that about trusting me?"

"It still holds," Hearne said. "I do trust you, but I've also heard that Americans are very independent people, and like their own way best. Perhaps you might begin to think once more that you could manage better by yourself."

"Perhaps I could."

"Perhaps. But it would be better to avoid all risks. You are much too important at the moment."

"I don't think I like being important," Myles said, but he was not displeased.

"It has its disadvantages," Hearne agreed, and gave his customary bow. That always amused Myles. At least, Hearne thought, the temperature had risen again. Tonight's journey would not be such an unpleasant task after all.

"When do we start?" the American asked.

"At sunset. Meanwhile I'll see my mother and work over some maps."

"And I'll rest my feet, I suppose?"

"That's the idea," Hearne said. He paused with his hand on the door. "And I really do advise you not to leave the house until we both go. It will be dangerous not only for yourself, but for all of us here. There are Germans in the village. The soldiers are coming here in some numbers tomorrow, but there are others already in the hotel. They probably call themselves a Commission for Economic and Educational Understanding. I think Gestapo is simpler to pronounce, don't you?"

Myles gave a short laugh. "So *they*'re here," he said as if to himself. "I might have known it."

"Well, I'll see you later," Hearne said, and moved into his own room. He closed the door behind him. Already, he could feel the numbered lists, which Corlay had hidden so securely, being turned over in his hands. If they were half as good as he hoped, they would still be dynamite.

They were. He spent the next two hours happily copying the names of these men on the German payroll, noting their districts and headquarters and meeting places, memorizing as he read and solved and wrote. This, he thought, as he finished his last entry, would be a nice little surprise packet for Matthews: a sort of bonus on the side. It would be useful for the agents whom Matthews had sent into Northern Brittany to know just what peaceful citizen was a dangerous enemy. And it would be particularly useful for the French who were fighting on. They would have a special interest, a special bill to settle. What was more, if the key map and its accompanying lists had been drawn up so methodically for Northern Brittany, it also existed for the other districts of France. Hearne imagined perhaps twenty of these map sections, fitting neatly together into one large expanse of intrigue and infiltration. Now that they could be considered an actuality, the search could start for the others. Most things could be discovered, provided you knew that they did exist. That was the snag in this kind of work: there were so many possibilities that you wasted ingenuity and effort, time and trouble, just looking for something you hoped would be there. But once you had a reality to deal with, that was quite a different cup of tea. Then you could stop worrying about fifty problematical ways to be explored; then you could start working, with the added zest of knowing that you were on the right road.

Hearne folded the sheets of paper neatly. Later he would add the information which Elise had left for him at the Hotel Perro, along with a coded summary of his own observations. Together, they would all sail for England.

He was debating in his own mind whether he should make the coded summary now, or visit Madame Corlay to break his news of Myles's departure to her, or slip down to the village for Elise's instructions, when voices from the stairway decided him. Women's voices. He listened to Albertine's solid footsteps followed by lighter movements. There was a rustling outside his door, but the room they entered was Madame Corlay's. He stood with his hand on the door latch. And then, as he heard Albertine come out of Madame Corlay's room, he opened the door, quickly and silently.

Albertine had started back at his sudden appearance.

"Who?" he whispered, pointing towards the closed door of Madame Corlay's room.

Albertine was shaking her head unbelievingly. "They've turned her out of her farm."

Turned out . . . turned whom out? . . . Hearne said, "Anne?"

"Yes." Albertine was still shaking her head as she started downstairs. Only God could know where people could sleep or eat; it was beyond any human being to imagine. . . . Hearne watched her go. He thought grimly, she doesn't know the half of it; in another six months, or in a year, she may begin to understand. And there would be so many Albertines, so many simple hearts and simple minds whose orderly unimaginative lives had left them ill-equipped to grasp what was happening to the world. There was the tragedy of it: if only they could have realized the danger while there was still time, while they were still free to carry a gun and still free to make guns for themselves. Instead, they would now find that it costs three times as much to retrieve a position as it takes to hold it. And the reckoning had not yet begun. In another year, or more, the full cost would begin to be realized. Hearne suddenly hoped he wouldn't be in France at that time. He had always liked France too well to watch it weigh the load of chains it had helped to fasten on its own neck.

"Chuck it, you damned fool," he told himself. "You aren't here to worry about people who just wouldn't believe that such things could ever possibly happen to them. The first job is to worry about those who are still holding on. You're here to find out what you can to help them, and to keep your skin whole. Fat lot of use you'd be to them, if you didn't."

His face was quite expressionless as he knocked on Madame Corlay's door. "Bertrand," he called, and then entered.

Madame Corlay sat bolt upright in her chair. She was angry. If I were a German, Hearne thought, she would have struck me with that stick.

"Albertine told me," he said, and looked at Anne. Her face was quite white, and it seemed thinner, but there were no tears.

"It had to be someone," she said. Her voice was low, but Hearne felt it was being tightly controlled. "It would be much worse if I were a man with a wife and children. There are some in the village for whom it is much worse."

"But your family have lived and worked on that farm for two hundred and forty years," Madame Corlay exploded. She was taking it much less philosophically than Anne. Hearne suddenly remembered that Madame Corlay had planned that the two farms should be joined: in that sense, she no doubt felt that the Germans had taken possession of something connected with her. "Can't you *do* something?" she went on indignantly. "Can't you say Anne is betrothed to you? Can't you—" She halted. Possibly the words had sounded more distasteful than the impulsive thought. When wild ideas surged through your mind, you couldn't often tell how cheap they were until you put them into a sentence. Anne was looking at her in bewilderment.

"Why," she asked, "should the Germans pay any attention to that? They think we are lucky to be left alive at all."

Madame Corlay's face had reddened. Hearne noted the shining eyes, the trembling lip. She's going to burst into tears, he thought, and the idea so startled him that he walked over to Anne and took her hands.

"You can live here with us," he said.

"You've no reason to be so kind," Anne replied stiffly. "Not after what I said to you last time we met. And if I say I am sorry, you will think it is only because I need you now."

"No, I shan't. I believe you were sorry in the ten minutes after you left me."

Anne looked at him for a long moment. She was even smiling now. "But, Bertrand, I was."

Hearne became very aware of her hands and let them go suddenly. He faced Madame Corlay. Her eyes were fixed on the floor at her feet, but her lip had stopped trembling.

"It will be all right for Anne to stay here?" he asked.

"Of course. But the American?"

"He's leaving here tonight. I was just coming to tell you about that. I think it is safer if he leaves tonight." He turned to Anne. "We've had a man staying here. He's trying to reach the coast."

"And you've been hiding him? Oh Bertrand, how wonderful." Anne's eyes were larger than ever. "But he mustn't leave because of me."

"He has to go. The Germans will be here in greater numbers, tomorrow."

"I know. The village is being made ready for them. Half of them are to be garrisoned in the empty houses or billeted with families. The rest are to be together on the meadows beside the church."

Hearne nodded. "Trees there," he said.

"Trees?" Anne looked puzzled.

Hearne smiled. Trees were natural camouflage, just as the Romanesque-Gothic church would seem so disarmingly innocent from the air.

"Who told you this?" he countered.

"Kerénor. He came to see me as soon as Marie went into the village and told them what had happened to our farm. I've brought Jean and Marie with me." Her voice was apologetic and anxious. "They are old, and they don't eat much, and they'll help Albertine. They had nowhere to go. . . . They couldn't stay on the farm. The Germans wouldn't let any French stay around it." She looked at Madame Corlay. "Jean and Marie are so old. They are so alone."

"They can stay here," Hearne said quickly. "But what part is Kerénor playing?"

Anne smiled sadly. "He has declared war."

"What? The pacifist?"

"But he has changed. Believe me, Bertrand, he has. He has been worried about his ideas for months now. He still believes that they are the right ones, but he says the time is all wrong for them. And now he is going to—" She halted.

"Tell me, Anne." Kerénor's name hadn't been on that Nazi pay list. Elise considered him a fool who had lost, who was beaten even before he ever fought. Kerénor was just the man Hearne needed.

Madame Corlay said unexpectedly, "You can tell Bertrand. I have talked with him and he has changed in many ways too. Our enemy is his enemy."

"Kerénor wouldn't talk very much. He only hinted. . . . And I said I would keep everything secret, as his friend."

"He was right to ask you not to tell," Hearne said. "And don't tell anyone else. But I've got information I want to give Kerénor. Information which may save St. Déodat from making some mistakes. But I can't give you any information for Kerénor until I am sure that he is willing to take risks against the Germans."

Anne looked at Hearne for a moment. "I see," she said. "Well, I am sure he's already taking risks. He has a wireless set, and he hid it when the Germans were inquiring about them yesterday. He listens to London. He's making a report each day, and he has already chosen the men who are going to pass the news by word of mouth. Then we'll all know the true news. He says that is important. He says all the little things are important. Little things, he says, would add up to something bigger." Anne's voice held a note of wonder which once would have made Hearne smile. But now he knew the value of little things in the smothering blanket of enemy occupation. Anne was still talking. "He heard from London that there are

Frenchmen who are calling themselves Free Frenchmen. They are fighting on, and they've their own ships and their own army. And some of the colonies are going to join them."

Hearne, watching Madame Corlay's expression, had his belief in little things such as wireless sets strengthened.

"I've got to go to the village, now," Hearne said. "Will you come with me, Anne?"

"Me?" The gray-blue eyes widened. When she smiled like that the expressionless mask vanished, and her face was suddenly and charmingly alive.

"Yes, I want you to help me, Anne. I cannot be seen talking to Kerénor for certain reasons. And yet, I want to give him a message. So, when I am in the village, will you try to see Kerénor, and tell him some things?"

The smile on Anne's face faded, but the eyes were watching him gravely and honestly. She hid her disappointment well.

"Now, listen carefully, Anne. Tell him he is right: that the little things will grow into big things. Tell him he must get the men together whom he can trust, and as long as the Germans think they are holding Breton nationalist meetings they will be able to get together quite safely. Tell him that he must be careful, for the Gestapo are watching him; and if he doesn't seem to co-operate he is in danger. And tell him·that, although he has always hated me and I've never liked him until now, this is what the Nazis want. They hope we'll hate and distrust each other, so that they can rule us easily. And if they rule us easily, that helps them in their fight against the rest of the world which is still free. So Kerénor's big job is now to unite everyone in the village. All their differences and quarrels must be forgotten if they are ever to know freedom again. When he has united the village, he can start uniting people in other villages. He must choose men who can be *trusted* to help him. And the movement will spread. And the Germans won't be able to kill some of us, without reprisals being taken against them. If we are united, they have more to fear and to worry about. Can you remember that?"

Anne nodded, and repeated his words quickly in obvious willingness to help. What he had said had excited her. She added, "Perhaps I can be of help too!" Her eyes were shining at the thought.

"But always be careful, Anne. We are fighting against a stranglehold. One slip, and we shall have our necks broken. And there is one thing more which you must remember. Never forget this." He paused to let his next sentence have added emphasis. "Do not trust Elise, or any of her friends. She is in German pay."

He might have overturned the cabinet which held all Madame Corlay's treasured crystal. The effect on the two women was as spectacular.

"Elise. . . ." Anne's soft childlike face had frozen; her nostrils dilated. And it wasn't only the fact that Elsie was a traitor which had transformed her. It was the fact that he should have mentioned the hated name, mentioned it so coldly and so damningly.

"We must leave now for the village," Hearne said. "Might the American come in here to talk to you? Keep him with you until I get back. It would be dangerous for us all if he were to go out for a stroll. And don't tell him that I've gone to the village. He might get worried and come after me. He is getting restless, now that his feet are better."

Madame Corlay could only nod her answer. The name of Elise still held her silent. In condemning Elise, Hearne had condemned Bertrand Corlay. Now she knew everything. Anyway, thought Hearne, even if something goes wrong tonight and I don't get back to St. Déodat, I have warned them of their greatest danger there.

He looked at the faces of the two women. He knew that he had given his warning to the right people. They would not disbelieve it. They would not forget it.

CHAPTER **14** COLLABORATION

It was a strange walk to the village. When the stone bridge was crossed, Hearne breathed a sigh of relief. He felt he had performed just as neat a piece of imaginative realism as ever in his life. For Anne had asked about Dunkirk, and as they crossed the calm fields he had answered with a description of the Bordeaux evacuation (which he *did* know, at least), and multiplied its horror by ten to achieve the chaos of Dunkirk. Judging from the look in Anne's eyes, and the tightening of her lips, he had succeeded well enough. After that, they finished their journey in silence. Hearne found himself admiring a girl who had the sensibility neither to exclaim nor to commiserate.

They halted awkwardly at the corner of the market square. Anne seemed to realize that this was where he intended to leave her. She smoothed her hair nervously with her hand, half-smiled, took a hesitating step away from him. Hearne felt he was being inadequate. He reached out and touched her arm lightly. "I must try to get some brandy for my mother," he said, "before it all disappears. I'll see you later, Anne." He was relieved, and yet somehow dismayed, to see her smile become wholehearted.

"Yes," she said. "Later."

And then he noticed the appearance of a frown between the level eyebrows, and his eyes followed the sudden shift in her glance. Outside the Hotel Perro, a small thin man was standing. He was soberly dressed in black. But neither by his clothes nor by his sharp features could Hearne identify him. Perhaps he was one of Corlay's so-called "negligibles" in the village. Whoever he was, he had noticed them too. He spat out the cigarette stub from between his lips, stepped on it deliberately, and then with his hands still in his pockets and his eyes on Hearne, he sauntered into the hotel. Hearne was left with the feeling that the man had known him. He kept his worry out of his eyes, looked questioningly at Anne.

She shrugged her shoulders. "He doesn't look like a Boche," she said, "but who can tell what kind of visitors we have nowadays?"

So the man was a stranger to St. Déodat. Hearne's worry increased, but he shrugged his shoulders too and said, "Well, I'll see you later. Take care."

She laughed suddenly at the seriousness of his face, and then became dutifully grave. "You must take care, yourself," she answered, and for a moment Hearne's breath stopped. "We all must take care near this place," she added, nodding over her shoulder at the hotel. "Why don't you send Henri for the brandy? He's too old to be recruited for a labor squad."

Hearne smiled and said, "Last time he came down here, he got drunk." She laughed at that, and then she was walking quickly across the square towards the Widow Picrel's shop.

Hearne's pace was slower. There was danger in the hotel, more danger than Anne had even thought. But once he faced the yellow-screened door, he pushed it quickly open, as if by hurry he might get Elise's message and leave before he met that man again.

The bar was empty. As Hearne's footsteps sounded on the bare floor, a door behind the counter opened and Madame Perro appeared. She was as completely waved and corseted as the last time he had seen her. She concealed her welcome as efficiently as her surprise. She reached into the pocket of her apron and produced an envelope. As she handed it over the counter, she unbent enough to incline her head towards the restaurant.

"He's in there," she said, and then turned back to the doorway through which she had entered. It closed decisively behind her spacious hips. She thinks that Corlay is too insignificant for her Elise, Hearne guessed: she sees bigger fish floating round the hotel, now. He looked down at the envelope. In the same square, back-sloping, thick down-stroked letters which spelled Corlay's name was an urgent command across the top of the paper. *Open at once!* It was the Elise touch, all right.

Hearne obeyed. Inside the envelope were the new names he had been promised, along with the numbers which represented their districts on Corlay's map. But what held his attention was the hastily written postscript. *Number 8 is here unexpectedly. See him before he leaves.*

Well, thought Hearne, well. . . . He wished to heaven he were now walking across the stone bridge. If only he could have sent someone else down to the hotel for this envelope, if only— But what was the good of thinking all this? It only wasted time, and he knew it was short now. *"He's in there." See him.* He half-closed his eyes to recall the list of numbered fifth-columnists which he had found in Corlay's bookcase. Number 8. That was Dol. The name was . . . and then his memory, perhaps because he was urging it so strongly, went blank on the name. It stayed tanta-lizingly on the tip of his tongue. It began with B. B . . . Dol was Number 8, Number 8 was B. . . .

And then he heard the parrot-like screech of the restaurant door. He thrust the letter into his pocket, and turned round.

The small man in the black suit was standing there. He still had his hands in his pockets. A fresh cigarette drooped from the corner of the thin lips which stretched tightly between the long jaw and the pointed nose. His head motioned back over his shoulder. Hearne nodded, and came forward. The man let the door, held open by his elbow, creak into place as he turned back into the restaurant. Hearne dodged the swing of the door in time, and pushed it open for himself. Charming fellow, he was thinking as he reached the table, and sat down to face the long jaw over the checked cloth. The man had chosen a table set in the corner of the wall, where no one looking through the door or the window would see them. But that wasn't the only good thing about the table's position, Hearne thought. In this corner, none of the direct light from the windows would reach him. He sat with his arms folded so that the size of his hands was hidden. He kept his feet well under the table and pretended to study the salt shaker and the advertising ash tray. The man's eyes were so deep a brown in color that some of the pigment from the iris seemed to have spilled over and turned the white into yellow. Above the eyes, the fore-head was high and slanting, the hair was dark and receding. The sallow face was watching Hearne with distrust. There was no doubt of that. Hearne restrained himself, and went on looking at the ash tray impas-sively.

"Well," the man said at last. "Surprised?" The voice was high-pitched, almost fretful.

"Yes," admitted Hearne with considerable truth. He was fascinated by the cigarette, still held in place by the colorless lips even as they moved.

"So now we are having our first meeting under the new régime. It is certainly safer, anyway."

"Yes," Hearne agreed, "but is it wise to have one here at this time? I thought we were to avoid being seen with anyone at the hotel, meanwhile. We aren't to come out into the open, yet. Later, but not yet."

"Wise? Sitting in this dump in this God-forgotten hole? No one comes in here any more. They are even avoiding this side of the square. And why do you think I didn't talk to you when you were out there with that girl? Who was she, anyway?"

"Anne Pinot."

"Oh." The truculence in the man's voice gave way to interest. He had obviously known something of Corlay's private affairs. How much? And was that a sign of real friendship with Corlay, or did the man's knowledge come from gossip? His next words with their undisguised sneer gave Hearne a clue. "Oh, your fiancée?" The man was obviously no real friend.

Hearne remained silent, his brow in the frown which Corlay had adopted whenever he was reluctant to talk.

"Still unwilling to take a joke?" The man laughed maliciously, showing an uneven row of fine pointed teeth, complete with handsome gold patchwork. The cigarette clung to the moist lip. "Clever chap, aren't you, Corlay? We always used to laugh at the way you played up to the women. But you got results." He looked round the empty restaurant with undisguised scorn. "You got *this* made the headquarters!"

So that was what was annoying this man. He had, no doubt, thought that his own district would have made handsomer headquarters. Instead, he now felt subsidiary to Corlay, and he didn't like it.

Hearne watched the spreading brown stain on the chewed end of the cigarette. "There are more important reasons than that," he said coldly, "or this place would not have been made the headquarters. Why did you come here?"

The man accepted the change of subject quite as unsuspectingly as Hearne had hoped he would. A change of subject was only natural after the implied snub which had just been administered.

"I came to verify the points in a letter which I received yesterday."

The bitter voice told Hearne as much about the letter as he needed to know. The points in the letter had so confounded this man that he had come here at once to make quite sure there had been no mistake. He couldn't quite believe that the headquarters of the organization, which Hans and Elise had been so skillfully nursing, should really be established here.

Hearne said, "I hope the trip has been worth your while. What instructions did you get?"

"Plenty." The man jabbed the sodden cigarette end into the ash tray, and lit another cigarette. He didn't offer one to Hearne. "Plenty. Including the instructions to wait for you here until you came down this afternoon so that we could compare notes. What are your plans?"

"Just what I've been told. I'm working towards results by stimulating a series of Breton nationalist meetings, and by accenting the importance of co-operation for the achievement of our ideals."

"That would carry you through here, all right," the man assented gloomily. "But down in the towns, it is going to be more difficult. Here, the people are half-asleep. Here, the Germans haven't interfered much with the life of the district so far. But in Dol, it is different. They have been there for some weeks now. They are using many of its people in construction work, and the women don't like it any more than the men. And then I'm told to gather them all together under the banner of co-operation! I tell you, that can't be done unless the Germans don't inter-fere with the people's existence; and they cannot but interfere in impor-tant centers, where large-scale preparations have got to have extra labor. We'll have to use other methods in those towns, I tell you."

Hearne checked his first impulse to soothe the man. Why should he? It would be the best thing he could do if he could encourage a feeling of in-justice and jealousy among Hans's chosen band. He smiled condescend-ingly, tilted his chair back against the wall, and watched the man through half-closed eyes. His obvious enjoyment of the man's predicament infuri-ated the thin nostrils.

"You think it's easy?" the man demanded.

"If you don't, someone else will."

The man stared. "So," he said softly, "if I don't find it easy, someone else will?"

"No doubt," Hearne said placidly, and yawned.

"Do you realize how important my district is? Do you realize how I have worked there for nearly two years? No one else knows all the diffi-culties, the peculiarities, as I do."

"Really?"

"Yes, my fine friend, really. You sit up here with your head in the clouds, thinking out grand phrases for your next speech. But it is I who work."

"And just what gives you the impression that you work more than I do? Just what makes you think Dol should be so much more important than other districts?"

"You must come and visit me some day. We shall make a little tour of the new airfields, of the new underground stores, of the new roads, of the— But what's the use? Nothing I have ever said ever convinced you."

"On the contrary. I am delighted to hear your news, for it shows our strength. As you know, I have just managed to get back to St. Déodat, and until this talk with you I wasn't sure of the progress that has been made during the last month. I used to think that Brittany would only be of political value to our friends. Now, I see that we have still a greater role to play."

"Yes, and more difficult."

"Then all the greater credit will be ours."

"Yes." The man's tone was not wholly confident. "If the right people get the credit," he added spitefully.

"That's to be seen, of course," Hearne said callously, and watched the man's reaction with a good deal of pleasure. "But why worry if *you* don't get the credit, provided the cause is victorious?"

That silenced the thin face opposite him. It was Hearne who had to speak first, after that. He said casually, "I suppose all this preparation is for attack?"

The man looked quickly up at him. "Why do you ask?" he said sharply.

"Because I prefer to be on the attacking side in this war. Defense is unpleasant since the perfection of the bombing plane."

"Oh, you can sleep in your comfortable bed without fear of bombs. We are on the attack."

"Good. The sooner the better."

"It will be quite soon. In six weeks' time. That is definite. England is beaten already. In six weeks' time, the army of occupation will be over in Britain. That will make things easier for us, then."

"You feel there will be nothing to fear here, once the Germans are occupied elsewhere?"

"Nothing to worry about, nothing that can't be taken care of by the Gestapo and a handful of planes. Some will be relieved to find they are on the winning side, although they hadn't the courage to fight for it like you and me. The others, they'll have all the heart taken out of them. That is why Britain must fall. She's the rallying ground of those who want to fight. Once she's gone, they'll be left hopeless, and when they are hopeless, they can be persuaded."

"And that's our job," Hearne said. "How are the rest of our organization? Are we meeting soon?"

"I shall call a meeting for five of them this week, and tell them what I have learned today. Then they will each hold their own meetings, and pass on my report and recommendations. In that way, we will co-ordinate our campaign, although we shall have to use our individual judgment in dealing with the particular problems of our districts. We don't all live in pleasant villages, and plan speeches, you know."

Hearne hesitated, as if he were weighing something carefully in his mind, and then he said quietly, "Are they all to be trusted?"

The man paused in lighting another cigarette. The flame from the small wax match reached his bitten thumbnail, and he dropped the smoking stub with an oath.

"Why shouldn't they be?" he said slowly. "They've all risked death for the rewards they will now get. Rewards never dulled loyalty."

"That's the point. Rewards. There may be a division of opinion about these. After all, you and I understand each other. You have a difficult, and an important, district to organize successfully. I have to make important speeches. We aren't competing. We are each sure of the rewards for our loyalty." Hearne watched the man's eyes and was content with the uncertainty which he saw there. Hearne continued calmly, "But the others may not be so sure of the results for themselves. They may be impatient. Be very careful with them. They may interpret our efforts in a wrong light, even carry tales to our German friends in order to discredit us."

The man said nothing, but there was a look of speculation in his eyes as they stared at the wall above Hearne's head. The idea which Hearne had sown was firmly planted. It would bear sour fruit.

Hearne became businesslike. He talked of the next meeting, of the problems which must be covered before it would take place. The man from Dol listened, and made his counter-suggestions as Hearne had guessed he would. That type always had a counter-suggestion ready. Then counter-suggestion gave way to detailed instructions, which were obviously pulled out of his memory. He repeated them too glibly not to have heard them only some hours before. Some of the phrases he used might have come straight from Elise's mouth.

"Good," Hearne said at last, "now, what about a date for the next meeting?" As the man searched through a small diary of closely written pages and licked the point of a pencil, Hearne was thinking of Kerénor, of Kerénor and the use to which he might put the nationalist meetings which the Nazis were going to encourage. Kerénor, if he could get his warnings to the various districts about the true meaning of these meetings, if he and other true Bretons could use these gatherings for their own purposes, could start the beginning of a powerful movement against the Germans. The Nazis would regret some day that they had encouraged the Bretons to get together. And the Bretons would play their own secret game very well. Hearne smiled to himself as he thought of the enjoyment they would get out of duping the Germans.

"What about the twentieth of this month?" the man asked. Hearne made a great pretense of concentrating.

"Good," he agreed at last. "Now where? In Dol? Café de la Grande-Rue, as usual?"

The man was pleased at the choice of locality. He nodded almost amiably, and marked a neat cross in his diary. "I'll inform the others," he said decisively.

I bet you will, thought Hearne. He said, "Any other particular news? You must have been busy in the last month."

The man nodded, holding his head to one side so that the curling cigarette smoke would avoid his eyes. Then suddenly, he began to talk. The temptation to show the speech-making Corlay just how little he knew about what was going on couldn't be resisted. He plunged into long details mixed with complaints and boasts. Hearne listened, his face set in an expressionless mask. Whenever the man slackened in his descriptions, Hearne would look only half-convinced, even skeptical. That was enough to start the flow again. But at the end, he gave the man the satisfaction of seeing a Corlay who was visibly impressed by the importance of the small town of Dol and its surroundings.

At last Hearne rose. "Mustn't stay too long in the hotel, meanwhile," he explained.

The man nodded. "It is sort of funny too, to see you again. We all thought you were missing for good. Marbeuf said the last he saw of you was someone dying on a wharf at Dunkirk with a couple of English soldiers lying beside him."

"Marbeuf? And how did he get away?" Good old Marbeuf, Hearne thought, whoever Marbeuf was. But he obviously wasn't someone who had stopped to see how he could help Corlay.

"A French boat took him off. How did you get away?"

"On the next French boat. I wasn't so good at using my elbows as Marbeuf. And tell him I wasn't dying. A shell exploded too near me, but I was lucky and the most I got was a bad shock. Sorry to disappoint you all."

"Same old Corlay, aren't you?"

"Only more so." Hearne stared fixedly at the small thin man.

"All right, all right," he said hastily. "Believe me, I am delighted to find that Marbeuf was wrong."

"You aren't half as delighted as I am."

"All right, all—" And then the restaurant door was opened, and two German officers marched in. They halted their stride as they saw the two men at the table. The smaller officer was Traube, the auctioneer's clerk who had surveyed the Corlay farm. He was peering uncertainly through his glasses, and then nodded as he recognized Hearne.

"Good afternoon, Lieutenant Traube," Hearne said confidently. "I hope you are well, and Captain Deichgräber, too."

"Yes, yes. Captain Deichgräber is away at present, but he will be back shortly. I see you and Vuillemin have been taking the opportunity to have a little talk."

"Quite right, Lieutenant Traube." Vuillemin, Vuillemin. . . . Something was wrong somewhere.

The other officer didn't trouble to conceal his impatience. He said quickly to the strangely silent Frenchman beside Hearne, "You are leaving now? Good. It would be better not to come to St. Déodat again until you receive definite instructions to do so." He nodded abruptly, and continued his way to another table. He slapped its top with his gloves. "Service!" he called loudly as he sat down, seemingly quite unaware now of the two Frenchmen. Traube nodded in turn, looked embarrassed, and joined the other officer.

Hearne noted that all the confidence had left his companion. As he rose to leave the restaurant and the loud foreign voices, he was still silent. Hearne glanced at his face, and felt satisfied. The small thin man had not failed to mark the Germans' contempt for an ally. He returned Hearne's look, and that seemed to depress him even more, as if Hearne's set expression only verified his own fears.

"So then, until the twentieth!" Hearne said at the door.

The man nodded. He looked smaller, thinner. He wasn't paying any attention to Hearne. His eyes were fixed on the restaurant door which he had closed behind him.

By the time Hearne had reached the end of the hotel street, the Frenchman had disappeared. Hearne paused. And then, quickly, he turned and retraced his steps.

In the restaurant, the two German officers halted their conversation only as he reached their table. Hearne stood beside them and waited for them to finish their phrases. Traube cocked his head inquiringly.

"Herr Lieutenant Traube . . ." Hearne began in a low voice.

"Yes?"

The other officer wasn't even looking at Hearne.

"That man from Dol . . ."

"Yes?" Traube blinked his eyes anxiously.

"He's behaving strangely. Doesn't like taking orders."

"So." Traube glanced nervously at his companion, as if asking for help.

The other German poured himself some more wine. "I had noticed that," he said in his precise voice. "I had noticed that. Pity he should be at Dol, of all places. How long can you control him?"

"How long do you want him to be controlled?" Hearne's voice was that of a dutiful, eager and ambitious man. But he still kept his words low. Hurry, he was saying to himself; hurry, or that little shrimp from Dol will be in here on top of you.

It was Traube who said quickly, "Until the fifteenth of August. There must be no trouble before then. After the fifteenth we shall have more time to deal with him, if he doesn't behave more rationally."

"The fifteenth," Hearne said thoughtfully. "The fifteenth . . . it isn't so long until then."

"It isn't so long," Traube's companion said. His lips were actually smiling. Then he was serious again. "But if you have definite suspicions about that man, then remove him at once. We can't risk any treachery."

"I've no proof. I only had a feeling today that he was a waverer. With the proper supervision, he should be safe."

"Well, give him that supervision." The German's voice was irritable once more. "See that he's satisfied." He turned to Traube. "Would it be difficult to replace him now?"

Traube said, "Well, he knows a lot. He's been trained under us for two years. And he has done some good work in the past."

"In that case, keep him working with us. Promise him anything. Later, when we are less occupied with important plans . . ." The officer removed a thread from his sleeve.

Hearne knew he was dismissed. "Very good." He clicked his heels as he took one step back. "Then you suggest I should pay an unexpected visit to our little friend at Dol? I shall make a report on that visit."

The captain nodded. Traube, watching him anxiously, said, "Yes, yes. You will be held responsible if you cannot control him. And when you visit Dol, see Major Kalb of the Schutzstaffel. He is in charge of the organization of that town."

Hearne raised his arm in the approved salute, barked the magic words, wheeled neatly towards the door.

The captain's voice, speaking in German now, carried farther than he had intended. Or perhaps he thought that this man Corlay wouldn't know much German, anyway. ". . . set a Frenchman to catch a Frenchman," he was saying. "But I advise you to set one of Ehrlich's men, too, Traube. And advise Deichgräber on his return, of course." Traube was mumbling a reply. "Deichgräber . . . Ehrlich . . ." was all that Hearne could catch, as he stepped out into the deserted street.

Hearne walked quickly back to the farm, arranging in his mind the information he had learned in the last hour, so that the facts which he had sifted would go neatly and easily down onto paper. It was at the dovecote that he halted, as he suddenly remembered. His subconscious had at last yielded up the name which had been haunting him. "Vuillemin," he repeated. It wasn't Vuillemin. The man was Number 8 from Dol, and the name was Bruneau. Bruneau, not Vuillemin. Vuillemin was Number 9. Now the reason for the man's worry became quite clear. The German ally had not only shown his contempt: he had even not considered it necessary to learn the right name. And the fear which Hearne had sown in the man's mind would be strengthened. What chance was there for proper rewards and recognition for Bruneau, when he was just as easily called Vuillemin?

But Hearne hadn't time to be amused. He was too busy thanking his stars that his caution with names had prevented him from imitating the German. "So then, Vuillemin, until the twentieth." That would have sounded well enough at the time. But it would have been an unsatisfactory way to end one's career.

He was concentrating on the facts he had learned from Bruneau as he climbed towards the Corlay farm. That was one way to stop thinking about the thinness of the ice over which he had performed such an elaborate outside edge. And then he realized that it wasn't his stars he should thank: it was Matthews.

CHAPTER 15 THE GOLDEN STAR

As the crow flew, it was fourteen miles to St. Servan, sixteen to St. Malo. But it took Myles and Hearne from sunset in St. Déodat to the cold gray sky of the heartless hour before dawn to reach the outskirts of St. Servan. They had avoided the villages and the roads, had skirted farms and isolated houses.

It had been a strange journey, with the tall American, dressed in the corduroy trousers and blue smock and round black felt hat of Madame Corlay's uncle, plodding determinedly beside an equally silent Hearne. When they had to speak, they spoke softly, abruptly and in French. That had been Hearne's advice. He had also stipulated that, if by some stroke of bad luck or piece of carelessness they were intercepted, the American must then forget he had ever seen the Corlay farm. He would have to produce his own story. Hearne, in his turn, would have to admit that he had never seen the American before: that they had met only by the sheerest accident in that field or that wood over there. With Bertrand Corlay's name attached to him, they would eventually believe him; and the excuse to Elise for this night journey would have to be tied up with the name of one of the men on Corlay's list. He was to have a free hand in his decisions, she had said. He was to keep his business meetings secret from the Bretons. Elise would believe him, too.

But he felt a wave of relief when he saw the spreading estuary of the River Rance flowing towards the Channel coast. Ahead of them should be the straggling outskirts of St. Servan, forming a kind of suburb to the old walled town of St. Malo. Here, where the two men had halted, the dismal string of small houses and small shops and flagrant billboards had not yet begun. Here, the fields and trees still met the steep banks of the river. Here, where the tides had swirled out a muddy inlet, there were still small groupings of simple houses, with their inevitable jetties and anchored boats and drying fishing nets. They could be called fishermen's villages, if barely a dozen cottages could be said to form a village. Hearne and Myles had passed two such communities, scarcely a mile apart.

"We should be almost there," Hearne said, more to reassure himself than to encourage Myles. "There are only seven houses and a pub. It's called the Golden Star. The pub, that is. We *must* be almost there." We've got to be, he added to himself, as he looked at the sky.

"Perhaps we are." Myles pointed to the fishing nets stretched between the tall poles just ahead of them. Down on the river, two black shapes of boats with furled sails pulled against their moorings. Three other smaller boats lay drunkenly on the smooth mud, where the tide had abandoned them. And then they saw the row of houses, built at the very edge of the riverbank. Some of them had ends which overshot the bank and were supported by props driven into the shore itself. At high tide, the water would lap under these gable ends themselves. Now, they looked as hunched and precarious as a man slumping over his crutches.

Myles and Hearne strained their eyes.

"Can't be sure, in this light," admitted Hearne at last. "You stay here, well in the shadow of this tree. I'll have a look."

"Sure." Myles sat down thankfully. His voice was cheery enough, but there was a drawn look in his face.

"Feet?"

"Blast them."

"Wait here."

"Sure."

*   *   *

The houses hugged each other tightly as if to give themselves courage. Even so, the only word to describe them was "dejected." They needed plaster and paint: that was obvious even in this half-light. In their sleep, they looked as sluttish as a sagging woman with twisted rags in her hair. Hearne counted them carefully. They looked like eight altogether, if they began and ended where he thought they did. That was the difficulty with a row of houses: it would have been simple if they had been clearly separate. One was a pub. That at least was definite. Despite its lack of paint, the lettering was still visible: faint but visible. "Etoi . . . 'Or." That must be it. Etoile d'Or. That must be it, although the three middle letters had given up all hope, and faded away entirely. Like the other houses, the Golden Star was dark and silent. It stood at the end of the row of buildings, and in its dark side wall was an insignificant door. Hearne took a deep breath. He had found the name *and* the side door. This was the place. It had to be.

He tried the handle. It turned easily. So far, so good. Inside, another door faced him. That was correct, too. He let the outside door swing behind him and stood in the dark coffin of space between the double entrance. This time he knocked: three short raps, two long. Pause. Again three short, two long. It was so dark that he couldn't even see his hand. All he was aware of was the smell of fish and decaying seaweed which still persisted here, and mingled in its own peculiar way with the stale odor of fried oil and damp walls. He knocked again in the same way. Wish to God that Basdevant would come, he thought desperately. Apart from the nausea which gripped him, he was haunted by the thought of the steadily approaching dawn, spreading inexorably from the east. As

for the possibility that Basdevant might no longer be functioning here—
well, that was something he couldn't even start worrying about. Without
this Basdevant, there was only a long dangerous walk ahead of them towards Mont St. Michel and the archeologist Duclos. He waited, rehearsing
the phrases which that worried French Intelligence man in London had
taught him. Basdevant would be six feet and broad-shouldered. He would
have black hair, black-brown eyes, an aquiline nose, a red complexion,
strongly marked eyebrows and a bottle scar on his left temple. What the
hell was keeping Basdevant?

And then the door opened suddenly and a lamp was held in front of
his face so that it blinded him. He stood there, with his eyes screwed up
tightly, his hands half-raised to shield them from the glare. He cursed his
over-caution in not carrying his revolver: he had thought that his name
of Corlay would be better protection than bullets as long as Elise and
her Hans could vouch for him.

A deep voice said truculently, "What do you want?"

"This is an inn, isn't it?"

"Yes. But it's closed."

"Well, it's open now. I've money to pay for what we eat." Or rather,
Myles had. The few francs which Madame Corlay had given him might
be needed for the return journey.

"We?" The man's voice was friendlier. He shifted the weight of the
lamp, and Hearne had a chance to see him.

"Two of us." Hearne could make out the man's face. Yes, this must be
Basdevant. Fournier had indeed given an accurate description. At this
moment, the man's black hair was ruffled, his feet were bare, his clothing
consisted of a shirt.

"It's cold here," Hearne said suddenly, remembering Fournier's careful
coaching. He spoke slowly. "We could talk better in front of your fire, if
the wood is still burning."

"The wood is still burning." Basdevant stepped aside to let him enter.

Hearne hesitated a moment. Perhaps the man was getting careless, or
perhaps the identification formula had to be shortened to suit the memories of his new clients. They wouldn't be only Deuxième Bureau, now:
probably most of them, if not all, were fugitives.

"I'll get my friend," Hearne said and turned towards the door at his
back. The man hurriedly blew out the light. There was darkness behind
Hearne as he descended the three stone steps into the road, and Basdevant's voice, low, urgent.

"Hurry," he said, "hurry. Daylight is breaking."

The American was still sitting as Hearne had left him. He rose stiffly,
clumsily, to his feet. He was trying to stop himself shivering in the raw
morning air.

"All clear. We'll get something to eat and drink," Hearne said, and helped the limping Myles to hurry his steps. He, too, felt suddenly pretty low in the water. He blamed it on lack of sleep. Lack of sleep, he thought. Two nights over hills and fields, two nights scrabbling under hedges, two nights floundering through muddy paths. Two cold dawns with needle rain which stung your skin and froze your blood. Two waking nightmares, he thought.

"We'll get something to eat and drink," he repeated. And then as they were almost at the door, he remembered to add, "Don't say what you want to eat or drink. I'll do the ordering."

Myles nodded. His face was colorless and lined with fatigue.

"Cheer up," Hearne said, "you won't have to walk over the Channel." If Myles could have given a smile, Hearne would have had one.

The outside door opened easily and again Hearne noted that the hinges had been well-oiled. But this time, the inner door was open too. They closed it behind them, and stood together in the darkness. Hearne unconsciously kept hold of the American's elbow.

Basdevant's deep voice said, "Is that door closed properly?"

"Yes."

A match grated and flared. The lamp was lit once more. Basdevant smiled amiably and spoke again. "This way, gentlemen. Had to make sure about the door. The night air is treacherous." He was standing at the other end of the short corridor; behind him was the entrance to a room. He had added a pair of faded red sailcloth trousers to his shirt. He jerked a large thumb over his shoulder. "There's a fire in here," he said, and led the way into the room.

The ceiling was low, so low that the Breton only had to sling the handle of the lamp over a hook in one of the wooden beams just above his head, and the room was lighted. And there was a fire, with flames leaping comfortably on the wide stone hearth. Myles sat down heavily on the wooden bench at one side of the fireplace. Hearne stood in front of the blaze and held his numbed fingers out towards the heat of the newly added log. He heard the sound of a bottle knocking against a glass. He took the thick tumbler which Basdevant held out to him. The raw brandy stung his throat, but it was what he needed. Myles had emptied his glass too; perhaps it was the warmth of the fire, or the fact that his weight was off his feet, or that he was becoming accustomed to the strange smell of the house, but he suddenly seemed cheerier. Or, thought Hearne, perhaps he just needed that brandy as much as I did.

Basdevant was moving skillfully about among the disorder of the room. He noticed Hearne's expression. "This is my own corner," he said with a broad smile. "It's warmer here than in the front room. You see I like to live comfortably." He swept his powerful arm round the unbelievable chaos. "Now, what would you like to eat?"

Myles looked at Hearne, and then bent down to unlace his boots. Hearne said slowly and distinctly, "Cold mutton and some goat cheese."

"And to drink?" A still broader smile was spreading over the Breton's face.

"Water."

Myles paused in the unlacing of his boots and looked sadly at Hearne. The Englishman looked as if he meant what he said, but he was thinking how very unpleasant it would be if Basdevant were to take him at his word.

"Dry your clothes on that line," Basdevant said as he picked up a smoke-blackened pan from the table and set its chain handle on a hook over the glowing log. He was pointing to a dirty piece of rope which was stretched across the front of the stone mantelpiece. Like all of Basdevant's arrangements, it was practical even if it wasn't beautiful. It looked worse when their bedraggled clothes were strung over the sagging piece of rope. Hearne had hung his jacket carefully, so that the two neat packages in his inside jacket pocket wouldn't be dislodged. He resisted the impulse to take them out and hold them in his hand: better, he decided quickly, to leave them where they were, to let the others think there was nothing of value in his pocket. He ostentatiously removed his penknife, his few francs, and the map. He opened it up to dry it, so that Basdevant could see what it was. But he remained standing at the side of the fireplace, watching the oil crackle in the heated pan. Even when the Frenchman handed him a red-checked tablecloth with which to rub himself down, he didn't move away from the fire and the drying clothes. Nor did he step aside when Basdevant tossed some fish carelessly into the pan. This time, the odor which filled the room was not unpleasant.

"Sorry," Hearne said, as Basdevant bumped against him. "This fire is too good to leave." As he finished drying himself with the tablecloth, he was looking round the room. The door by which they had entered was on the same side as the fireplace. Opposite them was a crumpled bed. In the wall which probably overhung the river was one small window, heavily curtained, and a flight of stairs leading to the rooms overhead. Opposite that was a wall filled with wardrobes and chairs, and in that wall was a second door. Hearne guessed that it might lead into the front room: bar was probably its real function.

Basdevant was watching him. "Cosy here, isn't it?" he asked. "How do you like the decorations?"

There was something in the big man's voice which impelled him to look at the calendars and advertisements hung on the walls. Cinzano . . . Byrrh . . . Quinquina . . . Berger. . . . From this distance they all looked equally gaudy, equally innocuous.

"Very pretty," Hearne murmured. Basdevant was still looking at him. Hearne's eyes flickered again over the dim walls to see what he had missed.

Two small pieces of paper were pinned up over the bed. The Breton had left the fireplace and was now clearing a place for their meal at the table by raking his forearm across one of its corners. Hearne crossed the room towards the bed. Two pieces of paper: two certificates. One was birth, the other first communion. Both belonged to Louis Basdevant.

Hearne came back to the fireplace. "Cold away from the fire," he said. The Breton had found the plates he was looking for. As he came over to the cooking fish, he smiled at Hearne and nodded as if to say, "You see. I'm your man all right." Hearne smiled back. He was as amazed as he always was whenever he saw someone so big and powerful as this being so incredibly naïve. It amazed and pleased him. But that was the natural reaction, he reflected, of someone who only measured five feet ten.

"Now we can eat," Basdevant said. "And drink. And then we can talk, if you're still awake."

"Which reminds me," Hearne said, "have you a room we can rent?"

"And have you some clothes?" It was Myles who spoke, rising slowly from the wooden bench. He said in English to Hearne, "It's no fun being a nudist. I just about left half of my skin on that chair."

"What did he say?" Basdevant was looking with interest at Myles. Hearne translated freely. The Breton threw back his head and laughed. With a pair of gold earrings skewered through his ears, he would have made a fine corsair.

"Of course," he said. "I forgot." Now, did you really, thought Hearne and looked at Basdevant's broad back reflectively as he carried the fish to the table. "Take a blanket from the bed. Hurry, or the fish will be spoiled," the Breton called over his shoulder.

"And so," he continued, as they held a dark gray blanket round them with one hand and ate the fish with the other, "and so, you are English?"

"American," Myles said quickly.

"We haven't sailed anyone as far as that yet." Basdevant laughed again. There was a gold tooth in the back of his mouth. That was what had started thoughts of earrings, Hearne realized. He saw one of Myles's eyebrows raised. This unexpected mention of sailing had probably interested him. It certainly interested Hearne: everything was being made very easy for them. It must be pleasant working in the Deuxième Bureau.

Basdevant was talking volubly, with smiles and quick gestures and a general air of comradeship. They might have known him for years. Myles and Hearne found themselves smiling and nodding at the right places as they listened. "It's strange," Basdevant was saying, "very strange. Once we used to fish over towards the English coast. But did the fishermen in Cornwall welcome us? Not they. You'd have thought we had been fishing right within their waters! Well, that didn't worry us. Who's to say where one bit of sea ends and the other begins? It all flows together, doesn't it? So, when we were right close to the shore, we'd pay a little visit to these

Cornishmen. Just to show there were no hard feelings on our part. And we'd get some food, or a sail patched up, or a net mended when we were there. I remember a place called St. Ives. . . . Ever been there?" Myles and Hearne shook their heads. But for Hearne there was a tingle of pleasure as he heard the name, even pronounced as it was. "Well, in St. Ives there was an inn just down by the harbor where they used to sell their catches of fish. We used to go there for a drink, perhaps two, perhaps three. And as we were very sorry for those poor fishermen in Cornwall, we'd tell them how to catch fish. Well, then there might be a fight. These Englishmen used to lose their tempers very quickly. But they didn't fight as well as we did. They used their fists, or perhaps, when they got very angry, a bottle. But that's no way to fight."

"Knives?" suggested Hearne with a suspicion of a smile. He remembered some of the scenes in St. Ives when the foreign poachers (every Cornish fisherman swore they poached) started drinking in the local pubs. First, wary silence; then boasts; then arguments and loud oaths; then blows, and knives, and broken bottles. It was always the same pattern. It ended with the Bretons slashing their way to their boats, cursing the English vividly as they ran; with the Cornishmen shaking bruised knuckles after their visitors, yelling to them to bloody well stick to their own bloody side of the bloody fishing grounds. And then three weeks later, the Bretons would be back, smiling their way towards a bar, talking loudly of the good catches they had had, in their perfectly understandable form of English. The strangest thing of all to Hearne was to know that the Bretons were more closely related to the Cornishmen than they were to other Frenchmen, or than the Cornishmen were related to other Englishmen.

"Why didn't the Englishmen stave in your boats?" asked the practical Myles. Hearne watched Basdevant's face in amusement.

"Stave in our boats?" he shouted incredulously. It was obvious that the idea had never occurred to him. Fishermen didn't take away each other's life, that way. Poach? Yes . . . but not destroy.

"You were saying something was very strange," suggested Myles.

"Ah, yes." Basdevant relaxed again. He would be an ugly customer in a fight. Whoever had given him that bottle scar was a brave man, if he still lived.

"Yes, it's strange. For now, when we go, we are given a fine welcome fit for a prince. You should see the way they welcome the lobsters we bring over, now." He paused, as if to let his words sink into his guests' minds. "When do you want to sail?" he asked suddenly.

"Tonight," Myles said.

Basdevant thought for some moments. His heavy eyebrows were bushed over his brown eyes. He said at last, "The tide will be difficult. What about tomorrow night?" He didn't wait for a reply. "Fine," he said. "Tomorrow night."

Myles looked quickly at Hearne, but he was picking the last bones carefully out of his piece of fish.

It was excellent fish.

CHAPTER **16** TRIAL FOR A TRAITOR

It was cold in the room upstairs in the Golden Star, and it seemed all the colder because of the bareness of the place. Three narrow beds, a mattress on the floor, a rain-spotted window overlooking the river, a chair. That was all.

"Why did you bring the clothes up here?" asked Myles.

"They were dry." They damned well weren't dry, thought Myles, and Hearne knew it as well as he did. He spread his trousers and shirt flat on the wooden floor, thoughtfully.

"We'll sleep well," Hearne said very clearly in French, and sat down heavily on the nearest bed. It creaked satisfactorily. "There are enough blankets, anyway. We have thirty-six hours for sleep. That should be enough." He yawned loudly.

Myles finished arranging his clothes and his boots. He looked towards the door and pointed silently. One eyebrow was up.

Hearne nodded. The American sat noisily down on the bed next Hearne's and yawned in turn. The two men rolled the blankets tightly round themselves, and then lay still. The rain had stopped. There was morning sunshine outside the window, and a smooth stretch of blue sky.

When they at last heard the sound of Basdevant's large feet moving about in the room below, Hearne raised himself on an elbow. He whispered, "We'll sleep in relays."

"You can begin. I got some shut-eye yesterday. It is only my feet which worry me. What's wrong, anyway?"

Hearne considered for a moment. He owed the American a warning. He couldn't expect any intelligent co-operation if he kept Myles completely in the dark.

"What do you think of all this?" he asked Myles.

"I liked the fire and the food."

"And Basdevant?"

"He's a big fellow, very big."

"That's just about what I thought."

The two men looked at each other and grinned.

Hearne said, "To be quite frank, I don't like it."

"Strong smell of fish," agreed Myles. And then, he was suddenly serious. "Isn't that buzzard all right? You should know."

"I thought I did. He's certainly the man I was looking for. I got his name from someone reliable." Or was Fournier reliable? God, nowadays you had even doubts of your own grandmother, Hearne thought. Or was he being too jittery, worrying over trifles, finding suspicions where there should be none? Lack of sleep, probably: perhaps if he got some sleep he would stop seeing mysteries.

The sky outside the window was a pale, ruthless blue.

"Well?" the American asked. "I'm old enough to know."

The footsteps still moved about downstairs.

Hearne spoke quickly. "This is the place, and that is the man. He's probably just careless, or simple, or good-natured. I'm probably dizzy with sleep and cursed with a doubting mind. But, first of all, he let us into the house without proper identification. He seemed eager to get us inside. He was eager to identify himself. He was eager to get down to business. He made all the moves. And then he didn't like our idea of bringing our clothes up here. It was he who suggested we should dry them at the fire, but he didn't rush to offer us any others, although he was a good host in every other way. Last of all, he said the tide wouldn't be right: that was an excuse for a couple of landlubbers. We seemed that, all right, by suggesting something about a hole being knocked in someone's boat."

"That explains a lot," Myles said. "Now, I'll add my nickel's worth. He lives too damned well. Did you notice the oil he wasted when he fried that fish? I'm telling you there hasn't been a farmhouse in my travels which slopped the oil about that way. And there was butter, even if it did taste like a goat. And cheese, a big one at that. And brandy, and red wine, and good coffee, and cigarettes. It's what I would call pre-armistice standard. Look, you've a farm and the Germans have only started to penetrate your district, but you live more carefully than he does. He's slap bang beside St. Malo, and the Germans have settled nicely into the place by this time: I bet every inch of bread, every spoonful of oil in the district is noted down in their little black notebooks."

"We are making a nice case out of very little," Hearne said. "He may smuggle a lot of things in here, by his boat. He seems to enjoy poaching. He may even—" He paused. The room below was silent. There might have been a movement at the foot of the stairs.

Myles had noted it, too. "Sleep," he whispered.

Hearne added a few snores to that advice. He felt warm and comfortable. The food and wine and brandy were doing their work. Another five minutes of pretending, and he would act himself into sleep. He heard the door open slightly. Myles stirred, turning in the way which light sleepers do at the suspicion of a noise. Then the door was closed again; careful footsteps descended the steep wooden stairs.

"You sleep," Myles whispered again. "I'll keep watch."

"Half an hour. Wake me then. We may have to be ready to move on."

Myles nodded his agreement.

The blue of the sky was bolder.

Myles was wakening him, shaking him lightly but determinedly.

"Sorry," the American was saying, "but I thought I'd better let you in on this. I can't get the hang of the accent."

Hearne sat up in bed, shaking his head to waken himself fully. The room was now warm with the sunlight which streamed through the window. *Later than I meant to be,* he thought. The clothes stretched out on the floor were crumpled but dry enough.

He looked at Myles and grinned. "That's better," he said. "I feel much better."

"I thought you needed more than a half hour. You'll be able to run all the faster, if we have to. But look!" He pointed to the half-open door. Standing in the shadows was a thin boy in Breton fishing clothes. "I've been struggling with his language for five minutes. He's nearly bawling because he can't understand me."

The boy spoke, his dark, anxious face looking at Hearne expectantly.

"The gentleman speaks French?" His accent was pure Breton.

"Yes. What is it?"

"My sister sent me."

"Well?"

"She says you are to hurry."

"Where?"

"You must go away."

"Now?"

The boy nodded.

"Why?"

The boy looked anxiously over his shoulder.

"Please," he said.

"Where's your sister?"

"Downstairs in the bar."

"Where's Basdevant?"

"Big Louis has gone to St. Malo. He will be back in an hour, perhaps more, perhaps less. My sister is in the bar."

A sudden light dawned on Hearne. "You mean she's in charge?"

"Yes."

"Who else is there?"

"The others."

"What others?"

"The men who live here: all except big Louis and Corbeau."

"Who's Corbeau?"

"Big Louis takes him on his boat now. He's his cousin."

"And your sister sent you up here. . . . Did the others know she sent you up?"

"Yes."

Hearne bit his lip. Myles, watching the boy's face intently, said in English, "He's scared stiff at what he's doing."

Hearne suddenly got out of bed. "We'll dress and go down and see this sister. Better hurry. How are the feet?"

"Could be worse."

They dressed quickly and silently. The boy's face relaxed. His brown eyes were smiling now.

He led the way down the rickety stairs. In Basdevant's living room, he halted and pointed to the door by which they had entered this dawn.

"No thank you," Hearne said, "we want to see your sister, first." He moved towards the door which lay opposite the window in the room. His guess last night had been that it led to the bar. He had probably been right: even now, with his hand on its latch, he could hear voices arguing.

The boy tried to catch his arm. "Not that way. This way." He pointed again.

"It's all right, sonny. We're friends," Myles was saying. "We only want to thank your sister." As the boy turned his head to answer the American, Hearne opened the door.

The noise inside the little room with its four marble-topped tables, its dark wood counter, its brightly colored calendars and paper flowers on the walls, ceased abruptly. Five men, their faces bronzed and lined from sea and wind; three boys, large-eyed and alert; a dark-haired woman leaning over the counter. That was all. They seemed to be one person as they turned and looked at Hearne and Myles. However divided had been the opinions which had caused their violent discussion, they were now united in thought and reaction as they faced the strangers.

"Pierre," the woman said angrily, "I told you—"

"We insisted on coming to thank you," Hearne cut in. "This isn't Pierre's fault."

Someone cleared his throat, feet shuffled, but no one spoke.

At last the woman said, "You've thanked me. Now go as you came."

"In this daylight?"

"It is safer now than at night."

"But we have a bill to pay," the American said.

"We don't want your money."

"Big Louis will."

The woman shrugged her shoulders. "Go now," she insisted.

Myles exchanged a look with Hearne. "You handle this," he said in English. "The smell of fish is stronger."

Hearne nodded. He put his elbows on the counter of the bar, and leaned forward so that his face was no more than a foot across from the woman's. She wasn't so old as he had thought. Her resemblance to the boy Pierre was extraordinary: there was that same thin, high-cheeked shape of face, the same broad brow and deep-set brown eyes. The fine black hair was smoothed into a knot at the nape of her neck. There was color in her cheeks, and her skin was tanned as deeply as the men's. She wasn't so old after all; probably not even thirty. The lines and little wrinkles on her face came from strong sun and sea wind, not from age. The large eyes, fixed on him so intently, were young, and so were her strong arms and hands. It was the severity of her hair, the seriousness of her face, the fine lines on her skin which had made her seem more like Pierre's mother than his sister. He kept his eyes on hers, and a smile on his lips, as he fumbled in his mind for a beginning. A dull red flush mounted over the color in her cheeks and surged down into her neck. She moved a step backwards from the counter, and stood under the vase of paper flowers which had been hooked to the wall. But her eyes were still fixed on his.

"Please go," she said. Her voice was quieter, now.

"Yes, we are going. And we thank you for warning us. But we must find out why you warned us, so that in turn we can warn any others who might come here, as we did."

"You could stop them from coming?" The woman's face was suddenly animated with relief.

"We could stop many."

She turned to the boy quickly. "Pierre, go down and wait at the jetty. When you see him coming, let us know." Pierre left the room obediently. Myles and Hearne exchanged glances. So it was big Louis, all right.

"We'll have a drink," Hearne said. "We'll all have a drink." The silent men behind him were beginning to worry him. "What about a drink?" he said to them. Two of them came forward, the others hesitated and then followed.

The woman uncorked a bottle of a white colorless liquid. She shook her head as she said, "You are in danger by staying."

"We'll be all right. We wakened and came down for a drink. If he comes, then we pretend nothing has happened, that you didn't warn us. And we'll leave at the first chance we get." That seemed partly to satisfy her: she was pouring the drinks carefully into the small thick tumblers.

"Tell us one thing," Hearne said. "Would it be impossible to sail from here tonight?"

The men were amused: he must have said something highly funny.

"Is the tide unfavorable?"

The men were trying to hide their laughs. One of them failed. It was the seaman's prerogative over the stupid landlubber.

"Stop that," the woman said sharply to them. She turned towards

Hearne and Myles politely. "The tides never prevent us from sailing on this part of the river at any time. There's a deep channel in the middle."

"Big Louis said the tide was wrong tonight. That was why we must wait until tomorrow."

The men were amused no longer. The mention of big Louis had frozen them into silent watchfulness. Again Hearne had the feeling that he was facing an individual, and not five men and one woman. Myles was pretending to concentrate on his drink, but his eyes were missing nothing.

Hearne went on calmly, "Are there any German-lovers here?"

The effect was electric. The woman's eyes dilated and then narrowed. Two of the men slipped their hands into their pockets. Myles reached for the bottle casually as if to pour himself another drink, but he paused with his fingers round its neck. One of the younger men suddenly cursed, spat into his drink and pushed it away from him so violently that the glass upset.

"I knew you weren't," Hearne said in the same unhurried tone, "but I had to make sure. You do not look like the type of men who would lick the soles of the Germans' feet. Some do; and some even like the taste of it."

"So what?" the young man asked, his cold blue eyes hard with anger. He looked as if Hearne's words had soured the saliva on his tongue.

"What will the other fishermen on this river begin to say about you when they learn that big Louis sells their allies to their enemies? And they will learn some day. You can't hide such things: they come out."

"That is our business." It was the oldest fisherman who spoke. The others nodded. Only the woman and the man with the angry eyes looked as if they didn't agree with that, but they said nothing. Those Celts, thought Hearne irritably: clannish was another word for them. He was the stranger sticking his nose into their business. They could say what they liked to each other about Basdevant, but they would have no foreigner criticizing him for them. And a foreigner was anyone who had not been born and brought up in this little village of eight houses.

"That is your business," Hearne agreed. "You must deal with him yourselves. But what if other men come here for help? Will you stand aside and let the Boches catch them? And what is going to happen to you if Basdevant quarrels with any of you and informs the Germans that you helped men to escape from him?"

"He wouldn't do that," the old man said, but his tone lacked conviction.

It was the woman who spoke next. "I'm sick and tired to death of hearing you men talk. Shall we do this, shall we do that? You argue yourselves into your graves. First, let Jules tell what he knows, what we all know. Then these two men will go away, and we alone shall deal with big Louis and that Corbeau he brought here to help him. This man is right: big

Louis is on trial. I didn't lose two brothers and my father in this war for other men to grow fat on the leavings of their murderers. Jules, tell what you know."

The young man with the angry blue eyes said, "At first, everything was as it should be. When I got back from the war, I helped with the others. We'd sail out to fish, and we'd take any man who had come to big Louis, and we'd meet the English boats, and sometimes we'd land them in England ourselves. We know places on that coast like the back of our hand. We didn't ask for money. If they had any, they gave us it. If they didn't, well that didn't matter. We helped nine men to escape. Some were French, some were English, one was a Pole. Five days ago, we no longer had to sail so far. Big Louis said he and the Corbeau could do it by themselves. It was safer that way, he said. And then he seemed to have money, and food. He gave us good reasons. We could say nothing."

There was a general murmur from the men, and a shuffling of feet.

"But two days ago I was in St. Malo, and there I saw something." Jules paused. He looked gravely from Myles to Hearne as if to warn them to listen well. "Three days ago, two Englishmen were brought here by a man from Dinan. Big Louis sailed with them that night. There was also Corbeau, and young Yves from the next village."

The woman explained, "Young Yves is the son, the only son left, of Yves who is the head of that village." She smiled as if to excuse this interruption. Anyway, thought Hearne, she is really anxious we shouldn't miss a trick. He smiled back and nodded. The only son left . . . something important was behind that.

"But why did young Yves come here to sail for England? Couldn't one of the men from his own village have taken him across the Channel?"

"Old Yves had forbidden it. This was his only son, now that the other two had been torpedoed in the war."

"And young Yves was determined to join the Frenchmen in Britain, even against his father's will?"

"Yes, and he had come to Basdevant for help."

Hearne and Myles exchanged quick glances. If Basdevant had betrayed young Yves, then here was the makings of a blood feud between the two communities; if the boy's father ever learned of the betrayal, that was. And the woman realized this. Hearne could see that in her eyes.

"Go on, Jules," she said impatiently.

"Well, two days ago I was in St. Malo. Some prisoners were being marched through the street. We stood in silence and watched them go. There weren't very many, and all were wearing civilian clothes. Among them I saw the two Englishmen: the young one, and the big one with red hair. And I saw young Yves."

No one moved. The dark, silent faces of the fishermen stared into emptiness. The woman's eyes were fixed, unseeing, on the pool of alcohol from Jules's overturned glass.

At last Hearne said, "Yes, you must deal with him yourselves. And if any others come here asking for Basdevant, will you help them?"

Jules nodded slowly. "If we see them arriving. We would not have known that you were here if you hadn't been late this morning, and I saw you by the gray light. We help anyone who hates our enemies."

Hearne thought, now there's the explanation for Basdevant's haste to get us indoors. He said, "And you hate anyone who helps your enemies?"

The men were still silent. At last, the oldest one said, "He is a good fisherman, the best on the river. We'll never find another like him."

"He is brave," agreed another, "and he is clever."

"He was a good man before the Germans came," the oldest man went on, "and perhaps—" He stopped and looked at the others.

"Another drink?" asked the American suddenly. "Open another bottle." Out of the side of his mouth he said to Hearne, "These damned appeasers."

Hearne was thinking, it's no good: the older ones will remember big Louis as he was to them; they'll remember his good points, his leadership, his comradeship. They'll begin to believe that he might be the same again, if only no more refugees come to tempt him. They may even end by blaming it all on the fugitives, and they'll turn their anger against Jules for disturbing their peace of mind.

"Yes," Hearne said, "I could do with another drink myself."

The woman was listening to the reminiscences of the other men. She looked at Hearne and shook her head sadly. "You see?" she seemed to be saying. She began to wipe the counter where Jules's glass had been upset, and then she paused suddenly, her brown eyes looking at Hearne and Myles in dismay.

"Do you hear that?" she began. "It's Pierre. He's running. I told you you would be too late. Get back to your room, quick. I'll think of something else to help you. Quick."

Pierre burst into the room, incoherent in his excitement. They understood the reason for it when they at last could make sense of his news. It wasn't Basdevant or Corbeau who had arrived. It was old Yves, and young Yves, and all the men from their village. They had sailed down as far as the little bay above the jetty; they must have left their boats there, for they had suddenly appeared on the river path. And they were walking towards the Golden Star.

Even as Pierre finished that last detail, the sound of men's feet could be heard on the roadway outside.

"If they want a fight, they can get it," said the old man, and drew a knife from his pocket. The blade snapped back into readiness. Other knives were coming out.

Hearne cursed this misplaced bravery under his breath. That old fool
appeased when he should fight, and fought when he should reason and
explain. "Gentlemen," Hearne said. "I think this solves your problem. It
is Yves and his friends who will take action against big Louis. Obviously,
he has escaped and his village knows all about Basdevant. If you defend
him, the whole river will judge you were guilty along with him. Your
names will stink worse than the mudflats at low tide." It was his last
desperate effort to cut through the dangers with which they were binding
themselves.

And then the door of the bar was flung wide open, and there seemed
to be a mass of brown faces and red sailcloth trousers wedging the narrow space. A tall, broad-shouldered man with red hair slipped through the
sullen group of fishermen. A thin young man followed him.

Hearne put his glass slowly down on the counter, and stared.

"What's wrong?" asked Myles. The spoken English reached the ears
of the thin young man. He turned his head sharply and stared at Myles
and Hearne, and then at Hearne.

"Well," he said. "Well. Look, Sam, who's here!" He came forward with
a smile on his haggard white face, brushing a lock of hair impatiently back
from his forehead. "I must say we *do* meet in the oddest places, don't
we?"

Sam came forward unbelievingly. "Can you beat that? It's his nibs,
himself," he said, and his slow Yorkshire voice filled the room.

It had a remarkably comforting sound.

CHAPTER **17** FIRST BLOOD

Hearne looked at Myles, and then grinned. If he had seemed a funny
kind of farmer before, God knew what the American was thinking now
behind those alert eyes. Alert, but tactful. He was pretending to be interested in the newcomers, and only a shadow of a smile twisted the corner
of his mouth. Hearne turned quickly to the two Englishmen and spoke
in his own voice: there was no need now for his Corlay imitation.

"Better get between them, tactfully. There's no good in a fight starting
now. They'd only knife each other instead of big Louis."

"You know him?"

"We all know him," Myles said.

The three Englishmen and the American grouped themselves not too
noticeably across the middle of the room. This separated the two parties

of Frenchmen. There had been enough interest and surprise over the foreigners who knew each other to ease the initial tension just a fraction. That, and the fact that big Louis was not here, explained the feeling of indecision in the air.

Hearne seized his advantage. "Jules," he said, "tell them how you have judged big Louis." There was a stirring at the mention of the name.

"Yes, Jules, go on," the woman said quickly. She was standing beside the young fisherman. Her hand touched his arm for a moment.

Jules looked at the men in the doorway. "We have learned what big Louis has done. We shall deal with him. It is our business." The men around him echoed his words: ". . . our business."

"It is also ours." This time it was the black-bearded man standing in the doorway who had spoken. That must be old Yves. At his shoulder, there was a young man with the same high aquiline nose, the same black hair and eyes. Young Yves, obviously.

There was a silence except for the marked breathing of the men.

"We shall deal with him," Jules said with finality.

Again that ominous silence.

Hearne spoke, wondering if he'd get a knife in his back for his trouble. "Jules, why not invite them to wait to see how you deal with big Louis?"

"They are already invited," Jules said, with unconscious dignity.

"And we accept the invitation." The black-bearded man nodded to the men behind him. They entered the room singly. But the knives were no longer visible.

"Order another bottle, for God's sake," Myles said to Hearne. "At this rate, I'll have no money left to take me to England."

"Don't worry about that." It was the thin Englishman who spoke. "Old Yves is going to take us, and he will take you too. We sort of helped his son to escape. He says he would take us to South America for that."

"England will do, this time," the American said with a smile.

"It bloody well will," said Sam.

"Looks as if they'll be ready for a fight by the time big Louis arrives," Myles suggested.

"Yes," Hearne agreed, and looked round the room, too. The two groups of men had sat at the farthest separated tables. They sat in silence, their thin cigarettes drooping from their lips, one hand round their glass of crude spirits, the other hidden by the table. The woman served them, quietly, watchfully. It was only when her eyes would turn towards the door and she would listen that Hearne could see how nervous she really was.

Myles and the three Englishmen moved back to the counter of the bar. They could relax for a moment. The young officer was looking at Hearne once more. He was the first to speak.

"Well," he said again, "you do get about, don't you? By the way, you proved to be a very good doctor. Thanks for that. I'm almost cured." But Hearne noticed that he didn't touch the drink in his glass.

Hearne said quietly, "Why did you come back here after you escaped?"

"Safest place, at present. The Jerries would think we'd make a beeline for the coast. And then, Yves had a score to settle, and we felt like that, too. That blighter Louis, or whatever he's called, can't be left to run this show. By the way, my name is Townshend, and this is Walls."

Sam grinned, and said in a mock-Oxford accent, "Pleased tomeetyou, I'm sure."

"I am Myles, and this"—the American nodded towards Hearne—"is—" Hearne's glass unexpectedly emptied itself over Townshend's leg.

"Sorry," Hearne murmured. "Messy creature." Myles smiled gently and changed the subject.

"I've been wondering who is going to take big Louis on," he said. "Or is it a mass affair?"

Sam Walls looked at him with amazement spread thick over his good-natured face. "Who's takin' him on? Who d'you think?" He held out a large doubled fist, and a slow grin widened his mouth still more. Take a couple of pounds of good red meat; shape it roughly over broad round bones; stick a round lump in the middle for the nose; cut two creases for the eyes, and a wide slit for the mouth; add two twists of flesh for the ears, bending them forward slightly; fringe with thick red hair; forget about the eyebrows; and there you would have made Sam Walls. Not a work of art, thought Hearne, looking at the honest face in front of him: just the salt of the earth, that was all.

"It won't be so easy, Sam," Hearne said. "There's also a matter of Celtic pride and Celtic blood."

"What's that?" Sam asked bluntly, with fine Yorkshire contempt.

"These men," Hearne nodded to Jules and his comrades, sitting so silently and bitterly at their table, "these men feel it's a family affair. They want to deal with it in their own way, without any foreigner butting in. Even these men," he looked towards Yves and his friends, "are counted foreigners, although they've lived only two or three miles away from here all their lives. Do you see?"

"Can't say I do, lad."

"If you interfere first, they may gang up on you, on the four of us. Not because they hate us, although they don't like any foreigner very much, but just to teach us to keep our noses out of their business."

"They would, now?"

"Yes, they would."

Sam brooded over that. "Well, I've my own pride, too," he said at last. "I don't give a booger for this foreigner stuff. I'm after that Louis. There isn't a lad here big enough to deal with him."

"They are wiry and quick; they can use a knife as well as anyone."

"That's a bloody awful way to fight."

"Very bloody," agreed Hearne with a suspicion of a smile. "But don't start the fight, Sam. You'll never get to England without friends."

"I'll get there if I have to swim for it," Sam said.

"I think I heard aeroplanes," Townshend interrupted tactfully. "Hear them?"

"Third lot in the last two hours," Myles said.

"Plenty of them about. Boats too, and barges. You should have seen them in the water round St. Malo."

Hearne said quietly, "When you arrive in England, there will be some-one to meet you. Remember everything for him."

"How will they know we're coming?"

"They will. Get Yves to sail his boat towards Penzance. An aeroplane will be scouting for you, and a launch will come to meet you."

"Reception committee?" Myles suggested.

Hearne nodded. "And I'll give you a package. All of you are responsible for its delivery. You're to give it over to a man called Matthews: white hair, red cheeks, blue eyes, large straight nose, natty navy suiting sort of person. Scotsman. Matthews. Matthews. Got that?"

The three men beside him looked suitably impressed. They nodded their agreement.

"What about you? Aren't you coming, too?" Townshend's thin face was politely curious.

Hearne shook his head. "Damn those planes," he said. They all listened. Even the silent Bretons had emerged from their Celtic gloom. One of them said something. Another added to that. A third contradicted. The tension had broken. All of them were talking, it seemed, as if to make up for lost time; talking quickly, loudly, with much expression and many oaths and even an occasional laugh.

The four men standing at the bar looked at each other in a mixture of incredulity and relief. The younger Yves had left his table and sauntered over towards them. Jules, not to be outdone in politeness, had come forward too. Hearne talked to Yves, while Myles and Townshend listened intently. His father would know Cornwall? Penzance? Good. Could they sail tonight? Still better. Then they could use the darkness to run clear of the French coast, do some fishing, and get near the Cornish coast by tomorrow's sunset, when an English boat would meet them? And then his father could make a neat exit into the darkness and be fishing off the French coast by next day? Yves nodded his head gravely. Yes, that could be managed. It would be arranged that way. He had his father's permission to go now: he had to go, now that the Germans were searching for him. They hadn't found out his right name, or where he lived. But there was always the possibility of being identified by some quick Boche eye: his father had understood that danger, and so he could go to England after all.

"Excellent," said Hearne with so much warmth that Yves's serious face was suddenly wreathed in smiles.

Myles was less enthusiastic. Either his feet were starting to trouble him again, or the waiting was getting on his nerves. "Fine and dandy," he said. "Now, all we've got to do is to get out of this country. That's all."

"And settle with Louis," added Townshend.

"Aye," Sam said. They could see a thought forming in his mind. He stood in front of the two young Bretons. "Looey!" he said loudly. "Looey!" He held up his clenched hand. Some of the other Bretons had looked towards him. "Looey!" Sam repeated to all the room, jabbed the air viciously with his fist, and pointed vehemently to himself. "Savvy?" he added.

The Bretons looked at him with polite interest and amusement. One of them shook his head sadly, drew his forefinger along his throat, and clicked his tongue. There was a little wave of laughter.

Sam stood with his big hands on his hips and glared at them. "Look here, lads," he said, "you don't know my lingo. I don't know yours. But get this straight. I'm going to twist Looey's neck until it breaks." He acted his words with a good deal of feeling. The Bretons were watching without any laughter now. The words were unintelligible to them, but the realness of Sam's emotions had got through to them. The silence was broken by renewed arguments.

"What d'they say?" Sam asked Hearne anxiously.

"They see your point, and they are interested in it. But it's no good, Sam: their minds are made up already. Still, they enjoy discussing your point of view."

"Where's this Louis, anyway?" demanded Myles. He was beginning to show a surprisingly strong temper.

"I *wish* I had my gun," Townshend murmured unhappily.

Hearne thought, we are all getting a bad attack of jitters just because none of us want to see a man knived to death. Sam wants to use his fist, Myles is feeling truculent, Townshend wishes he had a gun, and I only wish that the whole thing could have happened in hot blood instead of us all waiting here so coldly for the kill.

He said, "Sam, what happened to that train?"

"Eh, lad?"

"You remember. . . . The train the Pole was going to drive?"

A slow grin replaced Sam's glumness. "Oh, that! Well, it was this way. The Pole got the engine movin' after fiddlin' with all t'nobs and buttons, and away we went like the hammers o'hell, and we skidded round t'bends, and we blew through t'stations like a nor'easter. Then train took notion to slow down, just gradual like, all by herself. There wasn't nothing we could do about her. We tried, but she was stuck fair and proper, bung in middle of bridge. We—" Sam halted, and listened, his head to one side. A car was passing through the village. It was slowing down. It braked suddenly outside the Golden Star.

They all looked at each other. They shared one thought: Basdevant would return by boat. Who was this? The windows were too high for the men to see what was happening in the street. Jules and two others moved quickly over to the door. They had just reached the three stone steps which led up to it. The door opened. They were pushed aside by the men who had entered with so much assurance. At least, two of the men were assured; perhaps their field-gray uniforms helped their confidence. But the third man's swagger was only bravado. Hearne watched the set smile on his face and thought, you didn't want it this way: you wanted to sail back quietly in your boat and pretend you were going to help us; you wanted to hand us over to the Nazis in the darkness far away from here, so your friends wouldn't see your way of making a living; you wanted it that way, but the Nazis didn't, and they are more interested in the catch than in playing the fish; they insisted on coming back with you quickly, by car; and here you are, Louis, with a bigger crowd to damn your treachery than you had expected; you hoped there would only be the women, and a boy or two, at this time of day; how do you like being a Quisling, Louis?— go on, look round, look at the faces, Louis; how do you like it?

Basdevant's smile had stiffened as his eyes rested on Sam, and then Townshend, and then young Yves. He had seen old Yves and the men grouped round him too; you could tell that by the way he wouldn't look at them. He descended the three steps slowly. The Germans, a non-commissioned officer and a private, had drawn their revolvers. It was obvious that they, too, had not expected to encounter so many men.

"Where are they?" It was the sergeant, speaking painfully accurate French.

Big Louis scarcely hesitated. There was a kind of fatalism about the very movement of his arm as he pointed towards Myles and Hearne, and then to Townshend and Walls.

"You said two," the German said angrily. "You didn't tell us there were four of them."

"And what about me?" Young Yves's voice was as contemptuous as his face.

Basdevant's eyes flickered towards old Yves, sitting so grimly among his men.

"What about me, Judas?" Young Yves spat out the words.

The sergeant was angry. "Why didn't you tell me there were more than two?" He was not only angry, he was worried. So, thought Hearne, there were only the sergeant and the uncertain-looking soldier, fingering his revolver unnecessarily. He had lost his assurance: he obviously couldn't

understand much French, and these silent, dark faces smoldering round
him had their effect. He kept his face rigid, but his eyes shifted round
the room with the same nervousness which his fingers on the revolver betrayed. Even the thickest German hide must have felt the hate which
poured towards the two uniforms.

Hearne suddenly relaxed. This was all going to take care of itself. He
needn't worry any more. He caught Jules's eye for a moment: Jules and
his friend standing strangely motionless and silent behind the two soldiers.

"What about me, Louis the Great?" Yves was challenging Basdevant
boldly.

"Is he another?" the sergeant demanded. "Is he?"

Basdevant's smile had evaporated. He looked again towards old Yves,
still motionless, still watching. The silence in the room was like the deep
vacuum before a typhoon.

"Yes, I am," young Yves answered. "He would have told you if I hadn't
brought my friends along with me."

Basdevant took the sneer with the same fatalism he had already shown.
His authority had gone, and he knew it. But he still felt he held the ace
of spades: he still was on the winning side.

It was at this moment that Hearne chose to pour himself a drink.

"Put that bottle down," commanded the German who was doing the
talking. Hearne put the bottle down just beside Myles's hand, lying so
negligently on the bar.

"Put down that glass!" The German was losing all patience.

"Why?" Hearne wasn't even looking at the sergeant.

"At once! Outside! You and these four men. Outside. With your hands
raised. Hands raised!"

Hearne took a step forward. Seven feet away, he calculated. "Let's go,"
he said. He threw the glass of spirits at the sergeant's eyes, and dropped
to the floor. Jules and his friend had moved even as he threw. The Nazis'
necks were drawn back in a throttling elbow grip. The two shots echoed
through the room. Townshend clutched his shoulder and swore earnestly
in his light thin voice. A Breton had fallen face forward on a table. Two
shots; that had been all. The revolvers clattered jarringly on the wooden
floor. The two uniforms, once the Bretons' arms had released them,
folded heavily forward like two sacks of flour. Jules wiped his knife on his
trousers and exchanged a small thin smile with the man beside him who
was cleaning his knife too.

But Sam wasn't watching Jules and his friend or the dead Germans in
front of them. His eyes were on big Louis.

Myles had caught up the bottle by its neck; one smash against the
counter's edge, and it became a jagged threat. Hearne picked up a chair as
he rose to his feet. They, too, were watching Basdevant.

The Breton saw his only chance: it was speed. His only hope was to escape, to inform. Whirling on his heel, even as the Germans dropped, he had knifed the man who was still exchanging a smile with Jules. And as quick as Jules was, big Louis was still quicker. He knocked Jules sideways and slashed him as he went down. He had reached the foot of the stone steps.

"Throw a knife someone!" yelled the American, and flung the broken bottle at Basdevant; it struck the back of his shoulder, but the gash didn't stop him.

Then Sam moved. The shouts of the Bretons were cut off short as they saw the redhaired man launch himself head first through the air. His outstretched arms encircled Basdevant's legs, and the weight behind his dive knocked the Breton off his feet. He fell forward heavily, his head striking against the top stone step. Young Yves's foot was grinding the wrist which held the knife. The shouts broke out once more as the mass of dark-haired men surged forward.

Hearne had headed that rush. It was Sam he wanted. Myles, hobbling over to the milling group, cursing his feet, cursing everything and everyone and his lack of a weapon, saw the two men suddenly being ejected out of the crowd like a football out of a scrum. He steadied them as they slipped on the blood on the floor, and pulled them back towards the safety of the counter where the woman, large-eyed and tight-lipped, was standing. She was watching the men round the door. The glass, which she had been wiping on her apron as the Germans and Basdevant had entered the room, was still in her hand.

"You were damned lucky to get out of that, if you ask me," Myles began, and then a smile broke over his face as he looked at Sam. "That was a lulu. Boy, that was a lulu."

"You blasted fool, hanging on like that," said Hearne, regaining his breath.

"I was winded," Sam said. All the sulkiness and anger had gone, now. He was smiling to himself. "All of eight feet that was, lad. A beezer."

Hearne relented. "More like ten feet. It was a beezer, all right. A bobby-dazzler and all, Sam."

"The best yet, Sam." It was Townshend, looking whiter and younger than ever. His right hand held his left shoulder; the fingers were red.

Sam's pleasure was gone. "Hurt bad?"

"I was lucky." Townshend nodded to the table over which the Breton fisherman had sprawled. The man lay as he had fallen. Townshend looked round the room and shook his head incredulously. "It was less than five minutes ago that the car arrived," he said.

The car, thought Hearne. He looked quickly at his watch. There was much to be done in the next five minutes, too. The bodies, the cleaning up of this room, the car . . . yes, there was much to be done.

"Dead as mutton," the American said suddenly. Like the woman, he had been watching the group round the door. "And some of the others seem to have been getting in the way."

The woman's face relaxed. Hearne followed her glance towards the men who were now coming towards the bar. Jules was among them. His arm showed a long red cut where he had warded off Basdevant's lunge. But he was safe. The woman finished wiping the glass which she held in her hand, and set it down slowly on the shelf behind her. When she turned round again, she could smile back to Jules. It was a pity, thought Hearne, that he would have to interfere at this moment, but someone had to take charge. Old Yves and his men had kicked Basdevant's body away from the door; some of them were already moving out into the street.

Young Yves walked over quickly to Townshend. "Come now, we are going."

"At once?" the American said blankly.

"At once." The boy pointed towards his father waiting at the door.

"Better take this chance," advised Hearne. "They'll get you safely to their village, and it's better for us all to leave here as quickly as possible. I'm leaving too."

"It's sort of sudden," the American said awkwardly. Hearne handed him an envelope for an answer.

"Heavy," Myles observed in surprise.

"All ready to sink, if need be. Take care of it. Remember everything I've told you?"

"Yes." The American placed the envelope carefully into a deep pocket. "I'll keep one hand on it until I hand it over to Matthews. That right?"

Hearne nodded. "For heaven's sake, see you get it across." He looked at Townshend and Sam.

"We'll get there," said Townshend, and started to move towards the door. Old Yves watched them impassively.

The American hesitated. "Perhaps I'll be seeing you some day," he said, "so you may as well know my name. It isn't Myles: that was just my subconscious coming out. I'll explain it to you some day. I'm van Cortlandt, Henry van Cortlandt. We'll get together sometime and you can tell me how this ends for you, and I can tell you how it all began for me last summer. Right?"

Hearne nodded. Van Cortlandt stepped carefully over the bodies. "What about these buzzards?" he said. "What about the car?"

"We'll take care of that."

"I hate to go while the job's half-finished," the American grumbled. Hearne gave him a grin and a wave of the hand. "Hurry, you idiots," he told the three loiterers. "What do you think you're doing? Sightseeing?"

"Well, good-by, and good luck," Townshend said abruptly, making the decision for the other two.

They followed the Bretons into the street. Sam's face turned to give a last enormous grin. He jerked his thumb up, and held it that way for a moment. And then they were gone.

Hearne wished he could have gone too, could have seen them safely onto that boat tonight along with his precious envelope. But events had moved too quickly, and that always meant plans had to be scrapped and reshaped.

He turned to Jules. "First, we must get rid of these bodies. You can put them where they won't be found?"

"When they are found, they will not be recognizable." Jules's voice was as businesslike as Hearne's.

"This place will have to be scoured: all traces of the fight must be removed. And no one must keep any of the Germans' equipment. That might mean death for the village."

The woman, standing now beside Jules, nodded. "I shall see to all that," she said determinedly. "We've had fights here before. I know what to do."

"Then there is the man Corbeau."

"He was probably left to sail back the boat safely from St. Malo. He will be late, he will be drinking. We know him."

"You will take care of him, when he returns?"

Jules nodded. "He isn't one of us," he said.

"I shall take the car and abandon it as far from here as possible. That will keep the village safe. You must look after the rest; you know what to do. And if the police come asking questions, then you will say that big Louis left to buy provisions this morning at St. Malo, that he hasn't returned. That's all you know." He looked round the set faces. "Is that clear?" They nodded. Hearne realized that what he asked of them was something they considered not so very strange, something they could do much more efficiently than he could plan. There had been no fear in their eyes when he had spoken of police: they would take a pleasure in outwitting any policeman, and there would be all the more pleasure if he were German.

"You must act quickly," Hearne said, looking at the bodies.

"Some will clean this room. I shall go with Philippe, Jean-Marie, Henri, to set some nets." As he mentioned their names, the men came forward. Jules nodded his head towards the bodies, and the men moved over to them.

Jules went to the table where the Breton had been killed by the wild bullet.

"It is sad about Robert," he said, his tone altered. "Robert was always friendly to big Louis."

Hearne looked again, and saw that Robert had been the man who had tried so hard for appeasement. "Too bad," Hearne said sadly, and shook his head slowly. The woman lowered her eyes so that he wouldn't surprise the smile in them. The men went gravely on with their job.

Hearne paused to pick up one of the revolvers. "I'll leave this with the car," he said to the woman. "But don't let anyone here keep any souvenir."

"I understand," she said, and turned to take the pail of water which one of the young boys had carried in.

"Good-by," Hearne said, and the Bretons nodded politely. It seemed as if they had forgotten he was even there. He moved towards the door. It was just as mad as that, he thought. You left a woman scrubbing blood from the floor, men moving four corpses into the back room, and you stepped into the street, and got into the car. You drove it straight ahead, so that the wheel tracks would look as if they had passed right through the village. You saw two middle-aged, tight-lipped women at the door of a cottage; and they didn't seem to notice you, just as they hadn't seemed to notice the uproar in the pub, this morning. Behind you was the Etoile d'Or, and floors being cleaned, and bodies being weighted for their last dive. It was all as mad and as simple as that, he thought.

He swung the car into a small road leading away from the river. Behind him, Yves and his men would have almost reached their village. Tonight, a few fishing boats would set sail and creep silently out into the estuary to reach the Channel. It would be pleasant to be in one of these boats: however great the danger, it would be pleasant. He discarded the thought of the English Channel abruptly. He'd come to that in good time, unless he ended up against a stone wall. But there was no use in thinking about that either. The job, now, was to get to Mont St. Michel, to his friends Pléhec and Duclos with his nice little wireless transmitter.

Strange how seeing men die so suddenly made you start thinking of death. Not the best frame of mind for the work on hand, he decided, and increased the speed of the car. A few more miles on these side roads were all he could risk: as it was, he had already come farther than he had intended, but the farther he went the safer were Jules and his people. Van Cortlandt and he owed a lot to the woman's courage and to Jules's frankness. As the car swayed on the road's hard stone surface, he suddenly remembered Sam's engine and the Pole who had driven it so dangerously. Perhaps it was the memory of Sam's solid voice and equally solid face, or it might have been his idea of the Pole's vocabulary when the engine halted so determinedly, but Hearne's spirits rose. He would hear the end of that story yet, even if he had to scour all Yorkshire to get it. He stepped on the accelerator to pass a detachment of German soldiers, and flipped his hand codfish-wise as he had seen it done from a high flag-covered platform in Nürnberg. The junior officer saluted back. Either the car had passed too quickly, or it, itself, was a guarantee of authenticity, for neither these soldiers nor any of the other detachments had challenged him. But of course all the French walked or bicycled these days, unless they were in the proud position of being trusted by the Germans. He had been taken for one of these, and he was allowed to pass with the usual German contempt for an ally. An ally won sneers just as an enemy won relentless hate. The Germans alone were beyond sneers, and worthy of love. Hurrah for the master race, goose-stepping so neatly to the fulfillment of their conquering destiny. He pressed the horn viciously and watched a small column of soldiers scatter obediently to the side of the road.

He curbed his enthusiasm for this kind of sport: he had had just about enough good luck for one day. He knew when to stop. But it was with regret that he abandoned the car, in the ditch running along a lonely stretch of winding road. It had been a pleasant journey after all.

There were no houses, no civilians, no soldiers in sight. Even the sky was clear of planes. This was the moment. He pulled the German's revolver from his pocket and aimed for the petrol tank carefully. Quickly he felt for his matchbox. Four matches inside. Enough. He lit one carefully and held it to the stalks of the others. As they sizzled like a firecracker and then flared into life, he threw them at the growing pool of petrol and ran as if the whole German army were at his heels. He had reached the small road at the edge of the wood. Beyond it were fields and more twisting roads and a ditch whose long weeds hid the gun. Any curious people within these two square miles wouldn't be interested in him: the car which had become a flaming torch would seem much more important. His run slackened to a walk. He was near the coast, now. Ten more miles, perhaps even less, and he would be at the island of Mont St. Michel.

He was still thinking of the last half hour: it had been a pleasant journey after all.

CHAPTER **18** ST. MICHAEL'S MOUNTAIN

The road to Mont St. Michel was simple, for it stretched in a series of straight lines over the flatness of the reclaimed sea land. But it was just this simplicity which added to the danger of the journey, which forced Hearne to follow the road itself and not trust himself to the emptiness of the miles of open grass and vegetable fields. Flat as a pancake, he said to himself in disgust, and there was just about as much cover as a fly would find in a stroll over a pancake. One thing he could be thankful for: he wasn't the only person on this road. Here and there was a lonely figure trudging patiently along with a heavy basket for company, or a small family group of fishers and oyster gatherers.

In front of him, a woman thickly bundled in black petticoats had halted to rest. The little boy in his faded and patched blue dress waited patiently beside her. As Hearne drew level with them, the woman lifted the basket slowly onto her back.

Hearne slowed his pace. "You've a heavy load, there," he said.

The woman gave a final heave to the basket, settling it as comfortably as it was possible between her shoulders. The black blouse was threadbare and sewn into a patchwork of mends. She was eyeing his dusty crumpled clothes, probably trying to place him within her limited knowledge of people. But at least he couldn't have seemed dangerous, even if he was filthy, for she at last gave him an answer.

"Yes," she said, and plodded on with the child half-walking, half-running at her side. He was a thin little thing, probably no more than five years old although he had the face of a child of ten. His closely cropped hair, as if shaved for scarlet fever, bristled thinly over the egg-shaped head and made his large, dark eyes larger, darker.

"I'll take the basket," Hearne said, "and you can take the child. He looks tired."

The woman didn't answer, but she had heard him for she gave him a long sideways look and tightened her hold on the basket.

"I said I'd carry the basket for you," he tried again, and again there was silence. He was only frightening the woman into tight-lipped distrust.

Hearne smiled. "Well, I'll carry the boy," he said. The child would be lighter than the basket, but if the woman was afraid to trust him with the oysters, then that was her lookout.

The child's body stiffened as Hearne picked him up. And then, as he felt himself quite safe on this strange man's back, with his two thin hands tightly clasped under the funny man's chin, with his bony little shanks held firmly by the big man's arms, the rigor of his body disappeared. He was speaking in his thin hoarse voice after they had gone only twenty steps: he was saying, "I've got a horse! Look, *maman*, I've a horse!"

The mother didn't speak. Her mouth had tightened as if to say, "Such like nonsense: teaching the boy bad habits, that's what you are." But their pace had noticeably quickened, and she was pleased in spite of the will to be displeased.

She asked at last, "Where are you from?"

"St. Malo. And you?"

"This side of Le Vivier." The admission was made grudgingly, but after all she had started the questioning. And an answer deserves an answer.

"Where are you going?" she said after a pause.

"Beyond the Mont. Where are you?"

"The Mont."

Hearne's technique had the desired result. There were no more questions. What's your business, were you fighting, are you married, what was your father, where were you born, how old are you, why are you going beyond the Mont—all these and more were stillborn on the woman's tongue.

"It's a long way for the boy to walk," Hearne said at last, looking at the island of Mont St. Michel still three miles distant.

"He is used to it." The woman wasn't being callous: it was the calm statement of an economic fact. She had to make this journey to sell the oysters; and either there was no one with whom to leave the boy, or she preferred to have him beside her.

"We come twice a week," the hoarse little voice announced from behind Hearne's ear.

"You're a clever boy," Hearne said.

"I can walk more than that."

"Then you're a very clever boy. What's your name?"

"Michel."

"That's a good name." Hearne turned to the woman, who was now listening with a half-smile. "How is the price of oysters today?"

"Bad. But it keeps us alive." And then, as if to explain why she had to provide for herself and the boy, she added quickly, "My husband is in a prison camp. It will be easier when he comes home. He was coming home, and they caught him. My brother was with him, but he got away then." She was silent for a moment. "Do you think they'll let them come home, soon?"

"I hope so." Hearne tried to make his voice confident.

"The war's over," the woman said, as if that were reason enough. "The war's over."

"So they say," Hearne said bitterly.

She halted and put down the basket to rest. Michel slipped unwillingly from Hearne's back. "So they say," she echoed dully, and looked across the flat fields on their right. Hearne followed the direction of her eyes.

"Big guns," Michel said. "Big guns. They will go boom, boom. My uncle works there."

The woman hushed the boy sharply, and then, as if afraid that this stranger would think she was related to a German, said quickly, "That's my brother. He had no job, and they took him away to work for them. Him and the others who had just got back from the war. First, they took away his boat. Then they said he had no job. Then they took him to work for them."

"And he's there, digging?"

The woman didn't answer, as if she were afraid of her information. She spoke angrily to the child. "Stop kicking up that dust, Michel. Stop it at once, do you hear?"

Michel heard.

"I suppose we are to be blind to what is going on around us," Hearne said. At regular intervals along the flat fields, about a mile or so from this shore road, were clumps of what seemed bushes or thick trees. He tried out his idea. "What do they take us for, anyway? As if we didn't know camouflage when we saw it!"

The woman nodded, but said nothing, and bent to pick up the basket again.

"I can take it this time," Hearne said. "Just for the last mile. I won't bruise the oysters."

His attempt at a joke was rewarded with a smile, and Michel laughed so much at the silly man that he forgot his disappointment at losing his horse, until it was too late to complain. His mother and the man had already walked on.

Hearne looked again towards the concealed gun emplacements. The row of scattered shrubbery stretched back for miles. "Can't see any men working," he remarked.

"They are there, all right. They are all screened from the road. Can you think of it? Such madness."

Skillful madness, thought Hearne, and thanked heaven that he had had sense enough to stick to the road. Cross-country would be impossible in this district. But in one way the woman was right: it was incredible to what lengths of ingenuity the Germans would go. Like that batch of specially circumcised, long-nosed Nazis which had been dumped across the Dutch borders as pitiful refugees, in the days before their comrades came over with flame-throwers and parachuting nuns. The gift to see ourselves as others see us was definitely one which God had not included in the make-up of Nordic Aryans.

They had passed other Bretons, walking on this road which skirted the bay of Mont St. Michel. But now they heard, and then saw a long column of motorcyclists. They stood in the ditch until the speeding unit had swept contemptuously by. And then came half-a-dozen lorries, each filled with soldiers sitting proudly erect. Or perhaps they enjoyed that attitude, as they pretended not to notice the French who plodded on foot or were driven into the ditches, who were smothered by the clouds of white dust which rose from the conquering chariot-wheels.

The woman's face was tight-lipped. Hearne spat the dust out of his mouth; and her eyes, as she watched the expression on his face, were suddenly friendly. They went on in silence. There was no need of words. The heart should have no witness but itself.

The road, as it neared the island in the bay, swerved farther inland. They left it, as it curved round to the right, and cut across the salt meadows instead, following a well-worn track which was obviously used by the fisherpeople or those who looked after the sheep which scattered over these strange fields along the shore. The feeling of unreality grew as they neared the Mont St. Michel. There it was, rising, like a mystic mountain of medieval fantasy and delicacy, from the strength of the granite rocks which held it secure in the surrounding miles of golden quicksand. Now the tide was out, and the long narrow causeway, which was the only connecting link between the continent of Europe and this island of tiered turrets and pinnacles, looked forlorn and purposeless. Hearne looked over his shoulder to reassure himself: he always felt the beauty of the island had to be diluted, to be swallowed with any conviction. Behind him lay the seemingly unending road, with the flat grasslands mixed with bog; and the hum of bees; and the scattered sheep; and the occasional *estaminet* advising the passer-by, with a rain-swept girl's smile on its gable-end, to drink more Cinzano; and the few indigent houses huddling together in stray groups. This part of the land was "new," and there were none of the solid, and yet romantic, old villages which covered the rest of the Breton coast. Here, it was as if the shrinking houses knew how fragile their foundations were. For to the north of the road lay the sea and the flat shore of long green-gray grass, its color sapped by the seeping of the tide as it surged hungrily towards the stolen land. Without the gray Germans, and their hidden guns and serf-labor toiling behind camouflaged screens, this would seem a fantastic place enough. With them, it was incredible.

The track through the salt meadows turned away from the shore line now, in its turn; but it was only to pass over a canal and through a small collection of houses commanding a long straight avenue of trees which led directly onto the long straight causeway. The woman halted, expecting Hearne to put down the basket.

"This is my way and that is yours," she said.

Hearne hadn't paused. He turned to the left into the straight avenue of trees, keeping to the left of the tramway lines which had appeared with the canal. The woman and the child followed.

"I can carry it more quickly," he said. "Are you walking back home this afternoon?"

The woman nodded. "It will be easy with the basket empty."

"Don't you find a better market in St. Malo?"

She shot a quick glance at him. "You know the reason," she said. "You know what happened to the fish market there."

"Yes," said Hearne, and wished he did. Too many Germans, probably, with the usual story of forced sales at their price, and payment in occupation marks.

"Aren't there Germans here?" he asked, remembering the three soldiers in the village square which they had just left.

"They have a garrison. And there are tourists. I sell these oysters to a restaurant: the owner's wife is the cousin of my godson's uncle."

Hearne tried to calculate, but gave it up. "And they pay you a good price?" he asked sympathetically.

"Fair."

"They must make a lot of money from the tourists."

The woman gave a short laugh. "Bad money. Tell me, how is it going to end? They pay money, these Germans: they don't steal. But the money will mean nothing when they are gone. Why don't they steal? It would be just the same."

"But then they couldn't say they were being 'correct.'" The Teutonic genius for self-justification was obviously unappreciated by this woman's simple, direct mind.

"It would be just the same," she repeated, stubbornly.

And then, as they stepped onto the causeway, Michel pointed to the sand stretching on either side of them.

"My uncle got drowned there," he said proudly.

"Quicksand?" said Hearne. Even men who knew their way about these sands made grim mistakes.

"Tide," the woman answered placidly. "It's coming in now. Do you hear?"

Hearne listened. His eyes followed her arm. He had seen the phenomenon before, but it still made him hold his breath. From the distance came a low continuous rumble, at first scarcely noticeable, and then surprisingly clear. The rumble became a growl, growing in intensity as the sea moved in over the flat six miles of empty sand. The growl became a tattoo of drums, a fanfare of trumpets, and then the moving mass of water at last swept into sight. Its long line rushed smoothly towards the island ahead of them. It formed one stretch of wave, always about to break, and then rolling over to let another powerful sweep of water take its place, so that the line never seemed to halt.

"There are two men on the sand now!" Hearne exclaimed.

"German soldiers," the woman said calmly, shading her eyes. "Tourists. They see the priests and the fisherwomen on the sands, and they will have their try, too."

"I wonder if they'll make it?"

"Some don't," the woman said, almost hopefully. "The path from the causeway to the front gate will be covered. We must hurry too." They quickened their pace.

The two men were running hard, but the tide was moving still more quickly. Hearne watched the greedy surge of rapidly moving water gaining so inexorably, so triumphantly.

"They are too near the walls. They'll escape," said the woman. She didn't sound as if she were rejoicing. "Unless they walk on the quicksand," she added. "Their boots are heavy for quicksand." Both she and Michel were staring at the running figures. Hearne averted his eyes: he looked at the maze of towers and turrets in front of them. From the highest spire soaring on the pinnacle of the rock which formed this island, the lacework of chapels and abbeys swirled down to the pointed roof-tops of the crowding houses, to the thick turreted wall, which encircled them all. There were soldiers on the wall, all looking towards the running men. Otherwise, it seemed an uninhabited medieval fortress.

"When I am here, I may as well visit my mother's late cousin's husband," Hearne said. "We haven't heard from him for the last two months."

The woman was scarcely listening. Her eyes were still on the two running men, as she pulled Michel quickly along the paved causeway. "They will reach the wall. A boat will be sent round to get them off the rocks," she said resignedly. And then, unexpectedly, "What's his name?"

"Pléhec."

"He keeps the restaurant next to my godson's uncle's cousin's husband. It is a small restaurant." Her pride in even remote family connections asserted itself.

"Yes, I know. He is a poor businessman."

"But it is good enough for him now. He doesn't have so many of the Germans as customers. They like the bigger places."

They had reached the rampart and followed a wooden footpath branching off the causeway. It led to a first gate, and then to a second. The two sentries stationed in the small courtyard between the two gates let them enter with no more than a cursory glance. That wasn't so surprising, thought Hearne. With his face streaked with sweat and dust, his clothes muddied and crumpled and torn, he would have passed for an oyster gatherer. And the guards must know the woman and child by sight. It wasn't so surprising—but even at this stage in his experience, it amazed him to find how unexpectedly simple it could all be. And the simplest things were often the most successful. He never could stop being amazed at that. It was too impudent, somehow.

He bent his back lower as he climbed the steep cobbled street. It was only broad enough for four men to walk abreast. The shops and over-hanging houses closed in on either side. Curios for sale, mementos of St. Michel, outmoded intimations of good things to eat, postcards, painted shells, religious relics, good-luck charms—all pathetic reminders of the Mont's one-time summer trade. Behind him, the tide had reached the walls, and the sea had become a caldron of boiling water.

The child trotted ahead. Perhaps he knew he would get some scraps to eat in that genealogical restaurant. Hearne was content to follow. Up the street they went, then suddenly they turned to the left, along a twisting alley which led them to the back courtyard.

Hearne let the basket slide off his shoulders and straightened himself, painfully. Houses all around them, two- and three-storied houses, so that they seemed to be in a maze of man-built canyons. He hesitated. Which side was Pléhec's back entrance? Last time, he could walk in at the front, but that had been almost two years ago. An army of doors and windows faced him. He wondered again just how many people could be crowded into this half of the small island. Certainly the inhabitants of Mont St. Michel had tried their best.

"They seem empty," he said, pointing to the windows.

"Many people have gone. Only a few remain."

"To feed and entertain the Germans?"

"Yes, these were allowed to stay. Pléhec is there." She pointed to a narrow door in a corner of the alley.

"Thank you."

"It is I who should thank you."

"It was nothing."

She bowed and smiled gravely, with that dignity of the Celt which is so unexpected and yet so natural that you are surprised at your own surprise. She pulled the basket over the worn threshold, and smiled good-by as she pulled. Michel was already inside.

Hearne turned towards Pléhec's doorway. He entered quickly. Behind him, the alley and the street outside were silent. The turbulent waves and jostling currents beyond the ramparts had suddenly eased into smooth noiselessness.

A man was sleeping beside the open hearth in the kitchen. At each side of the fireplace, there was a stone oven with a heavy iron door. From either oven-wall an iron rack stretched over the flames. Two brown earthenware pots had been placed in its center to catch what heat there was in the low fire. Hearne advanced quietly over the stone-flagged floor, and passed the large white-scrubbed table with its few bowls of half-prepared vegetables. From here, he could see through the half-open doorway into the front room. Checked tablecloths on small round tables, spindle-legged cane chairs. This was the place, all right. He didn't need to see the

screened shop window with **PLÉHEC** crudely spaced on the glass. This was the same place.

The small round man in the high-backed wooden chair stirred; and said, without opening his eyes, "Closed until six o'clock."

Hearne suddenly realized by his relief that he had been more worried than he had been willing to admit. He still felt sick, though, but that was probably hunger after all. He wondered if Pléhec's skill with omelettes was still as unchanged as his slight lisp, and those two deep furrows between his heavy eyebrows. There was gray beginning to show now in the thick black hair growing in the peculiarly straight edge round the sallow face. Hearne remembered he used to wonder if Pléhec shaved that hairline. Then he noticed that the man's right hand was resting inside his loose shirt. Hearne said quickly and softly in English, "Even for friends?"

Pléhec raised one eyelid slowly. The eye, small in the heavy folds of his face, seemed reassured, for his right arm relaxed and the other eye flickered open too. Hearne waited patiently while Pléhec identified him. Each minute was sixty hours. Either lack of food, or too little sleep, or the fact that he had been living in tension ever since he had left St. Déodat, was beginning to tell. I can't have changed as much as all this, he thought dully, and pulled a wooden chair in front of him. He sat down heavily, straddling it, with his arms and chin resting on the high back.

"It just needed that," Pléhec said as if to himself in his thin light voice. When he was excited the lisp was more noticeable as he hurried his words. "It just needed that . . . the archeologist who told stories."

"Not archeologist," Hearne found himself saying. "Ethnologist." But what the hell did that matter now? Stories . . . had he ever told stories? They seemed as dim a memory as the ethnologist.

Pléhec nodded his head with surprising energy. "Yes, you always made that distinction. July, wasn't it?"

Hearne repressed a smile. The Frenchman knew quite well when he had visited Mont St. Michel.

"October," Hearne said gently. "October 1938."

"And are you to be with us for another week, this time?"

"I leave tonight."

"So?"

"So."

"No archeology this time?"

"In a way. . . . How is Duclos?"

The Frenchman looked at the large nickel watch tucked into a pocket at the waist of his tight black trousers. He had lost weight already, Hearne noticed: he could slip the watch out easily now. Once Hearne had been amazed that anyone so solidly constructed round the waistline should choose to keep a watch just there. Pléhec was speaking. "It is now almost five o'clock. He will be sitting at the table in the corner, as usual, in just one hour and twenty minutes."

"I must see him. You are sure he will be here?"

"Unless he has been arrested. And, then, it wouldn't do you any good to see him." Pléhec was laughing. He noticed the look on Hearne's face and he became serious. "Yes, I know; it's a bad joke. But we must laugh at something, these days."

"What I really need is something to eat," Hearne said. "That always improves my sense of humor."

"Of course. Of course. You must forgive my thoughtlessness."

Pléhec rose, a short round figure in tight black trousers and an open-necked white shirt. He picked up an apron from the chair, on which his black jacket and ready-made bow tie were neatly lying. "Once," he said, "I should have thought it impossible to make an omelette with two eggs. Now I can even do it with one, and I can see the day coming very quickly when I won't be able to make any omelette because there will be no eggs. You would think the hens knew that there's no use in laying, for a Boche will be there to catch the egg as it falls."

"One egg will be enough for me," Hearne suggested politely; but he was relieved to see Pléhec shake his head at that, and smile.

"And I can offer you some soup: thinner, to be sure, but still soup. And a slice of bread, and some cheese which I managed to hide in time. The coffee is unspeakable. I insult the word 'coffee' by using it to describe what we now drink. Our supplies here were requisitioned, and we have been most generously allowed to buy this." He thumped the brown coffee-pot so heavily down on the wooden table that Hearne thought he had smashed it. "*Filtré,*" Pléhec added bitterly, and gave that short laugh of his. He suddenly halted, one hand holding the long twist of bread against his chest, the other's thumb ready to drive the sharply pointed knife into the loaf. "How," he said, suddenly halting and looking up at Hearne, "how did you get here?"

"Walked in."

Pléhec sawed a slice off the loaf of bread and handed it over to Hearne on the point of the knife. "Begin with that," he said. "Now, when did you so calmly walk in?" There was a mixture of amusement and irony in his voice.

"About half-past four. When the two Jerries had to run from the tide."

"Then the others would be crowding onto the wall at that side of the Mont, in order to see them. But the guards? They didn't stop you?"

"I was carrying oysters. For a woman. She went next door, by the way."

"Mathilde?"

"I don't know. Her little boy was called Michel."

"That was Mathilde." Pléhec paused, and traced an imaginary line with the knife on the table. He suddenly went to a small door in a corner of the kitchen, and called abruptly, "Etienne!"

A boy's voice answered him; there was the sound of a creaking bed and then slow footsteps.

"Is it six, already?" the boy asked as he came into the room. He smoothed back his dark hair and yawned audibly. He scarcely paused to look at Hearne. "Another?" he said.

But Pléhec had his own question to ask. "Mathilde usually leaves after five o'clock?"

"Mathilde? Oh, they try to get her away before supper begins."

"See her. . . . Say I want to know if she can bring some extra oysters when she comes next week."

The boy nodded, and slipped out of the room as quietly as he had entered it. He had an infinite capacity for not being surprised, it seemed.

Pléhec was still silent as he handed Hearne a bowl of soup. Hearne took his cue, and didn't speak. But now he was worried about Mathilde, too: he must have endangered her; there must be some regulations about which he knew nothing. He had finished the soup, and the omelette was rising on the flat brown earthenware dish when he heard the footsteps on the stone-paved yard. Pléhec folded the omelette quickly and slipped it hurriedly onto a plate. He was still holding the brown cooking dish and the fork in his hands as he reached the door. He moved with surprising lightness and speed.

"Mathilde," he greeted the woman standing outside, "can you bring a few extra oysters for me when you come next time? What is the price, now?"

Mathilde talked volubly and practically. The boy who was called Etienne had come back into the kitchen. He nodded to Hearne pleasantly, took an apron from a hook in the wall and tied it round his waist. He picked up a bowl of green peas from a side table and began shelling them. Hearne began the omelette: Pléhec would never forgive him if he let the two eggs spoil.

There was only a murmur of voices now from the doorway. Then, suddenly, Pléhec's voice was normal once more as he stipulated the price. The door closed. Mathilde's footsteps faded.

"Well, how did you like it?" Pléhec asked. He was smiling again as he looked at Hearne's empty plate. "Once I should have thought it impossible to cook an omelette without one of my copper pans." He pointed to the row of empty hooks above the fireplace. "But of course, you saw that?"

Hearne nodded. He hadn't, but he now remembered that the omelette had looked strange cooking slowly in the earthenware dish, and that its texture had been drier and spongier. "It was excellent," he said, and he meant it.

Pléhec said, "I'm afraid you must lose your jacket. Would you take it off?" He handed it to Etienne. "Wear this, and go with Mathilde as far as La Caserne. There you will go on towards Pontorson, while she will take her usual path home. Get rid of the jacket when it's safe, and come back here. We'll need you later."

Etienne grinned and took off his apron. The jacket fitted him loosely, but convincingly enough.

"Mathilde?" Hearne asked quickly.

Pléhec spoke without turning from the small curtained window looking out into the courtyard. It was so high that he was standing on tiptoe to bring his eyes above the level of the sill. "She realizes that the son of my late wife's cousin wants to stay longer with me, that it would be dangerous for him to stay without permission—and so Etienne will wear his jacket and carry the basket, and the guards will notice that a man who came in has gone out again. That's all we have to worry about."

"And little Michel?"

"He doesn't know Etienne. He will remember the strange jacket as much as the face." Pléhec was suddenly silent. His eyes were on the court-yard. Hearne thought he heard voices, and then footsteps.

Pléhec turned back into the room. "Front door, Etienne. She's just gone. Quick."

Etienne moved quickly and silently. They didn't even hear the door close.

"Well, that's that. He'll catch up with her on the Grande-Rue, and if Madame of the long tongue from next door was watching to see anything she could see—for her eyes are as sharp as her tongue is long—she will be disappointed." Pléhec rubbed his hands with the pleasure of frustrating Madame, the cousin of Mathilde's godson's uncle. "Well, that's that," he said again, and picked up the apron which Etienne had thrown on the table. He handed it and the bowl of peas to Hearne. "Something useful for you to do. Very useful, if anyone should come in."

Hearne smiled and rolled up his sleeves: first oyster gatherer, now pea sheller and potato peeler. It was all in the day's work.

Pléhec carried two pails over to a small side table. "You'll find it easy enough," he said consolingly. "Our catering has become very simple. Just so many customers, just so much to eat for each customer, just so little to cook." He picked up a fish out of one of the pails, and slapped it onto the small table. Slitting it carefully up its belly, he raked out its insides. There was a grim smile on his face. "Do you know who I like to think this is?" he asked suddenly, one hand ripping out the last piece of gut.

Hearne nodded. "I can guess."

"And there were those among us who would say 'What are we fighting for?' The rich said 'War means revolution: we will lose our possessions!' The workers said 'Patriotism is for the rich: war means we will lose our new privileges!' Well, they know now: they got their peace, and they've lost everything. 'What are we fighting for?' Bah!" He chose another fish, and beheaded it neatly with one blow of the knife. "That," he said, "for all traitors who think of their own private interests first. And this"—he selected another fish "—this for the politicians who play with their country's enemies for the sake of power; and—" He halted as he saw Hearne's expression.

"Don't worry, my friend," he said. "This is a little luxury which I permit myself each evening. *This* is not rationed. The choice is either thoughts such as these, or a chloroformed sleep. I prefer to keep awake."

Hearne nodded sympathetically, and finished the shelling of the peas. They were pitiably few.

"How many customers?" he asked.

"Exactly seven. Duclos and Gouret from the Museum; Guehenneuc, Brault, and Boulleaux, the guides to the Abbey; old Dr. Fuzet and Picquart the notary. Yes, exactly seven. But it simplifies things for me. It gives me a lot of free time for more urgent business."

"Can you trust them?"

"The customers? But of course . . ." He smiled enigmatically. "They come to eat here, and talk, and get through one more evening."

"What about meeting Duclos?"

"I shall forget to lay a glass before him, and the way to the lavatory is through here." He pointed to the door through which Etienne had first emerged. Hearne was satisfied, and nodded. He mentally blessed the peculiarities of the ancient plumbing on the Mont St. Michel.

A cool draft swept into the kitchen from the restaurant. The front door was open. There were voices.

Pléhec hurriedly wiped his hands. "Put these in the pail: tomorrow's lunch," he said, nodding towards the fish guts on the table; then clipped the bow tie round his neck, before picking up the glazed black jacket. He reached for a white linen cap, and, with a smile, placed it on Hearne's head. He was still smiling as he closed the door leading into the restaurant behind him.

Hearne settled the cap more securely on his head. *Well*, he thought, and took a deep breath. Well, here he was, in a half-lighted eighteenth-century kitchen, clearing fish guts carefully into a pail. Here he was, with a cap a foot high on his head, waiting for a white-haired archeologist to pass through to the lavatory. In his pocket was that folded wad of paper with its neatly coded phrases. Tonight, Duclos would send them out into the air.

He wiped his hands on his apron, tilted the starched cap securely over one eye, and casually turned his back to the restaurant door as it was swung open. It was Pléhec. He bustled over with quick short steps to the soup pot hanging above the driftwood fire.

"I gave him the sign," he said in a voice so low that it was almost drowned in the ladle of soup which he held to his lips. He nodded his head as if satisfied. The lines at the side of his mouth had deepened: there was perspiration on his brow and upper lip. He worries more than I do, thought Hearne: he's worried and he's nervous. Hearne looked at the anxious brown eyes. "Two lousy Boches just arrived," Pléhec muttered; and then, as he handed the ladle to Hearne, he added, in an attempt at a normal voice, "It is as good as it ever will be. Three platefuls, Etienne. Two small ladles and no more, for each person."

The door opened again. Hearne's hand tightened on the ladle.

Pléhec spoke hurriedly. "Ah, Dr. Fuzet. I am just about to bring the soup."

An old voice said, as though from a great distance, "Good." Old feet shuffled across the stone floor behind Hearne. He measured the two small ladlefuls of soup carefully into the plate, and handed it to Pléhec. Two more plates to be filled, and then the tired feet shuffled back across the kitchen floor. Pléhec followed them into the restaurant. The door swung open once more. Hearne slipped his hands into his pockets. I am near enough to the fire to drop the wad of paper into the flames, he thought. But the footsteps were light, and the hand which touched his elbow was friendly. The white-haired man with the sallow skin scarcely flickered his drooping eyelids, as Hearne turned to face him. Like Pléhec, he had aged. Like Pléhec, the lines in his face were more finely drawn, and the shadows under the half-veiled eyes were deeper. As he recognized the Englishman, his smile changed from politeness to pleasure. But he said nothing.

He pointed. Hearne followed him silently into Etienne's room.

CHAPTER **19** CONTACT

It was a dark little room, lighted only by one high narrow window. Duclos gripped Hearne's hand.

"It's good to see you, my friend," he said simply, and then suddenly put both arms round Hearne's shoulders; and their cheeks touched for a moment. Hearne was silent, but he clapped Duclos' arm. It was good to see him.

"Well," Duclos said, "we must be quick. Two Germans in the front room. And we've been watched for the last two days. You want me to send a message?" He was unlacing his boot as he spoke.

"Yes," said Hearne, and handed the wad of paper to Duclos. It was a duplicate of the paper he had given Myles—no, van Cortlandt. His observations and notes, and the list of names and other details of Elise's organization. The Frenchman took it silently and slid it into the sole of his sock. He pulled on his boot again and laced it methodically.

"First of all," said Hearne, "zero date is August 15th. August 15th. Then tell them that a fishing boat must be met off Penzance tomorrow at sunset. Penzance. Tomorrow at sunset. American on board has vital information. Got it?"

Duclos finished tying a loose knot. "Fishing boat. Penzance. Tomorrow at sunset. American," he repeated.

"Then, after that, send the message I've given you, if you have time."

Duclos smiled at the last phrase. "If I am not interrupted, you mean," he said calmly. "First, August 15th; then the fishing boat; then your information. And then?"

"You've reported about the gun emplacements along the coast?"

"I've only heard vaguely about them. We aren't allowed to move about freely, you know."

"Who's covering this territory?" Hearne was half-incredulous, half-angry.

"Dunwoodie was. Haven't heard from him for two weeks. I fear—"

"Jimmy Dunwoodie?"

Duclos nodded sympathetically. Hearne paused. Jimmy Dunwoodie. Another good man . . . no time for thoughts. He shook himself free from them.

"Well then, fourthly, if you still have time: guns are being mounted along this coast, between Le Vivier and Pontorson, about two miles from the sea. Possibly to guard aerodromes, which are also under construction." Must be for the aerodromes, he thought. Large batteries would be pointless here. This part of the French coast was about a hundred and fifty miles from Southampton. Big guns, Michel had said. But all guns seemed big to a child. "Further information regarding aerodromes will follow," he ended.

Duclos repeated the sentences in his low, calm voice.

"That's all," said Hearne. He looked at the Frenchman. "*Au revoir.*" And for God's sake take care of yourself, he added in his heart.

"*Au revoir.*"

Tonight, the customary phrase had a literal meaning which lifted it out of its usual offhand triteness. They meant it, both of them.

Duclos had gone, back to the dining room and his meager supper. Hearne picked up the cook's cap which had fallen from his head, and slipped back into the kitchen. Duclos would finish his dinner unhurriedly, as if he had all the time in the world; and after making his quiet good night to the others, he would walk slowly up the hill in the gathering dusk. He would pause, perhaps for the view, and certainly for breath, on each stone platform as the street became a series of steep twisting steps; and at last he would reach his narrow little house and its quiet garden under the walls of the towering Abbey. There he would settle in the high-ceilinged room at his book-littered desk. And there he would work until the dusk had become night, until it was safe for him to move quickly and silently through the garden, through a door hidden under climbing roses, into the thickness of the garden wall—and then into the base of the Abbey wall itself. The medieval mind which had designed that passage had no doubt pleasanter purposes in view: but now, six hundred years later, medieval ingenuity and secrecy had perhaps their greatest success.

Hearne stood watching the peas swirling in the boiling pot on the iron rack. The acrid smell of vinegar came from the flat dish beside it, where the fish were steaming placidly. Oil must be scarce, he thought: too scarce for fish. He looked at the pail of fish offal. Tomorrow's lunch . . . We'll never know the half of it, he thought: those of us who lived through this war in safety will never know the half of it. Even if we can imagine all the stark bloodshed which peacetime prophets foretold, we shall never guess about the little things, the little things which add up to a horror of their own.

He looked impatiently at his watch. In four hours, perhaps even three, Duclos would send that message. He remembered his last visit here, when Duclos had led him one night into the dark narrow passage within the walls. Then it had been a kind of joke, a strange and rather mad kind of joke. But he also remembered the awe which had silenced his amusement when they at last emerged from that dark journey and found themselves inside the Abbey. They were standing in the shadows of a narrow, half-ruined courtyard. Above them, soaring into the night's soft moonlight, were the delicate spires of chapels, the crenelated edge of terraces and twisting flights of stairs, the crowding walls of mounting churches and Gothic towers. They seemed to stretch up the steepness of the rock as if to reach Heaven itself. It had been a subdued and silent Hearne who had followed Duclos into recently restored cloisters, and from there into a decrepit passage leading down into the depths of the Abbey's foundations. Above their heads, men had once prayed and sung, had feasted and fasted, had fought and lived. But down here, where Duclos was now leading him (with a torch to light up the blocks of stone in their way), men had welcomed death to release them from their tortures, men had gone mad in hidden dungeons, men had been entombed alive in oubliettes. It was one of these, a hole in the wall where men could be forgotten by their enemies, that Duclos had discovered in the course of his excavations.

Pléhec bustled in and out of the kitchen. There was the clatter of plates. Hearne still stood in front of the fire—as if, there in the flames, he could see Duclos making his way so carefully and quietly to the secret oubliette. There had been two iron rings in the wall, at shoulder height. Beneath them lay a small heap of dust and fragments of bone. After the flesh had rotted away, the skeleton's wrists had slipped free from the iron manacles. Death had given a double release. Hearne wondered whether Duclos had buried them when he set up the transmitter that he had smuggled there, piece by piece. Or had he left them to remind himself that others had died for their beliefs—as a savage warning against carelessness? That would be like Duclos, strange mixture of idealism and practicality.

The door of the dining room opened. The firm hard step on the stone floor gave warning. Hearne carefully stirred the soup, all his attention fixed on the hanging iron pot. Light hurried footsteps followed. Thank heaven, Pléhec was watchful.

"Where is it?" It was a voice used to command and demand.

"Through there," answered Pléhec. The confident footsteps resumed their march. A door banged. Pléhec began arranging some food on the two plates which he had placed on the table.

"Less for us all tonight," he grumbled under his breath. He was grudgingly doubling the quantities on the Germans' plates. "Same price, double helpings!" The curses which moved on his lips were as blistering as they were silent.

The door crashed once more: again the steps rang on the floor.

"Such filth," said the German, with characteristic tact. He paused in his stride. "How long must we wait for the food?"

"Coming. This instant," said Pléhec.

The footsteps passed into the restaurant. Pléhec finished arranging the fish and peas on the plates. Then he spat on the fish, and smeared them carefully with his thumb. "*Garni!*" he said, grimly, and carried the plates into the restaurant.

Hearne, concentrating on the soup as if he were preparing the most difficult soufflé, could hear only the voices of the two Germans. The Frenchmen were sitting in complete silence. "How long must we wait for the food?" There was something familiar in that voice. Or perhaps every German talked French with that accent. "How long must we wait for the food?"

Hearne took off the cook's cap and walked silently to the screened restaurant door. By standing at the side of it and gently moving the pleated curtain half an inch, he could see well enough into the front room. The two Germans were at a table near the window. One was a dark-haired young man with a high thin nose and tight eyes. He wore a uniform, but he wasn't a soldier. The other man had his back half-turned to Hearne. Tall; powerfully built. An officer. For an instant, his head turned to watch the silent Frenchmen. For an instant, Hearne could clearly see the even features, the colorless face, the smoothly brushed fair hair. He remembered the fluttering white curtains in Madame Corlay's room, the immovable soldier at the door, the young captain who hadn't enjoyed his visit. The ditch-digger . . . that was it! Deichgräber. If it wasn't Deichgräber, then uniformity was still on the increase in Germany. Deichgräber . . . what the hell was he doing here, anyhow?

Hearne moved quickly back to the table and began shifting some plates about. Pléhec returned, fussed about the pots and the table, and then he was back in the restaurant once more. So it went on for half an hour, and by that time the seven customers had all arrived and been served. By that time the Germans had finished their meal and left.

"They've gone next door. They'll get wine and music there. They didn't think much of this place," Pléhec said when he returned with the news of their departure.

Hearne sat down on the nearest chair. He was tired and hot; his worry over Deichgräber wouldn't go away. It cut through his head like a saw. "Any guess?" he asked Pléhec.

"—Why they were here? Oh, just the usual: they come to look us over about once every week."

"You know them by sight?"

"No; these were new ones. Picquart says they arrived yesterday evening. You'd enjoy Picquart, by the way. Pity you can't meet him this time. He sits at his window next the Hotel Poulard and watches the visitors in its garden. We have many visitors, you understand. We are now a Boche playground. Sometimes it is interesting. When Reichsmarschall Elephantiasis was here, for example. Unfortunately, the little bomb was not expert enough: it didn't go off. But the Reichsmarschall left at once, and two men who had nothing to do with it were executed. That depressed Picquart. Still—it is war." Pléhec hunched his shoulders, and cut himself a slice of bread, and poured himself the last cup in the coffeepot. "It's war. Those who can help must keep alive, even if others are killed. Only those who try to help are any good to France. The others are bilge-water, not even ballast."

"Does Picquart know the names of the visitors?"

Pléhec, his mouth full of bread and the remains of some fish, nodded.

"I'm interested in the names of these two men."

Pléhec rose and wiped his mouth on a corner of his apron. "Must see if Picquart needs some more water to drink." He disappeared through the screened doorway.

He came back soon, licking his lips like a cat. Evidently Picquart's system did work well. "The dark one is secret police. Hans Ehrlich. The other is a captain. Joachim Deichgräber. Both arrived last night by car— with a lady. A Fräulein Lange. You look surprised? I assure you that we have our feminine visitors too. That is quite usual."

Hearne wasn't listening. Hans Ehrlich . . . secret police . . . Hans Ehrlich along with Captain Deichgräber, whom he had seen only a few days ago in St. Déodat. Hans . . . Hans . . . It couldn't be. He was just at the stage of imagining things, of inventing suspicions.

"What's the woman like?" he said suddenly.

"Young and beautiful. They always are."

"Red hair? Dark red—almost brown?" Like the glint of autumn leaves in the evening sun, he thought bitterly. He was being a complete fool: the girl was haunting him.

"Is it important?" asked Pléhec.

Hearne reflected for a moment. "No," he said; and then, "Yes!"

Pléhec looked at him curiously and once more pulled himself out of his chair.

He came back into the kitchen, carrying some dirty plates. "Red hair," he said.

Deichgräber—St. Déodat—Hans—Elise. Hearne's intuition had completed the circle before his mind had dared. "Fräulein Lange," he said aloud. Could that possibly be her second name? Lang-e. Two syllables. And then it dawned on him. "Mademoiselle Lange." This time he gave the French pronunciation, making it one syllable. It sounded convincing.

Pléhec finished lighting the second candle before he looked up. "What does it matter?"

"A lot. If she is the girl I think she is, then she and the dark-haired Hans are responsible for counterespionage in this district."

Pléhec had closed the shutter over the small window. "So?" he said slowly. His eyes moved quickly towards the back entrance to the kitchen. His attention was divided: he was listening.

Hearne said, "They may be here for a short holiday; or they may be here to investigate. There is plenty to investigate." He thought of Duclos and Picquart, the notary; and Pléhec himself. The Frenchman read his thoughts.

"Others too," he remarked. "Guehenneuc has a small printing press. He prints sheets, and then Boulleaux smuggles them out into the mainland. Such things as the truth about Dunkirk, and about Oran. But it would be difficult to guess they came from here. And Dr. Fuzet—"

"So all your customers are in it together?"

"They don't know that."

"But you do?" Hearne grinned at the little fat man in front of him. So here was the real center of all this resistance. Pléhec had understood him. He said simply, "They don't know that either." Again he listened, his eyes slanted towards the back door. The moisture on his pale face gleamed in the light of the candles. His face seemed whiter, his hair darker. "Etienne," he said.

It was Etienne. He locked the door carefully behind him. He no longer wore Corlay's jacket.

Pléhec spoke again. "I've kept you some food." He turned to Hearne. "And you should eat some more too. There's little to offer you but scraps. But even the best people are eating pot scrapings these days." He and Etienne sat down at the wooden table with its clutter of dirty plates and emptied pots. The two plates which the Germans had used were noticeable: they still contained food. Pléhec emptied their leavings into the fireplace. "It would poison even the pigs," he said scornfully.

In the front room, French voices were again talking with their quick staccato accents. There was silence in the courtyard outside the shuttered window. The rejected food hissed and spluttered in the dying fire.

CHAPTER 20 QUICKSAND

If he were to be killed, thought Hearne, then he couldn't have chosen a more beautiful place to end this life. It would be almost worth dying to draw a last breath of this silvered air; to see, as his final glimpse of this world, the fragile spires and curving walls etched against the dark blue sky. The moon was crescent; the stars shone all the brighter for its half-light. Any other visual memories would be bathos after this: this was the ultimate perfection. From behind the shower of stars there should have come the soaring of pure voices in Debussy's "Sirènes." That would have the magic of this picture. Thoughts of death and sirens and glamourie. . . . Hearne smiled to himself as he stretched his body tightly into the shadow of a house wall, and waited for Etienne's touch on his arm to move on again. Thoughts of death and sirens . . . he must be pure Celt after all. This proved it. Only the Celts had thought of this island as the Mountain of the Tomb.

But he wouldn't die tonight: not here. That, Hearne suddenly knew. If you were willing to die, then you didn't. Death liked to snatch you when a hundred reasons pressed on your mind why you must live. He glanced at the thin serious face of the boy who touched his arm so lightly, who now walked so quietly beside him, matching cautious footsteps to his. The boy felt that look, but he still said nothing. Only when assured German footsteps sounded on the stone of the street and its steps would he halt Hearne with his calm grip, guide him unhurriedly and cleverly into deeper shadows, into the labyrinth of passages and alleyways which crisscrossed the Grande-Rue.

They had already passed the parish church and the gardens of the fourteenth-century houses beyond it. Above them, to their left, towered the walls rising from the central peak of the island to guard all the spires and chapels which formed the Abbey. Down to the right would be the ramparts along the sea edge. They were walking northwards on the east side of the island, moving farther and farther away from the gateway by which Hearne had entered the Mont that afternoon. And it was the only entrance and exit. But Etienne must know another way: he was traveling too confidently and easily. Again they halted in the black shadows of the high crowding houses. This would be the fifth time they had taken cover.

Two figures stood on the terrace of the street. They were looking down towards the ramparts and the sea on the east side of the island. The one

nearer Hearne was the dark German who had visited Pléhec's this evening. And then the figures moved, turned to walk down the short flight
of stairs to a new level of the street, and Hearne saw them both clearly.
They were walking towards him, a man and a woman. Hans Ehrlich and
a woman with a gray cloak thrown round her shoulders. As they crossed
a band of soft moonlight, flooding a short stretch of the roadway where
the house walls were lower, the woman's hair caught the faint rays and
held them prisoner for a moment. Hearne couldn't even feel himself
breathing. His arm, resting under Etienne's gentle grip, tightened. The
boy felt, rather than saw, the direction of his eyes, for the darkness of
the empty house, against which they sheltered, was as deep as the plunge
of the Abbey wall down into the street. Together, they watched Elise pass.
Elise, or could it have been Lisa when necessary? Elise Lange: Lisa Lange.
One soft and sibilant: the other, flat and two-syllabled and clear. The
French and the German of it, as it were. Paris, she had said. Paris . . .
so she couldn't even trust her Corlay. She probably trusted no one except
herself. Even Hans would find he had known little of Elise when she
found a *Gauleiter* of a bigger province.

They had passed. The perfume, which Hearne had noticed on the evening Elise had first appeared before him, still clung to the air.

Etienne shivered, as if he were awakening from sleep. Hearne whispered
"Gestapo!" and this time it was the boy's arm which tightened. And then
they were moving along the narrow alley which skirted the open stairs
of the street, moving towards the town ramparts where they joined the
Abbey walls.

For a moment, Hearne wondered if Etienne intended to scale the steps
to the top of the rampart and climb down its north face. But that seemed
madness, for there must be patrols on top. And then, as the boy pulled
him under the shadow of the rampart's tower, he suddenly knew that the
boy would never have entertained such a dangerous idea. They remained
motionless there for two minutes—time enough for Hearne to feel foolish
at the way he had underestimated the boy. Strange, what wild ideas came
to you when you found yourself out of your own particular field, as if you
instinctively feared others' judgments. Hearne stopped worrying, and
decided to let Etienne do the thinking. The boy knew his way about these
walls and ruins. He had played there as a child, and now he was using his
play to outwit those who had invaded his home. When Etienne touched
his arm again, Hearne moved quickly and obediently.

He could feel Etienne leaning his weight against a part of the wall.
Hearne heard the strained breathing, saw the droop of the boy's head between his shoulders as he pushed with the side of his body. A panel of
stones, narrow and low, opened as suddenly as a fissure in quake-racked
earth, opened only enough to let them slide through. Again Hearne felt,
rather than saw, that Etienne was leaning his thin body against the

cemented rocks, and then they were shut into the darkness which lay inside the hollow of the ramparts. Etienne's torch flickered and then held its beam steadily as it swept over the wall six paces in front of them. High above their heads was the rampart walk with its guardhouses. Outside, up there, the Abbey soldiers had once patrolled; and later, tourists had walked and exclaimed; and now soldiers had come back, soldiers with green-gray coats and streamlined helmets.

Etienne's torch picked out the stones he had been seeking. They were easy to find, for they were not the depth of the rest of the wall, and they formed a deep alcove or recess in the tremendous thickness of stone which supported the rampart walk. Hearne, looking quickly over his shoulder, noticed that behind them was a similar recess through which they had entered. It seemed as if there might have been a small gateway through the ramparts at this point once; as if it had been blocked up, but not with the same thickness as the walls themselves. Etienne was advancing over the thick white dust on the ground, the round circle of light from his torch growing larger as he neared the stones on which it was aimed. He beckoned Hearne to follow closely, and placed his shoulder against the stones as he gave his first word and smile. "Swivel," he explained politely, and then the torch was switched off and there was no smile to see, only the darkness. And there was only a feeling of effort as the thin body strained. There was only the dead smell of forgotten space, and the sound of a stone as Etienne's foot slipped gratingly. And then the narrow slab of rock moved slowly aside. The cool clean breeze from the sea ended the feeling of suffocation. In front of them was a panel of night sky, and the gentle movement of small trees swaying like black-shawled women at a funeral. Etienne knocked Hearne's arm impatiently. They stepped over the rough threshold of stone onto firm earth, where the dust had been molded by rain and wind into something solid and clean.

Hearne took a deep breath. They were outside the ramparts. For the second time that night he was thankful for the medieval mind and its love of mysteries. Perhaps it had been the repression of the Middle Ages, its secret opposition to authority, which had created these ingenuities.

Etienne led a careful way through the wooded grove, sloping inevitably towards the sea. Judging by the stars, they were curving round to the west as they approached the north shore of the island. Hearne tried to recapture a visual image of the map of Mont St. Michel. As far as he remembered, the southern half of the island consisted of the houses and shops and was guarded by the ramparts rising from the rocky shore. In the center of the island were the spiraling buildings which formed the "Abbey," enclosed by steep walls of their own. And these walls joined the ramparts of the little town, so that the Abbey and its walls formed its northern boundary. Beyond the Abbey, towards the north shore, were only small trees and shrub falling away to the sea, where the precipices and rocks of the island met the treacherous sands. Small wonder that for seven hundred years no invaders had ever captured this island. No invaders. . . . Hearne thought of the silent, darkened houses behind the ramparts, of the Germans taking their evening stroll while the half-fed Frenchmen were locked indoors. Only invaders, he qualified, who had been handed the keys of the fortress on a silver platter. That was why Pléhec's hate had only been equaled by his bitterness; that was why this boy of sixteen had the eyes and mouth of a man of forty.

Etienne spoke in a whisper. "Soon we shall strike the path of steps from the Abbey's north wall. They will lead us to St. Aubert's spring at the edge of the shore. There is an easy way there of getting onto the sand. The rest of the shore is too steep and dangerous." Hearne nodded, and concentrated on following. The ground was difficult, but if any sentry was looking down from the heights of the deserted Abbey the shadows of the trees and bushes would camouflage their progress. It was with considerable relief that he at last saw the stone staircase. Follow that, and they would reach the shore.

But Etienne had no intention of doing anything as simple as walking down the steps carved out of the rock. He used them only for direction, it seemed. And then Hearne had to admit to himself that the ground was easier, too, at this part. By following the staircase, Etienne was saving them a good deal of effort. That was something to be thankful for, anyway. It was then that they heard the footsteps.

Etienne grasped Hearne's arm as he halted, and pulled him under the cover of a bush. They lay still, their ears straining for every sound. Yes, it was footsteps all right, Hearne decided. Two people. Not guards or sentries: the pace was too broken, too leisurely. Two men talking. Germans, of course; and Germans with special privileges too, to be walking through the Abbey groves at this hour. For no one lived within the Abbey: it was only a museum and showpiece, closing its gates to ordinary mortals each evening. Hearne waited, wondering.

At last the two men came into view: first, their heads; and then their uniforms, as they slowly climbed the stairs back to the Abbey. Two officers, Hearne could see, but that was as far as he could identify them at this distance with the tree shadows blotting out the steps as they did.

A high-pitched voice was saying ". . . fantastic. Pity you couldn't have been here when the moon is full and the tide is phenomenal."

"I can imagine it." This voice was polite, but assured. Hearne's eyes narrowed.

"The Reichsmarschall himself would like to take the whole place and set it up on the Rhine."

"Not on his estate?" The sarcasm in the second voice ended in a laugh.

The high voice laughed too, and turned the conversation. "Interesting what you've been telling me, but I assure you this place is as dead as its

buildings. Have you seen its inmates? They are part of the Museum! Your
—your friends have brought you on a hopeless hunt: there's no game here
for them. I've seen to that already. How long are you staying?"

"Until tomorrow. I must be back then."

The men were almost level with Hearne now. His guess about the
second voice had been right. It was Deichgräber, himself. The high voice
belonged to an older man, a major, Hearne noted.

He was saying, "Are the others leaving with you?"

Deichgräber was answering, "No. They will probably stay longer."

The high voice hardened. "I suppose they don't trust our efficiency in
these matters. How did you get mixed up with them? And what use is a
woman in such things?"

"Headquarters," Deichgräber said briefly in answer to the first question.
But about Elise he made no reply.

The two men halted and turned to watch the sands once more.

"Pity you couldn't have seen high tide at nighttime," the major said. And
then, unexpectedly, "You might at least tell me what brought them here."

"I assure you, Herr Major, that they only tell me as much as they've told
you."

"That English agent . . . he was caught on the mainland. Why do they
come here? Had he friends here?"

For a moment, Hearne's heart had stopped. He didn't hear Deichgräber's reply. And then he realized that the major had used the past
tense. *Had he friends here?* He thought of Dunwoodie, whom Duclos
hadn't seen for two weeks. Something which they had found when they
had searched Dunwoodie or his room had directed Ehrlich to Mont St.
Michel. That must be it. So Duclos had been right about Dunwoodie.

Hearne heard the major say with some bitterness, "I resent this intolerable interference." He had started to climb the steps once more.

"What is it like at high tide?" was Deichgräber's answer. The two
voices faded with the footsteps. Hearne drew a deep breath as the major's
explanations blurred in the distance. Etienne touched his arm. Together
they slipped from the cover of the bush and began the last part of their
journey to the sea. Hearne looked back over his shoulder. The two figures
were still climbing the staircase, their heads bent, their hands clasped behind their backs. It was a scene of touching peacefulness, with the warlike
Germans indulging in the relaxation of a moonlight stroll and a chance
for the practical major to mingle a few off-the-record remarks with his
eulogies on nature.

Either the major's eloquence was effective, or it was just one of those
damnable pieces of luck, but Deichgräber halted suddenly and turned
round for his last view. Even as Hearne caught Etienne and pulled him
into the nearest shadow, the German's arm stretched quickly towards the
major, and pointed. The two men seemed to hesitate, and then Deich-

gräber was leading the major back down the rocky staircase. They were hurrying, but they were taking no special care to walk quietly. So perhaps Deichgräber hadn't been sure that he had seen anything at all, or that there really was someone. And the major was obviously under the belief that his guest was suffering from a moonlight hallucination. Even at this distance, the note of his voice was one of amused annoyance.

Hearne's eyes looked despairingly towards St. Aubert's Well, from shadow to shadow, to see where Etienne and he might slip unobserved away from the determined Deichgräber and the reluctant major. Or could present cover be trusted? Was it better to lie quietly here, or to crawl cautiously into further shadows? And what about the matter of time: could they afford to wait, for the tide wouldn't? This was really Etienne's problem; he knew the ground they would have to cover. The boy seemed to sense Hearne's impatience. He motioned with his head and moved stealthily towards the next tree. By drawing *nearer* the steps, they could follow the almost continuous line of bushes which edged the staircase at this point. And so, mad as it seemed, they crawled through the undergrowth fringing the steps, while behind them the footsteps came nearer. Hearne judged by the desperate quickening in Etienne's pace that he was trying to reach a hiding place before the footsteps caught up with them.

They could hear the words now. ". . . assure you . . . Captain Deichgräber. . . . It would have been seen by my sentries from the Abbey walls. They are constantly on watch. And how do you suppose that anyone could get here? The ramparts on the east, and the rocks on the west are well guarded, too. Where was it you saw this shadow?"

The footsteps halted. "Just over there."

"Can't see a thing," the major grumbled. "Shadows everywhere. Remember how you admired the shadows playing over the sands?"

"I saw something." Deichgräber was obdurate.

"I assure you, the sentries—"

"There should be searchlights."

"There are." The major's voice tightened. "There are, when the danger is *real*, such as at high tide when boats might slip in to help someone to escape. At present, no one would venture on these sands. All that searchlights do is to make this a perfect beacon to guide English planes." He obviously didn't like this interference, and interference by a junior officer, at that. Deichgräber's officiousness was going to be a useful ally to the man and the boy who had now reached the last of the bushes. Before them, the rocky ground dipped suddenly, and they could see the wet sand gleaming darkly. Using the outline of the bush to blot out their movements, they slipped cautiously in turn over the edge of rock. Etienne's arm steadied Hearne and encouraged him. This sudden dip in the ground would shield them from the men behind; unless, of course, the two Germans were to retrace their steps right down to St. Aubert's Well. The stone platform on which it stood was just below this hiding place. From the well, the Germans could look back up the hill and see them.

"I trust you are satisfied?" the major said at last, breaking the silence which had become oppressive. There was a cold sweat on Hearne's brow. His tensed muscles cramped under the strain of crouching.

Deichgräber's voice was deferential but determined. "With your permission, Major, I shall continue my walk to the Chapel."

There was a silence.

Hearne suddenly realized that if Etienne didn't know much German, then the strain must be doubled for him. He clapped the boy's shoulder gently, reassuringly. That might have been a smile in reply through the blackness of the shadow. Hearne was wondering if he dared shift his weight onto the other knee, when the major answered.

"Very well," he said stiffly. "Report to me in my quarters in half an hour." The voice was as controlled as a refrigerator. The reprimand was not lost on the younger man. There was a clicking of heels, and probably an efficient salute to match, as he acknowledged it. Then they heard the major's footsteps climbing away from them. Still Deichgräber hadn't moved. Hearne imagined him standing half-angry, half-worried, looking at the wooded, rocky slope around him with impatience and distaste.

It was then that Etienne's hand grasped Hearne's arm again. This time, Hearne followed unbelievingly as the boy led him forwards, and obliquely away from the steps. But there was nothing else Hearne could do except follow. The boy was far from stupid. He couldn't have thought that Deichgräber's steps synchronized with the major's. There was only one pair of footsteps climbing towards the Abbey: that was obvious to anyone who listened well. And Etienne was a good listener. Hearne had had that proved to him, tonight.

Even as Deichgräber started to descend the staircase, Etienne reached his goal. It was a deep narrow fissure, a slit through the plunging rocks of the cliff. Hearne's hands rested against the cold granite walls which rose above his head on either side of him. His feet fumbled cautiously for the roughly hewn steps. At least, there was no more crouching. Etienne's arm was the guide. He would pull Hearne's shirt gently for each step forward; for each pause, his hand would press against Hearne's chest. The seeing eye, Hearne thought grimly, and stepped and paused and stepped obediently. That blasted ditch-digger couldn't see them anyway. The only danger now was that he could hear them, and that accounted for the slowness of their descent. Cautiously they worked their way down through the cleft, originated by nature, improved by man. Deichgräber's footsteps, quieter and more cautious now that he was alone, had passed well to the left of them. He should be almost at the little stone house built over the well. Yes, he must be there: his footsteps no longer grated against the stairs.

Etienne seemed to pay little attention to the German now. Their journey through the cleft in the short cliff was almost over; the rocky walls on either side of them rose higher as they neared the shore level. Hearne found it difficult not to think what happened if a fat man had to make his escape through this narrow passage. He would probably come out corrugated, if at all. But at last, he felt softness under his feet, and Hearne knew he had reached the foot of the cliff. In front of them, and to either side of them, stretched the miles of flat sand; stretching like a sheet of watered silk under the perfect sky. Too perfect, thought Hearne. A few nice deep banks of thick cloud would have been a help. These little puffs of smoke up there might be highly ornamental, but they only served to float chasing shadows on the brownish sand. Still, even a few shadows were not to be despised. And the moon was young enough not to illuminate the whole place in efficient floodlighting. "But just where do we go from here?" Hearne said to himself. They must reach solid ground again before daybreak: apart from the matter of light, there was also the tide to guard against.

Etienne kicked off the thin leather shoes from his feet. Their lack of heels and toe caps made them look like a sort of slipper, but they had carried him easily and lightly over the worst ground. It was surprising how securely they had clung to his feet like a *torero's* shoes, stamping, running, side-stepping on the arena. Hearne, sitting on an outcrop of rock, resting his cramped back against a dank wall of cliff, followed Etienne's example. He flinched as his feet sank into the sand, for here it was thick and moist, and, without the sun to give it surface warmth, it was as cold as . . . as cold as . . . He finished tying his boots carefully together, and draped them by the laces round his neck. As cold as a grave, he decided grimly, and rolled his trousers up under his knees as Etienne had done.

The boy stood with his back pressed against the cliff. He nodded as Hearne finished, and pointed to the left. They moved, keeping close to the shadow of the rocky precipice. There was no need to worry about the sound of their steps, here. The sand deadened all noise. Once they skirted this northern shore and slipped round to the west side of the island, they would be safer, for at present it would be heavily in shadow. By the time the moon, or what there was of one, sailed over to that side of the Mont, they should be safely on the mainland. From where they stood now, it was about half a mile to the causeway and entrance to Mont St. Michel. And from there, it was just over another mile to the flat shore of the bay. Hearne remembered the little river which flowed into the Bay of Mont St. Michel, just to the west of the Mont itself. Now that the tide was out, it was only a thin line of shallow pools, a skeleton river spreading forlornly towards the sea between banks of sand. He believed he could now guess Etienne's plan. They were to reach this ghost river at the northwest corner of the island, and, by following its course to the mainland from which it flowed, they could use its banks of sand as cover. It was shallow cover certainly, but still it was cover. The danger would now not be so much from the sentries on the ramparts as from the wet sand. That was why Etienne was going barefoot. That way, even if they stepped into a quicksand, they would have a chance. With boots, there would be no chance at all. And that, too, was why Etienne was starting their journey at once; that was why he wasn't going to wait under the northern cliffs until Deichgräber had returned to report to the major. For high tide would come again in all its terrifying speed about half-past four. These seven miles of sand which stretched out to sea would be swiftly covered by the rush of waters, and the channel of the river bed would be hidden, and the sea would sweep up the river into the mainland as far as six miles deep. Hearne looked at his watch. Yes, there was no time to waste. The distance which they had covered from Pléhec's restaurant to this point was not much over a mile, perhaps even less. They had taken one hour and three quarters to reach here. It was a record of caution. He looked at the dark, thin-faced boy beside him, so silent and calculating. It seemed incredible that anyone so young as this should have such patience and restraint. War was a hard schoolmaster.

From the rocks above them came no sound of footsteps. The German must be standing quite still beside the well, searching this side of the island with his eyes. Hearne suddenly wondered if a direct path led from the well down to the shore. If there was one, they'd have to pass its mouth, and that wouldn't be a pleasant two minutes. If there was one . . . There was.

They saw it after they had gone less than fifty paces. Etienne's speed slackened, and he stood with his head slightly tilted to one side as if to hear better that way. His eyes flickered impatiently. From where they stood in the safe shelter of the rocks at the mouth of the path, they could see along the first ten feet. The track must curve round towards the terrace on which the little stone building was built over the spring, for they couldn't see St. Aubert's Well from here. If they couldn't see, they probably couldn't be seen. The man and the boy listened. But nothing stirred. It was uncanny: they had heard no footsteps climbing back to the Abbey on the hill. But at last Etienne seemed satisfied. His hand flicked impatiently towards the other side of the path. Hurry, it seemed to say: hurry! Without further delay, or even a glance up at the path, he had slipped across its entrance. Hearne followed as quickly. They seemed a ghost and its shadow.

No one had been on the path. That, Hearne had verified. The danger point was passed. Their speed increased. Three hundred feet ahead of them was the northwest promontory of the island with a chapel on its rocks. Three hundred feet, one hundred yards, and they would be on the darkened west side of the Mont. The sand was firm enough so far, and the walking was easy. But farther out from the rocks, the sand's color changed in light and dark patches; and even on its apparent flatness there must have been hollows, for the inches of water which still lay in them spread like black shadows. Hearne was wondering which were the danger spots, the dry or the wet sand. . . . He thought he remembered something about wet sand, but it was only a vague memory. If it were true, then the journey back to the mainland under cover of the flat banks of that stream would be no picnic. It would be a hopeless attempt without Etienne as guide. Even as Hearne worried to himself, the sand's consistency changed under his feet. It became a soft rubber sponge, letting his weight sink for a good six inches into it, oozing quickly over his instep and round his ankles. It wasn't a quicksand: it was just a hint of what they would have to deal with if Etienne were to lead them into one. But it wasn't pleasant. Hearne stepped carefully, so that the half-sucking, half-sobbing sounds, when he drew each foot out from the semi-liquid surface, would be minimized. Again their pace slowed. Etienne gave one of his rare smiles, and pointed to the stretch of sands to their right. He emphasized the direction by shaking his hand warningly and then pointing it quickly downwards. The gesture was explicit enough.

He would be glad when he got out of this, Hearne thought. It was the highest piece of understatement which he had ever committed. If anyone could have listened in to his emotions at that point, they would have heard one long despairing groan. He tried not to look at that smooth treacherous surface. Ten feet away. Much too near for his idea of comfort. Perhaps it was only imagination on his part, but he really felt that the give of the sand under his feet had increased. It swallowed more than his ankles now. Then suddenly it had become firm again, and Hearne breathed more naturally. But Etienne still motioned towards their right, still shook his hand, still pointed downwards. He was a nice boy, but Hearne wished he would stop the hand effects. After all, that idea didn't need to be driven home twice. He kept rigidly behind Etienne, almost treading on his heels. If the boy had been afraid that Hearne would step out to the side to walk abreast, then he had won his point.

They were almost at the promontory. Thirty feet, or less, still to go. Then these cliffs to their left would swing round almost at right angles to face the west. From here, they could already see the shallow pools which traced the course of the stream.

And then, from the shadows of a jutting rock, stepped Deichgräber. He had a gun in his hand, a smile on his lips.

"Up!" he said. "Up!"

They raised their hands above their heads, Etienne still holding his shoes.

"Drop them!"

Etienne did. They landed at his feet.

Deichgräber's smile changed. He had half-recognized Hearne. He narrowed his eyes for a moment and then he said triumphantly, "My friend on the farm! Well, now! Corlay is the name, I believe?"

Hearne tried to make his voice sound natural, even amused. "Captain Deichgräber, of course. Well, now we can take our hands down."

"Keep them where they are! I was just about to waste a bullet on each of you, but now I think you will be more interesting as prisoners than as corpses. Will you tell me why you are here, or do you prefer to wait until I signal for the guards?"

"Don't be a bloody fool, Deichgräber. Do you want Ehrlich and Lisa to laugh behind your back?" Hearne spoke as if he had the rank of general, at least.

"What has Ehrlich to do with this?" Deichgräber was angry, but he still kept the smile which was not a smile in place.

"Ask him."

"I shall. Turn round, and start walking back. Any suspicious move and—"

"You will apologize handsomely for this," Hearne warned indignantly. "Why don't you summon the guards now, so that we can end this farce quickly? It would be simple enough. A couple of shots—"

"If you are as innocent as you pretend, there will be no need to summon the guard. If you aren't, they'll hear the couple of shots when they strike your bodies."

Hearne shrugged his shoulders. "By this time, the men I am after will have heard us and escaped. Fool," he said venomously.

Deichgräber ignored that. He pointed to Etienne.

"And who's this supposed to be?"

"He's my informant. You could do with one yourself, couldn't you?" The savage sneer, the authoritative tone, had some effect, but not enough. "Wait until the major hears about it," Hearne went on. "The new broom sweeps clean, too clean. I hope you'll enjoy your new command after this." That was a double-edged barb. Deichgräber as visitor to Mont St. Michel had not even the privilege of being a new broom.

"We'll get back to the Abbey," he said, but the calculated smile had vanished.

Hearne stood very still. He seemed to be listening intently, his eyes fixed anxiously on the stony promontory behind the German's back. "I thought I heard them," Hearne said, as if to himself. His voice was a mixture of anger and savage disappointment. "Our voices must have carried. They'll get away."

"Just where are these mysterious people?" The voice was contemptuous, but Deichgräber still watched Hearne, still pointed the revolver.

"At that small chapel on the promontory. You saw it, didn't you? But let's get back to the others. Perhaps it won't be too late even then, to catch these men. Come on, Pierre—" he spoke to the boy beside him, who was standing motionless, his eyes on the ground—"we may get some results if we hurry."

Etienne had flashed a glance at Hearne at the mention of the false name. With his hands still held high, he slipped his right foot casually into one shoe. Deichgräber hadn't noticed anything strange about that. Hearne drew a deep breath.

"We'll have to hurry," he said to the German, holding his attention by the urgency of his voice and eyes. Etienne was fumbling for the second shoe; and when his foot couldn't find it, he knelt quite naturally to pick it up, his eyes still on the German, his free hand still in the air. He straightened slowly, both hands in the air now; he looked as if he were very bored.

Etienne's leg moved so quickly that even Hearne was surprised. His right foot struck the German sharply on the wrist, with a savage side-kick which sent the arm high and the revolver flying. It fell somewhere in the rocks behind Deichgräber, as the shoe from Etienne's left hand caught him across the mouth and silenced the shout from his opened lips. Hearne closed in, and the German warded off his blow with a kick from a heavy boot. The kick was sufficient to throw Hearne sharply against a low rock, and the jagged edge caught him beneath the knees like a knife: he lost his balance, falling backwards on the hard sand with a thud which smashed all the wind out of him. He lay still for a moment, his eyes closed. The German must have thought he was knocked out, for he turned and struck at Etienne. The boy slipped from his reach, twisted and turned, and ran back towards St. Aubert's Well. He looked easy to catch. The German, not even pausing to shout, was on his heels. Etienne side-stepped, was missed by inches, started running out from the shore as if he had lost his head. The watching Hearne, picking himself up dizzily from the sand, smothered a shout in his throat into a hoarse croak of warning. Again Etienne side-stepped. But this time his arm was raised. Hearne saw the gleam of a knife as the boy's arm struck at the German's neck, saw Deichgräber plunge heavily forward. He landed on one knee, his hands on the sand before him. And then the knee and hands disappeared. Deichgräber struggled, tried to shout, but the struggles became a spasm and the shout was only a whisper. The sand sucked more deeply; the grip was firm.

Hearne sat down on the rock. "God in Heaven," he was saying to himself. "God in Heaven."

Etienne came running lightly back, Etienne whose feet hadn't paused for a moment even when he had stabbed. He was searching for his shoes, picking them up carefully. He was waiting for Hearne. "Come," he said, "we've little time, now."

Hearne hesitated and looked towards the lump in the dark sands. Only twenty feet away . . . the strangled shout had given way to a moan, and then there was nothing to hear. Etienne must have read his thoughts. He

said to Hearne, "He will soon be under: he struggled too much. It was
either him, or us and our friends."

"Yes," said Hearne, "it was either him or all of us." But he didn't look
back, as they walked on in silence. Not even when they had reached the
promontory did he look round. He was thinking, Deichgräber must have
gone right down the stone staircase without waiting at the spring; he must
have followed the path directly onto the shore while we were still coming
down that cleft in the rock. He must have guessed that if anyone was
escaping, they would make for the sand. And then he had explored it as
far west as this promontory; he must have been on his way back when he
saw us coming. Probably he was going to explore the east part of the north
shore then. He was thorough, all right. And he was ambitious. Too ambitious. If he hadn't thought he could torture more information out of us
as prisoners, he would have shot us dead on sight. But that was one way
of dying which they didn't teach him in a Death-and-Glory academy.

Hearne followed Etienne automatically. Even when searchlights suddenly blazed over the north-shore sands, even when one of them swept
round to the west while they both stretched flat on the mainland shore,
Hearne was apathetic. Emotionally, he had reached saturation point. He
just lay patiently, and waited until the beam of light was switched away.

"They can't risk it for long," Etienne whispered consolingly.

Hearne nodded. "They are worried about him," he suggested. "He's
overdue. Search parties out now, probably."

"They'll find nothing. *Les lises.* . . ." The boy shrugged his shoulders.

Les lises. Water holes. . . . So that explained the quickness of Deichgräber's end. Hearne remembered Pléhec's vivid description of them one
evening during his last visit to the Mont. Water holes, they were: water
holes covered with a deceptive layer of sand. Just another of Mont St.
Michel's little surprises, Pléhec had said. *Spécialité de la maison*, Pléhec
had added, and they had all laughed.

"No," Hearne said. "They'll find nothing."

"And by the time the light is good enough to search properly, the tide
will be in." The boy's voice was unemotional. He was neither triumphant
nor fearful. He noticed Hearne's curious stare.

"My father was killed. That was in the war, and that was what one
could expect. War is war. But two weeks ago my brother was shot. Shot
for something which he didn't do, didn't even know about. He and another, just chosen blindly, just pushed against a wall and shot in cold
blood." He paused, his voice still unemotional. "*Merde, alors!*" he said
suddenly and buried his face in his arms.

At last Hearne said, "I'm all right, again," and the boy rose silently to
lead him over the salt-meadows. Clouds had blown up. A wind ruffled
the trees lining the bank of the small canalized river, which Etienne now
followed.

"I go this way, my friend," Hearne whispered as they halted near a road. He swept his arm to the south and the west.

Etienne smiled. "Soon the tide will come in. This river will be flooded and the boats will leave from Pontorson. Pléhec said you might as well sail."

"To where?"

"Past St. Malo. Anywhere up the River Rance towards Dinan, if that suits you."

Hearne was smiling now, too. "Can I sleep on that boat?" he asked.

Etienne was politely amused.

"Sleep, and rest these blasted legs?"

Etienne was still amused, but he nodded reassuringly. "After we get there," he added cautiously.

"We shall," Hearne said with unusual confidence.

And they did.

CHAPTER **21** THE AWAKENING OF
ST. DÉODAT

Another dawn was breaking when Hearne came back to St. Déodat. This time, he did not walk through the village. This time, he did not trouble to count the Picrels, the Guérins, or the Trouins. In these gray-stone houses now slept gray-uniformed men. Yesterday had been the day of their coming. Yesterday had been the day for Nazi flags and, no doubt, a Nazi band playing in the market place. Hearne wondered if they had had the insolence to play Breton songs. Yet that had happened in other places. Anyway, the Picrels, the Guérins, the Trouins must have laid themselves down to sleeplessness with bitter thoughts last night. Grim as were his own at this moment, Hearne wondered just how he would feel if the names had been Jones, Brown, Robinson. Maniacal, he decided: without either exaggeration or heroics, quite simply maniacal. He looked down the hill at the dim shapes of the quiet houses round the towering church, and he remembered the third tree in the seventh row in the Corlay orchard. There would be many third trees in these farms in this hill and valley, and in all the other hills and valleys of Britanny. "*Ni zo Bretoned, tud kaled,*" Henri had said.

Hearne found himself quietly whistling the refrain of "*Bro goz ma zadou,*" the Breton national song, as he crossed the stone yard of the Corlay farm. The kitchen door was closed, but unlocked. Henri was kneeling beside Albertine, helping her place the first log of the new day on the glowing embers in the hearth. They turned round as Hearne entered. They waited until the last line of the song was completed, and then they came forward together, came forward almost quickly.

"You're home," said Albertine. Her voice was roughly kind. Old Henri grinned through the gaps in his gums. He said nothing, but reached up with his thin, corded hand to pat Hearne awkwardly on the shoulder.

"He's ice-cold," Albertine said. "Henri, get that fire going. Do you want him to starve?"

Henri obeyed with unaccustomed willingness.

"What's happened to your clothes? Where did you get that hat?" Albertine looked at it unbelievingly. "It smells of fish."

"All of me does," Hearne said. He felt pleased by their welcome—pleased and yet worried. Had Madame Corlay talked more than he had expected? He watched Albertine as she bustled about the kitchen. She asked so many questions on top of one another, not even waiting for his answers, that he was spared the agony of conversation. Where were his own clothes, was that nice young American safe, how were his feet and the trousers which Albertine had sewn to fit him, had they seen any Boches, were they caught in that rain, why didn't he get home yesterday? That last question was the key. They had begun to get alarmed. This sudden friendliness was chiefly due to relief. And she still called him Bertrand quite naturally: so if Madame Corlay had told, she still hadn't told everything. Hearne ate and watched the simple face under its white-starched cap, looking anxiously to see if he enjoyed the food, if it were enough. He judged from the quantity she had placed before him that she had included her own share, and perhaps even Henri's. Hearne ate the amount he was usually given, and refused the rest, saying that that was all he could eat. By the sudden light in Henri's eye, he knew his guess about the food had been right. He gave the old man a grin, and Albertine a hearty clip round the waist, as he rose and walked over to the fire.

Her severe face relaxed. "You'll spoil my apron," she said, but color had flooded into the patch of red veins on her cheeks. Henri and Hearne both laughed.

"God," he said, "it's good to be home," and stood with his back to the fire.

Old Henri nodded. His fingers were tapping out the rhythm of "*Bro goz ma zadou*" on the wooden table. The sound drew Albertine's attention.

"Henri!" she said sharply. "Your work. Jean and Marie will be almost finished." The old man rose and moved slowly to the door leading into the byre. He gave Hearne a side-look and an unmistakable wink. Hearne grinned: in every language it meant the same . . . anything for a quiet life.

"What is it?" asked Albertine, sensing the conspiracy.

"Good to be back," repeated Hearne cheerfully. He heard light footsteps coming down the staircase into the hall. Yes, it was good to be back.

The door opened and Anne came in. She had dressed completely, to the last button of the tight-bodiced dress, to the last smooth braid round her head. For a moment, watching the simplicity of her smile, the honesty of her eyes, Hearne wished he really were Corlay. It would be something to have a look like that for one's own.

She said, "I knew it was you. I was listening and I heard you whistle. I knew you had come back."

There was the same directness in her speech that had greeted him the first time they had met. Then, she had told him she couldn't marry him. Now, she looked as if she would marry him tomorrow. It wasn't, he thought, as he watched the neat weave of plaited hair, it wasn't that women were fickle. They were completely loyal: either to themselves, like Elise, or to others, like Anne. But when they made their illogical leaps and still managed to balance themselves neatly in reverse, it wasn't because they had changed. They were still the same: it was only the outside influences which had changed, and by some strange alchemy made them feel like saying *Yes* when they had once said *No*. Madame Corlay had only to say "He has changed"; he had only to prove it; and above all he had only to show his distrust of Elise. That was all—and Anne's doubts and fears had vanished. The icicles had melted. In some curious way, which he couldn't manage to analyze, he felt pleased. But it would have made things easier if she had still distrusted him; now he would have warmth and affection to deal with. Thank heaven that Anne was Anne, that complications could be kept as simple as possible. He looked at her. She was unique, in a certain sense. She was shy without affectation or awkwardness: she was innocent without being ignorant, modest without being stupid. He almost laughed at that—modest. . . . It had been a long time since he had thought of that word.

"Why are you looking at me like that?" Anne was disturbed, as if she feared she wasn't pleasing him.

"It's nice to relax," he said. It was true: for the last ten minutes, he hadn't even thought of a bloody Nazi.

Albertine said, "Get those clothes off, and I'll wash them. They are smelling up the whole kitchen," and then to Anne, who was listening with a smile, "Did you wake Madame when you rushed down here?"

Anne shook her head, and the color came into her cheeks. Not, decided Hearne, because she might have wakened Madame, but because the rushing had been so obvious. He looked down at his clothes. After the second hour on that boat he must have lost his sense of smell.

Anyway, relaxing was over for the day. Albertine was in charge.

His room had been scoured and polished; otherwise, it was untouched. The bookcase still held its secrets. The books were in the same order, even to that upside-down volume which he had left to test any curious fingers.

It seemed strange not to have the American next door to his room. In the short time he had been there, he had become a part of this house. Strange not to hear the limping step, or the deep voice talking its own variation of French. As Hearne washed and changed the disreputable blue shirt and corduroy trousers for something cleaner but less comfortable, he wondered how van Cortlandt was liking Matthews. Van Cortlandt . . . why had he called himself Myles? Probably some psychological impulse when he was forced into the danger of giving his real name, some impulse rooted in that story he had promised to tell later.— Here I am, Myles from home, he would think. Well, that made two stories Hearne owed himself when he got back to Britain. When . . . Myles's—no, van Cortlandt's; and Sam's. That would be a fair do, that would. And they would make it a night, lad. His attempt at Yorkshire was more than the razor could bear. He sighed, and patiently washed the streaming blood off his chin. By the time the flow had become an ooze, and the last slow drop had hardened into a clot, he had next week's plans fixed, with the help of his map. A week was all he could depend on, now. Elise was due back from her trip to "Paris" on the twentieth of July. Ten days, she had said. That gave him just seven days more of this kind of thing. He might even have to work in daylight to get all the information he wanted. For when these seven days were over, he might find little time free for himself and his work. Then he would simply have to seize any chance he could: for with Elise's unexpected demands there would be an end to systematic observation.

When he went downstairs, Anne was alone in the kitchen.

"Albertine's gone to Mass," she began, and then she was looking at his chin.

"What about you?" His voice was half-teasing.

"I wanted to see you alone. Look, I must get you something for that cut." She didn't wait for an answer, but ran lightly into the storeroom. She brought back a bottle of colorless liquid.

"Please don't trouble," Hearne said, but inside he felt rather pleased at her solicitude. She dabbed the liquid lightly over the cut. She was so absorbed in everything she did, he thought, as he watched her eyes fixed so intently on his chin. The cut stung into life again, and he grinned as he saw the look of dismay on Anne's face when the blood trickled over his chin once more.

He jammed a handkerchief hard against it, saying, "Thank you. That will cure it, I'm sure," and wondering if Adam's rib had been better left in place. But it was difficult to feel irritated with Anne: not when she was still trying to look dismayed, when she was trying so hard to keep from laughing.

"You wanted to see me alone?" he suggested.

She nodded, and put the offending bottle down on the table.

"Yes. I went down to the village yesterday, and—" He touched her arm and silenced her. He pointed towards the thin wooden partition which separated the outbuildings from the kitchen. She lowered her voice. "Only old Jean and Henri are there," she said in surprise. "Marie has gone with Albertine."

"They'll soon be in here for breakfast. I'd like to walk in the high field. Would it be too cold for you?"

She shook her head and lifted a black shawl from the back of a chair. In silence, she walked up the hill beside him, her arms crossed under her breast to hold the shawl tightly in place, her smooth head slightly bowed, her full skirts billowing out like a black umbrella in the morning wind.

When they reached the high field, and walked on open ground with no bushes or trees near them, Anne halted.

With a smile, she said, "May I talk now?"

Hearne laughed, and nodded. "Let's keep near the cabbage patch," he answered. "We ought to have a good excuse to be up here, even at this hour."

"Excuses for everything," Anne said with surprising bitterness. "Excuses for just being on our own land, or for standing in our own market place, or—"

Hearne interrupted. "It isn't ours at the moment, Anne. They are the men in possession, whether they call it protection, occupation, or conquest. All we can do is wait, and live our own secret lives and make our own plans. They haven't possessed our minds; and they won't, unless we let ourselves be deluded. How is it in the village?"

"As you would expect. You remember I went down with you to the village on the afternoon before you left with Monsieur Myles? I didn't want to make people think I was looking for Kerénor. I walked about and visited different friends. I couldn't find him. I went to see Monsieur le Curé, but I couldn't find him either. Then when I came home, you were upstairs in your room with Monsieur Myles, and Albertine said you were both too busy. I waited, but you didn't come down; and then I had to go upstairs to read to Madame Corlay before bedtime. And then we went to bed, and I never saw you before you left. It really was such a disappointing day: nothing had come right, and I was very angry with myself."

Hearne nodded. "Too bad it happened on your first try, but don't blame yourself. It's often like that."

"But I went down to the village yesterday afternoon." Anne was smiling now, so the disappointment couldn't have been repeated. "And this time, I did see Kerénor. He was sitting on the stone bridge, alone with old Monsieur Guézennec and young Picrel. He said 'What are you doing here? Don't you know the Boches are arriving, and no one is going to be in the streets to welcome them? I'm taking you straight home.' You see, he and the others were turning back anyone from entering the village at that end. And he had men at the other end of the road to stop people coming from the farms on that side. And there *was* no one in the streets, not a soul to be seen. Even the older children had been taken care of. You know how children run out to see motorcars and soldiers? Well, Monsieur le Curé had taken them all for a picnic to the ruined castle, and he wasn't going to bring them back until the early evening; and then he was going to march them straight home—no playing on the pavement or in the market place. That's why I couldn't find Monsieur le Curé or Kerénor the day before: they were arranging all this."

Anne was excited over her story. She paused to see its effect on Hearne. But he was chiefly interested in the last sentence. "Monsieur le Curé and Kerénor—were they always friendly?"

"No, not at all."

"What is Monsieur le Curé like?"

"He's not very big. He's sort of fat. He has a deep laugh. And he's kind. Everyone likes him. Even Kerénor used to say that, as a man, he wasn't bad."

Hearne, rather impatiently, said, "Yes. But what does he feel about the Boches?"

Anne looked at him in surprise. "Why, he feels as we do."

Hearne was thoughtful. The Breton priests had the reputation of being brave men. Few of them were given to equivocation and appeasement. They belonged with the people; but he wanted to be quite sure. He asked, "What did he say in his last sermon, for instance? Were you there?"

"Oh yes, everyone was there. Even Kerénor. Strangely enough, Monsieur le Curé said something very like what you told me."

"I told you? When?"

"Just five minutes ago . . . you know, about not letting them conquer our minds. He said we must help each other to keep our minds free from lies against ourselves and our true friends: that as long as our minds were free and we had courage and faith, there was hope. *He that leadeth into captivity shall go into captivity: he that killeth with the sword must be killed with the sword.* And then we sang our hymn—the one you were whistling as you crossed the courtyard this morning. When we got to the refrain, many men couldn't sing any more, and the women were crying quietly." Anne's voice trembled, and she turned to look at the trees which sheltered the back of the village.

Hearne kept silent. *As long as the sea is its rampart, may my country hold its head high in freedom,* he remembered. Now the sea was no longer the rampart of Brittany's freedom; now it was the only road to freedom.

At last he said, "What about Kerénor?"

Anne was looking at the ground, digging the toe of her black leather shoe gently into the rich earth, watching it fall in thick moist lumps from the leather as she tilted her foot.

Hearne tried again. "What did Kerénor say about my message?"

She faced him so suddenly that he knew she had been trying to find courage to tell him. "He wouldn't believe me."

"Wouldn't believe you?"

"No. He said you were a Fascist; that you would do as the Germans told you, and enjoy it."

Hearne said to himself, "The damned fool, the bloody idiot." And then he remembered that, if he had really been Corlay, Kerénor would have been right. He met Anne's gray-blue eyes, anxious, worried, apologetic. "I see," he said calmly.

"Of course he doesn't *know—*" Anne began, and then halted.

"Know what?" he asked quickly, almost sharply. Anne's eyes flickered.

"Know that you've changed," she said in a low voice.

He looked at her searchingly. Did *she* know? Had Madame Corlay told her everything? He could read nothing in the calm gentle face except trust and loyalty and—he shook himself free from these thoughts. Now *he* was being the damned fool: what on earth had almost made him say "admiration"? How could she find any admiration for a Corlay who had treated her and his own country so abominably?

"So he doesn't believe me," he said and laughed bitterly. He still couldn't conceal his disappointment. "Did you tell him what I said about Elise?"

"Yes."

"And even that didn't convince him I might have changed even as he has changed?" Strange how an intelligent man could always admit his own change of faith, and feel honest and brave about the admission, and yet could go on distrusting any change professed by another man.

Anne shook her head slowly. She seemed to be fumbling for words. Watching her, Hearne knew that Kerénor's comment had been bitter. I bet it's a corker, he thought. It was.

"He—well, he laughed. He said that was the joke of the year. And then he said that it just needed that touch to convince him completely that you were a—a Fascist liar."

Hearne looked so blankly at her that she rushed on, "You see, he thinks you have always been a bad influence on Elise. And he says that Elise is vain and weak and may be pleasant to the Germans, because that kind of person always is. But it is quite impossible for her to have any power, or to be dangerous except to herself."

"I see. And I suppose I was only accusing Elise, so that by sacrificing her I could prove how truly I have changed?"

"That was what he thought."

Hearne looked at the large, serious eyes: in the early morning light they were gray, a soft clear gray.

"And what does Anne think?" he asked gently.

Anne smiled. "I think that Kerénor is being too clever. He always did think too much. He'd find reasons behind reasons, and all he did was to make himself feel clever and unhappy. He really did love Elise once; now, I think he despises her for what he calls her 'weakness.' But he is still infatuated. She is very beautiful, isn't she?" There was an anxious look in her eyes as she waited for his answer.

"Yes, she's beautiful, Anne. But it's skin-deep. She'll need something more than that when she is reaching the age of forty."

Anne smiled again, this time a strange little smile, but didn't reply. She was looking at the earth once more. She was probably thinking that forty seemed much too far off to be of any consolation to the women Elise was going to hurt before then.

Hearne was making a pretense of studying the rows of vegetables. What, he was asking himself, what are we to do now? Just leave St. Déodat to its fate at the hands of the sweet Elise and her gentle friends? Or should he make one more try? Monsieur le Curé . . . would he listen, or had he his own distrusts of Corlay? Hearne walked among the rows of round fat cabbages, and wondered. After all, this wasn't his job. . . . His job was to report on the traffic on the roads and railways and canal. His job was to get information liable to form a patch of the crossword puzzle which Matthews and these other blokes in their hush-hush rooms could fit together into a pattern of German intentions. His job was to do a microscopic piece of the groundwork for future bombing raids, for the upsetting of carefully laid invasion plans. He halted and looked at the sun's broadening rays flowing over the hillsides, over the sheltered village and open farms. By God, he thought, anything which hurts the Nazis, anything which helps their enemies, is also part of my job. He could always argue that with Matthews, and he knew that, if his real mission was well done, Matthews would listen and even agree. *If* his real mission was well done. Matthews was a Scot.

His best plan would have to be this: to wait until the time came for him to start his last walk to the coast. Then Madame Corlay, after he had left, could tell Monsieur le Curé everything, and by that time his warning would be believed. If, he thought in sudden gloom as he looked towards the hidden houses of St. Déodat, if it were not too late for some of them by that time.

Anne had come up to him. Her hand lightly touched his arm for a moment. "Marie and Albertine are home now," she said. "They've just entered the house. I think I must go back."

"So she bullies you too?" Hearne said teasingly.

"Albertine? But she's so old, and she works so hard, and she deserves some kind of—"

"Respect?"

"Well, yes. Why are you smiling? Do I seem so stupid?"

"You seem just the way I like to think of you, Anne." He paused. "Anne—" He paused again. Hell, he kept saying "Anne, Anne, Anne." Was it an easy name for his tongue, or what?

"Yes?" she said, and halted with her head slightly tilted to one side. Not coy. No, she wasn't coy. She was just Anne.

"Never mind," he said abruptly, and began walking quickly down to the house. She was hurrying to keep up with him.

"What shall we do about Kerénor?" she asked.

"I'm still thinking about that. Don't risk anything, Anne, and don't worry." And then, almost as much to change the subject as to solve a problem which had suggested itself to him, he said, "By the way, I've been calling you Anne all the time. But you haven't mentioned my name once today. And you call me *vous*, I notice. What's wrong? Don't you trust me, either?"

"I trust you." Her voice was very low. There was a hint of a smile in her eyes, now more blue than gray. "But, you see, I don't know your name."

He checked his pace, and grasped her arm. "What?" he said.

"I don't know your name."

He glanced towards the house. They were too near it. He turned, and, still holding her arm, led her back up the hill.

"Now, what on earth do you mean by that?" he managed to say with a show of injured innocence. So Madame Corlay *had* told her. Perhaps, as a woman, she had thought it only fair to tell the girl who thought she was betrothed to this man. Women were like that. Not that Madame Corlay need have been wary of him: not much, anyway; not as long as he was worried stiff by the job he had on hand. Then, Anne was Anne. Only swine like Corlay would hurt a girl like Anne. Elise, now—well, that was another cup of tea. She would deserve anything that was coming to her. She was just one of those bitches who went about asking for it.

Anne said again, "But I don't know your name."

It was no good evading it. That would only lessen her trust in him, and that was no good either. In one way he was glad she knew. In one way he felt relief. "It still must be Bertrand," he said slowly.

There was a shadow on her face. "You, perhaps, don't trust me," she said.

"I trust you, Anne. It just isn't safe for you to know me as anyone but Bertrand Corlay."

"Oh."

"I mean that. We are all in great danger, Anne. You and Madame Corlay must never know. Then, later, if there's any questioning, you will be able to say truthfully that you did think of me as Bertrand Corlay."

"Later?"

"Yes." Quite baldly he added, "When I have left here."

"When you have left—" Anne's voice was low enough to sound like a faint echo.

"You see?"

"Yes, I see."

"So Madame Corlay told you?" He was almost speaking to himself.

"Only," said Anne, "after I had guessed. There were little things . . . things which I had missed in the real Bertrand." She paused as if she couldn't go on. "Oh, this is all silly. And she didn't really tell me: only hinted, so that I was sure my feeling was right. And then this morning, you whistled 'Bro goz ma zadou.' "

"Didn't the real Bertrand know that song?"

"Yes. But he *couldn't* whistle. That was something he was very touchy about. He just sort of blew." She laughed in spite of herself. He caught her arm again and swung her round on the path.

"Home, this time," he said. "Albertine will begin to get her suspicions aroused, too. And two women are enough in one secret. I must say you kept it well, yesterday, when you were arguing with Kerénor."

Anne's answer ended his new worry. "I didn't tell him. I'll tell him only when you think I should."

"Two women are enough," Hearne repeated. "Good girl, Anne," he added. Something in his voice surprised himself. Anne was smiling again. In the warm sunlight her eyes were quite blue, her cheeks were flushed.

They walked in silence back to the house.

Seven days, Hearne was thinking, seven days—and he might find that not only was it difficult to continue his work: he might find it too dangerous even to continue living on this farm. He looked at the neat fields around him, at the slate roof gleaming blue in the sunshine. Seven days weren't much. . . .

He was right about the danger. But the time was even shorter than he thought.

CHAPTER **22** CAPTAIN RIEDEL
TAKES CHARGE

On the next day, while the people of St. Déodat prepared to go to church, Hearne paid his official visit to Dol. It would have to take place today, he decided that morning, for he had his own extremely unofficial business planned for the rest of the week. He hadn't forgotten Traube's parting shot about Agent Number 8 from Dol. "You will be responsible," Traube had said. Nor had he forgotten the German words which had followed him to the restaurant door. "Set one of Ehrlich's men, too. Advise Ehrlich." No doubt the movements of Bruneau from Dol were already being noted. And if the supposed Corlay didn't appear in Dol, then that would be duly noted too.

But there was a third remark in that short interview in the restaurant of the Hotel Perro which Hearne had not forgotten. As he cycled through the small side roads, through the thick dust of their loose surface, he was repeating to himself, "Kalb, Major Kalb. Kalb of the Schutzstaffel. Kalb, organizer of Dol. *Heil Kalb! Heil Deutschlands teurem Kalb!*" For it was Kalb who had got Hearne into this Sunday suit of Corlay's with its tight waist and flaring shoulders. It was Kalb who had got Hearne onto Corlay's decrepit bicycle, patched up yesterday afternoon with old Henri's help. It was Kalb who was drawing Hearne to the small town of Dol on a hot Sunday morning. Such an opportunity as Traube had given Hearne with that brief reference to Major Kalb was not to be missed. There were plenty of risks attached, but such risks were not only to be taken: they were to be welcomed.

There were but few travelers on the narrow, twisting roads, and they were all Bretons. (The Germans would travel by the large, first-class road where there was less dust or roughness.) Some cycled like himself, their shoulders and heads bowed over the low handlebars, their feet rotating continuously. Others plodded along between the green hedges and scattered orchards, a basket or a bundled cloth over an arm, their best black clothes already coated with the fine dust. They looked as hot as Hearne felt. Even a shimmer of heat was rising from the green grass.

When he at last reached the main road, he found his map calculations had been adequate enough. The towers of Dol's cathedral welcomed him, pointing towards the blue sky and the hum of planes. It was strange, thought Hearne, how people had come to accept that mechanical drone above their heads, as if it were as natural as the wisps of white cloud. He watched the people walking in the streets under the balconies of the old houses. But no one looked upwards; no one shaded his eyes to see what planes could be seen. In the little square which led to the Grande-Rue, the sun baked the cobblestones, and the heat, thrown back in Hearne's face, stifled him. He dismounted and walked at the edge of the narrow slope of pavement, noting the uniforms. There were more uniforms than Breton costumes in the Grande-Rue. Air Force Personnel. Air Force. Transport. Air Force. Air Force Personnel. Transport. The Bretons he saw were either middle-aged men or young boys. The younger men might now be conscripts in the "labor volunteers," like Picrel's son at St. Déodat. But it wasn't only Hearne's age which made him seem conspicuous. Some of the uniformed men who brushed him aside into the flat gutter had looked pointedly at his natty gray suiting. Hearne wondered how long he would have to wheel this bicycle along the street before someone would stop him. It wouldn't be long, he guessed.

He propped the bicycle against a café wall, and entered the airless room. He brushed the flies away from a ringed table, and ordered beer. He might as well wash out the taste of dust from his mouth before he was picked up by a curious Nazi. He settled himself as comfortably as possible on the narrow chair, ignored the proprietor's curiosity, and returned the stare of the only other customer. The man went back to his newspaper.

It wouldn't be long, he had guessed. He was right. The light beer was only half-finished when the loud step of solid boots on stone broke the drowsy silence of the bar. Hearne, his back to the door, saw the tension on the proprietor's face. The man at the corner table, after one look at the doorway, was still more engrossed in his newspaper. Hearne had only time to notice that the paper wasn't held so steadily as it had been, and then a loud voice said in atrocious French, "Whose bicycle?"

Hearne swung round to face the two men. One was moon-faced, broad-shouldered; what hair was left on his head was very fair. The other, if he had had a clubfoot, might have been Goebbels' twin brother. He had the lean and hungry look, all right.

"Whose bicycle?" It was the bald-headed man.

Hearne rose. "Mine."

"Your papers," the large man demanded. Curlylocks wasn't wasting any time. Hearne searched quickly in his pocket. He brought out his identification card and Corlay's list of his fellow traitors' names. To the top of that list, Hearne had pinned a sheet of paper. In square letters he had printed clearly: TAKE ME TO MAJOR KALB. DO NOT SPEAK MY NAME IN FRONT OF FRENCHMEN.

The bald-headed man passed over the collection of papers to the thin, dark man. Both faces were quite impassive.

It was the little Cassius who spoke next. "It is against the regulations to leave a bicycle blocking the narrow pavement. You will accompany us. There will be a fine to pay."

Hearne looked towards the corner table and the bar. The proprietor was busy with some glasses. The other man was reading as if his life depended on it. Perhaps it did.

Hearne held out his hand for the identification papers, but Cassius placed them in his own pocket. His smile was as false as his face. The risk had begun, Hearne realized. He shrugged his shoulders, and fell into step between them. The quicker he got through this episode, the sooner he would see Kalb.

The black-haired man walked with Hearne on the narrow pavement. He kept one hand on his revolver. He certainly wasn't the trusting type, Hearne thought. Curlylocks followed, officially wheeling the offending bicycle. In this way, Hearne retraced his steps on the Grande-Rue. There were fewer people on the street now. The distant sound of singing came to them as they crossed the narrow entrance to the cathedral. Noonday service, Hearne calculated. And then the voices were hidden by the cluster of old houses, and they were passing under medieval gables and balustrades into the small square. It was at one of the larger houses here that the Nazis halted him.

"Inside."

Hearne obediently entered. A broad curve of staircase faced him along with its two S.S. men standing on guard.

"Inside." It was Cassius, again. This time, Hearne was guided by the arm into a small square room at one side of the hall. It was shuttered and cool, but that was all that could be said for it. He was alone, with the small table and two chairs for company, and with the two Schutzstaffel men thumbing their belts outside. Through the shuttered windows he could see the square, and then the bright blue blouses, all the brighter in the glaring sun, of three young Breton boys. Then the splatch of color was gone; and Hearne was left wondering just how comic it would seem to his friends when they heard he had walked of his own seeking into this dark house, out of the sunshine, never to see it again. His friends would never know, in that case, he reminded himself. That would be a bitter joke for only himself to enjoy.

Ten minutes. Fifteen minutes. Hearne paced the little room. He rehearsed his story carefully. That kept him from thinking about the chance that he might never be able to use it. Eighteen minutes. And then he heard the quick, precise footsteps of the dark-haired man.

"This way," he said. The smile was still inscrutable.

They mounted the stairs. The guards stood immobile. Hearne breathed more easily. His confidence in his plan returned. The dark-haired man pushed a door open on the first landing they reached. By its size and magnificence, Hearne guessed this must be the most important floor in the

house. His confidence increased, and he entered briskly. The man closed
the door behind him, and again he was alone.

But this time, the room was large. There were pictures on the walls, an
abundance of delicate furniture neatly arranged over the thick carpet.
Flowers to match the long yellow silk curtains were massed at one corner
of the large writing desk. Elegant, Hearne thought, and moved his eyes
from the desk on which lay his identification papers, thrown on top of a
large glass-covered map. And businesslike, he added, noting the row of
card-index boxes, the three telephones, and the large safe half-hidden behind a carelessly draped tapestry on the paneled wall. He was sure now
that the waiting period in the depressing room downstairs had seen a lot
of activity in this mixture of office and boudoir. The telephones, the card
index. . . . A lot of activity: enough to let him stand here, anyway.
Hearne smiled to himself. The papers so openly displayed on the desk, the
half-disclosed door of the safe, were rather touching in this supposedly
empty room. Even if they thought you were their friend, these chaps
couldn't stop selling their little traps it seemed. He sat down on the
nearest chair, a gilt-edged affair with spindle legs and a satin seat. The soft
notes of a tremulous song filled the room. "Holy Night." . . . Hearne
dropped the magazine he had picked up, and looked around him in amazement. And then the delicate sound gave him a clue. He stood up, and
the music ceased.

There was a laugh from behind him. Hearne turned round; the young
man in officer's uniform closed a side-room door, and came forward.
"Amusing, isn't it?" he said in excellent French. "But not all my visitors
are obliging enough to choose that chair."

Hearne nodded. He was annoyed, and yet more relieved than annoyed,
that he should have furnished the Nazi with some amusement.

The officer's face was impassive now. "You wanted to see me?"

Hearne noticed the captain's insignia on the man's uniform, and felt
his irritation increase. He kept his voice smooth. "I came to see Major
Kalb, on the orders of Lieutenant Traube, stationed at St. Déodat. There
were instructions, I believe, which Major Kalb was to give me. I am Bertrand Corlay of St. Déodat, in charge of—"

"I know. I know." The young man silenced Hearne with his hand. "Why
didn't you come direct to this house? You knew the address."

So that was something Corlay must have memorized and never entrusted to his private notes. Anything with direct reference to the Nazis
had been carefully omitted from Corlay's documents. Even the man Hans
Ehrlich had only been recorded as H.

Hearne said quickly, "I arrived at an awkward time of day. I thought I
would make myself presentable first, for as you see I have been traveling;
and I thought I would have something to eat so as not to disturb you at

lunchtime. And then, there is the man Bruneau. I wanted to find out how his work was going, before I had the honor of seeing Major Kalb."

The explanation wasn't questioned. "Sit down," the German said, and took his place at the desk. "Major Kalb has been called away very suddenly. I am his deputy, Captain Riedel. What did you want to see him about?"

"I wanted to discuss the work of Bruneau with him."

"It is satisfactory. As Lieutenant Traube noted in his very full report, Bruneau has a tendency to grumble. But he can be kept in line with adequate rewards."

"That is what worries me."

"What?"

"Adequate rewards. The fact that we have achieved such results as we have, the fact that the fifteenth of August and victory are so near, is sufficient reward for anyone who is wholeheartedly with us."

The Nazi nodded. Hearne's earnest eyes waited. Black hair, he was noting; brown eyes; mole on left cheekbone; heavy eyebrows; tanned skin; long upper lip; undistinguished nose and chin. It was a pleasant enough face, except when the eyes were wary and the lips were tautened. But now the mouth had relaxed and the eyes were approving.

"Yes?" Captain Riedel said.

"On the other hand, Bruneau is a good worker. He will work very well, if only he is promised enough. And as he has been well-trained for the last two years, it would be difficult to find someone with equal knowledge of this town and its surroundings. The data he has accumulated in the last two years are particularly necessary to us at this time."

"I agree," Captain Riedel said. He had relaxed against the back of his chair. His fingers were playing with Corlay's papers. He suddenly added, "What made you think of this?" He picked up the sheet with the printed instruction TAKE ME TO MAJOR KALB.

"The chance that I would be questioned. I wanted no fuss over any arrest. The less my countrymen notice, the easier it will be for my work."

"True. Now tell me, what else did you come to see Major Kalb about?"

"So far, the only general instructions which have been given our organization are to prepare for founding a separate Breton national state. I have been told, of course, about the fifteenth of August. But it seems to me that our organization could be of some use to you about that date."

"In what way?" There was a hint of amusement in the German's voice.

"For counter-sabotage. Some soldiers must have been talking; some quick French ears must have been listening."

The implication was not lost on Riedel. The amusement left his voice. "So."

"So. There are rumors among the people that something very big is about to happen. The date of August 15th is beginning to be mentioned, here and there. That rumor will spread. As the movements of troops and supplies, as our preparations increase in the next few weeks, even the skeptical will believe. You know the Bretons. You know what they will do."

"Sabotage? But I assure you, Corlay, that Ehrlich's men will find out all we need to know."

"The only men under Ehrlich who will find out anything from the Bretons will be those who are Bretons themselves. You know these people. They distrust even a man from Normandy, or Bordeaux, or any other part of France."

Riedel nodded. "I see. Then you suggest that Ehrlich should use your particular organization to discover any plots which his own men may fail to detect?"

"Only if you agree with me that non-Bretons may fail to discover what is going on in the Breton mind."

Riedel was silent. His lower lip protruded and cupped the upper one. "I am inclined to agree," he said at last. And then suddenly— "Curse those Breton swine! They respond neither to smiles nor to kicks. They live within themselves, behind a prehistoric stone wall that nothing breaks down. There's only one thing they hate as much as a German, and that's a Breton traitor. Be careful, you Corlay. I shouldn't like to be in your place if they find out about you."

"They won't." Hearne's jaws hardened. "And I don't consider myself a traitor, Captain Riedel. I'm a true patriot. I *know* that the only good for Brittany is Germany's friendship and guidance." His voice rang earnestly through the high-ceilinged room.

Riedel's anger had gone. He stared morosely at the map of the Channel coast resting under the glass top of the desk. "These cursed Bretons," he said. "When will they learn?"

"With time and patience. We shall try that first. Later, when the war is over, we can try harder discipline. But now, there is first the problem of their autonomy; and secondly—and I think this more important—there is the complete success of our undertaking against the British. For without that, the war will be long. And of all the invasion coast, we are responsible for the most difficult area to control. If we fail in Brittany, if sabotage hinders any of the Führer's plans, not only will you and Major Kalb and Ehrlich be called to account, but, Captain Riedel, I and my friends will be held responsible too. For that reason, it is necessary that we know just *where* we are to guard against possible sabotage, just *where* the danger points are, just *where* materials and men are being assembled. Then I can warn the rest of my men." Hearne pointed quickly to the map. "Look, Captain Riedel. Here is Number 8 in Dol, Number 6 in St. Malo, Number 5 in Rennes, Number 9 in Combourg, Number 3 in Paimpol, Number 4 in St. Brieuc, Number 10 in Dinan. These alone could find out a great deal, if they were only told what they were to guard against. But now, all we're told is to get the Bretons to vote the right way. They may vote the way we want them to, but that won't prevent them conspiring to sabotage. They just couldn't resist the chance if they got it! And even a small piece of sabotage can dislocate a railway, a canal, a main highway, an aerodrome, just on the very eve of its usefulness."

"Why don't you tell this to Ehrlich?" There was a touch of a sneer in the German's voice. Hearne remembered Tacitus and his observations on the Germanic tribes. *Invidia*, spite, was their worst fault: that, and the baseless fear of being encircled. Tacitus, or was it Caesar? Not that it mattered. Only the observation mattered, now.

Hearne, concentrating on *invidia*, said gloomily, "Oh, he isn't there. Nor is Lisa Lange," and watched Riedel innocently. "Now I hear from Traube that they may not be back for another week or so."

Riedel rose abruptly. He paced the room. "Ehrlich has summoned Major Kalb. Dragged him away from some trouble at the coast."

"Do you know when the Major will return? If only we had more time before the fifteenth, we could wait for his advice."

Riedel looked angrily at Hearne. "I am in Major Kalb's place at the moment. I know what he knows, and I can make any necessary judgments." But he still paced the room.

Hearne said slowly: "And Traube won't be any help to us. The army has its own job. The detection of sabotage is left to Ehrlich's department, or to your own. It is the Gestapo and the Schutzstaffel who will be blamed by the High Command if we overlook any dangers."

Riedel shook his head impatiently. "I know. I know," he said irritably. But his decision was almost made.

Suddenly he halted, and then moved quickly to the desk. He was now a man of action. "Where did you say these men of yours were stationed?"

"Here," said Corlay, "and here, and here. . . ." He pointed to the map, town by town.

"Well, as you've already been told, the zero date is August the fifteenth. Aerodromes are now almost complete along this part of the coast . . ." the captain's finger swept across the flat plains north of Dol . . . "and from them will develop Phase Two of our attack: Bristol, Plymouth, and the southern ports will be destroyed. Phase One, the attack on the Channel shipping and the Channel fleet, has already well begun."

"But the British aerodromes?"

"Attended to, from further north. But here, what we have to worry about is the maintenance of a steady flow of material and troops to the north coast of Brittany from the Paris–Rennes–Brest railway. Our men are already arriving, and concentrating west of St. Brieuc. Others must be enabled to reinforce them continuously. Barges and light craft are being assembled. Tidal seaports along these miles of sand have to be guarded with particular care. So far the enemy has concentrated his attacks on the

Norman and Belgian coasts. So far, our shipping has been safe in the small harbors of Northern Brittany. Southern Brittany's better harbors are more under suspicion." Riedel jabbed at the map of the northern coast, angrily. "At *these six points*," he said, "your men must take special precautions to maintain order. Under protection of the aerial attacks of Phase Two, our barges and ships will sail. Phase Three . . ." His finger swept up towards the Southwest of England, and into the Bristol Channel. His eyes were fixed on the South of Ireland. He flicked his fingers over Cork. "If need be," he said, and disposed of the Irish problem.

He added, "That is sufficient for your purpose, Corlay."

"Yes, Captain Riedel. I'll direct my men immediately as you suggest, and as soon as they learn of any possible sabotage, I'll inform you at once. And, of course, I'll inform Ehrlich. Then you can instruct your men to contact my informants and go to work. This plan of yours, Captain Riedel, will be a double safeguard. The army will be in your debt, more than they will ever know."

Riedel was pursing his lips at the map. "Just what are you going to tell your Breton agents?" he said suddenly.

"Only to ensure that there is no disturbance in those particular areas. I'll put the fear of death in them, without telling them the reason why. That is your suggestion?"

"That is my suggestion." Riedel folded the identification papers and pushed them across the desk.

Hearne buttoned his jacket. He was a very serious, very exalted member of the chosen band. He gave their masterful salute, and uttered their brief confession of faith.

"One more thing. How are you returning to St. Déodat?"

"The way I came. It isn't far. And a bicycle will arouse no suspicion among the Bretons."

Riedel nodded, and looked at the map. Hearne repeated the salute. Outside the door of the room, the sardonic man was waiting for him to conduct him downstairs. The bicycle was in the hall.

Outside, he paused to run two fingers round his sodden collar. For a moment, he halted and leaned on the bicycle; then he was painfully negotiating the cobbled surface of the square.

The towers of Dol's cathedral dropped behind him. Hearne, keeping his eyes fixed on the white road ahead, only saw a map under glass and the nervous forefinger which had tapped so peremptorily. Here, and here, and here . . . six points to remember.

In the week that followed, Hearne made good use of his time. Afterwards, he wondered just what it was that had impelled him to work so constantly and so hard, almost as if he had foreseen dimly what was going to happen. Then he would laugh at himself, for no one except the most second-sighted Celt would have foreseen that. But there was no doubt of the solid fact—he had made good use of his time.

Each morning he would drop his damp, muddy clothes on his bedroom floor, and then drop his numbed body onto the thickness of his bed. When he awoke, his clothes would be gone, and later he would find them dried and brushed, or even washed, in the kitchen downstairs. At first he thought it was Albertine who was responsible. Then one morning when sleep was difficult—the morning after his visit to the aerodromes outside Dol, where he had almost been caught by a German patrol—he had awakened at the sound of the carefully opened door. It was Anne who came in so quietly and gathered up the filthy clothes. He hadn't moved, pretending to be asleep. She had gone as quickly and silently as she had come.

When he rose and dressed, it seemed as if his footsteps overhead had been the signal for Anne to have hot food ready for him. He wondered just how she had silenced Albertine, who scarcely raised one of her meager eyebrows when he came down so late. Normally, there would have been a feeling of thunder in the air at such nonsensical upsetting of routine. But instead, the weather continued fair and warmer. Albertine, eternally busy, would work about the kitchen while Anne, after she had served his meal, would sit across the table from him, and talk. Never anything about themselves or the farm, never a hint of a question about the mud on his boots or the tired look on his face. She talked about the village, which she visited daily—as if she had guessed intuitively that that was what he wanted. And Albertine would join in the conversation too, telling what she had heard that morning after Mass. In this way, Hearne knew almost as much about the village as if he had been staying next door to the Hotel Perro and the Gestapo.

Kerénor had been turned out of his room at the inn. And he had gone to live with Guézennec, of all people! It was as much a symbol of the burying of old quarrels and jealousies as anything. Guézennec, the old schoolmaster, and Kerénor, his successor, were now together under the same roof; and Hearne was willing to bet their conversation wasn't entirely scholarly, either.

The Trouins had opened their kitchen as a free house: there was no room in the small bar of the Hotel Perro for any of the villagers. Instead, they brought their cider along with them to the Trouins', and sat round the large wooden table in the evenings until nine o'clock came and it was time for all Frenchmen to be off the street.

On the day of the weekly market, the Bretons were amazed at the quickness with which their produce was bought. The market was over before it was begun, and the farmers found themselves with the right number of "occupation marks" (printed, it was whispered, in a van which stood with the trucks and tents on the green meadow below the church) in their hands, but with none of their usual purchases. For there was nothing left for the Bretons to purchase or to barter with. One large farmer, Laënnec, hadn't liked the set prices: his vegetables were a bigger and better crop than those he had sold last month for more money. He insisted on an increase in price, or at least an equal barter exchange, and had gone so far as to argue. He wasn't good at keeping his temper. Before Monsieur le Curé could reach him and lead him away to discuss the new regulations, he had thrown the worthless marks in the face of the nearest German soldier. By the time Monsieur le Curé had pushed his way to the spot, all he saw was hot-headed Laënnec being marched to the small town hall at the side of the market place. From there he had been transferred to working on the roads. Quite a number had been "recruited" for that job; but it was particularly hard on the Laënnecs, for (unlike Picrel's son and the others who were now working on the road which led through St. Déodat) Laënnec himself had been sent to some foreign country. No one knew where, although the guesses were as wild as they were numerous. Not even his wife knew. Old Madame Picrel had closed up her shop—she said her son could take care of anything left to sell—and had gone up to the small Laënnec farm to help. It was difficult for Marie Laënnec, with three small children and a baby still to be born. Even old Monsieur Guézennec had left his books to go up there to help with the digging. The German Colonel-in-Command of the district announced that he had been extremely lenient.

Otherwise, as Albertine said, things were as normal as you could expect. As normal on the surface, Hearne amended to himself. The Germans were being rigorously correct. No incidents, no Frightfulness, so far. Nothing like the last German invasion. Hearne, watching Albertine's relief, didn't voice his thoughts. What was the good of saying "Just wait until they are retreating: wait then, and see how they leave you"? Instead, he listened to the description of the band which played each day at noon in the market place, of the quickness with which huts were being built to replace the tents under the trees below the church. Even when Albertine marveled at the fact that some houses in the village had been left unbilleted while German soldiers were sleeping in wooden huts, Hearne kept silent. It would only worry her to realize the true meaning of that fact. The Colonel had decided to keep a good portion of his men together, and not let them be scattered. Then he could use them for quick action if that were necessary. Careful man, the Colonel: thoroughly realistic. *Praktisch.*

But the news which seemed most extraordinary to Albertine and Anne was that the annual *Pardon,* the procession and fête in honor of Saint Déodat, had not been banned. It was to take place as usual next Sunday. This year, the village had decided not to have any festivities after the religious ceremony, when offerings were carried to the church and those taking part in the procession mounted the worn stone steps on their knees, up to the sacred shrine preserving the bones of their Saint. On Sunday, all the people from the village, from the farms on the hillsides, would be in the market place. All would be dressed in their complete national costume. All would bring what they could spare from their fields and kitchens. Everyone was pleased, Albertine had said. Except Kerénor, Anne had added—he was worried. He couldn't guess why the *Pardon* had been permitted, and that worried him. Again Hearne could have given them all an answer. The *Pardon* had been permitted because it suited Hans and Elise and their present policy: the Breton nationalists were to be "persuaded" into accepting a separate Breton state. How could any Bretons be persuaded into co-operation if religious traditions were to be banned? And why the importance of this separate Breton state to the Nazis, except that it would be the beginning of the skillful disintegration of France? Alsace; Lorraine; Brittany; the north, with its coal fields and industries; the Mediterranean south. . . . So Hearne listened, and said nothing. What was the good?

When the women's news was exhausted, he would go back to his room. There he worked on his notes, listing his findings of the previous night, copying them into his own shorthand, adding careful diagrams or neat two-inch-scale maps when it was necessary for extreme accuracy. Then the sheets of thin paper joined the others behind the false panel in the bookcase, and he would pay his short daily visit to Madame Corlay. After that, it was a matter of preparing with the map for the journey he would make next night. He had to know each mile of ground forwards, backwards, and sideways.

It was a simple enough routine, but it was producing results. The railway, the roads, the canal—all these had repaid his visits. Trucks, oil tanks, barges, concentrations of material and troops, construction work, all found their place in the notes on the square miles which formed his "district." And above all, the airfields which were being built to the north of Dol. He could feel some pleasure as he looked at the bookcase each morning. "Thank you, Captain Riedel," he would say, and he would salute it informally with one finger and a wide grin. That was how he was feeling these days. He ought to have known that the luck was too good to hold.

Especially after that long night near Dol, when the patrol just missed him by so little . . . just by a bullet grazing his thigh. He ought to have known. Perhaps, deep underneath, he did.

For when the Germans came, he rose to his feet almost calmly. No time to move, no time to get away by the back door. There were footsteps in the yard. Anyway, he thought, there was nothing left lying about upstairs to incriminate him. He even gave Anne, her eyes wide with fear, a smile of encouragement.

It was Albertine who had voiced their thoughts as the pounding came to the front door and they heard it open.

"The Boches," she had said, and crossed herself as if the Devil himself had arrived. Anne rose from the table where she had been sitting as he finished his bowl of soup. She had been laughing at something he had said. Her lips were still parted, but the laugh had died in her throat.

He was on his feet too. And yet he was calm enough, as if he were only reacting to something which he had been long expecting.

He had only time to say to the two white faced women "Keep silent!" and then the German lieutenant walked into the kitchen. His hand was on his revolver. Two armed soldiers were behind him. Two more entered from the back door.

"Corlay?" In appearance, even in voice, the man was a duplicate of Deichgräber.

Albertine's hand had gone to her mouth as if she were holding in a scream. Anne stood as still and white as a statue. She hardly seemed to breathe.

"Yes. What do you want?"

The officer pointed with his revolver to the door. "At once!" he said.

"Why?"

"At once!"

Hearne shrugged his shoulders. He left the two women standing beside the table. Albertine was crying silently, her hand still held to her lips. Anne was as rigid as if she were facing a firing squad herself. He felt her eyes follow him into the yard.

In the high field old Jean and Marie were standing, watching. Henri had gone.

Past the heap of hay on the cobbled yard, past the pool of water which gleamed beside the well, past the empty cart lying backwards with its shafts pointing into the air. And then they were round the corner of the house. He looked up involuntarily at Madame Corlay's front window. She was there. She had left her chair; and she was trying to pull the window open. She must have succeeded, because as they took the path to St. Déodat, he could hear her voice. Perhaps the solid Germans grouped round him didn't know Breton: for Madame Corlay's sake, he hoped not.

And then he saw Henri. Henri had reached the orchard. He was standing there, near the third tree in the seventh row. And then there were only the fields, and the dovecote, and Anne's farm, and the thin fringe of trees. . . .

Today was the nineteenth: Friday the nineteenth. Tomorrow Elise should arrive. So it couldn't be that Kerénor had told her about his warning. In any case, Kerénor was not a teller of tales. No, it couldn't have been that. Or was it that Deichgräber had been found still alive? Or that Ehrlich's mission to Mont St. Michel had resulted in the arrest of Pléhec and Duclos? Or that Captain Riedel had become suspicious? Or that Henri had got drunk and talked about the American? Or had the boat which sailed for Penzance been captured? Or what? If only he knew, then he could muster up some kind of story, perhaps even be able to deny enough to give himself a brief respite, a chance to collect his notes from the bookcase and head for the coast tonight. He cursed silently to himself as they crossed the stone bridge into the village street. Even if he could only get a chance to make for the coast, he could always leave his notes behind. He remembered enough of the main details to do without them if necessary. But the real problem was letting Duclos know in time, so that he could be picked up on the French coast as arranged. For originally, before van Cortlandt blew in on the scene to alter things, Hearne's plan had been to visit Mont St. Michel just as he was ready to leave. Then Duclos would have sent out the chief items of his information—to make sure of its arrival—and then let Matthews know from where and when he was leaving. Matthews had given him the choice of three suitable places. Well, now, it looked as if he couldn't use that choice. Now he wouldn't even be able to get word in time to Duclos by the boat which had brought him back from the Bay of Mont St. Michel. He didn't fancy spending any extra days or nights on the shores of Brittany, waiting for his message to reach Duclos and then Matthews: not with the Gestapo hot on his trail. Now he'd better just try to get *any* boat and sail across the Channel, alone if necessary.

They had left the road and turned west into the market place, following its south side and the narrow pavement leading to the Hotel Perro. This was the way he had come when he was looking for Henri, on the day the Gestapo had first appeared in St. Déodat. The Nazi flag was still there, but now there was also a detachment of soldiers in fatigue uniform with spades and picks over their shoulders. They swung through the square. They were singing, loudly, carefully, operatically. A few civilians, their eyes averted, hurried on their business, or stopped to speak quietly and briefly to one another. The German words marched in perfect unison. They flattened your feelings as if they were a steam roller, Hearne thought. Even when the hard sound of exact boots had blurred in the distance, the chorus of voices remained like a bitter echo in your heart.

They passed two men: one old and white-haired, the other short and fat with his priest's hat squarely set above a kindly face, now more stern than good-humored. The Curé and his companion looked at Hearne with only half-interest, and backed against the wall to let the officer, the four soldiers, and Hearne pass.

They mustn't get the wrong idea, Hearne decided. He wasn't coming to visit his Nazi friends with a bodyguard to protect him. He pretended to step out of line towards the priest. It worked. The soldier behind him caught his arm roughly and forced him back into his place. There could be no doubt at all of the way the soldiers had crowded more closely around him, no doubt at all of the lieutenant's animosity in the quickly barked command, the sudden movement of hand to revolver. He didn't object even to the way in which two soldiers held him with unnecessary vehemence as they urged him into the hotel. Behind him, the two men were standing motionless against the wall: but their eyes had followed him with an interest which had become real.

Now, thought Hearne savagely as he was pushed through the restaurant, Kerénor will perhaps believe my message. But at the moment that was cold comfort.

They had crossed the floor of the empty restaurant. To their right, the bar seemed empty too. It was quiet enough. The lieutenant halted at the back of the room, and knocked neatly and politely on a door.

A voice said "*Herein!*" And again two of the soldiers gripped his arms and almost ran him through the door after the officer. Just inside the room they halted, still gripping his arms.

There were people in the room. He could hear movements—a cough, two men talking quickly to the lieutenant. But he could not see any of them, for a large draft screen stood across the entrance, shutting off the room. The two soldiers holding him had halted behind it. All he could see was a side view of some heavy furniture backed against the wall at this end of the room. Not Breton furniture, either. Probably this had been Madame Perro's living room, and the furniture had been brought with her when she came to the village. He noted some cheap prints in massive frames on the plaid wallpaper: they were views of towns. By stretching his neck, he could see the three nearest—views of *one* town, he corrected himself. Views of Strasbourg. So that was where Madame Perro and her charming niece came from—Strasbourg. That was quite possible. That explained a lot of things, quite a lot.

One of the soldiers had noticed his interest in the pictures. He knocked Hearne's head to face the screen, with a side blow from his fist. Charming fellows, Hearne thought, and then the voice which had given the command "*Herein!*" spoke once more.

"Bring him forward."

Damn it all, you don't need to shove me about with so much relish, Hearne thought savagely, and checked the impulse to hit the short nose of the long-chinned private who had taken a particular pleasure in a heavy grip on his arm. The two soldiers let him go so suddenly that he almost stumbled. He caught his balance, straightened himself in time, and looked at the table in front of him.

Three men faced him across it. Only one of them was a soldier: a captain. There, but for the grace of God and a quicksand, would probably have sat Deichgräber. The other two men, watching him intently with that close-eyed tight-lipped look peculiar to their breed, didn't need their darker uniforms to identify them. So the boys themselves were here, thought Hearne: the perverts, the sodomites, the torturers. Pleasant time he was going to have. The young lieutenant saluted smartly and turned on his heel. The soldiers followed him out of the room. He could hear the sound of heavy boots diminishing through the echoing restaurant.

And then a door, which must have led from the bar itself, opened, and closed. The girl who had entered paused, with her shoulder leaning back against its panels as she looked round the room. There was an amused smile on her lips, a tilt to her head which showed the line of her neck, a flicker of black eyelashes veiling the green eyes.

Hearne felt a stab of admiration. The timing, the gestures, the entrance, were all so perfect. It was a pity that the three men were absorbed in watching his face. He took a step forward.

"Elise," he said, with sufficient enthusiasm and relief and surprise.

She walked across to the armchair beside the window. She settled herself on one of its arms, curving her legs to the side like a ballet dancer, one arm stretched along its back. She looked at him directly for the first time. Her eyes widened.

"Well," she said, "and how are you, Mr. Hearne?"

CHAPTER **24** ONE MORE DAY

Hearne was conscious that the eyes of the three Germans had never left his face. He forced himself to watch Elise, to keep his look of enthusiasm and relief and surprise in place. Now he added blank amazement as well. "Elise!" he said again. And then, "Is this some kind of a joke? If it is, then it's a poor one."

Elise dropped her posing along with her pseudo-amusement. She was sitting very erect now, looking at him quite coldly. "Is it, Mr. Hearne?"

"Is it what? What's that you keep saying? Mistererernmisterem." He ran the words quickly together to form a meaningless jumble.

If he was really lost, really discovered, then he was taking the risk of adding a lot of amusement to their present pleasure. He had always promised himself that, once he was hopelessly caught, he wouldn't give his captors the joy of watching him invent. But now he was finding that the word "hopeless" didn't have much authority. He was caught, yes; but until he knew more about the evidence he wasn't going to admit he was hopeless. It would have been just as easy for a strong swimmer to commit suicide by drowning: even as his mind was telling him to sink, his subconscious struggled to keep him afloat.

Hearne looked angrily at the men. "What is all this about, anyway?" he said.

One of the shark-jawed men spoke for the first time. His remark was not addressed to Hearne. "I told you this was the wrong treatment for this man. Now, perhaps, you will let us follow our own methods."

The German captain moved impatiently in his chair. "The colonel has ordered this examination," he stated abruptly. He narrowed his eyes at a sheet of paper in front of him.

"Your name?" he said to Hearne. There was only hard efficiency and determined routine in his voice.

The shark-faced Gestapo man caught his breath audibly. He was watching the officer now with barely concealed amusement. The captain ignored the byplay, and proceeded, with at least outward calm, through all the stereotyped questionnaire. Date of birth, place of birth, mother's name, father's name, education, religion, attendance at university, date of father's death, date of uncle's death, other relatives living, income, political activities, career in peacetime, army service. Hearne, keeping his mind alert, concentrated on the questions, on the way they were asked. He replied easily and assuredly. But he knew that, although there was an undercurrent of friction between the army officer and the Gestapo man, it did not mean the officer would be easy to deal with. He was apparently some kind of liaison or military intelligence man, who came into contact with the Gestapo side of the occupation forces in cases of common policy, or of certain aspects of army morale, or of citizen morale when it interested the army. He was probably Deichgräber's successor: that he obviously enjoyed his work less than the late unlamented ditch-digger didn't mean that he was disposed to any kindness for the prisoner under interrogation. He was only determined that the Gestapo was to be kept in its proper place, that the army's power would be unrelaxed. And so the dry impersonal voice continued with the endless questions. And so Hearne concentrated and replied with all the strength of the details he had so painfully memorized. The way in which he acquitted himself, down to a concise account of his rescue from Dunkirk by a French trawler which had brought him as a shell-shocked casualty to Brest, didn't have any effect on the hard businesslike tone of the captain. But the two other men were now watching him thoughtfully; and it gave Hearne some pleasure to see a puzzled look on the girl's face when he answered one question directly from Corlay's secret diary. She hadn't expected that.

The captain asked his last question. Hearne gave a straight answer. The German hesitated for a moment—his first sign of uncertainty—and then looked at the two others.

The shark-faced one said, "We expected something like this. We'll continue the investigation—with your permission, Captain Holz."

The third man, who had been silently examining his finger nails, looked at Elise and said, "In my opinion, all form of oral investigation is useless." His voice, like his face, was razor-edged. He was the lad who would now spend his time in thinking up variations of torture, instead of inventing filthy jokes—as he no doubt had done before he had turned political. Razorpuss was going to supply several bad quarters of an hour before he had finished. He could hardly wait to get his innings, Hearne thought; that was obvious.

Elise came forward and leaned against the end of the table. She smelled like a flower garden on a hot August morning.

"I'd like to know what all this is about," Hearne said petulantly, and looked angrily at the girl. "This is really intolerable, Elise."

She smiled with little sweetness. One eyebrow was raised, the eyelids were half-lowered. "Very pretty, so far, Mr. Hearne. But your feat of memory is unfortunately in vain. Here is something which arrived yesterday. Captain Holz—may I?"

She stretched out an arm, and Holz placed a sheet of paper silently in her hand. He looked as if he would be much happier sitting at his desk, planning the occupation of the Isle of Wight by parachute troops as an advance base against Southampton.

Elise looked at the sheet for a moment, as if to tantalize Hearne. He was keeping the same look of indignant annoyance on his face for the benefit of the others' watchful eyes. He took the piece of paper when it was at last handed to him with an air of unconcern. He looked at it and thought, they can see my face but thank God they can't feel my heart. He said, a treacherous tightening in his throat almost spoiling his attempt at anger, "What the devil is this?"

It was a small sheet of paper with rough scallops edging one side where it had been torn from a loose-leaf diary. It was dirty, and creased with many folds. The writing was in pencil, small, scribbled, spilling over into the margins; but it was undeniably the writing of Bertrand Corlay.

"Elise, my own," it began, "you may be in grave danger. I am here in England at the Downside Hospital near Bath. Was brought here after Dunkirk with shattered thigh, nearly dead. Only thoughts of you kept me alive. A man, looking like my image in the mirror, came to visit me constantly. I answered all his questions, told him many details of my life but nothing about us, because I knew I must prove I was Bertrand Corlay and not a German. The English are much afraid of Fifth Columnists. I haven't seen this man for a month. He *may be now* in St. Déodat, for at the last I found out that was his purpose. He looks like me, his voice grew like mine, but he is English. I asked cautiously for my friend who had visited me. Only two days ago, I asked a young doctor. That way I found his name is Hern. Yesterday, Jacques Lassarre came to see me before he sailed. He came here from Dunkirk too, but is now going back to France. I have asked him to send you this note when he arrives in France. Am writing under difficulties. All letters examined, but L. will smuggle this out. I shall return soon. Still two boatloads of wounded to sail to France. Lying here tortured to death with thoughts of you."

Then followed two lines over which Hearne had shuddered when he had first seen them in Corlay's diary.

> *"Tes beaux cheveux, couleur du soleil riche et sombre,*
> *Ils seront mon abri, me pâmant dans leur ombre."*

And then the signature: "Bertrand Corlay."

Hearne looked up at the four intent faces. His eyes were incredulous. Damn that pip-squeak of a doctor, he was thinking. It must have been Paton, who had known him at Cambridge, who thought he had a nice cushy job in Whitehall and used to greet him when they accidentally met by saying, "Well, how goes the rubber stamp, these days?" And Paton, out of ignorance and genial bedside manner, had answered Corlay's innocent question. Blast Paton and blast the fates that had stationed him at Downside Hospital.

Hearne looked down at the sheet of paper again, and then quickly back at Elise. "What the devil is this?" he asked.

"What do you suppose?"

"It's a letter from me to you, but I never wrote it."

"No, *you* certainly did not," the shark-faced man said and laughed at his joke.

"It's no laughing matter." Hearne was indignant and angry. He read aloud thoughtfully, "Elise, my own, you may be in grave danger. . . ." He looked again at Elise. "Indeed you may, and so may I, and all those who work with us." The intensity and urgency of his voice silenced even Shark-face.

"Whoever wrote this," Hearne went on, "knows about us, and is trying to upset our plans by the only means he has: by sowing suspicion. Cleverly done, too. See, he scribbled it hurriedly, so that if he made any mistakes in copying my writing then you would only think it was due to haste."

"And just where would he learn your handwriting?" Sharkface asked caustically.

"Only one place possible. The poem proves that. I had it written down in my diary. I was working over the last couplet. He has copied it down the old way." Hearne quoted the lines:—

> "Your tresses fair, like the sun's gold at setting,
> Bring me sweet shelter, languorous forgetting.

"I was changing that to

> "Your golden hair, like the sun's rich setting,
> Brings me sweet peace and deep forgetting.

"But he couldn't guess that. . . ." The injured poet threw the sheet of paper contemptuously on the table.

The Germans exchanged amused glances. Good, thought Hearne: the more of a fool they think me, the more chance I have.

"And just where would this man find this interesting diary?" Sharkface prided himself, it seemed, on heavy sarcasm.

"I don't know. . . . The last time I saw it was before Dunkirk. I lost everything there."

"Do I understand you mean to say—" began Sharkface with bogus politeness.

"I mean what I say," cut in Hearne angrily. "Enough of this foolishness. We are obviously in danger."

Sharkface turned a dull red. He leaned forward, opening his mouth to shout—

"One moment." It was the captain. "Who is the man Lassarre?"

"There was a man of that name in my unit," Hearne guessed wildly. It did well enough to fill the gap at the moment. But only for the moment.

"We shall find that out," Captain Holz said, and settled calmly back in his chair. Sharkface made a note on the pad in front of him.

"In my opinion, all form of oral investigation is useless." It was Razorpuss again. He was a man of one idea, it seemed. Hearne could make a good guess at that idea, too, looking at the tight eyes and spade-cut mouth, the sleek hair, sloping brow and high thin nose.

"There's still one thing, gentlemen," Elise said slowly—but her voice had lost something of its confidence. Gentlemen. . . . Hearne smothered his smile before it reached his lips. He looked reproachfully at Elise, in as good an imitation of a hurt dog as he could manage. She moved quickly over to the door which led into the bar.

"Hans!" she called, and there was the sound of footsteps. Several footsteps. So that was it, so that was it. Hearne felt a surge of excitement as his fears over this last test gave way to relief. So that was it! The real Corlay knew Hans, the false Corlay didn't. At least, that was what Elise believed.

Three men followed each other through the narrow door, and stood there in a group. All wore ordinary lounge suits. All looked at Hearne with the same blank look. He let recognition come into his eyes as they fell on the dark young man who had been Deichgräber's dinner companion in Pléhec's restaurant, who had walked on the ramparts of Mont St. Michel with Elise.

"Well, Hans," he said, "and so you've got back from Paris. Had a nice trip?" His voice was acid. He glanced at Elise. There was veiled jealousy in that look. And then, he turned on Hans.

"You wouldn't know, would you, my dear Hans, about a letter supposed to have been written by me?" His tone was vitriol itself.

The attack took the Nazi by surprise. Then his face reddened with anger and he came quickly forward into the room. Elise was sitting quite still on the edge of the desk.

The underlying suggestion had not been lost on Captain Holz. He rose abruptly to his feet, marked distaste in every movement. "Enough!" he said in German, and he did not add "gentlemen." "Enough! This is developing into a servants' brawl."

There was a cold silence. The others hadn't liked that: Elise least of all.

Holz spoke again. "Have your men, Captain Ehrlich, been detailed to search the farm?"

Ehrlich answered, "They have not yet returned with their report, Captain Holz."

Holz nodded thoughtfully. "We must find this Lassarre. What was that postmark?"

"Bordeaux." Elise's voice was toneless. She didn't look at Hearne. He was thinking. Bordeaux was a big place. At least, he had some kind of breathing space until Lassarre was found. Even allowing for the Gestapo's loving care, there was still that breathing space. As long as there was no wall behind your back and no firing squad facing you, there was still a chance. It wasn't hopeless, yet.

The men had risen.

"Elise," Hearne said in desperation. "Elise. What has happened to you?" But he was damned if he was going to fall on his knees and plead with her as the emotional Corlay probably would have done.

Her eyes wavered, and then she walked to the window. She had made her decision.

"Take him away now," she said. So she was clever enough to know that she had lost his loyalty. Whether he was found guilty or innocent, she couldn't command his blind obedience after this. "At once," she added over her shoulder, as if she were ordering a table to be cleared of soiled dishes. Her profile against the light from the window was as perfect as she probably hoped.

Razorpuss motioned with the fingers he had examined so thoroughly. The two men beside Ehrlich advanced, grasped Hearne by each arm, and propelled him towards the screen and the restaurant door. Behind them came the man with the razor-face. He had drawn his revolver. They were taking no chances, it seemed. Hearne relaxed, and walked easily. He wasn't going to give them the slightest excuse.

In this way they left the hotel.

There were silent groups of people in the square. The news must have traveled fast. Under one tree, Kerénor was standing, and with him was a girl whose soft fair hair gleamed in the sunlight striking through the thin branches. They stopped talking as Hearne was marched past. He didn't look at them. But he knew they were still watching him as he was led into the group of buildings on the opposite side of the market place to the hotel. As he ascended the steps of the little town hall, a Nazi flag swung confidently overhead.

Inside, there was a large desolate room with a few rows of cane chairs facing an empty platform. The table on the platform had been decorated. At one end there was the tricolor, at the other the arms of Brittany—the black cross and ermine fringe on silver—and in the middle, separating and dominating in ironical symbolism, was a giant swastika. There was a doorway beside the platform. This was where he was to be taken.

The doorway led to a dark narrow corridor, and in turn the corridor led to a flight of wooden stairs, circling down into the basement of the building. The stairs ended in the largest room of them all. It was the central cellar, and the darkest. Round its flanks were small boxlike storerooms. The only light streamed through their opened doors, from their small windows set almost at roof level.

Hearne stumbled over a pile of papers in the darkness of the central room, and was encouraged by a kick to keep his footing. It seemed as if the smaller rooms had all been cleared out. There wasn't even a stick of furniture in them now. But the floor of the central room was littered with piles of books and ledgers and papers. As his eyes grew accustomed to the half-shadows, he could also see the dark shape of a table and two benches. More papers were stacked on the table. The archives of St. Déodat were in process of examination, it would seem.

They had halted him at the entrance to one of the small rooms. The smell of dampness and stale air hung round him. After the warmth of the sun in the market place, the chill of the basement struck at his bones. He shivered in spite of himself. So this was to be his lodging. The ground certainly looked cold enough. Two kicks confirmed his guess. He picked himself slowly up from the middle of the floor. There was no hurry: there were plenty more where those had come from. He turned to face the three men standing at the doorway of the small cellar. Behind him the small high window half-lighted the room. Outside there was sunlight. He heard the clear voices of children, raised in the excitement of some game.

The man with the tight eyes and spade-cut mouth nodded. The heavy oak door was closed. It shut with a deep thud, almost blotting out the hard voice.

"Now," the man was saying, "now, we might get the truth."

No use of backing away, thought Hearne: it would only be worse if they were to get him up against the stone wall. He stood in the middle of the floor and watched the three men advancing.

When Hearne regained consciousness, the half-light from the small high window had faded. It was almost dark in the improvised cell. He lay for some minutes on the stone floor. When he tried to raise himself, it was too unpleasant. He gave up; and lay as he had fallen. He didn't even think. He felt better after the second spasm of vomiting.

At the end of half an hour or so he tried again. This time he managed to stagger to the wall. Why should he try to stand anyway, he suddenly thought, and let himself fall and slide to the ground. Why should he even sit? He wanted to laugh at himself for his subconscious attempt to assert the natural dignity of man. There wasn't much natural dignity left after three men had kicked the daylight out of you. He lay on the floor, watching the fading light. He felt the crusts of blood on his face with his left hand, and he thought of Anne. He remembered her dismay when the razor cut had opened afresh. . . . He began a smile, but his jaw wouldn't let him finish it.

Well, his face wasn't too bad. Not too bad, considering. It wouldn't look exactly pretty, but at least it still felt recognizable in parts. His left hand went slowly over the rest of his body. Right collarbone gone. Well, he could have got that in a Rugger scrum any day. Probably something wrong with a rib too. He felt the sore spot gently . . . yes, probably a rib. The rest was bruises, and probably a kidney afloat. If ever he reached middle age, he'd find out. He could feel the differences in the consistency of his flesh even under his clothes. Legs were all right, though. Bruised and scraped, but no bones broken. And they were the most important for him. Without his legs he could never reach the coast.

He lay and looked at the window. The bars were hardly needed. It was at least ten feet from the ground, built into a smooth stone wall. No footholds, no reach. And not a piece of furniture in the room to climb on. From somewhere in the large central cellar outside, he heard a movement. He felt his muscles tighten, and sickness once more strike his stomach.

But no one came in.

He relaxed again, and wiped the cold sweat from his brow. They weren't coming back yet. Not yet.

He licked his dry lips and moved his throbbing jaw onto the coldness of the floor.

The trouble with him was that he didn't enjoy triumphing over pain. The trouble with him was that he wasn't a natural hero. He hadn't given Razorpuss any satisfaction so far, in the way of information, but after the first ten minutes he had grunted and groaned enough. He grimaced as much as his face would let him, at the thought of that last yelp they had wrung out of him. Not very pretty, he decided: not the way you like to think of yourself behaving. Indian braves did it better. At the stake, they laughed and mocked. The worse the torture, the louder they laughed. But they didn't keep silent either, he added as an afterthought: no, they didn't keep silent. Well, he could try laughing, too. Perhaps if he used up all the air in his lungs that way, he wouldn't have any left to talk with.

When he was kicked awake, it was quite dark. The full moon's light shunned the cellar. But they had brought outsize electric torches as well as rubber clubs. Ehrlich was there, too, and the man with the shark's mouth. This time, Hearne didn't try to fight back. He let himself pass out as quickly as he could. As after-dinner entertainment, it must have been disappointing.

When he revived, there was light again from the window, the cold gray light of a morning still being born.

There was a lot of blood on the floor.

After lying staring at it for some minutes, he realized it must be his own blood. His right arm was more useless than ever, but his left could still move. Slowly, this time; but still move. He held it painfully up in front of his half-closed eyes, and moved its fingers one by one. And then the wrist, and then the elbow. Yes, the left arm was still all right, and so was the left shoulder. Back was bruised, thighs probably blue and purple by their feeling, leg bones still unbroken. Slowly he made his inventory, slowly took comfort. It might be worse. He didn't let himself think long that it *would* be worse. No good thinking about that. He lay and tried to will his strength back into his bones and muscles. No good, either, in just lying still. He had been wrong yesterday when he thought he would just lie on the floor. That way, he wouldn't ever get out of here, until he was walked to a firing squad.

He raised himself on his left elbow, and rested. Then slowly onto his knees, and rested. Then, by holding onto the wall, he was on his feet. After a pause, he felt his way along the wall. It was a slow job but, just as he had hoped, his body obeyed his mind. He could move. He could stand upright—almost. He would walk round the four walls of the room before he would let himself sit down.

"You are not the only one," he said to himself. "At this moment, in Europe, you are not the only man forcing himself to walk round a cell. Not by a long chalk. So drop all your self-pity. You are lucky, compared to some."

As he almost reached the window, there was a slight sound above his head. A sound almost like a crack. And there was a small white ball on the floor behind him. He glanced up at the window. In one of its small panes, there was the smallest puncture. Slingshot, he judged, and turned uncertainly to retrace his steps. This time he didn't hold onto the wall with his arm. When at last he reached the little wad of paper wrapped round the ball bearing, he didn't know whether he was more pleased at feeling it hidden in his hand, or at having walked by himself without any wall to prop him up. He lay on the floor, his back to the door, and unwrapped the scrap of paper.

One more day. Courage.

That was all it said. One more day. One more day.

God, he suddenly thought, at least I've got friends: at least, I'm not alone.

He tore the paper into four small pieces. They made a poor breakfast, but the hope they had given him helped him to swallow them.

Footsteps outside the cellar door made him alert. But no one came in. Changing guard, probably.

He felt the lead shot in his pocket, and it cheered him. How had they known he was in this cellar? Had they been watching all last night from the meadows behind the town hall? Had they seen the dim light which the electric torches would send into the darkness? That must be it. . . . Anyhow, that meant he had friends, and patient friends. He felt better every minute. Whoever had written that note was a good psychologist, or perhaps just someone with a heart as well as a mind. It came to the same thing.

As he was slipping into sleep, he remembered that this room, at the back of the building, faced not only meadows and trees. There was also the road to the right, the road leading north. That was where he had entered St. Déodat when he had first arrived. And the two houses nearest the market place along that stretch of road belonged to Guézennec and Trouin: Trouin, who now kept open house where the men brought their drinks to sit and talk together; Guézennec, who now gave shelter to Kerénor. These two houses were together. From their backs one could watch this cellar. Then he thought of the tree in the market place, yesterday, as he had been marched into the town hall. Kerénor had been there, and he had been with Anne. Anne, he thought: it was Anne who was at the bottom of all this. He was convinced of that in his own mind as he fell asleep. His sleep was all the deeper for that last thought.

This time he was awakened by a heavy, dull, distant noise. An explosion. It could only be an explosion. It wasn't likely that British air raids were being carried out in broad daylight: not yet, anyhow.

After that awakening, he couldn't get to sleep again. He limped once more round the room. He kept thinking about that noise. Perhaps two or three miles away. It might be on the railway, or on the main road down in the valley. His mind was racing now. The explosion might be accidental. But there was just a chance it had been carefully engineered.

If it had, and if it had been arranged by anyone in this village, then there was only one object in it. It was a diversion to keep Sharkface and his friends occupied elsewhere. *He* wouldn't seem so important to them today, with an explosion for them to investigate. He didn't let himself fully believe this wild hope. Yet, through the long day, as he was left alone, he kept finding explanations to justify such an idea. The explosion wasn't in the village itself, so that no one here would suffer direct reprisals. It was down in the valley within reach of twenty villages, so that the investigation would be more complicated, would take greater time. Whoever had engineered the explosion had wanted the Huns to be occupied today. Perhaps he only believed all this because he wanted to believe it, because the belief gave him courage for one more day; but he believed it.

In the late afternoon he thought he heard a distant sound of many footsteps, from somewhere upstairs. But, down here, no one came.

By the time the evening light waned, he was convinced that his guess must have been right about the explosion. Without that, he would have had an unpleasant day.

When Ehrlich, Sharkface, and two others entered the cellar late in the evening, he learned just how unpleasant the day might have been. But still they didn't get any information. The bad temper which they had been unable to conceal when they entered the room must have been considerably increased by the time they left. But long before then, Hearne was insensible.

He was becoming accustomed to the painful awakening from unconsciousness. His first worry was how long he could keep up this business of passing out before they twisted any information out of him. Next time, he was sure the technique would be changed to keep him from being completely knocked out. They would find a way, all right. He lay and worried in the darkness. He looked at the patch of window, at the strong silver of the moon. He didn't even bother to count his wounds this time. He was a bloody mess: that was what he was, a bloody mess.

And then, in the middle of his depression, he remembered that the day was over. *One more day*. And it was over. Painfully, agonizingly, he crawled across the dark floor. It was sticky; it smelled foully. Hunger was the least of his troubles: even this thirst and the swollen tongue were little enough. He had to get on his feet, he had to be able to move his body as if it were one piece, instead of the twenty throbbing nerve-ends it had become. He touched the wall and slowly pulled himself to a kneeling position against it. He felt a cool sweet sagging. When he became conscious, he found himself lying again on the floor. Once more he pulled himself onto his knees. This time he was at last on his feet. He clung to the wall in the darkness. It's getting late, he thought despairingly. *Courage, one more day. Courage;* but it was getting late. There was not much courage in the feeling of a stone wall in a bloodstained cell.

He must think of something to stop this attack of nerves. If he let his mind give way, then there was no hope at all for him. Despair never won any game. Defeat came quickly to those who thought of it.

He stood in the darkness, his weight sagging against the cold wall. Outside, the moonlight was fading. He thought of the curve of hills . . . cloud shadows weaving over furrow-stitched fields . . . the smell of hay and clover under the sun's warm rays . . . the hum of bees and the clear note of a girl's gentle voice laughing . . . a light clear voice made to sing. Made to sing *"Au clair de la lune."* Gray changing to blue, as the sky changed above her. He thought of the blueness of her eyes and it was the blueness of the sea, changing like the sea in shade and sunshine. He could feel their soft coolness, their warm clearness as if they were the gentle waves of the sea itself. He clung to the wall, and thought of the sea's blue depths.

And then he was walking round the wall, feeling his way in the darkness, and the despair had been washed out of his heart. If no friend came, he was thinking, then he would have to work out his own plan of escape. He must do it at once . . . a few more days of this and he wouldn't be able to escape at all. Now his mind was busy thinking of chances to take, of ways to get the guard to come into this cellar.

From the darkness outside came footsteps on the village road. There were voices, the sound of a cart. People were moving about, out there. For a moment he wondered if he had already begun to imagine things, and then the melancholy ringing of the bells in the church tower reminded him. Today was the dawn of Sunday, today there was to be the *Pardon.* The people were coming in from the farms and the small hamlets round St. Déodat. He could almost see them coming to the church, the women in their elaborate lace caps and black velvet-trimmed dresses, with their stiff shawls and aprons, the men walking carefully in their best clothes. They were coming through the night to gather in the market place, in time for the first Mass at dawn. He listened carefully, and knew he must be right in his guess. There was the sound of feet, slow hesitating feet, or the sound of wheels. But there was no laughter, no talk. Even the children were silent. Only the bell sounded its solemn note. Now, now, now, the notes hammered into his brain.

He turned towards the door. Now.

He could hear a movement from the cellar outside. He had reached the door and flattened himself along its left side: that was the way it opened. That way he could perhaps surprise the man who would come in.

He filled his lungs with air and let out a yell. His throat didn't let him make much of a noise, but the guard would hear it. "I'm willing to talk," he would say, and the guard would halt in the doorway. That was all he wanted. It would be interesting to see if one-armed jiujitsu would work.

His breath gave out, and he listened. There was a movement from outside, the sound of a key in the lock.

"Keep quiet. Quick. Can you walk?" The voice was urgent, and it was Breton. A dimmed torch searched the room anxiously.

"Here," he croaked and put out an arm to the two figures in the doorway. "Here."

"Quick."

He needed no more urging. As he came out into the large cellar, lit feebly by a lamp on the table, a third man brushed past him. He was dragging the guard. The limp body was flung into Hearne's cell. Its swollen face and protruding tongue thudded on the stone floor. The third man locked the door, straightened his large back, and started after the other two who were helping Hearne to climb the stairs. As he passed a large stack of papers and books in the corner of the cellar, he stooped quickly and thrust the keys under the heap of documents. They were well lost. And then he was behind Hearne, pushing him up the stairs. Strong hands he had. Hearne thought of the German's twisted neck. Yes, strong hands.

"Quietly," whispered one of them, and they halted in the narrow passage. This was how he had been brought by Razorpuss, Hearne remembered. Ahead of them would be the large meeting hall with its flag-draped platform. There were footsteps, either in that hall or beyond it at the front door. The Bretons had heard them, too. Moving silently on their bare feet, they pulled and pushed Hearne, through the unobtrusive door in the passage wall to their left. He didn't even remember seeing it last time he had been taken through here.

Now they stood in another long passage, listening as they paused. The insignificant door was silently closed behind them, and then they were moving down the gentle slope of the floor. Hearne, concentrating painfully on each footstep, had only time to think, we've doubled on our tracks; we've traveled to the other end of the building—to the west, farther away from the road and church; the bells are just so much fainter. And then they were through another doorway, heavy, thick, resisting. They were back in a large room: a storeroom. It smelled like a grocer's shop. After the bleakness of the cellar it was warm and friendly, and yet nauseating. There were too many odors for an empty stomach to digest. Its comfortable stuffiness smothered. One of the men felt Hearne's weight sagging.

"Just twenty paces more," he urged in a whisper. Hearne nodded, and moved desperately forward with the two unseen and unknown friends on either side supporting him when his body faltered. The third man, the man with the strong hands, held the torch. Its dim light flickered their way through the islands of barrels and sacks. Once, when footsteps overhead halted them, the large man pointed upwards, caricatured a salute, and grinned. So upstairs in this part of the building, soldiers must be quartered.

They had reached the far wall of the room. Hearne, his sense of direction still alert, guessed this must be the outside wall of the building. His cell had faced north, the front entrance to the town hall had faced south. Then this wall would face west: it would be near the village school, for the school stood in the fields behind the northwest corner of the market place.

The torch picked out the broad double door in the wall. The large man was slowly lifting up the crossbar until its end was free of one half of the door. Supporting it there with one hand, he pushed the free side of the door slightly open, as the torch was switched off. He stood there, waiting, listening. Hearne could see the black shadow of a tree, could feel the night air whip the gashes on his face, strike his naked shoulders. The Breton motioned quickly, and one of the men holding Hearne leaped down into the darkness. The other shoved him forward, and jumped behind him so that they fell together. They were lying in the shadows of a deep cart track, on grass edged with deep ruts. Above them, the large man edged his way out of the door, one hand still above his head holding the crossbar in place until the last minute. Then he jumped, thrusting the opened half of the door back in place as he leaped. The door stayed shut. The crossbar inside had fallen of its own weight and held it secure.

To the south of them was the square, and the movement of people grouping under its trees. Harder boots struck the pavement, round the corner from where they lay Patrol or sentries . . . Hearne didn't care. The jar of the six-foot drop had seared his like a flame. His body couldn't seem to obey him: it wouldn't rise at the touch of his companions' hands; all it could do was to lie and tremble, like a moth after its wings had struck a lighted candle.

"Quick!" The large man's whisper was urgent. Hearne stifled his groans and raised himself slowly. They half-carried, half-lifted him into the darkness of trees and bushes. Ahead was a small square house, the schoolhouse, thought Hearne. But that was no good—it was one of the first places the Boches would look for a hiding man. Dismay and desperation gave him strength. The quicker they reached there, the quicker he could get away from it. For one thing seemed absolutely certain: the three men were determined to take him there.

They almost ran over the last twenty yards of grass. But it wasn't the schoolhouse to which they led him. They halted in the trees at the edge of the children's playground, moving cautiously into the three-walled shelter at its side.

From the darkness at the back of the shed, a voice vaguely familiar said "Splendid." Hearne, swaying on his feet, looked at the three dark shapes beside him. Even now he couldn't see their faces properly. The man who had spoken limped forward, and held his arm to steady him.

"Can you walk? Try, please." It was Kerénor, all right.

"Yes."

"Good." Kerénor was slipping a long loose piece of clothing over his head, pulling it down into place on his shoulders. When Hearne's face had struggled free from the folds of the material, he was alone with Kerénor.

"The others?" he whispered, as Kerénor wrapped a cloak round him.

"Gone to change their clothes for the procession. You and I will walk together." Kerénor had thrust some kind of hat on his head. As they moved out of the shed, towards the path which would lead them into the market square, Hearne saw, even as he felt the long skirts pull round his knees, that Kerénor was dressed as he was. They followed the line of trees across the school playground, back towards the market place. They were two priests coming to join in the celebration of their people.

The first bright streaks of light were breaking in the east. The bells halted, and then swung into a changed rhythm. The people, waiting in small groups in the market place, began to move towards the church. One of these groups, standing at the northwest corner of the square, moved forward as the two priests passed them. Hearne noted the three grim-faced men, the two white-capped women, as they walked slowly to join other equally straggling groups, walked silently with bowed heads towards the steps of the church. They would hide the two priests from the town hall and the sentries patrolling its front. Hearne's head bowed too: no one, not even those who were his friends, must see his face. He walked slowly and draggingly, his chin resting on the black cloth covering his chest, Kerénor's hand comfortingly at his elbow. He felt as old and as weak as he must have looked.

They had left the market place and crossed the road. The two Romanesque towers soared above them. The thickening stream of people paused, and moved, and paused, as those in front began to climb the stone steps to the vaulted doorway. Hearne felt Kerénor's guiding hand keep him to the edge of the crowd, close to the base of one of the towers. The group of three men and two women still shielded them. Now, as they started to mount the stairs, their bodies formed a screen behind which Kerénor opened the narrow little door in the wall of the tower.

"For the clergy," murmured Kerénor, and stood aside to let Hearne enter first, as was fitting for his marked age.

Inside, it was as cold and dark as the cellar in which he had lain.

Hearne took three steps after Kerénor, fumbled, and then fell. Kerénor had him on his feet again, urging him through the blackness. Hearne went forward blindly. All that mattered was to get one foot before another, one foot before another.

Then at last Kerénor said quietly, "Now you can faint as much as you want."

CHAPTER 25 SANCTUARY

At first, he thought of his bedroom in Cornwall. It was his birthday, his fifth birthday, and his father had hung up a Chinese lantern in the window. The air blowing against the thin, flat pieces of glass which dangled from the lantern sent them swaying and striking their tinkling tune. He was lying in his cot, and he had wakened to hear the pretty colored thing sound its gentle song. The fragile notes would halt in the middle of their harmony as the wind drew new breath; they jangled into silence, and then began all over again. It seemed to him then that it was the loveliest kind of song, for it had no real beginning and no real end, and even the notes were as indefinite and vague as a song should be.

Hearne shook himself fully awake. The notes haunted him. He could hear them in their clear faintness. Perhaps he was really going mad. His eyes searched the dimly lit stone walls around him. The ceiling was of stone, rough and uneven. The floor on which he lay, wrapped tightly in a heavy blanket, was of stone too. It was dark, with shadows deepening in the corners: the only light came from a carefully trimmed lamp standing in a niche chipped out of a wall. No windows. No doors in the proper sense: just two arched openings in opposite stone walls. This wasn't a room in a house. Dismay seized him, and he struggled to raise himself on one elbow. It was more like a dungeon . . . a prison. . . . And then he saw that the rough blanket was an army blanket, and an old British army blanket at that. His right arm was bandaged with clean linen, his face felt sticky with some grease. He wiped some gently off his sore jaw with his free left hand. Yes, it was ointment: a thick, black ointment smelling of tar and sulphur. His body felt clean. It was still sore, still heavy to move, but the blood and the dirt from the town-hall cellar floor had been washed off, and there was a clean white linen sheet wrapped round his body to keep the coarse blanket off his flesh. He relaxed again and lay back on the thin straw mattress. He wasn't in Nazi hands, that was certain. He looked at the faint yellow light burning so steadily, and listened. Gently, the dripping dropping notes sang through the rough vault above his head. It was water. That was it; water trickling, falling slowly. He smiled, and now his face didn't hurt so much.

He must have fallen asleep again, and he must have slept for a long time. He could tell that by this feeling of expansion which his body had: a nice, warm, comfortable feeling, a clean feeling. He closed his eyes and listened to the distant trickle of water, as he tried to fit this jigsaw puzzle together in his mind. This place wasn't a house. It hadn't been built by man, but rather by some long, patient process of erosion. The ceiling was too high for a mine: a cave, or a series of caves perhaps, would be nearer it. But just whereabouts was this cave? He tried to remember what had happened after he had crossed the market place and the road in front of the church. There had been people crowding slowly towards the steps. . . . Kerénor had pulled him into the shadow of the tower, had opened that small door in its base. Then there had been darkness, and the sound of bells and the chanting of a choir had grown more distant. He thought he could remember another door, some steps, another door. He couldn't be sure. It had been too dark, and suddenly he had felt too tired. One step before another, stumbling, hesitating, leaning on Kerénor, reeling like a drunk on a Saturday night, one step before another. That was all he could remember. Then there was Kerénor's voice, no longer whispering, no longer strained. "Now you can faint as much as you want." And, by heaven, he had.

And now he was here, wherever that was.

He lay and listened to the trickling water. It must be falling into a pool in one of the next caves. There was a series of drops, which kept repeating the same notes like the strings of a violin being plucked. They almost formed a tune, but before they resolved themselves they halted, and the first notes sounded all over again. Like the tone signal of a radio station, like rain from the roof dripping into a barrel of water, like a Chinese lantern swinging at an opened window.

Then he heard the footsteps, at first an uncertain hint, then marked and sure. He kept his eyes closed as they entered the cave.

A light clear voice said, "He's still asleep!" A cool hand was on his brow, and the blanket was smoothed where he had disarranged it.

"He needed it." That was Kerénor's voice. "I don't think you have to change the bandages again. They look all right to me."

Hearne opened his eyes. Anne was kneeling beside him, and Kerénor was standing behind her. It pleased him somehow to see them both looking so anxious.

"Hello!" he said.

Anne smiled with her lips and her eyes and her voice. "He's awake."

Kerénor's twisted smile wasn't disagreeable. "Evidently," he said briefly. "How do you feel, now?"

"Not so bad."

"Good. You were beginning to worry us. I told you that you could faint, but I didn't expect quite all this."

"How long has it been since?"

"Since you collapsed? Two days and two nights."

"Was this where I passed out?"

"No. Further back there." Kerénor pointed to the opening through which Anne and he had entered the cave.

"Are we in a mine?"

"No." Kerénor's voice became informative: you could have guessed that he was a schoolmaster by trade. He sat down on the ground beside Hearne. "These rooms and passages are caves, discovered by the founding fathers of the church, no doubt, and used by them to escape from the pagans when they were searching for a suitable sacrifice on their stone altars. Later, the caves were useful against roving bands of northern raiders, and still later, against the English." Kerénor paused to let that sink in. He was smiling. So he knew now, too, Hearne thought. The schoolteacher was talking again. "Then, about four hundred years after the English, the caves were used during the Revolution, during La Vendée to be precise. That was the Breton counter-revolution, and there was much bloodshed here." Yes, Kerénor knew that Hearne was English: he was explaining French history politely for the benefit of a foreigner.

Kerénor was still talking in his matter-of-fact way. "Those of the inhabitants who managed to survive La Vendée did so by living down here along with the treasures from the church. After two months, they went above ground again, but they didn't put back the gold plate and silver candlesticks on the altar for almost thirty years. Cautious people. Now we may find these caves very useful again."

"Who knows about them?"

"The priests. The villagers had heard the stories about the caves, of course, but somehow they believed that they were either filled up, or destroyed, by Revolutionary soldiers. Certainly, all entrances from the fields have been completely blocked and forgotten. I myself didn't believe that the caves existed at all, until three days ago and a little conversation with Monsieur le Curé. The Church remembered how well the caves had sheltered its people—and its treasures—and it kept the secret, believing that the less others knew about it, the more valuable it would be."

Hearne was about to speak, but Kerénor interrupted him quickly. "I want you to answer some of my questions later, so don't tire yourself now. I'll explain as much as I can." He moved to a more comfortable position and cleared his throat. "I've been thinking what I should like to know if I were you." He rubbed the bridge of his nose reflectively as if arranging his thoughts into the neatest order. Anne was sitting motionless on the ground, her full black skirt spreading circlewise round her. When Kerénor spoke again, he counted each point briskly on the fingers of his left hand. He was a good schoolteacher.

"First, the Curé and Guézennec saw you were under arrest. Second, Anne arrived and confirmed that rumor. She had come down into the village—the Boches sent to the farm, to question Madame Corlay and to search the rooms, didn't think she was important: she wasn't one of the family; she was just a visitor to them; and no one at the farm enlightened them—and she went at once to the Curé for help. Third, the Curé sent Guézennec to bring me to the square, and I was there talking to Anne when you passed on your way to the town hall. We were discussing, actually, how any escape could be managed. Fourth, Monsieur le Curé went up to the farm to see Madame Corlay. He sent Guézennec over to Anne and me, with the news that there *was* a place which could hide you for days or even weeks, *if* you were to escape. Fifth, we met in Guézennec's parlor that evening, and perfected our plans. It's next door to Trouin's house, where the men come to drink together, and we know all of them and they know us. Anyone who seemed most suited for what we were planning was sent in to see Guézennec by Trouin. All very quietly, all very simply. That's how we completed the plans. It gave us good practice for the future."

"What about Anne?" Hearne said. "This must be dangerous for her."

Anne smiled, rose quickly, lighted a second oil lamp, and moved into the next cave.

Kerénor waited until she had gone, and then said, "She's living here. . . ."

"What?"

"Easy, easy. Don't put your temperature up again. Someone had to be with you; and no one else could, without their absence being noted. So Anne is visiting her aunt at St. Brieuc. She left on Friday, after you had been arrested and everyone at the farm had answered the Boches' questions stupidly and satisfactorily. What else was there for a girl to do, whose fiancé had turned out to be quite another man in disguise? Very embarrassing for any girl living in a village like St. Déodat. Her decision to go didn't need any explaining, I assure you."

Hearne ignored the raillery of Kerénor's voice. He said, "What about a permit to leave?"

"She's had that for some time. She got it the day she was turned out of her farm. They told her she could go and live with her relatives, and graciously gave her a permit to do it. No extra charge. That was an easy way to lease a house, so thoughtful, so generous." Kerénor's voice rose in savage imitation of a German accent. "Anne Pinot, born in Brittany, educated and living in Brittany, will be allowed by our gracious German permission to travel by foot (all trains being occupied by us, all buses being used by us, all petrol being commandeered by us) the distance of some eighty kilometers to the town of St. Brieuc, carrying one bundle of her possessions not larger than six kilos in weight, and there in St. Brieuc she will find a roof to put over her head (provided that the roof has not already been blown to bits or occupied by the soldiers assigned to that district) to replace the roof of her Breton farm exploited unjustly by her Breton family for two hundred and forty years and now in the rightful occupation of

Brittany's friends and saviors for the essential defense of Brittany and the Reich." He had risen to his feet, and was now limping up and down the rough floor, pausing here and there to accent a phrase with two uplifted fists, raising his voice in the crescendo of unmistakable parody as he reached the end of the peroration. He ended abruptly on the highest falsetto screech. "Bah!" he said in his normal voice. "Carpet chewer!"

"They'll hear us," Hearne warned.

Kerénor shook his head with a mystery which he obviously was enjoying. "Do you know where you are?" he asked. It was strange to see him become so much the archconspirator. Queer fish, thought Hearne: he seemed to pass from sarcasm to mockery, from emotional animation to calm disinterest, as easily as clouds changed their color at sunset. You could never tell what he was going to say next, whether his face would freeze into remote coldness or liven with expression, whether he would be serious or amused. And in spite of all these variations, you knew you could trust him: you might not like him, not at first anyway, but you could trust him.

Hearne replied, "We are under the church." It was as much the obvious answer to Kerénor's question as the answer was obviously expected.

"No." Kerénor was delighted with his secret. "No. Under the marching feet. Charmingly symbolic."

"Under the tents and huts?"

"Yes. Under the meadow lying in front of the east Gothic tower of the church. That water you hear is a small stream draining out of the pond in the meadows."

Anne was coming back, walking slowly so that the pitcher of water which she carried would not spill over. There were two pink spots in her cheeks. She had heard part of their conversation about her, no doubt. Hearne was about to say, "Anne, why didn't you tell us about the permit?" and then didn't, as he noticed the way she avoided his eyes. She was raising his shoulders so that he could drink, but she was watching the level of the water in the jug. If she hadn't told him about the permit, then she had her reasons. If she didn't want to explain them, then it was none of his business. Or, at least, he had no right to think it was. Perhaps she had preferred to stay at the Corlay farm rather than face the long journey to her aunt's house, perhaps she had felt that Madame Corlay's invitation would have been less warm if she knew about St. Brieuc as an alternative haven for Anne, perhaps it had been an oversight. And yet, he found himself entertaining the fantastic hope that none of these explanations was the right one.

He said, "Enough, Anne. Thank you." She still avoided his eyes. She lowered his head gently onto the mattress again, and pretended to smooth the blanket. The pink spots deepened in color and flowed over her cheeks. Hearne was suddenly aware that Kerénor was watching them both, with a strange un-Kerénor look on his face. There was a pause in which each could feel the words they were all avoiding.

Hearne said quickly, "Think I'll try to walk." He raised himself on his left elbow, disarranging the blanket which had just been so carefully smoothed.

Kerénor was smiling openly, now. "Better not," he said. "You've no clothes, anyway. I had to cut what was left of them off you. We'll have to find new ones. In any case, I want you to lie still today and save your strength for talking. I've some questions to ask you." He was serious again. The amused smile twisted off his face, and his eyes watched Hearne anxiously.

"I haven't finished my own," Hearne replied. "How many people know about me?"

"Madame Corlay and Anne, Monsieur le Curé and myself."

"How many know I am here?"

"The same again. We had to tell Madame Corlay. She was on the point of sending old Henri and his blunderbuss to rescue you. Much good that would have done, but both Madame Corlay and Henri were all set for action. So we had to tell her."

"What about the three men who got me out of that hell-hole?"

"Back working on their farms after attending the procession."

"And the three men with the two women?"

"They know nothing except the Germans weren't to notice you going towards the church. They are the rest of our committee."

"What committee?"

"Committee for the Preservation of Liberty, Equality, Fraternity." Kerénor was tensely serious. If Hearne had even looked about to smile, Kerénor would have struck him. But Hearne didn't smile . . . there was something pathetically courageous in the formation of a committee for the preservation of France in this remote Breton village. Yet, great oaks from tiny acorns . . .

Hearne said, "Good."

Kerénor relaxed again. "Is that all you want to know?"

"I'd like to know what happened when the guards were changed in the town-hall cellar."

"We were coming out of the church at the end of first Mass. It was almost six o'clock. Then systematized pandemonium broke loose. Squads of soldiers were summoned and herded us into the market place. We were counted and listed like sheep. Just when I thought we were all to be arrested—and that would have been an interesting experiment, but the Germans unfortunately thought better of it—we were all sent back for second Mass, and sentries were posted all round the church. When they let us out at last, they had decided on their course of action. A large reward was posted for your capture. Grim warnings were published about the fate of anyone who helped or harbored you. Houses were all searched from cellar to attic. Patrols are everywhere: there's a curfew for us all to go to bed early like the bad little boys we are. Then there is talk of hostages. But the only trouble is that, at present, they want to keep us co-operative—until the end of this month, anyway. You were right about the warnings you sent me through Anne. We are being maneuvered. I want you to give me the details about that."

"I've still a question. How did these three men get into the town hall? Its entrance was heavily guarded."

"As part of this German co-operation plan, a meeting had been planned for late that afternoon. If you hadn't been arrested, you would no doubt have had to speak at it. We were all told to attend, and in accordance with our own private plan, we all went. The place was crowded. No Boches were present. Elise was there, and she had got Picrel to speak along with her. He's trying to save the remnants of his business and to get his son out of the road gang. He didn't know what he was doing. Elise had persuaded him it was the only sane and sensible thing. The trouble with Picrel is that he has got accustomed to having more than his share of the village wealth and power; and he's hanging on to what he has. He's willing to be persuaded of anything which will let him hang on. It was a lively meeting. Then our Committee crowded round Elise and questioned her on the way out. The three men who had been chosen hung behind, and hid. Under that table on the platform covered by the draped flags. They just lay there and waited all through the night until the church bells began. That was their signal. I am sorry we had to arrange it so that it looked as if you had killed the German, but we must safeguard the village. You understand?"

"The village has done more than enough for me," Hearne said quietly. "How did they get into the cellar?"

"You want to know everything, don't you?" Kerénor looked at him warily.

"As someone who would like to perfect his own technique."

Kerénor's suspicion ended as quickly as it had begun. "It was simple. There might have been the noise of a movement from upstairs. The guard came to the foot of the staircase. Silence. He came up the staircase with a torch and the gun. Then he turned to go back downstairs. The door in the corridor, through which you escaped, opened. Our man came forward. In the old days he was the best smuggler in the district. Bare feet make no noise. Neither do large hands wrapped tightly round a German's throat."

"But what if there had been a second sentry?"

"One of the other men came into the corridor. German hat, German coat. Enough to pass in the dim cellar light (we are so backward here, no modern conveniences!), enough to pass for a moment. That was all we needed. From then on, he was to improvise, while the third man guarded the corridor with his knife. That was why we chose three men."

Hearne's look of admiration stopped Kerénor.

"That's nothing to what we *can* do," he said modestly. "After this war is over, the tales we shall have to tell will make strange listening. Nothing that art can invent is so wildly improbable as what happens in real life. Art and fiction are only imitation. Life is truth, and stranger than either of them."

Hearne nodded. "So I've found," he said. "There's one last thing. There was an explosion."

Kerénor said, "Yes, there was, wasn't there?" His eyes were mocking, and Hearne knew he would be told no more than he had guessed already. But, looking at Kerénor's triumph, he knew his guess had been near the truth.

"Here is your information," Hearne said. "I can give it to you as far as I can remember it, but the full proof is in my room in the farm. Who can go to get it?"

"Anne is out. I am out too—for I never went near the Corlay place, and if I were to go now, it would seem strange. There's only Monsieur le Curé left."

"Will he?"

"If he can act without being told the facts."

Hearne said, "My head is dull today."

"Take these caves, for instance. Monsieur le Curé told Guézennec about them. At the same time he suggests it would be a good place for anyone to be safe from the Germans. Then he says no more, except to tell me about the history of the caves, and he doesn't come to see you. Again, he doesn't notice that the clothes belonging to his young assistant—at present in hospital somewhere in Germany—were borrowed. But the vestry where they were stored was left open all yesterday afternoon. Again, in a few minutes I shall go back up into the church, and from the church I shall take the private way to his house. When I return I shall carry a basket of books, with food underneath for Anne and you. This afternoon when I see Monsieur le Curé we shall talk of other things, but not of a depleted larder."

"Here are the facts: I shall let you suggest them to Monsieur le Curé." Hearne's voice was beginning to tire. His head was beginning to throb again. He felt hot. Quickly he told Kerénor about the bookcase in his room. Two notebooks, two sets of papers clipped together, a map, a French service revolver, a silencer, a pocketknife, an envelope. Kerénor listened intelligently. At the mention of the gun, he shook his head slowly.

"The arsenal will need some careful suggesting," he said, and rose slowly to his feet. "I think I'll see Monsieur le Curé right away. I'd like that list of names . . . before I keep an appointment."

There was something in his voice which roused Hearne.

"What appointment?"

Kerénor was dusting the seat of his trousers. He seemed interested in the weave of the material. "After the meeting yesterday, Elise spoke to me. It's most unfortunate that Picrel turned out to be such a bad orator. There was only one thing Corlay and I had in common—the ability to talk."

"She asked you?"

"Sideways . . . nothing definite. For the sake of Brittany and the chance of a really worth-while career. If I feel the call, I am to let her know, and we can meet. Added bait, of course . . . the lovely Elise and a moonlight meeting. The first she's ever given me . . . such an honor, such promises of delight. Three days ago even, I should have been struck dumb by an invitation like that." His mouth twisted bitterly as he laughed at himself. "But three days ago is three days ago." He looked at Hearne. "Damn you," he said abruptly. "Why did you have to be right?"

He limped towards the passage.

"I'll bring the food," he called back to Anne.

"And the clothes," she said quietly. She looked towards Hearne. "You want the clothes, don't you?"

He nodded. "Most of all," he said. There was something else he had meant to ask . . . what was it? . . . But he was too tired: he gave up the effort.

Kerénor's limping footsteps had dulled into an echo. Once he had the clothes, Hearne thought, he would make his plans and start the journey. Meanwhile it was pleasant to forget; to watch Anne's quiet movements about the room; to feel her bandage his arm and smooth the sheet over his shoulders; to close his eyes and listen to the distant water-music.

CHAPTER 26 "WHITE IN THE MOON THE
LONG ROAD LIES"

Perhaps Hearne had slept enough, or perhaps it was just that his mind wouldn't rest. During the night, he woke five times in all, and each time Anne came forward out of the dark corner where she rested. She was beside him again when his broken sleep ended at last. Her heavy round gold watch, which she had fastened by its brooch to the blanket when he had started worrying about the time, told him it was almost six o'clock.

"Six o'clock when?" he asked her, as she carried in a basin of water.

"Six o'clock in the morning. Kerénor should soon be here." She gave him water to drink, and bathed him gently.

"What day is today?"

"Wednesday, I think." She smiled. "I lose count too, you see." He looked at her pale cheeks and tired eyes.

"I owe you a lot," he said. "If I hadn't had someone to nurse me so carefully as you have done, I should still be only half-recovered. I feel I could get up today. And then tomorrow—"

"You mustn't hurry too much."

"Not too much, but I must hurry."

She felt his brow and his pulse. "You *are* much better." Her bright smile made him feel better still.

"How did you learn all this?" he asked, pointing to the bandage she was cutting from a piece of linen.

"Because of Kerénor. He was going to start a kind of clinic for the school children, but the people against it were too many for us. He wanted me to help him. He was teaching me astronomy, and his fee was that I should learn first-aid."

"Astronomy!" said Hearne in amazement. "In heaven's name, why?"

"I wanted to learn," Anne said simply.

Looking at her calm face, he knew she spoke the truth. There was nothing behind her words. She had just wanted to learn. "You certainly learned how to nurse."

Anne smiled. "Oh, I've nursed animals: they are much more difficult to take care of than people." She finished changing his bandages, gently wiping his face clean of its black grease. "Now you do look better," she said. "You are healing nicely."

Hearne's spirits rose. "When will the clothes come?" he said.

"Today. And your map and your papers too, I should think." She saw the relief in his eyes. She gathered up the basin and the towel and bandages quickly, and hurried towards the other room.

Now what had he done? he wondered. Then the excitement of the plans already half-forming drove all other thoughts from his mind.

It was nine o'clock, however, before they heard Kerénor's footsteps and saw the round circle of light from his torch coming towards them.

He settled the basket clumsily on the floor beside Hearne and said, with a pretense of lightheartedness, "Food, what there is of it. Clothes, rustic but useful. Map, holding miraculously together. Clasp knife. Gun, very much loaded and complete with a peculiar object. What is it, by the way?"

"Something to take the noise out of shooting. A silencer."

"Careful kind of fellow, aren't you?" And then Kerénor dropped the amused tone as he picked up a neatly folded handkerchief, and handed it in silence to Hearne. The small bundle had weight. Hearne looked at Kerénor in surprise.

"What's this?" he asked.

"From Madame Corlay," Kerénor said shortly, and bent over the basket again.

Hearne unwrapped the handkerchief. Inside its folds was a silver watch of an old design, with fine engraving on its cover. Within the tracery of the pattern were the words *To Bertrand Corlay on his twenty-first anniversary, 29th January, 1868.* Hearne opened the watch in silence. The thin Roman numerals were delicately painted on the yellow face: the slender hands still moved on their dutiful way. He closed the cover gently, placed the watch carefully under his pillow.

"Would you give Madame Corlay my—well, please tell her that some day I shall thank her properly. Now I can only—" He stopped short. He was thinking, that watch was one of Madame Corlay's few treasures. He was thinking, that watch has seen three invasions of France by the Germans. Anne was watching him. He shook his head, as if he did not know what to say.

Kerénor nodded. "I'll tell her you felt you couldn't find words adequate enough to appreciate her kindness." Hearne looked up quickly at the Breton, but he wasn't laughing. For once he was being quite simple and direct.

Anne said, "Just tell her what he did say. She'd like that better."

Kerénor looked amused now. "I was just trying to help," he said. He looked at Anne teasingly. "Why do women think all other women like what they like? Men, at least, know better than that. Now, for the last things in this basket. Here's an envelope, bulky; and sheets of paper with excessively neat scratchings." He was watching Hearne's face. "Will that do?"

Hearne, his hand reaching eagerly for the envelope and sheets of paper, nodded. He looked through them quickly, but carefully. It was all there, everything he had noted and copied. He took a deep breath. God, he was feeling better every minute. He looked up to see Anne watching him again, this time with that little smile on her lips.

"All right, now?" she asked, trying to keep her voice disinterested. "I'll give you something to eat, and then you can try to dress."

Hearne nodded his answer, and patted the papers lying under his hand. Then suddenly he asked Kerénor, "Where are Corlay's original lists, and his diaries?"

Kerénor, limping back and forward restlessly across the cave, forced a twisted smile. "Under study. I thought the Committee should know just what they had to fight."

"You've seen them yourself?"

"Yes."

Hearne, watching the white face, the gaunt cheekbones, said nothing.

He thought: masochist is the word. He's made himself read every word of Corlay's diary and poems, and they are eating into him.

"Well?" demanded Kerénor truculently, as if he had guessed Hearne's thoughts.

"Well?" said Hearne.

Kerénor halted. He controlled his voice with difficulty. "In a France ruled by Frenchmen, Elise would be given a trial and shot. It is the only France I recognize! Because of the Germans, we cannot give her the trial she would otherwise have had. But we can complete the rest." He paused. "I shall accept her invitation when it comes. I shall bring her here."

Anne's face had whitened. "Jean," she said, "remember that if she comes here, she cannot go back."

"No, she cannot go back. That will be definite, Anne. You needn't fear. For once I am not letting arguments and hair-splittings prevent me from acting in time. This time, I shan't reason away my anger. One learns."

There was a silence.

Anne hesitated. At last she said, "I don't trust her. She'll be the one who will do the shooting. You'll be in danger." She was looking at Hearne, her eyes wide; Kerénor noticed the look.

"Charming," he murmured half-seriously, half-ironically, and silenced her effectively. "Now eat," he said to Hearne. "And I'll get you into these clothes. What were your original plans to escape?" Except for the nervous tension of his constant pacing, he had buried his own emotions deeply enough. But he was scarcely listening to Hearne, and the Englishman was glad of that. For then the omissions in the plan he was sketching wouldn't be so noticeable. After his own practical experience of the Gestapo's persuasive powers, he wasn't going to burden his friends with much knowledge. He touched briefly on the boatman who had brought him back from Mont St. Michel, and who would take a message so that his friends in Britain would know he was coming. All Hearne wanted was to reach Dinan and give that message to the boatman. All his plans depended on that. Then he realized Anne's occupation with the food which she was dividing into two portions was only a pretense.

"You've kept too little for yourself," Hearne said, to interrupt her thoughts.

"I can't eat any more," she answered. "If you want to get dressed before Jean leaves, you ought to finish your breakfast quickly." He wondered whatever had given him the first impression that she was a simple creature. Perhaps it was her gentleness and her direct honesty which had made him think she was easy to estimate.

"You're a determined woman, aren't you?" he asked.

She laughed, wrinkling her nose. Anyway, she seemed to have forgotten to worry about his plans for escape.

But when Kerénor had gone, and Hearne paused to rest after his first attempt to walk round the cave, she suddenly sat down beside him, and said, "Wouldn't it be better if someone could go to Dinan in advance, and see that boatman, and give him your message to take to your friends to send to Britain?"

"You like your questions long," he said, and then as she laughed, "Why do you always wear your hair so tightly braided, Anne?"

The two pink spots were coming back into her cheeks, but she wasn't to be dissuaded.

"I mean," she said slowly, "if someone could go in advance to Dinan, while you were still getting stronger here, then the message would sail back with that boatman to the Bay of Mont St. Michel, and he could send it to your friend, and it would go to Britain, and then you could get away from here with all the preparations made, and you wouldn't have to wait at Dinan for all these things to happen before you could reach the coast."

"Breathing helps," Hearne said. Anne laughed in spite of herself.

"But wouldn't it be better?" she insisted.

"No doubt. But after Sunday's excitement, every man in this village will have to keep close to St. Déodat for a while, and appear to be leading a normal life."

Anne said slowly, "I suppose so. But it would have been such a good idea. It would have made everything quicker and safer for you. You could go straight to the coast without going near Dinan yourself."

"I'll manage well enough, once I'm feeling all right again. Come on, Anne, give me a hand round this room."

She smiled. "You looked like a newly born calf, at first."

"I'll be less like one this time. Just you see."

When he sat down to rest again, she said, "That must have been a nice old man who brought you back in his boat."

He had been thinking of something else, and looked at her blankly.

She explained, "When you came back from taking Monsieur Myles to the coast; when you wore such funny old clothes all smelling of fish."

Hearne smiled. "Yes, he was a nice old boy."

"Can he be trusted, really trusted?"

"Yes."

"Then why don't you tell us his name? When you are gone, there may be others from this village who want to get to the coast. He could help them too, couldn't he?"

"Yes, I suppose he could."

"Perhaps someone may be desperate and need help. Perhaps Kerénor or one of the others . . ." Her voice trailed off.

It seemed, thought Hearne, as if he had now three different jobs to worry over. There was his real job, information. It came first: it had to. Then linked with that there was the safety of the men like Duclos and

Pléhec who were working with him and the other agents. And thirdly, there was the beginning of secret resistance in the villages: he had to help St. Déodat, even apart from what he owed it himself. He thought of L'Etoile d'Or and of Jules, who would have taken the place of big Louis. Jules was to be trusted, but the Golden Star itself might be dangerous: too much had happened there. He couldn't send anyone there when he was unwilling to try it himself. The only really definite source of help was the boatman to whom Etienne had led him, the boatman who sailed from the canalized river on the Bay of Mont St. Michel along the coast and up the River Rance to Dinan. The boatman knew nothing about the activities on the Mont St. Michel: all he knew was that the boy Etienne and he were serving in the same cause. So Pléhec and Duclos and all their plans would not be in danger if he were to tell Anne the boatman's name. That was the main thing, that Pléhec and Duclos should be safe to go on with their work.

Hearne said, "I know him only by a nickname—Le Trapu. He is about fifty years old, short and broad-shouldered, with black hair and blue eyes. He has a boat and a sister called Marguerite. The boat has faded red sails with two brown patches. The sister has a *bistro* on the wharf at Dinan, just where he moors the boat, and anyone who is looking for Le Trapu can wait for him there. Tell Monsieur le Curé about this: he will know when a man really needs help, and he can send him to Le Trapu. But *you* mustn't, Anne; you must leave that to Monsieur le Curé. And tell no one else. Promise?"

Anne nodded, her eyes wide and serious, her lips grave.

"And also tell Monsieur le Curé that if any interesting information should be found in this district, then a man could be sent with it to Le Trapu. He will pass it on, and it will reach Britain. That may be important for us all. Can you remember that?"

"But of course." She sat silently, thinking over what he had said. "How do you feel now?"

"Not so bad."

"Should you sleep, perhaps?"

"I'll have another try on the old legs, first. You don't need to hold me, this time."

She nodded and watched his slow progress with anxiety. After twice round the room, he was forced to give up.

"Not so good," he said bitterly as he straightened himself on the mattress.

Anne brought him water to drink. "It will be easier when you try again tomorrow," she said. "You can't expect miracles."

"This afternoon," he corrected her. "I can't wait until tomorrow." He moved restlessly on his bed.

"When do you want to leave?" she asked. "Saturday?"

"Too late. Le Trapu doesn't sail on Sundays." It had been the twelfth, a Friday, when he sailed back from Mont St. Michel. Mondays, Wednesdays, Fridays from the Mont; Tuesdays, Thursdays, Saturdays from Dinan.

He said, "I must be in Dinan by dawn on Saturday. Better leave here no later than sunset on Friday." He swore to himself. "If only I could have left tonight, I could have reached Dinan tomorrow."

"No, you'll only add to your dangers if you aren't recovered enough. You'll manage Friday, all right," said Anne. "Then Le Trapu will deliver the message on Saturday night. And you can be at the coast by Sunday night. . . . Which part of the coast?"

He looked at her suddenly. Her wide eyes returned the look candidly: her face was eager and sympathetic. "Why do you ask, Anne?" he said slowly.

"I was wondering if it were near St. Brieuc." She bent down and picked up the blanket which he had thrown aside. He looked at her with a dawning suspicion.

"And why?"

She pretended to be folding the blanket.

At last she said, "I am traveling to St. Brieuc. Remember? I thought I might go with you, to look after you."

"*You* look after *me*? Out there?" He was shocked, incredulous; he stared at her. Then as he saw her face tighten and the light go out of her eyes, he reached up and caught her hand. "Anne," he said, "I'm sorry if I hurt you. You're kind and you're brave. But you don't know what you are letting yourself in for, if you were to travel with me, or even be found with me. You cannot go with me. It would be dangerous—impossible."

She stood, saying nothing, her eyes downcast, her hand lifeless in his. He saw he had really hurt her. "Anne," he said gently, "Anne. Anne, darling."

She flinched and tried to draw her hand away, but he held it tightly. His resolution melted. "Anne, you've got to get to St. Brieuc safely. You've got to stay there safely. You've got to keep safe."

She was looking at him now. "Others take risks. Why shouldn't I?"

"Because I don't want you to." He spoke sharply—but she was smiling now.

There was a silence. "Is that all?" she asked at last.

"Yes."

She drew her hand slowly out of his. "Do all Englishmen behave like you?" she said.

He took a deep breath. For their own mental happiness, he hoped they didn't.

"What are you thinking of?" she asked.

"I'm thinking of a poem I once knew."

"Tell me it."

"It's in English."
"I want to hear English."
He spoke it slowly, softly.

> "White in the moon the long road lies,
>   The moon stands blank above;
> White in the moon the long road lies
>   That leads me from my love.

> "Still hangs the hedge without a gust,
>   Still, still the shadows stay . . ."

He closed his eyes, trying to catch the next phrase. Strange: when he was young and only imagined himself in love, how he could recite yards of such poems and bury himself in thwarted gloom. Now, when he really knew what the poem meant, he was forgetting it—forgetting not its feeling, but the words. He tried once more:—

> ". . . Still, still the shadows stay:
> My feet . . . my feet upon the moonlit dust
>   Pursue the ceaseless way.

> "The world is round, so travelers tell,
>   And straight though reach the track,
> Trudge on, trudge on, 'twill all be well,
>   The way will guide one back.

> "But ere the circle homeward hies
>   Far, far must it remove:
> White in the moon the long road lies
>   That leads me from my love."

It was Anne who spoke first. "It is a sad poem."
"How do you know?" he asked quickly.
"Because your voice was sad. . . . Will you translate it for me?"
Hearne shook his head. "Some day, Anne. Not now. Later." He roused himself once more, and rose slowly to his feet. "Now *you* are looking sad. Where's that smile of yours?"
She found it with difficulty.
"What's wrong, Anne?"
"Nothing. At least not much. I'm worried, that's all. Brittany's coast is treacherous. I know it quite well, and there are many places with bad tides, currents, rocks. You may choose one of them." She was walking beside him, watching his steps with a careful eye.
"So we are back there, again?"
"Yes."
"Would it make you any less worried if I were to tell you that the place

I shall go to has been chosen because it is safe? You wouldn't know it; it's quite small, just west of Dinard, but it is certainly safe. As safe as any place is, now."

Anne said quietly, "Is it St. Lunaire?"

He checked his pace, and looked at her with a mixture of annoyance and amusement.

"I noticed your map," she explained quickly. "I noticed a light pencil line. Or shouldn't I have?"

"No, you shouldn't." He was half-angry. Women always wanted to know everything. But even if Anne had seen any of the other papers, she couldn't have understood the coded shorthand.

She had guessed part of his thoughts. "I only looked at the map. It was lying on the ground beside the mattress. I picked it up and put it safely with the rest of your things. I am sorry if I shouldn't have looked at it." Her tone was stilted, her face was flushed and her eyes were bright. She looked so much like a worried child that he relented and smiled. After all, no harm was done. And she had obviously thought there was nothing wrong in looking at a map: if she had had a guilty conscience, she would never have told him about it. His annoyance and suspicions melted, and he was left with a feeling of being mean and ungrateful.

He smiled again. "Well," he said, "does all that make you feel better?"

Anne nodded. "Much better. The coast at Dinard is dangerous, but further west there are safer places." She didn't mention St. Lunaire again. She stood smiling at him, and the smile was real at last.

Kerénor came again in the evening, bringing food and little news. Things were as they had been, he told them gloomily. In that case, Hearne thought, he ought to be more cheerful. Things might very well be worse: the Nazis might have discovered the real story of the escape from the town hall, its cellars might have new guests within their walls, and Sharkface and Razorpuss might very well be striding into the cave at this moment. Hearne watched Kerénor as he paced the floor, and wondered just what conflicts raged in the Breton's mind. Elise's influence wasn't so easily removed as Kerénor had pretended to believe, yesterday, when he had pronounced his judgment. Or perhaps, by making an open declaration to Anne and Hearne, he had hoped to keep his decision strong. He had probably feared he would hesitate, if he hadn't witnesses to challenge his pride. And now, even with witnesses, he was losing his determination. The coldness of reason was strangling the will to act. Kerénor was the kind of man who had to strike when his anger was at white heat; when it cooled, then his purpose wavered and the will to act became frustrated cynicism. He would always give Elise a last chance, not from kindness of heart but from intellectual self-hypnotism. Hearne looked dispassionately at Kerénor . . . *the native hue of resolution is sicklied o'er with the pale cast of thought,* he repeated to himself. Yet, who was he to criticize Kerénor? He thought of Anne. Yes, anyone looking into his mind would think he was another kind of fool. Plenty of people would judge him equally harshly, either because he had smothered his own emotions too much, or because he hadn't smothered them enough. But what the hell could he do? This wasn't a case of doing what he wanted to do: it was a case of what he had to do. Personal feelings didn't enter into it at all. He recognized that, and yet he couldn't stop himself from having them. So, who was he to criticize Kerénor? A typical Nazi would sneer at Hearne for his sentimental weakness: a typical Frenchman would think he was cold and hard. That's the trouble, he was thinking, he was neither of these. He was just a compromising Englishman.

Kerénor noticed his silence. "You are tired. I'll come back in the morning when you've had a good sleep. You can tell me then about your plans for leaving. You've made them?"

Hearne nodded, but said nothing. Yes, they were made, and he wasn't going to let anything change them, either. On Friday he would leave. Not tomorrow, but the next day he would leave. He looked again at Anne. How long, he wondered, before this bloody war was over? How long before he could come back?

Anne was restless. She was waiting impatiently for Kerénor to go, and when he did she went with him. "I'll walk to the tower steps," she had said, and had lifted the smaller lamp to light her way back to the cave.

Hearne watched the entrance to the cave blankly, and listened to the limping footsteps mingling with the light crispness of Anne's heels. Then the following echo died away too. He stretched himself gloomily on the straw mattress. If Anne wanted to walk and talk with Kerénor, then it was nothing of his business. He, himself, had chosen to make it none of his business. So why the devil was he feeling like this? It was all the fault of lying cooped up in a stone coffin: living in this cave made you imagine things. What on earth had ever given him the idea that it would be any good coming back here when the war was over? She was still betrothed to Corlay, wasn't she? And if she weren't, then there were others. She had been kind and gentle to him because she was kind and gentle. What was there for her to see in him, anyway?

When she returned, he was lying staring up at the rough ceiling of the cave. She didn't explain anything, and he wouldn't ask.

They ate the food which Kerénor had brought them, with little to say. The strangeness of the silence between them struck Hearne: he hadn't realized before just how much they usually talked when they were together. When Anne changed the bandages, she fastened them with special care, and she examined the cuts and bruises with capably cool hands and eyes. Nothing escaped her, tonight. At last, everything was done to her satisfaction. She lowered the lamp, smoothed the sheet under his chin.

Standing beside his bed, she looked tall and slender. The smooth fair hair seemed almost silver.

She spoke softly, her voice clear and low. "Good night."

"Good night."

Well, he thought savagely as he heard her footsteps moving quietly in the cave next door, that was just as neat a piece of emotional bathos as he had ever had. The sooner he was out of here, the better.

CHAPTER 27   THE DARK WOOD

When Hearne awoke, Anne must have already risen. The blanket in her corner of the cave was folded in a neat square on the thin mattress. Then he heard a movement from the inner cave. Blast, he thought: he had wanted to go in there for a drink— He interrupted his thinking to listen to the footsteps. They were limping. Hearne, lying rigid on his mattress, said, "Hell, what's going on here, anyway?"

It was Kerénor, all right. He was standing in the entranceway now, with a lamp in his hand and a twisted smile on his face.

"You waken early," he said.

Hearne didn't answer.

"Do you want anything?"

"A drink—I'll get it later."

"Why not now?"

Hearne rose stiffly and went towards Kerénor.

"Walking more easily? Take this." He handed the lamp to Hearne.

"Yes. Thanks," Hearne said briefly and passed into the other cave. It was empty. Only the the thin cascade of water, falling into the pool, made any sound. Only the little stream, flowing in its miniature canal, made any movement. He paused uncertainly.

"What's wrong?" asked Kerénor. Hearne wished he would wipe that grin off his face.

"Nothing." He drank from the pool, cupping his hands and letting the cold water splash over his face. His body was certainly better. He could even move his right arm as far as the elbow without any pain.

When he came back into the cave where he had slept, Kerénor was sitting on his bed. "I'll go and get our breakfast soon," he said. "Might even find some nice hot soup waiting in Monsieur le Curé's kitchen this morning. He thinks a man who might be recovering from Nazi treatment might need more nourishment. Funny thing: I am getting quite attached to Monsieur le Curé."

Hearne stood in front of Kerénor. He was listening, but not to the Breton.

"What's wrong?" Kerénor asked again.

"Nothing."

Kerénor was enjoying himself immensely. "Don't tell me you are missing Anne already."

Hearne felt his face flush, but he didn't speak.

"She's gone, you know."

"Gone?" Hearne echoed. But of course, he thought, she had to leave sometime. She had already delayed her journey to her aunt long enough for safety's sake. "How long will she take to get to St. Brieuc?" he asked more casually than he felt.

"She hasn't gone to St. Brieuc." Kerénor was watching him with a mixture of amusement and clinical interest.

Hearne said slowly, "You can stop playing for effects. Where the hell is she?"

"By this time she should have reached Dinan."

"Dinan?"

"I said Dinan." And then Kerénor relented. "She wouldn't tell me very much. She just said I was to tell you that she would see 'him' and give 'him' the message. That she might shelter with 'his' sister before she continued her journey. Does it make sense to you?"

"Partly." Hearne's voice was grim. "What message? Did she say?"

"Saturday at the seaside. Not very exciting. Or is it?"

"Exciting enough." Hearne began to pace about the cave. Anne must have gone last night after he had fallen asleep, so that she could be in Dinan before dawn, so that Le Trapu would have the message before he sailed this morning back to the Bay of Mont St. Michel. That meant Etienne would get the message today or tonight; and by tomorrow night, Friday night that was, Duclos would send the message out from his oubliette in the Abbey. Perhaps, if Le Trapu saw the boy Etienne in time, the message would even be sent tonight. Saturday at St. Lunaire. She had planned everything as neatly as he could have wished.

"But why didn't she tell me?" Hearne said at last.

"Because she was afraid you would have forbidden the idea. Anne is a well-brought-up girl. Her father's word was law. If you had forbidden her to go, she would have felt the compulsion of the old instincts to obey."

"I'm not like her father," Hearne said irritably.

Kerénor smiled, as if to himself. "No. But you seem to have a lot of authority over her. Now don't go asking me why. If you can't understand that for yourself, then it isn't worth explaining. Here, you'd better sit down and rest."

"I'm all right. I need to walk." Hearne's excitement was fading, and in its place was worry. He thought of Anne alone at Dinan, on the dark road to Dinan. She might never have reached there. His face was hard as he halted in front of Kerénor. "You shouldn't have let her go."

"I?" asked Kerénor, in mild surprise. He was no longer smiling as he looked at Hearne's face. His voice lost its raillery. He said gently, almost sympathetically, "I assure you I have no influence over her at all. She's my oldest friend here. She would talk with me when the others were still watching me with distrust, because I come from another part of the country—from the South of Brittany. But she talked with me, partly because she doesn't like to hurt people, partly because I could converse about the things she was interested in, partly because she liked me, partly because she pitied me. But the chief thing was that I was someone to talk to. You see, her father had her sent to a good school at Dinan, but he wouldn't let her go on to Rennes University as she wanted to do. He brought her back to live on the farm, and betrothed her to Corlay. He thought he was doing the best thing for her. If Corlay had been a different sort of chap, no doubt these simple-minded plans wouldn't have been so bad. Most girls would make happier women if their personal ambitions were sublimated. Well, anyway, we'd talk, Anne and I. I would preach and she would listen or argue gently. But she never took my advice unless she wanted to take it. Last night was one of the times when she just listened to me and did the other thing. You don't know Breton women when they have all their plans made."

"She couldn't have had them made, if I hadn't talked so damn much," Hearne said savagely. "She got me into the state of thinking aloud yesterday. I never guessed . . . she seemed so simple . . . so . . . I've been thinking of her as a—well, look at her! She fitted into the background of St. Déodat so well that I never guessed she would do anything mad like this."

"She seemed to me to be very sane."

"But she doesn't know what she's up against. What the devil was that message for me, again?"

Kerénor repeated it slowly. "She was going to see this 'him' and give 'him' the message, and perhaps shelter with 'his' sister before continuing the journey."

"Shelter with his sister . . ." Hearne exploded: he cursed fluently and vividly until he had to pause for breath. "Shelter with his sister!" he repeated. "I've never been there. For all I know, the sister may run a brothel."

"You are worrying too much," advised Kerénor. "Anne is no fool. She knows Dinan and has friends there. That is where she went to school. And she has her permit with her. She thought of everything, including leaving Jean's permit for you."

"Jean?"

"Yes, the old man who worked on her farm. Both he and Marie had permits too; but when you were arrested and Anne came here to nurse you, Anne sent them up to the Laënnec farm to stay out of the way for a while. They will be useful there, too: Laënnec is dead. The news has just come to his wife. Anne gave the old couple's permits to Monsieur le Curé for safekeeping. Last night, she told me that perhaps you could use Jean's permit, if we could change the age in it from eighty-two to thirty-two. I think I can do that, all right."

Hearne sat down at last. "And I thought Anne needed protection," he said with a wry smile.

"That's one of her greatest charms, and it is completely natural, too. It appeals to our masculine vanity. Do you know Latin? Remember what the Censor Metellus said in the Senate? 'Nature has arranged that we can live neither with women nor without them. If we *could* live without them, then we should not have all this trouble.' "

"You forget to add that the Censor Metellus was happily married."

"I suppose satisfied men can afford to be critical: it adds to their feeling of superiority to know that what they criticize doesn't really apply to them." Kerénor was bitter once more. He didn't mention the name of Elise, nor did Hearne; but the name was there between them all the same.

Kerénor rose suddenly. "Must get the food before it is too late. Then after that, I'll have to leave you. I am to appear before some Nazi committee for instruction on what I may teach in the village school."

"How are things up there?"

"According to plan. Trucks have visited the farms, and the shops, and the houses even. We might have had a plague of locusts. We never knew we had so much until we saw the truckloads driving away. What is left can only be bought and sold at fixed prices, fixed for everyone except the Boches. They are scattering worthless marks about like confetti. And there are some among us—not many, but still some—who are selling to the Boches. They know the marks mean nothing, but they think Nazi good-will means a lot. We've got a little list starting. These false Bretons will get paid in full when we start marching towards Berlin. Even Picrel's son agrees that there can be no pardon for his father. He's first on the list. We are deeply ashamed of him."

"Picrel, the man who owns so much?"

"That's why, I suppose. Strange, isn't it? He's a great Christian by his way of it, and I have never professed to be one. Yet the one aim in his life is to hang onto the possessions he has got. Worldly possessions. If I remember my New Testament correctly, worldly possessions weren't held in great esteem. In fact, if a man gives up honor or humanity for the sake of what he owns, then he is betraying the principles of Christianity. When I watch the Picrels scrabbling at German feet for the sake of their property, do you know what I believe? I believe that if Christ came back today and preached to the people, the Picrels among them would have him shot against a stone wall as a revolutionary."

There was a pause, and then Hearne said, "Yes, I think you are right. And now, having disposed of Picrel, what about the others in the village?"

"Standing fast. Before, there were two types of people in the world. People from St. Déodat, and foreigners. Now there are people from St. Déodat, foreigners, and filthy Boches. You can rest about your escape, by the way. The Boches are now convinced that you called the guard in on some pretext, throttled him, and made your escape. They don't think you could go far, and they keep seaching all the neighboring farms. All they've discovered so far were two escaped prisoners of war, poor devils. The Boches have offered a stupendous reward for you. They describe you as an Englishman under the assumed name of Bertrand Corlay."

Then the Germans had found Lassare at Bordeaux and questioned him, Hearne thought. He said, "What do the people of St. Déodat believe about me?"

"They still think you are Bertrand Corlay, and you have become a sort of village hero. Those who have seen you swear that you *are* Corlay, and that the Boches are lying so that someone might be tempted to betray you, for the Boches know that Bretons don't betray a Breton. Anne suggested that we should just let the people go on thinking that you are Corlay, because that would make up to Madame Corlay for what she had to suffer before. Monsieur le Curé agreed to that, and so, there we are. To St. Déodat, you are still Bertrand Corlay, the reformed. They'll probably carve a memorial to you in the church, when the peace comes. I've always wondered who chose national heroes: it's interesting to find out."

"If Corlay comes back after peace—"

"Then he will reform with great sincerity to live up to the character you have left for him, as soon as he finds it gives him enough esteem and power. That's all he wanted, anyway. He backed the wrong horse, that was all."

The idea of Corlay returning vindicated, accepted, conforming, depressed Hearne still more. Once it would have amused him as Kerénor was amused. But now he thought of Anne, of Madame Corlay and the two farms which she would like to see as one.

Hearne rose and walked round the cave. Eleven paces by thirty-six paces: eleven by thirty-six.

Kerénor paused at the entrance. "Don't walk much," he advised.

"I'm all right." And then as Kerénor still halted, watching him, "I am just getting ready. I am leaving tonight."

Kerénor said, "Anne thought you would leave tomorrow."

"I'm leaving tonight."

Kerénor was smiling again. "If you hurry, you may even catch up with Anne at Dinan."

Hearne halted. "Who said I was going to Dinan?"

"There's got to be some limit to your sense of duty. Even an Englishman must be human, sometimes." Kerénor started to limp away.

"One moment," Hearne called after him. "That's what I meant to ask you two days ago. How did you and Anne learn I was English?" He watched Kerénor's face, half-turned over his shoulder. I wish to heaven, Hearne was thinking, I didn't always seem to amuse him so much.

"You were unconscious, weren't you, for over two days?"

"I talked?"

"You did."

"In English?"

"Mostly."

"What about?"

"Partly nonsense, partly sense."

"What about?"

"Yourself. Don't look so worried, even if Anne sounds the same in both languages. She knows only schoolgirl English. She couldn't understand everything."

Kerénor enjoyed his exit. He was a last-word man.

They stepped out into the shadows of Monsieur le Curé's sheltered garden, and felt the real air with its cold sharpness encircle them again. Kerénor, who had led Hearne through the caves and passages up into the ground floor of the tower, through the silent church, out through the Curé's private door leading to the shrubbery and his house, now grasped the Englishman's arm. They halted. They listened, and when they were satisfied moved quietly on under the shadows of the trees beyond the house. Then the garden ended.

Ahead were fields. West of them, to their right, lay the road and the last houses in the village and the stone bridge and the path to the Corlay farm. On their left were the meadows and trees under the east spire of the church, and the rows of neat huts filled with sleeping soldiers. The last quarter of the moon was in the sky, with clouds and the feeling of rain to come. They saw the shape of a patrolling sentry, and then he was hidden by the corner of a hut. High above them was the intermittent drone of planes.

"Many of them in the last week," whispered Kerénor, pointing upwards. "We hope they may be British, because they fly to the northwest and don't come back."

Hearne said nothing. They weren't returning British planes. Their engines hadn't the right sound. They were Ju 88's. He thought of the aerodrome he had found on that last journey towards Dol. The planes were no doubt flying to its well-camouflaged fields, while the former French airport had its quota of dummy planes and visible hangars. He smiled in spite of himself. This war had its childish aspects. . . . If the results weren't so grim, you would laugh at them. He looked at the darkened village over his right shoulder. You would laugh, if the results weren't so grim.

He followed Kerénor, who was moving with surprising speed and silence on the smooth grass. They had crossed the stream flowing to the pond down in the meadows. Kerénor, using the scattered groups of trees for cover, was circling at some distance round the Germans' camp, to enter the wood beyond the pond. From that point, he had explained with the help of the map in the cave, he would leave Hearne to strike northwards until it was safe to turn west for Dinan. This was how Anne had gone last night. It had been, and ought to be, simple.

Hearne felt in the pocket of the worn French army-jacket, with all its markings ripped off: watch, map, matches, gun, silencer, knife, some small money forced on him by an embarrassed Kerénor, and the sheets of neat notes. He pulled the old cap still further down over his eyes. He was glad now that he had rejected the offer of Jean's permit and the fancy dress of an old peasant. If he were caught, Jean's permit would only lead the suspicious Boches to Anne. It was better this way. It meant he would have to keep hidden in the daylight, and move only during darkness. But that was something he could do. And ahead of him were only two night journeys. Dinan was roughly ten or twelve miles away to the west. From there, northwards to the English Channel, was slightly more than that distance. He could manage it. His legs were strong again, and all that was left of the Gestapo's attentions was a stiffness in his back, a carefully bandaged right shoulder, some bruises, and a tenderness in the stretch of the skin forming over the cuts. He could manage it, not exactly comfortably, but sufficiently capably if he didn't meet downright bad luck.

"How are you feeling?" Kerénor whispered.

"Unbelievable." It was true. The strange freshness of the air made him feel as though he could walk thirty miles before sunrise.

They were at the wood. The trees were neatly spaced, and there were winding paths beneath the branches. Here and there they passed a stone bench. It was the kind of place in which lovers walked in every country, escaping from the hard eyes of their parents and the ridicule of their friends.

It was Hearne who gripped Kerénor's arm, this time. His quick ear had heard the light crack of some twigs. They halted behind the tangle of a thorn bush, with its vague sweet scent encircling them. At first Hearne thought the man on the path ahead, with his arm coupling a girl, was some young Breton who had risked the Nazis' anger to walk with her here.

And then, as the two figures crossed the patch of faint moonlight on the path, he saw the man's uniform and the girl's gleaming hair. He knew by the sudden intake in Kerénor's breath that he had recognized them too. It was Elise, with the man Ehrlich. But Hearne no longer saw Elise. He was staring at Ehrlich. The expression on the German's face was very different now, very different from that he had worn in a cellar of the town hall. Hearne's hand tightened on his gun: he fitted the silencer carefully over it, his eyes still on the German's face.

And then, as they passed a stone bench, Ehrlich pulled the smiling girl down onto it. Her head was thrown back and the hair was loose and soft, its thickness catching the stray beams of light through the leaves overhead. She was laughing now.

Kerénor stiffened. His lame foot slipped and a twig snapped. Ehrlich looked quickly towards the bush behind which they were hidden. His hand left Elise and went to his holster as he rose, peering into the darkness.

Kerénor stepped silently out of cover. Perhaps he felt discovery was inevitable and had decided to give Hearne the chance to get away. He limped slowly forwards. Ehrlich's gun was out. Elise had risen, turning as she started to her feet. Hearne, still standing behind the thorn bush, saw the loose coat swing open as she turned, saw the whiteness of her body. Kerénor had seen too. He halted, and his low voice lashed her dispassionately. The German smiled, and pointed his gun; but Kerénor's savage words didn't halt.

Hearne moved slightly to one side so that his aim might be completely accurate. The pang at his shoulder as he raised his forearm was an unnecessary reminder of the cellar, of the torch which had lighted him as the three other men had held him down, of the amused face of Ehrlich beind the torch. There wouldn't be any more cellars for Mr. Ehrlich to preside over. There wouldn't be much more of anything for Mr. Ehrlich. His love-making was as practised as his torture, but there wouldn't be any more of either for him.

The German was still grinning. He motioned impatiently to Elise to stand away from him, as he raised the revolver.

His voice was as low as Kerénor's. "Trouble-seekers find trouble," he began, and the girl laughed softly, her head thrown back, the white curve of throat outlined against the loose thick hair.

There was a thick hiss, a stiffening of the German's shoulders. He was a marionette whose strings had been cut. He sagged, slipped slowly to the ground. He lay as he had fallen.

Elise's soft mocking laughter had halted. The parted lips stiffened to scream as terror gripped her throat, but the limping footsteps had already reached her, and hands stronger than terror strangled her cry. Even after the last vague attempt to free herself from the death grip, even after the frenzy of her struggles had given way to limpness, Kerénor still held her

Assignment in Brittany   541

crushed in his hands. The coat slipped from her bare shoulders. He
dropped her suddenly, stood motionless, looking down at the red gold
spilling over his feet.

Hearne came forward from the thorn bush. He touched Kerénor's arm
gently. Kerénor did not move.

"Hurry," Hearne said. But Kerénor didn't hear.

"Listen," Hearne whispered urgently. "How near are we to the north
edge of the wood?"

Kerénor looked at him dully. All emotion had left his face. "Another
five minutes." His voice had all feeling cut out of it.

"You get towards that side of the wood. When you hear a pistol shot,
start running, keeping to the shadows, using the trees. Get back to the north
end of the St. Déodat road and reach your house. Now hurry. If you don't,
there will be hell to pay in St. Déodat."

The last sentence roused Kerénor. "No. It will be simpler than that,"
he said. "I killed them both."

Hearne's patience was wearing thin. "Don't be a bloody fool. We don't
need martyrs, we need live men to fight."

"What else is there to do?"

"You'll hear. Hurry. Make for the end of the wood. Keep on the grass.
Don't step on any earth. I'll see you, some day, when I can get back here.
Go on. I can't get started until you are at the edge of the wood. I'll time
you."

Kerénor moved hesitatingly.

"If you don't," Hearne said, "we're all lost. You, and I, and Anne, and
all of us. Go on!"

Kerénor disappeared into the shadows of the trees. Thank God he had
enough sense left to move quickly, Hearne thought. He waited for five
minutes, his back to a tree whose branches shaded him. He was probably
as big a fool as Kerénor, with his noble offer to take the blame and the
punishment. As if, thought Hearne, one victim would satisfy vengeance
for the death of one German: ten for one was nearer it. Yet he himself
was probably as big a fool. It would be easy to walk away through the
night and leave St. Déodat with hell to pay: it would be easy, if you could
think that way. But you'd have to be one of the new super-race to be
able to do it.

The five minutes were up. The wood was silent. Hearne moved quickly
from the shadow of the tree. He bent over the German and lifted the gun
still gripped in the stiffening hand. It was the usual ugly hole-tearing
Lüger. He twisted the Nazi's arm and aimed the revolver at the neat
puncture ringed with a dark-wet stain on the Nazi tunic. This time the
report seemed like a crack of thunder in the quiet woods. Its echo hit
the fields. Hearne only paused to note that the Lüger had lived up to its
reputation, and then he was running swiftly, silently along the path which

Kerénor had taken. He could see the fields once again. In the half shadows of the clouded moon, they seemed empty. Kerénor must have got away. Thank God for that, anyhow.

But at the edge of the wood, Kerénor was waiting. He gave one of his old smiles as he saw Hearne, and then he was half-running, half-hobbling by his side. Behind them, on the other side of the wood, the alarm had sounded in the camp. Hearne made for the first tree in the field. At least, they were free of the wood. It would soon be surrounded. But once they were far enough away from it, it would be a help to them. There was plenty of searching to be done there. They hurried through the night, black peace in front of them, danger behind them. Kerénor's numbness had given way to grim fatalism. He was keeping up the pace he had set himself, pausing, halting, running, crouching as Hearne did, across the sloping curving fields with their scattered trees and rambling hedges.

At last they had circled round the village and climbed the steep fields on its west side. Below them was St. Déodat, and Guézennec's house lying at the end of a row of black shadows.

"Waste no time. Get indoors and stay there," Hearne said between the heavy breaths which tore his lungs.

Kerénor nodded. He was breathing with difficulty too: drops of sweat clung to his eyebrows.

"*Au revoir.*"

"*Au revoir.*"

There was a fumbled handclasp, and then Kerénor was following the path down towards the road.

Hearne climbed higher on the hill. The clouds were piling up, hiding the quarter moon. When he turned to watch Kerénor, he couldn't see him, but he knew the Frenchman was making his way along the backs of the buildings to reach the house of Guézennec. Hearne listened. There was no sound from the roadway or from that row of houses. Kerénor must be safe.

He looked towards the meadows beyond the church. After the first alarm, the Germans had been quiet enough. First, they would encircle the wood, for the sentries in the camp would identify it as the place from where the sound of a shot had come. And then, they'd have to start searching carefully, working inwards from the edge of the trees. If they did it as thoroughly as he expected, then they would probably now be finding the bodies. There would be something of a scandal, too. The men who found Elise would have something to talk about for the next few weeks. Hearne's lips tightened. Well, she had earned it, and there was a kind of poetic justice in the fact that the body she had loved so much had earned it for her. He was beginning to believe that Kerénor had still clung to the futile hope that, in some way, she might be innocent, that she had been misled by Corlay. Kerénor had held to his wishful thinking, until tonight. And then, there had been no doubt left.

Hearne paused as he reached the crest of the hill, and looked back at St. Déodat. It was a group of vague black shadows clustering under the proud towers of the church. This was the way it had been when he first crossed this hill four weeks ago. Then he had believed it incapable of change. It still looked the same, but the changes were there, as deep and powerful as they were invisible.

The clouds had spread into a dull gray coating over the sky, and the first fine needle-spray of rain stung his cheeks.

He left St. Déodat and crossed over the hill.

CHAPTER **28** FISHERMEN'S REST

The greater part of the town of Dinan stands securely within its walls, high on the edge of an escarpment above the gorge of the River Rance. But outside the walls, down at the water's level where the boats trading from the coast come to anchor at the small wharves, there are old houses beside the Gothic bridge, and expensive restaurants placed to catch the superb view. Marguerite's café did not belong to that class. It was one of the smallest and oldest houses, whose front room served as an informal club for the men who worked on the boats.

So the bargewoman had said, pointing to the quay. It wasn't far: just across the cobbled wharf. There were one or two men loitering there already, waiting either to load or to unload some boat. If he hurried now, he wouldn't be noticed in this light. The men, he saw, wore old army jackets to shield them from the rawness of the cold dawn. This added to his confidence. He chose his moment, stepped quickly onto the wet paving-stones from the barge, and moved boldly towards Marguerite's house.

The barge, too old and too decrepit to have been commandeered by the Nazis, rested quietly and innocently at its mooring place. Already it had forgotten it had carried him four miles down the River Rance to the Dinan quay. The woman who had helped him to cross the river was still standing on the deck of the barge, waiting for the restaurant keepers to come down to buy her small stock of produce. For the smart restaurants now had their clientèle of German officers, and the vegetables and butter had to be fresh every day for them. Hearne turned as he reached the narrow little house which the barge owner had pointed out, and looked back. The woman moved as if to let him know she had seen him. He pulled his cap further down on his head. But neither of them waved. He wished she had taken the few francs Kerénor had given him; heaven knew she needed it, working that old tub by herself, with her husband dead and three children to feed. Her husband had been killed, she had said simply. In the war, Hearne had guessed, for when she saw his stained tunic and battered cap, she had given him shelter at once. Another barge was slipping into its place beside the woman's. It would have helped him too, she had said, as if to explain why he mustn't pay her. The barge owners were now so accustomed to picking up stray men wandering near the locks on the canal that they kept a watch for them. It seemed as if many of the escaping men struck naturally towards the Rance, knowing that its waters would lead them to Dinan, and then from there by wooded riverbanks to the coast.

Over the door of the house were slanting fading letters, but they still spelled *Marguerite*. Hearne turned down his jacket collar, wiped his face with his sleeve, and pulled the door quickly shut behind him. The square room was small and dimly lighted. It smelled of stale tobacco smoke and vinegar. Two men were sleeping slumped across one of the half-dozen small tables which had been jammed into the available floor space. A bar faced the door. Behind it were empty shelves, a fly-spotted mirror, a vase of large yellow paper daisies. On its left there was another door. On its right, a staircase.

One of the men half-raised his head from his arms, his eyes scarcely open, and then slumped back across the table. The other still choked and snored alternately.

The door beside the bar opened, and a woman stood there. This must be rising time for her: she was still fastening her dress. Her black hair was plaited into two thin pigtails falling over each shoulder. She fastened the last button, twisted the meager plaits of hair into a knot behind her head, and jammed them into place with the large hairpins which she had been holding in her lips. That let her talk, anyhow.

"No food for an hour," she announced. "You can sleep at one of the tables." She pointed a square hand to the two men.

Hearne made his way past the crowding tables and stood in front of her. She was a short broad-shouldered woman, almost as square in shape as her brother. She had his blue eyes, too, and the black hair without any grayness showing, although she must be fifty at least. She even had the same laugh-wrinkles round her eyes and mouth, grooved deeply into the coarse tanned skin. She waited for him to speak, her hands on the place where her hips might once have been.

"Marguerite?" Hearne asked.

She nodded, watching him closely. She couldn't quite place him, but she would certainly know him again.

"Le Trapu told me to come to his sister if I needed a place to rest."

"Where did you meet him?"

"Sailed with him two weeks ago from the Bay of Mont St. Michel."

"He's not here."

"I know. But he will be here tonight."

Her eyes flickered towards the table with the two sleeping men.

"Did you come here for breakfast?"

Hearne shook his head.

She nodded over her shoulder, and he followed her through the door into the small room, which was a mixture of kitchen, bedroom and sitting room. It was surprisingly clean and neat, but the faint smell of vinegar still persisted.

Hearne sat down on the wooden bench at the side of the fireplace. He looked at his filthy boots, the stained corduroy trousers.

"Are you waiting for him to arrive?"

Hearne shook his head again. "Not exactly. Tonight I must travel again, and I wondered if I could stay here."

"This isn't a hotel."

"Your brother said—"

"Him!" she snorted. "The trouble he gives me!" But her voice was less annoyed than her words.

"He said you could beat trouble any day," Hearne said with a smile.

"That man!" The tone was amiably contemptuous. "He's a sailor, and as stupid as they are made. He wouldn't know trouble if he was to meet it."

"He's a very good sailor."

"Him!" Her sisterly admiration was amusing enough, Hearne thought, but he hadn't come here to be amused. He said, suddenly serious, "I sent a message to Le Trapu. It should have reached him here yesterday morning before he sailed."

"You did?" The voice was noncommittal, but the clever eyes were watching him curiously.

"Yes. And I wondered if the message reached him."

"My God, how should I know? He never tells me anything." She turned abruptly and began to fuss with a coffeepot.

"Perhaps you know if the girl bringing the message arrived safely?"

"A girl? What are you worrying about that for? You look to me as if the only thing you should worry about is the Boches. You're as bad as—"

"Him," Hearne finished quickly. "But *did* this girl arrive? And has she gone?"

"You're all the same, you men. A girl's a girl. There's a dozen of them hanging round here every day. Can't get the place cleared of them. How should I know what girl?"

"She should have arrived in the early morning." Hearne's voice was worried. Anne hadn't got here; he was almost sure of that now.

"They often do."

"She has fair hair . . . blue-gray eyes . . . a short nose with freckles: seven freckles." He stopped short in embarrassment. God, he thought, such abject foolishness. What had happened to him? Blithering here like an idiot to this old pot, who wasn't even bothering to listen to him.

She finished cutting the small loaf of bread and dropped the slices into a shallow basket. "Sounds as if that might be the same girl," she said casually, but there was a gleam of laughter in her wrinkled eyes.

Hearne sat quite still. He felt hollow inside. Some day, he thought, as he looked towards the solemn Marguerite, some day someone who needs sleep and food and information is not going to appreciate your sense of humor. Some day someone will— He restrained himself, and played her game. At least, Anne was safe so far.

"Here's all the money I have," he said with excessive calm. "Will it buy me something to eat, and a place to rest until the night comes? And while I eat, would you tell me what you know?"

Marguerite looked at the money thrown on the table, and then looked at his white face. The calmness of his voice stung her into remorse.

"I don't need your money," she mumbled. "You'll need it yourself before you reach the coast." And then she grew angry. "What's her name, you who come into my house and ask me questions and try to make me tell you things I'll tell no one?"

"Anne," said Hearne, and he was smiling now. "Anne."

"And what is yours?"

"She didn't know my real name."

Marguerite had recovered her humor. "That's what she told me. Strange thing, I told her, to go gallivanting over the countryside for a man whose name she didn't even know." But her voice was kindly, and her eyes laughed at Hearne's expression. "Cheer up," she said, "I don't blame you for getting angry with me. You don't know my little ways. Take your money before I change my mind! And here's something to eat. You need it, I'm thinking."

"How did you know I was going to the coast?" Hearne rose stiffly and went over to the table.

"Well, she's gone there."

"She's *gone?*"

"Yes. Where did you think she was? Hiding under the bed?"

Hearne looked at her bleakly. "Please tell me," he said, "just what happened when she came here. Was she all right, why did she leave so quickly, where did she go? Did she see your brother?"

Marguerite relented and forgot her little ways. "I just had to know whether you were the man she told me about. I didn't want to give the right information to the wrong man. You've got to be careful these days. Now, here's what happened . . ." She cut him a thin slice of sour cheese and poured some brown liquid into his cup; then she began the story—it was long, but neatly told.

Anne had arrived, had seen Le Trapu and talked alone with him in this room. Then she had rested and changed her clothes, for her dress was covered with mud and dirt. She had left that dress here, and Marguerite's niece had given her a blouse and skirt and wool jacket in exchange, for the dress was good rich cloth, and not the kind of material you could buy nowadays. Then, with some food wrapped inside her shawl, she had insisted on setting out again. It was all right to travel in daylight, she had said, for she had a travel permit and money enough. She had even insisted on leaving money to pay for the food she had had. She wanted to go away at once, it seemed, because otherwise she couldn't reach the coast in time.

Hearne rose, and walked across to the fireplace. "Just where, at the coast?" he asked. He thought, St. Brieuc, no doubt: where else?

"She didn't tell me that. You can talk with him about it—she discussed a lot of things with him in the hour before he sailed. He always had a soft spot for blue eyes and fair hair."

"I wonder if your brother will be here before I leave?"

"He told me to keep you here until he came. He thought you would be here."

Hearne looked up at that. "He did, did he?"

"He did." She watched him curiously. "Better come and finish your breakfast. Then you can sleep upstairs."

Hearne came back to the table. There was still one important thing to ask. "Have you had any visits from the Boches?"

Marguerite allowed herself another half-cup of the tasteless coffee. "Patrols look into the bar every now and again to check up on the men they find there, but they haven't found anyone yet who couldn't be accounted for. The Boches don't come as customers, not after the first week. Our drinks didn't agree with them. The other restaurants are bigger and smarter, and they get good food there. Here they have to eat what we've got to eat, and they don't seem to enjoy it." She suddenly laughed, and plunged into a long story of what had happened that first week when some soldiers had bought drinks at the bar. She had mixed them, herself. The soldiers gulped almost half the drink before they realized how bad it was. Then they swore she was trying to poison them.

"Me!" Marguerite said, and picked up the last crumb of a crust with her wet forefinger. "Me!" She looked so outraged, so indignant, that Hearne grinned.

"What then?" he asked.

"Things looked bad. Yes," Marguerite admitted thoughtfully, "it was as dangerous as facing a herd of mad pigs in an orchard. Especially when a sergeant was called in. He took a swill, and then his face puffed up till it looked as ugly as his other end. It was hard to tell the difference: you couldn't tell whether he was coming or going." She shook her head slowly, smiling broadly as she enjoyed the memory.

"And then?" prompted Hearne again. This was one story he was going to hear the end of, anyway.

Marguerite shrugged her broad shoulders. "Well, I pick up their glasses, one by one. And I empty them slowly into three clean glasses, see? Then I hand two of them to Jacques Hémar and Yves Andhouard who are standing there at the bar watching everything. And I take the third glass myself. And I say, 'Jacques and Yves, show them how Bretons can drink!' And, before their very eyes, the three of us swallowed the stuff down·to the last dreg."

"Yes?"

Marguerite looked at him quizzically. "The Boches went away."

Hearne's disappointment was her reward. She loved it. She cracked with laughter, smacking her hands in delight against her thick thighs. When she had quietened, and wiped the tears from her eyes, she said in a casual voice, "But you should have seen Hémar and Andhouard and me standing in this kitchen ten minutes later, spewing our guts out." She paused, and admired the effect on Hearne. "Sh! Not so loud," she warned. "But God knows you look as if you needed a good laugh. And sleep, too. Here, get upstairs before these men outside waken and start shouting for something to eat."

Hearne followed her quietly upstairs. The small square room showed by the gray light from its narrow window a welter of acquisitiveness and thrift. He picked his way through the empty boxes, casks, bicycle parts, wine bottles, piles of newspapers, and broken ornaments; and looked carefully out of the window. Back yard, he decided.

"If you leave by the window, there's a vine to help. But don't go upsetting my hydrangea pots on the ground," Marguerite said and opened a panel in the wall, to reveal a concealed bed.

"You should be as safe here as the others," she said. "Come on, get in. I've no time to waste."

Hearne looked doubtfully at the box bed, in spite of its cleanness, and climbed in obediently. He put out his left arm instinctively, as she shut the door.

"Don't worry," she said. "You can open it from the inside. You can breathe too. See?" She pointed to the decorations across the top of the panel, carefully carved to make the ventilation holes look artistic.

Her voice came through the panel. "I'll lock the room door, and I'll make a holy row on the staircase if anyone who shouldn't tries to come up here. All you've got to worry about is the fleas the last man left behind him."

But if there were any, he didn't notice them. He thought, sleep is impossible here, lying like a sardine in its tin. Yet it seemed only ten minutes later when Marguerite's large-knuckled hand was shaking him impatiently to rouse him.

"He's here," she was whispering. "He's down at the boat, waiting to sail. The weather's just right for it. Hurry." Her words awakened him as thoroughly as a bucket of cold water.

He stumbled cautiously across the room. By the light from the window, he guessed it must be almost night. Probably about nine o'clock. "What—" he began, but she silenced him with a finger at her lips.

"He'll explain when you are safely away," she said.

At the top of the narrow wooden stairs she halted him again. "I'll go down first and start serving at the bar. Then you just come down quietly and walk out. Don't stop for a minute."

Hearne listened to the loud voices coming up from the room beneath. "Won't it be dangerous for you if someone sees me?"

She shook her head impatiently. "A man coming down these stairs doesn't surprise them. They've come down themselves." She smiled and patted his shoulder. "Now get to the boat. I'll have some more stories for you next time you come back. And you can bring me some real coffee." And then she was moving silently down the staircase, her weight balancing from side to side as she placed one foot carefully in front of the other.

He waited until he heard her voice raised in a shout of laughter and the sound of glasses being clanked heavily down on the bar. A heavy blue haze of smoke filled the little room. But no one turned to watch him slip out of the door, cutting off the warm thick air and Marguerite's storytelling as he closed it behind him.

A cold wind ripped the darkness. He paused in the shadows of the overhanging eaves of the last house in that row. Across the narrow cobbled street was the wharf. From the large restaurant further along the riverbank came the ebb and flow of music. His eyes searched for the outlines of the boat. There she was, pulling gently against the mooring rope. He gauged the distance with his eye. It would take only ten seconds of quick movement. He gathered his confidence and a deep breath, and walked smartly across the quay.

There seemed to be no one on board, but a hand pulled him down behind a heap of sails and covered him loosely with their folds.

"Half an hour," Le Trapu whispered, "and it will be dark enough to sail."

Hearne pushed aside enough of the sail to breathe. He lay and listened to the rise and fall of the violins from the restaurant, the lapping of the tide's ripples against the boat's sides. Once he heard marching feet, and held himself ready to slip into the cold water. But the feet marched on, and his tense muscles relaxed again.

Before the moon had risen, the boat was moving gently into mid-channel. The dark banks of the river rose steeply on either side. The wind which had cut through his jacket, as he had left Marguerite's house, now filled the sails. It was only then that Le Trapu left the other man to steer the boat and came forward to talk to him.

He gave Hearne a nod of recognition, and sat down silently beside him.

"Where are we bound?" Hearne asked.

"*You* ought to know."

Hearne looked at the square-set face with its thick growth of hair on the jaw. "Do you?"

Le Trapu raised his eyebrows and shrugged his shoulders. "The boy Etienne brought me back an answer to take you to St. Lunaire."

Hearne relaxed. *Brought me back,* Le Trapu said. That meant Anne's message had got through to Etienne. Hearne asked, "Answer to what?"

"If I should sail you there."

Hearne was silent, trying to puzzle that one out.

Le Trapu spoke again. "It was the girl's idea. She said you were hurt, that the Boches had got you for a while. She thought you might come to Dinan, although she hadn't wanted you to come, because you'd want to make sure of that message. So I asked the boy Etienne what was I to do. And he came back with the message to take you to St. Lunaire if I found you."

"Did the girl say where she was going?"

"To the coast."

That was as much as he knew already, thought Hearne. He stared moodily at a patch on the sail. After the strain of worrying about these last miles, it was a strange feeling to sit in a boat and feel them floating past. That was like life . . . you worried and you schemed, you sweated and you suffered, and then something quite different happened, and all your careful plans were just so much sawdust.

"I'm giving you a devil of a trouble," Hearne said.

"No trouble. It's quicker this way. Three hours, four hours perhaps in all. It is simple. No trouble." The Breton was equally awkward. He rose and moved to the stern, as if he were afraid of further thanks.

Hearne lay still, his eyes watching the riverbanks, his mind filled with crosscurrents of emotion. The wooded gorge gave way to sloping fields and woods, and small dark huddling villages. As they passed them stringing along the riverbanks, Hearne remembered L'Etoile d'Or. He wondered how Jules was getting on. He'd make a good boss if he married that girl behind the bar: she was the one to give him the confidence he needed. It was strange to think of big Louis' body anchored in the mud and slime at the bottom of this river. It was strange to think that they might even be sailing over what was left of it—for the estuary was now broadening, the banks were widening, and there was the hard square shape of the first big town on the right bank. Hearne, stretching his cramped legs painfully in the bottom of the boat, felt the spray sting his face, and smelled the first real saltness.

Le Trapu came forward, and pointed to the distant bank.

"St. Servan, and then St. Malo," he said. "From now on I'll be busy. Once I get her out between St. Malo and Dinard, I'll talk to you again." And then he had gone back to the tiller.

Hearne, remembering the picturesque shapes on his map of this river's estuary, felt a chill going through his body which didn't come from the wind. In this darkness, with white clouds chasing each other across the sky, with the slice of moon and scattered stars still struggling to break through the heavy drift of mist, he didn't feel like talking much. He only half-smiled at Le Trapu's canniness: no chickens being counted here before they were hatched. *Once I get her out, I'll talk to you again.* Anything they planned before this getting-out business might be just a waste of breath. It might, thought Hearne, as he felt the boat rise and fall and shiver as the strong currents tried to pull her their own way. It might, but it wasn't going to turn out like that. He concentrated on that thought, as if by keeping his mind fixed on arriving at St. Lunaire the boat would be bound to get there.

He could see the black shapes of curving rocky peninsulas, of scattered islands like so many boulders dropped into a pool of racing currents. Once the moon struggled free of its shroud long enough to throw a sickly gleam on the water. Hearne wished it hadn't, for the *Marguerite* appeared to be heading straight into a whirlpool, and between them and the cliffs of the shore were needles of rock round which the cross-currents fought and slavered. If he only knew more about sailing a boat, he thought, he wouldn't need to imagine himself as a steersman. Perhaps he could relax then, and let Le Trapu manage it all by himself. There was only one thing which gave him any pleasure: the little boat's speed had increased. At this rate they would soon be in the open Channel and then St. Lunaire was only three or four miles to the west of them. The salt spray covered him as the *Marguerite* suddenly plowed across a stretch of broken water. Hearne was relieved that the moon hadn't tactlessly emerged at that point, to show him just how broken it was. And then the boat plunged forward again: the water against its side stopped jabbing at the planks, and hissed as it streamed smoothly past.

Hearne was startled to hear a voice bellowing in his ear.

"We're out now," Le Trapu explained.

"Thank God," Hearne said, unclenching his hand from the mast and relaxing. "I'm all worn-out, steering. I'd rather meet a German patrol, any day."

That amused Le Trapu. "Each to his own job," he said politely.

"Didn't know a boat was so damned noisy," Hearne said. "All creaks and sighs and groans."

"Nice little breeze. And nice moon. It was bad for us when it came out for a few moments."

"When do we reach St. Lunaire?"

"Very soon. If the light were better, and thank God it isn't, you would be seeing the way the rocks stick out between the two bays. I'll take you to the west bay."

Hearne nodded. "That's the one further away from the town," he said. "That's the one."

"We'll run in as near the coast as we can. You can wade ashore. Good sand, big dunes, and no houses. You can lie up there quietly all to-morrow."

"Yes," said Hearne. That waiting wasn't going to be much fun. He couldn't allow himself to sleep. He'd just lie and worry about this job: worry how he could have done more, or could have done it better. Not that it mattered now at this stage, but at least it would keep him from thinking about himself. And his personal thoughts were far from pleasant at the moment. It had to be this way. The job came first: it had to. Damn it all, he said to himself, why do you have to keep persuading your-self about that? You know it's first. You can't think of Anne or yourself until it's all over. When you chose this kind of work, you were choosing a moment like this, even if you didn't know it. He looked at the black streak of coastline, with the darkness hiding the arcs of sand pointed by cliffs. Perhaps Anne would follow that shore road to St. Brieuc, perhaps she might even think of him as she looked over the waters. Shut up, he told himself savagely, shut up. She had only been kind to him because she *was* kind. She couldn't help but be sweet and gentle. If she had felt the way he felt, then she would have waited at Marguerite's house in Dinan. She would at least have said good-by. Shut up, he said to himself again. He should know it was better that she didn't wait, that she didn't say good-by. Now he could stop sentimentalizing, and prepare for a cold swim. That would cool his brain for him.

"St. Lunaire. East bay," Le Trapu said, pointing. Hearne looked, but there was nothing but blackness, perhaps at the most a faint smudge of gray where the sand of the bay swept out to the sharp teeth of the rocky peninsula. There was no doubt about that spine of rock. Its cliff rose darkly up in a savage line against the sky, as if to protect the town shel-tering back in the mainland.

Le Trapu's man was bringing the boat in a wide sweep round the head-land now, into the second bay. Le Trapu was working swiftly and furiously with the sails. Their speed slackened. They drifted towards the long gray curve of sand, growing grayer and wider. Behind it was a stretch of soft darkness. Golf courses, Hearne remembered from his map. Miles of them. This was the place.

Their speed slackened still more, they were almost drifting in.

Le Trapu was beside him again. "Can't risk any further. Can you swim?"

"Yes."

"Good. It's very shallow. Stay in the dunes all day. Don't leave them. They're safe."

Afterwards Hearne remembered the insistence of the Breton's voice. But at the time, he only nodded, and slipped over the edge of the boat, holding his gun in his right hand. Only the left arm was good for swimming, anyhow. He hung onto the side of the boat for a moment, Le Trapu bending over to hold the left hand secure.

"*Bonne chance alors. Au revoir,*" he said, and released his grip on Hearne's hand. Hearne drew his knees up to his chest, his feet against the side of the boat. He shoved against it, and felt himself glide out into the water free of the boat. He paddled softly with his left arm, as he felt for the sand and touched nothing. Six strokes later, he felt again and touched bottom. He waded slowly in over the long stretch of shallow water, keeping only his head and his right hand above water until he was forced to change to crawling on his knees. At the water's edge, he came in with a curling breaker, and rolled flat on the sand. The waves' last flow licked his face as he turned his head to watch the boat. He could see it only because he knew it was there. Already it was swinging out. Soon it would be just another fishing boat crossing the bay.

He gathered breath, and started the long slow crawl over the cold sand. When he got back to Britain, he could start thinking about the pain which gripped his right shoulder, about the spasm which dragged at his back muscles. He lay over on his left side and wrung the water out of his jacket pocket and slipped the gun back into it. He needed his right hand free— such as it was. Then, with his face muscles set in an ugly grin which had nothing to do with amusement, he pulled his body over the shore.

It was heavy going, for the dripping clothes and swamped boots had the weight of lead; and he was weaker than he had thought. In spite of the constant effort and movement, he was deathly cold and shivering uncontrollably by the time he reached the first curving bank of sand. He rested there. Then he pulled himself up over its soft face towards the waving spikes of grasses. Twice he slipped, and dug in with his knees and elbows to stop himself from sliding back to the shore. But at last he had his left hand round the toughness of the grasses. They cut into his flesh as they took the weight of his body, but he was over the last lip of the dune and he let himself roll gently down its grass side until he rested at the bottom of its hollow. There were bushes near. He crawled over to the largest clump. Gorse bushes. Painful, he thought, but at least safe. He groaned to himself, and looked for the easiest entrance to the sweet-scented tangle.

And then he heard a step. A careful step, as if someone had halted uncertainly.

Oh God, he thought despairingly. He forced his right hand into his pocket. He rolled over quickly on his side, aiming at the half-crouching figure. It moved forward as he steadied himself.

The whispered words were like the touch of the wind on the tall grasses round him.

"I was watching for you."

That was all; but his heart leaped, and he forgot the throbbing shoulder and the coldness and the numbing sickness.

"Anne," he whispered.

And then she had slipped, as quietly as she had come, down to where he lay. "Anne," he said, and gripped her so that he felt her bones yielding under the pressure of his arm and heard the short gasp as the breath left her body.

"Anne," he whispered again, and kissed her.

CHAPTER **29** END OF A MISSION

The spreading gorse bush grew at the foot of a short, steep bank, bearded with tall, waving grasses. Its heavy branches swept to the ground at its front and sides; at its back, they clutched the top of the bank and trailed beyond. They formed a perfect, but painful screen, Hearne thought, as he forced the stubborn branches apart and held them that way until Anne, her hair protected by her rough woolen jacket, could reach the free space of ground between the roots and the bank. Then he entered the thorny tangle, letting the branches fall to the earth again behind him. They had torn his hands and lashed his shoulders, but the shelter they offered was safe. Anne was lying on the sparse, stubby grass which forced its way up through the sand. He stretched himself carefully beside her. It was too dark to see her face, but the arm which he had thrown round her measured her heartbeats. His left hand pulled the jacket back from her hair. It was no longer tightly braided; its soft, loose silk covered his fingers.

"I can't even see it," he said bitterly. "And I can't see your face properly. There's only a black outline which is you. And we'll have to talk in whispers, and we dare hardly move in case we lose an eye." He looked up at the dark mass of branches sweeping arc-wise above their heads to reach the steep bank behind them. "Hell of a lover I am, bringing you into a place like this."

She laughed softly. "I like it," she said. "I feel safe here. And I feel so happy." Suddenly the laughter in her voice stifled, and he knew she was crying.

"Anne darling," he said. "Anne!"

"I'm just so happy," she repeated. "I thought Le Trapu was never coming, that he had missed you after all, that you had both been caught. And then the light was so bad, and the clouds made so many shadows on the bay that there might have been fifty fishing boats there or none at all. Then the clouds thickened and a mist moved in from the sea. Even at the very end, I wasn't sure it was you. By the time I left the dune where I was lying, and hurried along to where I thought I had seen you go, I began to imagine that I had been dreaming. And then, I found you."

Hearne, his lips touching the smooth cheek, didn't answer. He was thinking of the danger Anne had been in, of the risks she had taken. At last he said, his voice now normal, "How long did you wait?"

"I came this afternoon. There were others walking on the sands of the bay, so it was quite safe. Near the rocks beside the town there were German soldiers." A hint of laughter entered her voice. "They were trying to learn to swim. I watched them from the dunes, as some other people were doing. I just sat down there, and the tall grasses were higher than my head, and no one noticed me. After an hour, I moved further back into the grasses, and I lay there in the sunshine, waiting for the darkness."

"Any other Germans?"

"Some on leave from the town were walking along the sand. They kept looking at the sea."

"What about the golf course?"

"Some Boches were playing there. Madame Chevel said they were staying in the big hotels, and in the villas the Parisians used to own. The Casino is filled with them every night. People believe something is going to be started here very soon, because a lot of boats have been bringing loads to the small quays on the other bay. Some say it's ammunition, and some say building material. But everyone seems to think the Germans' holiday will soon be over, and that there's going to be work here for them. There are a lot of soldiers in the town, and on the beach in the other bay in front of the Casino."

"Who is Madame Chevel?"

"I stayed with her last night. When I arrived in St. Lunaire, I was hungry, so I joined a queue outside a baker's shop. There was a woman like Albertine standing beside me. That was Madame Chevel."

"You've only to smile and wrinkle this nose of yours, Anne"—he kissed it and won a little laugh—"and even the Albertines offer you shelter."

"It wasn't my smile; it was what I said to her when three soldiers marched past the length of the queue, went into the shop, and came out eating the last pies."

Hearne laughed too, and ran his hand over the soft hair lying so close to him. "And where is Madame Chevel now?"

"Asleep in her little house. And I am on my way to my aunt at St. Brieuc."

Hearne was silent. He was wondering if all women were naturally adept at this kind of game. First, there had been Elise, and now here was Anne who, for a different cause but with much the same skill, had managed to plan her way to the coast. Plan his way too: he owed much to her cleverness and foresight.

"What's wrong?" Anne was asking. She stretched her free arm across his shoulders. "Oh," she said, "you are cold, so cold. And you've let your bandage slip out of place." The concern in her voice pleased him.

"I'm warmer than I was. I'm feeling better every minute." He tightened his grip on her waist. "Darling, why did you come here?"

"I wanted to see you." Anne so direct, so honest. No hedging. Just *I wanted to see you*. There was a pause, and then the whispered voice was so low that he could hardly hear it. "I had to see you leave safely. If I had gone to my aunt's house, I should never have known that you had even reached here. I should never have known what had happened to you."

"And what happens to me . . . does it mean so much?"

Anne was silent.

"Does it mean so much?" he repeated.

"I kissed you," she said, in a very small voice.

His left arm, encircling her waist, pulled her closer. "Darling," was all he said.

And then, later, "If kisses show how much, then you know now how much it means to me, too." He kissed her once more. "I couldn't be sure, Anne. I'm a jealous kind of chap. I worried about you being engaged to Corlay. You aren't the kind of a girl to let herself get engaged to a man without having liked him enough at one time. Then I thought you had been kind to me because you were sorry for me, or because you hated the Boches so much, or both. It wasn't until I saw you out there among the dunes that I let myself think of anything more. Even yet, I can't quite believe that you love me; you'll have to say it, to make me believe it."

"Why do you want to believe it?" Her cheek was warm with the hot blood under the fine, smooth skin. Her heart was pounding again against his arm, her voice was half-laughing, half-serious.

"Because," he said simply, "I am coming back here after the war ends. And if I'm coming back, I want to know you'll be here."

"Yes," she said slowly. "I'll be here. I'll stay at St. Brieuc and watch for you coming from England. After the war . . ." This time, the tears which came could not be controlled or explained away. She caught him convulsively and buried her face in his shoulder. It was his right shoulder, and it hurt like hell, but Hearne found a fierce pleasure in the pain.

"After the war," he said firmly, "I'll be here even if I have to swim across." His voice was calm, determined.

Anne had stopped crying. "Your arm!" she said, suddenly remembering. "Your shoulder!" Her hands were gently feeling for the bandage, gently arranging it to make his shoulder more comfortable.

"I'd rather have your head than a bandage," he said. "Leave it, Anne. There's still one question I'd like to know the answer to. It keeps haunting me. Were you ever in love with Bertrand Corlay?"

Anne's words were clear and direct. "I wanted to fall in love with him, at one time. I thought I could. But I didn't."

"Why did you want to fall in love with him?"

She bent over suddenly to kiss his cheek. "Because I was young, and he was so very good-looking."

"What? Corlay? He's as ugly as—well—" He halted in embarrassment.

"Then only you think so." She kissed him again. "You are the strangest man."

"Why?"

"You keep silent when I want you to talk. And when you do talk, you ask questions."

"Do I?"

"Yes."

"But I've so much to find out about you. There's so much I want to know. First tell me how much you love me, then tell me about you . . . everything you can remember, little things, anything."

"First, you must tell me how much you love me. You will teach me how to say it. That will give me courage."

He said seriously and gently, "Do you ever need courage, Anne?"

"Sometimes."

He kissed her. "I don't think words are very adequate for this moment."

"No?" She was half-laughing.

"No." He was half-serious.

Later, she said, "And I can't even say your name. You've never told me it." It wasn't an indirect question: it was a simple statement, tinged with surprise and melancholy.

"Martin," he answered. "Martin—" He halted. "The other name you will know later, Anne. Later, when it is safe for you to know it. Now, I must just be Martin."

"Martin," she repeated, giving it the French pronunciation. "Martin." Her finger traced a line across his forehead and down the side of his cheek.

Hearne stiffened suddenly. He laid a finger across her lips. They lay in silence, straining to catch any sound. At last Hearne relaxed. "Thought I heard feet crumpling shells on the shore," he explained. They listened again.

At last, Hearne spoke softly, "You didn't know my name, you still only know half of it; you don't know what kind of job I have, or how much money I make or don't make; you have scarcely seen me except when I was worried, or tired, or smelling of fish, or all bloodied-up. And now I've chosen a gorse bush to drag you into, and my wet clothes are leaving a damp trail of sea water over you, and the sand is still sticking to a week's growth of beard, and yet you say you'll marry me. God, however did I have the luck to find you?" His eyes, now accustomed to the blackness round them, tried to see her face more clearly. His lips touched her eyes and hair.

"There are so many things to—" he began and then halted. "We've so little time left."

"At least we've until dawn, and then through the day, and then through the evening, until darkness comes again."

"No, Anne. You can't wait all that time. You must go before light breaks. You must be on the road to St. Brieuc by morning. You must."

She lay very still.

At last she said, "Can't I even wait on the dunes, just to see you leave?"

"Anne, darling, I'd only worry about you. Better reach your aunt. If I only had time I'd take you there and see you into her house."

At first she didn't speak. And then the soft voice had tightened. "How long have we together, then?"

Half an hour, or an hour at the very most, Hearne thought, with his heart as cold as the damp clothes clinging to his body. He said, "Not long enough for any more talk, my love," and kissed the smooth outlines of her face. "Not even for the reasons why I adore you." Her skin was soft as a child's. Her hair smelled of sunshine and fresh winds.

They both flinched when they heard the explosion. Anne had instinctively tightened her arms round his neck, wincing as one of them scraped against the sharp-edged spines of gorse.

"Something's gone up," Hearne said. "Something's blown sky-high. About two miles away, beyond the town. What the devil could that be?"

"The little docks on the east bay, where the river runs into the sea," Anne suggested. "Madame Chevel said that was how they were bringing the ammunition—by boat. But it's all guarded: there are soldiers there."

Hearne nodded. He was alert, listening.

"What's that?" Anne asked, flinching again.

"Rifle fire over there. Sounds like machine guns, too. What the dickens *is* this, anyhow?" He struggled to a kneeling position, his head and shoulders bent, his hands still holding Anne.

Then they heard the footsteps, running footsteps, footsteps coming near them, footsteps coming from the golf course behind them. Again there was rifle fire, but this time stray shots sounded from this side of the town in counterpoint to the continuous staccato beat from the east bay.

"Hell's broken loose," Hearne said. "I'm going out for a look-see." He started to crawl forward to the place where he had found their entrance.

"Perhaps your friends?" Anne said.

He shook his head. "They wouldn't make all this racket. They do it very differently. Sounds to me like a raiding party." He thought grimly: it would be just my luck to have chosen to leave St. Lunaire on the night after a prearranged raid.

The footsteps were further away now. As Hearne parted the branches cautiously, he heard someone fall, and then there was a torrent of descriptive adjectives.

"British," he said to Anne. And then, in alarm, "They're going away." He stooped down to help her rise. He ripped her cardigan from the thorns. To their right they saw the disappearing heads and shoulders of the two last soldiers, as they jumped down onto the shore.

"Hurry, darling, hurry," Anne said, "quick, quick." He took her hand and together they raced for the edge of the dune. From somewhere behind them, perhaps from the hotel across the golf course, came a furious burst of firing.

"Keep low!" he urged, and slid over the end of the dune, dragging Anne with him. She was talking so quickly he could hardly separate the words.

"Good-by, darling, good-by. And come back. Martin!" But even as she was speaking, he had to whistle shrilly to the running figures. Three boats near the beach. From the other side of the rocky peninsula, flames were rising, and the firing was heavier.

One of the soldiers had heard him. He stopped and half-turned. Hearne waved his left hand, and whistled again. The officer bringing up the rear also halted and looked round, and then waved in turn. Urgently. The rifle shots were coming nearer now. A machine gun crackled on this side of the town, too. The rifle shots were coming nearer.

"Go on, darling," Anne said. "I'll be waiting at St. Brieuc." The officer waved again. Hearne could hear him swearing as he waved. He crushed Anne's hands convulsively. He couldn't speak. He turned and ran towards the four soldiers who were waiting for him.

He remembered her as he ran, standing quite still, her back against the dune, her hand frozen in mid-air. She would be smiling. If he could see, she would be smiling.

Hearne turned to look towards her for the last time. She hadn't moved. Her hand was still upraised.

And then, from where he now stood, he could see the moving shadows as well as hear the sound of their rifles. They'd get her. If she stayed behind, they'd find her. The moving line spread thinly, unevenly, but still dangerously, towards the shore.

Hearne started to run back to the dunes. Behind him, he heard the officer's voice raised angrily. The bullets were finding range now. Sand spurted to the side of him. "Anne," he called. "Anne. Come. Quick." And she was running towards him. She seemed to stumble just as she reached him, but his arms were ready and caught her, and then holding her round the waist, her arm resting on his shoulder, he pulled her with him towards the four waiting soldiers.

"What the bloody hell do you think you're playing at?" said the officer. He looked at Anne. "But what's all this?" Then, looking at Anne, he was suddenly silent, and stepping to her other side crossed arms with Hearne to sweep her along between them. They were in the water now, the surf round their feet, the breaking wave catching their waists. Beyond the waves at the edge, it was shallow and smooth.

The officer was talking all the time. "Good show!" he was saying. "Not bad at all. We gave 'em a pincer movement all right. Pinced them with their panzers down!" He looked approvingly towards the red semicircle of sky beyond the rocky peninsula. "I wonder how many the others got on that side," he went on. "We nabbed three officers from the hotel, and disposed of the rest. They are in that boat moving out there, trussed like hens. But of course that other bay's the really exciting one." He nodded casually to the east. "Casino's over there, jammed full of them. And there's the town too. Well, we'll soon know what happened." His calm voice had brought them to the boat, and the bullet splashes were now behind them.

The boat curved out into the bay to follow the others.

The roar of its engine hid the clatter of machine guns from the beach. The water shoreward was cut and furrowed.

"Jeez, throwing stick grenades and all," a soldier said. "Everything but the kitchen sink." A second voice said "No good!" with mock concern. "Wouldn't they like us to fire at them and show them what to hit? Poor old Jerry can't get on the target . . . what a blee-ding shame!" Other voices were talking too, counting wounds, remembering jokes, now that they were leaving the bay with a flaunting trail of foam behind them.

But Hearne, kneeling beside Anne, heard neither the roar of the engines, nor the broken rhythm of the machine guns on the beach, nor the jubilant voices of the men. He only heard the strangled breathing of the girl, only felt the warm trickle of blood from her mouth. He watched the face of the man who had pushed him aside, watched the skillful fingers working by the ghastly light of the flares straining their way up into the sky.

The officer returned from his tour of the crowded boat. "Worst is over now," he said as he looked down at Anne. "We got her in time, I think. By the way, do you happen to be Matthews' young man who was to be picked up on Saturday? Matthews was fuming when he found we had this operation all planned for tonight. Might have been nasty if you had crossed the Nazis' trail when they were on the warpath."

Hearne shook his head. Better that, than this. Better that than Anne lying at his feet with a bullet in her lung. He pressed her hand convulsively.

She opened her eyes, and he knew there would be a smile in them if he could see clearly.

The last flare filtered away. Above them was the drone of planes, searching in vain. The stark coast of Brittany had darkened into the night. But the coldness had left his heart. Within his grasp, Anne's hand moved gently, hopefully.